Dedicated to the real-life *Calvin*.

You were supposed to stay while I saved myself.

But you left.

JAMIE CORRIS
INFERNO

Printed in the United States of America

First Printing, 2025

ISBN 978-1-958919-04-0

Library of Congress Control Number: Pending

Crimson Folio
publishing

Inferno (noun):

a place or a state that suggests Hell

I don't want you to save me.
I want you to stand by me as I save myself.

- Sushil -

Jennie & Calvin's Playlist

Fresh Out The Slammer – Taylor Swift

All You Had to Do Was Stay – Taylor Swift

Let It Go – James Bay

The Night We Met – Lord Huron

Say You Won't Let Go – James Bay

18 – One Direction

The 1 – Taylor Swift

Take a Bow – Rihanna

Lose You to Love Me – Selena Gomez

Tell Me That You Love Me – James Smith

Apologize – One Republic

Hear You Me – Jimmy Eat World

Hold On – Chord Overstreet

Try Sleeping With a Broken Heart – Alicia Keys

Better Man – Taylor Swift

Us – James Bay

Jennie

Wednesday, April 11ᵗʰ, 2007

I hate you. You are nothing. I wish I never met you. You should just go fuck Glen and leave me alone. You make me sick.

The sound of my alarm clock wakes me. I'm drenched in sweat; my forehead, my lower back, my armpits, even in between my toes. I turn off the beeping, checking the time.

7:45 AM.

I flop onto my back, staring at the ceiling. I pull pieces of wet hair from my forehead. Thankfully, insomnia didn't keep me up all night. I somehow got a solid three hours of sleep.

The nightmares keep me awake. The words he said to me stay on repeat in my head. It's a record player, over and over, and I don't know how to turn it off. Those were the last words he ever told me before he vanished. It's been one-thousand, three-hundred, thirty-one days since I've seen him.

I turn over to face the window, not surprised to see it full of water droplets. The sound of the rain makes me drowsy, but not enough to fall back asleep.

My boyfriend Calvin got arrested three and a half years ago after a camping trip that went to shit. They sentenced him to five years in prison. I don't know much about what he did to deserve such a lengthy sentence, but I hate him every day for it. Thought I could handle the separation. I'd imagine I'd finish college, get a degree, save some money for us to find a house together. When he got out, I wanted everything to be perfect for him. He's supposed to come home next year sometime. Each day, I wonder if I should pack a bag, buy a plane ticket, and go to South Carolina to see him.

I just can't, though. It's been hard to keep the happy memories at the forefront of my brain because all I hear, every single day, are the last words he said to me. If I were to see him, I'd probably want to spit in his face or kick him in between the legs. God, I hope I have more time to get myself prepared before I see him.

1

Three months after he left is when things got bad. I had more panic attacks; I contemplated dropping out of school, and I had nobody to turn to. I spent most of my time sitting on my couch, crying and watching our favorite movies. They didn't bring me any joy, just complete misery. The numbness, emptiness, and depression were too much. The black shadow in my life was getting darker and darker. I couldn't let myself go under... Not when I knew he was still floating on the other side of the country, waiting for me to save him. But I was slowing sinking.

I had an accident last May that put me in the hospital. That's when I started medication and therapy. Things felt really great for a while. I got married and started my internship. I made peace with grief. I felt that happiness was still possible for me.

However, I haven't been going to therapy or taking my medication in the last five months. I've been lying to my loved ones that I'm taking my pills and still going to therapy because I'd hate to disappoint them. To be honest, I've been avoiding most of them because they would know that something was off about me.

When I realize that a few tears have slid down my cheek, I wipe my face with both hands. I have my last final today and that's the only reason I get up.

The three hours of sleep have helped with my energy level. Seattle is usually chilly and rainy in April, so I find a pair of army green leggings and a black sweatshirt. I try to pick outfits that are cozy enough and if I sit on the couch and cry, I'm not uncomfortable in jeans or a nice shirt. I brush my hair, which I haven't done in days, and spray a small amount of dry shampoo to my roots. Since seeing Cal, I've let my hair grow out past my bra clasp. Running my fingers through my hair, I make sure to remove all the tangles. Unsure of the last time I showered, I make a mental note to take one when I get home later. My makeup is probably expired, but I apply some mascara, blush and Chapstick.

I groan when I throw my clothes onto a pile of dirty clothes. At least, I think they are dirty? This semester has been my busiest one yet. Laundry is usually my last priority. My internship, coffeeshop job, and classes overwhelm my schedule. The clothes pile looks like it's composed of my nice clothes for Hilltop, my only pair of jeans I wear to the shop and a mix of Calvin's and Jonah's shirts.

"Jen, just put a load in now." I grumble softly. I hate when I argue with myself.

I grab my laundry basket and toss the pile in it.

My washer and dryer are hidden at the back of my kitchen, inside a small closet. I'm getting irritated on not only how many clothes I own, but why I let myself wait so long to do laundry!

Today, being Wednesday and my final week of classes, I'm content with my leggings and sweatshirt. My final today is Clinical Assessment.

I decided to take a semester off to sort of get my shit together. My bosses, Max and Lydia, who own Hilltop, which is where my internship is, and Pat, who owns the coffee shop, *Coffee & Honey*, saw how much stress I was under the past few months. Without my medications, my life has been chaos—only they don't know how bad it's gotten.

After my hospital visit, I got behind in my classes. When I signed up to take extra winter classes, I still had my head on straight. I busted my ass to get all my credits done in time. Lydia, Max and Pat told me I deserved a break.

Well, that was before I got the news...

Coincidently, it was December 26th-Calvin's birthday- that I received a text from an unknown number he was getting an early release. The date remained unknown, and I fell apart from that moment. Calvin was coming back home, and he was going to know that I was on prescription medications and going to therapy and meeting with a dietitian. Hell no! I wanted to be the same girl he knew before he left.

Filing the detergent and fabric softener, I start the washer. My clothes will be ready for next week. Starting next week, my schedule will finally slow down. It's a bittersweet thing—I'll have more time to think about Calvin's arrival back in Seattle, but I also won't be constantly on the go. Max and Lydia hired me part time at Hilltop. I'll be with them on Mondays, half days on Tuesdays and Wednesdays. I'll work at the coffeeshop on Fridays, Saturdays and Sundays.

I leave the laundry basket in the kitchen, so I remember to move the clothes to the dryer. I head back into my bathroom to finish getting ready. To conserve energy for the rest of the day, I brush my teeth slowly. I reminisce about what happened to me last week, and ever since then, the blackest cloud has been hovering over my life.

I was walking to my car from class and I thought I heard his name. I swear to God it was his name. It paralyzed every muscle in my body. My heart felt like it stopped beating. My incoherence led to me dropping my keys in the parking lot.

I didn't even flinch when horns started beeping at me to move. Someone pulled me out of the way and when I stared up at this figure, my world crashed.

Callen. I recognized him from my theories class. He kept quiet most of the time, and I only knew of him because of first day introductions. He sat close to the front, but there was nothing about him that resembled Calvin—except his name. Someone must've been calling his name. I couldn't even speak when he asks me if I'm okay, so I shake my head. He hands me my keys that fell on the ground, holding onto my arm to keep me up. I couldn't get over how much I missed hearing his name—or something similar. As soon as I got into my car, I cried the entire way home. I haven't fully recovered from that moment yet.

I'm stuck in this humiliating bubble where God just wants to punish me. The constant reminders of *him* are brutal. I see red trucks everywhere. His favorite song always seems to come on the radio. It feels like every male human I pass smells just like him. It's a constant torment. I wish I knew when he'd make his arrival. He's kryptonite, though. He always comes back and blows up. I'm waiting for disaster to strike my life, as if it hasn't been a disaster for the past three and a half years.

Since my experience in the parking lot, I've been trying a new self-care regime to help get out of this funk. I've tried so many things to feel better, and I already know this won't last, but it's worth a shot.

My routine consists of trying to wake up early, if I sleep at all, and drive to Whole Foods before my class. It's simple, but it requires a lot of energy. I usually only drive to Hilltop since it's on the other side of town. The coffeeshop is only a few blocks away that I walk there most of the time. It almost feels like exposure therapy-having to put myself out there for the world to see. As much as I don't want to be exposed, I'm trying to get myself in a better mindset for when he comes back. I've only been doing this for two weeks, and I don't drive every day, but I'm trying my best.

The walk from my front door to my car is not far. It's misty outside, but I figured a rain jacket was excessive. I take the same route to get to Whole Foods. It's about a fifteen-minute drive.

I'm pissed off because someone parked in my spot. The angry part of me wanted to park next to this asshole, enough that they couldn't open their door.

I decide to take the advice of my psychiatrist and park a couple of spots further from the front door.

Sixty-two steps today.

Someone is playing a sick joke on me and there aren't any hand baskets available. *Guess you get to carry your snacks today.* I'm still trying to let things roll off my shoulder, so I roll my eyes in annoyance and follow my imaginary line.

Following my trail, the first stop I make is my protein shakes. I discover they are out of the strawberry banana.

Fan-fucking-tastic. We are 0/3.

I grab a mango peach shake this time. Thankfully, my popcorn, fruit and carrots don't leave me with any surprises. I decide to get a gallon of water today too. Carrying the water to the checkout, my arm aches, and I'm still anxious about picking up an item that wasn't on my mental grocery list.

Drinking water is beneficial for your health.

Jesus, how many times was Dr. Beckett going to tell me what to do today?! I haven't seen her in months! Why am I still allowing her to control my thoughts?

I let my unconscious drive me to the checkout lane, number 4, his favorite number. I don't hesitate; I never do.

It's giving obsessive compulsive vibes, but I'm learning to be in control of my life.

After everything that happened with Calvin, feeling in control is equivalent to bungee jumping. I get to decide how high to jump, where I want to jump to, when I want to jump. I've never been bungee jumping in my life, but I figured you either have lots of courage or none. The courage to go out in public, and shop, and interact with people requires a lot of self-control.

The cashier, Eddie, has become a part of my routine. He's an older gentleman and walks with a limp. He has those old school 70s glasses that are too big for his face and he's balding on the top of his head. Despite his unappealing outside, he always smells nice. I wonder if he has a girlfriend? It's nice to interact with him because he doesn't know the part of me that is spiraling and hates the world. I put on a good front for him by giving him a fake smile and setting my items on the side of the self-checkout machine.

"Good to see you this morning. Your water is new today."

Eddie walks behind me, his cologne overpowering my senses. I think he was going to touch my arm, but shoved his hands in his apron instead.

"I figured I should stay hydrated."

If Eddie knew how many times I've considered drowning myself, he'd probably suffer a stroke.

"Well, I hope you have a pleasant day today." His voice drifts off as I realize another customer needs help.

I'm not sure I will, Eddie, but I will try. As I swipe my card, I say "you too", then shove the receipt in my bag. And just when I wasn't ready for it, someone pushes me off the ledge to bungee jump.

"Jen..."

I stop in my tracks because I know that voice. The voice that has haunted my dreams for months. It can't be real.

There's only person on this planet who calls you by that name.

I want to move, but I can't. Psychology teaches you about flight or fight, but rarely do they mention the freeze. All my muscles tense, like I'm getting electrocuted. My heart and mind are attempting to sync together. They are both trying to be powered by my defective power supply that has been offline for over a thousand days. I can feel a spark in my chest at the sound of that voice.

I try to swallow to keep breathing, but my autonomic nervous system fucking breaks. Or malfunctions. Or disappears.

"Jennie, hey..." The voice talks to my back, and I'm trying my hardest to ignore the feelings happening around me. My eyes are filling with water and for the life of me, I can't move my feet. I move only my eyes towards Eddie who is still assisting someone. *Why can't he be Superman and fly me away?* I've scrunched my fists so tight that my fingernails are creating crescent moons in my palm, and I'm sweating again.

Here was my kryptonite.

I'm unsure if I should be happy or fearful. All I know is I'm walking back into the flames, ready to burn again because I'd do anything for this man.

There's a warm sensation on my upper left arm.

The voice is touching me.

Please don't be real. I'm not ready for you to see me like this.

"Jen, it's me." And with that, my tears fall.

I'm not sure if my bungee cord snapped or if someone let go, but I'm falling. The hand that has hold of my arm is tugging me to face this person. I'm trying to keep my head down, but there's a force in me that has to look at who's been talking to me.

Devil. She's been my trusty sidekick. She's forcing me to look at him. Forcing me to come face to face with my kryptonite.

I'm not ready to blow up yet.

Please don't be real.

Calvin

She's here. Right where Lydia said she would be.

Her scent is invigorating. Even though I'm barely moving her to face me, my hand feels like I'm on fire. She's so fucking close to me—I can see all the little details I remember about her.

She has only become more magnificent. Literally the best Christmas tree I've ever seen in my life. Her hair is longer and lays perfectly down her shoulders. She isn't looking at me yet, but I see her eyelashes are layered with mascara and she's wearing pink powder on her cheeks. Or I've really made a good impression on her. Facing me now, she's always been the perfect height where my lips could kiss her forehead. I feel like a dog with a choke collar on, being restricted to kiss her. Her outfit is adorable and comfortable, perfect for Seattle weather. I'm not sure if that's my sweatshirt, but I like how it's positioned to show off her curves. My eyes move down her face so I can see the small beauty mark on the base of her neck. Good God, I miss kissing that part of her.

Stealthy, I move along with her as she does her grocery shopping.

The popcorn does not surprise me. Her favorite, although I can't tell if she got the extra buttery bag. If she did, she has changed little. Her fruit tray consists of watermelon, strawberries, and blueberries. She hates everything else. The carrots are a funny story. That made me chuckle when she picked those up. She only eats carrots with ranch, but she doesn't have any in her basket, but I would presume that wherever she is going has some. I'd buy her all the ranch for all her carrots. The protein shakes caught me for a surprise though. She used to drink coffee, granted we worked at a coffee shop together and it was the only beverage available. Caffeine affected her too much, and water was never a suggestion. She looked irritated when she tried picking up the water with her hands full. Why didn't she get a basket? I want to jump out right now and help her, but God knows it would end in a messy way.

I watched her interact with the cashier, who seemed a little creepy. He smiled when she got to the checkout lane, and my temper flared when I saw him almost put his hand on her.

It was probably just a kind gesture, not a possessive gesture, you idiot.

Her interaction with him was strange. Her smile was different, though, not the one I remembered when I left. It was... sad and forced.

I had to be smart about my re-appearance. There wasn't ever going to be a good time for this, but she's been hard to find. Almost non-existent.

She's here now. I'm here *for her.*

Jennie

"Calvin, is it really you?"

My body is trembling as he spins me around, and I find the courage to look at him.

And for the first time in over a thousand days, sunshine peeks through my dark clouds. I missed the sun. So damn much.

Calvin

The time I spent waiting for Jen to get to Whole Foods, and allow her to get her items, gives me time to reminisce about my release and journey to find her. Fuck, I didn't think this moment would come.

I got an early release from prison ninety-five days ago. When I left South Carolina, I took a taxi to Charlotte Douglas airport, and booked the quickest flight back to Seattle.

The layover in Chicago was fucking agonizing. I spent three hours of Google searching for private investigators in Seattle. I found a guy who had agreed to meet me on short notice, as in the following morning. Guess there wouldn't be any sleep for me. Not that I wanted to sleep anyway. I was on my way back to *her*.

Waiting in Chicago was also a good time to call my brother Lincoln and ask him to unlock my door and gauge the weather so he could turn on my A/C or the heat.

I'd been in contact with Linc since I'd been gone. He was five years younger than me and was the best secret keeper. I'd hire him as my private investigator if he was old enough and had the proper qualifications. Upon hearing my request to check up on Jen, he decided to, and I quote, "stalk" her during my time away and fill me in on everything. It was the first and only time I laughed so hard in prison. My mom would kill him and me if she knew what he was doing.My mother hated Jen.

When I went to jail, Linc was only thirteen. He would turn seventeen next month, and I didn't want to be the culprit of Linc's criminal record at such a young age. My mother was already ashamed of my actions.

Chicago was a good first attempt to showcase my renewed patience and lessened irritability.

It didn't get renewed, and I was more irritable than any other day in my life. I hated I had thoughts of wanting to punch every man and woman at the airport.

I felt I wasn't ready to be released if I was having such thoughts, but I'm glad to be a free man. I did my due diligence of being on my best behavior and completing my program ahead of time. The prosecutor of my case was a real dickhead and I thought I had no chance to get out early.

Something noble in me considered it wasn't the best thought to punch the shrieking baby crying two rows behind me. It gave me plenty of time to work on my breathing techniques.

To hold my breath maybe...

I'd been to Sea-Tac a few times with my dad to travel for his fishing excursions. I was antsy to get off the plane and make my way to find a taxi. Thankfully, I had no baggage to pick up, besides the mistakes I was carrying on my back.

By the time I got to Seattle, I had a migraine from the lack of sleep, lack of normal food, the screaming baby, the turbulence, and my anxiety to want to get to *her*. My stomach was twisting in knots.

What if she wasn't here?

I lost track of her whereabouts for several months, so I was walking into darkness. She could've followed me to South Carolina, but there's no way she would've known where I was unless my folks told her, and I find that idea unlikely.

After I track down a taxi, I give him my address. It was too late to stop at *Coffee & Honey,* thinking she would've burned that place down after I left. My mouth salivates at the thought of dark roast coffee hitting the back of my throat. The coffee during prison meetings tasted like cold hot chocolate with a hint of gasoline. It was fucking putrid.

It wouldn't surprise me if she burned everything that brings her thoughts of me. I'm surprised the state of Washington wasn't in shambles.

I didn't arrive home until close to two in the morning. My head was throbbing.

My brother was a good kid. The door to my apartment was unlocked, and he had turned the heat on. It was nice and warm. Everything looked the same. Nothing looked touched. Three years of my life that stood still. It felt like I was revisiting an old camp room. The same sheets, the same furniture, the same smell. I got my first apartment a few weeks before the camping trip. Jen came here only a handful of times because I didn't have much. My parents looked after my place once they knew I'd be gone for a while. There are a few pieces of new furniture and as much as my parents were disappointed in me, I'm beyond grateful for them. It was well over five grand I'd plan to pay back, but I'd figure it out later. I had more pressing matters.

My mom had placed a candle on the stove, so I lit it to create some new aroma. It smelled stale and musty from Seattle's constant rain.

A shower. I wanted to take a shower. A long, hot shower. Wanting to remove all traces of my past life, I dispose of my shirt, pants, boxers and socks that were returned to me yesterday morning.

Linc, you could've at least put a trash liner in the can. I leave the clothes near the trashcan to take care of them later.

The shower helped a bit with my migraine. Showers in prison weren't terrible, but showering in private was a dream. Showering in private *and* with silence was just heaven. I stood under the water just listening to the sound of the water pressure coming from the shower head. No other sounds.

Being a young guy, it was not the most comfortable of situations. The other inmates were always calling out vulgar shit, making inappropriate comments to each other. If they only knew how much I loved saying the word *fuck*, I'm sure I would've been best friends with some of them.

The first time I showered in the community bathroom, I thought I wasn't going to make it out alive. I tried my absolute best to not show any emotions when a gang of guys approached me, taunting me with taking my soap and towel away. In the moment, I wasn't sure if I was supposed to fight back or just let it be. I didn't befriend a lot of other inmates, but this one guy, they called him *E*, he took a liking to me. Not in a perverted way, but he kept a close eye on me, making sure people steered clear of giving me a hard time.

He had a group of guys that stayed close to him. E was a short guy, completely bald and had a full-grown beard. I had learned he was an alcoholic and was serving a forty-month sentence for driving under influence, child endangerment and failure to appear. He was married and had a set of twin boys. His wife wanted things to work out between them, so he got himself some help. They talk every day, and it's nice to see him show emotion when he's on the phone with her. For the most part, E stays out of trouble. He's trying to win an early release and talks about taking his family to Disney.

I really fucking hope he was able to do that...

After my hour-long shower, I sifted through my clothes. Hardly anything fits, but I found a shirt and some shorts. They didn't feel like mine, but it was better than an orange jumpsuit. I will burn everything that I own that has orange on it. When I get dressed, I stood at the end of my bed and stared at it.

"I have missed you." I was hoping to save those words for Jen instead of my bed, but we all couldn't be winners.

Falling face first onto my bed, I let out a loud groan. Holy fuck, I wasn't laying on cardboard and it didn't smell like sweat.

It was heaven.

The private investigator wanted to meet at eight in the morning at some doughnut shop off 70th Street. I had set an alarm to make sure I found a taxi in time. Shit, I'd meet him in the landfill as long he could help me find her.

My eyes were heaviest they've ever been, and before I had time to think about her, I fell into a deep sleep. At least I was dreaming of her. I had been dreaming about her for over a thousand days.

Tuesday, January 16th, 2007

The sound of my alarm startled me. I was used to shouting from guards and banging on the cells. I preferred my alarm. It was annoying, but at least I had control over it.

My eyes felt like concrete bricks. The time change was horrible. I swear it felt like I only slept twenty minutes. My body felt a million times better, even if it was three hours of sleep. I felt like I was sleeping on velvet sand. I stayed in bed for a bit to savor the feel of my mattress and sheets and fresh air.

As I laid in bed, I contemplated my game plan. If the private investigator couldn't help me, I had to think of a Plan B. The thought circled my mind like a school of piranhas—*what if she wasn't here?* I didn't pray, ever, but for this one time, I hoped God was on my side to keep her here in the city. It would make my payment to this PI a helluva lot cheaper. Rubbing my hands over my face to wake myself up, I breathed deep. Even though I wasn't having a panic attack, I did the 54321 method, Jen said it was called the grounding technique.

Jen taught me about it at the coffeeshop when she was working on her AP psychology homework in February 2003. It was only a week after she started working. God, one of the best memories I have of her.

Five things I could see was the first step. I usually couldn't find four more things because I only stared at her. She was the center of my vision. I remember her reaction to me watching her. She blushed immediately and I don't know what was holding me back from diving my mouth to hers. She was so fucking beautiful. The first time I saw her right dimple, I thought I was going to die. From then, it was constant mission to make her smile or laugh just so I could see that perfect imperfection. I'll never forget the first time I looked at her eyes. They were a shade of green that I've never seen before, and they were a potent drug that I was hooked on.

We kept trying until I was able to focus. I wasn't focused for long because she would do something that overwhelmed my senses and I got distracted.

I'm thankful by the time I left, I could get from steps five to one.

Five things I see. My carpet needs vacuumed. My recliner in the corner of my room with clothes piled up–Lincoln's clothes? The most beautiful and candid picture of Jen from her birthday in 2003 is on my dresser. My sunrise peeking through my window blinds, giving my bedroom a golden feel. The dust accumulated on my ceiling fan. I'll have a chat with Linc about that...

Four things I can feel. The softness of my jersey sheets. The shirt Jen left here years ago that must've been laying on my bed this whole time. (I don't just touch the shirt, I clench it for dear life). The sweat forming on my forehead to find Jen today. The knot in my stomach to meet with the PI.

What if he couldn't find her?

Three things I can hear. My empty refrigerator running. Car horns outside. *I've missed that sound.* My breathing intensifying.

Two things you can smell. A burnt smell...

SHIT. I left the candle burning all night.

One thing you can taste. Nothing yet, but I hope it will be Jen soon.

"Let's do this. Go find her."

My pep talks weren't the best, but I was running on low fumes and high adrenaline. Not the best pairing.

As much as I don't want to leave my bed, I scoot off and walk down the hallway to inspect the candle. There wasn't much wax left, so it must've gone out by itself.

I showered again, hoping to make a good return statement to Jen. Plus, I just could.

I trim my beard a bit, hoping not to scare her away with my lumberjack appearance. The last time I saw her, I had just a stubble of hair. Would she like the amount of facial hair I have now? My arms and legs were bulky, because I'd taken quite a liking to the prison rec room. I put on a few fresh shirts, only to find most of them didn't fit anymore. One of my larger sweatshirts fit just enough, and I paired with my khakis. They were a little tight around my quads, but it would have to do. New clothes would have to wait. I tied my laces of my suede Vans and took one last glance at myself.

Lincoln was bringing my truck by later, so for now, I'd walk down 35th Ave. It's about a fifteen-minute walk from my apartment to the doughnut/diner place. Plus, I'm not against a pleasant morning walk. The freedom felt unusual, but ultimately very freeing.

Henry, the private investigator, was sitting in the corner booth of Top Pot Doughnuts.

The smell was fucking intoxicating. Coffee overwhelmed my senses with so many memories and flashbacks that I contemplated ditching this guy and going to Pat.

Stay here and do this.

Henry had sent me a description of what he was wearing, and I probably didn't need that information because he stuck out like a sore thumb. His black ball cap covering his eyes made him sketchy as hell. He sported a dark beard, surrounding his lips and connecting with his sideburns. His dark brown eyes could give someone nightmares. An oversized navy jacket and black jeans were his attire, and he was wearing large combat boots.

This guy looked more like a drug dealer than a PI.

I took my chances by paying him everything I had left to my name. I glanced in the other direction, hoping by some coincidence that Jen was here, too. She wasn't, so I walked to Henry.

"Hey man, I'm Calvin."

He sat in place in the booth while I held a hand out to introduce myself.

"Henry."

He took a bite of his doughnut and shook my hand. He motioned for me to sit on the opposing side of the booth. The dozen doughnuts that sat in the middle of the table made my mouth water.

"I was going to order ya a coffee, but wasn't sure how ya took it."

His intimidating face eased a bit.

"Oh no problem, man. Let me grab one really quick."

I shifted out of the booth to the counter. This coffee was probably trash compared to Pat's coffee, but it was a million times better than prison coffee.

The service was quick, barely waiting a minute at the counter. I returned to Henry, who left me the remaining doughnuts.

"All yours."

Henry pushed the box closer to me.

"Thanks. So, how does this process go?"

I devoured into the first doughnut.

"Straight to business kind of guy." He leaned back in the booth and crossed his arms. I got a better look at his face from this angle. He had a large scar that faded down into his facial hair on his left cheek.

I think that was supposed to be a question but came off as a statement.

Dude, I'm not here to be your friend, sipping my coffee.

"Sorry, is there another way to go about this?"

I was hoping he didn't need a backstory about our relationship. Hopefully me telling him I wasn't trying to stalk by ex-girlfriend, no, current girlfriend... friend? would be acceptable. Besides, I wasn't *stalking* Jen. I was merely using resources to capture what was mine. Right? It was a game of hide and seek. I was hiding in South Carolina for three and a half years, not sure if Jen was ever seeking to find me. Now it's my turn.

Henry sets his empty coffee cup down on the table, angles his head to stare at me and chuckles.

"Well, first, is this a chase for hate or love?"

I lower my eyes, trying to hide my answer. If I say hate, will the rules be different? Of course, I didn't hate Jen, I could never, even if I did tell her that. But I was slightly confused why she never came to bail me out of jail or visit me or send me anything. There had to be some slim chance that my parents told her where I was.

Someone had to tell her I didn't just leave with no explanation... how fucking broken and messed up she would be if that's what she believed?

I clear my throat. Sitting with your feelings for over a thousand days makes you real fucking sentimental.

"Love."

"That makes it easy, then."

Henry responds. A feel a flicker of spark ignites inside me. *That makes it easy.*

"How will this be easy?"

My voice cracks as I tackle another doughnut.

If it's so easy, let's get started.

"For one, our relationship is already ten times better since I can tell this will not be a murder heist. I hate getting involved in that shit."

Henry shakes his head, like he's shaking off terrible memories.

"Second, you seem like a decent dude. Tell me a bit about you."

He crosses his arms over his chest, fully expecting me to tell him my life story.

"Look, Henry, I appreciate you meeting me and wanting to help me, but aren't we wasting time sitting here chit chatting about useless information about me?"

He just stares at me, offended. I'm almost waiting for a slap across the face or for him to walk out of me. He just keeps staring. Intimidation factor of this guy–check.

"Fuck, fine. I just got out of prison. Like as in yesterday. I was in South Carolina serving a five-year sentence. Got out early for good behavior and because that was my first offense. I tried to get probation, but the victim's family insisted on at least five years."

"Victim, eh? Have you already completed a murder heist?"

The veins stretch in my neck. My fists tighten and my stomach distorts into cartwheels and flips. My appetite has disappeared, and I want to drown myself in hot coffee.

Almost...

After a couple of minutes of not responding and my body stuck, Henry asks a different question. A better question.

"Who is she?"

He uncrosses his arms and leans across the table. He's interested now. At the mere thought of her, my body relaxes. I don't think he has enough time for me to explain who she is.

She's everything.

I look down at the table, fiddling with my thumbs. A grin appears on my face, lifting my eyes to look at Henry. He smirks. He knows this is about to be good.

"Her name is Jennie, but I call her Jen. We met at a coffee shop a few blocks away. Fell in love with her at first sight, really. She was beautiful. No, she was more than beautiful. She was a fucking goddess. I cursed at the Heavens for bringing this angel into my life because she was so distracting, but man, I thanked them every single day I saw her."

I chuckle at my cheesiness of trying to describe Jen to a stranger. There were no words in the dictionary to give justice to how stunning Jen was.

"So yeah, we just worked a lot together and over time, just liked being with each other. I guess we fell in love pretty fast. We were together every day. She was my haven. Life was fucking pure bliss for several months. I thought I would take our relationship to the next level and book a weekend away with a couple of our friends."

A wave of nausea is washing over me. My nose feels itchy. I feel tears swelling up. My voice breaks, and I straighten up in my seat, feeling Henry watch my every move.

Give him all the details.

"Um, one of our friends was there, well not really my friend. But he was just giving me shit. His name was Glen. He used to date Jen in middle school, and they just stayed friends, I guess? Well, he was there and my good friend Anna and her boyfriend, Andy. Things were just not in my favor. Long story short, Glen and Jen kept flirting in front of me. So, I said things to Jen... cruel, terrible things. The plan was for them to leave early so I ditched them and went to bar in town. Some guy started mouthing off to me and I just couldn't hold myself together and one thing led to another. I found myself hungover and in jail. I fucked up and I'm just trying to find her because that wasn't how things were supposed to end between us."

My counselor told me to not sugar coat our experiences. I've retold this story so many times, trying to come to peace with my actions and hoping to reconcile the future. I don't know if I trust Henry and I don't want to become vulnerable and allow him ammo he shouldn't have. He's doing me a simple favor. Sure, if we decide to become friends, then maybe I'll share the gruesome details. Not today though. A sly grin appears across his face.

"She sounds great. Question though, what's your friend's name? I could do some digging into him." I laugh enough for my head to fall back. A genuine laugh since being out of prison.

"Don't worry about him. He'll get his fucking karma someday."

Fucking Glen.

"So have you tried calling or text Jennie, Jen... which do you prefer I call her?"

Henry's humor disappears, and his business act is back on.

"She's Jennie to you. I uh... I can't bring myself to check. If she changed her number or if she didn't answer me, it would just ruin me."

Henry nods his head like he understands.

"So, there's a possibility. Give me her number. I can check into her phone records."

I glare at Henry. Not sure if it's because I don't trust giving Jen's number to *this guy* or because I don't need a full-blown investigation.

"Henry, I'm sorry if I never made myself clear about this. I don't want to know what she's been up to. I couldn't care less who the fuck she's been texting or calling. I just need a location. I just need to know if she's here in Seattle. If she is, then I'll handle the rest. If she's not,

then I guess I owe you a lot more money."

My insides flinch at the thought of paying more money to Henry, but more so at the thought of tagging him along in my mess to find my love.

Henry stares at me for a moment like a bomb just went off. He leans forward, taking in a big sigh. He stretches his arms above him, then places them on the table.

"Calvin, if I have her phone number, I could look up some sort of phone bill which would have an address. If you don't want to give her phone number, that's okay, too. I can find other ways to get an address."

His whisper haunts me. I don't take my eyes off him.

I daydream about working together with Henry. He's tall, intimidating, charming. All the exceptional qualities I have. We could do some damage if we tag teamed together. Henry clears his throat, bringing my attention back to the conversation. He's also impatient... bonus.

You're a fucking idiot, Calvin. A phone number would connect to a phone bill, which would lead to an address.

There's something holding me back from giving her phone number away. She no longer trusts me. I want to salvage what I can and make things right. I don't know what kind of reaction she would have if she knew I gave her phone number to a stranger. The answer to her whereabouts could be right in my pocket and I feel a hole burning through my pants where my phone is sitting.

"I can't do it. I can't give her number away. What's our second option?"

I feel instinct relief at my words. *Proud of you.*

"No problem, man. I understand. We try to protect the ones we love. I've dealt with many clients like that. So, have you been to a house of hers while you guys were together?"

Her dad's house was off 38th Street NE. No. 41st Street? 45th Ave? Fuck, I can't remember.

"Yeah, she lives with her dad. I can't remember which street but it's near Jackson Park, in Lake City."

I hate that the once cherished memories of being with Jen and her father have faded.

"If you drove there, do you think you would remember which street or how to get there?"

"I don't know. What if she walks out and I drive by? I'd drive into something and die on impact. Then it would all be for a fucking waste."

Perhaps this was a bad idea. I should just let Jen go, let her live her life.

"Woah, woah slugger. Calm down. Nobody is going to die."

Henry gives me a strong, comforting grip on my arm.

"Look, I'm not saying you need to do it today, but just try it. Start at your place and see if your memory remembers how to get to her father's house. If you remember, all I need is the address and I'll look at the details. If you forget, then it's okay. We'll do plan C. We're screwed if we reach plan Z, Calvin."

Henry's demeanor is admirable. He makes it sound like driving to a past lover's house is normal.

He's right. I should start with that.

"Yeah, yeah, I can try that."

Hope fills my heart.

"Okay, great. Let's start there. I'll give you a couple of days to try it out. Call me if it works out or if it doesn't. There has to be something."

The next day, I remembered how to get to Jen's father's house. I asked Henry to meet me there for moral support. When I knocked on the door, a younger woman answered. She said the house went up for sale a couple years ago, and she never met the seller.

Then I remembered Rosie, the neighbor. Henry followed me to the house to the left. Feeling nervous that Rosie might not be here anymore, I knocked. I heard a woman yelling in Spanish, then the front iron gate opened.

"Yes?" It wasn't Rosie. Similar descent of a Latina woman, she had her hair in a tight bun. She was wearing cleaning clothes, a dark maroon scrub of some sort.

"Hi, um, hello. My name is Calvin. My girlfriend and her father used to live next door, and I was wondering if you knew where they moved to."

From the other side of the door, Henry and I towered over this lady. As I noticed more features of this lady, she had pieces of grey hair falling from her bun. She looked to be the age of a grandmother, but I didn't want to insult her. She had crow's feet on the outside of her eyes.

"ROSIE!" This lady turned her back to scream. I jumped a bit, and I heard Henry snicker behind me.

"¿Por qué estás gritando?" I swallowed hard when another Latina woman appeared at the door.

"Sh, nobody is screaming. This boy is looking for your neighbor. I know nothing about that." The older lady walked further back into the house, leaving Rosie by herself.

"My neighbor?" Her accent was much thicker than the other's. She still looks the same from when I saw her the last time-right before Jen and I were leaving for the campsite. Tight curls surround her hair, almost perm-like. Freckles went from one cheek to the other and her brown eyes were hardly visible from her large, framed glasses. I got a good whiff of cilantro and lime through the door.

"Yes. Jennie Helton and her father, Don."

Her face almost instantly showed a recognizable expression. She brought a hand to her mouth, hiding a gasp.

"I haven't seen either of them in a few years. The end of 2003 was the last time I saw them. I'm sorry, mijo."

Crushed. My chest is being slammed with a sledgehammer.

I don't say anything for a couple of minutes, until I feel Henry approach me to offer his presence as support, putting his hand on my shoulder.

"Thank you so much, ma'am. We appreciate your help." Henry's hand slightly grabs my shoulder blade to move me from the door.

"I hope you find them, and if you do, tell them I say hello. I miss their faces."

So do I.

Henry guides me down the driveway to our cars. Still in shock that Jen and her father left this place. This was my greatest fear.

"What do we do?" Staring at the ground, I whisper to Henry.

"Next plan. We'll find her, okay?"

A couple of days later, Henry learned she was enrolled at the University of Washington. He gave me her schedule and I navigated through campus several times but had no luck finding her. It took me a few days to figure out how to read college campus signs, especially with 33,000 other students in the fucking way. I was pissed as hell when I realized her winter break was approaching, so I had to take a week off from exploring. When classes started up again, I found her classrooms and waited for her to appear.

But she never did. I thought for sure I would spot her, but it's like she blended in. I wanted to keep waiting for her, but I waited for two weeks after all her classes, and I had no luck.

We were in the middle of February when Henry asked if we could check out *Coffee & Honey*. I thought he was joking around, but when I faced him, he was dead serious.

"Dude, I cannot show my face around there right now."

We were at the diner, drinking terrible coffee.

"Why not? It's highly likely she'd be there. I'll go and see if she's there."

"Fuck no, you won't. You look like a drug dealer. She'd probably knee you in the dick. Besides, I still have a score to settle with Pat and I am not doing that until I know Jen is here."

Henry did a low belch, and I crossed my arms, irritated at the fact that Henry might be right. She could be there, and I'm just too scared to show up.

The entire month of March went by with nothing. I swear if I didn't have a record, I could kill Henry. We were together every day, going through our next plan. It felt like we were on plan double Z. I could feel my grip slipping from her.

Most days, and nights, I stayed at his place. It was the beginning of April, and I was lying on his couch while he typed away on his computers in the front foyer. Staring at the ceiling, I was feeling so much in my body. Anger was the heaviest. Not only at Henry, but at me. If she moved away *because of me*, I could never forgive myself.

Angry that she left no traces behind. So much of me thought she wanted to not be found, but there was something in me, our invisible string, that was connected to her.

"Hen, I think you're a scam." I blinked aimlessly at the ceiling, wishing a pile of bricks would crash on me. If for some reason Jen wasn't alive, I wanted to be with her.

"The fuck did you just say?" From my peripheral, Henry stands up from his desk. My body was so tired. I don't think I've slept since the first night I got back. My thoughts were constantly spinning, wondering if I should walk the city for her.

"I don't even know what I'm doing here. You're so full of shit." Part of me didn't realize what I was saying; my paranoia speaking nonsense. I sprang to my feet, facing Henry, when I felt him tug my shirt. He was pissed.

"You are so lucky I enjoy your company. I would punch the living shit out of you for saying that."

Then it's like all my emotions poured out of my chest.

"Then what the hell is happening, Hen!? We have nothing. I don't know what I'm waiting for. It's been three months, and if she knew I was back, she would make herself known, but Christ, she's a fucking ghost!" The back of my throat tightens as I put my hands behind my head and pace the living room.

"This shit doesn't happen overnight, Calvin." Henry's voice, calm as a kite. That was the first time he's ever laid his hands on me. I knew I hit a sensitive spot about his investigative capabilities. He was determined, smart, and loyal as hell. Three months and no sign of her, and he still wants to keep going? I don't deserve his friendship, but I'm grateful.

"You are not the only person I'm helping right now. This shit takes time, and there are loopholes I have to get through without getting caught."

I continue pacing, trying to regulate my breathing. I'm feeling too much and a shot of whiskey sounds good right about now.

"Besides, if you sit down, I can tell you I think I may have something."

"What is it? You found her preschool? Awesome." My sarcasm makes Henry sigh.

"No, asshole. I found her employer. But if you want to be in a bad mood, I'll just keep the information for myself."

He's back at his monitors and I slowly approach him.

"Tell me. Where is it?"

Henry glares at me as he twists hairs of his beard in between his fingers.

"Hilltop Psychiatry. Owned by Max and Lydia Byrd. It's on the other side of the Interstate. 5th Ave."

"Let's go now, c'mon." Without thinking, I march towards the door, feeling full of optimism.

"Calvin, it's almost eight o'clock. Looks like their hours are eight to six. We'll go tomorrow, okay? Just relax. Get some sleep or something, you look like shit. If she's there tomorrow, you look like you just crawled out of a hole. She'd run away." I punch his shoulder as I walk to the kitchen to get a snack.

He's right though. I was so irritable at every sound, at every push-back, at every person who got in my way. If these people were successful doctors, they probably have good lawyers. I wasn't trying to get into more legal trouble.

Making my way back to the couch, the sound of Henry's clicking in the background helps me drift off to sleep. I dreamt of finding Jen at Hilltop.

Tuesday, April 10th, 2007

At eight o'clock, I arrived at the address Henry had sent. This had to be where I find her because I was running out of hope. I push through the brightly colored yellow door and check out the waiting room, using all my senses to know that she's here.

Evana asked how she could help me. She had a black pixie haircut that left bangs falling along her forehead. She had thick, black-framed glasses and dark red lips. She was wearing a black t shirt with a black cardigan. She looked older than Jen.

"Does Jen Helton work here?"

"You mean Jennie Helton? I am not at liberty to confirm nor deny. I'm sorry."

She wasn't going to make this easy. Little did she know that clarifying her name gave me the answer.

"You don't understand! I need to know if she's here!"

I didn't mean to raise my voice, but my temper was flaring. *Please, just help me.*

"Sir, I will call law enforcement if you don't calm yourself."

Don't threaten me with the police. As much as I don't want the cops involved, I couldn't care less if she called the police. There was a sixth sense brewing inside me that knew Jen had been here.

"Eva, what's going on out here?"

A blonde woman comes from the side door. My eyes scan her from foot to head. She's wearing bright red heels, a mid-length black skirt, and a fluffed red blouse. There's some sort of ID badge dangling from the waistband of her skirt. Her blonde hair is curled and stops above her shoulder, and her bangs stop right above her eyebrows. She barely had any makeup on besides some blush and mascara.

I turn my attention towards her. *Maybe this lady can help.*

"Is Jennie Helton here today?"

My voice is raspy and my adrenaline is pumping as someone adds a new chess piece to the mix. *Please help me. Help us.*

"What's your name?"

Her voice is soft, just like her features. If I'm annoying her, she sure isn't reacting that way. I still don't know what kind of practice this is, but if she's some sort of doctor, she's got a calm personality for whatever she does.

"Calvin. Calvin Klenn."

Weirdly, her eyes widen as if I was a secret popstar or something. That's when I notice how delicious looking her eyes were. Two chocolate Hershey kisses. I realized how stunning this woman was.

"Eva, cancel my next appointment and see if Max is available."

She looks over my shoulder to talk to the receptionist.

At this quick moment, I take in the lobby area. There are kids' pictures everywhere. Positive quotes everywhere. The walls are a bright blue. In the corner, there's a small table and some toys. There is a couple next to the kids' table watching me. A few seats down, there is a teenager playing on his phone next to his mother, if I had to guess. The teen seems annoyed to be there. As this blonde lady talks to Eva again, the door opens and a young red head girl with her father walks through. She's holding his hand and carrying a small brown bear. She seems nervous.

"What kind of place is this?"

I try to whisper to the blonde lady, but she just smirks at me.

"Calvin, why don't you come back to my office?"

What? No, I want to know where Jen is!!

"No. It's a yes or no if Jennie Helton works here."

I look at Eva to see if she's willing to answer me yet. She stays silent, watching the interactions unfolding in front of her. I look back at the blonde lady, who is still smirking at me. With her arms folded, she looked impressed by my demeanor.

"Calvin, I'll tell you everything you need to know. We just need to leave the lobby area. You are frightening my clients."

I don't want to go without an answer, but I can sense she's hiding something from me.

"Fine."

The blonde lady taps her badge on a scanner and when the light turns green, she pulls at the door. She holds it open for me and I walk through first.

"Just down the hall, first door on the right. My husband's office is the one on the left."

Her voice is pleasant. I try to justify with Devil that we may have someone who wants to help us. I follow her directions and keep walking down the hallway. Several doors are visible as I look down the hallway. It's very quiet.

The blonde lady's door is already open. I hesitate at the door, waiting for permission to enter.

"Please. Have a seat, Calvin."

Why does she keep saying my name?! I sit in one of the oversized chairs across from her desk, looking around, trying to find clues or answers. This lady has her diplomas hanging up and several wedding pictures of her and her husband. I see nothing relating to Jen.

"So does Jen work here?"

My patience is at a two percent. When the blonde lady walks around to her chair, her soft features are gone. She's scowling at me, holding her fingers to her mouth. Her soft features have vanished.

"Calvin. Why should I help you?"

What is happening? Did this lady just trap me in her office?! Maybe it's the distance between us, but those lovely eyes seem to have more black to them now.

"Who are you?"

I'm leaning forward in the chair, trying to appear unintimidated by this lady.

"I'm Lydia. Lydia Byrd."

She stands and hovers over the desk with her hand out, waiting for a handshake, like I'm supposed to know who she is.

Trying to cut the bullshit and move this conversation along, I shake her hand.

"What kind of place is this?"

"My husband, Max and I, started this practice about five years ago. Hilltop. It's child psychiatry."

She falls into her black faux leather chair. Her softness slowly reappears, clearly proud of what she has created.

"Jen is a doctor here?!"

The news left me speechless with disbelief. This is what Jen has been doing since I've gone? Getting her shit together and making something for herself?

Lydia laughs, and I bring my gaze back to her, confused by her reaction.

"No. Jennie works the front with Eva two days a week. Unfortunately, today is not a day she'll be in."

I roll my eyes and bring my heads to my cover my eyes.

"Thanks anyway. I appreciate your time."

I stand to pull my phone out to contact Henry that we have a good starting point. Right place, wrong day. No problem, I can come back every day if necessary.

"Wait, hold on a second. You just got here. We have lots to catch up on."

Lydia swings her leg over the other and puts a finger under her chin, trying to figure me out.

"No, really, I should get going."

"Calvin, sit, please. You don't want me bringing Max into this."

Her softness is gone again. She's good at that. Not wanting to piss off this lady, Jen's boss, I reluctantly sit back down.

"When did you get back?" Lydia asks me, with a smile back on her face.

"Look, I don't know what you think you know about me, but I don't have time for small chit-chat. I'm just trying to find Jen."

Lydia moves her leg off the other and rolls her chair forward towards her desk, laying her hands on her desk. She stares at me and chuckles, not sure if it's directed at me.

"What's so funny?"

"She told me you're the only person to call her Jen. It's just interesting to hear someone call her that."

She smirks at me, like she's giving an approval look of her nickname. Jen talks about me, but I'm unsure whether it's good or bad, leaving me with mixed feelings.

What does she say about me? There's a tightness in my chest that signals my brain that it's time to leave. I push myself off the chair again.

"Slow down, tough guy. I know all about you, Calvin. The one Jennie talks about. The one she cries about. The one she gets angry about. The one she avoids."

I lift my eyes towards Lydia's. First, I felt irritated, but now I'm intrigued. It's hard to swallow, and I'm getting weak knees.

"What do you mean, avoids?" Lydia licks her lips, looking guilty, caught in a terrible truth.

"Calvin..." She leans forward on her desk. "Jennie knew you got out early. To be honest with you, it's made her...different. She's been on edge and I hate to see her like this."

I think if someone just hit me with a barbed wire bat to the face, I wouldn't care.

"What do you mean, she knows I've been out?" *That's the information we needed.* I sit back down, resting my elbows on my knees, leaning forward to Lydia.

"I don't know much about all of it, but she got a text message from someone that said you'd be getting out early. So, I don't know.., It's almost like something triggered inside of her the past few months. She stays mostly in her apartment and only comes to work."

"I tried to find her at school. Waited by her classes, but I couldn't find her."

Lydia bites her bottom lip. I notice this immediately.

"What?"

"She thought she saw you. She wasn't sure, thought maybe she was having a hallucination, but she came into work that day and it was hard for her... She asked her professors if she'd be able to complete the rest of the course online."

Holy. Shit.

She saw me.

"Does she ask about me now?"

"She hasn't mentioned you since that day. I'm worried about her. Max and I weren't around when she met you, but we've met Pat from the shop. He's told me a bit about your guys' relationship and the aftermath of Jennie. Poor girl breaks my heart."

I'm desperate for Lydia to reach out to Jen so I can provide her with comfort. I also want to shove shards of glass into my ears to punish myself for hearing that Jen has been struggling since knowing I've returned to town. I was supposed to bring her comfort, not anguish.

My mouth feels like it's filled with glue, so I continue looking at her for more information.

"She started working here in the fall, October, I believe. My husband's niece was her professor. During family dinner one night, Sarah, our niece, started talking about this student of hers. Don't repeat this, but Sarah showed us some of her writing assignments. Sarah showed us this one particular assignment about marriage. She wanted the class to explain, hypothetically, if they were to have children in the future, what they would want their children to think of their parent's marriage. That was the first time I saw your name. She talked honestly and sweetly of you. How marriage to you would be the most magical thing ever. Better than Disney, and to some people, that's shocking. Anyway, I asked Sarah more about Jennie. I wanted to read more of her assignments. She was interesting to me. She seemed so lost. So in love with this mysterious boy." Lydia winks at me. I can tell she's trying to lighten the mood, but I'm struggling with feeling anything happy.

"When she came in her for interview, I asked Max if I could have a few minutes without him."

Lydia pauses the story here and takes a drink from her tumbler. *Keep talking, woman!!*

"I was candid with Jennie. I told her I read some of her assignments and I asked her to tell me about this boy named Calvin that appeared in her writing. And she fell apart in front of me. I tried to comfort her the best way I could. I want you to know that I gave her this job because I thought we could grow together, not because I felt sorry for her. I believe Jennie will make a brilliant partner here with us someday."

With tears forming in my eyes, I look away from Lydia. For her to confide in a stranger is not typical Jen. Either she was lonely and needed to lean on someone or she's just changed that much since I've left. Either way, the story breaks my heart.

I am not worth her tears. So many fucking tears she cried for me...

"Did Jen ever know where I was?"

I have so many questions for this person. I hate finding out information behind Jen's back, but it feels like she has a treasure of all the answers I need.

"She never mentioned it to us. Where were you exactly?"

Angel and Devil debate about telling this stranger where I've been.

She doesn't need to know your business.

This person is close to Jen, be kind to her.

I clear my throat. "Prison. South Carolina."

"Oh boy. That's far."

"Yeah, not one of my finest moments."

I ease into comfort talking to Lydia. I probably owe so much to this woman for taking Jen under her wing–to save her.

There's silence between us for a while. I'm pondering on whether to ask more questions.

"Do you have any of her writing?"

"Hmm, Max may have a couple of pieces in his office. Let me check." She moves around her desk, her heels clicking along the tile.

I can't wait to tell Henry what I've found in the last ten minutes. I should mess with him and tell him that all we needed to do was find Lydia Bryd and all our prayers would've been answered.

Her heels enter the office, and then the door shuts.

"This one is special. Sarah, she teaches marriage and family dynamics if I didn't mention that, wanted them to write about how they think they would do as a partner. Pretty much speak to their strengths. This is what she wrote." Lydia slides a paper on the table. Jen's handwriting makes my stomach twist. I see my name written multiple times, making me nauseous.

"Should I read it out loud?" My voice cracks.

"Up to you."

I lick my lips profusely. My hands are sweating and it's becoming uncomfortable to sit in this chair, but I lean back anyway.

"I think I would fail as a wife. I want to marry my best friend, Calvin. He's perfect in every way. He's funny without even trying. He's protective of me, like a grizzly bear. He knows the little things about me like that I like ice cold water, and I enjoy holding hands in the dark so I don't get lost. He's incredibly smart, that I think he knows a little bit about everything. Even though he's fiery, I love when he takes control of situations. I wish I had time to tell him those things. That's why I think I would fail, because I don't speak up enough. He deserved to know how amazing he was-and still is. I want to save him, the same way he's been saving me."

I throw the paper on Lydia's desk and jump off the chair. I sniffle and wipe the corner of my eyes. *Damn you, Jen. You would be the most perfect wife, and to be my wife, it would be the best honor in the world.*

"God, I left her in such a shitty position."

"She's been getting better."

"Do you know where I can find her? Do you know her schedule?"

"Yes, I know her schedule, but why should I tell you?" She scolds me.

I thought we were friends here, lady.

Her question catches me off guard.

"Uh, well, I guess you don't have to help me. I have help in other ways. Just figured you want Jen to be happy."

"And you're going to make her happy?" Lydia retaliates.

Fuck, she sounds like my mother.

"I want to try again."

I watch Lydia take in my answer. She spins from her chair and stands up. She moves to her wide window, approaching me. Her scent is intoxicating, almost like mixed berries. *What is taking so long to answer me?* My patience is so close to maxing out.

"Lydia?" Unable to contain my impatience.

"She'll be at the coffee shop later. I would highly suggest not showing up there, though. Book club thing and it gets busy. Max and I learned the hard way that visiting her on Tuesdays is not a good idea. Tomorrow, she has a final in the morning, but she stops at the Whole Foods. You might be able to catch her there. She'll be here on Thursday to help for a couple of hours. I can't promise I won't have Max standing guard at the door. Don't come in like a lunatic like today. Then Friday's, she's at the coffeeshop again. I hope that helps."

I mentally log all the information I was just given. She can't possibly still work at *Coffee & Honey* after all this time?

The goddamn book clubs. Pat didn't learn his lesson?!

If Lydia thinks I shouldn't see her there, I will attempt to keep myself away. This lady seems to know what's good for Jen.

"What time does she get to Whole Foods?"

"Hmm, I think her final is around 9, so she'll be there early. Probably around eight-fifteen."

Tomorrow, I'll find her at Whole Foods.

"Thanks, Lydia. I appreciate the information. Sorry for harassing the girl up front." She waves her hand towards the front receptionist area.

"Oh, Eva has dealt with a lot." Pushing my phone out of my pocket, once again to call Henry and update him.

"Calvin..." Lydia calls after me.

"Please don't break that girl's heart again. Max and I feel she's finally headed upwards, to something good and happy. She wasn't always that way. Please be gentle with her." The only thing I can do is nod.

I know I broke her once, but I'm determined to fix this.

"It was nice to meet you, Calvin." Lydia says. She follows me out the door, likely going to gossip to her husband about me.

"You too, thanks again."

I turn the corner and head down the hallway, back to the front room. The lobby is clear this time. I pass the window where Eva sits, and she looks up at me.

"Sorry."

Walking out of the front doors, I take in the biggest breath of fresh air.

She's still here.

I've been waiting at Whole Foods since eight. I was one of the first "customers" who walked in.

I barely slept last night, knowing I finally had a location. Henry barricaded himself in his room because I was so excited to know she was here. Three cups of coffee have spiked my nerves with ecstasy. Henry was nervous I might wreck on my way here because my adrenaline was so high, so he offered to drop me off. I told him to come back in thirty-ish minutes. He had to go do some digging around for another client, anyway.

Will she remember me? Has she forgotten about me? What will she do when she sees me?

It's eight twenty-eight. I hardly notice it was her when she walks in at eight fifteen.

My biggest concern is the fact that I look like a voyeur, peeking through certain items to prevent Jen from noticing me.

Please don't let anyone call the cops on me. That's the last thing I need is a big scene for me to be taken away again.

I watch her closely, planning for my resurrection. She bags her groceries, slips her card back in her purse and proceeds to walk towards the front door.

This is it.

Jennie

"It's me, Jen."

If it is him, I'm not ready to face it. I thought I had more time to prepare myself, more importantly, more time to prepare my heart.

All the blood is rushing to my heart, trying to resuscitate it. My body feels paralyzed. Thankfully, the stranger twists me around and I try to keep my eyes from looking up. My eyes are blurry from moisture because it all feels so recognizable.

When I'm turned around, I'm looking at the stranger's feet. Those shoes are another trait I recognize. Grey suede Vans and khaki pants. Slowly, I let my eyes wander up, taking in very single inch of him. The scent is far too strong to think it's anyone else.

It's him.

When my eyes reach his, he's staring at me. A smile plays on his lips as his burning hand moves from my arm to my face, setting it ablaze.

I want to smile. Cry. Slap him so hard I leave a mark. Run away. I want him to hold me, but I continue to stand there, in the middle of Whole Foods with my ghost lover holding my cheek, waiting for me to speak.

"It's me. I'm here." He responds.

The influence that had me in its grip is gone, allowing me to confidently retreat from him. His hand drops from my cheek.

"How did you find me?"

I don't know why I ask that question first, but I'm surprised to find him standing here at Whole Foods with me at eight thirty in the morning. Stalker.

He laughs and looks down at the ground.

"I had some help. Been trying to find you for a couple of months."

What the hell does he mean he had help? He nervously put his hands in his pockets, but I remain completely captivated.

"Jen, I uh, I want to talk. I know it's not a good time right now. Will you meet me at *Coffee & Honey* tomorrow at 8?"

Completely forgetting my strict routine, or what day it is, or where I am, I nod my head up and down. The desperate part of me wants to beg him to stay. The irrational part of me is suggesting I skip all my obligations and talk right now.

His voice reminds me of whiskey–my poison. His words intoxicate me; I want him to continue speaking. It's been a long time since I've felt that feeling. Drunk.

"Great. I'll see you then." He lowers his head and walks away from me.

Get me drunk with your words, Cal.

"Calvin, wait..."

I didn't think there was enough oxygen in the air for me to get those words out. The two words I should've told him a long time ago. Cal stops moving and turns around to face me again. I still feel unable to move towards him. He moves to me, grateful for our unspoken communication.

"Yeah?" I watch his throat bob, looking uneasy and uncomfortable.

God, he looks incredible. Healthy and strong.

Licking my lips, every word in the English language seems to disappear from my mind.

You have a final in an hour, there isn't time to talk.

"Um, I'm sorry. God, I just can't believe it's you. I think I saw you a couple of months ago."

"It was me. Like I said, had some help to find you, and I've been hunting for the past three months now. I'm so glad you're still here. Thought you left the city."

I watch him look at me like a treasure. The look I used to love. Sucking on my bottom lip, I look away because it's just too much for my heart to handle. The boy I used to be in love with is standing right in front of me. The boy who left me.

"Look, I'm sorry again about harassing you here. I just... I just needed to find you."

His nervousness is so out of character that it's making my insides hurt. Am I having that much of an impact on him?

"Can I ... um..." Doing a mix of licking my lips, rubbing my lips, and biting my lips, I stare into his chest. Do I really want to finish the question?

No. You should leave.

"Can you what?"

And then as he caresses my cheek, my soul cracks open with light. For the first time in three and a half years, the same person who made my heart black and soulless, has cracked open the dark, callus shell I've created around it.

"Hug you?" I feel like a toddler, spitting out a couple words out for what I want.

I need to feel it. To feel him again.

I don't watch him, but I feel his hands brush through my hair, around my neck and tug me towards him. The minute my cheek reaches his chest, my soul illuminates.

Odd as it is, I'm holding my tears back. His smell. The sound of his voice. His touch. It's what I've dreamt about for months and months. There was always a part of me that thought I would have to forget, but all the parts of him I would recognize anywhere.

I can feel his fingertips indent on my shoulders, holding me so close to his body. I lock my hands together on his lower back, wishing that I didn't have to let go. My head rests on his chest hearing his heartbeat. The best sound in the world. I've always been the perfect height for him, that his chin rests perfectly on the top of my head. His whole body feels like armor, encapsulating me. I desperately want to know what he's thinking, but I'm still trying to process this moment myself.

I just let him hold me, not sure how much time has passed or how many looks we're getting. Bliss has overtaken me, and I don't want to move.

I hate myself for unhooking my hands. As I step back from his chest, he looks more relaxed. He does the unthinkable and moves a piece of hair behind my ear. A tingling sensation creeps down the back of my legs.

No, it's time to leave now! You are going to get lost in his spell. I clear my throat.

"Okay, well I have a test to get to, but I'll see you tomorrow, Calvin."

I grab my bags from the ground and walk around him. My body feels so conflicted. I'm hoping he'll grab my arms and whisk me around and continue holding me. I'm hoping he'll stay away. As I round the corner through the automatic doors, I peek over my shoulder, finding him staring at me.

Why are we leaving?

I don't know if it's a sign, but when I walk outside, the sunshine is peeking through. It feels nice on my skin, even though most of my skin feels like it's on fire. Calvin's scent lingers on my clothes, and I don't know if I want to throw my clothes in the incinerator or hide them under my pillow to smell later.

I stop on the sidewalk, unconsciously waiting for Cal to walk up behind me. Someone beeps their horn at me to cross the parking lot. I decide I should go back to my apartment, but remember I have a final.

"SHIT!"

I hardly curse, ever. Calvin ruined this day. There is no way I'll be able to focus on this exam. Throwing my snacks and purse into the passenger seat, I hold my face and cry. An angry cry. Why today???

Irritated, I find my phone and text Lydia.

Jen: He found me.

Within a minute, she responds,

Lydia: to get from a miserable place to a happy place, you have to be brave enough to travel through a scary, vulnerable, lonely place called uncertainty. Having the courage to choose uncertainty over certain misery is a happiness decision that will transform your life.

Lydia: stop being miserable and go get your answers!!!

I laugh through my tears. Miserable is a complete understatement.

Jen: I have a final in twenty minutes. How am I supposed to focus?

Lydia: you have done far more intimidating things. Turn off your brain to him, focus on your work and then turn your brain back on to him. It won't be easy but I KNOW you can do it. Good luck!

I'm partially irritated by her response. This is Calvin. How am I supposed to turn off my brain when I just found out he's back in Seattle? I'm always thinking about him.

The lingering scent of him on my clothes, along with his fingerprints etched on my cheek, neck, and body. There have been so many circumstances where I had to force myself to stop thinking about Calvin. I don't want to; that's the unfortunate thing.

Another ping comes from my phone.

Lydia: Don't bother coming in tomorrow. Spend time with him. We'll see you Monday (:

Thank God, Lydia. Sighing in relief, I'm barely going to get through my final, let alone having my full attention at my job.

I think about the exam. Mental status of an individual. Types of neurological tests. Behavioral analysis. I'm sure there will be plenty of questions regarding antecedent, behavior, consequence.

Like a switch, my confidence sings in my ear. *You know all of this. Think about where you'll be in the next couple of years. Once you've completed your Psy.D, hopefully you'll be kicking ass with Lydia and Max.*

The ten-minute drive to campus, all I think about, is my future. I've started feeling excited about the future. The future without Cal. A guilty feeling overcomes me as I walk towards campus.

There is no future without Calvin.

Calvin

The completeness I feel in my body is overwhelming. I text Henry to tell him I'm going to walk back to my apartment, needing some time to clear my head. Plus, I don't want to be slammed with a million questions from him. The obsessive stalker in me wanted to follow Jen out the door and beg her to let me tag along with whatever plans she had for the day.

Her scent clings to my sweatshirt and it's suffocating me. Still the same scent from almost four years ago.

Jasmine and peach nectar. I'd have a secret cabinet filled with vials of her scent. My personal drug.

I feel the outline of her and can't help but smile at her request for a hug. I could've done so much more, and God, I wanted to. But didn't want to push her away, no more than I already have.

Jennie has been waiting for you... Angel says.

Not she hasn't, she's just too stuck to leave this place. Devil responds.

Angel and Devil have been on my shoulders since the camping trip. They are constantly chatting in my mind, and I wish I had duct tape to shut them up. At least for Devil.

Angel is my second favorite girl in the world—my supporter of Jen. Devil, on the other hand, is anti-Jen, sneaking her way into my head to tell me I'm better off without her. It was Devil who I blame for everything that happened between me and Jen at the campsite. Even though Devil lives in my body, and I was the one who did the actions and said the words, I hate that she's still around. She deserves to be poisoned for her shit. I tend to tell Devil to fuck off a dozen times a day.

Not realizing how close my apartment was to Whole Foods, the walk felt shorter than expected. I question where in the world Jen lives now? She could be my next-door neighbor for all I know. Entering my apartment around ten, I can feel sleep overcome me. What the fuck am I supposed to do now?

You wait.

Stupid devil, always with the obvious answer.

You can rest now. We found her.

See why Angel is my favorite?

Jennie

Thursday, April 12ᵗʰ, 2007

I wasn't lucky last night to get sleep. Insomnia kept me up all night. This couldn't feel real. I thought about calling him, just to hear his voice again. I thought about walking to Whole Foods, just to see if he was still there. I spent so much time trying to disconnect from him, but I've learned that our connection remains, regardless of time passed or our last meeting.

Coffee & Honey was **our** coffee shop. This is where it all started. Of course, this is where he wanted to meet me. I've been here since I was 18–with Cal. This is where I first met him. So many hours were spent here together.

Walking into *Coffee & Honey* is both haunting and refreshing. It smells like it always does–fresh roasted coffee. My favorite. I'm here early because I'm anxious as hell. About a year ago, Pat wanted to open the shop at six AM. Convinced he was trying to kill me with waking up that early, I worked the late shifts. It's been a couple of weeks since I've worked (because depression and finals), and knowing I'm walking into a conversation with Calvin and not for a shift seems odd. I don't come here for pleasure anymore.

It's rather dim inside from the lights and the gloominess from outside doesn't help either. Low music comes from behind the counter. There are pictures in every crevice of the walls. It's old-fashioned in the way where Pat connected a bell to the door every time it opened and closed.

At first, I despised that bell. It rang so much! I never realized how many people needed coffee.

Then I grew to love that bell. Especially when Cal was running late, and he'd come in a slight jog, hoping Pat wouldn't notice. He'd quickly put on his apron and start making orders. Pat would ask him when he got in and Cal and his wit would say, "I've been here, man."

Ugh, I loved his sense of humor. He was so funny that I felt he always wanted to see my smile or laugh.

When Cal left, that bell and I were not good friends. Every time the door opened, accompanied by the ring of the bell, I looked up.

Every.

Single.

Time.

Whether I was on my break in the corner booth that Cal and I unofficially made ours, or taking an order, or with my back turned behind the counter, I hoped Cal would come through the door.

I never went to the bathroom during my shifts, afraid that he would come through while I was peeing. My neck hated me for the next six months. The constant jolt of my neck from around the counter, or over the expresso machine, or back from taking orders from the table in the corner. It was months and months of the constant wonder.

I stayed late most nights, helping Pat clean up but also waiting for Cal.

Pat wasn't surprised when I told him I needed some time away from the shop. It was the end of my summer of 2005 when I started working less. We had been cleaning the coffee cups at the end of the night, standing side by side.

"Pat, I think I need some time from here. The memories are becoming too much." My voice cracked, and I tried holding back my tears. A lot of shifts were spent crying to Pat, or just completely on edge that I thought I was going to cry.

At first, when Cal was here, he was our fun, overprotective uncle. He let us get off the hook with things like the register being short a couple dollars or not putting the coffee cups in a certain order. Then he was on our asses about cleaning the expresso machine a million times before we closed, or how we should never touch his precious coffee cup that sat next to the register for his morning dose. Other times, he would be a paranoid boss. He hounded us because we talked a lot. Coffee wasn't going out quick enough and customers complained their drinks were cold. We apologized to Pat and made a truce to do our work when customers were around.

He caught on to me and Cal early on. I started working in February and Cal started full time in January. He graduated a semester early, so he was saving up for trade school. We were extremely flirtatious by the end of February, but it wasn't until March that Cal and I had been sneaking around.

A memory that sticks out most is when I had been keeping a graduation present a secret from him. Pat had let Cal close the store, and I liked to close with him because we were alone. I reached for his hand to follow me to my car, but he insisted I worked too hard and gave me a piggyback ride instead.

Cal and I were really into horror movies, like the classics. I had done some antique shopping and found the best, most exceptional classic horror action figures. He had received Hellraiser, Freddy and Jason. He already had Leatherface and Michael.

When he picked me up and kissed me, I didn't realize Pat was sitting in his car, watching us.

Shrieking, I swatted at Cal to put me down and turned so red. It was a triangle of looks between us.

It was hard to tell because it was dark, but we both swore we saw Pat smile. Moments later, he backed out of the parking lot and left us. It felt almost as if he wanted to catch us and confirm we were together.

The next day, he mentioned nothing, but he knew.

Pat gave us a deal that once customers left, he'd let Calvin and me be "together." He would let us take out the trash together and take our time washing the dishes together. He became our secret admirer, telling us now and then how much he enjoyed seeing us together.

"I understand, Jen. I don't think it's been healthy for you to be here. You need some time to get away from this place, as much as I hate to admit that."

That was the only time I let it slip for someone else to call me Jen. My mind was too exhausted. He was so supportive of my decision. I wanted to stay and help Pat, plus the shop was comforting. But there were many things that became triggering for me, and I was constantly crying. When Cal left, Pat was my only shoulder to cry on. And I cried a lot. Almost every day for months.

Pat stopped giving me a shift because he knew I would be here from open to close. I told Pat I would come in when I could, even though he pressured me to take a couple of weeks off. It was hard for him too because I was practically a veteran, and I knew the little details that what Pat liked and disliked.

Pat was the most sincere, kind-hearted person you could ever meet. Although he'd deliver unpleasant news, his approach was gentle. I met him when he entered his thirties. Owning a coffeeshop in the city must age you. He's got a few gray hairs now and substituted his clean face for a solid salt and pepper mustache. He's been trying to go for the hipster look. Pat was about six feet tall, a little taller than Cal. He always been a good Christian man. Didn't have tattoos, didn't drink or smoke. He only cursed rarely, usually just a "damn" if the espresso machine burned him. He was smart and witty, always making people feel welcome. He visited each table to make sure everyone was well-cared for. I think that's why he installed that stupid bell, so he wouldn't miss anyone coming in. He just cared a lot.

I remember when it was my sophomore year; it was midterm week. My schedule was so busy that I didn't even have time to think about Cal at that point. My schedule allowed me to have no classes on Wednesday and Friday, so I worked at an adolescent clinic from eight to five as a registered behavior technician. Most weekends, I was at *Coffee & Honey*. I was always keeping my mind off him.

It was Saturday morning at the end of finals week, but I felt like a walking zombie. My life revolved around working. Around five AM, I arrived at the shop and was about to pour myself a cup of coffee. Pat came from the back room, surprised to see me.

"Jen, hey. I'm sorry to do this, but I've had Brooke training a few girls this week and wanted to give them a shot to work with the Saturday morning rush. I'm going to let you head home. Go get some sleep, relax. You look dreadful. Again, I'm so sorry. I know you just got here, but I don't need the extra coverage today."

I made a mess from the coffee spilling because I laughed so hard in his face.

Oh Pat.

I could barely keep my eyes open; my hair was oily, I was breaking out, and hadn't eaten in hours (maybe days; I didn't even know what day it was). Turns out, it wasn't the best decision to send me home early because I had a panic attack at home and Pat had to come over to help me recover.

Anyway, there was once a time where the bell on the door was just background noise, then it became a trigger, and I cringed at the sound of any bell. As I walk through the door now, I don't know whether to stop and cry, thinking of Cal, or walk happily to the counter to talk to Pat.

I feel unsettled. The bell sends a shrill down my back. *The next time this bell rings, it might be Cal. Don't give me false hope.* Awkwardly walking through the door, I immediately see Pat.

He about overfilled an expresso when he saw me walk in. Laughing as I approach him, he's probably really confused why I'm here at eight in the morning on a Thursday. I don't work Thursdays, and he knows I was going to help Lydia and Max today. His Adam's apple bobs, and concern is plastered on his face.

Once Pat got himself cleaned up, he brought me a chai latte and sat across from in the furthest table.

"Jennie, whatcha doing here? It's Thursday. Are you okay?"

Instead of a causal "hello", I stood up to give Pat a hug. Pat's hugs are the best. He's tall and I was short, so his arms wrapped around my neck, pushing my face into him. He always wore a subtle cologne that smelled manly even though the coffee roast overpowered it. Although Pat was my boss, he was currently fulfilling the role of the big brother. He's been playing this role for a while now.

"Geez, good to see you, too. Am I bothering you?"

I was feeling anxious about telling him the reason I was here. After my hospital visit, we agreed the only time I could talk about Calvin was in therapy.

"Stop it, you know I love to see you. What brings you here? You don't look like you're ready to work."

His grin was so wide and real; his joy in seeing me was clear. He cupped his hands together on the table, relaxed as always. Pat never worries about anything, besides when the expresso machine breaks.

I hesitate and look out the window. *Coffee & Honey* is off 55th Ave, and I can picture Easton in the far distance.

Oh, heartbreak.

I clear my throat to get rid of the forming tears. *Don't hate me, Pat.*

"Cal's back. He wants to see me."

Pat releases his hands and his eyes widen. As he tries to speak, we both watch Cal stroll on the sidewalk, the tinted window being a barrier between us and him. His red truck parked behind him makes my face turn red.

"I didn't realize he was back. Better get out of his spot. I'm sorry for intruding. We'll talk tomorrow, or later. You know I'll be here if you need someone." I grin at his brotherly response. When I look down at my hands, I'm shaking.

Quickly, I frown.

I notice all the changes in my body.

First, I notice the goosebumps that have formed on my arms and the back of my neck. Second, I notice how my leg bounces. Third, I notice how my hands get clammy. I am profusely rubbing them against my pants to eliminate the moisture. Fourth, I notice my throat is getting dry and my nose is getting tingling, which happens right before I'm about to cry.

I look over at Pat, who is perched behind the counter for the ultimate reconnection of his two favorite people. He's leaning against the counter with his hands together. He sees me struggling to swallow and gives me a nod.

You got this, he mouths to me. I drop my head, looking at my fingers and twisting the ring that sits on my right hand.

For the millionth time, the bell rings above the door, but my head doesn't move. Pavlov would be disappointed.

I move my hands to my coffee cup first, then bring my eyes to look at him. He's standing at the main door, looking at me.

I hear Pat say, "Calvin, hey man." But he doesn't respond. He's focused solely on me. He's different today.

Determined. Focused.

I find another burst of courage to grin at him. He's even more beautiful now. The stitches in my heart make me flinch, almost as if they are saying, *do you remember what he did to you?*

I can tell he's nervous. He bypasses Pat and walks over to me. His hands are in his pockets and his shoulders look tense. His complexion is flushed, like he's seeing a ghost. He hasn't stopped making eye contact with me. When he reaches the table, I'm still sitting, looking up at him now. As much as I want to hug him like I did yesterday, I can't.

I stare into his dark blue eyes. His eyes, once full of kindness, joy, and love, now appear empty.

He's got a good beard forming, leaving his lips to be barely noticeable. His hair is a dirty blonde color, reminding me of wet sand. He's wearing a backwards Nike hat, and it makes me want to fall out of the chair. I love when he wears his hat like that.

Then I notice his body. He's wearing an identical outfit from yesterday, khakis and his grey suede Vans, but he's wearing a solid black sweatshirt.

Those arms. They are... large. He's gotten buff. His sweatshirt looks tight and uncomfortable on him. I'm sure there wasn't much to do in prison besides go to the library or use the rec-room. Knowing Cal, he would never choose the library.

Thinking of all the kids I've worked with, and how surprised they were when I had them shake my hand the first time we met, that's what I do. I stood up, never losing eye contact, and held my hand out.

Back in the day, we would've made a bet on who would look away first. He always won because I would get self-conscious. He told me he could stare at me all day without looking away. I was that beautiful to him. I wonder if he still feels the same way.

Catching Cal off guard and making him look away first, he stared down at my hand. One point for me.

Confusion written all over his face, he removes a hand from his pocket and fits it in mine. We move up and down a moment... or two... or three... I think I lost count.

We probably look bizarre if I were watching us from afar in the coffeeshop. Just standing there, looking at each other and shaking hands for minutes.

WHO SHAKES HANDS FOR MINUTES?!

His hand electrifies me. It just felt like he and I were the only ones in the room.

"Hi, Jen."

He whispers my nickname, and I think I gasped. I'll never get over hearing him call me that. He breaks hand contact first. Another first loss for him. I would always let go of his hand first because my hands got sweaty fast.

Two mental points for me.

"Hi, Calvin. Sit down. You want a coffee?"

So many questions are filtering through my mind-questions that kept me up all night long. To where I made myself sick and wanted to bail on him.

I sit back down and place my hands in my lap and cross my ankles under the table. My shoulders hunch forward, and my hair falls forward as I let my head fall, looking down at my ring again. I think Cal mutters no to coffee and I feel him sit down across the table, probably still staring at me.

I look up from my hands for a quick moment because I miss looking at his facial features. His torso and shoulders are upright. His chest is buff, too. He doesn't look like a boy anymore. He's a man. A gorgeous man that, at one point, used to be mine.

His hands are in a ball on the table and his eyes are looking right at me. I look away quickly to get not get caught, but I can feel his stare. He's intimidating me.

"Cal.." I don't realize I call him by his nickname. It just felt natural to do. I'm the only one who calls him that.

At least, I *was* the only one.

There's so much we don't know about each other now. Does he have someone else in his life that calls him Cal? Is he here to tell me he has a wife? I have hope that my heart will be strong enough for whatever he says.

He takes notice of it and blinks twice. He moves his chair closer to the table...

Closer to me.

"Calvin..." I start again, using his complete name. That feels wrong.

"I wasn't sure what to think when I saw you yeste..."

His elbows rest on the table, shielding his face from me. Closing his eyes, he brings his balled hands to his forehead. He remains that way for a few seconds.

"Are you okay?"

With his hands still on his forehead, he peeks one eye open at me. Then his hands fall onto the table. His eyes are open and full of ....

Yearning.

"God, you are so beautiful, Jen." He looks out the window, almost to give his eyes a breath of air.

I can feel my cheeks get hot and my fingers intertwine in my lap. I realized I uncrossed and recrossed my ankles at least four times. Looking out the window, I also recognize our reflection. Of me.

He's been staring at me in the window.

"If you'll excuse me, I'll be right back." Impatiently, I stand up and run to the bathroom behind our table.

For a moment, I feel a shadow behind me.

Please Calvin, don't follow me. I need my own breath of air.

Part of me wants to leave because being with him is too much right now. I wish I had brought my phone with me so I could call Pat and tell him to get rid of Cal. Part of me wants to throw up at the best compliment I've heard from the man I loved. Jonah compliments pretty much everything I do, but it doesn't feel the same. Part of me wants to cry at the fact that I've been trying to fight my feelings for Cal, but now that he's here, I can't resist. I've walked straight into the sunlight with no protection.

I know this feeling inside my stomach though, and I need to get my panic attack under control before I decide what part of myself I will follow.

Thankfully, the bathroom is empty, and I grasp the sides of the sink to hold myself up. Needing to center myself before I crash, I do the 54321 technique.

5 things I can see.

The soap bubbles dissolving in the sink.

The blinking light on the automatic paper towel dispenser. Blink. Blink. Blink.

The speckles of grey and black paint on the stall wall. It looks like wet concrete.

The framed newspaper article of the opening of *Coffee & Honey*. Pat had me hang it here two years ago.

Myself. Watching my chest rise and fall unsteadily.

4 things I can feel.

The coldness of the sink.

The air conditioner fan at a slight angle, moving a few strands of my hair.

The itch right above my right sock.

Goosebumps from Cal.

3 things I can hear.

Beeping from the coffee counter.

A toilet flushing from next door in the men's room.

My breathing becoming regulated.

2 things I can smell.

Coffee.

Cal.

1 thing I can taste.

The cinnamon Pat secretly tried to put in my chai latte.

"You're okay," reminding myself. That's been the ninth one since getting that text message. Despite standing tall, my head drops. I fix my hairs messed up by the air, then open the door.

God, he is kryptonite.

He's standing right in front of me. Well, he's leaning against the wall, but it's close enough. I hold the door open awkwardly and stare at him, embarrassed.

"What are you doing?" I question him. Despite my efforts to get past him, he stays put. I appreciate his presence—it's reminiscent of the past—but I'm uncomfortable with how close he is. I just want to run into his arms and have him hold me.

"You still have them? The panic attacks?" he asks me, worry forming in his voice. My eyebrows furrow inwards and he's biting his bottom lip.

I look down, ashamed. My first panic attack in front of Calvin happened here at the coffeeshop. It was my second week.

On Wednesdays, there was a book club that occupied much of the shop from six to eight at night. A regular, Marley, wanted his usual. A cappuccino. Instead of adding milk, I accidentally added hot water.

"You bitch!" Marley was back at the table when I looked over at the outburst. I watched him spew his drink out and cover his mouth.

"Are you trying to burn my throat!?" Marley looked at me this time.

I felt horrible. I had yet to mess up an order. The coffeeshop was so busy that night. I dropped the cup I was working on and felt my breathing intensify. My chest was on fire. From behind the counter, the shop felt dizzy and almost as if the shop was closing in on me. I ran out from the counter and into the bathroom. I slid down behind the door, sweating, clenching my arms and crying.

I was so consumed by anxiety that I couldn't think straight, and I ended up collapsing on the bathroom floor in a fit of tears. My body shook for minutes, going through its own earthquake. Opening my eyes, I saw a few stars in my vision. It seemed my heartbeat was normal I had no sense of time, and it only felt I was in the bathroom for a few minutes. I gathered myself together and got off the floor. When I opened the door, Cal was leaning against the door frame. His arms were crossed over his chest. The moment he saw me, he jumped off the frame.

"Are you okay?!" he asked me.

"Um, yeah, I think so. Sorry, I don't normally go through that." I lied.

"Pat said the book club needed to end early tonight, so that douchebag is gone." He tried smirking to lighten the mood. I smile at his defensiveness towards Marley.

"Oh, cool. We should clean up the mess."

I moved out of the bathroom and towards the counter. The chairs were all overturned on the tables, and someone had cleaned the counter.

"Pat and I cleaned everything up." He said from the bathroom. I looked back at him.

"How long was I in there for?"

He glanced at his watch. He hummed.

"Close to an hour. 50 minutes, maybe?"

I grabbed my chest again, but Cal grabbed me, holding me up for support.

"Hey, you're okay. Pat said we can leave once you were out of there." I didn't realize I was bracing myself against his arms. The feel of his hands on me gave me instant comfort.

"Do you want me to drive you home?" Cal asked me.

"No, no, I'm good." I pushed myself away from him. I started walking behind the counter to grab my stuff.

"I guess I wasn't really asking. I want to drive you home, Jen." Again, Cal stayed in his place and talked to me from a distance. That was the first night he called me Jen. Pat always called me Jennie, and that's what everyone else called me. I did a double-take at him for calling me by a nickname.

I stayed silent as I picked my nails.

"Please, Jen. I want to make sure you get home safe."

As I bent down to pick up my bag, the thought didn't seem too bad. I was beginning to like being around Cal. He was funny and thoughtful. He was tall, which made me feel safe. Plus, he stayed to wait for me tonight. That had to mean something. I didn't hear him move closer to me, so when I turned around, he was leaning against the counter. His gaze held a hopeful optimism that tugged at my heart. I couldn't resist. I just wanted to spend time with him.

"Please." It was so cute to watch him beg to take me home.

"Fine." I grinned as I walked past him towards the front door.

Opening the door this time, though, Cal wasn't leaning against the door frame. He leaned on the adjacent wall, giving me space to walk out the door without him badgering me. His arms are crossed with his ankles crossed over each other. He's lost in thought again as his eyes move down my body.

"Cal, I'm fine. Let's go sit back down."

On instinct, I hold my hand out for him to grab, but then pull back before he notices. He lets me walk first, then I feel his presence behind me. I settle back in, waiting for him to do the same.

But he doesn't.

Instead, I look over and see him getting a glass of water from Pat. He walks back over to me and places the glass in front of me.

"Drink." His demeanor changed. Very authoritative.

"Cal, I'm fine." I look down at the water. *It sure would make my chest feel better.* The ice cold moving down my chest...

I pick up the water and drink half of it in one gulp. Putting the glass down, Cal is smiling at me, satisfied with himself.

I clear my throat and wipe my lips.

"Thanks. I guess I needed that."

"It's about time I did something right." Cal leans back in his arm and props his arm onto the chair next to him. He's comfortable now.

"Jen, what I said before. I meant it. You are so breathtaking. It was hard to focus on the words you were saying to me, if I'm being honest. You've changed so much over the years."

First, I caught the fact he still calls me Jen. My nickname, the only person who calls me that. He still, is in fact, the only one who call me that. It made my heart jump.

Second, he speaks with such confidence and sincerity to tell me how beautiful I am. He would tell me I was beautiful as often as he could. Whether it was a text or a phone call, or if we were working. He would walk behind me as I would take an order and whisper, "you look so beautiful." I was never expecting it- even now, I'm trying to hide my face.

"So should we talk about where you've been or keep sitting in awkwardness?" I ask him.

"No. I'd rather sit in the awkwardness and stare at you." He brings his arm off the chair and looks out the window. He's trying to deflect the conversation.

I stay silent, hiding the information that I knew where he's been. I've known for three and a half years. All the waiting, and this is the bullshit lie I get? He peers back at me and realizes I'm not letting up.

"Jen, I um..." He's uncomfortable, not wanting to tell me where he's been. I can tell he's getting anxious, running his finger over his love line on his palm. The number of times I traced that love line.

Unable to fight the feeling of staying away, I slip my hands into Cal's. Feeling our fingers connect feels like the time Cal kissed me under the fireworks. My missing piece. I'm trying hard to stop my bottom lip from quivering because this is all too much, but my job has always been to comfort him.

"Hey, look at me." I whisper to him, but quickly wish I hadn't asked him to, because his eyes are filling with moisture. It's like I'm looking in a mirror. His bottom lip is quivering, and he's biting his bottom lip. He looks like he's in pain.

I don't force it, but I try to telepathically tell him I can handle whatever he's about to tell me. He needs to know that I've had knowledge of his whereabouts. I don't know all the pieces, but I've known. There is something holding my tongue to prevent me from bridging the conversation. Instead, I squeeze his hand. That was a nonverbal movement to show each other we were here, and that the other person was safe.

He was safe with me.

Calvin

I thought about all the years I lost with her. She still doesn't feel real. This moment doesn't feel real. She about sends me over the edge when I feel her fingertips walk into my palms, and then fully into my hand. I was not expecting that from her. When I look at her, I can't keep my gaze on her for too long because her piercing emerald eyes are just full of abandonment. Abandonment from me.

"Jen, I was in prison." It was vomit. Like eating bad bread. Hard and flavorless and stale. Not enjoyable.

I expect her to stand up and storm off. I let a few silent moments pass for the words to dissolve until I look at her again. Her hands are covering mine, protecting them. Her face is stoic, not really showing any emotion. She just looked at me. Then, with no inkling, a single tear falls from her eye.

I pull my hands away, unable to keep myself together. My hands cover my face, which ultimately covers my emotions. Taking a deep breath, I fight back tears. I wish I could take it all back. Why was this so hard to tell her?

My body reacts to her touch like I was getting into an ice bath. I tense and make a little jolting motion. She grabs my wrists and takes them off my face. She's so fucking gentle with me-I don't deserve it. I deserve a slap in the face or her ice-cold water poured down my back. With her hands on both of my cheeks, I'm forced to look at the girl I abandoned. And she's face to face with the boy who left her.

"Don't shake your head like that. Or put your hands on your face. That's the same thing you did last time I saw you, before you left."

She only remembers me as 'that' guy.

The one who hurt her.

The one who left her.

God, I don't even remember what my face looked like on that night. Angry probably. I was absolutely livid that day.

Unable to control my urge to touch some part of her, I take charge to untwist her hands from my face and lay them flat on the table, her palms facing up. I place my hands on top of hers, entering bliss. Our hands look like we were going to start a hand slapping game. But I was gentle with her, because I knew she was still damaged from what I had done. I had missed her touch. So goddamn much.

When I place my hands on top of hers, I lean forward to the table to put my elbows on the table, needing the extra stabilization.

At this point, she has several tears falling from her eyes, and makes no attempt to wipe them away. She wants me to see how much she was hurting. How much she missed me! How much she lov...

No, she didn't love me anymore.

"Why are you crying?"

What the hell?! She's crying because you are a piece of shit. You left her with nothing. As Angel shouts internally, I choke as I try to swallow.

Jen shakes her head, thinking hard. "This is just...a lot."

"Jen, I am so sorry. I want to tell you everything. I want to tell you what happened that day to me. Where I was. How shitty life was without you. Until yesterday, life has been my worst enemy. I wanted to talk to you every single day. But I couldn't... I just wanted to find you. Before I go on about my hiatus, it wasn't a coincidence that I was there at Whole Foods yesterday morning at eight thirty in the morning. I had to find you..."

My hands feel sweaty, and I'm hoping she doesn't notice. She keeps her hands still on the table while I kept mine on top. Tears still forming in her eyes, and it was too painful to watch.

She breaks eye contact with me to look over my shoulder. Probably at Pat. She sniffles and then she slides her hands into her space. She grabs a napkin off the table and wipes her tears away.

Two points for me. She looked away first and took her hands away first. *Asshole, we aren't counting points right now. We are dealing with the aftermath of telling your girl that you were in prison.*

"Who told you where I was?" she asks me.

Angel whispers *your lovely boss who cares about you almost as much as I do, but less.*

Devil says, *don't fucking lie to her. Tell her who it was.*

Okay, so they both agree I should say it was Lydia.

"Lydia." I see Jen's eyes go wide, and she tries to pull her hands away from me. Quickly, I grab them.

"Don't, please. Don't take them away." My voice is at a tremble. I hate the hurt I just caused her.

"Cal, you cannot go back to my job. Ever. I may not have rightfully earned a job there, but I have worked hard to keep my reputation good. Lydia and Max have been nothing but incredible for me. We've been talking about me starting as a doctor there once I'm done with my doctorate. You cannot jeopardize my future."

Jen is quiet as she yells at me. I want to smile as she yells at me because it's a character trait she is not confident about, but I remain neutral. I won't argue with her about my desperation to find her. Once she's done, I nod, so she understands I will comply.

"Can I say something else?" She whispers. As if I didn't think my heart could break anymore, it shattered into another piece from the sound of her pathetic voice.

"Yes, please. Say whatever you need to."

She takes in a deep breath and looks down at my hands. *There is nothing you could say that could make me hate myself any more than I already do.*

"Cal..." she starts. She looks back up at me. She rests her hands back on top of mine. Moving only my eyes to witness the connection of our hands again. I about lose my center of gravity when I see the ring on her finger...

The ring I was supposed to give to her.

Has she been wearing it this whole time, or did she put it on just for today? Fuck, my insides shake and I don't know if I can look at her without completely losing myself.

"Wait, have you been wearing that ring since I've been gone?" My mind is going into overdrive.

Please say no... please say you only wore it today. Her face moves to look down at her ring. The ring that ruined everything...

"Ever since the day we got back to the house, I've worn it." She twists her ring for a moment.

You suck, motherfucker. You gave her a part of you she held onto for years.

"Why, Jen? Why didn't you take it off and throw it at my house or in the fucking river? You have no idea where I've been or what I've been doing. You must've lost faith at some point that maybe my promise was a lie? Why would you purposely brand yourself?"

"First off, I never lost faith in you. In us. You had to come back to save me. I want to hear what you have to say, I really do, but before we have that conversation, though, there's something I need to give you. You need to understand something before we continue this."

A wave of confusion hits me. What does she need to give me? This is all I wanted—to have her back. She takes her hands off mine again and digs into her bag. She pulls out a stack of ... papers?

No.

Letters.

"RETURN TO SENDER" is stamped on the top envelope. I bite my bottom lip, holding back the second round of tears, and turn my head to look out the window before she notices my eyes. Luckily for me, her reflection hits from the window, so she still provides me comfort.

"Cal, I wrote you. For three and a half years. Whether you want to call it intuition or faith or stupidity, there was something telling me to not stop reaching out to you. I just felt I needed to tell you what was happening in my life, so that when you came back, all you had to do was read these, and life could pick up where we left off. When everything happened, yes, it was messy and scary, but it also didn't feel like it was the end. Our story isn't over yet. Before we have the talk about how you ended up in prison, I need you to read these." She scoots them towards me, nicely wrapped in a red piece of ribbon–my favorite color. Not sure if that was intentional.

Forgetting my bad habit, I place my face in my hands again and shake my head, feeling so overwhelmed. *Was this a mistake to meet with her?* There had to be 50, 75 letters?

Her touch on my wrists electrocutes my skin, and she pulled my hands down off my face.

"Sorry... bad habit." I barely whisper. My throat is so unbelievably dry. "Jen, why did you keep writing to me after the first letter came back?" I can't stop staring at the top letter, bothered by the content.

"You'll find out." For the first time since being at the shop, she grins. And it's a devilish grin that makes me want to jump across the table and kiss her until she can't smile anymore.

"Look, I know this is a lot. Hell, this entire morning is a lot, but I think you'll understand some things before we have that talk. Just please promise me one thing."

"Anything." I hush.

"No matter if you are angry, sad, disappointed, confused, whatever you are feeling, call me when you are done with them." Her emphasizes on the words *call me* send a shiver through my spine. Those words stab through me like the sharpest blade I've ever known. I let her grab my hands to prevent me from shielding my face. Her hands were so soft, but they trembled. *Do I still make her nervous?*

After our fight years ago, we were both supposed to cool off after everything went down. I told her I needed some space because everything that happened over the span of those two days was traumatizing.

I never called.

"Jen, Jesus Christ..." My antsy-ness catches up with me, moving my hands from hers. I pace around our table, back and forth, squeezing the bridge of my nose, holding on for dear life for the tears to stay inside. I say nothing for what felt like minutes. Then I bend down on one knee next to her and grab her hands as tight as I felt safe.

My mouth was salivating now, and my voice cracks.

"If for some reason I'm hit by a train, you'll be the first person I'll call." She looks down at me with no fear or caution. It's the look that said *if you don't call me, never find me.* I couldn't lose her again.

She pulls me up by my elbows.

She doesn't believe you because you never keep your word.

"Listen, I have to get going. It was so good to see you again and I hope we can talk soon." She gathers her used tissue, even though her face is mostly dry now. She drapes her bag on her shoulder and stand to face me. Her hand caresses my cheek and my God, does it feel like the elixir of life.

"I missed you, Calvin." It was so quiet, almost like it meant just for me. Like she had been holding on to those words for a long time.

Because she was.

I can't suppress my need to touch her. My hands cup her cheeks and my fingertips sit underneath her ears. She's reserved now, not giving me all of her. There isn't the same glint in her eyes she adored me like all those years ago. Her eyes looked up at me, the light giving them a speck of gold within the emerald.

Breathtaking.

"Jen, I missed you more than anything in the world. I promise to read these and call you soon."

More than anything did I want to kiss her.

I couldn't, though.

Who knows what I would read? Perhaps she already started a second life for herself, and her husband was waiting outside for me with a baseball bat?

Instead, I move my hands around her neck, pulling her close for the long-awaited hug. A three and a half-year hug. This differed from the hug from yesterday. I want to pick her up and twirl her around like I used to, but again, it's not the right time. The possibility of her rejection terrified me. The letters felt ominous. Her alluring scent fills my senses as her hands envelope my lower back and tighten. She always fit perfectly under my chin. With her head against my chest, I feel her breathe in. I wrap my arms around her neck and, as perfect as it felt to have her in my arms, I had to be the one to let go. It's almost impossible to let her go.

I clear my throat as our bodies separate, then she walks around me. Through the window, I watched as she wiped her face and got in her car. Not once did she look my way and that broke my soul.

Exhaling, I place my hands in my pockets. I contemplate reading these letters here so I can order another coffee but decide against it. Having no idea what to expect, I grab the stack of letters, avoiding eye contact with Pat, and walk out to my truck.

The anticipation is unbearable. I unravel the ribbon and toss it to the side. Reaching for the top letter, I ravenously rip it open.

My heart isn't ready.

August 17, 2003

Dear Calvin,

I just got dropped off by Glen. We didn't talk much. I slept most of the way. When I woke up, he asked me if I was okay. I shrugged and told him I wasn't sure. I want to be okay. I want us to be okay, but you really scared me this weekend. I want to understand what happened to you. If your "episodes" had anything to do with Glen, he's nothing to me. He was part of my past, and nothing more. You are my future. I'm sorry if having him there was awkward, or just too much. I should have told Anna that it wasn't a good idea.

I'm lying in bed, probably going to take a nap soon. I care about you a lot and don't want anything to happen to you. I hope when we talk, we can sort everything out and we can go back to being silly and lovey-dovey and watch movies together.

Waiting,

Jennie

P.S. My clothes smell like fire. YUCK

A sharp pain enters on the left side of my chest. If I had to guess, she probably hated her first camping trip. I made it terrible for her.

Instead of walking through the woods trying to find gnarly bugs so I could hear her squeal, she cried in the tent.

Instead of sitting on the lake together looking into the horizon at the endless possibilities of our future, I looked at the horizon by myself.

Instead of smearing ketchup on her after grilling hot dogs, she didn't eat a single thing.

Instead of driving home with me, reminiscing about the memories we just made, she went home early. With Glen.

Fucking Glen.

The fifth wheel that tagged along with us. He dated Jen during middle school, or so that is what I've been told. I think he and Andy became good friends when Andy transferred here, and they were on the basketball team together at the beginning of tenth grade. I grew up with Anna, and she and I spent a lot of time together, really just helping each other with homework. No extra benefits. Andy and Anna started dating quickly after he transferred, and that was annoying as hell.

Jen and Anna became friends when they worked at the daycare during junior and senior year. Jen was the only one out of all of us that went to a different school. Her dad lived on the North side of the city, and we lived in the South. It was a small world, really. I met Jen at the coffeeshop, but all along she was friends with Anna. Jen dated Glen, who was friends with my best friend the whole time. It's a messy spiderweb.

He was going through some relationship issues during that time. I'll always hate that he took my girl home. The entire weekend he was always trying to move sly moves around her. He enjoyed making me jealous, and fortunately for him, it worked. Despite everything, Jen's unwavering devotion never faltered. She always came to my side. At least, years later, that's what I should've believed. Back then, I didn't think she wanted me. She really shot my self-esteem down, making me compare myself to Glen.

The night Anna told me Jen wanted to leave early, I didn't even bother to offer to drive her back home. I offered nothing. The only thing I saw was red, I was full of fury. It would not have been a good idea for me to drive, with the culprit in the passenger seat.

A peek of sunshine comes from behind the clouds and my mind wanders to that conversation with Anna all those years ago.

"So, Jennie doesn't feel comfortable staying the rest of the weekend. She's scared of you, Calvin. We all are. You've never done something like this before. She wants to leave tomorrow morning. What do you want to do?"

I was sitting by myself on the outskirts of the lake, watching a guy struggle with his bait. She didn't sit down, and now that I think of it, she kept a rather large distance from me. I had scared her too. I shrugged my shoulders but said nothing.

"Okay, well, we are going to head out tomorrow with Glen. Let us know if you want us to wait for you or if you'll drive back by yourself."

That was the last time I spoke to Anna. I'm sorry I ruined your trip.

I'm sorry, Andy. They needed that weekend to mend their relationship.

I'm sorry, Glen. These weren't your pieces to pick up and try to put back together.

I'm sorry, Jen.

I decide to read the next one.

August 18, 2003

Dear Calvin,

I'm trying to not be upset that you haven't called me yet. I know sometimes you need more time to simmer down than I do. I'm writing in this journal I found under my bed. I used to write letters in here to God about you. Figured maybe he's punishing me somehow.

Today I didn't feel like doing anything without you so I hung out with my dad for most of the day. I thought about driving to your house and talking face-to-face but I know that you'll come around when you are ready. Whatever it is that is bothering you, I am sorry.

I saw another trailer for the Freddy vs Jason movie. I can't wait to see it with you and steal your popcorn and have your sweatshirt on and hold your hand. It's going to be an amazing night!

I hope you'll call soon.

Waiting,

Jennie

I think I'm going to be sick. We were going to the movies that Friday.

I never saw that movie. Never showed. Never called.

August 20, 2003

Dear Calvin,

I probably shouldn't have, but I went to your house today. Your truck wasn't in the driveway so I figured you weren't home. I knocked on the door anyway. Lincoln was confused why I was there. Then I was confused. I guess he thought we were still in Easton because you hadn't come home yet. My heart felt like it was trapped with barbed wire. I had to hold onto the door frame because I was going to fall over.

You didn't come home...

Calvin, wherever you are – I will come find you. When will you let me save you?

I asked your brother if your parents were worried. Or if they heard from you. He said no, and that pissed me off. How long did you tell them we'd be gone? It was only 3 nights. I wanted to call your mom and tell her. I was worried something happened to you and we needed to go to the police. But then Lincoln said you had called your mom. So Cal, I'm confused because you called your mom but not me? I'm sad because you aren't here with me. I'm angry because you still aren't calling me. Please tell me where you are.

Waiting,

Jennie

August 21, 2003

Your first two letters were sent back. A small scribble of "does not live here" was marked on the 17th letter.

It was your mom's handwriting, I could tell.

What is going on?!

August 22, 2003

I gave our movie tickets away because I haven't heard from you. Are you avoiding me? I guess I must've really pissed you off. I decided to go to Coffee & Honey tonight instead and talk to Pat.

Hoping you'll be back soon for a new movie,

Jennie

August 24, 2003

Dear Calvin,

Something doesn't feel right. I went back to your house on Sunday and your mother answered the door. She was pissed off that I came by but she told me you got arrested.

On August 17th. The day we came home early home Easton.

What the hell, Cal?! That's why you never came home. Because you were sitting in jail!!! Why didn't you call me... were you that mad at me that you couldn't call me? I would've saved you.

Your mom .... ugh – she didn't hold back. Your mom said I wasn't worth it. That I didn't deserve you. She didn't tell me a lot but she told that I'm a monster for making you feel like you had to almost kill someone. She said I should move on and leave you alone and leave your family alone. Whenever you'd come home, she would make sure you never saw me again. Then she threw a box of my stuff out the door. Everything I gave to you was in that box... she wanted you to forget about me.

Cal, my sweet, I cannot and will not let you slip away. Your mom is a bitch.

I wish I knew where you were.

This past week has been absolute Hell without you. I don't like the feeling of not having you around. I haven't smiled or laughed or slept or watched horror movies. I haven't stopped thinking about the camping trip and I regret not driving home with you. I think about how that conversation would've gone but if I would've known our last conversation was going to be "I hate you", I would have sacrificed anything to drive home with you and hear anything else. Who knows, maybe you would've said "I don't hate you." I would've felt fifty times better.

Cal, I know your mother does not speak for you. You are clearly very outspoken. I will wait for you to come home. I will wait for you to come find me. No matter how long it takes, I will be waiting here. Come back to me.

I love you & I'm waiting,

Jennie

I scrunch this letter up close to my chest, breathing heavily. My throat was parched. There was an excruciating tightness in my temples. I don't even notice how brightly the sun is shining on my face, but I'm sweating.

She was waiting for today. Or yesterday, perhaps.

She was waiting for me.

She would never give up on you.

August 25, 2003

Calvin,

I'm not sure when you'll read these so I intend to write you everything that is happening. You always wanted to know how my day was—so I'll do my best to tell you. I think it's probably best to not mail them to your house either, or else your mom will literally kill me.

I'm still trying to process you are in jail, so I'm trying to find a new hobby.

I'll let you know what I find. First on my list, rollerblading. Remember when you rode your bike, and you pulled me on my skates? I held on by a piece of rope. It took us <u>at least</u> 2 hours to get back home. We only stayed in my dad's neighborhood! My feet kept moving outward so I would pull on the rope to keep my balance but then you would toggle on the bike, making you drift. Oh my gosh, so fun! Hopefully when you come back, I'll be able to keep up next to you.

I hope you are okay. I miss you.

Waiting,

Jennie

Rollerblading. That's what she's been doing with all her time? Wouldn't be my first guess, but I'm happy to hear she tried to keep her mind busy.

I feel the sun beat on me and I forget I'm sitting in my car. I trace over her handwriting–it was one of my favorite things about her. Her words just flow with ease on paper. She left notes on my windshield all the time. I think I have them somewhere. There should be a box at my parent's house with all our mementos.

The box my mom threw at her...

Jesus Christ, why does she always have to ruin everything?

August 28, 2003

Dear Cal,

I miss you. It's been 11 days since I've seen you. 12 days since I laughed. I would've done anything to make you laugh on our last day together. The memories are starting to keep me up at night.

The looks you gave me all weekend, like I was some sort of enemy to you.

The words you said. Oh my god, the words never leave my mind. It's never-ending ribbon floating throughout.

The violence when we got back to the campsite.

No, I have to stop myself from re-telling that story. I want to remember the good times.

Do you remember when we made breakfast for each other? That was after I got plastered, and Anna was a bitch.

You decided to go fancy with crepes and strawberries. When we were cuddling on the couch, I heard a video on how to cut the strawberries into a rose. Then you curled pieces of chocolate around the strawberry rose.

It was perfect.

I, however, decided to make you waffles with pieces of butterscotch in it because that's what you liked. You didn't like the sugary syrup, so I had to drive out to get the old-fashioned syrup. I poured into a small cup next to your waffles because you liked to dunk them. I put blueberries on your plate and spelled out 'I like u'.

I liked that morning. That was a good memory.

Waiting,

Jennie

She's going to crush my heart. Literally.

I remember that day, Jen. We had gone to a friend's house (I think it was Andy and Anna's friend, but we got invited) for a bonfire but she drank a little too much. I hardly drank at all. I remember asking Anna if Jen could stay at her house, but her brothers were home, and she didn't want to "babysit." Her words, not mine. I could've strangled her if I could, but I was also thankful that she came up with the idea of taking Jen to my house instead. So I did. I snuck her in because my parents would KILL me if they knew a girl was in my room overnight. Her laughter filled the foyer, and I tried to keep her quiet, but I loved hearing her laugh. I asked my brother if we could hang in the basement, until the morning. He hated us for it, but he left us alone. Now that we were in a private setting, I let her laugh her ass off. I couldn't get enough of the sound. We weren't really talking about anything funny, just talking about the basement and she thought it was neat. Then she sat next to me and leaned into my shoulder. She drifted off, and I tried to get up to find a blanket. She didn't let me up, which made me laugh. Frantically, she grabbed my shirt collar and told me to stay. I repositioned us on the couch so we were laying down. With her in front of me, I wrapped my arms around her to keep her warm. Before she went asleep, she mumbled to me, "I want the best breakfast tomorrow." And then she fell asleep, and I started watching rose-shaped strawberry videos.

That memory brings me peace.

She deserved good things.

God, I wish we could've been pen pals. I would've written her back to tell her my version of the story. She would've giggled, reading how embarrassing she thought she was. She wasn't, though. She was perfect.

My heart hurts as I look down at the pile of letters in my passenger seat. It almost felt like a version of Jen was sitting with me. It pains me she's not here with me.

I haven't even made a dent. She's already missing me on day 11. What could these letters possibly say on day 200? 500?

1,331 days.

That's how long I was in prison. On the other side of the country.

Part of me hopes she didn't write 1,331 letters. The stack doesn't look that large. Part of me hopes some of these letters only have one word in them. I could not imagine her pain when the days passed.

I missed her voice. She asked me to call after I finished reading, but I can't wait. The sun makes me feel like I'm getting burnt, but it feels so nice to feel the warmth. I take it as a sign from the Heavens that something good is happening in my life.

Folding the letters back into their envelopes, I pull out my phone. The picture for her contact picture makes me smile, filling in the empty spaces of my soul. God, she's perfect.

Please be the same number.

It rings. And rings. And rings.

"Cal?" When I hear her voice, I sigh with relief. My head falls back on the headrest, already feeling a million times from her saying my name. I think back to giving her number to Henry. *We could've found her earlier.*

"Hey, are you okay?" Then I sense the confusion in her voice.

"Jen, hi. I'm sorry. Just needed to hear your voice."

"You're a fast reader."

"No, I didn't finish them. I just finished the one where I made you breakfast after the bonfire. Didn't realize you were awake when I was watching videos!" I want to reminisce with her. Just to hear her laugh would brighten my mood.

"Finish all of them, please. Don't call me until you've read them all." *Click.*

I stare at the phone, dumbfounded at her quick dismissal of me. There has to be something she's hiding from me. Something that is written in this journal of hers. Is she married? Does she have kids? Has she started drinking?

Then I think to myself...

No, she better not have.

Sweat is glistening off my forehead and my beard itches as I look at myself in the rearview mirror. My fingers shake with adrenaline as I call her back.

She answers on the first dial.

"Cal, I'm serious. Do not call me back until you've read each letter. Please. You'll understand."

"Wait, Jen. Wait!" I'm frantic. The line hasn't ended yet. I need to take off this sweatshirt or I'm going to pass out from heat exhaustion. Turning my key in the ignition, I roll down the window.

"You haven't been hurting yourself, have you?" There was such a long silence that I wanted to punch the steering wheel as hard as I could. *You probably could've asked that in a different way, idiot.*

"Jen..." panic set in. There's no way she has been hurting herself the whole time I've been away. Not for three years. I'll drive my truck off a cliff if that's the case.

"I'm not." And the phone line ends.

"Fuck!" I scream out loud.

I want to read the last letter in the stack. Hopefully, it will help to put the pieces together.

I throw my phone down and pick up the stack of letters. Even if it's only for a few seconds, my hand cramps at trying to hold the stack together. Keeping them in order, I pick the bottom one, hoping they were in order. I tear it open like it has the answers to the most important test of my life.

April 11, 2007

I start scanning for words. Until I realize the date.
She wrote this today. How is that even possible?

Cal,

I can't believe you're back. I can't even begin to tell you how much I felt like I was in a twilight zone. The amount of butterflies that filled my stomach yesterday – those butterflies typically never go away cause you're always on my mind, then about a 1,000 more came when I saw you and when I left, there was a million more. I can't begin to explain to you how hard it was to watch you leave. Again...

Well, I guess I walked away first.

This hasn't been easy Cal. I am writing this at 4:30 in the morning because my body is not allowing me to fall asleep. I just keep thinking about you.

I've thought about you every day since the day you left. You have no idea how debilitating life has been without you.

I know it won't be easy reading these letters. I'm sure at times, you'll want to burn them. But I also hope there were ones you'll want to keep forever.

There are things you are going to hate me for. There are things you will wish you didn't know. There are things you'll want to stop reading because it's too painful.

Here's the thing though Cal, I'm not trying to be malicious for you to experience my pain. I so badly want to hear your stories and experiences I already know it was painful without me. I could see it clear as the moon in your eyes. As you can tell, life hasn't been easy for me.

When we have our next conversation, you'll know what I've been through and what's been happening. I'll get to hear what you've been through.

So please read them.

Jennie

Wow, I'm more upset than what I should be. My shoulders are tense and the muscles around my eyes hurt from squinting, trying to keep myself together. I should just let myself cry for a moment. I fold this letter back the way Jen did and place it in the envelope. Sniffling, I wipe my eyes, then curse out loud. Replacing the letter on the bottom of the stack, I scowl down.

The stack of letters looks back at me with devilish eyes. Her words spiral through me.

There are things you are going to hate me for. There are things you will wish you didn't know. There are things you'll want to stop reading because it's too painful.

What the Hell does that mean? I want to call her to ask her what she means. She will only have one answer for me.

Read the letters.

I figure I can't stay in this parking lot forever, so I decide to pile up the letters in the passenger seat and drive. I need some air, so I go towards the highway. Moving my windows down, the cool breeze feels so nice on my skin.

The desire to drive to see her is overwhelming. I need to make sure she is okay. Being less impulsive than I used to be three years ago, I want her to know that I made changes, and I can listen to her requests.

I'm a better man now because of her.

Jennie

How could he think he can call me already, wanting answers even though the answers were in his hands?!

Because it's Cal... and he's impulsive.

Everything he'll ever need to know is in those letters.

I'm annoyed at myself for telling him I had things to do when I really didn't. Being in his presence made reality not feel real. I contemplated going to Hilltop to tell Lydia and Max about my encounter, but didn't want to drive that far. Instead, I've been sitting in my car, watching people walk by along the street of the coffeeshop.

Jonah's been texting me since last night, but I haven't found the courage to tell him Calvin is back.

I'm irritated at why he asked me if I was hurting myself? There's no way he would've known. That letter doesn't come until 2005. He barely just got through one of our first nights together. Maybe he's being paranoid.

I lean my head towards the window to feel the breeze, wondering if he read the last letter to magically discover all the answers.

I never realized what a void he left me with. It felt like no time passed at all. Part of me wishes we were still at *Coffee & Honey*, discussing everything. Prison, life, school, family. I wanted to leave the letters in my bag and forget they were a thing.

Currently, time is an enemy. How much time does he need to read all of them? I feel I've been waiting days for him to call me back and tell me he's finished. That he is ready to talk. That he is ready for us to pick up where he left off.

It's only been an hour and thirteen minutes.

I HATE YOU TIME.

Calvin

I return to my apartment after a couple of hours of driving around and plop myself down on my balcony. The afternoon coolness is helping me feel better.

Starving for answers, I bring the stack of letters outside with me along with a case of Bud Light. It helps with the nerves. Not to mention the taste of beer after three years is incredible. The letters I have opened are in the back of the pile, the flap clearly demolished. The next one stares at me-September 3rd, 2003.

There are things you are going to hate me for. There are things you will wish you didn't know. There are things you'll want to stop reading because it's too painful.

"What are you bound to tell me?" Speaking to the letter, flapping it back and forth against my hands.

The faster you read these, the faster you can see her again.

September 3, 2003

My Cal,

I spent the weekend with my dad. He's been asking why I've been home so much recently. I haven't told him where you are. I just tell him I'm tired after working with those bratty kids all day and the quietness is nice. We decided to see Mount Rainier. Oh Cal, you would've loved it. I took some pictures to show you when you get back. We did a small walking trail. I thought I was going to be able to do it since it kind of reminded me of the woods where you left me, but the trail was wide open. It didn't feel suffocating.

Anna, Andy, and Glen have been asking me about you. They haven't heard from you. I wish I could hear your voice so you could tell me what to tell them. You know I'm not good at keeping secrets. I should be good to keep it from my dad. He isn't super interested in my life. Those three though... I don't know how long I can keep a secret from them. Especially Anna. I'll do my best to keep your secret.

Speaking of secrets, good memory time.

I tried SO HARD to keep your graduation party a secret from you. Your mom was a pain in my ass for a month! She wanted to do everything and if I even put my finger on a decoration, she probably would've burned it. Instead, she just scowled at me and asked me to not touch anything. At least she let me be there. I had just finished making your picture collage (which was so enjoyable to peek through all your baby pictures!!) and brought it to your mom. Calvin, she YELLS at me to make sure I used tape and not glue to attach your pictures to the poster board. She really thought so little of me.

*I had to drive to **Coffee & Honey** that night but was ten minutes late. I had tried to tell you I was working on a paper for school but you knew I NEVER did homework before work. You were constantly pestering me all night trying to figure out where I was. Finally, I told you that your mom needed my help with something. And you said, "my mom hates you. What help could you possibly give to her?"*

Ouch. But it's funny now. I didn't totally give away your graduation party but there had to only be one reason why your mom and I would be working together. Your birthday wasn't until December. I hope you liked your party.

I'm already planning your welcome home party.

Waiting,

Jennie

Ah. My mom and Jen. They were like water and oil. They did not go well together. My mom wasn't overprotective of my life, especially since she knew I was with Anna most of the time. She hated Anna, too. She thought I was hanging out with too many girls and wasn't focusing on my future. Little did she know that spending time with Jen, I was with my future.

This letter jogs my memory back to the first time Jen met my mom.

Jen and I went to see a movie after a shift on a Thursday in late February. *Final Destination 2*. I was leaving Friday morning to go on a fishing trip with my dad for the weekend, so we were wanting to hang out. My dad told me we had to be at Sea-Tac by six forty-five.

We didn't mean to choose the last showing of the night, but it just meant more time with her.

I left my car at *Coffee & Honey* for the weekend since I didn't need it. Jen was going to bring me home and I would have my dad drop me off when we got back. Jen pulled into the driveway a little after one in the morning. We had been flirty with each other all night. When she got out of the car, we hugged goodnight, like we usually did. The porch light blinded us as my mother stood in the doorframe, her night robe and house slippers on. Her eyes were so tired, I could tell as I walked towards her.

"Who the hell is this, Calvin?" My mom whispered loudly.

Jen stayed near her car but politely waved to my mom. I stood right in the middle, glancing back and forth between them.

"This is Jennie, mom. We work together." Suddenly my mom stepped down onto our porch and again loudly whispered, "Get over here, young lady."

I stayed put as I look over at Jen, hinting caution, but she passed in front of me, our fingers grazed over each other. Jen approached my mom on the steps on our porch.

"This fishing trip for my husband is one of the most important times of the year for him. He always takes Calvin and Lincoln.

Always. If Calvin is even in the smallest bad mood tomorrow or this weekend, I won't hear the last of it. Don't ever jeopardize him being late again. If I need to start a curfew, I will." She hovered over Jen and intimidated her. God, why didn't to swoop her away that night and tell my mom to go away?

"Calvin, get inside. We're finished here. Tell her goodnight and be inside in thirty seconds." My mom turned and closed the door, making sure to not wake my dad. I know she watched through the blinds to make sure we abide.

Jen released her breath and turn towards me.

"I'm sorry, Cal. That won't happen again."

"Hey, don't be sorry. She pretends. She wouldn't hurt a fly." To ease the discomfort, I offered a smile and pull her into me for another hug.

"Thank you for the movie and for bringing me home. I'll call you soon." I kissed her cheek, feeling its warmth.

"Have the best trip. Get lots of fish!" Letting her go, I snicker, and she laughs, too. I move a piece of hair behind her ear, and she stares at me.

I laugh after reading that letter. The first time Jennie met my mom. All it does is make me chuckle.

September 4, 2003

Calvin,

I have some bad news. I had to tell Pat what happened. Where you went. Even though I don't really know where you are. I just told him we had a fight. Something happened and you went to prison. I mean, that's all I really know. He wanted to make sure this 'fight' between you and me wasn't physical, therefore resulting in you going to prison. I told him absolutely not. You would never hurt me that way. Although, there were times on our camping trip that I thought you'd have the capacity to maybe hurt me.

I stop there and open another beer. Standing up to stretch out the tension in my back, I leave the letter down in my chair and look around from my balcony. I need a distraction from reliving that damn camping trip.

Every mistake you've made is from that camping trip. You ruined so many things.

I'm pissed off and heartbroken that she would think I would hurt her. And Pat, too. What the hell?

There are things you'll want to stop reading because it's too painful.

Painful, yes. I'm so glad she never has to see the damage I did to the guy who I went to prison for.

I take a few more swigs of my beer and pick up where I left off.

Pat tells me he would never ever think you have the capacity to hurt anybody. Ugh, Calvin he is so distraught about this. We talk a long time about you. He tells me how much he has enjoyed watching you become an amazing worker. An amazing friend. He says you are a good listener. There must've been times when I wasn't around or didn't work that you guys had some meaningful conversations. We talk about the time you told him you were having feelings for me. Pat can hardly get through the conversation without crying because he just thinks you were perfect.

You are perfect.

Fuck, this letter is hard to get through.

Pat and Jen. The two most amazing people I have ever known.

Pat knew where I was and why. After I called my mom from jail, I called him. I practically begged him to take care of Jen while I was away. Told him to update me every week about how she was doing. But I made him promise me to not tell Jen that we were talking. I hope to God he didn't go back on his word.

I know you're going to disagree because you are your own critic, but I mean it. You're perfect to me.

Anyways, Pat is in with me to start planning your welcome back party. He says we can have it right here at Coffee & Honey !!

We hope you'll be home soon. We miss you.

Waiting,

Jennie (and Pat)

I finish the beer and toss it on the ground. Leaning forward, I grab my forehead and think of Pat. He stopped answering my calls last May. For months, I didn't know where she was or how she was doing. He starved me of the only thing that was keeping me alive. I was paranoid about leaving South Carolina because I wasn't sure if she was dead. My vendetta against him still pains me because I trusted him. All he needed to do was protect her.

I knew he was at the shop yesterday. I could feel him staring at us. When I went to get a cup of ice-cold water, it felt like I was talking to a stranger. He tried to make small talk with me, but I wasn't ready to listen to his excuses.

He let me down.

I put the letter back in the envelope and grab the next one.

September 7, 2003

Calvin,

College sucks. The freshman fifteen is a real thing and I'm so glad you aren't here to see me wear sweatpants everyday. It's not attractive. It's only been a few weeks into the semester but I want to drop out already. It's been hard to focus, and I'm already missing assignments. Pat thinks I'm depressed but I tell him to shut up and bring me more coffee. I think coffee is the only thing in my system.

Thankfully my last day at the daycare was right before the semester started which means I've been at the shop more. Because I'm on the struggle bus, I asked Pat if I could take a couple weeks off to trying to get myself together.

I'm hoping you'll be back by the time the holidays start. I'd hate to think I'll have to spend the winter doing things alone. We had so many plans this winter -- going to your grandparent's lake house, ice skating (even though I hate to do it). We were supposed to look into new cars for me. I have my dad's car anyway, so I guess I can cross that off. Oh, and movies. So many horror movies together! I'll keep praying that you'll be back soon.

Waiting,

Jennie

Jen wanted to work with kids as a career.

On Sunday mornings before church started, kids were everywhere in the shop. It felt like a freaking playground. I handled the coffee orders and Jen handled the kids. She was a natural with them. She colored pictures for some of them, she would dance with others, and she'd always hug them goodbye. Every single one–the familiar ones and the rare ones. She found comfort and security in hugs.

I was in awe of her. Watching her be so nurturing. I'd picture her with our kids. How lucky they would be to have her, my Jennie, as their mother.

She clearly attempted to persevere through the tough times, knowing she's working alongside the Byrd's. Not to mention Lydia offering her a position with them after her degree.

When we met, she had been a daycare worker with Anna. It was senior year for her, so she only had a couple of credits left. After school, she would spend her mornings and early afternoons there, then come to *C&H* in the evenings with me. There were days I could tell where the kids had overwhelmed her. She'd walk in, barely able to hold herself together because she looked pissed. I'd wait at the counter to let her tell me what the kids did to her. She would ramble on and on for several minutes.

"HE DIDN'T WANT APPLESAUCE ON HIS PLATE, HE WANTED IT IN A BOWL!"

"SHE FELL DOWN OUTSIDE AFTER I TOLD HER OVER AND OVER TO WATCH WHERE SHE WAS GOING!"

"THEY JUST KEEP TALKING TO EACH OTHER. I HAVE TO GIVE THEM AT LEAST 3 WARNINGS BEFORE I TAKE STARS AWAY!"

I didn't mind, though. I got to hear her voice, and be the one to make her smile after she released her stress. That was my favorite part. Watching her run her fingers through her hair, clearly tense and trying to savor the peace and quiet of the shop. Then I would do what I did every time–I'd tell her the corniest joke.

"Why do ghosts ride elevators? It lifts their spirits."

"Why did the cookie go to the doctor? It felt crummy."

"Why don't animals play poker in the jungle? Because there are too many cheetahs."

Oh, she would laugh every time. Enough to make her cry and hold her stomach. After a few days of the jokes, I started complimenting her. It wasn't intentional. She was just so goddamn beautiful when she laughed. She has the cutest dimple that sat on her right cheek.

I smile while I open another beer, picturing her smile.

Doing a quick count of the letters I've read already, I'm at ten.

I take a long sip and prepare myself for the next one.

September 17, 2003

My Cal,

I'm sorry it's been a while. Today has been hard. Ever since I woke up this morning.

It's been a month since you've been gone.

I miss you so much it hurts.

She didn't sign her name. I sensed her struggle in writing this letter. Her handwriting is different in this letter. Messy and rushed.

It was a hard day for me too, baby. I should've never been gone that long.

Jennie

What Calvin didn't know is I knew everything about his case. Pat's parents worked for the government. They were now retired, and when I asked Pat about their help, he hesitated. I didn't talk to him for a couple of days because I didn't understand why he didn't want to help me. At the beginning of October in 2003, he allowed me to talk to his parents about finding out information.

Pat's parents lived in Tacoma, so he let me off early to go down there to see them. His dad was a defense lawyer and his mother worked as a county court clerk.

I couldn't keep my emotions together when I arrived at their house. Its secluded location in the middle of the woods evoked memories of our trip's house.

"Hello, you must be Jennie." Pat's mom, Cassandra, wrapped me into her. It had been so long since a woman held me, and I missed the feeling.

"Thank you for wanting to help me."

Pat's father, Clint, stood in the front foyer as I walked inside. Talk about a splitting image of Pat.

I was desperate, explaining everything to them. All the dirty details of the camping trip, without skipping any of it. Details I didn't even know I remembered or noticed. My mind was working faster than my words were able to speak. I told them about driving home with Glen and not knowing where Cal went after we left. His impulsive tendencies and irritability were new behaviors. His anger problem and how frightened I had become to be around him. I told them how I went to his house and his mother said he went to jail the night we were supposed to come from Easton. And how his mom left me with no information. I had to bite my tongue to call his mom names.

When I finished talking, I thought I was having a panic attack. My face felt like a rotten tomato; tears stuck to my face. There was barely anything in my stomach and I felt like I was going to faint.

"Jennie, I hear you. I need you to take a big breath right now and just relax, okay? We will help you. We will find him, okay?" I had overworked myself by retelling the story. This was the first time I had told the story to someone who wasn't involved in the trip.

.

Calvin

I finish the pack of Bud Light. Luckily, there's another pack in the fridge. I leave the stack of letters on the balcony and walk into my apartment. It somehow feels like I was being arrested all over again; those letters being shackled to me. I lean my back against the counter and cover my face with my hands, taking in a big breath. This wasn't the homecoming I was expecting. To be fair, I wasn't sure what to expect. Did I expect for Jennie to welcome me home with open arms and kiss me over and over? Did I expect for us to come home together? Did I expect for us to eat pizza in the late hours and then complain about stomach-aches because that's what we used to do? Did I expect for her to make love to me and then stay the night in my bed?

I guess, yes. I expected some of that. At least, let's kiss and stay the night together. I miss her company so much it hurts. The conversation from this morning was not nearly enough time with her. Prison was lonely and with each passing day, it only became lonelier. Even though there were others around, it felt like total confinement. I could not even imagine how lonely she felt.

It makes me wonder what she's doing right now...

I forget that I have my freedom back, and also that I have a cellphone. Jen is just a phone call away. My phone is on the table and decide to text her this time. Even though her voice would temporarily soothe me, she told me not to call until I finished the letters. I will keep my promise to that. She said nothing about texting, though.

Calvin: Hey. What are you doing?

Jennie: I'm sitting in my car. What are you doing?

Calvin: I'm taking a quick break from the letters. I wanted to make sure you were okay.

Jennie: which letter did you just finish?

Calvin: I just finished the 1 month I was gone.

Jennie; Oh, well the next letter is a happy one. You'll enjoy it (:

Calvin: what is it about?

Jennie: HA! No, it doesn't work that way.

Calvin: Why did you keep writing me... you knew I wasn't going to write back, right?

Jennie: Of course I knew. I guess it was just comforting to write to you. I didn't feel like our story was over.

Calvin: it's not over.

I'm happy she kept an ongoing conversation with me. She didn't respond to my previous text so I walk back to the balcony to read this anticipated "happy" letter. Then my phone pinged on the table. I turn around to check it.

Jennie: Waiting... ♥

September 20, 2003

Dear Cal,

I want to refresh your memory with a happy moment. A moment that I love. I want to tell you my version of the night at the shop when I had a panic attack. And then you drove me home...

But I want you to know that you drove me somewhere else instead. To wonderland. A place that was perfect and beautiful and where I wanted to be all the time.

I get distracted when my phone vibrates and rings on the table. I contemplate ignoring it, knowing I have a happy letter to look forward to. But it might be Jen, wanting to see me so put the letter down and grab my phone.

It's Jen.

"Jen, are you okay?" My voice is in a panic. Why is she calling me?

"Hey." I can hear a smile form on her face. "You read the last letter, didn't you?"

I run my chin, twisting pieces of my facial hair between my thumb and index finger. I can't lie to her and find a smile forming on my face as well. She knows me too well.

I clear my throat and try to act causal, "Yes..."

"Well, two things to say to you. First, still impulsive, as always." I can picture her smile widen. I can't seem to get this grin off my face, and I'm so glad I answered the phone. Her voice brings goosebumps to me, and a feeling in my stomach that I've missed.

"Yeah, I'm sorry. I couldn't wait and thought I didn't have to read these letters in misery."

"Hey!" she exclaims. "Not all those letters will put you in misery. I promise. That brings me to why I called. You mentioned you were about to read the letter after you were gone for a month. And I said it was a happy letter. I want you to know that while there are letters that are painful and will want to make you stop reading, there are letters you will fall in love with. Such good, happy memories that you may have forgotten or didn't realize how pure blissful it felt."

Her voice is calming. Her words only made me want to read the next letter right now. I want to read the letter to her and laugh and sigh in awe of whatever it is she has to tell me.

"Will you stay on the phone with me while I read it?" I take a chance to see if she's willing to play along. Does she have enough resistance to hang up the phone?

I wish I could see how big her smile was. It would probably break me.

"I can't. It's only fair that you relive it again, too." As much as I wanted to read this letter in peace, I'm still disappointed her voice would not be accompanying me.

"Call me when you're done with them. All of them." And the phone goes quiet.

Why does she always do that–hang up without letting me say anything? Probably so she feels in control, and she can have the last word. The last day we were together in Easton, I said the last words.

I hate you.

I'll let her say whatever words she wants to say if it means she never has to hear me say those words again.

Unconsciously, I bring my hands to my forehead and shake my head. I'm getting pissed at myself, so I decide to go back on the balcony and enter this so-called-pure-bliss. I pick up the letter, position myself in my chair, and open another beer.

I don't want to start this letter talking about the attack itself because it was embarrassing enough and that wasn't a happy moment. I want to tell you my version of what happened afterwards.

I remember how you so badly wanted to take me home. I gathered my bag from under the counter and my heart was beating really fast, but it wasn't from the panic attack anymore. It was a different feeling. An excited feeling. I said okay because I wanted to spend time with you.

I was starting to really like you at this point... I had known you for a couple weeks, but it was the best two weeks of my life so far. You made me smile, the cheesiest smile I never knew I had. I smiled around you all the time, I smiled when I drove home thinking about you, I smiled when I woke up knowing I'd be seeing you later. I smiled the biggest when you asked me for my number on my first shift. One of my very best decisions. Anyways, we walked outside, and I waited for you to lock the door. I stayed close to you, maybe an arm's length away. Pat had left you with keys and allowed you to lock up. You looked so confident and sure of yourself. I was in awe of you. For a couple reasons,

Your patience – you stuck around to wait for me until while I got through my longest panic attack ever,

Your generosity – pleading to take me home to make sure I got there safe,

Your kindness – you brought me the best tasting water after I opened the bathroom door,

Your chivalry – opening the passenger door for me and making sure I was warm enough.

My favorite part of this moment was when you asked to hold my hand. You were so nervous, I could tell. I didn't even have to answer because I immediately opened my hand for you.

My hand fit into yours perfectly.

And you held it with such gentleness and care. My heart felt like it was going to burst out of my chest.

I was curious when you started driving because you hadn't asked me for any directions on how to get to my house. I didn't question it though because I was thoroughly enjoying my time. We had talked about our future plans. I knew you graduated a semester early and was deciding to work until fall for college courses to start. You were still trying to decide if you wanted to explore being an auto mechanic, IT or the military. My heart felt sad at the latter – thinking about you leaving and being in some serious situations. Then my mind wandered to you being "my hero."

At the thought of you being mine, my hand became sweaty, and I had to take it from yours to reduce my level of embarrassment. You asked me if I was okay. To quote myself, "yes, I get sweaty hands quickly so if we ever hold hands again, I might have to let go because of that." You looked straight forward and then started laughing... I didn't find it funny. Then you said, "if that's the case, we should start a competition of who lets go of holding hands first. See if we can make it longer and longer each time..." You looked over at me and squinted like it was a fair challenge and then you smiled. My heart skipped a beat knowing you wanted to hold hands with me again. "Deal" I said.

You asked me what I wanted to do with my future. I said I wanted to work with kids. I wasn't sure in what capacity yet, but I wanted to look into child development or child psych. I talked so much about my future, only because nobody had ever asked me, and I had so much to say about it. I wanted to stay in Seattle, maybe Portland to be close to my dad.

Then we started talking about my dad. Without realizing it, you had somehow grabbed my hand without me noticing. Our fingers were intertwined resting on the cup holders. I felt a squeeze from you when I mentioned that I have a special relationship with my dad and didn't want to be far from him. When I got sight that you were holding my hand, you looked over at me. You said, "you have to beat 8 minutes..." Again, all I could do was smile. You made every part of me smile.

You finally asked for directions to get me home and instead of being only twenty minutes away if we first started at C&H, we were somehow forty-five minutes away. But I didn't mind.

You made me feel special.

We talked more about Pat and, the future. How exciting the future felt.

I felt my stomach drop when you parked in my driveway. I hate that the night had to end. Neither of us moved yet which felt...nice.

We still held hands, but I could feel the moisture beginning to set it. I didn't want to let go. I wanted to keep talking to you. You wanted to keep listening (I think...) you told me you had a really nice drive with me. You somehow let go of my hand and reached up to move hair behind my ear. I looked down and smiled, of course. "Point for me." I looked over at you and you were smiling too. At me. You gave me so many butterflies, Cal.

I thought out loud "how I was going to get to work the next day." You dropped your hand from my hair and grabbed both of my hands. Your thumb grazed over my knuckles, so lovingly. "I guess I'll have to pick you up then." You would think my cheeks would've been hurting by the amount of smiling I did that night but nothing in the entire world compared to that smile.

You were going to come back.

I felt giddy and just said "okay." I wanted you to kiss me that night, Cal. I felt in the past forty-five minutes of you driving me home, my level of attraction to you amplified. I'm glad you didn't kiss me because our first kiss was... perfect. I had to find the willingness to open my door and get out. I pulled my hands away from you and by the time I stood out of the car, you were already there.

You walked me up to my door, and we were both smiling like idiots. Ugh, such idiots.

Then you hugged me. Your hug has no words. It was safe. It was clear you wanted me to feel safe in your arms. And I did. I didn't want to leave your arms. I remember you rested your chin on the top of my head and I found the courage to bring my arms around your lower back. We scooted a little closer. We stayed that way for a few moments. Few of the best moments in my lifetime. It took everything in me to pull away. Again, we both smiled. Again, I was hoping you would kiss me. Instead, your moved hair behind my ear and you said goodnight, and that you would see me tomorrow. I never knew what butterflies felt like until you looked at me when you said those words.

I couldn't wait to see you again. And currently, as I write this memory, I feel the same way. I can't wait to see you again, Cal. I can't wait to feel safe in your arms again and for you to move these pieces of hair from my face.

One of my favorite stories to share.
Waiting,
Jennie

Fuck. That was a mix of happy and sad, and I'm smiling and crying at the same time. Her version slightly differs from mine. Protecting the words in this letter, I refold it and place it back in the envelope. I laugh to myself, thinking how innocent her thoughts were about me. I wanted to do so much more than just drive around that night. Trying to fight the temptation to call her, I wander inside for another beer but pick up my phone instead.

"Hello?" Her voice gives me goosebumps. Every time. There was a long period of time that I didn't think I'd hear her voice again.

"Hey. I uh, finished that letter."

'Yeah? And what did you think? Are you happy now?"

"Well, I definitely smiled... and cried. Not that you need to know that. That was a special memory for me too."

I look down at the stack of envelopes, wondering how many happy memories there are. We had some amazing times together. Then her words pop into my head again. *There are things you are going to hate me for. There are things you will wish you didn't know. There are things you'll want to stop reading because it's too painful.* I don't want to read those times.

"You still there?" Jen interrupts my thoughts.

"Yes, I'm here." Guilt rising in my throat for her to ask that.

"I wanted to share my version."

"I want to hear it, but when you are done with all the letters."

I'm not a fan of the stubborn Jen.

"Jen, please. Let me just say this memory and I'll leave you alone." I immediately jumble over my words to finish my sentence, "Until I'm finished reading so I can call you back."

"Nice save." She's referring to my phrasing. I know she doesn't want me to leave her alone. I've already done that. For three years.

"Please, can I proceed?" On my couch now, I get comfy by putting my feet up on my coffee table, tilting my head back and close my eyes to remember that night.

"When have you ever been one to ask permission to do something?" She laughs out loud, and I think I'm getting kissed for the first time because a rush of blood drains in my face and moves in between my legs.

"I'm a changed man, Jennie." Holding my hand over my mouth, embarrassed someone is going to see me so giddy.

You're an idiot. You are here by yourself. Nobody is going to see you.

"Fine."

"Jen... I never realized how breathtaking you were until that night. You're right, I don't want to talk about the panic attack as much as I want to tell you how scared and at a loss I felt. I wasn't sure what to do to make you feel better. It was a nightmare to hear you sob through the door. What you didn't know is I sat on the other side of the door, waiting for you to get done. I was in no rush. Pat told me he had something urgent to take care of and threw the keys at me. Told me not to leave until you came out. I had no plans of leaving you behind anyway. I kept thinking about how I wanted to make sure you never felt like that again. I also thought about why I didn't punch that guy in the face. I could've easily destroyed him..." I clear my throat, going off tangent.

"So I waited for you. The moment you went into the bathroom, I was going to be the one to take you home. It wasn't up for discussion. I usually got my way." I smiled, waiting for her to say something about that comment, but she remains silent. It was agony not being able to see her face, to see her reactions to my version.

"You were right, though. I was so nervous to hold your hand. My attraction to you was almost too much to handle, hence my quick forthcoming to introduce myself and show you around the shop. But that night, your eyes were just...special. Not that I ever want to see you cry, but the way your eyes looked after you cried, I can't explain it. I'll do my best here. Forgive me, though, you've had more time to write your words than I have." Closing my eyes to visualize hers, well it doesn't take long. My insides are screaming with sunshine.

"You already have the most perfect emerald eyes. When you came out of the bathroom, they were glossy. Reminded me of plants almost like right after it rains. How steady the raindrops sit on the petals, just waiting to be evaporated. I love the look of water on plants. And that whole night, I just wanted to look at your eyes. They are still so fucking special." I pause to regain myself, still hearing nothing.

"I wanted to just drive with you. No clue where I was going, but you didn't seem to mind. I remember driving around in high school and thinking how cool it was going to be having no curfew and doing whatever the Hell I wanted. I loved listening to your voice. About the kids, your dad, the future. I was hopeful about your future, especially if I thought I could be part of it." I pause to decide where to take my story.

"You okay?" She was still there.

"Yes, sorry. Just memories. I want to tell you my version of dropping you off. So yes, I parked the car in your driveway, and we sat there in silence. Gosh, I didn't want you to leave. I contemplated asking you to come over to my house for awhile, or if you wanted to keep driving, or if I could come inside. But I didn't ask for any of those things. Instead, I looked at you, at your special, beautiful eyes. Jen, how badly I wanted to kiss you. From the very beginning, I wanted to kiss you. I never wanted you to think I was taking advantage of you because you had a panic attack only hours before, but I wanted you to feel safe with me. You opened your door, and I wanted to be right there for you. Then I don't know what came over me, but I engulfed you. I felt you could use the hug, and what better person than me, of course."

Finally, I hear her laugh, and it's pouring rainbows and confetti on me. I'm at ease knowing she's still listening. *You have so much making up to do.*

"I wanted to pick you and spin you around the first time right then and there. I'm glad the next time we hung out, I found the courage to do that. It's one of my favorite special things we do. Or I guess did..." Picturing myself picking her up so many times before and spinning her around like we were on Broadway, ugh, it made my heart cracked.

"So, I guess in my version, I want you to know how beautiful you were. And still are. How I fell in love with your eyes right away, and how I wanted to be the only one to make you feel safe. No one else could replace that feeling."

With a burning passion, I hate I'm on the phone with her. That I can't see her face, and just grab her and tell her I'm sorry.

I hear a sniffle through the phone. *Please be happy tears...*

"I like your version." I sigh with relief.

"Every word is the truth."

It sounds like she's trying to get herself together—sniffling harder and breathing quicker.

"Ugh, this is why I needed you to read all the letters, so we don't get lost in you calling me after certain letters to hear your version."

"Why?"

There's a long silence. Each second is a break in my heart. *Please don't tell me there's someone else.*

"It just makes me fall in love with you all over again."

To hear her say she's falling in love with me again makes me grab my chest, right above my heart, because it sounds like she doesn't want to. *When did you her words become so painful to hear?*

"Can I please see you?"

"It's not a good idea right now." Disappointment and hurt enter the cracks of my heart.

"How many more letters do I have to read until I *can* see you?" She likes games. Let's see if this one works.

I hear her smile.

"Ah, your ultimatums." She knows my game.

"So... how many?"

"Finish the rest of 2003." I remember the stack of letters is still outside on my balcony. Frantically, I say, "how many is that?!"

"Well, you just finished letter thirteen. You have ...." She pauses. I think she's counting?

"Fourteen left. If you read another one, you'd have read more than what you have to finish. That's exciting!" Her sarcasm is real, and it's real annoying.

"Jen, c'mon, you can't be serious."

"One hundred percent serious." I stand off the couch and pace around my living room, running my fingers through my hair.

Is she worth it?

I hate that she's calling the shots, but I guess I deserve that. She's learned to stand on her own two feet.

Because you left her with no other option.

14 letters left.

It's taken me most of the morning and all afternoon to read thirteen letters. If I continue at this rate, I'll be reading into the middle of the night. Maybe into the early morning because I'm almost out of beer and need to make a trip to the store to get more.

"Are you serious, though? If I finish 2003, I can see you?" She needs to be serious. I will illuminate my entire apartment to keep myself awake to finish those letters.

"Can I tell you a secret?"

Is she deflecting? Does she not want to see me? Just because I want to hear her voice, I play along with her game.

"Sure." I bring the phone away from my mouth, so she doesn't hear my frustrated sigh.

"I've been sitting in the parking lot of *Coffee & Honey* since this morning. I watched you stay at the table for a bit, then I watched you sit in your truck and start reading the letters. I kind of saw your reactions, your expressions. I watched when you called me. From twenty feet away, we were talking to each other. I watched you laugh and smile. You got overly frustrated, and I think it was the last letter. But, um, I just haven't been able to move. This place has always felt safe for me. It was a thousand times more safe when you were here... with me. I guess that's why I didn't want to leave. I wanted to follow you to wherever you were going to go because I feel like I have to, considering I don't know if you're more or less impulsive in the past three years. It seems like you've been at home, which is good." She's crying now. Hard tears coming from her eyes, making me visualize the plants.

"I saw you leave." My voice says it as a question.

"I just drove to the other side of the parking lot."

"I'm coming to you." Finding whatever shoes I can, I slip them on and grab my keys.

"I wouldn't do that. Because now that you know where I am, I have to leave."

I don't like this fucking game.

"Jen, why are you doing this to me? Why are you punishing me?" Turning my back against the door, I barely have enough energy to hold the phone up. She's exhausting.

"Read the fourteen letters. Then I'll come back. Read them at your apartment, at the lake, in the mountains, at *Coffee & Honey* in Easton. I don't care where you read them. But please, read them and I'll find you." Then the call ends.

I throw my phone across the room. With my elbows on my knees, I grab a handful of my hair. And then I fucking scream. Panting to regain my breathe, I do the 54321 technique.

5 things I can see.

The letters sitting in my chair on the balcony.

The dust piling up on my tv stand.

My phone lying helplessly on the floor.

My hands, clenched into two fists.

A picture of me and my dad, the first time I got my swordfish.

4 things I can feel.

The tension in my shoulders.

The slight breeze of my back door being open.

My left sock is scrunched in my shoe, so that's uncomfortable.

Hmm, I'm hungry.

3 things I can hear.

Traffic.

A dripping from my shower.

Jen's voice, telling me she's been sitting in the goddamn parking lot this whole time.

2 things I can smell.

Pineapple.

Vanilla.

1 thing I can taste.

Beer.

I'm centered. I'm good. *You're okay.* I've watched Jen give that whole spiel a million times. Although she's frustrating, of course she's worth it, and I'd do this method over and over to keep my composure for her.

I get off the floor, pick up my phone and place it on the table. My body needs more energy, so I head out the door to get more beer and food. She makes me ravenous. Not to mention, it's going to be a long night.

Jennie

I hate playing this game. I never enjoyed being in control with Cal. He always made the first moves, the decisions. It was easy to be his mannequin. But since he's been gone, I had to figure out how to make choices on my own. It's still uncomfortable, but I'm enjoying this small leash I have on Cal.

He'll never understand the loneliness that accompanied my life when he left. People asked if I was okay, but after a time, they stopped asking. Anna and Andy stopped asking me to hang out. Glen stopped coming over. My dad... well, he wasn't around. Pat was the only one.

I thought about going back inside to talk to Pat about what just transpired, but God, he's been listening to me for three and a half years. He probably hates the sound of my voice by now. Hates the sight of me coming around every day.

I think of the letters remaining in 2003, what all Cal has left to endure. He'll have to read about Glen. That's going to hurt. He'll have to read about me going to Crypticon by myself and how I reveal to him that I know where he was. He'll have to read about the stupid costume party Pat insisted on. That will be a real treat for him. The beginning signs of my depression. The time I said I love you, which is not a happy letter. And he'll have to read about how I spent his birthday. The last letter in 2003 is our first kiss.

I get choked up thinking about why I wrote so many sad letters in the beginning. A deep, unending sadness consumed me. Every minute of every day. And he gets to read about it.

I decide to head home. For two months, I have harbored negative feelings about my home. Barricading myself inside my home, I isolated myself from the world. I wanted to venture out, but knowing Cal was home made me fearful. But there's nowhere else to go. As soon as Cal finishes with 2003, I'm leaving. We can meet somewhere that isn't this depressing hellhole.

September 25, 2003

It's Anna's birthday today. I told her I wasn't feeling well but she knows why and thinks it'll be good for me to get out. I haven't left my room since the 17ᵗʰ, a month since you've been gone.

I'm hopeful you'll be home soon.

I'm torn between my lavender jumpsuit or flare pants and a crop top with a sweater? What would you say...

Calvin

She'd be wearing my shirts because they were her favorite.

You'd probably say either nothing (because you'd convince me to not go if you were here) or your shirts or sweatshirts. I think I'll do the flare pants, tank and sweater. It's kind of chilly today. We are going to a comedy club off Roosevelt. You'd probably hate it. We are supposed to do dinner before, or after, I'm not really sure.

You aren't going to like this, but Glen is picking me up. He lives closer to me, and we figured it would be fine to just carpool together. I think he's supposed to be here at 7:30? I hope he doesn't ask to come inside, especially with my dad.

By the way, he asks every day about you. He says he misses your face and hopes you'll come by soon to visit him.

I'll write you tomorrow to let you know how terrible tonight was.

Waiting,

Jennie

I consume a whole beer during that one letter.

Fucking Glen.

There's a strong feeling I'm not going to like where this goes. A letter concerning Glen is forthcoming; I may get nauseous, so I'll keep a bucket handy.

I try to look on the bright side of these letters. If I were there helping her pick out her clothes, I would've told her to wear the pants, tank top and sweater. She owned this oversized beige sweater that had these large, chunky buttons. I reminisce, holding her with that sweater on and playing with those buttons. No distraction was never big enough from her eyes. She probably looked perfect for Anna's birthday. She always did.

Anna. I never missed saying happy birthday until I was gone.

I found a silver lining in that letter, and I'm proud of myself for it. I'm hopeful I can continue for the remaining 13 letters.

"If you read another one, you'd have read more than what you have to finish."

I've read 14 and I have 13 left. Over halfway done.

I've retreated to the comfort of my bedroom recliner. The bright overhead light helps me concentrate on reading every word in these letters. My spacious side table holds all my beer and takeout containers. I lift the next envelope, my heart racing in dread of the news it holds.

September 26, 2003

We stayed the night at Anna's after dinner. That was always the plan Anna made with me, just so I wasn't alone that night. We weren't expecting Glen to invite himself in, but he did. It was uncomfortable, Cal, I hated it. Anna and Andy ended up going to bed early and I was making myself a bed on Anna's couch. I don't know what else I could've done for Glen to get the message that I was just trying to sleep. I went to change my clothes. I was not expecting him to still be there, but he was and then I came out of the bathroom in my silk pajamas – a peach tank top and shorts. You would've liked them...

Oh, I wanted to hide myself from him.

I sat down the couch, covering myself with a blanket. And he leaned back on the couch, then faced towards me.

I want to call Henry and accept his offer to find my "friend". I'll break his fucking neck if she mentions anything close of touching her. Trying to stay calm, cool, and collected, my hands grip tighter on the paper.

It was awkward for a few minutes. He started asking about you. I started crying, of course. And then I grabbed his hands and kissed him. It wasn't anything special or magical – nothing like your kisses. But I just needed to feel something. I don't what Glen's feelings were towards me but then he grabbed my face and started kissing me hard. We just got lost. I was kissing him for the wrong reasons. To fill the void that you created. I wanted the emptiness to go away.

Glen was caring and smart. I never realized how different he was from you. Not that you aren't caring and smart, but he was just so serious about everything. I never once saw him laugh at the comedy club whereas I was laughing my ass off. It felt so nice to laugh. You would've been embarrassed of me, laughing at the corniest jokes but I think that's why I was laughing so hard because it reminded me of you and your jokes...

We just kissed; I promise you. There was nothing else. I had to stop myself from making a huge mistake.

There was only you to make me feel that way.

Glen was pissed when I told him to leave. He pleaded with me to stay the night, to keep me company. He said it would make me feel better. I said no. I wanted to be alone. Or at least be with Anna. He huffed and I held my breath until I heard his Jeep down the street.

I fell asleep crying. That isn't unusual. I had been crying for days, Cal.

Anna heard me. She told me she heard everything, between me and Glen. She told me about her diabolical plan.

She had asked him to pick me up. She had told him to hold my hand during the night. She told him to sit next to me at dinner, and not next to Andy. She told him to willingly come into her house to spend time with me. She felt awful. She didn't realize it was going to end that way.

I cried more. I told her, "I don't want Glen. I want Calvin."

I wasn't even upset that Glen's motives weren't authentic because I wouldn't have cared anyway and would've continuously pushed him away. I was upset that Anna felt she needed to force Glen to like to me to make me forget you.

I couldn't forget you. And I wouldn't let myself forget you.

So, in this letter, Cal I am sorry. I shouldn't have done it. My lips and body were only for you, always.

Waiting,

Jennie

The urge to call her sets in. She doesn't need to be sorry. I understand the need to find someone to fill the void. At least she had other men around her. It was torture to not even interact with women at prison. Not that I wanted anyone to fill my void, expect Jen. Her temptation was more prominent.

I want to call her and thank her for only kissing. It pains me, but I don't know what I would've done if that letter read anything more than a kiss.

I, however, don't want to call her right now because I need to calm myself about Glen. How could that fucking prick make her feel that way? How could you not fall in love with her?! He was an ugly mutt during the camping trip, trying to do everything and anything in his power to make her look at him. He followed her around as if chained to her. But he was disgusting. I look back now and realized how much of the time she spent looking at me. He wouldn't stand a chance against me. I'm disappointed in Anna, too. She knew my feelings for Jen were real and how I would do anything for her. To put her in such a vulnerable spot to get over me... with GLEN?!

These people haven't changed. They pulled the same shit with me in Easton, and it pisses me off.

September 30, 2003

Cal,

My rollerblading hobby didn't stick. I got defeated. I'm sure if you were here, I would've been able to do it. But I just couldn't do it. I'm on the hunt for a new hobby. I'm going to try knitting. I've been watching a lot of videos and it seems simple. I just came back from getting yarn and needles. I got red yarn for you – hopeful to make you something. I don't know yet. So when you see it, I need your best compliment! I bought blue yarn to make my dad a hat.

He hasn't been doing well.

Waiting,

Jennie

Henry has been blowing up my phone. *Did you talk to her? Does she look okay? Are you with right now? Let me come over.* Bypassing his thread of messages, I click on Jen's name.

Instead of calling, I text her.

Cal: So did you ever knit me something?

Her response is almost instantaneous. It makes me wonder if she's still in the parking lot.

Jen: HAHA! What do you think?

Cal: Well, there's one side of me that thinks you did because you wanted to make me something special. There's another side of me that makes me think you didn't because you got defeated...again.

Jen: you're right.

Cal: About which one?

Jen: I got defeated. The needles and I did not become friends.

Cal: That's a shame. I was looking forward to giving you a compliment.

Jen: That doesn't mean you still can't compliment me...

She was always a good flirt. It was so natural, almost like she didn't need to do any work to show much she liked me. I try to think of the best compliment she would want to hear right now.

Cal: I wanted to tell you that even though I couldn't see your smile when we were talking on the phone, it's still one of your best qualities. Second best to your eyes. I love them so much.

Oh god, Cal please don't scare her away. You said the L word.

Jen: (blushing) I was smiling like an idiot.

Cal: Me too, just a couple of idiots.

Jen: Get back to reading.

I like how she didn't completely dismiss me. This conversation gives me hope and confidence that she's okay with texting regularly.

I set my phone down, ate some chicken, took a couple of sips, and then grabbed the next letter.

October 1, 2003

BEST MONTH OF THE YEAR HAS ARRIVED.

I'm making us an itinerary of the upcoming weekends filled with the best Halloween-related spooky adventures. This weekend there's a cool ghost tour we can take. It starts at 9 and it's a walking tour. You can meet me at the Four Seasons Hotel – that's the meeting point. I already got our tickets. I'm already excited to hold hands for a whole hour. It'll be a new record for us!

There's a neat Day of the Dead festival at the end of the month. I figured I could do our makeup and we can find some cool costumes. That sound fun to you?

Next weekend is Crypitcon I feel excited about something for the first time in the past few weeks. I hear there's going to be some pretty awesome booths there. We'll escape into our world.

Pat just announced he wants to start doing a costume party every year on Halloween. I'm trying to decide what we should be... Bonnie and Clyde? Zombie bride and groom? Vampires? Hopefully you'll be back so you can decide for us. You always have the best ideas.

I'll be waiting at the hotel on Friday for you! That will be a really really nice surprise, don't you think?

Waiting,

Jennie

Painful. Heartbreaking. Excruciating. Unpleasant. Upsetting. Whatever word you want to use. I sweat after that letter. So many fucking questions.

Why did she buy tickets? She had to know I wouldn't be home in 2 days.

Was she in denial that I wouldn't be coming home? Is that the point of this letter? She wanted to create this great itinerary plan to make herself believe I was coming home? Why did she do this to herself? I pick up my phone and text her again.

Cal: That letter makes me mad.

Jen: Let me guess, you just finished October 1st?

Cal: Yes.

Cal: Why would you do that to yourself?

Jen: I didn't want to do things we had talked about alone. I wanted you to be there with me. I pretended you were there with me...

Cal: But I wasn't, Jen. I couldn't be there. I already hate myself for it. I don't want to hate you for it too but I'm having a hard time.

Jen: you should hate me. It was a miserable month. You'll see.

Jen: there's only 4 letters for October because I was so depressed. Each day that passed was a reality check that you weren't coming home.

Cal: Baby, I'm sorry.

Jen: you have no reason to be.

Jen: keep reading.

My heart hurts. My heart hurts for her. She put herself in so much goddamn misery, and I hate myself for it.

You did this to her.

Jen: don't hate yourself.

Was she reading my thoughts?

Not looking forward to reading these next three letters in October, I decide to take a breather and stretch my legs. Where did the delusion come from? Did I really mean that much to her she pretended I was with her during these "adventures"? These weren't adventures. They were fucking hallucinations. I can picture her waiting at the Four Seasons Hotel for me... did she even go on the tour? Did she pretend to hold my hand but was just holding air?

I pace back and forth in my bedroom, asking myself the same questions.

Why would she do that...

Then her fucking words surround my questions.

There are things you are going to hate me for. There are things you will wish you didn't know. There are things you'll want to stop reading because it's too painful.

I can't be mad if she gave me a warning, right?

This is painful, though. To listen to her life without me.

Without sitting down, I pick up the next letter and read.

October 3, 2003

Calvin,

It's almost two o'clock in the morning and I just got back from Crypticon.

Best day ever.

I watched a prosthetic tutorial by a girl named Claire. She made an incredible werewolf transformation. I took a few pictures of it so I can show you. Can you believe she only took 50 minutes from start to finish? You know how much I love the makeup application process, so it was just really cool to watch it up close and personal.

Then I got my caricature done. The artist, Dan, made me a super gothic witch. He drew an incredible witch hat with spiderwebs but he made have large green eyes, a dark winged liner, my lips were covered in black lipstick. I can't really describe the facial expression he gave me. Almost devious, deceptive? A good poker face?

He asked me to think of a secret I've been hiding. He needed some inspiration.

I told him my boyfriend was in prison for the next five years. In South Carolina. Kersaw Correctional Facility. For assault charges.

Wait, what?

What the actual fuck.

I run into my bedroom and pick up my phone. I don't care enough to debate if I should call her—I do it anyway.

It rings. And rings. And rings. Until I get her voicemail. This time her voice doesn't give me goosebumps. It makes my blood boil. I toss my phone, not bothering to leave a message.

Anger is penetrating my soul. I turn back to continue reading, grabbing my chest and completely flustered by her honesty. Or dishonesty? I don't even fucking know.

It felt like a wave of relief to tell someone. Even if he was a stranger. He kept drawing and I started talking. I started telling him how I found out where you were. How long you were going to be gone for. Why you were gone. I don't have all the details of the why you were charged but I can put your temper and irritability together to make a pretty interesting story in my head.

Your mom only told me you were arrested. No other details. I thought you'd be gone for a couple of days. Figured your impulsive tendencies got you in some trouble but then a month went by... I knew something wasn't right.

I begged Pat to let me talk to his parents about finding some information on you. At first he wasn't on board and so we didn't talk for a couple of days but then he came around. I was so grateful for him.

When they found out more information and told me where you were and for what, I cried hard. I thought my chest was going to collapse. It was so embarrassing to meet his parents and I'm hunched on the floor, sobbing. But then I realized that I was crying happy tears. You were alive and you were somewhere safe (at least I hoped you were safe...) I prayed to God you played well with the other inmates. I hoped you weren't stupid.

SWEAT IS POURING DOWN MY BACK AND MY INSIDES ARE ON FIRE.

I WANT TO PUNCH A FUCKING BRICK WALL. HELL, I'LL PUNCH ANY WALL!

SHE KNEW THIS WHOLE TIME. IT ONLY ADDS AN INSANE AMOUNT OF QUESTIONS.

WHY DIDN'T SHE LET ME GO? SHE COULD'VE LET ME GO...

So now you know. And every letter after this, you will know that I know where you are.

You should know that I've started a countdown. 2008. I don't know a day or anything, so I'll just keep the year in mind.

I'll wait until then. I can wait for you. And even though I know where you are, I won't be sending these letters because Cal, if I were to EVER read a letter from you while you were in prison, I probably couldn't get through it without crumpling it up and lighting it on fire. My heart could literally not handle that. I will keep writing to you in this stupid notebook and when the time is right, you can read my letters.

I'm sorry I can't send these letters to you. I'm going to stay in this fantasy, pretending you'll be back in no time.

Waiting,

Jennie

P.S. I also got a tattoo. Of a black widow. Not only your favorite spider but to give me hope. A black widow can represent that even during darkness and solitude, wisdom and strength can be found deep in one's soul.

I WANT to crumple this letter up and light it on fire.

Rage boils inside me. Am I angry at her? Am I angry that I wasn't here? Am I angry with myself? Yes, to all of it.

If we could've just gotten through that night at Easton, I would've been here the entire time. One fucking night ruined the next three years for us.

I let my anger take control of me.

There is no positive about this letter. I crumple this letter into a ball and throw it on the couch. It's not one I want to re-read. I walk back to my room to find a text from Jen. She must've responded while I was reading.

Jen: I'm sorry.

I want to punch two brick walls at reading her apology. I am fuming with irritation knowing she looked me straight in the eyes at the shop earlier that she knew where I was!!!

"Jen, give me a happy letter. Please." I beg out loud. Calling her and talking to her feels impossible right now. My anger is spiking, and she doesn't deserve that.

I'm in the wrong. Not her.

I need to see her. I want to grab her face, look deep into those perfect emerald jewels, and tell her I'm here now. That I'm real. I'm no longer a piece of paper. Her fantasy can end now. She can kiss me, or she can punch my chest over and over and tell me how much she hates me. Whatever she wants to do, as long as I'm standing in front of her.

The time is approaching 8:49 pm. I saw Jen almost twelve hours ago and heard her voice three different times. We've been talking on and off throughout the day. But God, I miss her face. I miss her smell. Her fucking eyes. I miss her submissiveness. It was never a weakness to me. I loved taking the lead for us. She had faith in me.

Nine letters left, Calvin Louis. You can do this. Pound through these letters and see the woman you left behind. The woman you want to see in the future.

I decide to take a shower to wake myself up even more, but because I need a break from these letters. I wish the hot water would cascade the guilt off me.

I knew it was going to be hard to see Jen again, to hear her voice, to feel her pain, just didn't think it was going to be this hard. I left her...broken.

Turning off the water, I scream in the towel, dry myself off and change into gym shorts and a plain white tee. I turn on the fan to help me relax my anger, hopefully. The next nine letters are the only ones I bring to the dining room table, leaving the stack in my bedroom.

This is all I need to focus on for now.

Instead of a beer, I grab a bottle of water. It'll be easier to clean up in case I need to throw something.

I breathe in and out, then run my finger under the flap.

October 18, 2003

Dear Cal,

Halloween is in less than 2 weeks. I want to be Elizabeth Swann from Pirates of the Caribbean. Do you remember when we saw that movie? You didn't want to admit it and I kept giving you a hard time that you had a crush on Keira Knightley...I mean to be fair, Orlando Bloom was really hot in that movie!

I like the part where Elizabeth thinks Will dies on the interceptor and she attacks Barbossa. Then everyone in the theatre gasps (including me) when Will jumps on the Black Pearl and saves her! I I wanted to feel beautiful like that. I imagined you were Will Turner, willing to do anything to save his one and only lover. I know you won't be here but I'm holding on to hope that maybe, something miraculous will happen and you'll show up and save me from this misery.

Pat says he's dressing up as Wayne Campbell from Wayne's World. Pat hired Joey to take your place as assistant manager. He's dressing up as Garth. He's definitely got the look. He'll have to wear a blonde wig because he has really short hair. But he wears those exact frames that Garth wears and he talks kind of funny. I think they'll make a good combo. You've got some competition when you come back (winks).

Maggie is dressing up as Lara Croft. Badass.

Angelina is dressing up as Lydia from Beetlejuice. I was so jealous when she said that. We love that movie! That would've been a cool duo to do with you, Lydia, and Beetlejuice when they get married at the end. Maybe next year?

There are going to be so many Freddy and Jason's. I'm already not looking forward to it. Each one of them will remind of you.

I asked Pat if I could leave early on Halloween. I don't have classes on Friday but I just need time to be myself on our favorite holiday. It's depressing that I don't get to share it with you.

I wish I could hear your voice. It was two months yesterday and everything around me still reminds of me of you.

Waiting,

Jennie

That wasn't so bad. Still heartbreaking, but at least she didn't reference the fact that I was coming to this party as her date. Maybe this is the year we dress up as Beetlejuice and Lydia.

I've calmed down from earlier, so I find my phone to text Jen. It's close to ten at night, so I'm hoping for two things. One, she's awake and two, she still isn't sitting in the parking lot.

Cal: So how many compliments did you get on how beautiful you looked like as Elizabeth Swann?

I fall back onto my bed, still pleasantly surprised at the softness. A few minutes pass by and my eyes feeling heavy. I sulk she might be sleeping. I'm about to open the last October letter when my phone pings.

Jen: HA! Quite a few, but you didn't see me so how would you know?

Cal: I don't have to be around to know how beautiful you are, Jen.

Cal: Wish I could've been there.

Jen: Me too.

I hate I get sucked into wanting to talk to her instead of reading these letters. If I just finish them, I can talk to her face to face and for however long I want to. I don't want to stop talking to her, so I keep texting her.

Cal: I hope you still aren't in the parking lot...

Jen: What would you do if I was?

Don't tempt me, Jen. I am wide awake now, and I'd be there before she even responds to my text. She doesn't know how close I live to *Coffee & Honey*. Walking distance, about 20 minutes, but if I run, probably 8 minutes.

Cal: Then I'd have to come save you. I don't think you want to break the rules of your game. You don't want to see me before I finish these letters. That would be cheating.

Jen: you have no idea how badly I want to see you.

I stand up from my bed, pacing my room. Fuck. Do I go or not go? Is she toying with me? Her flirting is getting very close to the line of mind-fucking. We are playing her game with her rules. No matter how badly I want to see her, I will abide by her rules.

Cal: 8 letters left.

Jen: Waiting...

Walking down the hallway to the living room, I chuck my phone on the couch, pissed off at myself that I let her win...again. I should've told her I was coming. This dominant personality is not my favorite. Putting my hands on the back of my head, I stretch my shoulders and pecs. From the couch, I hear my phone ping.

Jen: By the way, I'm at home. I have been for a couple of hours now.

Cal: Good. Stay there until I'm done.

I can at least give her a little of my old dominant self.

October 31, 2003

Happy Halloween, my sweet Cal. I'm writing this at 11:30 at night, almost November 1ˢᵗ. I want to tell you all the things I <u>almost</u> did today...

I almost got out of bed early to make pumpkin waffles.

I almost made it to the shower to wash my face and body.

I almost wore my favorite skeleton sweater.

I almost wore our matching shirts we found in Tacoma – his boo, her boo.

I almost ate lunch today.

I almost went to buy cheap candy to give out to the kids tonight.

I almost went to see Pat.

I almost ate dinner.

I almost watched Halloween.

But I didn't any of those things today. I couldn't do anything today. I feel very numb. I feel so empty. This our supposed to be "our" day – our favorite day. We were supposed to start so many traditions today. We had talked about this day for weeks. It was one of my favorite things about you, that you L-O-V-E-D Halloween as much as I did.

After today, Calvin, I'm not sure I'll ever love Halloween again.

I wish I had more happy things to say.

Waiting,

Jennie

November 20, 2003

Cal,

I'm sorry I haven't written in in a couple of weeks. I've been kind of busy with school and work. Just trying to keep my mind occupied so I don't have to think about you.

I found this pediatric mental health facility where I'll be a child specialist. According to the owner, each child has a specific individual plan they follow which includes certain social skills they need to excel at and so my role will be coming up with certain lessons to teach them, so they grasp the concept. I'll have to teach the lessons a few times so we can become familiar with the expectations. It sounds exciting and I'm hopeful about it. I started last week so I've been doing some training here and there when I don't have class.

I've been doing better with my classes. I'm getting the hang of my schedule. Just taking the standard introductory courses- English, Math, and two electives – poetry and child development. English and math take up most of my time after work to complete all the assignments. I've been having some pretty late nights.

I've been working here and there at the shop, but been trying to put some space between me and Pat. I asked him if I could just work on weekends for now. Of course he was fine with it. Pat kind of stopped talking about you to me a couple weeks ago, before Halloween. He felt like I was getting sadder alking about you and he didn't like being around sad Jennie. He likes to keep me busy when I'm there, so he's got me taking on a few more responsibilities on the weekends. I'm supposed to start closing the store by myself this weekend. I don't think I'll be able to close the store like you did, so effortlessly, but I'll try my best. Maybe when you come back, I'll take over Pat's position. Could you imagine? There is no **Coffee & Honey** *without Pat.*

So yea, my weekdays just consist of school, then training from 3-6 usually on Monday, Tuesdays, and Thursdays. Wednesdays I don't have classes, so I spend most the day doing homework. Friday, Saturday, and Sunday I work at the shop.

Just trying to get through the days, really.

There's a lump in my throat as I consider something. This isn't a conversation I should text about, so I pick up my phone off the floor and call Jen.

She answered immediately.

"Hey. Everything okay?"

"Jen..." I whisper her name ever so quietly. Almost inaudible.

"Yeah?" She doesn't know I've put the pieces together.

"Jen, what happened to your dad?" My voice cracks. My heart cracks. Every bone in my body cracks.

There's absolute silence until I hear her sniffle through the phone. I close my eyes, already knowing the answer. I let my head rest on my arm.

"When?"

"Beginning of November." Her voice is distant and bitter. God, how I want to be there for her.

"Why didn't you write a letter about him?"

"And say what? Dear Cal, my father died." She chuckles, thinking that the letter would have any importance. It would've been important to me.

"I'm sorry, baby. When you started talking about how you were doing school and working all the time, you didn't mention him. What happened afterwards?" Clearing my throat, I give her the time to process that we are talking about this now.

"He wanted to be cremated. He didn't want me to go through the hassle of a funeral and all that shit."

"Where is he?" I shut my eyes tighter, hoping, praying, she doesn't have her dad in the same house as her.

"Boston. In the water." I breathe out a sigh of relief.

"You've been living by yourself all this time?"

"Yes. I moved out in the beginning of 2004 with the money I got from his will. I moved closer to the shop. Pat helped me sell the house too. I couldn't stand to be in there without him. On top of already being without you, it was too much to deal with."

I put the pieces together of visiting her father's house with Henry when I remembered the address. Rosie said they hadn't lived there in a while.

"Everyone left." She finishes, then cries.

My heart feels like there's barbed wire wrapped around it. I can't fucking breathe. My sweet Jen. The loneliness must have been deafening. I struggle to hold back my own tears, pinching the bridge of my nose.

"I'm so sorry, Jen. I'm so fucking sorry." The fan is not helping with my rising temperature, so I move to the balcony for some fresh air.

There's silence between us. She doesn't need my sympathy. We stay on the phone for a few minutes, saying nothing.

"Can you tell me a joke?" She asks me.

"What?" I'm quite baffled at her request. But it makes me smile.

"Tell me a joke. The corniest joke you know."

"Okay." I think for a moment. Then I laugh out loud. She's going to hate this one.

"Do you know what the little mermaid and I have in common?" I smile through the whole thing.

"No," she giggles, and it's the most beautiful sound in the world.

"We both want to be part of your world."

Silence. Not even a chuckle.

"Oh c'mon, that was funny!" I tell her.

"That was so incredibly cute. But you know Ariel is not my favorite princess..."

"That's right. You're the closest thing to Belle as they come."

I'm the worst Prince Charming if there ever was one.

I walk back inside, down the hallway, and plop down on my bed.

"Jen, can I please see you?" I can't handle the temptation anymore. Leaning over the ledge, I hold the phone close to me. My head has been throbbing for a few minutes. Too much reading. Too many emotions. Too much Jen. I want her to say yes, but I think if she says no, I'm going to sleep. I'll be more emotionally available if I get enough sleep.

"Jen..." the silence is longer than what I thought. I sit up on the side of my bed.

"Where do you want to meet?" Her voice is quiet. I walk into my closet to grab a sweatshirt, but I don't put it on because I'm burning up. I wasn't expecting her to break her own rules.

I can't have her come here. I've been stuck in this apartment for hours surrounded by trash.

I know she's itching to get out of her house, granted she sat in the parking lot for a couple of hours.

Coffee & Honey is closed.

I don't know any other option unless we just drive around like we used to.

"I wasn't expecting you to say yes."

"I'm not saying yes." She's blunt with it. She sounds tired, and it makes my stomach hurt. *Come over here and let me hold you while you sleep.*

"But I'm tired of waiting for you. I've been waiting for three and a half years. You feel like a stranger, but I know you're not. Seeing you and feeling you around my body yesterday and today, God, it reminded me that you know me better than anyone. You know all the little things about how to make my body react."

What the Hell would happen if we saw each other right now... after today...

"Jen... I don't think we should. We've had a long day. Lots of emotions and feelings. Can we make it a date tomorrow night? I'm almost done reading. I swear I'll finish reading these. Plus, I need to sleep. I think you do too." I just crushed my soul, but I need to remain level-headed about this decision. We can't let emotions lead us to bad choices. This wouldn't benefit either of us.

"I'd sleep better if I had you next to me."

Fuck.

"I haven't slept in a long time, honestly."

Her pure, genuine flirtatious self is so tempting. All I've ever wanted is to sleep next to her.

"Jen, believe me, I want nothing more. If we feel comfortable to stay with each other tomorrow night, we'll do it. Not tonight, though, okay? It's not fair for us, especially being so vulnerable. And like I said, we've had an emotional day. I want you to fall asleep thinking about me. I want you to picture me kissing your lips and looking into your heavenly eyes while I move hair behind your ear. Can you do that for me? Can you wait one more night for me?" I should just stab my heart for doing this. Better yet, I should call Henry and have him do it, because I know he wouldn't hesitate.

No, Cal, you're doing the right thing. This meet up would not be good. My counselor would be proud.

"I've only thought about you today, and every day since. I won't stop now. See you tomorrow. Goodnight."

Click.

Annoyed as I fall backwards onto my pillow, I text her after she ends the call.

Cal: You've got to stop doing that.

Jen: It's easier than saying goodbye.

Cal: You don't want to say goodbye to me?

Jen: I guess I just believe goodbyes mean it's the end.

Cal: there will never be a goodbye from me.

Jen: I hope not.

Cal: is goodnight the same as goodbye?

Jen: I don't think so.

Cal: Then goodnight my beautiful Jen. Think of me.

I lay my phone on my nightstand. I want to stay awake, but my eyes are so heavy. Thinking of Jen is my reason for wanting to sleep. She was always in my dreams. It seems surreal that she's here now.

I get off the bed to splash some cold water on my face, grab the next letter and lay back down.

November 27, 2003

Happy Thanksgiving my Cal.

What's the purpose of Thanksgiving really? To be with family? To be gluttonous? To gather with family and friends? What if we don't have anything? What if there's nothing to be thankful for?

It's pathetic, really.

I'll call it hatesgiving. I hate it all.

I sit up, trying to allow more oxygen to enter my lungs. It's hard to breathe because she's alone now. My heart aches for the letters I have to read, now that I know her father has passed away. All she has is Pat. And God knows, sometimes he can't be reliable.

Her mother left when she was little—too little to even remember any details about her. It's always been her and her dad.

I should've been there.

She should've been happy that she was *with me*.

I can already feel the depression getting worse. Her penmanship is tainted with hopelessness. And I just want to fucking erase all of it.

If that's what I'm supposed to do on Thanksgiving, then I'll give it a shot. First, there's no one at my table.

One of my favorite memories with my dad was visiting Boston when I was twelve. He was the best tour guide and there was just so much life and joy in his face. He was so happy to be home. We drove past a couple of his childhood homes. It was one of those looks on his face that you just wish you could never erase from your memory. Nostalgia. I could tell he yearned to be a little kid again, playing outside, getting in trouble. You never realize years and years later how life can quickly change.

You want to know my favorite memory? This past March. You came over to meet my dad and I was so nervous. Your temper...his temper...I thought I was entering Hell.

It was one of his better days. He was in good spirits that day. You gave him hope that I was going to be okay without him. My dad was starting to get his cold spells, so I went to grab his sweater and I came back to you and him at the kitchen table, looking at my photo album. I hid behind the wall so you guys wouldn't see me and completely embarrass me. I overheard that whole conversation though.

"She sure is beautiful, isn't she?" my dad was looking at my junior yearbook photo. I could tell by the cover of the book.

"She is. The most beautiful girl I've ever met." You were looking at a different photo, not even motioning to my dad. It was hard to catch a glimpse of what picture you were looking at cause you were sitting at an angle. I squinted hard to figure out which picture you were awing over. Then I saw it.

My prom photo. The most recent picture of me. That picture was only a couple weeks old. The one and only time I felt beautiful. My dad caught sight of what picture you were looking at and agreed.

My dad and I didn't have a lot of money so I got my hair done by a volunteer organization at a church up the street. I didn't normally curl my hair because I didn't know how to, so I let the volunteer ladies have a stab at it. I felt them do their magic as they twisted and curled each strand of hair. When they handed me the mirror, I didn't even recognize myself. They had formed two twisted braids that eventually formed one perfectly loose braid down my shoulder. They had added some glitter spray, and the reflection of the lights made the glitter shimmer. Step one was complete and I already so excited to finish the rest of my transformation.

Another volunteer girl, much younger than the ladies who did my hair, stepped in to do my makeup. She touched my face a lot, stroking my eyebrows, tilting my face from side to side to get a better view of my strong points. If there were any.

I didn't think she'd be able to cover up my hideous genes. She put powders on my cheeks, pencils on my eyes, mascara on my lashes, lipstick on my lips. I seriously thought she was making me look like a clown. I was so nervous when she handed me the mirror.

I wasn't hideous.

For the first time in a long time, I was impatient to get my dress and for you to see me.

Everyone in the room gasped and awed at me as I took one last look at myself for picking a dress.

That dress. It was everything.

Of course you chose the color and we decided to do a navy. I shifted through the hues of blue dresses for what felt like an hour.

And then that dress had a magic spotlight hanging over it, singing only to me. I was beaming was I pulled the hanger off the rack and looked at it. Several of the volunteers expressed that dress was perfect.

And it was perfect.

Two ivy inspired thin spaghetti straps. Perfect A-line with a stunning lace pattern that flowed into a tulle ball gown. Corsage styled back that I knew would make a statement with my braid off my shoulder. Ugh I was so excited to get it on!

"That's my favorite picture. I want you to have it." My smile quickly faded.

"No, no Mr. H, this belongs to you." I didn't see you caught off guard many times, if ever. He got you this time. You were frazzled. You quickly put the picture back in the sleeve.

"Calvin, please. It's forever engraved in my memory. You take it. You make new memories with her. Make the best memories with her. I have never seen her so happy. She smiles all the time. Please don't hurt my baby's heart. I know I'm already slowly breaking it for her. I need you to be the one to repair the damage I've done. Can you do that for me, Calvin? Can you be the one to keep her together?"

Ugh, my dad looked so fragile in that moment. His glasses were falling off his nose and I could start to see him shiver. I forgot I was holding his sweater. I needed to hear your response first.

"I will do anything to make her happy. I will protect her like you have, if not more. You won't ever have to worry because I will keep her safe. I promise."

I walked out with his sweater and started looking at the pictures with you guys, my soul gripping onto your words.

So you tell me, Cal. Did you keep your promise? Do you think I'm safe sitting in this house by myself without my father and boyfriend?

Wait, you aren't here to answer. I'll answer for you.

No. You broke your promise like you broke my heart.

Jennie

Not only is she turning depressed in these letters, but she's also getting angry.

Rightfully so.

It was only a matter of time. I fear how she'll express her anger. I hope to God it's nothing like how I do. *Please don't do anything stupid to put yourself in prison.*

I try to find the positive of this letter as I fold it up and laugh. She thought she would hurt me with this letter.

Ah Jen. This was a fantastic letter.

I push myself off the bed and walk into my closet to check my coat pocket. That coat I wore during my arrest. The coat I wore as I was charged and processed. That contains her prom photo. The only physical thing I have that reminds me of her father.

You were always with me.

With that, I lay her photo on my pillow next to mine.

Dreaming of her.

There are letters that you will fall in love with.

December 1, 2003

Happy birthday month, my love.

I want to celebrate you every day for the rest of my life. Ugh, I'm so in my feelings today. Isn't it weird that I never spent a birthday with you? It makes me sad but it also makes me laugh. I want to know if you like vanilla cake or chocolate cake. Do you like sprinkles? You didn't eat a lot of sweets when you were around so I'm thinking you aren't a cake kind of guy, but maybe you'd surprise me.

Friday, April 13th, 2007

I snap awake, the sound of paper crinkling on my chest. Shit, I didn't finish this letter. I squint at the date to remember anything about the contents. Oh, my birthday month.

I slept peacefully. My heart felt full, and all I could think about was Jen's laugh.

I toss the letter and envelope on my side table and switch it for my phone.

Cal: Good morning. How are you feeling today?

I lay my phone on my chest and rub my eyes. The brightness of the sun has caught me off guard. I've slept so much of the morning and early afternoon away. I contemplate falling back asleep when I read the clock saying 12:45 PM.

Shit.

The plan was to wake up early to read the rest of the letters before seeing Jen today. I smile at the thought and rub my face, my heart feeling excited.

Even though I just saw her yesterday, today will be different. I have gained a great deal of understanding. I hope she's willing to spill her heart out to me because I'm ready to take it.

I just want things to be how they were before Easton, before I left.

We were so in love. There is so much love I have left to give to her.

My chest vibrates and Angel cheers inside my head.

Jen: Hi (: I feel like I've been run over. How are you feeling?

Cal: Run over by??

Jen: A hurricane of emotions. How are you doing this afternoon? (; Thought maybe you left town again.

Cal: Ouch!! There's no way I'm leaving you behind. I'm good. I'm annoyed that I slept in so late. Need to get up and start reading. What time did you wake up?

Jen: I didn't go to sleep.

I re-read that text over and over. There's no way she's been up all night. While I slept peacefully, thinking about her, she was awake in misery and loneliness...again.

Cal: What? You had to have gone to bed. You mentioned you hardly slept the night before yesterday.

Jen: Yeah, insomnia and I have become best friends. I try to get a couple naps here and there but haven't had solid sleep in a couple of weeks.

Cal: Jen, that's not good. You need to sleep.

Jen: I get to sleep next to you tonight. Right? Is that still our plan?

I grin at this message, needing to call her. To hear her voice.

"Hey, that was quick." She laughs. She doesn't sound tired at all.

"We are absolutely seeing each other tonight. Where do you want to go? What do you want to do?" I should be the one to make the plans. I hate that I just tossed the ball into her court.

"I was hoping you'd pick." She requested. Thank God, the ball is my court again.

"I would love to."

"Cal, I hope you know this shouldn't be something romantic, okay? There is still so much you don't know. I am, in fact, breaking the rules for you. But I'd do anything for you."

I'm heartbroken that I can't do this big romantic gesture for her. There is so much making up I have to do for her. There is so much trust I have to win back from her.

I get where she's coming from. I still have no idea what kind of life she lives now. For all I know, she could bring her beef head boyfriend who wants to axe my head off.

"We can just do dinner and a drive? How does that sound?" Slowly, I sit up in bed, my back against the headboard.

I must've gotten hot during the night and stripped off my shirt. Curling my shirt into a ball, I look down and her prom picture that is still resting beside me. I pick it up and stare at it awestruck but with so much wonder.

Who are you now, Jennie Marie? What secrets are you hiding?

"Hey, where did you go?" Listening to her voice soothes and

thrills me simultaneously. I trace over her picture and mutter, "I'm sorry, baby. I got distracted."

I can only imagine her reaction to my charm. Her cheeks flush as she tries to hide her smile.

"So, what do you say about dinner and a drive?" I lay the photo on my chest and close my eyes, soaking in the memory of her that night.

"Yes. I'd like that."

"Do you want me to pick you up or do you want to come here?" I'm torn between playing the Prince Charming and letting her take the initiative.

I hate to ask these questions.

Four years ago, I would've made a promise to her dad to have her back by midnight. She would have trusted me with a plan–any plan that involved just her and me.

"I um... I don't know." I can hear it in her voice, the uncertainty.

"Do you still live in the same apartment near that pizza place we went to?"

"Yeah. Where do you live now?"

"Like ten minutes from the shop. By the water. I usually walk to *Coffee & Honey*, so I could meet you there?"

"So we're pretty close. That could be dangerous for me..." I bite my bottom lip, allowing my charm to be present.

"Yes, it could be."

"What would make you happy?" That's all she deserves. Whatever happiness I can give to her, I will give to her.

"I want you to pick me up in your truck." She doesn't hesitate to answer.

"With flowers, or no flowers?" I like this game, picking her mind of what she wants.

"No flowers. Just a passionate kiss and a hug."

"A passionate kiss? I thought we weren't doing anything romantic?" I stand off the bed and walk to my closet, deciding on what to wear for this evening. This smile feels permanent, and it feels so nice.

If she wants a passionate kiss, she'll get the best freaking kiss she's ever received.

In my soul, I can feel her smile.

"I think you owe me a kiss. It's all I've ever wanted."

"Is there anything else you want tonight to make you happy?" I leave my closet and walk to my kitchen to start a pot of coffee.

"Just to be with you." Her voice is so heartbreaking.

She has been waiting for this day.

To go on a date with me.

To start over again.

I know Jen and she's been a part of me for the past four years, but I'm also going on a date for the first time with her, both damaged and flourishing at the same time. I get the spend the time learning about *this* version of her.

Devil pulls at my heartstrings like a fucking violin. *We could be playing with fire. Don't let your walls down yet with her.*

"You'll have the best version of me tonight." Telling Devil to shut up, I lean against the counter and watching the coffee pot brew. It reminds me of *Coffee & Honey.*

"Have you read any more letters?"

"I tried starting December last night, but I fell asleep."

"Oh, boy... you're in for a treat." Her voice, that was just happy and excited, falls flat and sarcastic.

"What secrets are you keeping from me this month?" I smirk, trying to lighten the mood. I hear water in the background; a shower starting?

Oh God, don't picture her getting in the shower... we are not that far along yet, big guy.

"No secrets. Just lots of heartbreak, so prepare yourself. I'm kind of hoping you would read those letters after our date."

I lean my head back and laugh. I leave the kitchen and open my back door to stand on my balcony.

"Oh, Jen... you are something."

"What does that mean?"

"After every conversation, you hang up on me, forcing me to read these letters before you'll see me. Then you say you want to see me before I read these next letters. I just don't get what you're trying to do." Leaning forward on the balcony, I listen to the traffic. I hate to banter with her, but I'm not used to this confusing version of her.

She exhales and I hear the water turn off.

"I'm sorry, Cal. I'm trying to understand myself. I want to pick up where we left off, at least before Easton. I want those days back with you. With the version of you I remember, that I'm in love with. I try to forget that almost four years have passed without you. But shit happened to me during those years. I'm sure shit happened to you, too. We are different people now."

Since receiving her letters yesterday morning, I've been wanting to ask this question.

"Why did you give me the letters to read? We could have made a date to re-learn each other, couldn't we? You're leaving me with so much secrecy about what has happened to you." I sit down in my chair on my balcony.

Coffee sounds nauseating right now. I hate we are having this conversation, but I need answers.

There's silence. I pull back my phone to check my screen to see if she's still on the line. Call hasn't ended yet.

"Jen."

"I want you to read them to decide if you still want to love me." Her voice cracks.

"I do love you." I lean forward, becoming frustrated.

"You love the old me. And I love the old you. I know you would not read the letters in a couple of days. There's a lot to process, and I'm sorry for that. I thought I had more time to prepare myself to see you. I thought I had more time before I gave these letters away. I made mistakes, Cal. You didn't have that opportunity when you were in prison. But I made horrible mistakes. I always knew in my heart you were going to come home to me. I never knew when, but I always knew that, Cal. It's not fair for you to think I was going to be the same person when you left. I'm not. I'm so fucked up. I *needed* to give you the letters and the time to process if you wanted to love this fucked up version of me." She's gasping for air.

I pinch the bridge of nose, feeling that tickling feeling that comes right before I cry. My stomach is in knots. My heart is in unbearable pain. I have countless questions running through my head.

"Jen, I will never forgive myself for what I did to you. That will be a mistake that will haunt me forever. When they charged me, I felt some excitement at the thought of you finding someone better than me. You were going to be better without me. I don't know what mistakes you made while I was gone, Jen, and right now I don't care. I want to be in love with you until I make that decision to love you more or love you less. You don't get to make that fucking choice for me!"

I don't mean to yell. It's not an angry yell. I'm frustrated that she thinks I should stop loving her because she tried to move on from me. That could've been the best thing to happen to her.

"I'm sorry. I don't want to upset you." She mutters quietly, trying to swallow her tears.

"Baby, you aren't upsetting me. I'm upset with myself. It seems you weren't better without me, and I hate that. I wish we could pick up where we left off, but you're right, we can't. But I am begging you, please let me love you how I want to."

"I just don't know how I... I don't know if I'll be able to continue living if you decide you don't want to love me. And that's not a position I want to put you in."

My stomach drops. What does that mean?

She's everything to me. From the moment I met her, I knew she was going to be different. No matter what happens between us, part of me will always love her.

"Jen, part of me will always love you. Right now, it's a huge fucking part, okay? I want to pick up the pieces that I've shattered and try my damn best to put them back together for you. Please let me try. I'll keep reading your letters to understand your past, your mistakes. But it's going to be my decision of when I want to talk about certain things. I need to process this with you."

"As much as it kills me to answer your questions about the letters,

I'll keep doing it if that's what you want." The calmness in her voice is helping to lower my boiling point.

"Yes, please keep doing that for me. I want you to answer my every phone call, my every text. Jen, a game that I don't want to play, is figuring out why you didn't answer my messages. Never let me play that game, okay? Stay here with me because that's what I want right now." My dominant tone ends that conversation.

"Okay." Submissive.

"I'll pick you up at 6:30 in my truck with no flowers and a passionate kiss." I remind her.

"I'll be waiting." Her voice sounds better—it's hopeful.

"Have a good day, Jen." I smile on my end of the phone. Walking back inside, the aroma of my coffee makes me want it now.

"Have a good day, Cal?" She laughs over the phone, instantly bringing my spirits up.

"Well, you said you don't like goodbyes, so have a good day and I will see you later." I open my cabinet and pull out my largest coffee cup. It's going to be a long day...

"See you then."

Click.

This girl INFURIATES me.

But God, I love her so much. She was never this complicated...

Why did I have to make this complicated for her?

For us.

Jennie

I'm sitting on the lid on my toilet, waiting for the bathtub to fill up. I drop my phone on the floor and cry.

One thousand, three hundred and thirty-four days I have spent crying. I was hopeful the tears would disappear once he came back, but I was mistaken.

The last time I saw Cal, he hated me.

He said he hated me.

He showed he hated me.

I believed nothing else.

We had no exchange of words for three and a half years. As much as I tried to live in the past before Easton, I couldn't get past that day.

His face was so angry.

He was cold and distant, like I was the ugliest flower in the garden.

His words were poison, and I had no choice but to drink them in.

I would never tell Cal this, but he killed me that day.

I never wanted him to hate me. To be honest, I never knew what I did wrong. He had such a short fuse.

When he was overprotective, it was the most charming thing about him. He loved when he protected me, and his temper made him all sweaty and hard-headed.

This was the one and only case when his short temper was not attractive. It was terrifying.

I've spent the last three years wishing I'd asked him for a ride home from Easton. He would've done it. And maybe our ending would've been different.

No, not maybe. Definitely.

I cradle my head in between my hands and rock back and forth, desperate to get the what-if visions out of my mind.

This is the life we have now. We pick up the pieces and keep getting better.

Getting myself together for tonight means that I can't dress too sexy for Cal. He wouldn't be able to take his hands off me.

Although, a little touchy-feely wouldn't be so bad, right?

I ended my last relationship about five months ago. Squashed him like a bug. I even went to this job to tell him it was over. My heart breaks at the memory. It breaks even more knowing Cal had no other options for someone to please him.

Was I the last girl he was with? I had to be. *What if you weren't? What if there were others?*

I cry harder as my mind wanders to him being with someone else.

"You're a hypocrite, Jen." I get off the toilet and strip off my clothes. Tiptoeing in the bathtub, my head rests against the ledge. I splash water on my face to not only wipe away my exhaustion, but to get rid of my tears.

I feel I haven't slept in days, and the last thing I want to do is look at myself in the mirror. I need as much time as possible to fix the terrible mess I've made of my life.

Pull yourself together. You can do this.

Letting the water relax me, I let my mind drift off to imagining a perfect night with a perfect man, and for once, our time together is perfect again.

Calvin

I drink my first cup of coffee with no distractions. Back outside, I ponder if I was too harsh on Jen.

I think I'm just frustrated with the whole situation that I've put us in. I didn't think it would be this hard to come back to her.

With every fiber in my body, I am allowing Devil to curse my soul that I've left Jen uncertain about my true feelings for her. I hate with a burning passion that she has the last words I told her on replay in her mind.

When I was gone, I felt depleted of my drug. It was like entering rehab that I never signed up for. Two mornings ago, seeing her for the first time revived me. All I needed was a small dose of my drug to feel alive again. I'll do whatever I need to do to keep feeling this high.

I glance through my open back door at the stack of letters that I set on the coffee table, looking at them with pure hate.

What do those letters contain that make Jen believe I no longer want to love her?

I loathe the life that Jen had to create without me.

We were supposed to save each other.

You can still save her.

I set my coffee on the ground on my balcony and walk inside to grab the next letter.

"Just rip it off like a fucking Band-Aid." I mutter under my breath.

December 6, 2003

Cal,

I am warning you as I begin to write this letter, this one will hurt you. I know because it hurt me. I can't possibly fathom how painful this is going to be for you to read, so many years down the road. So please don't hate me. Don't hate yourself. Hate time because that's all it was... just bad timing.

Of course, the first letter of the day is a letter that is bound to "hurt me." I breathe deep, using all the energy in me to stay calm.

Do you remember the carnival?

No, no, no. Please fucking God, no.

Don't tell this story, Jen.

My frustration is already causing me to feel uncomfortable, and this is the letter she wants me to start out with?!

This memory **will** absolutely hurt me.

It still hurts. It always has.

I grip this letter and crumple it, feeling goosebumps form on the back of my neck, and I'm tempted to rip this letter in half.

Just do it. Just fucking read it. Devil says to me.

I don't know why I started thinking about the carnival. That was at the end of April. It's held every year at WGM Park, right beside Lake Washington. I had gone a few years ago with my dad and you had to take your brother there the year prior. This was our first and last time going together, which is kind of a bummer to think about.

You picked me up that night and gosh, I was feeling good. The weather was a little warm than the days prior. I wore a pair of washed-out jeans and a red crop top. I asked you if I should bring a sweater when you came up to my door. You told me not to because you had a sweatshirt in the car, in case I got cold, I could wear it. I decided to straighten my hair and put some blush and lipstick on that night. I'm not sure if you noticed but I never wore that much makeup. Tonight just felt different.

You held my hand to your truck. You looked good yourself. If I remember correctly, you wore a plain black shirt with khaki pants. You smelled so good too – just like your shampoo. I also noticed that you hadn't shaved in a few days so you had some stubble on your chin and cheeks. Ugh, you were perfect.

You still are.

You opened my door for me and helped me in. I had gotten into your truck every day at the point, but you were so generous that day.

The park was about thirty minutes away from my dad's house, but the time felt endless. Was it me, or were we both nervous? I couldn't even hold your hand in the truck because my hands were so sweaty. I didn't want to embarrass myself. You kept both of your hands on the wheel, which was something you didn't normally do. You usually held my hand and drove with one hand.

We had to park about a mile away, which wasn't bad. The weather was nice. You told me to wait in the car until you came around to open my door.

My knight.

Because I couldn't pass up the chance to show you off to everyone, I grabbed your hand. You smiled down at me and gave my hand a squeeze. It was pretty crowded, but we didn't care. At least, I didn't care.

We started off with getting a funnel cake – obviously. We shared one and you dipped powdered sugar on my nose. Then you kissed it off. My stomach had so many butterflies.

We decided to play the water gun race. You had yet to see my competitive side, Cal. I was ready to take you down!

And I did. After we played 4 games of that... I was not about to get beat by a ten-year old. I don't even know if you noticed that we played five games? It was worth it. I was content.

You wanted to play the basketball game. You said you would win me the biggest prize they had. Fortunately for me, they had a giant stuffed animal giraffe. I told you I want that and pointed to it. You wrapped your arm around my shoulder and brought me closer, kissing me on the temple and promising to get it.

There's no way to describe how you played that game without getting slightly aroused. You were so confident and so good at it! I happen to look around at a group of people who formed to watch you! I was so proud to stand next to you, to grab your arm and shoo off any girls who thought they had any chance.

You were mine.

And you won me the best prize. I was annoyed you only had to play that game once to win, but I was fine with the outcome. I carried that giraffe around with such pride.

You grabbed my hand and asked if I wanted ice cream. You didn't really like ice cream but you offered to buy me some.

I said yes, of course. I only like vanilla ice cream with sprinkles and that's exactly what you got me. We walked up the path to get to Sand Point. We found a quiet place to sit by the water. The quietness was peaceful. I was all alone with you. The sun had died down and you brought your sweatshirt. Once I finished my ice cream, I put it on.

It smelled like you. It was so warm, and I felt absorbed by your presence. It was like being in a cave, completely surrounded by your aroma and warmth.

You wrapped your arm around me and brought me close. And we stayed like that for a while. I tucked my head on your shoulder, and you laid your cheek on top of my head.

It was pure elation.

After a few minutes, I moved my head off your shoulder and looked up at you. You looked back at me.

"Cal, I think I'm falling in love with you."

I thought you were going to say it back. I thought you felt it too. But you looked away from me and didn't say anything.

You never said anything back.

I guess you did say, "we should get going."

The whole way back to the truck, tears were stuck in my eyes. I looked out the window and cried silently. I hoped you hadn't noticed. I was already embarrassed enough.

I felt like an idiot. I thought you falling in love with me too...

The whole drive home felt the same as coming to the carnival – quiet, not holding hands, tense.

You pulled into my driveway and I couldn't get out of your truck fast enough. You followed me, all the way to my front door.

"Jen," you said. "I'm sorry." You looked so pathetic, like you were the one whose heart just got shattered.

I whispered to you, "its okay." I left the giraffe in your truck, look off your sweatshirt, feeling exposed, and handed it back to you. You grabbed it reluctantly.

Then I went inside and cried some more.

I'll have to write a letter about what happened next because I like what happened.

I hope this letter wasn't too painful to relive. Sometimes we don't know when we love something, or if we are supposed to love something.

I wasn't sure if you were supposed to love me, Cal. I wasn't sure I was the puzzle piece you were searching for to feel complete. At least in my life, your puzzle piece was exactly what I was looking for.

Waiting,

Jennie

Second to what happened in Easton, not saying I love you back to Jen on that day is my second biggest mistake.

God, I loved her.

I just don't think I knew how to get the words out. I felt it so much in my veins, in my heart, in my head. The words were just stuck in my throat. She was always taking my breath away that I never felt in control enough to tell her I loved her.

Guilt is rising through me right now. I head back inside and find my phone off the counter.

Cal: Ever since the first day I saw you, I loved you.

There were no other words I needed to say to her at this point. She just needed to know–she deserved to know then. I will never pass the opportunity to tell her that.

Folding this letter back into the envelope, my phone pings.

Jen: I know. I hope it stays that way.

Without questioning her, I open the next letter.

December 7, 2003

I just got done re-reading the letter from yesterday. It hurts every time. Reliving it, imagining it. But I get to write a happy letter. I get to write about the poem you wrote me. Before I write the poem back to you, I should refresh your memory of what happened after the carnival.

God, the next day was awkward, wasn't it?! I got to work early to prepare for the morning rush, making sure cups were cleaned and the creamers and sugar bowls were filled. I heard the bell and looked up at you. You didn't smile at me, just gave me a half grin.

My heart broke a little bit. You didn't seem excited to see me.

I didn't realize you were hiding daisies behind your back. You approached the counter, acting like a customer. You handed me the daisies and attached was a small purple envelope that had my name on the front.

Happy tears formed.

That was the first time you bought me flowers.

You finally came around the counter, hugged me like you hadn't seen me in weeks, kissed my cheek and put on your apron.

I remember catching Pat smiling at me. I was already smiling – at the daisies, at this secret letter, at you? All of it.

I put the flowers under the counter and took the letter outside to a table.

I still get butterflies after all these months.

I never meant to hurt you,

Or make you second guess,

I understand where you are coming from,

But I'm not like the rest,

As the weeks go by I wondered,

Where our relationship would go,

Our conversations got deeper and more intense,

"In time it would show",

Communication is number one,

And trust is not far behind,

Without these two components,

They may lead us to be blind,

I knew my actions seemed like the same,

But trust me when I say,

I promised I would never hurt you,

And that's the way it's going to stay,

Since you have been in my life,

A day has never passed,

Where are you are not on my mind,

And I want these thoughts to last,

My Jen,

I'm going to tell you something that you need to hear,

It's the truth that I was scared to say,

I love you too, and I will year after year.

This was a good letter to write at the time of the year. I'm happy you wrote me that. I hope you don't like not hearing about the carnival memory because it leads up to that moment. One of my favorite moments.

Waiting for my next poem,

Jennie

Reading this letter makes the anger dissolve quickly. She remembered everything I ever did and said. For some relationships, that may be a good thing. It can appear sweet and thoughtful. For Jen, though, to remember how distant I was the next day after she told she loved me? I've killed her a thousand times. I just know I have.

I put down the letters and pick up my coffee, cold and unappetizing now, but it gives my hands something to do.

Why does she have this effect on me where she can make my blood boil in a quick second?

I think about Easton and wish my coffee was scalding hot so I could "accidentally" spill it on me. I deserve any pain from that day.

I place my coffee down on the side table and lean forward to cover my face. Humiliated by the sheer stress of just two days of meetings with Jen, I let out a loud sigh. She didn't have to give me these letters. Our conversations are so much better without having to bring up these letters.

Trying to catch myself before I enter the hurricane of unanswered questions and constant why's, my mind thinks about tonight.

It's almost like I get to get a do-over for our first date.

I'm struggling to decide if I want to keep her close to home or if we should go somewhere further south. She said on the phone this shouldn't be anything romantic, but how could it not be?

We are staying the night with each other after three and a half years apart. She could snore now. She could sleepwalk. She could hog all the blankets. She could sleep with the fan off. She could honestly not want to be in a bed with me at all.

Do I find a hotel with two beds? Do I suggest bringing her back home to make sure she's comfortable?

God, I want this to be special for her. This is my opportunity to repair the damage. To silence the doubts for her. To eliminate the fear that I would not come back to find her. To show her much I loved her, and still do.

Jennie

I'm frantic. My anxiety is taking me to new heights I've never experienced before. This date is more nerve-racking than the first time I went out with Cal.

I take my time in the bathtub, sulking in depression. Thinking about Cal sleeping in so late, but it made me happy that he was catching up on his sleep because he deserves it. Maybe he was having a pleasant dream...a dream about me?

I completely rid my body of all fatigue. I wash my hair at least three times to get rid of the oil, then I shave and re-shave my legs until the smoothness resembles ice. I wash my face until I feel it getting dry.

I was desperate to get rid of my scars.

How badly I want them to disappear...

Even though Cal could already see through my cracks, I ached to look in pristine condition. This felt important for both of us.

I had prepped my hair with a collection of argan oil, leave-in conditioner, frizz tamer and rosemary oil. Finally, with some heat protectant, I spent the next twenty minutes blow-drying. There were several hair styles that I thought would be sexy or romantic for Cal, but I remembered *this isn't supposed to be sexy and romantic.*

Brushing through my now dry hair, I think my hair being straightened would be most acceptable. It's the hairstyle I did most frequently on the days I worked at Hilltop. It made me feel pretty. There were a few pieces that needed the help of my straightener, so I turned it on and finished with my hair.

I checked the time on my way to carrying my makeup bag to the bathroom. 2:34.

Holy shit, you aren't going to have enough time.

As I feel my chest cave in, I think about sending a text to Cal, sharing my nervousness. In doing so, he could reassure me he still wanted to see me.

He wants to see me still, right?

I pick up my phone from my nightstand and find his name. My fingers are shaky. This is the first time I've started a conversation with Cal, and I'm fearful he won't respond. I had trained myself not to text him, even though our sporadic conversations from yesterday have gone well.

Jen: I'm getting more nervous by the minute to see you again.

Jen: Even though I saw you yesterday. And the day before...

GET YOURSELF TOGETHER. YOU SOUND LIKE AN IDIOT.

Thanks Devil, you are doing the best job at making me feel better. I roll my eyes at the evil monster talking in my mind.

Cal: I'm not nervous at all. In fact, I'm on edge over here wishing I picked an earlier time.

Cal: Wow, two days in a row of seeing my face–you aren't tired of it yet?

I smile at his insult to himself. I love talking to him. Tonight, I'm looking forward to talking to him as much as I want.

Jen: Never.

Cal: Can I pick you up earlier? I'm dying over here.

This time, I laugh out loud.

This is old Cal. Impatient Cal. The Cal who loves being in control of everything. The Cal I loved and fear isn't the same person anymore...

Slowly, I frown and respond.

Jen: No. 6:30 still. No flowers, a passionate kiss, your truck and you.

Cal: UGH

Cal: Fine. See you then (;

I hold my phone close to me, enjoying the temptation I still have on him. Angel gives me a quick pep talk.

He's already excited to see you. You're going to look irresistible.

I smirk at the comment and pick up my makeup bag. Dropping my phone on my bed, I head into my bathroom.

The lighting is so much better in here than doing it in front of a mirror using the natural sunlight. Jonah put up vanity lights around my mirror, which makes it bright and studio-like. I wipe away the sweat beads forming at my hairline, both from my nerves and the work of straightening my hair.

I look like a vampire, and that was not a good look on me. *A vampire with good hair.*

I'm afraid my makeup will turn out terrible if I put more effort into it. I let my hands do their thing. Even though they are shaking, like I haven't had caffeine in days, I try to be patient with myself. Moisturizer. Foundation. Blush. Bronzer. Concealer. A small amount of brown, sparkly eye shadow. Top winged eye liner–not too much wing (I'm not a bat). I curl my lashes and apply the four coats of mascara. It's a bit much, but the feeling of knowing Cal is going to compliment my eyes AT LEAST ten times makes my stomach flutter. A little lip gloss, then spray the setting spray.

I walk to my standing mirror in my bedroom, and the sunlight is coming through my window.

Take a look.

Even with my Vancouver Canucks shirt, black yoga pants and purple fuzzy socks, I am looking like a 7.5 out of 10. Not too bad. I run my fingers through my hair once more and get closer to inspect my makeup using the natural sunlight. My eyes shimmer like green crystals. The sparkly eyeshadow was a good choice. I almost don't believe it when I smile at myself in the mirror.

I haven't enjoyed looking at myself since the weekend at Easton.

Before things went to shit.

Right now, I feel on top of the world. I turn around with hands on my hips and sigh at the mess I've created.

There are clothes everywhere. I've thrown all my shoes out of the closet to complete an outfit. I don't know how much time has passed, so I nervously check the time.

3:58.

Crap, I've wasted almost an hour just *looking* through my clothes.

I run my fingers through my hair to rid the tangles. It's also a nervous tic for me.

Be in control.

What do *you* want to wear, not what would *Cal* want you to wear? I ponder over all the clothes. I decide to give myself three choices. Then I'll send a picture to Lydia, maybe Anna too, and ask their opinion.

First option, a lilac jumpsuit. Thin spaghetti straps, loose-fitting and the pants are long enough to not show any leg. I've always been self-conscious of my legs. I could wear my white Keds. It would be easily accessible to slip off in case...

Nope. Stop.

Second option is a satin, form fitting red dress. It has a low V neck, long bishop sleeves and a slit on the left side. I could pair my black heels with this. It's been a looooong time since I've worn this dress, probably even before I met Cal.

I hope it fits because it's a good contender. Red is the Devil's color, and boy, is she ready to play. The high slit makes it easy in case Cal wants to touch my smooth...

Stop it.

Third option is an oversized white t-shirt with light blue jeans. I could wear a black or gray cardigan and my black Vans. It's simple and sophisticated. More of my style, but I'm craving something more powerful. There wouldn't be anything special about this outfit, except I'd feel confident because it's what I would wear with anyone. Cal isn't just anyone, though. He's special. He deserves something special.

I fold the option three clothes and place them back in their original spot.

My eyes bounce back and forth between the jumpsuit and the dress. I find my phone again and send a picture to Lydia. I decide to not send a picture to Anna. She would be so disappointed that I'm going on a date with Cal. Especially after everything. She would hate it, and I don't need her negativity at this moment.

I pace my room a few times, my eyes locking onto my phone screen. While I impatiently wait for Lydia's response, I make myself another pot of coffee.

4:31.

Okay, I can't wait too long, but I'll wait for her input.

I head to the kitchen to make a small snack. All the adrenaline and excitement has actually made me hungry. I haven't felt hunger in months, so I let the ghrelin hormone enter my system with open arms.

I wish I could call Jonah and tell him I was right this whole time. He thought Cal being gone had nothing to do with my appetite, depression, self-injury.

It was my mental health pulling me down.

I appreciate him sticking up for Cal, regardless of his intent, but Cal's absence paralyzed me. I want Jonah to know that my mental, emotional, physical health deteriorated *because* of Cal.

Stay in the happy. All that matters is you get to be with Cal after all this time.

I cut an apple and dip it in peanut butter while I wait a few more minutes.

My phone rings from my bedroom. I simultaneously feel terrified and thrilled at the possibility that it's Cal.

Is he calling to cancel? Did he make other plans and can no longer see me tonight? Was all of this a mistake?

I lift my phone, preparing myself to see Cal's name, but I see Lydia's instead. My sighs stammer.

"Hey!"

"Hi hon! So, you guys are going on a date tonight? That means the meetup went well then?" I didn't tell Lydia anything besides the two pictures I sent, asking *which one?*

I almost choke on my apple. "Well, I guess. We talked on and off all day yesterday. He was struggling to get through the letters, so I told him if he finished the rest of 2003, he could see me. And well, he finished them." My cheeks blush.

"Yay! Oh, I'm so happy to hear this! Okay, let me look at these pictures again and let me talk out loud while I do." I laugh because Lydia is the Queen of this. She has a hard time using her internal voice, if it's even existent.

"I love the jump suit! I could see you wearing that. It seems like it would be a bit form fitting to show off your curves. The straps are dainty and cute! But my eyes go straight to the red dress. Fiery!!!! The V cut is nice and sexy, enough to show some cleavage. Hmm hmm. I like the flowy-ness of the sleeves since it has the tight wrist cuffs. What do you think about the length?" My eyes move down the length of the dress. It would stop a little above my kneecaps. I rub my hands over the dress, feeling the satin run across my fingers. I daydream about Cal moving his hand up and down my leg...

"Um, I, I don't know... it feels kind of short, but..." My cheeks flush again.

"There is it!! But what, Jennie?" I hear the giddiness in her voice.

She wants me to say it.

I could talk to Lydia about anything, but we've never discussed how provocatively to dress for a date. Jonah and I hardly went on dates. I was too busy trying to get myself out of bed most days. The conversation is giving me butterflies, knowing I am dressing up for a date with a man I've been in love with.

"It's short, but I think I might like it. It would expose a lot of my lower body. But then I feel like the jumpsuit shows more of my upper body." The confliction hits me.

"Well, what part of you do you like more?"

Oh Lydia, no, don't ask that question.

I need to decide because I'm running out of time. Whatever outfit I choose, I need to make it sure it's flawless. I've been pointing out my flaws for three and half years because Cal was the only person to point out my good traits.

He never mentioned my flaws.

It's been exhausting to pinpoint all my imperfections. Cal would be so proud of me if I saw the good parts of me.

My eyes bounce back and forth between purple and red. Between long pants or long sleeves. Between spaghetti straps or a low cut V. Between pants or a short dress.

"Red dress." I say confidently.

"Hell yes to the red dress!!" I hear a deep chuckle in the background.

Max. Oh my god.

I cover my face in humiliation as I recall the conversation we just had about my curves and feeling sexy. I'll never be able to look at him the same again.

I laugh into the phone and pick up the red dress. Holding the phone in between my shoulder and cheek, I hold the dress up my body while I stand in front of the mirror.

A million times, yes.

"I think it's going to look great." I tell her.

"Your curvy butt better send me a picture of you!" My cheeks darken.

"Oh my god, Lydia, can you stop talking about my curves in front of Max please? He is my boss."

"So am I. He's barely paying attention, anyway. Listen, you get yourself together, send me a picture and please, with sugar on top, have the best, most amazing time. I can't wait to hear about it Monday." Lydia is so excited for me, it's making me feel excited for myself.

I'm ready to change out of my clothes and into this dress. The final touches are approaching. I picture Cal's reaction in my head, hoping it's one I'll store in my long-term memory forever.

"Okay, I will. Thanks for your input. Bye. Bye Max!" I throw my phone onto the bed and remove my socks, pants and shirt.

I wore this dress to my dad's early retirement party. That was five years ago. Cancer rapidly ravaged his body, and his days were numbered. When Cal left, I knew my dad was leaving soon, too.

The very idea shattered my world.

I had reached out to my dad's work and asked for this one thing. For him to feel accomplished and appreciated. My dad worked fifty-two years as a software developer. It may not have been much, but he did the single father thing effortlessly. I had no regrets of what I wish my life would've been like if she were still around. My father was a true saint.

I have my back to the mirror when I zip up the back. It feels tight around my waist, but not uncomfortable. I glance down and notice my breasts protruding like little peaks. My smaller stomach makes me happy, even though I used unhealthy methods to achieve it. Leaning forward, I see my glossy legs still look rather dazzling. The lotion session was much needed. I stand back up fully and let myself turn around to look in the mirror.

I make a noise that comes out like a laugh. Some people laugh when they feel hideous or silly. Some people laugh when they don't know how to take a compliment. I, however, laugh because I'm in shock at transforming myself.

I look pretty.

I know Cal won't use that word, but I can't think of anything better at the moment.

Staring at myself in awe for a few minutes, I run my hands over my stomach. Turning to the side to get a view of my "curvy butt", I smirk when I hear Lydia's voice because, yeah, it's looking pretty good in this dress. Facing forward again, and run my fingers through my hair to loosen the tangles. But because I'm getting more nervous. My makeup still looks fresh and not over-done. There's no way Cal will be able to keep his hands off me.

Is that what you want? My confidence gets punched by the comment from Devil.

Well, I guess it's my fault. Red is the Devil's color, and she is, in fact, here to play.

Was this the plan–to convince him to see you so you could take advantage of him? He's broken too. You don't get to play with his heart.

I'm taken aback by Devil's thought. I promise to not bring up anything of the past or the future, but just to live in the now. It'll be fine if we just pretend that things are normal.

I check the time once again. 5:13.

I reach for my phone off the bed.

First, I pull up Lydia's number and snap her a picture of myself. A genuine, happy smile spreads across my face.

Then I click Cal's number.

He answers on the first dial.

"Hi." I can tell he's smiling. I blush so hard that my cheeks are probably the same color of my dress. This seems unreal. To have another first date with Calvin.

"Hi." I say back to him, bringing my fingers to my lips.

"What are you doing?" His voice sounds different this time. It's excited and hopeful.

I've had Cal's anger tone stuck in my head for the past three and a half years. I almost forget what his soft, husky, loving voice sounds like.

Sitting down on my bed, I savor this moment.

"I just got finished getting ready." I bit my bottom lip, hoping to send him telepathic thoughts of what I want him to say.

"Oh yeah? You're an hour early..." He chuckles a bit. My stomach is filling with butterflies, and God, they are ready to fly.

"Well, I was wondering if I could change my answer." Nerves are vibrating throughout my body.

"What was the question?" I roll my eyes at his humor. I know what he's doing. He's seeing this out.

"Cal, don't make me say it." I'm not afraid to ask him if he could pick me up. I just want to hear his dominant self, the one who always had everything planned for us.

I hear nothing for a couple seconds and when I check my phone to make sure he didn't hang up, I see a text from Lydia. I hurry and check what her response was to my outfit.

Lydia: OH. MY. GOD. YOU LOOK AMAZING <3

"Jen?" My body shakes as I hear Cal's voice through the phone.

"Yes, I'm here. What did you say?"

"I didn't say anything. You weren't saying anything." I nip at the inside of my cheek. Ugh, to hell with it.

"Cal, will you please pick me now?"

"Ah, I thought you'd never ask! Be there in fifteen. Still no flowers, right?" I chew on my cheek harder. *Flowers would be nice... but no.*

"No, no flowers."

"Okay, I hope your lips are ready, then." And somehow, he ends the call.

I'm left trying to catch my breath. I text him my address as I try to determine if I should open the window to get some air. When did it become so hot in here?!

I push myself off the bed, grab my black heels, and strap them around my ankles. I haven't worn heels since Jonah and I got married.

Not that we had a wedding, really. We went to the courthouse, but I still wore a dress and these shoes.

Walking laps around my apartment, I try to get the hang of putting one foot in front of another until I feel like I'm a model. I walk to the bathroom, inspecting my makeup for the last time, then add a touch of lip gloss and rub my lips together.

C'mon Angel, talk to me.

You've been waiting for this moment. It's everything. Stay in the moment. Don't bring up the past and don't worry about the future. This is the second chance you've been dreaming of.

Gratitude fills me as I close my eyes. I hear a horn when it's directly outside my apartment. I look at myself in the mirror one last time.

From my closet, I pick up the small wristlet that I shoved with the necessities. Taking in a deep breath, I fill my lungs as I press my hands to my stomach. I've come to terms that the nerves aren't going anywhere. He's here. This moment is here. I close my eyes as I let myself exhale through my nose.

I untwist the doorknob and feel the cool air of Seattle rush through me. Cal's headlights are off to the right, but I don't see him. My unsteady walk on the sidewalk nearly results in a collision with him. He holds me by my elbows and looks down at me, speechless. Surprised?

"Jen, holy shit." The look in his eyes makes all the butterflies in my stomach emerge from the conservatory.

I hate that the sunset is happening now, knowing Cal can see my cheeks blooming.

"Hi." I say to him. This time feels even better than the first time. He takes one hand from my elbow and touches my cheek. This feeling is new.

Fireworks are exploding in me. Extra blood is running through my veins, making me feel hot everywhere.

"Jen, you are stunning. Wow." He runs his thumb along my

cheek, and I feel I'm about ready to catch on fire.

A smile appears on my face and when I feel Cal's finger run along my lower lip. I thought my legs were going to give out.

We could just stay here in this moment. I would be fine with that.

"You really think I can take you out to dinner and not get in a fight with someone for looking at you? Let alone trying to talk to you? You must have a lot of trust in me because I don't believe I'll be able to control myself." I'm staring at him in a way that doesn't feel real.

Is he real?

Is this moment real?

I feel my smile fade, worried this is a dream. Shutting my eyes, I bring my head down, trying to conjure Angel to tell me this is happening right before my eyes. I feel the touch of his hand leave my face and my arm.

Open your heart and stay in the moment.

I find the willpower to open my eyes, hoping that he's here with me. With scrunched eyebrows, hands in pockets, and tense shoulders, he looks back at me. I take the quickest moment to take a mental image of him, to cherish this moment.

God, he's so beautiful. He doesn't have a hat on like he did the last time I saw him at *Coffee & Honey*, but that's okay because I like the way he's styled his hair. His hair is shorter on the sides and longer on top, so he could tousle the top of his hair. His appearance is so attractive, extremely sexy, that I'm fighting to bite my lip.

A bit of beard trimming has made him appear older than twenty-one. He's wearing a dark blue polo shirt on with the sleeves rolled up. When I run my eyes over his arms, I can see his veins popping out from his forearms and I'm ten times more attracted to him He's tucked his shirt into his khakis, and as I look down his legs, I see his suede Vans.

"Are you satisfied with how I look?" His voice startles me. I bounce my eyes back to his, where he's smiling at me. Reciprocating his behavior, I bring my hands to cup his cheeks.

Be real.

I feel the warmth of his skin. He was always like an enormous bear. He brings his hands over mine, giving me extra evidence that he's touching me.

"I'm sorry. This doesn't feel real. It feels like a dream. I can't believe you're here." My voice comes out like a whisper, not wanting to share my truth.

He brings his forehead down to mine and I can feel the heat of his breath as he speaks.

"I'm here, baby. I'm here for you." I can smell the mint from his mouth, and it's tempting to be the first one to give in for a kiss.

I drop my hands from his cheek, making his fall too. Falling into his chest, he pulls me close, resting his chin on my head and wrapping his arms around me. His fingers leave imprints on my lower back.

The feeling is like hugging Santa when you're five. The person who has the power to give you everything you ever wished for.

It's like hugging the Genie who you thought was ignoring all of your wishes–even though the only wish was to be with him again.

It's like hugging the doctor who told you your chances of living were minimal, but for some odd reason, a miracle happened, and you get to live longer.

When the curse breaks and Beast changes back, I feel like Belle at the story's end.

I feel whole. Complete. Happy.

I shove my face into Cal's chest, hoping to God that I keep my tears inside. I spent too much time fixing my makeup and we haven't even left the driveway!! Cal moves his hands to touch my hair and grapple my head, as if he's protecting my thoughts.

"Are you ready to go now, or do you need more time to check me out?" I laugh in his chest, thankful for his wit to always make the mood brighter.

I'm thankful for *him* to make my life just a tad brighter. It's so been dark for so long.

"Yes, I'm ready." I give his body a squeeze and then release him. Thank God my eyes are dry. He still looks so handsome. He holds his hand out for me to grab, and we walk down the sidewalk to his truck. It's crazy how so much time can pass, but behaviors are so habitual. And how our reactions are so involuntary.

My hand fit in his, like it was sculpted just for him, and for a moment, I felt a piece of my heart restored.

He opens my door and, as happy as I am to be preparing my body for an actual date, I am hit with instant sadness.

Sadness that overwhelms me. It makes my heart feel cold and I can feel my body shake with anxiety. My chin trembles and I'm fighting the urge to cry.

"Hey, what's going on?" Cal can see the distress in me as he turns me around by my waist. He puts his hands back on my cheeks, forcing me to look at him. I could get lost in the ocean forever.

"I um, I'm sorry..." It feels like someone is choking me.

Please don't begin a panic attack!!

"You don't need to be sorry, baby. Tell me what's wrong." My body is struggling with how to react. I've been on my own to handle these difficulties for three years. Sometimes it just takes me a moment to figure out my course of action.

Jonah would be disappointed to hear me say that, but emotionally, caring for me was a struggle for him. I've let the emotions come through me, do their thing, and let them leave. They are unwelcome visitors, but it's like not I've been checking the lock.

This isn't Jonah. This is Cal. He doesn't know how to respond or handle my emotions.

The memory of him leaving me is overwhelming, and I can't articulate my pain to him. In the hospital, doctors diagnosed me with post-traumatic stress disorder. There would be things, memories, even people that would trigger a painful event. And it was Calvin's truck that made me want to die.

Part of my heart will probably always live in Easton, and I've come to terms that I will never get that piece of me back.

I try to find Angel.

He's here. Talk to him.

I look up in his eyes, which brings me comfort. My shakiness minimizes and my heartbeat is trying to slow down.

"This truck." I move my eyes to the truck, where I look inside the open passenger door. The same seats with the same smell, the smell of Calvin. His rearview mirror has the same fishing pole keychain hanging from it. For so many drives, the same console supported our hands. The radio system still lights up red and the same rock music comes through the speakers.

Cal looks to the truck, then back to me. Sometimes I would surprise him with how messy my thoughts were. This was one of those moments. Confusion is clear on his face.

"This is what you asked for. Do you want to drive instead?" His voice breaks my heart, as if he's taking the blame for his truck's actions. I touch his arm.

"No, no. I want to go with you. Just give me a moment. It's just a lot of memories." I try to regulate my breathing, but Cal suffocates me as he pulls me in for another hug.

"We'll wait however long it takes, okay?" I'm comforted by his reassurance; it reminds me I'm not alone. Yet, hearing those words from Cal creates a shield around my heart, one only he can penetrate. He has a way to melt me and make me feel full in a matter of seconds.

My mini-panic attack may not have lasted long, but being comforted by Cal was incredibly overpowering. It hadn't registered that Cal was now in the passenger seat, holding me between his legs. I break out of my trance when I hear a car door slam nearby.

I don't think any girl, no matter how old they are, will never not get woozy from forehead kisses. My knees about buckle underneath me. And just as I thought my kryptonite had exploded with love, patience and encouragement, he nearly detonates my heart.

After he kisses my forehead, he takes my face and brings his lips to mine.

I dreamt about this moment for years... and I don't care if this is real or fake. I'm letting it happen.

His lips are so soft. They are as strong as they look. His mouth is so minty, it's even more enticing. I move further into the opening of his legs, and I think it makes him more... smitten. I remember the feeling of kissing those lips. Finding the courage to open my mouth, I breathe in and reveal my tongue. A sound escapes from his mouth as our tongues collide. He grabs the back of my head, adding more pressure between our mouths. He moves his head from side to side, getting new angles of my mouth. God, it feels like a grenade is going off in my mouth. He takes his time feeling my tongue and then kisses my lips, slowly, like he's savoring my taste. It's no longer the truck that will kill me, but lust.

I can feel so much of my body awaken with glitter and confetti and serotonin... so much serotonin. My brittle, lifeless bones are getting revived with oxytocin and I feel like I just got injected with cocaine. There seems to be a reason to keep my heart alive.

I don't want to stop kissing him.

He reminds me of whiskey.

It's so damn good and I want a bottomless bottle. On our last connection, I let my lips sit on his for a few moments. And as painful as it is to move away, I do. But I don't feel my heart breaking. When I open my eyes, my Cal is still here, gawking at me, touching his lips as if they had a speck of dusting on them.

Calvin

Are you kidding me?

If anyone has a time machine to take me back to the first time I kissed Jen, please take me there. There is such a small, very fucking small, part of me that is glad I was gone for so long because that was the best kiss in my entire life.

My mouth feels like it's full of cotton balls, even though we exchanged a hefty amount of saliva. I can feel my body shake with excitement and nervousness and happiness.

She pulls back from me first, and as much as I hate it, it allows me time to really soak her in. Jesus, did she wear my favorite color on purpose? My eyes can't help but dip down to peek at her chest. Her legs are displayed for me, and they look flawless. I want to run my fingers down her skin. My eyes work their way back up her figure to her face. I wish she didn't wear so much makeup for me, but my God, she looks beautiful.

It's almost as if I've met three different versions of Jennie in the past three days. The first version at Whole Foods. She was shy and quiet. Clearly very surprised to see me, and just very reserved. I wasn't a fan. The second version was at the shop yesterday morning. Still reserved, but I got to notice how mature her features have gotten. She was honest and just pure. Then, I get this version. A supermodel who is confident and perfect in every way.

I can't believe she's mine.

She used to be yours.

Nope, I'm not letting Devil get in my fucking head.

I pull at my bottom lip-the remnants of Jen's taste lingering. I smile at the ground and chuckle.

"Well, that was nice." She giggles, looking down at her feet, blushing. Not wanting to lose this version of her, I pull her chin up to look at me.

"That was perfect. I have missed you so much." Then I allow

Angel to work her magic inside me. We pull Jen into my chest and I swear to God, her scent overpowers me. I rest my chin on her head and my eyes roll back as I get my dose of her. I felt her arms move up my back. Not even three seconds pass and her hands connect, pulling me in closer to her.

I don't know how much restraint I'll have for the rest of the evening, but so far, it already feels very minimal.

Jennie

I'm so glad he hugs me. It gives me a moment to let the blood disappear from my cheeks. He stared at me like I was Kiera Knightley. Like I was the only girl in the world.

Holding him, I grin like an idiot in love. Is it possible I can still have a fairytale ending?

"Geez, Jennie Marie, I didn't realize you stalled this long for a date with me.... I guess there's a first time for everything." He pulls me away to look down at me, but when I see that dimple on his lower cheek appear on his face, I'm fighting vengeful demons to resist kissing him again.

I tilt my head back to stare up at the sky, letting Angel do her victory dance.

"Yeeaaah, I don't normally take this long, do I? You distracted me." I let my forehead rest against his chest.

"C'mon, hop in. We'll make this memory a good one, okay?" He takes my hand to hoist me up to the passenger seat. My chivalrous Prince, melting my heart. I watch him, smiling, walk around the front of the truck and hop into the driver's seat.

"Do you want to talk or listen to music?" Cal kept the truck running that entire time. I pull my seatbelt on, feeling déjà vu of so many times of my life.

"I want to talk, but I made a promise to myself that I won't talk about the past or the future. Just want to try to stay in the present with you." Sitting down, I noticed my dress is much shorter than I thought. The slit is centimeters away from showing my underwear. I pull at the hem a bit, hoping to give a bit more length.

Cal doesn't notice my wardrobe flaw. He changes the gearshift into drive, then reaches for my hand and interlocks his fingers through mine. Angel sings loudly in my head.

SHE IS IN LOVE.

"I'm good with that plan." Squeeze.

"So, what did you do after I called you this morning?" I internally beg Angel to lock Devil up for the rest of the night, so nothing depressing comes from any of our conversations tonight. Cal is driving along my street, heading south towards the city.

"Well, I took a long bath, hoping to wake myself up from not sleeping. Then I've been getting ready all afternoon." Looking out the window, I give a nervous laugh. I'm nervous to look over at him, even though I've looked at him a million times in his truck. My hand is so incredibly sweaty. I try to wiggle my fingers free from his, but he grasps my hand harder.

"Hey..." he says first. His voice was almost a whisper at me, and I can't help but look over at him.

"Please don't let go." I lick my lips and nod, obeying his request.

Stay in the moment.

"What about you, did you read any..." As soon as I feel the word *letters* hit my tongue, I feel like I'm swallowing tacks. Okay, so Angel did not get my message to take care of Devil.

"Shit, I'm sorry." I say again. Great, now I'm just talking too much.

There's another squeeze. "Look at me. And for longer than five seconds, please." His soft plea makes my heart burst. Trying to hide my disappointment, I look over at him.

"It's okay, baby. I know how hard this is. I'm part of the story, too." His voice is low and reassuring.

I've been trying to keep this part of my life a secret. To reframe from telling someone the broken story of a boy who left me for dead. The daunting part is the person I'm keeping a secret from and the boy in the story are the same person.

Calvin.

And he knows it too. I look over at him while he drives and see the distress forming on his face. *I don't want to hurt you.* Hoping to erase his distress, I squeeze his hand this time. He doesn't look at me this time, but I watch him smile, and my eyes dart to the perfect dimple on his lower cheek.

"So, where are we going?" Changing the topic seems necessary. Cal merges onto Interstate 5, taking us towards Seattle.

"There's a place Henry suggested called the Corson Building. It's on the south side of the city. Is that alright?"

I haven't ventured anywhere from Laurelhurst since the camping trip to Easton. My life works in a triangle—home, *Coffee & Honey*, and Hilltop. I've been too scared to go anywhere else. My post-traumatic stress response makes me feel like something terrible is going to happen, which typically leads to a panic attack. Tonight though, I'm content to go wherever. It's exhilarating.

"Sounds good. Um, who's Henry?"

"Oh, uh..." Cal laughs. "He was my private investigator. To help me find you. Once we found you, he became a friend. Keeps me calm. At least he tries to." My stomach does a flip. I didn't realize Cal had a private investigator.

He told me Lydia gave him my whereabouts. I find myself in awe of the stretch he went to find me.

He looks over at me for a quick second, keeping his eyes on the traffic. Usually, we pulse each other's hand as a non-verbal gesture for comfort, but he keeps a firm grip on my hand this time. I don't care how much moisture has formed on my hands; I never want to let go.

"Hey..." He says when he squeezes my hand. I peek my eyes over at him, trying hard not to cry. The back of my throat feels tight as I feel a hint of sadness overwhelm me. The tip of my nose is tingling too.

What are you about to cry for?!

"I would have done anything to find you."

A celebration happens in my head as I feel dizzy from the sweetness coming from Cal's mouth. Wishing I could kiss him as hard as humanly appropriate; I opt to kiss the back of his hand. He's pleased with my choice, and I see his dimple form again on the cheek closest to me.

There's no way to describe how a heart regenerates after being stagnant for so long. Before I heard of Cal's release, I pictured life with a black, soul-less, useless heart.

I'm so thankful I don't live in that headspace.

We drive for about thirty minutes until we reach Beacon Hill. Corson Building is right off the highway, so it doesn't take long to park. Cal parks with one hand, then turns off the engine. Our hands feel stuck with glue (it's probably sweat from me). Neither one of us wants to let go. We are looking at the inevitable, our hands.

"You stay in the car, I'll run around the front to get your door and we'll hold hands again. Maximum of five seconds. Ready?" I missed Cal's controlling tendencies.

Despite its obviousness, I wouldn't have found that solution. I would've suggested staying in the car and starving, continuing to hold hands. I like his idea better because I'm hungry.

I nod my head in agreement with his plan. I pick up my wristlet off the seat and watch Cal run in front of his truck; it gives me five seconds to run my fingers through my hair. My door opens as my fingers reach the ends. He's already reaching for my hand.

Every part of me is smiling—my face, my heart, my soul, even Devil. I let him hold me up as I finagle myself out of the truck. I am one-hand short as I glide my wristlet down my arm, pull my dress down, finally, and stabilize myself as I step on ground and try not to twist my ankle in these heels.

"This night is going to be such a disadvantage for me. I apologize now for any destructive behavior or cruel words I have to say to any sleaze bag. We probably should've come up with a Plan B in case I get us kicked out of here." We walk to the front doors, hands swinging back and forth.

I laugh for the first time tonight. No other male stands a chance against Cal. He's vicious when it comes down to things that belong to him, and I remember he doesn't play fair.

He opens the door for me, letting me pass first. We wait at the hostess stand, and he catches me off guard when he whispers in my ear, "your laugh is so beautiful but tonight, your ass is even better." I can feel my cheeks turn into a combination of pinks and reds. He stands behind me, very close to me. I feel something semi-hard poking me in the back, and I try to hide my smile, but I can't.

We get seated at a far corner table. We stand awkwardly for a moment, realizing we have to let go. I exaggerate my frown to him, and he runs his fingers over my pouty lips and kisses me.

My stomach does cartwheels and somersaults. I scoot into my chair and Cal pushes me forward, grazing his fingers over my shoulder and then positions himself on the other side of the table, looking harmless.

The things he is doing to your body should count as a crime.

I'm facing most the dining area when I see this broadly, tall, blonde gentleman, who is wearing all black with an apron, approach our table.

I wish I had telepathic powers to tell him to not approach. I pinch my lips together when the server reaches our table and I look at Cal.

His gaze flips as he looks at the server, who is looking at me, and I'm looking at Cal.

It's a messy triangle.

I'm hoping my gaze will keep Cal calm and collected and he can continue making tonight perfect. He clears his throat and turns his body towards the server, then stands up. I hadn't realized how much taller Cal was than the server, but he's almost a foot taller. Panicking that a brawl is going to occur, I can't help but enjoy the show. I'm not sure if I intervene or let things play out.

Cal *did* apologize for his pre-actions in the truck, so whatever happens, it's not like I didn't expect it.

"Look man, three things. One, I'm going to need a waitress. Two, stop staring at my girl. And three, if I find you waltzing over in this area again, I will knock your teeth down your throat. I have a record and I honestly don't want to add more to it right now." The server looks petrified. He rapidly shakes his head back and forth and walks the way he came.

Cal and I stare at him as he stops to talk to another server, an older lady, who looks back at us and waves. Cal sarcastically waves back and then sits back down.

"Okay, that's taken care of. Now where were we?" I can't help but smile like an idiot at him. His anger has subsided significantly. If this was Calvin from three years, he would've done murder. He would do anything for me, past, present and hopefully future. He side smiles at me, taking a drink of water.

"What?" He leans forward, predicting that I might say something intimate or private? I shrug my shoulders. *Just impressed with you.*

"Tell me what you're thinking, please." He tilts his head to the side, trying to use his playfulness against me. I rest my elbows on the table and bring my hands to my lips, trying to decide how to put these words into a coherent sentence.

"Cal..." I start. I can feel Angel and Devil give me a thumbs down and stick their tongues out.

You can do better than that!

He brings his hand to mine and takes it, gently and delicate.

"I'm just going to spit out what is happening in my head." I shake my head, feeling flustered at my emotions hitting me like I'm the target.

"At least that hasn't changed about you." He grins, showing his perfect teeth. It's contagious and I smile back, squeezing his hand.

"You can tell me anything, baby. Just don't tell me you are breaking my heart."

"The opposite, actually. Cal, I don't want this night to end. I don't want to leave and go back to your apartment. I want to stay with you wherever that may be. This feels like a goddamn dream and please, for one night, I need to know this is my life again. That you are here when I fall asleep and when I wake up. It might be the biggest mistake because I'm sure we aren't the same people anymore, but God, I have missed every inch of you. If something happens between us, or to one of us, I just need one night to believe that you came back to me, for me, and you stayed for me."

I'm fighting back tears. Since leaving my apartment, I haven't checked my makeup, but I hope I still look good. I let my eyes move to the ceiling to hold the tears back. To regulate my breathing before looking back at Cal, I take a big breath in.

When I'm centered, and I look at him, he's staring at me. Staring deep into my soul. He bites his bottom lip and when he's about to speak, our new waitress approaches us. We leave our hands on the table and Cal looks down, disappointed at her arrival. I watch him, capturing all his behaviors and remembering all his quirks.

"Hello, folks. Welcome to Corson Building. I see you've got some water. Care to enjoy any wine?" I look at Cal, who doesn't look at me to decide.

"We'll do a bottle of Rosé. My lady here will have the..." He pauses and gestures for me to complete my order. I stutter, surprised.

"Oh, um, I'll have the steamed halibut. No cabbage for a side. Thank you."

"Lovely choice. And for you, sir?" The lady is looking back at Cal, but I can see her eyes moving back and forth between him and our hands. If only she knew our story of how we got to his moment.

"I'll try the roast pork belly."

"Also a lovely choice. Now, it is required of me to make sure you are at least twenty-one before I bring out your Rosé." She glances between the both of us. Cal looks at me, licking his lips mischievously.

"I am, ma'am. Let me get my license for you. My lady here turns twenty-one in eleven days. Now, I'm not going to BS with you, ma'am, but I recently got out of prison and this gorgeous, stunning, incredible girlfriend of mine has been waiting to see me for three and a half years. This is our do-over first date. So, I'm really trying to give her the best night here. I am at legal age for alcohol to be at our table, but it's our secret if you don't tell that my girl isn't legally there yet."

Holy. Shit.

He remembered when my birthday was?!

Gorgeous, stunning, incredible GIRLFRIEND?!

HE'S SECRETLY TRYING TO LET OUR WAITRESS SERVE ME ALCOHOL?!

As time passes, my heart is becoming more and more complete. Mending a broken heart is impossible, or so I thought, until now. Every action, every word, every look at me is making my heart recover. I cover my face at the blushing admiration of watching this new man display so many new qualities. I've missed his demeanor of watching him take lead, of taking care of us.

I peek over to see the expression on the waitress' face. I'm preparing for us to be excused from the restaurant. When I look at her, she has tears forming in her eyes. A puzzled look forms on my face. I didn't think Cal was *that* rude. I take control of the situation, knowing Cal isn't all too familiar with emotional women.

"Hey, are you okay? We didn't mean any harm. I apologize if my *friend's* spiel was...direct." I give a side eye to Cal when I say the word friend. The word boyfriend gives me poison vibes, and I'm not ready to die yet.

I place my hand over hers as she leans towards our table, trying to keep herself up.

"My son, Brady, has been in prison for a few months. Another DUI, for the millionth time." She rolls her eyes, but I'm attentive. "My daughter-in-law, Isabella, has been staying with me. They were living together for gosh, years. Even before they got married. They bought a house behind my back. But she struggled with keeping up with the bills and couldn't keep the house. I had to go with her to the prison to tell Brady the news. He didn't take it well. However, things don't always go as planned, a fact I'm sure you're all familiar with." She shrugs her shoulders, looking defeated.

"Bella and I have had so many conversations recently about their relationship. He has a twenty-four-month minimum sentencing, but he hasn't been doing well. Keeps getting in trouble, backtalking mostly. Bella is ready to start her life, you know? She can't keep waiting for him to get it together." Her posture falls forward as her shoulders slump.

Time is a thief.

"Anyway, I'm sorry. I didn't mean to blabber. It's just, knowing that you were gone, and she was waiting for you... and gosh, three years?!" She swings her head back, astounded. I glance at Cal, who is staring at our hands, lost in thought.

I would've waited a thousand years for just one more night with this man.

"Can you offer any advice that I can relay back to Bella, or even to Brady? Do they have a chance to make it?" She takes a napkin from her apron and presses it under her eyes. My healing heart breaks for her. *I know the pain.* Cal and I meet each other's eyes. It feels like we are thinking the same thing. He continues to look at me but talks to her.

"For Brady, I would say, if he has something worth fighting for in prison, then he could keep fighting for whatever that is. But if Isabella is fighting for something else, he can't be disappointed if she's gone by the time he's done fighting. Jen was worth the fight to get better and get out as soon as I could. I'm sure Jen here has better advice for your daughter-in-law. I wasn't the one waiting from a distance, on the opposite side of the bars." Tears trickle to the front of my eyes.

Every damn word that comes out of his mouth is like a luscious strawberry, perfectly plump and delicious as it already is, but adding the cute *Jen was worth the fight to come home* is like adding milk chocolate. It's divine.

I clear my throat, trying to swallow my tears. "Well, for Isabella, I would say..." I pause, feeling my breathing increase. My nose itches, and I take my free hand to pick up my napkin to bring to my eyes, which are filling fast with moisture. Cal's hand squeezes my other hand hard, keeping me in the moment.

"It's hard to be away from the person you love most. It's not even hard, it's draining. If she loved him, and if she wants to be with him, despite the trouble he's having, she'll wait for him. I will say, comparing to our story, I didn't have the courage to call or go to see him. I'm happy to hear she has that courage to visit him. It could be worth not visiting him, so she could decide if he was bothered by her absence. Sometimes we don't realize what we have until it's gone." Cal can tell this conversation is bringing up raw emotions for me. He leans forward, gripping my hand tight.

"Look, it's all about the fight. Every story is different. We hope they can pull through and create an incredible new chapter. I wish we could be more help, but we'd like to enjoy our time together."

The waitress can tell her story-telling time is over. She grins.

"Of course. Thank you for listening and the advice. I'll put your order in and bring over that bottle of Rosé." She winks at us, lays a gentle hand on my arm, and walks away. I turn my head to look at Cal, allowing his words to mesh into my soul.

"Ugh, how do I look?" With one hand, I dab under my eyes, praying that I haven't smudged my concealer or streaked my mascara.

"Absolutely beautiful." I bit my bottom lip, adored. Laying the napkin on my leg, I take a drink of water. Right on cue, our waitress comes back with our wine. Cal looks at me to give me a mental heads up; he has to let go of my hand. Internally, I frown, but I'm thankful for the air to breeze over my damp hand. I use the napkin under the table to wipe off the extra moisture.

A tiny squeal falls from my mouth as I watch my now grown, legal-age limit *friend* pour me a glass of wine.

He looks so good.

SO GOOD.

He hands me my glass but pours nothing for himself. I don't ask. Taking a small sip, my eyes widen, and I cover my mouth. I feel I'm drinking liquid cotton candy. It's delicious. Cal laughs at me, but I continue drinking. We've kept our hands to ourselves and the coolness from the wine feels so good on my hands. Cal leans forward, his hands in a ball on the table.

"We are only getting one bottle, so make sure you savor every sip." He winks at me as I drink the remaining bit in my glass. Cal already has the bottle in his hand to refill it.

"Can I ask you a question? About the past?" I watch the bubbles sizzle at the top of the glass as I take another sip. Cal looks nervous; he has a slight frown and brings his fingers to his lips.

"If it's about something that will get me angry, then no." Brutal honesty was never one of my favorite quirks about him.

"I don't think it will make you angry, but I can ask it, and if you think so, I will find another question." I also take another sip.

"Jen, I don't think I can focus on anything other than how breathtaking you look tonight, drinking fine wine like a grown-ass adult. It's distracting." He looks around him, probably checking for creeps and the first server. The compliments are getting to my head. Unconsciously, every word laced with ecstasy mends my heart.

"Fine, one question." And as if the stars align, our food arrives. It smells and looks delicious. We thank our waitress and devour. Cal's gaze doesn't leave mine.

"Why do you keep staring at me?" I giggle at him as I cover my mouth while I chew.

"That's your question? Well, shit... you got me excited." His eyes wander down to his plate. He smirks, showing his playfulness.

Under the table, I gently tap his shin with my shoe. I didn't realize his hand was in his lap, or waiting under the table for my leg? He snatches my ankle and holds it. I can feel him move his thumb in circles around my ankle. My heart is beating so fast, and I look around to see if other people's tables are *this* small. Cal continues to eat, not making known his sweet, secretive gesture.

"Was that the question?" He looks up at me. I'm in awe of the way he is caring for me right now. He's holding my leg under the table like it's a trophy. The way he's looking at me makes me feel like I have a spotlight on me and the way he talks to me is so gentle and kind. It's making me forget all his hurtful words that broke me years ago.

Nope, nope, nope.

STAY IN THE MOMENT.

I shake my head from side to side. "No. I want to know what prison was like." Cal lays his fork on his plate, creating a low, loud clack. He sits up in his chair like he's appalled I asked this question.

"Jen, absolutely not." I take another drink, realizing I've only gone a few minutes with tasting sparkles in my mouth.

"Hang on, let me elaborate because that's not exactly what I was asking." I placed my fork down and settled my hands in my lap. I don't know how far away I am from his leg, but I want to caress his leg, just the same as he's doing to my ankle. I don't want to look stupid by leaning forward too much, so I interlock my fingers together instead.

"The waitress said her son was having a hard time. It almost sounded like he wanted to stay in prison. He enjoyed it, maybe? I'm sure you didn't enjoy prison, but what was the hardest part for you?"

I try to keep my voice low and calm. I don't want to anger him and ruin this remarkable night. He looks at me, and I watch his eyes move down to my mouth. I feel the circles stop on my ankle. There is no touch from him, and I feel weird. He stares down at the table, trying to plan his answer, or maybe this is his answer–nothing.

I pick up my fork and look away from him.

"I'm sorry. I didn't mean to make things uncomfortable." When I hear him chuckle, I look at him again.

"Jen, when that lady said her son is having a tough time because he's fighting and talking back, I swear I could teach him a lesson or two. That fucking angered me. I couldn't imagine purposely trying to get the guards rattled up or making friends with the wrong guys. Jen, my biggest fear was that I was going to get caught in some fucked up shit which would cause me to stay there longer. I kept to myself. You know how hard it is for me to be so quiet, so I only spoke when instructed. I bit my tongue many, many times, but just had one goal in mind. I had to get out. I had to get back to you. The hardest part was just being away from you." I can hear the hoarseness rattle his voice.

I lose my appetite after another realization hits me. It was something I always wanted to believe but was never sure of. Cal didn't want to be away from me. Whatever happened to him, it was just shit timing for us.

I rested my fork on my plate and rubbed my lips together. Leaping across the table to kiss him crosses my mind, rewarding his good behavior with my presence. I want to ask more questions about prison, and about what happened before. Why he never made it home... but Angel scratches at my throat.

I look around the dining area, trying to avoid eye contact with him, feeling like I'll turn into a complete fountain if I look at him. His honesty is powerful. The Cal I used to know was impulsive and struggled with controlling his actions and behaviors. This new Cal makes me nervous and I'm struggling to fight the urge to throw myself at him.

My focus is back on him as he grabs both my hands. My vision is blurry from the moisture building in my eyes.

"What are you thinking about?" His voice comes as a whisper, and the atmosphere around us feels cloudy.

"Trust me, you don't want to know." I bite the inside of my cheek to keep my tears inside their home.

"Any other time, I would push you until you tell me, but I'll let it slide this time." He winks at me, squeezes my hands then resumes eating.

"I know a place we could stay tonight if you still wanted to." His comment throws me off guard and I feel I'm getting stuck in quicksand, only the quicksand is Cal. He's enclosing me, slowly and painfully but I'll gladly let him take me down. I only move my eyes up to look at him, grinning.

"That was the plan, remember? I get to fall asleep next to you." My heart is beating so fast, it feels like arrhythmia.

"I have to make a call real quick, so I'm going to step outside. Don't move. Keep eating, and so help me God, if that server stops at our table, he's dead." He pushes his chair out and kisses the top of my head. I watch him walk away, the stitches in my heart slowly coming apart because my heart is getting more full.

I get to spend the night with my Prince.

Calvin

I step outside not only for my emotional sake but physically I'm running out of oxygen. Jen is so damn beautiful. I almost feel like a creep staring at her.

Trust me, she craves your attention.

Over seventy-two hours, I've noticed more and more about her. Both the good and the bad.

I let Angel brag about all her perfections. The way her hair is so long and rests down on her shoulders. I swear I thought I was going to die when she moved her hair to lay it on her back before she started eating.

When I'm not consumed by all the little details, my eyes move down her chest to her low-cut V. It's tempting to not want to move a certain way so I can see more cleavage. I would never have guessed Jen would wear something so revealing. When I saw her in the truck and noticed how high her dress slit was on her leg, again, I thought I was going to die.

That dress. I don't know if she had help, but I don't care. She picked an excellent choice! I can't wait to touch her; to feel how soft she is under my fingertips. She gave me a little preview of how smooth her skin was when I grabbed her ankle under the table. I just had to feel her. I would have run my fingers up her leg, but I didn't want to scare her off.

Her ass is looking... just magnificent.

The best thing though, the absolute BEST thing about her, are those breath-taking eyes. When I'm not staring at her chest, then I'm staring into God's greatest gift.

Jen must've done something special with her makeup tonight. She's got sparkling powder stuff on her eyelids, but I'm happy with it because they remind me of shooting stars. They illuminate my heart and make me happy. Being with Jen makes me happy and my God, it feels so good to feel happiness again.

As I pace the sidewalk, I breathe deeply. Being here with Jen doesn't overwhelm me. I'm overwhelmed at how true Jen's words were to just stay in the present and not focus on the past or present. I didn't realize how tough that is...

I'm always open with Jen, and she can ask me anything, but her question about the hardest part of prison made my happiness vanish and instantly transported me back to Hell. It was true that I stayed on my best behavior. I have E and his friends to thank. I hate thinking about the time that passed since not being with Jen. So much time has passed between us and it's a fucking knife in my heart.

I'll do whatever it takes for Jen to feel comfortable with me. I could tell she didn't like being called my girlfriend, but she could be nothing else. We can't be friends. There's too much history and chemistry between us. The very idea of calling Jen my *friend* doesn't taste right.

I make my call and think enough time has passed for me, and for Jen too, to get our emotions in check. I don't want to, but I also check the time—7:13.

We've been in the presence of each other for almost two hours, and to think I still have the entire night with her.

I want to scream at the top of my lungs.

I pull the doors open and head towards our table, and it's like there's a spotlight on her. I notice her immediately, feeling lightheaded looking at her.

I pause, probably blocking the traffic flow, but I have to take a mental picture of this human being who has the honor of breaking and owning my heart, all in the same lifetime. She's running her fingers through her hair and she looks so beautiful.

God, I wish the English language had a better word for beautiful because she's more than that. Stunning. Flawless. Remarkable. Extraordinary. Striking.

She's all of those, but none of them do her justice.

My mouth curves up as I walk towards her. She finds me and mirrors my smile.

If I could choose my way to die, I'd pick this moment. With Jen just taking my last breath.

When I sit down, she props her hands under her chin, like I'm her trophy. It warms my heart but makes my blood boil because I'm not the hero in her story.

Stay in the moment.

I'm so caught off guard by her that I lose my train of thought. I'd get lost in those eyes forever.

"So, our place is ready whenever you are ready. I would assume we need to make a stop back at your apartment for bags and such?" I didn't think I said anything funny, but Jen busts out laughing.

Maybe it's the wine kicking in too... I laugh with her. She's so fucking cute. Aside from her eyes and the cleavage, her dimples are the next best thing to stare at.

"Cal, I don't always need several bags when I travel, okay?" She giggles at me.

I want to travel everywhere with you, and I don't care about many bags you bring.

"Well, bring whatever you think you need. Let me hunt down our friend." I twist my body around to search the dining area for our waitress.

She's bringing water to a table across the area.

For a moment, I feel bad about having her wait on us. Clearly, we are out of her parameters, but then I see the back of the head of our first server and I clench my fist. He makes eye contact with me, and I clench my other fist.

I dare you to come my direction.

Thankfully, the waitress sees me searching for her and walks towards me as the server walks in the other direction. My fists relax.

"Need some more wine, dears?" Jen laughs again. I look over my shoulder at her as she covers her mouth, like she said something wrong. I smirk at the waitress, who smirks back at me.

"Looks like your hands are going to be full tonight. Are you ready for the check, then?"

"Yes, please." I return my body to my normal position, so I'm facing Jen. She's flushed, and I'm sure if I bet her five-hundred dollars on my guess of what she wanted to do, I'd win. I'm not taking advantage of her, though. She doesn't deserve that. Merely, each other's company is what we need right now.

"I'll be right back."

I watch Jen dig through her wristlet for something. Intrigued, I watch her struggle.

"Looking for something?" I ask her. She swipes her hair behind one of her ears, and so help me God.

A feel sweat forming on my forehead.

I also feel a twinge in my pants.

"I thought I put my lip gloss in here." I crack a laugh and bit my lower lip when she looks at me, appalled to be laughing.

"I thought you lost your credit card or inhaler the way you were digging through that thing."

She slams her wristlet down on the table.

"Excuse you, sir. I just bought that lip gloss a few days ago and I like how it makes my lips look." Her drunken seriousness is making my stomach do flips. I can't stop smiling at her.

Our waitress comes back.

"You two have been so very fun and helpful tonight. It was a pleasure to meet you and serve you. I hope your love flourishes and you guys come back to see me soon. My name is Nancy. My daughter-in-law calls me Nan." She stays at our table for a moment.

I know Jen could say something more meaningful and sweet than me. She smiles at Nancy and then digs through her wristlet again. That thing has to be six inches long and maybe two or three inches deep. There's no way she'd lose a tube of lip gloss.

Smiling at the woman I get to take home tonight, I turn my attention to Nancy.

"Thank you for taking over to serve us. We really appreciate it. We hope things work out between your son and daughter-in-law. Love is hard, and it's hard work. I hope they keep at it, and they get a happy ending." I peer over at Jen, who has been listening to me. She holds my gaze, and I can't help but to look down at her lips.

They're glossy and I chuckle and look down at the table.

I take out my wallet and hand Nancy a hundred-dollar bill. I

didn't even check how much the meal was, but she deserves all of it. On the plus side, Henry never charged me for finding Jen, so having the extra cash is nice.

"Thank you so much. I hope to cross paths with you guys again. Have the best night." She lays a hand on Jen's shoulder and then places her hand on mine as she walks away. I stare at Jen again, who is rubbing her lips together.

"Would you be mad at me if I kissed you?" I ask her. She looks up at me with eyes wide, surprised by my question.

"What? No..." Her answer isn't very convincing. She grabs her hair and lays all of it on one side of her shoulder.

Holy fuck.

I clear my throat at the distraction.

"Well, I just figured it took you twenty minutes to find your lip gloss, so would you be upset if I kissed you just to smear it all off?" I'm hoping my flirting isn't coming across off as too much. She's so easy to play with.

She rubs her lips together some more.

"I can always re-apply, now that I know I have it."

Oh, an invitation?

I stand up from my chair and a hold out a hand for her to take. With hesitation, she grabs it, and we interlock hands.

Then, as an element of surprise, I swing her into my chest and take my other hand into her cheek and kiss her.

It's the worst-best thing I could do right now.

She hates when people watch her, at least I think she still hates it, but I know she would love a kiss from me. She groans a bit into my mouth, and I let go of her face.

We're in public, you prick.

With pride, I pull her behind me toward the entrance. I don't even want to look back at her reaction because I already know I earn a point. I'm clueless about these points, but I'll keep kissing Jen, regardless.

We get to the truck and she stops me as I try to open her door.

"What the hell was that?" I don't even have a moment to respond because she takes me by the shoulders and pushes me against the car.

At first, I'm wondering *what the hell is going on,* but then I don't even care because her mouth is on mine, and I just want time to stop.

For us.

She cradles her hands behind my neck, and I weave my hands through her hair. Our tongues tease each other again and I can feel her push her body against mine. Her breathing is heavy, and I when I open my eyes for a quick second, I see no remnants of gloss on her lips.

Fuck, I just want to keep kissing her. She tastes so good. Smells so good. Sounds so good. She feels so fucking good.

I don't want to, but I beg Devil to push me back from her. It's like an invisible force is pulling my hands from her hair and then suddenly I stop kissing her. She flutters her eyes open, disappointed at the discontinuation.

"Baby, I want to keep kissing you. So bad. Just not here. C'mon, let's go back to your place to pack some stuff and then we'll stop at my place, and we'll head to the cabin." I kiss her forehead and then open the door.

I feel like the biggest prick in the world.

This is all she wanted.

To just kiss me, for God's sake.

If our goal was to only stay in the moment, it would be easy, but we have a past to confront and future to decide. It's not always easy to stay in the moment.

When I get in the driver's seat, she's already re-applying her lip gloss. I chuckle as I start the truck. She looks over at me, curious.

"For next time?" I wink at her and grab her hand. She pulls her hand away, but just because she needs to put her lip gloss back in her bag. She re-grabs my hand and we rest them on the console.

"What flavor was it, do you know?" She looks out the window as she asks me.

"Hmmm, it tastes like orange."

"Good!" She squeezes my hand as an added layer of affection.

The drive back to Laurelhurst is easy. We talk about Jen's schooling and how she took a semester off. I ask about Anna and Andy. We reminisce about some of our date spots as we pass them on the highway.

We never let go of each other's hands.

We got caught in the city traffic for about ten minutes, so we arrived back at her apartment around 8:15.

I'm not sure she wants me to come in.

"No funny business, but you can come in." She points a finger in my face as she props the door open.

I follow behind her. My heart races and my fingers feel shaky.

Her apartment.

We should've had our own at this point.

Not the time to get sad, you pansy.

Okay, thanks Devil.

Jen finagles with her key and opens the door for me.

Clean. It smells like lemon. She has a large living room with tons of blankets on the couch. A medium sized TV is mounted on her wall next to a full length window and a couple of notebooks sit on the coffee table. I hear Jen toss her keys on her counter. Unlike me, she has a bar top, which creates an open concept from the kitchen to the living room. Her kitchen is tidy and large, especially for one person.

"You cook a lot?" I yell to her, noticing she's already in her room packing.

I hear one laugh. "No, my dad didn't teach me and then shit hit the fan for me to care about eating or food."

There are hardly any appliances in the kitchen, except an espresso machine. I smirk to myself, thinking that must've been from Pat.

I look at the photos that hang on the wall next to the kitchen that lead down the hallway.

There's her and her dad. Pat. Anna.

And so many of her and I.

My stomach twists into knots. Having to look at us every day?!

How fucking painful.

I quietly walk down the hallway to the door that's propped open—her bedroom. I stop at the entry and watch her. She doesn't hear me or notice me, so I take full advantage of watching her.

I notice she already has one bag packed with clothes, a blanket, and it looks like she's getting her toiletries from her attached bathroom.

That must be nice.

I startle her as she comes out of the bathroom and jumps to find me standing there.

"Welcome to my casa. Nothing impressive. It's boring and quiet. I'm not here a lot so..." Again, we come face to face with the past.

"Why aren't you here a lot?" I lean against the doorframe. My eyes go up and down her figure, enjoying the view.

"Um, I guess I don't like to be lonely, so I work a lot." She seems frazzled at the topic and swipes some hair behind her ears. She looks around her room, determining what else she needs to bring.

"Oh." It breaks my heart.

I don't like to be lonely.

With those words spinning in my mind, I walk towards her. She's facing the bed, and I put my hands on her waist to spin her around. She doesn't startle... it's almost as if she was waiting for me to come to her.

"You don't have to be lonely anymore." I give her a swift kiss on the cheek. I can't help myself but tangle my fingers through her hair after she rewards me with another kiss on the mouth. She does the same to me, grappling her fingers through my hair. After falling backwards on her bed, she straddles me.

IN HER LITTLE RED DRESS. SHE IS STRADDLING ME.

Game over.

I see everything that I want, and I can't stop myself.

I'm suddenly ravenous, and my hands are *finally* rubbing along her upper thighs.

Ugh, they're so soft and smooth.

She's pulling my face close to her, like she's depleted of oxygen, both of us groan and moan.

It's been a long time coming.

Again, I know she wants this, but it seems too fast. Believe me, I would lose myself to her in a matter of a millisecond, but there is so much disconnect between us we are both trying to ignore. I couldn't live with myself to let her fall apart to me, and then to watch her break down because of a memory or something I said.

Running my hands from her hips, up her waist, along her arms, I finally reach her shoulders and give her a soft push to create distance. I want to see her. With one hand on her shoulder, I use the other to brush hair away from her face.

"Finish packing. We still have to stop at my place." I avoid explaining my reasons for ending her seductive behavior. I *REALLY* want to, but I've got to keep some sort of impulse in check.

She doesn't look disappointed as she kisses me, then hops off me, pulling her dress down. I'm sure the wine is aiding in her good mood. I sit up on my elbows but stay on the bed to watch her finish packing.

"If you want to, we can stay at this cabin for the weekend. I don't know what other plans you have." She's folding a sweatshirt when she stops to look at me. She frowns, but then says, "All weekend?"

I shake my head and smile at her.

"Oh wow, yes! Weekends are the worst because I don't work, so I try to walk around the park or do some window shopping." She laughs at her despair. It breaks me, but I'm so glad I get to give her this.

"Why do you feel you need to bring so much stuff with you every time we go somewhere?" I ask her. She's folding the seventh shirt, at least and placing it in her bag. She glares at me.

"I don't know. I guess I just want to be prepared. But I've learned that you can never fully be prepared for anything." The comment sits in the air between us.

You mean you were never prepared for me to go awol and leave you behind?

We make no more of the conversation because we are trying so hard to stay in the present. I'm not sure about Jen, but I find it frustrating as hell to not bring up the past or the future. It's walking on eggshells but mixed with razor blades and shards of glass.

"Okay, I think I have everything. You ready?" She lifts her "weekender bag"–as she calls it–over her shoulder and slips her blanket over her arms. She picks up another tote bag full of.... What? I have no idea.

I stand from the bed and grab the larger bag that was on the floor.

When I stand in front of her, I smirk and lean in to kiss the corner of her mouth. The excitement is filling my stomach to spend the weekend with Jen. This is what I was praying for–to just pick up where things left off. To pick her up, have her pack her bags, and spend the night with me all over again.

She's bringing me back to life.

I wish we didn't have to stop at my apartment to gather my belongings, but I'm so fucking thankful we get to do it together.

I follow her down the hallway, keeping the space between us small. I stop by the kitchen bar and wait for Jen. She turns on her moon nightlight on the coffee table after closing her blinds and turning off the remaining lights. At the bar, she helps me open the door. She's had a grin on her face since we've left dinner, and the selfish beast in me is hoping that it's because of me. My ego needs some inflating. I walk out to the sidewalk as I hear her lock the door.

The drive from her apartment to mine was quick. She was only a few minutes away from me. The whole freaking time, Henry couldn't have figured that out?

We held hands the whole way and we reminisce when we pass the street where I got pulled over a couple days after my graduation. Jen was with me, of course. She complimented my assertiveness, even though it wasn't the best idea against a police officer, but Jen liked it, so I'd do it again.

Well, you did mouth off to an officer, but Jen wasn't around that time, and it landed you in prison, so.... you probably shouldn't do it again.

In my assigned parking spot, 404, which I consider lucky, I park my truck before heading to Jen's door. Her grin just keeps getting wider.

The differences between mine and Jen's apartment are obvious. Jen lives in a gated community with her front door being on ground level. She doesn't have to climb stairs, especially to the fourth floor, or fumble for ten minutes to get the key to latch on. God, I didn't miss this stupid doorknob. Jen has a freshly painted mailbox next to her front door where I have community mailboxes that were peeling with paint. Jen's apartment smelled clean of her jasmine scent and lemon. It's what I envisioned Heaven to smell like.

A whiff of vanilla, my shampoo and the stir fry aroma Henry and I tried to make last night exits my front door. Not as pleasant. Thankfully, I had plenty of time to clean up my apartment, not that I was expecting Jen to come over, but my lavish apartment looks in good condition. I hold the door open for her and flick the lights on behind me.

I finagle with the door because the side of the door scrapes against the doorframe. Shitty thing. We always talked about our getting a house with French doors and I smile to myself about our dream house we used to create together. When I turn around, Jen has her arms crossed and walks around my living room.

Unlike her, I don't have many pictures on the wall or things sitting around. I have a few trinkets that sit on my coffee table. My table is covered with a coaster set I made in wood shop class in high school, a glass figurine of a black bear, my favorite animal, my small collection of knives that need sharpening and cleaning, and a stack of letters. Like Jen, my tv mounts to the wall. A recliner sits in the corner next to my couch.

I usually keep my balcony door open to keep a breeze constant. Both our kitchens are similarly empty. I have a cheap coffee maker handed down from my parents when I moved in here. There's a wall that blocks my front door from the kitchen, so you have to take a few steps in to look into the kitchen. I watch Jen take in my life.

I barely got the chance to start my life with you.

"Well, make yourself at home, and I'll be out in a sec." I tell her as I set my keys down on the kitchen table and walk down my small hallway.

My closet, not attached to my bedroom, unlike Jen's, is also bare. With so much time that passed while Henry and I tried to secure a positive signal, I had a closet purge moment. It left very little. A few pairs of khakis, a couple of t-shirts and three form fitting sweatshirts.

I reach to the top of my closet to grab a backpack and start piling a couple shirts, one pair of pants, underwear, and a sweatshirt. From the bathroom, I also grab a couple of things. I finish in about five minutes. Prison helps you become a minimalist in a way. When I walk down the hallway, it's uncannily quiet that I fear Jen left. Instead, I find her sitting on the couch, holding something.

A letter.

My stomach drops and I don't know how to approach her.

Please don't be crying.

I sit my backpack down on the kitchen table, not wanting to bring attention to myself, then sit beside her on the couch. She doesn't look at me, keeping her eyes glued to the letter. I glance down and realize she's reading the last letter I read—the poem where I told her I loved her.

After the carnival.

Oh, thank God.

I'm silent, hoping she'll break the silence because I don't know what to say. I'm forming a complicated relationship with these letters.

"I could read this over and over." She finally says. She brings the letter to her chest like she's holding a precious puppy. I look over at her and she smiles at me, tears filling her eyes.

"That's the last one I read."

She folds up the letter and places it back in the envelope and lays it on top of my *read* pile. The pile next to it stands tall, *to be read*.

She leans back on my couch, looking comfortable. She crosses her leg over the other, allowing her dress to build up on her thigh. I eye her legs and it's tempting to want to run my hand over her thigh. I don't realize I bit my bottom lip, lost in my own thoughts of lust.

Don't touch.

She rests her head on my shoulder, moving closer to me. It makes me sad. How long has she gone without a decent night of sleep?

"I've missed you."

My dangerously spiraling thoughts thankfully came to a halt. I look up from Jen's legs and see her looking at me, her eyes glossy. She tilts her head, and her hair falls perfectly down her shoulders.

She looks like a fucking portrait. On the largest canvas, I would hang that portrait on my wall and admire it from dawn to dusk.

I turn my body to face her, and she repositions herself. She lifts her hand to touch my cheek. It's fire. Her touch is so foreign, yet so familiar. I would burn over and over if I could.

"Our weekend is only starting, baby." I remove her hand from my cheek and hold it tight between my hands. I kiss the top of her hand to ease some frustration happening in my head and my pants. It's almost like a magnetic force between us pulls us together. She leans into me, then I open my arm and she settles beside me. Her incredible smell has me wishing it were a legal drug; I'd be hopelessly addicted.

Her legs are on the couch, feet swung behind her, head perfectly nestled in my neck like a baby bird. From behind, I pull her hair from her neck and graze her jawline with my fingers. Her skin feels like velvet, the most expensive and precious kind of material.

We sit like this for a while–not sure how long because I can't see the clock from the couch.

I'm hoping time has stopped or, even better, my clock is broken.

It's just so peaceful to be here *with her* after all this time.

We both end up dozing off at some point because when I hear a door slam from outside in the hallway, I jolt up, jolting Jen as well. We both look at each other and smile. Kissing her is becoming natural and easy.

Even after a nap, she's still the most beautiful thing in the world. There is so much energy trying to keep me on the couch with her, but I fight through it to get off the couch and check the time. My oven clock shines a bright neon red 9:42.

I laugh as I turn the corner from my kitchen and find Jen has left the couch. My apartment is not big, so I check the front door to make sure she hasn't ditched me.

That would suck.

I hear a clink of something coming from my bedroom. I turn towards the hallway and see Jen's red dress take over my view.

To think this bedroom was boring and useless ten minutes ago when you were packing.

Damn right, Angel. This bedroom has now turned into the

Louvre.

"Whatcha doing?" Leaning against the doorframe, I admire a body shaped like an hourglass. She must've not heard me walking down the hallway, and she jumps to turn around, holding a picture.

"Snooping. Don't tell me you didn't snoop my apartment when I was packing?" She glares at me and I lose all temptation of staying away from her. I pull at her waist and I kiss her hard.

"No, I didn't snoop." I tell her in between kisses.

She's shocked as her mouth gapes open.

"Why not?"

"Well, I'd probably look through every shelf, every cabinet, hidden crevice to drive myself crazy thinking that something isn't adding up."

"Do you think there was someone else?" Her voice is quiet, almost secretive.

"Jen, c'mon. Look at you. You're fucking irresistible. It would not surprise me if there was someone else. It would absolutely kill me, but it just reminds me how lucky I am right now in the moment to have you, because I mean, any guy could have you." My words hurt. They twist my stomach into knots.

Please don't let there be someone else...

She hooks her arms around my neck and stares at me, searching for something. Or recognizing jealous Cal — the worst version of me. The most damaging.

She changes the subject by pulling away and showing me the picture she has. "I didn't know you kept this." It's her prom photo. Repair is impossible because it's badly crinkled and its edges are tattered. The same photo that was taped in my cell.

The same photo that gave me purpose, gave me a reason to do better and get home to her.

I chuckle even though there's nothing funny. Gently taking the photo out of her hand, I look at it. I have every centimeter of this picture memorized.

"This photo was in my jacket when I got arrested. I could take it with me once I got sentenced. I didn't care about any of my shit besides this. It was the only thing in my cell, right next to my bed. This, well you, got me through it. You helped me come home." Her eyes swell with moisture and I already have my hands cupping her cheeks to erase the tears as they fall. She drops her head to my chest and shakes it back and forth. I grab her head, kissing the top of her head.

"This is so unreal, Cal." She tells my chest. Her voice being so close to my heart that I'm getting goosebumps.

"C'mon, let's get going. I don't want to get there too late."

All I want to do is hold her hand. I want her scent to overwhelm my truck. I have the courage to run my fingers over her legs, and good God, I just want to carry her into the cabin and let her feel safe. The only thing I have ever wanted her to feel.

"Okay." She breathes into my lips as she kisses me. A kiss like she's trying to mesh our souls together.

She catches me off guard when I feel her tongue slip through my teeth. Something in me takes over as I grab a handful of her hair and push myself towards her. My moan is so loud and vicious. She's a poisonous snake right now, and the venom feels incredible.

It's the same desirable feeling of doing everything with Jen the first time, but it's only better. When I first kissed Jen, I felt like I was going to fall apart, and only she could fix me. Allowing her to fix me anytime, anywhere. That's what I feel right now.

I could barely stand as she creates distance between us. I find it hard to stop kissing her. She notices my turmoil and bites her lip.

"Thought we had to get going?" She's enticing. So goddamn enticing. I lick my lips and unravel my hands from her hair.

"Yeah, let's go." I don't know how I manage, but I pull away from her and walk down the hallway, reaching my hand back for her to grab. Instantly, I feel her warmth. Picking up my backpack and turning off my lights, I close the patio door. The next time I'm in my musty apartment, the claustrophobia will make me regret this decision.

I look forward to feeling refreshed upon returning home, confident that my weekend with Jen is the start of many new, exciting, and potentially risqué experiences.

Nothing will ever be the same.

Jennie

I wish I had a moment to recoup myself before we left his apartment. A sense of unease washed over me, though I couldn't confide in Cal. I know why, but it would destroy him. I stay quiet on the drive, but Cal notices my silence. He squeezes my hand several times to get my attention. I look at him but can only provide a sad smile. I lie and tell him I'm feeling tired. It's not entirely a lie, but I can't tell him the truth.

We decide to listen to music for the drive. It blocks the awkwardness, and it's soothing to have a break from kissing and talking, even though I want to. My mind feels mushy.

After what feels like an eternity, Cal shifts off the highway. We haven't been driving for long and we've been going north of Seattle.

"How did you find this place?" I ask him, taking in the new surroundings.

"Just a place I know of." His response sparks anxiety in me. *Why was his response short? Did something happen here?*

He drives for a few more minutes before he turns down a dirt road. I continue to blink, hoping Cal isn't planning on killing me in the middle of nowhere. Then a house, really more like a cottage, comes into view. It's small, but it's beautiful. It's a light tan color with white trim. The front door is a bright red color. *Maybe Cal painted this door...* The front steps are wide, almost cathedral-like, leading up to the front door. The spotlights shine down on the front garden, lined with wildflowers.

Daisies representing new beginnings and faith. Lupines symbolize happiness. The clusters of baby blue eyes showcase trust. My favorite, black-eyed Susans show strength and loyalty. But the variety of tulips that fill the garden, replicate how my heart feels—full of love.

Off to my right is a personal out cove to Lake Washington. There's some sort of picnic table and a shed near the water. Near the table is one large willow tree with a tire swing hanging down. How peaceful. When I look to my left, Cal is looking at me.

"Is this okay?" He pulls my hand to his mouth and kisses the top of it.

Please don't.

"It's perfect here. So quiet and isolated. Do you own this?" I'm eager to see the inside and to find the bed. More so for *my* personal benefit than for both of us. I open the door, but Cal is still holding my hand, so he jerks me back.

"If it's too much here, let me know. It reminds me of..."

"Easton..." I cut him off because I can feel the eeriness, too. Swallowing is painful; it feels as if I'm swallowing tacks. A black cloud is entering my heart, and I don't know where to run. My memories are torturing me that Cal is the bad guy and he's not safe. I don't have Anna or Glen to run to for safety. I'm left alone. My breathing intensifies and I grab my chest.

"Jen... hey." It doesn't even feel like a second has passed, but Cal is out of the driver's seat and standing on the passenger side of the truck. He's trying to move me to look at him, but I can't. I turn into steel the moment I think about what happened in Easton.

He is safe. This is present time. He won't hurt you.

Bullshit, he's a monster, and he's going to hurt you.

Stay in the present, Jennie!!

The conversation between Devil and Angel in my head becomes too much and I squeeze my hands against my temples.

I feel my body shake, but when I open my eyes again, I see Cal. His face is full of concern and worry. He has a hold of my face and I'm looking deep into the sea, trying to center myself.

"Jen, are you okay, baby?" I have an overwhelming urge to cry, so I do. I slam my head into Cal's chest and he consoles me the only way he knows. He just holds me and kisses the top of my head. My crying session lasts only a couple minutes, but enough for me to become twenty times more tired. *Stupid fucking emotions.* When I lift my head off Cal's chest, he frantically puts his hands in my hair and has a tight grip on me.

"Talk to me. What is going on?"

"I'm sorry. Just flashbacks of Easton and you and ..." I can't even finish because I know Devil will continue the savage cycle of recreating that night...

"C'mon, c'mere." Cal pulls me out of the truck and holds me. I shove my face into his chest and breathe him in. *He's safe now.* He holds me so tight, I felt like Rose when Jack was trying to rescue her from the back of the ship.

You can do this. You will be alright. Angel reminds me.

Cal guides me by the waist and pulls towards the house. I'm hit with a swarm of disappointment as I wanted to walk into this beautiful house feeling on top of the world, but now I feel like I'm falling.

Cal puts in a four-digit code on the door pad and an overwhelming smell of cashmere and vanilla escapes. The smell of Cal. Joy and happiness fill all my senses.

It could all disappear in a split second.

I wince at Devil trying to sabotage these precious moments. I want her to lie in her coffin and leave me alone.

Cal closes the door and the illumination coming from the kitchen draws me towards it. It's large and white and continues to remind me of the house in Easton. There's a small table that sits in the middle of the kitchen, but there are so many appliances on the counter. My eyes light up at the sight of the fancy, silver, simple looking coffee maker. The lights, I found, are coming from underneath the cabinets and create a warm, homey feeling.

Off to the left of the kitchen is the living room. There's a large, light brown sectional couch. A full blanket ladder catches my eye that sits next to the fireplace. The pictures on the mantle pique my interest, but Cal pulls me in the opposite direction before I can look at them. To the right of the kitchen, there are only two bedrooms. Well, one main bedroom and a tiny office.

The bedroom smells even more like Cal and I feel like I'm floating on the clouds, as he guides me into there. He lets go of me to start the shower, which is attached to the bedroom.

"Take a shower. I'm going to get our bags and we'll relax. Okay?" He pushes hair from my face and touches me so gently, as if I'm a China doll. *You don't know how damaged I am...*

I push the negative thoughts away and nod, even though I don't want to shower. When the bedroom door closes, I stare at myself in the large mirror in the far corner. My makeup no longer looks as great as it did when I left my apartment this afternoon. Streaks of mascara line my cheeks. My eyeshadow sparkles are scattered all over my face. My lips are no longer glossy. I run my fingers through my hair which is filled with tangles!! I guide my eyes down my body, chuckling at how hideous I look now. *What does Cal think of me right now?*

I turn off the water, conserving it. I put the lid down on the toilet and sit down as I claw my fingers through my hair. My plan is not going as expected, but I'm not failing...

Yet.

I heard a soft knock on the door and look over when Cal pokes his head through.

"Oh, no shower?" He fully opens the door and leans against the doorframe, as I've seen him do so many times. I detangle my fingers from my hair and look over at him, gawking. He's so handsome and perfect and dreamy and I don't know how in a million years, this man wanted to be better *for someone like me.*

"Cal, it's been years since I felt an ounce of feeling special and confident, so I want to stay in this dress for as long as I can. I'm sorry that my face looks terrible." I chuckle and look away, embarrassed. He comes into the bathroom and kneels in front of me, holding my cheeks to look at him.

"You look beautiful. No matter what you are wearing, where we are, what we are doing, or how long it's been since we've seen each other. My eyes always find you." I blush at Cal's affection. His lips find my forehead.

My head is spinning from everything that is happening. It still feels surreal that Cal is out of prison. His return was a blessing, and here we are, in the middle of nowhere, frolicking the night away; then I notice that bed behind Cal's head.

He wasn't messing around. We really are sleeping together in the same bed.

"Come on, come lay with me." He can read my thoughts now. He grabs my hands and tugs me off the toilet. I can't resist.

This is everything I've ever wanted. I don't care how I look, how messy my mind is becoming, what time it is, or where we are. Cal's arms are the only place I want to be.

Calvin

I'm holding her close, feeling her warm breath on my arm as I play with her hair. It's gotten so long over the past couple of years. We've just been laying together, nothing more, nothing less. Simply enjoying each other's company.

"Hey Jen..." I whisper in her ear, knowing she hasn't fallen asleep yet. She twitches when she's in a deep sleep—at least she used to. I've been in a deep thought, and it's been driving me crazy.

"Mhhm..."

"Can I ask you a question, and you promise to be honest with me about it?"

At the end of my question, she's already up and staring at me. I tousled her hair, and black streaks marred her eyes. God, she looks so broken and nervous. There are so many letters I haven't read yet and I know she doesn't want to give away information. My question relates to her past letters, so does this actually break the rules?

I turn my body to face her. Grabbing her hand to caress it, I try to keep her relaxed. I want to witness her expression when I ask this, to make sure she doesn't lie to me. Not that she would, at least the Jen I remember wouldn't like to me.

"Baby... how bad did you get?" I don't know where this question comes from but there's something in me that feels Jen suffered when I was gone. There is no confusion or shocked expression on her face because she knows what I'm trying to ask. Lost in her gaze, I long for a mind-to-mind connection instead of words.

Pulling her hands away, she shifts around on the bed. Clasping them together, she nervously rubs them. I can tell she's thinking hard, but I can't tell if she's thinking about the awful shit that happened to her or the way she wants to answer me.

"I need you to tell me, so I know what I need to do. I am here now. You are safe."

I want to pull her close to me. I want to console her so fucking badly that it breaks my heart that she is pulling away. She's rubbing her hands harshly, and I hate I notice all the little things, but I do. Her bottom lip quivers, and there's a small crinkle in her eyebrows as they crease together. She pulls the skin by her fingernails. She tugs at the sleeves of her dress, stretching the fabric.

"Pretty bad." She chuckles, but I don't laugh. If anything, I can feel my blood boil. *This isn't a joking matter, Jen.*

"What happened?" I move close to her, hoping she doesn't resist my approach. I run my fingers along her cheek. They glow with a gentle warmth. She looks up at me this time.

Wet plants.

I'm holding back tears of my own. I didn't think she could break my heart anymore, but I think she's about to. The thought of my Jen hurting herself, because of me, proves that I am going to Hell, or whatever is lower than Hell. I want to curse at the Heavens because she moves further away from me, making my hand drop from her cheek. She wraps her arms around her legs and sets her chin on her kneecaps. She's on the opposite side of the bed and it feels wrong for her to be so far away.

"I was in the hospital for a while. I wasn't taking good care of myself." Her words ripple through my chest.

She wasn't taking care of herself because you left her, you idiot. Shall we replay the words you said to her before you disappeared?

I can tell she wants to elaborate, but she won't do it willingly, so I press further.

"Why were you in the hospital, Jen? What did you do..."

"I was just so fucking lonely, Cal. You don't understand. There was nobody here." She dashes off the bed and jogs down the hallway, clenching her throat or upper chest, one of the two.

I get off the bed to follow her. She's at the kitchen table, her hands against her forehead. My lady in red is struggling to breathe normally. Her silhouette reminds of me how Devil would look, making me want to stay away from her sins, but fuck, lust in the best sin of all.

Her fragileness and hurt makes me feel sick. She's not even close to the Devil in my head and there is so much in me that wants to comfort her like the precise Angel she is. I inhale deeply to cope with the unexpected shifts in mood. I'll do whatever I can to protect her from the thoughts that have eaten her alive. Opposite her, I pull out a chair, reclaiming the air she breathes.

"Hey, we don't need to talk about it now, but I want to know what happened eventually, okay? Did you write a letter about it?"

I don't want to upset her by asking about the hospital, but I want to know if she's better. If she is or isn't, I'll take care of her. I have been waiting to take care of her.

She brings her hands off her forehead, and her touch electrifies me. I will never tire of feeling her touch me. I put my hands over hers.

"I was cutting. Really bad. I wasn't eating either. I had lost a lot of weight. Last May, I had made a cut that was too deep."

She takes her hand off my arm and pulls up on her left sleeve. I realize the first day I met her, she had a sweatshirt on. Yesterday at the shop, she had a jacket on. Even now, she wears a dress with sleeves.

My heart collapses. I bring my hands over my mouth and have no words. For the first time since seeing her, it's not for a happy reason. My stomach churns, goosebumps erupt, and tears well in my eyes. I need to shield my eyes for a moment. It's too fucking much to take in.

In the middle of her forearm was a two and a half-inch scar. The color is distinct from her skin. It's discolored, a shade of a light pink. She turned her left arm into a canvas of straight lines. Everywhere. Some are short, others are long. But the perfectly placed, imperfect wound is the most prominent one.

I run my fingers over it, as I feel Jen's fingers wipe away tears falling from my eyes.

Her eyes on me, but I can't bear to look at her right this very second. Her wounds are calling out for me. Pulling her around the table, I lift her arm so she stands between my legs. Beginning from her wrist and up to her inner elbow, I kiss her scars. I strive to give more kisses than there are of scars.

"Yes. I wrote you a letter. Several of them were when I was in the hospital. I'm sure you haven't gotten to those letters yet, but I want to start off with an early apology. It was never supposed to get that bad." Her voice cracks a bit. I feel her free hand run through my hair, comforting me.

It was never supposed to get that bad...

"Who brought you to the hospital?"

"I did. I never meant to cut that deep. When I got to the hospital, I was, um, I was worse than what I thought. Self-destructing badly. I hated myself for how disappointed you'd be with me. What's the point of waiting for you to return, only to hear that you no longer love this version of me?"

"Jen, I'm tired of hearing you say you were waiting for me. You didn't have to wait for me, you know that!"

I feel my blood boiling a degree or two higher. I don't even know why I'm getting angry, but I hate how she waited so long for me. It would've been so different if she didn't know I was in prison, but she knew. She knew I'd be gone for five years! She made the choice to continue being miserable without me. And at a cost of hurting herself.

I drop her damaged arm, but she continues to stand in front of me. She makes a ball with her hands, resting them on her stomach. I notice the ring still on her finger. Is this what it feels like to argue with your wife?

"You think I wanted to keep waiting? Jesus, Cal. All I ever wanted for the past three and a half years was to move on. The last words you said to me made me think you were done with me. And I tried to move on. I got married. But he was nothing, absolutely nothing compared to you." I stare up at her, alarmed and nauseated at the same time.

There it is. There is the someone she was hiding from me.

"You did what?" My voice is hoarse. I don't know if I want to cry or scream.

"His name is Jonah. We were married for six months. He married me as soon as I got out of the hospital. Our divorced finalized three months ago."

I let my thoughts speak, trying to align my life to hers. What was I doing three months ago?

"Three months ago I was..."

"Getting an early release." She finishes.

"Jesus, Jen. What secrets are you keeping from me?!" I stand up and knock over the chair. Needing air, I step outside.

I want her to follow me because I want her to stay close. I want her to tell me everything. How was she keeping tabs on me from the other side of the country? Nobody knew that I was getting out early. I surprised Lincoln when I called him from the airport, and I made him swear not to tell my parents I was coming home. The calls with Pat had dissipated several months earlier. There was nobody else that knew where I was.

At the same time of wanting to keep her close to answer all my questions, I want her to stay the fuck away from me for a moment. I don't know what kind of life she was living, but I don't appreciate the secrecy.

Marriage? I'm stuck on that part. There was another person in this world capable of loving Jen, my Jen. I'm fucking boiling with envy towards this guy. With disappointment towards him. With the utmost respect towards him. He had to pick up *my* pieces. Pieces that were broken into a million shards to fix her.

I go to the bench, hidden between bushes. Focusing on my breathing, I take a seat facing the water. I fight to suppress my tears, struggling to control the impulse to punch this tree.

WHAT FUCKING TWISTED GAME AM I IN NOW?

I'm trying with every fiber to keep my rational side of me stable. What would I practice in group therapy when I was feeling unstable? Breathing isn't doing a fucking thing right now. I'm breathing heavily like a dog.

Instead, I disassociate. It's not the best thing to do, especially in a situation like this. We learned in group therapy about depersonalization and derealization. I decide to take the derealization route and pretend to escape my body and look from the outside. I'm just floating through the wind, wondering when and where and why and how... So many questions flood through me.

Somehow, I'm back in the moment when I hear her voice. My eyes spring open, but I can't bring myself to look at her right now. *She was married to someone who wasn't you...*

"What are 5 things you can see?" Her voice calms me but annoys me at the same time. I can sense she's walking down the stairs from the front door. We are the only ones out here, and I think she realizes that.

I don't want to answer her. I want her to leave me alone. But her voice is so soothing. A voice I have missed so much. There is still a powerful urge to punch the tree next to me.

You've already done that once, you idiot.

I want to pull her close and never let her go. Never let her go *again*.

A sigh loudly, proving how annoyed I am to continue playing this messed-up game.

"The water. The tire swing. The sky is a black blanket. Two birds by the water. I picture how this Jonah guy looks with a broken nose and black eyes, but that isn't part of the technique, so... The last thing I see is the most beautiful and psychotic woman I've ever met."

I look over at her, and she's slightly illuminated by the spotlight from the front of the cabin. She has her arms crossed, disappointed in my comment about Jonah, or maybe the psychotic part. She's still wearing her red dress, and I have to bite my tongue to not tell her how devilishly sexy she looks in the dark. Her walls have been dropping all night and for a tiny fraction of a moment, I fear loving this version of Jen.

"4 things you can feel." Her voice is getting closer to me.

"I only feel you, Jen. You are everywhere." My voice is tired. Her game is exhausting. I don't know how she's been playing this whole time.

"3 things you can hear." She's right behind me. Still giving me space, but she's close. If I turn around and take a step, she'd be in my arms.

"Your breath. My breathing. The crickets."

"2 things you can smell."

"You, Jen. You're overpowering all my senses." That didn't mean to come off seductive, but it does. She wraps her arms around me.

"I'm sorry." She mutters into my ear.

The biggest relief falls off my shoulders. She can probably feel the tension leaving my body.

My girl. My Jen. So wounded and broken.

Reciprocating my seductiveness, she breathes in my ear again.

"1 thing you can taste." Without hesitation, and despite my boiling temperature still being in a danger zone, I turn around, grab her by the waist, and kiss her.

Every kiss felt like it could be our last. I kiss her as if my dominant, charming, overprotective alter ego comes out of me. I grab her face, then sink my hands into her hair and pull her even closer. She mounts my legs and the image I have of her right now is another photo I want framed to put in my living room.

She grabs my face with both hands.

She's wanting so much more.

She's been waiting for more.

I lift her off the ground, and she wraps her legs around my waist. I finally get to run my hands over her thighs and fuck, it's even better than I imagined. They're soft like butter, and I can't even remember what I stomped outside for, but I'm glad I did so I could pick her up and bring her back in. I'm holding the back of her neck when I lift her up and hold her ass for extra support. Her thighs tighten around me.

I haven't stopped kissing her. It's getting more wet. She's making more noises. My boiling temperature is quickly reducing. However, I enter a new danger zone. We've been playing with fire all evening, but now I'm ready to burn into flames. It's like looking at a solar eclipse. It's so mesmerizing and one of a kind, but for fuck's sake, I need to look away.

It's been so long. She tastes even better. Moans even better. Grips even tighter. I can feel it in her heartbeat that she has entered pure euphoria. This is all she wanted. All she needed.

Me.

"Take me inside, Cal. Please." I never thought I would hear her beg. The decisions were always mine to make.

I try to rationalize, but there's only one thing on my mind right now. Her moaning is only growing louder, and it's luring me in.

"I give you what you want, if you give me what I want." I gasp out at her while we get through the door.

"I don't care what you want right now. Please." We accidentally bump into the wall, but we don't flinch. Her kissing is becoming sloppy, but God, she tastes so good. There must be remnants of wine on her lips. We find the doorway to the bedroom, and I lay her down. I stand at the end of the bed, pulling off my shirt.

Like a dog, she pounces onto her legs and starts kissing me again.

She allows her tongue to play.

"Jesus, Jen." I smile as she kisses me with her tongue again. She pulls me by my arms onto the bed, on top of her. My body trembles from the sensual tension rising in me.

"I'll give you anything." She breathes out. I widen my eyes at her, realizing she's answering my request from earlier. I hope she understands what *anything* means.

She takes off her dress, revealing her topless body. Giving my eyes something to look at, I notice her tattoo on her ribs. The black widow from Crypticon. The tattoo that represents me. I ever so lightly trace the outline of it, watching the goosebumps form.

I lift her up a bit to put my hands under her back. To feel her bare skin is giving me tremors like the first time we ever did it. Once I have a good grasp on her, I kiss in between her neck and shoulders. I want to kiss every single inch of her body.

God, she's fucking perfect. Emotionally unstable, but perfect. I can help with the stability part—I hope.

She's been whispering my name this whole time. Digging her nails into my back only add fuel to the fire. I work my way down her chest until I'm hovering over her breasts. I stop and stare up at her. She's already staring back at me and smiling. She glides her hand under my chin and traces the outline of my lips. I take one of my arms out from her and take her hand, kissing her palm and placing her palm against my cheek.

"You have no idea how long I've waited for this moment." Smirking, high on euphoria.

"Believe me, *you* have no idea."

I let her leave her hands on my face while I kiss the top of her breasts.

Control your animalistic tendencies, Calvin.

I will probably lose myself if I continue kissing her breasts, so I lift my face and look at her. Her eyes are closed, which makes me frown, but that means I am in control of what to do next. Moving my hands down her body, I trace the shape of her. Her stomach going inward and then her hips protruding outwards. She is so sexy. I feel her move her hands behind my neck, which she uses as a stabilizer to boost herself up more on the bed. The push of her pelvis makes me groan.

I immediately grab a fistful of her hair. God, I have missed her touch. Her kiss. Her smell.

It's like falling in love all over again, only it's better this time.

Kissing her mouth, I feel her sweet saliva enter my boundaries, but I don't care. I wish I had more of that orange lip gloss to suck off her lips.

Striving to last longer, I leave her mouth and kiss her cheek, leaving a trail of kisses to her neck.

When I find her perfect sweet spot, I suck. Hard.

Like she has the worst kind of poison inside of her and I'm the only one who can remove it. I can't stop sucking, and I fear I'll make her bleed, or severely bruise her. The frenzy overpowers me. Luckily, Jen makes me stop before I hurt her.

That's until I realize what she just did. Or at least, what she's doing.

She just clawed my back. I think *I* could be bleeding.

"CAL!" I feel her body arch and her head lean back on the pillow.

Immediately, I remove my hands from her hair and stop sucking. I let my head hover above her neck, feeling the burning sensation of the air hitting my open wounds.

She **did** claw me.

There's a stinging sensation on my upper back.

"Jesus fuck, Jen. Are you serious?!" I bring myself up so I'm sitting on my legs, straddling her. My left hand crosses my chest to feel the damage to my upper right back. I check my fingers for blood.

Caught in complete distress, I hear Jen's giggle. No, not a giggle. A full out laugh. She's holding her hands over her face, making my heart return to its normal heartbeat. The tension in my shoulders drops as I hear the most beautiful sound in the world. I hardly notice the throbbing pain.

"Are you seriously laughing right now?" I bring my hand off my back and place them on her waist. I can't help but to let my eyes explore her body again. She's so delicious looking.

She removes her hands from her face, and her laugh subsides, but she's smiling at me, her head crooked in between her shoulder.

"I'm sorry. I didn't mean to hurt you. It just felt so good." She touches my cheek and continues smiling at me, like she was in pure dreamland. With me. I look down at her and couldn't help but smile back.

It's relieving that she scratched me because she was happy, and not because she hated me. I bend down and resume kissing her, placing my hands in her hair, picking back up where we left off. She wraps her hands around my neck, pulling me close. She's already moaning in my ear. I feel her hands leave my face and slide down my chest, then down my stomach until she reaches for my pants. I try to push away the temptation of sucking the other side of her neck, but realize my body can only handle so many scratches. Instead, I just kiss her repeatedly, each one feeling like it's the first time.

Without thinking, I lift my hips so she has access to unbutton my pants. I feel the button snap open and then feel my zipper move down. The instant relief of the pressure on my pants feels incredible. I should probably assist her in moving my pants down my legs, but that means I would have to stop kissing her, and I don't want to do that.

Pressing my body in towards her, I just want to fucking growl at her. I feel her hands on my chest as she pushes me away from her mouth. She thinks she can push me away, but my neck stays elongated to her mouth. I feel I look like a giraffe.

Finally, she gets a breath of fresh air.

"Calvin Louis." She gasps.

"What, Jennie Marie?" I lean in to kiss her for the sixty-fourth kiss.

"I am trying to take your pants off. You are not cooperating." She's trying to be serious, as I can tell by the straight line of her mouth.

I cannot take my eyes off her eyes. Her fucking beautiful eyes. I always feel like I'm about to enter the Hoh Rain Forest and God, how I just wanted to keep walking and never leave.

We just stare at each other for a while. Thinking to myself how lucky I am to have the most beautiful creature staring at me, wanting all the broken and damaged pieces of me.

Then I feel ungrateful.

She doesn't deserve the shitty pieces of me.

She deserves someone who is stable and dependable. I wonder if the man she was married to had his shit together. And if so, why would she give that up? I wonder what she's thinking. I move a piece of hair behind her hair and ask.

"What's going on in that pretty brain of yours?" She smiles back at me, putting her hands back on my face. I close my eyes at the feel of her touch. Her hands are so soft and warm. They feel like ten little rose petals that stick to my face.

"I have missed you. It just feels like my heart isn't breaking anymore." I close my eyes again, only this time, I wince. I'm filled with remorse for causing her so much heartbreak.

I drag my fingers along her hairline, by her ear and down her chin. I kiss her for the sixty-fifth time.

"Baby, I am so sorry. I am so fucking sorry." I lean forward so my forehead touches hers.

"It's okay." Her voice cracks on the first, second and third syllable. My heart cracks at the end.

It's not fucking okay.

"I think we've lost our momentum for tonight. Will you just lay with me?" She says again. With that, I move my legs from around her and settle on her right side. As I put my arm around her neck, she moves in close to my chest. I pull a blanket over her, covering up her naked body. She lays her hand on my chest, making shapes with her index finger around my pec. Her eyelashes tickle my clavicle bone when she blinks, but I try not to squirm because she feels content. I graze my fingers up and down her arm.

"So, does this mean I can't get anything I want now?" I smile but can't see her reaction. Instead, she chuckles and looks up at me, smiling, too.

Oh, thank God, I didn't piss her off by bringing up the stipulations.

She lays her head back on my chest.

"What do you want to know, Calvin?"

I hate when she uses my full name. She only uses Calvin when she is upset with me.

Breathing in deep, her body moves and down on my chest. I stop moving my hand along her arm and grab her hand.

"I have so many questions, Jen." I whisper, not wanting to upset her by starting this conversation again. Why are we entering this abyss again? I'm hoping this tunnel will end soon so we can see the light.

"Ask me what you want. I'm too tired to fight with you." Her voice feels cold, clearly not wanting to have this conversation. I should respect her wants but I can't help my impulsivity.

"Tell me about Jonah."

She's silent and remains motionless. Still laying on my chest, I pull her close to me. Then her hand goes to her face, wiping away tears.

Don't get angry, Cal. She is allowed to be upset. You asked the question, dumbass.

"What do you want to know?" She responds quietly, putting her hand back on my chest.

"Start from the beginning."

"We met when I was in the hospital. He was the nurse on my floor."

Don't get angry at her short answers. You asked the questions, you're lucky to get answers.

"Did he take care of you?" This question makes me shake a bit. I hate that someone else could care of her, but I'm so thankful that someone bit the bullet to do so. I wonder where this guy is right now, what he's doing, and if he still talks to Jen. Jealously courses through me.

Again, she takes a while to answer. I hate how she's contemplating her responses.

"Yes."

Jesus, I am going to go crazy here. But she's laying safe in my arms and she's willing to answer my questions without telling me to read those useless letters. I'm optimistic that my reaction to reading the letters about Jonah will be a little less explosive than my other reactions.

"Does he know about me?" *Why am I asking such stupid questions?*

239

I should ask how he took care of her.

"Yes."

Great, this guy somewhere in Seattle probably wants to break my nose and give me black eyes. He probably thinks I'm the worst monster that ever existed.

I try to think of a follow-up question, but my mind is foggy.

"I spent hours talking about you on my first night. He hated you for a long time. A really long time. He probably still does, knowing I left him for you. Once things got serious between us and he found some of our mementos in my house, he realized how important you were to me. I told him he shouldn't hate you. We were both in a messy place in our lives." I close my eyes and swallow, but I feel like there's a rock stuck in my throat. My Jen, defending me from a complete stranger.

"I was in the hospital for six weeks. He checked on me every day, even when he had days off, he would come see me. He worried about me a lot. God, he was a pain in the ass with making sure I was eating, but I guess it was sweet. He helped me get back to a healthy weight, so I should give him some credit. He helped me get familiar with my medications. Upon my release, he assisted me in establishing a new routine. He was very persistent about wanting to stay in touch with me when I got discharged. I was on the fence about letting him take me home because I thought I might like him, and I didn't want to move on. Forgetting you terrified me. I couldn't allow anyone to replace you in my heart and life. That spot was only for you."

She wipes her face again, and I wipe mine, too. I hope she hasn't realized a few tears have left my eyes. This guy is the definition of a fucking saint and he makes me feel like a fucking loser. I don't know what is holding my heart together after these past couple of days.

"What medications?" I wanted to ask this question ever since she mentioned it. *What secrets are you keeping from me?*

"Why does it matter?" I'm taken aback by her response. My tear ducts suddenly close and a crinkle in my eyebrows form.

"What do you mean, why does it matter? I want to know how I'm supposed to take care of you?" Her hand twitches on my chest, almost giving me a small squeeze that she appreciates my answer. She doesn't respond for several moments.

"I'm supposed to take 100 milligrams of Zoloft each day and 5 milligrams of Valium in the morning and evening."

"Did you take them today?"

She chuckles under me, like it was a stupid question.

"Yes, Cal. I took them earlier. I'm prescribed Xanax for my panic attacks, but the side effects were..." She pauses, and I can sense the hesitation for her to share the rest.

"Were what?" I pull her close to me, savoring all the words she is telling me. Although this sucks to hear how tormented her mind was, I'm glad to hear the answers to my questions right away without being told the answers are in a letter.

"I um, eventually got my attacks under control. I have the pills nearby, just in case."

"You never mentioned this before."

"Cal, you just came back into my life. There's so much you don't know. I felt so ashamed that I couldn't do basic things in my life. Once my dad died, the attacks got worse. Do you remember how depressing the December letters were? Each day that passed, my threshold just got lower and lower. Nothing was satisfying. Nothing was helpful. I was like that for an entire year. There was a party in November of 2004, and that's when things just got bad. Well, I guess things were already bad, so when things were at a point of no return." I ponder on all the information and try to make sense of it.

Panic attacks only got worse.

A reckless party.

I am not ready to read any letters from 2004.

There was a party that landed her in the hospital.

"Tell me about that night, when you did that." I trace over her scar.

"No, I can't tell you that story."

"Why not? You've been doing so well telling me about your life." I trace over her scar, imagining how much of a wreck she probably was and imagining my finger being an eraser to make it disappear.

"It's just a story I don't like to relive. I don't know what is lower than hell, but that's where I went. To the furthest, deepest, coldest place you could imagine."

Kissing the top of her head, I feel my floodgates open again. I stop tracing her scar, knowing she probably wishes it wasn't there either. Bringing attention to it was a mistake.

"Okay." I'll let that one go, but someday she needs to tell me that story. I've been to the furthest, deepest, coldest place too, and I wonder if we were there together.

We could've saved each other.

No, you couldn't save her because you were in prison, you idiot.

Devil is getting annoying, but more than usual. I am trying to be compassionate and understanding that she had reasons for all the things she did, but Devil isn't shutting up. It blames me, every single time.

"Done with your questions?" I must've been in a trance because she's looking up at me, her eyes red and wet. Like all the plants just went through the worst hurricane. I want to bring them sunshine.

I look down at her and kiss her. Number sixty-six.

She turns her body towards me and places a hand on my cheek. She presses against me. Is her momentum back already?!

She lets out a soft groan as I direct the back of her head towards my mouth, craving a more passionate kiss. There's a need in me to bring her the best fucking comfort and happiness she's ever wanted.

She is so fragile, so vulnerable. As much as it kills me, I bring my lips from hers.

"Well, I still have plenty of questions, but that's enough storytelling for now." I push some hair behind her ears and watch as she grins at me.

Knowing that I can be the safest place for her but give her the worst memories is such a tug of war. Do I brag that I can hold her close and kiss her and make her feel like nothing bad will ever happen to her again, or do I hold her and kiss her and tell her I am the culprit for ruining her life?

She eases out of my arms, quickly. Almost like she just heard the thoughts in my head and realizes that *I am* the culprit who ruined her life.

"I'm just going to get some water." She pulls her underwear up her body and grabs a shirt from her bag. "I'll be right back."

I hate to watch her go, and I hate this overprotectiveness to make sure she won't get a knife or walk into the lake or down a bottle of pills. Waiting just a minute or two, I move off the bed, put my shirt back on, and fix the button and zipper on my pants. I need to make sure she's okay.

Quietly, I move towards the door, remembering how creaky these floors are when I was a kid. I poke my head out the door and find her back to me. She's standing at the kitchen sink, with a glass of water on the counter next to her.

Thank God.

I watch her for a moment. She has her hands on both sides of the sink and her head hangs low, looking at the sink. Her shoulders slump, and she crosses her left ankle over her right one. She looks defeated. The armor she used to wear is broken, shattered, defective, almost nonexistent.

I can't take it.

The person she is today is because of you. You pathetic excuse for a human being.

The guilt is too fucking much to handle right now.

As quietly as I can, I walk out the front door and close the door behind me. Instead of returning to the bench, I go to the water. I don't even know what time it is, but the chill feels good on my boiling skin. My arms rest on the railing that barricades a ramp to the boat dock.

I mimic Jen's body language—I hang my head down and my shoulders slump. I try very hard to tell Devil to fuck off and jump in the water. Despite my efforts, my tear ducts refuse to stay closed. I let myself cry in peace for a few moments.

What kind of life have I created for her? Do I really want to re-enter her life to only fuck it up even more? How is that even a privilege? It's worse than prison. I will not stand by and continue being the criminal in her life.

I think about Jonah and how he could've done it. It was possible for him to save her. Unlike me, he was present through the worst of it. He saw her at the worst and still wanted to be her hero. Then I realized *this is probably her worst.* This version is Jen is confused, scared and trying to heal from the shit I did to her.

How confused she must feel to be here with me? Does she hate me or love me? Does she want me to give up on the letters, to give up on her? Does she want me to make a move that allows us to get completely lost in each other, like all those years ago? Does she still want me?

With a swarm of questions in my head, I hear it.

It was the most blood-curdling scream imaginable. The kind of scream you hear when you think someone is being murdered. The scream you hear during a scary movie scene you were NOT expecting. One you let out when you're going down the biggest hill of a roller coaster and you're scared shitless. The kind of scream that gives you nightmares.

I spin my head to see the house the scream came from. Pushing myself off the railing, I wipe my nose, lunge up the stairs, and bust down the door. Either I'm going to throw up or shit myself. Or both.

Jennie

I feel like I split my vocal cords in half with an axe and I think I'm swallowing blood. Pretty sure I just used up all the oxygen I'll ever have because my lungs are completely empty. My stomach feels like it expanded way more than it could. I could feel my bulging veins about to burst on my forehead and neck. And my heart... oh, how I thought my heart was breathing some sort of life. There have been a lot of things that have hurt in my life, 80% of those things relating to Calvin. I thought I had put my heart into a steel box and thrown the key away somewhere in Lake Washington, near enough for Calvin possibly to find it.

But nothing, absolutely nothing that has happened to me shattered my heart more than walking into the bedroom and Cal being gone.

He left me... again.

Because you're not worthy enough for his love. He deserves better.

Entering the bedroom, his scent fills my nostrils. I picture us intertwined on the bed, as if just moments before. The fresh wrinkles in the sheets and the blanket's position are evidence that we were together. Right? I walk over to the bed and still feel the warmth of our bodies radiating off the sheets. Calvin's duffle bag is still in the corner by the window, and it appears everything is still in there. I turn around and see my weekend bag on the lounge chair, untouched.

My heart is beating so much faster that I can no longer breath through my nose, and my body is trembling. It usually starts in my fingers, almost like a small earthquake is happening in my hands. The quake works its way up my arms and stop at my shoulders. My shoulders get tense, like a mass of unbearable weight is holding me down and I'm trying to resist. It moves down my throat, tight and dry, like I've been walking in the desert for days. Then it moves to my stomach... It's the worst kind of nausea you could imagine. It's like sitting with a ticking time bomb, just waiting for the bile to exit your body. But it never does... it just sits there, taunting you.

While the earthquake has been occurring in my body, I make

it to the bathroom where Cal's sweatshirt is laying on the counter. It's the same sweatshirt that I have so many beloved, heart-warming memories with. My heart doesn't get warm when I touch it, it stays ice cold. I wrap my fingers around it, gripping it firmly. Finally, as quickly as it begins, the earthquake moves down my legs where it ends there. I fall against the wall because I am weak. Confused. Broken. I will remain broken forever.

I stopped taking my Xanax because the earthquakes had just happened so fast. One moment, everything would be perfect. Well, maybe never perfect. But then something would remind me of him. His red truck. Halloween. Black widows. Zombies. Chinese food. My body would fail me. As much as I tried to control the switches of my brain, I realized I had no control.

Sitting with an overabundance of frustration from my body and the confusion on why Cal left, I can only scream. I scream so loud I hope people in Seattle can hear me. I hope wherever Cal went; he stops and turns around to come find me.

I don't even realize how long I held that scream for, but it doesn't help.

I knew he would not love this version of me. I knew I would not be enough for him.

Calvin

It's Jen screaming.

The spotlight helps me find the door. As a kid, the distance between the water and the door felt like miles. Right now, I could've joined the Olympic track team.

I bust through the door and dash through each room, trying to find her.

WHERE THE FUCK IS SHE?!

Down the hallway, I stop at the bedroom where we just were and find it empty. Allowing my predator tendencies to take force, I smell her scent and feel her presence, like she was just standing here.

Then I hear her cries.

"Cal... please..."

She's in the bathroom.

I push myself off the doorframe of the bedroom and about knock down the bathroom door.

There she is.

Holy fucking God.

She's on the floor, crouched with her legs in front of her. So many wet plants!!!!!! And she's holding my sweatshirt... no, not even holding. She's clenching it so that I can see her knuckles are turning white. She's trembling uncontrollably.

"Baby, what's wrong?" Squatting down to her level, I put my hands on her face. She looks at me like she just saw a ghost. A ghost from her past.

"Cal?" She whimpers as she says my name and puts her head in my sweatshirt she's holding.

"Jen, I'm right here." Awkwardly sitting next to her, I pull her into me. I don't know what is happening, but she is not okay. She falls into my chest and it's terrifying how much she is shaking. I pull her even closer, rubbing my hand on her arm, thinking maybe she's cold.

"Cal..." Her voice is so weak I can barely hear her say my name, even with how close she is to me.

"Baby, look at me." Tilting her chin towards me, it feels like she's not there. She needs to know I'm real. If Devil is on my shoulder, I ignore her because I know she would clip the last thread of whatever is keeping my heart together.

Her eyes. Her fucking eyes. They are full of...

Fear.

They are no longer a rain forest I wish to keep walking in. They are haunting me, and I need to find a new trail. Looking away, I scrunch my nose, holding back my tears.

You did this.

Fuck you, Devil.

"I thought y-you ll-left. I tho(sigh)ught you left me ag- gain." She weeps into a sob again. She buries her head into my jacket, strangling it into her hands. If that jacket was a person, it would be dead.

"Hey, hey I am so sorry, baby. I am right here. I am not going anywhere. I am so sorry. I won't do that ever again."

I'm such a fucking idiot to not even put the pieces together of why Jen would be so distraught that I stepped outside. It's no use to try to have her look at me because all she sees is memories. I feel so unbelievably useless that I can't comfort her right now. Her eyes are breaking my heart.

"Jen, let's do 54321. Okay, baby? Tell me 5 things you can see."

I don't know if this is going to work because I've never experienced this side of Jen. Two unbalanced people won't improve the situation, I know that. I try to keep my voice calm, to get her back to reality—back to me. She keeps sobbing, which makes me feel worthless that I can't console her. She takes a while to play along.

"You. The bed is behind you. The pretty flowers. The paint is peeling. The flickering light." Her voice is just as shaky as when she said my name a moment ago. I keep my hands on her cheeks for her to keep looking at me. My voice is filled with incredible pride because she succeeded in the first step.

"Good, baby, good. Tell me 4 things you can feel."

Please tell me you feel me.

"You again. The wall. Your clothes. The bath tub." I can hear her breathing slowing down. She's still shaking, but it's becoming less extreme.

Come back to me, baby. You're almost there.

Is this Devil talking or do I have a new Angel?

The bathtub, though? I hate to take my eyes off her to see how she can feel the bathtub. Following her distorted body, I see her left leg stretched out behind me, her big toe touching the tub's bottom. I sigh in relief.

"Good fucking job, baby. Tell me 3 things you can hear."

"You." I expect her to say three things, but I'm thankful she only says me. That means she is focusing on my voice. Good girl.

"2 things you can smell."

"I want to smell your chocolate chip cookies, but I smell you." I look down at her lap so she can't see my smirk.

Wrong time to be humorous, Jen, but I appreciate your honesty.

To be fair, there isn't much a smell here anyway, although I smell Jen. Her jasmine shampoo smells fucking divine. I can't help but to lay my head on her head to get closer to her smell.

"1 thing you can taste."

It's extremely difficult to ask her what she can taste, so I make it easy for her. Pulling her towards me, I kiss her. Knowing how fragile she is right now, I resist pushing her towards me to create more intimacy, but if there's anything more obvious to bring her back to the moment with me, it's kissing me. Her hands are on my cheeks, pulling herself closer. To keep control, I pull back from the situation. My eyes opened, but my hands remained on her face.

You were part of every sense.

She opens her eyes and looks back at me. Although her eyes are red and swollen, her rainforest is clear. Knowing she needs to rest, I pick her up off the ground and walk her over to the bed. I know how hard she is trying to enter a state of peace. Kissing the side of her head as I lay her down, her shakes are almost nonexistent. She's been holding on to my jacket during this transition.

"Are you going to give that back to me?" I sit down beside her and move the hair from her eyes so she can look at me.

"Will you keep it close, just in case?" Her answer is so innocent and it breaks my heart.

"There is no just in case, Jen. I am right here. I am not going anywhere. I promise."

"You said that four years ago."

She remembers every single promise you made to her, you prick.

There's Devil.

Lowering my head in shame, I bite the inside of my cheek because she's right. Jen probably remembers every word I've ever said to her. I'm surprised she didn't carve it into her skin.

That was a fucked-up thing to say.

I keep my eyes on her, and she keeps her eyes on me. Her eyes are getting heavy. There is no point in arguing right now, so I purse my lips together and give her a kiss on the cheek.

"I'm going to bake some cookies. I'll be in the kitchen." Unsure if I have the ingredients to make cookies, I'm not in the mood to bake, but I'll do anything for her to make her feel better.

"Leave the door open." She begs. I look over my shoulder at her.

She's like this now because of you. She was better before you.

I say nothing.

Sitting down at the table, I bring my hands to my forehead. Sadness takes over me. A scream is building inside me. I want to leave. I want to go back to the lake. Hell, I might even want to go back to the prison, just to create some space between us.

Silently weeping, I let the tears fall down my face.

Look what you've done to her.

Life was so easy for us before Easton. We were in love. Madly in love. We never wanted to spend time apart. We were constantly kissing. Everywhere we went, we held hands. She would laugh more times than I could count. I hardly ever saw her cry, only when we talked about her dad. Jen was happy. Not to mention, both of her arms were free of self-mutilation. God, she was so beautiful when she laughed and smiled. Where did she go? Why did I have to have such a temper? Why did I have to have such a smart mouth to that prick at the bar?

You should've walked away. You should've gone home to her.

I honestly don't know what is keeping my heart together. I was not expecting this night to go like this. It feels like a brand-new relationship. Arguing and making up. Questioning each other and then comforting. This isn't us, and I don't know how to handle it. I don't know how to handle the broken version of Jennie. The more I see how damaged she is, the more I break. I used to be her protector, her knight in shining armor. It was easy to protect her. She would just cow behind me when there was conflict. I'd protect her through it all because that was my job, to keep her safe. Trying to protect this version of Jen seems impossible. It feels like she doesn't want to be protected.

Unless she's being protected by Jonah, and she doesn't need your protection anymore.

Lifting my head up at the internal comment, I drag my hands down my face to get rid of the tears. I remember our conversation from this morning.

I wanted you to read them to decide if you still wanted to love me.

You love the old me.

The cabin feels like a fucking prison! Standing up from the table, I pace in the kitchen, feeling trapped. It's exhausting trying to calm her down. Then again, that was probably the third panic attack I've assisted with. I can't imagine how many times she had to calm herself down. How exhausted she must be...

Leaving the kitchen, I walk down to the bedroom to check on her. Her eyes are peacefully closed. I walk in and want to sit next to her, to comfort her that I'm still here. When I get close to the bed, she's holding onto something. I look over to the side table where I left my sweatshirt... it's gone.

She's holding on to it. Of course, she wouldn't believe me that I would stay close. She has no right to believe my words.

I pick up my duffle bag from the floor and search for my notebook. The notebook I wrote letters to Jen in when I was in prison. There's something I want to share with her, and it's best she's not awake to see my face as I recite a love-swoon poem to her. I flip open to the page and walk back over to the bed. Instead of sitting on the bed, I pull a chair next to her. Resting my elbows on my knees, I lean forward so I can whisper to her.

"Jen, I wrote to you too while I was away. I want to share something with you. Please don't laugh.

My sweet Jennie you

When I first met you, I was all in a trance

I told you my secrets, you told me yours

I bet you thought I would never like you

Who would of thought

We would be more than just friends

I got to know the real person, you

A soul so caring, a soul so dear

With a heart so true, your mind so pure

You are the wings that fly me to the moon

I'll never leave, I'd rather stay

Because of the feelings I have for you,

You're my shining star, in life's blue sky

And sometimes I wonder, is all of this true?

So I've decided, time will tell

If we're meant to be,

Time will reveal what lies ahead

But always remember what I'm saying,

Meeting you has changed my life

I truly care about you more than anyone

My sweet Jennie"

I want to kiss her so badly. Until all the pain has disappeared from every crevice of her body. Until she is free of my demons.

Brushing her hair back with my palm, I soak in the feel of her. I smile at the memory of her telling me she wanted to sleep next to me tonight. Her voice was full of happiness, like it was the only thing she needed. And here we are, arguing and making up twice already.

Now I realize why she made a promise to not bring up the past because it's damaging. There's a part of me that wants to wake her up to argue with her so I can feel her lips on mine while we make up.

That's a warped thing to say. This is real life, you ass. It's Jen's life, not a game.

Devil is right. This isn't a game. This isn't a game we know how to play, and we are continuously failing.

Just make her happy. What will make her happy?

"Cookies." I answer out loud to Angel. Brushing her hair one last time, I kiss her temple that's facing me.

"I'll wake you when the cookies are done." I whisper. As I push the chair back and approach the door, she speaks.

"Who did you steal that poem from?" Her voice was much more audible than before she went to sleep. I stop at the door and turn around, wanting to hide my embarrassment of my cheesiness. Nervously rubbing my beard, I smile at her.

"You heard that, huh?" She looks so beautiful, just lying there in peace from any arguments.

"Every word. I told you I was waiting for my next poem." She sits up now, putting my sweatshirt over her head and fixing her hair that was resting on the pillow. I bite my bottom at how fucking insatiable she looks with my clothes on and her panties showing underneath.

"I loved it." She whole heartedly smiles at me. The first time I've seen her dimples since picking her up this evening. I walk back over to the bed, wanting to be close to her again. To remind her I am real and I am here.

"I have a question." I say as I sit down next to her.

Ready to argue already?

"So do I." She fires back.

"Go ahead." She says again. Is this supposed to be part of the game? I didn't realize we were playing a tennis game of questions.

I laugh though because if this is a game, that's a stupid rule.

"Okay. Were you even sleeping?" I bring my hand to her upper cheek, tracing my thumb near the outer part of her eye. It's hard to look at her knowing if she feels refreshed because her eyes just make me lose all sense of where I am.

She lets her head fall into my palm, which brings me a sense of relief. Hopefully, she's moved on from the fact that she just had a panic attack because she thought I left.

She hasn't forgotten, dipshit. She'll never forget.

"Yes, and no. I closed my eyes for a while when you laid me down and I thought for sure I was going to fall asleep. My eyes were so heavy that I barely saw you leave the room. My PTSD woke me, so I grabbed this and waited for you to come back. When I heard you come down the hallway, my eyes were still closed, but I heard every word. Even the cookies part...which was random." She giggles, leans towards me, and places her hand on my knee. Gosh, she's very affectionate right now. I can't imagine how touchy-feely she'll be after a good night's rest. I drop my hand off her face and wrap it around her, pulling her in even closer.

"What's your question?" kissing her forehead.

"What did time say?" I furrow my eyebrows, confused as hell. Is she trying to say a corny joke to me? I lean away from her to see her reaction.

"What?" I chuckle. She's looking at me with serious eyes. Okay, definitely not telling a joke.

"In your poem, you said time will tell if we're meant to be. Did time say anything to you?"

Ah. It's clicking now. She's taking my words literally, not figuratively. In all honesty, I don't even know how to answer her.

Time is a thief, a villain, the scum on the bottom of my shoe for all I care. We fell in love for over seven months and then spent three and a half years apart. Time was not on our side. I want to be honest with her and hide no secrets.

I feel her hand move up and down on my knee to gain my attention. "Hey, where did you go? Did time take your tongue too?"

God, I love this version of her—the simple Jen.

"Can I be honest with you?" I'm still staring at her, hoping to

God she doesn't prepare her fight-or-flight to kick in.

Don't start a fight with her, dumbass. This is just a normal conversation.

"Absolutely. Always."

"I think time is a piece of shit who doesn't know how to stop when people are in love. Time has no business being part of our story. I would pause every moment you looked at me to fully enjoy it. If only time had frozen the moment you entered the car with Glen in Easton, allowing you to run back. I wish time had stopped when I entered that bar after leaving Easton, right before shit hit the fan. If time had been more generous, I would have remembered how long it had been since our last kiss and I would've found you. But time has not been kind to us–to me. So currently, Jen, I am begging time to be kind because I want it to stop right here, right now because it's the most calm we've been while being together and we aren't bringing up those letters or the past. And I just want to look into your eyes for as long as possible."

I have wanted to say that for a long time. Even though I feel this night has felt like a bipolar shit show, this right now is worth it all.

I have leaned forward with my elbows on my knees, and Jen starts caressing my back.

Please time, slow down. Let me savor this moment—it's peaceful.

I chuckle sarcastically before I speak again.

"Is that what you wanted to hear?", looking over at her.

She stops comforting my back and rests her head on my shoulder.

"Well, not exactly. I'm sorry time has not been kind. Trust me, I haven't been having a good time either." Her eyes look so sad. Of course, she would know that time is a fucking thief.

"If time were kind to you, what would you change?" I'm nervous about starting such a philosophical conversation with her. She's in such a tender place right now it feels like anything could break her.

With her head resting on my shoulder still, she grins at me. I can tell she's thinking of something happy. *Thank God.*

"If time were kind, it would've taken both of its hands and slapped me hard to bring me back to reality the day of the camping trip. There's so much I wish I could change. But you're right, time is a piece of shit and doesn't deserve to be part of our story. We've lost so much time." Her voice cracks and I can tell she's holding back tears.

Dear God, please no. Don't let her break on me again.

"I think I'm ready to go to sleep and enjoy the time we have left together tonight. I'd like you to take me home tomorrow morning if that's okay."

She lifts her head off my shoulder and stands up. My eyes follow her around the room as she opens her bag to get her sleeping clothes and then grabs her toiletry bag into the bathroom.

"What do you mean, take you home tomorrow? We have the entire weekend here." I try to keep my voice low, but here we are, talking about all the time we've been apart, and she wants to leave?

Instantly, my heart deflates. My memory jogs back to the camping trip when Anna told me they wanted to leave early. No, I can't let that happen again. I'll beg on my knees for her to stay with the entire weekend.

She disappears into the bathroom, but I see her shadow. Standing from the bed, I stop at the bathroom, holding onto the doorframe. I don't know how much more crying I can handle tonight.

"Jen..." She's clutching the sink, letting her head hang low. The exact position she was in when I saw her in the kitchen earlier. She looks so exhausted.

Just fucking comfort her. It's easy. Quit making it more complicated.

"Hey, you're right. Let's get ready for bed. Let me help you."

I don't want to fight anymore. We never used to fight, and it takes up 500% more of our emotional gas tank. We're finished fighting for today.

First, I pull my sweatshirt off her head, and I'm surprised she lets me. I keep my eyes locked on her. She stands in front of me with only her red, lacey underwear. She doesn't cover up for me and I try my damn best to not be a weirdo and look at her chest.

"I hope I can wear that dress again for you. Hope I'm still beautiful." Her sniffles are interrupted by a yawn. I look down on the floor at the dress crumpled on the floor.

"You are beautiful, always. You never have to worry about me thinking if you are or not. It's always a yes." Picking up a grey shirt she carried to the bathroom, I bite my bottom lip and grin. It's my Vancouver Canucks hockey shirt she stole from me the first time she stayed over at my house.

"You still have this?" Referring to the shirt as I poke her head through the top, allowing her to bring her arms through the armholes.

"It's my favorite shirt." She smirks and yawns again.

"We should go to a hockey game together." I wonder if this is how Jonah took care of her. It almost feels like changing a lifeless mannequin. Even though she's now 50% naked, there is no joy in changing someone who is so damaged. My eyes slowly move down her arm where she's damaged her perfectly-made body. I feel like I'm swallowing safety pins looking at her arm. To think that *I* was the one who did this to her... It makes me sick.

"We'll see if time allows it."

Touché.

"You brought shorts and sweats. Which do you want?"

I'm trying my hardest to not gawk over her half naked body wearing only my shirt and underwear, but it's almost impossible. She takes a long time to answer me, and I realize she's watching me through the mirror. I relax my shoulders in defeat, caught watching her admirably.

"I'm sorry. You're so beautiful, Jen." I try to hide my embarrassment, but she just looks at me in the mirror. She smiles at me, soaking in the compliment.

"I like the way you look at me." She bows her head at the sink, blushing. "Shorts."

I grab her shorts and she stabilizes her hands on my shoulders to place her feet through. She pulls her shorts up herself and ties the elastic into a bow.

"Thank you. I'm so tired." She turns towards me and leans against the doorframe, closing her eyes as if she could fall asleep that easily.

"I know, baby. Is there anything else you need to do?" I rub my hand on her cheek and wait for her response before I pull her towards the bed.

She shakes her head from side and side and there's my cue. With a little pressure, I push my hand from her cheek to behind her neck and pull her close to me so I can help her to the bed. I remember Jen hates to sleep near the main bedroom door, so I position her on the farther side of the bed. Pulling the sheets close to her, I throw over her blanket and give her two kisses on the temple and cheek. Her eyes are already closed.

"Are you going to sleep, too?" Only her mouth moves. I hover over her face and hesitate. I wasn't ready to lie down, but if it will ease Jen, then I will.

"Do you want me in here with you?" Her eyes slowly peel open.

"If time were kind, yes."

Ugh, my fucking heart.

"Let me change my clothes." That's all I can say. She doesn't need to hear anything else.

I don't think she was referencing time, but more like me. If *I* were kind to her, I will happily join her in bed and let her fall asleep in my arms. She needs kindness. She needs me.

With no need to go to the bathroom, I change my clothes by the table. I slip my shirt off and replace it with another, then swap my pants for basketball shorts. Pulling back my sheets, Jen's back is facing me. She is probably sleeping, and I could easily slip out of the room to clear my mind. My heart will thank me later for getting the extra time to lie with Jen.

I pull the string to turn off the light, and there's a small illumination from the window near Jen's side of the bed. Should I close the curtains to give her more time to sleep?

Yes, you idiot. She needs sleep after all the bullshit you've fed her.

Oh, I hope the Devil gets a good night's sleep too. I'm extra hopeful she never wakes up again.

Quietly, I move out of the sheets and close the curtains. Jen didn't move a muscle as I climb back into bed. I'm both thankful, but in agony.

I have a silent conversation with Devil in my head. Do I pull her close to me? Should I touch her at all? Do I stay awake until I know for sure she is asleep? I'm surprised when Angel answers instead.

You can't imagine the euphoria she will enter when she feels you around her. She wants you. Make her feel safe again.

With that, I turn onto my left side and use my right arm to bring Jen close to my body. It was like moving a lifeless body. She reacts to my touch but pressing her ass towards my groin and intertwines her fingers through mine.

"You can rest now, Jen. I'm here."

February 14, 2004

Happy Valentines Day handsome. Is it weird that the first thing I woke up to this morning was wondering how people in jail celebrate holidays? Do you have decorations around your common area and do the staff dress up? Probably not.

Pat had me stay late last night to decorate the shop. Surely being a single man, he does love the idea of love. I wish you could see my set-up. I decided to try to make a balloon garland around the front door and I think it turned out pretty good. It has red, light pink, dark pink and white balloons. Pat hasn't seen anything yet so when I see him later, I hope he likes how it turned out. I put a small bouquet of flowers on every table and printed off some love quotes. The coffee bar is just full of confetti – Pat is going to hate it!

Our first Valentine's day apart. It makes me sad. I plan on working most of the day today at C&H, just to keep my mind occupied. Currently, my plan is to get Chinese after work and watch Halloween. Two of your favorite things. I wish I could call you and tell you how much I miss you. Some days I want to give in and send these letters to you so I can be hopeful that you will send one back and I can see your handwriting and know that you are alive. Five years though... I couldn't bring myself to just look at your handwriting for five years.

Please do good in jail so you can home soon.

I miss you so much it hurts.

Waiting,

Jennie

I refold the letter and slip it back into its envelope. Stupidly, I have a giant smile on my face after reading that letter. Her curiosity makes me grin at whether or not the prison was decorated. *No... it was not.* I'm happy that she tried to bring light to herself to think I was having a good time.

I woke up pretty early and made some coffee to watch the sunrise. I brought a handful of letters with me and I'm not really sure why. It just feels like I have a ball and chain attached to them. There have to be answers to my questions. I realize I'm smiling wider because, although her paranoid hallucinations about my imminent return were messed up, she celebrated alone with my favorite things. It just makes me love her more.

Seattle's weather is so unpredictable. I didn't bother trying to slip my sweatshirt past Jen's arms this morning. She must've woken up in the middle of the night to retrieve it again. I grabbed a blanket to wrap around myself this morning while I sit on the front porch in a wicker rocking chair. My grandparents bought these chairs decades ago when they first renovated this place. The coffee is keeping my hands warm, but the cool breeze that sneaks through my exposed skin makes me contemplate going back inside.

Watching the sunrise takes me back to the time where Jen and I stayed up all night, just talking and watching movies and eating snacks. By the time we knew it, the sun was peeking through my window and we ran outside to watch it light up the darkness.

I hear the front door open and watch Jen come outside, with her/my Canucks shirt on, grey sweatpants and a blanket wrapped around her arms. She looks even more beautiful. More refreshed too. Instantly, I smile at her.

"Good morning." I say to her and sip my coffee. She walks to the other wicker chair and reciprocates her smile.

"Morning, Cal." I missed her crackly voice in the morning. She was right. Spending the night with her was more than worth it. I held her for most of the night. It was one of the best sleeps I've had in a long time.

"How do you feel this morning? You fell asleep pretty quickly." She's looking out at the view, and I knew she would find it just as serene as I do.

"Best sleep I've had in four years." Her gaze meets mine,

revealing her appreciation for us being able to stay the night together. I remember when I crawled in the sheets after closing the curtains, her body clung to mine almost immediately. And she stayed next to me the entire night.

"Me too. You still mumble in your sleep. It was cute."

Time, please stop. This is so peaceful right now.

"Oh yeah?" She brings her feet onto the seat of her chair and positions her body towards me, preparing to hear a good story.

"Did I say anything meaningful?"

"Oh, you know, just a fuck you, Cal, here and there." I try to keep a straight face and when I look at her, we both end up laughing.

"I would never say that." She smirks, enjoying my early humor. "Well, maybe not to your face."

We're quiet for a while. I'm enjoying her company and her saneness. Enjoying watching her be a complete bliss. While I found the sky beautiful, Jen's beauty is unparalleled.

"What's that?" Staring at the view, I look over at her and she's looking at the letter sitting on the table in between our chairs. She picks it up before I can answer. She opens it and I watch her eyes move from left to right as she rereads her torture.

"Wow." Refolding the letter, she places it back in the envelope. I haven't stopped taking my eyes off her. It's interesting watching her reaction to her words. Her forehead crinkles, and her bottom lip flips back and forth between pouting and grinning. She thinks too hard.

"What did you think?" I take a sip of coffee, and it's cold now.

"That Valentine's party at the shop was awful. Pat never let me decorate again." She talks away from me, avoiding eye contact, I think.

"Was the Chinese good?" I want to keep her in good spirits. She's still looking away from me, but then she looks down and blushes.

"Always the best." She readjusts her blanket around her.

"Read the next one to me." She has her hand resting under her chin, almost idolizing me.

"What?" I heard her, but want to make sure she's being serious. She knows what she wrote, I don't. She could either put us in a great mood, or a terrible mood.

"The next letter. Did you bring more?"

"Yes. I think I grabbed three." I put my empty coffee cup on the side table.

"Do you know what the next letter is about?" My nerves move quickly, and I doubt it's the caffeine hitting me. I look directly at her and she's already smiling.

"Yes."

Well, I can't deny that smile. If she knows it's a good letter, then I'll read to her. I brought all three letters outside with me, unsure how I'd feel after reading the first one. If Jen hadn't come outside, I probably would've read them. I'm nervous as I pick up the second letter and break the seal. I want to look at Jen to see her face right now, but I'm so fucking nervous. These letters make me feel queasy.

February 17, 2004

Dear Calvin,

I was re-reading another poem you wrote me. Probably my favorite one yet.

To describe the way I care about you, no words can do it right
The depth of the compassion is forever and despite
Though we argue, my love remains unending
I could never imagine the greatness of this feeling

You bring me such joy in a sense that I could never
Thank you enough for making me believe in forever
I find safety in your arms and knowing you're safe
You're able to make me laugh every single day

I think of you as a partner, one who cares, my best friend
The only part of caring so much for you is I hate it might end
Not today, nor tomorrow, but the day we die
Because no other circumstances will make me say goodbye

I believe in Heaven more than ever, if I didn't much before
You're nothing less than an angel and I care for you more
And more each day, my heart will eternally know your name
I hope I've won yours, do you feel the same?

I'm breathing heavily after re-reading my words to her. As I refold the letter back into the envelope, I tell Jen the story behind that poem.

"You know, I wrote this one for your birthday. I had intended to give it to you as a present, as I assumed you would love to hear those words back then."

"Why didn't you give it to me, then?" Jen's voice is sad. I don't even have to look at her to know that she's disappointed.

"I don't know. Guess I was just scared. Everything was moving really quickly for us and I wasn't sure you felt the same."

I find the nerve to look at Jen, but she's looking away from me.

"Jen?" Leaning forward in the chair, I place my hand on her knee.

Just comfort her, you prick. That's all she wants from you.

"Do you regret anything?" She asks me. When she looks at me, her eyes are filling with tears.

You should've just shut the fuck up and enjoyed the moment with her. You always make her sad.

"I regret nothing about what happened before Easton. Absolutely nothing. Please don't insinuate things moving too fast was a bad thing. I was loving every moment. I was finding new things to love about you. Loving every minute of being with you. I don't regret falling in love with you, if that's what you mean."

I feel I can never satisfy Jen. The words I say never seem enough. Every good memory is obliterated by a shitty one from Easton. Showing her I still care always seems to backfire. It's so difficult to love this version of Jen. I swallow her silence like I'm swallowing salt.

"Do you have regrets?"

You just opened a can of worms, you fucking idiot.

Jen wipes away her eyes and moves her knees up to her chest, forcing my hand to leave her leg. She lays her cheek on her kneecap and looks at me.

"Every day, Cal."

Told you, dumbass. You picked the wrong question to ask.

"Like what?" I know I shouldn't ask these questions because clearly Devil is provoking me, but my conscious has to know what she regrets. Was there anything I did right?

With her cheek still laying on her kneecap, she smiles at me. Not enough to show her teeth, really just a small grin.

"You tell me what happened to you after Easton and I'll tell you what I regret."

Immediately, my body reacts. My shoulders tense and my head drops. Shame. Anger. Embarrassment. Depression.

"Jen...." My voice cracks. "I can't tell you that fucking story." My anger frightens her as her head pops off her leg. I'm not angry at her, but with myself. Whatever Devil has to say about me is true. I'm a messed-up prick who left the love of his life behind because of jealously!

"I didn't think so. I'm going to go pack my stuff, and I'll be ready to leave in twenty minutes."

I sense Jen stand in front of the chair for a moment and then hear the door close. My eyes are watery, but I look over at where she just was and see the blanket laying on the armrest. I breathe out heavily, pick up the blanket, and find Jen.

"Jen, please. Don't do this. Don't leave yet. We can talk about anything else besides Easton, please. I don't want you to go." I talk down the hallway and stop at the bedroom.

She's sitting on the edge of the bed, clearly trying not to cry. She is so fragile. I walk into the room and kneel in front of her. Her eyes are glossy, but no actual tears have escaped yet. I place my hands on her cheeks and guide her face to meet my gaze.

"I don't want you to leave." I have lost so much time with Jen that no matter what we are doing, sitting in silence, arguing, reading letters together, kissing, I just want to be near her.

"I don't want you to leave either. But you have once already. How do I know you won't leave again? I think it's impossible for you to love this version of me, Cal. You left last night because I'm a ball of depression. I've seen you grab your hair, thinking hard about how to make me feel better. Nothing can make me feel better. I'm stuck, and I don't know how to get out. We should save each other the hurt and keep time on our sides by letting this go now. I'm ready to go home and try to move on with my life." She stands up, pushing my hands off her face.

Picking up one of her bags, she walks to the bathroom to get her things. I hear the sniffles from her.

"Let me help you get unstuck, baby. Let me save you." I face her as she looks at me.

"You tried, and you failed."

Her words crush my fucking soul.

Jennie

I don't know how many more times my heart has to break. Calvin has been the only one for me. I want things to work again. And I want him to love me as much as he did before, but he knows, just as much as I know, that we are both different people.

I don't think Cal can love me the way he used to. And that is killing me. Even with his hopeful optimism after the letters, he still won't love this version. I have to walk away from him, no matter how much it will kill me. I wish I had made this decision years ago, not only after he came back.

I catch my reflection in the mirror. My eyes have sunken in, looking like deep, dark black holes. Almost identical to how my heart probably looks. My cheekbones are prominent, sharp as a blade. My lips have turned a dark pink, licking them feverishly over the past forty-eight hours since I've known Cal has been back, and my body... my body just looks tired. Sleeping next to Cal felt like a dream last night. A dream I have had for years. I wish he'd returned to me that night rather than going to jail. Being held by him made me feel warm. His kisses have left marks on my skin, and I can feel them all over my body. Our feet playing footsies under the sheets. It was all so familiar and something I want to keep forever.

But I can't.

The thought of never being able to sleep next to Cal breaks my heart into more pieces.

Turning on the faucet, I run my hands underneath, then wipe my face with the warm water. The worst part about depression is the crying. I'm so tired of crying. Drying my face, I tossed the towel onto the counter. I take in a loud sigh and find my makeup bag. With a quick touch up of concealer and mascara, I zip up my bag. Looking around the bathroom, I pick up my dress, then double check I have all my belongings. Cal left his sweatshirt on the hook behind the door. Reaching out, I feel it, every memory of this sweatshirt. The first time he let me wear it after a shift one night, wearing it after the carnival, and all the times he offered it to me when I spent late nights at his house. I bring a sleeve up to my face and smell it.

Mhhm, it smells like Calvin. One of the best smells in the universe. It's a mix of musk and mahogany and his Old Spice body wash. It makes me feel safe and happy. Unhooking it off the door, I fold it as best as I can without Cal noticing what piece of article it is and shove it under my arm. I grab my makeup bag and dress and open the door, not ready to face the one who will have gotten away.

When I open the door, Cal isn't in the bedroom. I walk towards the couch to pick up my bag anyway, trying hard to not think that Cal has left again. If he left, it's probably for the best. There are only so many times someone attempts to leave before they decide they don't want to come back.

As I shove Cal's sweatshirt in my bag, followed by my makeup bag and pajamas I changed out of, dishes bang in the kitchen.

The magnetic pull to Cal activates. Turning down the hallway, his back is towards me. He's washing the dishes and the banging noise, I discover, is him putting the dishes on the drying rack.

"What are you doing?" I whisper to him. I have never seen him wash a dish in his life. The view is wholesome and cute. I picture this life with Cal for a moment until he glances over his shoulder to look at me.

"Just cleaning up the kitchen before we head out. Are you ready to go?"

I'm surprised by his solemn tone. It makes me sad I came up with this suggestion to leave so early. His despair is making it harder to say yes. I want to comfort him the same way he's been comforting me. I have mixed feelings about embracing him and holding him close. That was my favorite way to comfort him, from behind. I've always been a shy, submissive person. When I hold Cal like that, I feel in control. Like I'm protecting him.

I must've wanted to touch him. When he notices my presence, he turns around to face me directly.

My heart rate rises, and my desire to put my hands on him intensifies. He leans his hands on his sink, moving slightly back from me.

"What are we doing, Jen?" His voice is exhausted, almost as tired as mine.

His question catches me off guard. I don't know what we're

doing. I've never been more confused in my life. Unable to handle the temptation, I fall into Cal's chest. I cover the sides of my face with my hands to hide my humiliation, replaying the moments that have happened in the past couple of days. From me telling Cal that I want to see him before finishing all the letters, then I push him away by telling him about Jonah and the hospital, then we get very physical in bed, then he handles a panic attack of mine and consoles me deeply, then undresses me to fall asleep next to me. I can't decide what we are supposed to do.

I enter paradise when Cal's arms wrap around me. He pulls me close, and I let my hands drop from my face and wrap around him, pulling him closer to me.

"I'm sorry this hasn't been easy, baby." Cal mumbles into my hair. His apology continues to break my heart.

You shouldn't be apologizing.

Holding back my tears, I rub his back, consoling his words.

"I don't want to leave Cal, but I think we should. This has all happened so fast."

I'm lost in his aroma, but secretly grin at the fact of packing his sweatshirt. I am going home to put on that sweatshirt and enter a trance of the events that have transpired before us.

"I want to be wherever you are. I don't want to leave you again." His grip intensified around me. I try to put myself in his shoes, to understand his pain and loneliness, but I'm selfish and can only feel my only pain. As if there's anything left in my chest, I pull myself away from Cal and look up at him.

"Please finish the letters. I need you to decide if you can still love me." I try to keep my voice neutral, hoping to not stir an argument. It's clear to me how much Cal dislikes me bringing up the letters. After my comment, Cal looks over my head, looking down the hallway, probably trying to keep his cool about the mention of them.

"Jen, enough with the letters. I'm never gonna stop loving you, no matter what you say." He brings his gaze back to me, sighing.

"It's not just the things I have to say, it's the things I've done."

Oh God...

As expected, Cal removes his arms from me and turns back to

the dishes. There's only one person he hopes to never read about, I can tell by his posture.

Glen.

Figuring the conversation is over, I walk back to the room and finish packing.

Calvin

The fire inside me is brewing. Thank the Heavens Jen walked away. I know exactly what Jen is referencing when she said *it's the things I've done.* So help me God, if I have to read a letter about any sexual encounter with Glen, I might actually commit murder.

Fucking Glen. I hate that son of a bitch.

I put the last dish in the drying rack and dry off my hands. Letting my fumes simmer in me, I grab a bottle of water before heading into the bedroom to pack up my things.

Jen's back is to me as she makes the bed. Chuckling, she whips around, surprised to find me watching her.

"What?"

"You don't have to make the bed. The owners will just take the sheets off." The owners, being my parents. My mom would flip a lid if she knew Jen was the one I brought here. My bag sits on the floor. I feel Jen's eyes on me the whole time. She's trying to sense my odometer.

"Wouldn't the owners do the dishes, too?" I stop messing with my stuff and look back at her. She smirks.

I lick my lips to hide my smile, but fail. Usually my mom does the dishes, but I needed to do something with my hands besides punch a wall.

God, her beautiful smile. I have engraved it in my mind for years. I hate I haven't seen it enough since I've been back. Do I make her genuinely smile anymore?

"Hey, cleaning helps me calm down." I tell her matter-of-factly. Turning around to fumble with my clothes, I can't hide my smile.

"Mhm, okay sure." Playfulness escapes from her voice.

When she's done making the bed, I walk into the bathroom to retrieve my toiletries, then realize I brought nothing out of my bag. The bathroom looks weird without any of Jen's things in there. It reminds me of the first time Jen spent the night with me. I found her toothbrush in my bathroom. Little by little, the times she stayed the night, she bought more items with her. Hell, I didn't mind.

I close the door to get my sweatshirt off the hook when I notice it's gone. I thought I put it there last night. Maybe Jen saw it?

"Hey, have you seen my..." I stop talking when I realize I'm in the room by myself.

Angel tells me, *you purposely left it there for her to take. You knew she couldn't resist your favorite sweatshirt.*

I love Jen caught on to finding my Easter egg. It means I can heckle her later to get it back–hopefully.

Assuming Jen is already outside, I walk towards the door, throwing my bag over my shoulder. Jen is sitting in the passenger side of my truck, and I can't help but laugh again. She looks up from scratching her ankles and cocks her head.

"You still take forever to leave."

"Eager, are we?" I walk around the front of my truck and open my door, flinging my bag in the backseat.

"You know I'm not." I look over at her and find her serious face, one I don't come by often. Aware of her struggles, I'm unsure whether to ask if she really wants to go this early. I am too. Some space could help us figure this out.

I lay my hand on her leg, as she looks at me from looking back at the house.

"I know."

Wanting to give her some space, I rub my thumb to offer some comfort and then bring my hand back to the steering wheel. She grabs my wrist, not letting me go, and somehow intertwines her fingers through mine, then sets our hands on her lap.

"First one to let go buys the next dinner date."

Her words shock me. Well, double shock me. I'm shocked Jen could pull that sly move of holding my hand. Now she's trying to threaten me by not letting go of her hand. I grip tightly.

Oh, don't worry baby, I won't let go.

I'm conflicted about asking her again if she wants to go, but I can tell by the grip she has on my hand that she doesn't want to.

Do I take her back to my apartment for the rest of the weekend? Should I take her to lunch before dropping her off? Do I let go of her hand so I can pay to take her to dinner? I can't seem to be okay with dropping her off. There is so much uncertainty between us right now. I hate this feeling so fucking much.

I drive down the long driveway until I get to the main road. Checking the right side of the road, Jen is leaned against the window, sleeping. It hasn't even been five minutes, but God, I can't imagine how tired she must be. Even though her grip is loose in my hand, I still hold on to hers.

I reminisce for a moment, thinking about the drive to Easton four years ago, and how it felt so perfect. I had picked her up, wanted to make sure her father knew I wasn't taking her to a remote island to kill her. Plus, I wanted to see him. Little did I know that would be the very last time I would. I walked up to her front door and let myself in, as I did many times. Mr. H was sitting in his recliner, which was his usual place of comfort. He appeared to be sleeping and I must've startled him when I closed the door.

"Calvin, hey buddy. How're doing?" His voice was very weak. I sat on the couch next to him, unaware if Jen knew I was there yet, but that gave her more time to get her belongings together.

"I'm doing well. How are you doing, sir?"

Jen's dad intimidated me the first time I met him. Even though he had always been sick since I knew him, I always felt he could snap out of his cancer and kick me on my ass.

He should've.

I hate myself for how much grief Jen had to handle by herself. I should've been there.

Jen's dad wasn't big into heart-to-heart conversations, so after answering a couple questions about work and school, and reciprocating with asking questions about his health, we ended the conversation after a couple of minutes. Jen's quick reaction to falling asleep, I think, she gets from her father. By the time I make it to the foot of the stairs, which is maybe fifteen steps, I look over at Mr. H, who is sleeping again. My heart saddens, both in the past and in the present.

When I reach Jen's room, she's moving swiftly around. I can usually tell when she had headphones in because she dances around while she does her tasks. It was so adorable, so I just watch her from a small sliver opening of her bedroom door.

She's got her lavender duffle bag propped open on the edge of her bed and she's sorting through several shirts, probably trying to determine which ones she is okay with getting a little dirty. I try to hide my chuckle when she ends up packing all of them. I laugh louder, startling her as she turns around to find me entering her room.

"Jesus, Cal. What the hell are you doing?" She takes out her headphones and unplugs them from her phone.

"Just watching you in your element." I pull out her desk chair and sit down, nonchalantly look around to figure out how much more packing she has left to do.

"Oh, shut it! How long have you been here?" She still moves around her room, packing her toiletries bag and a towel for the lake.

"Maybe ten minutes. I was talking with your dad for a while." She emerges from her closet with her shoes on but laces undone. *Okay, we are getting closer to leaving.*

"Yeah, he's tired today."

"You sure you're okay leaving him for a couple of days?"

I try not to sound selfish, but I'm really hoping she's okay with it. This weekend is supposed to be special. It will be special.

"Yes. Our neighbor is totally fine staying over here with him. I told her he'll probably sleep most of the weekend, but just in case he needs some company or some food, she'll be here." She brings her feet onto her bed frame so she ties her shoes.

My heart flutters. She's okay with leaving her sick dad so she can spend time with me. That's not something I should be proud of, but I am.

"Well, if there's any point that she calls you or you feel you should be here with him, tell me so I can bring you home." Wrapping my lanyard around my fingers, my patience begins to spike.

"Hopefully, we won't have to leave early."

Present me whimpers at the memory.

"Okay, think I'm ready," she says again and looks around her room. It looks like a tornado, but she knows where everything is. I stand up to help her with her bag, but she walks over to me, wrapping her arms around my neck.

"I'll tell you again, I'm very nervous about this weekend, but I'm so excited to spend time with you." I run a hand over her French braid while my other hand rests on her lower back, pulling her a little closer.

"I won't let anything happen to you, okay? Promise." Kissing her, I unravel her hands from me to grab her backpack. She walks out of her room first, and I trail her with her bags on my arms.

We get to the base of the stairs when she turns to me and whispers, "I'm going to say goodbye really quick. I'll meet you in the truck."

She turns right to enter the living room where her father is still sleeping in the same position that I left him, and I go straight out the door. I'm walking down the pathway when I see Rosie coming from next door.

"Have a good time, hon! Bring my girl back in one piece!"

"Will do!" I wave to her as I open the back door to put Jen's belongings in. As I close the door and walk over to the passenger door to have it open for her, she's already coming out of the house.

"Alrighty, let's go!" She looks conflicted, like she wants to cry but is trying to smile.

"Everything good?" She hops in and looks down at me while I hold on to the door.

"Just always hard to say goodbye to him, but I'm trying to not be sad because I'll be with you. So yeah, I'm good." She gives me a genuine smile. Giving her a squeeze on the leg, I shut her door and head around my truck to the driver's side.

Pulling out of her driveway and out of the neighborhood, I grab her hand and look at her.

She's so fucking stunning.

Easton was about two hours from Seattle. Jen gets comfy by taking off her shoes and pulls them on the seat so they lean against the door frame. She grabs her blanket from the back and lays it over her legs. Once she's all adjusted, she reaches for my hand again. She never let go the entire drive, and I just drive in awe of her. I'm in awe of the love story we've created in just a few months.

Present me coughs, realizing I can barely see because my eyes are filling with tears. Without wanting to, I release Jen's hand to get a drink of my water. Jen notices and wakes up.

"Hey, are you okay?" She must've not been in a deep sleep. She runs her fingers through her hair. Her feet, resting on the seat, are still leaning against the door.

Now having access to both my hands, I reposition my driving hand so I can wipe my tears away.

"Yeah, I'm good."

Please don't ask me what I was thinking about.

"What were you thinking about just now?" She angles her body towards me, and she sets her feet on the ground.

I look out the window, hoping to avoid this conversation. Not knowing which version of Jen I have here in the car with me, I give in.

"Just thinking about our car ride to Easton. Sorry to bring it up, but your body language reminded me so much of how you slept when we drove down."

I change my driving hands again and let my right hand sit on the console, making it available for hand-holding again. I look over at Jen, who is no longer looking at me, but out the front window. Her hands are no longer available as she has them clasped in between her legs.

"You don't need to be sorry. We have to talk about it sometime."

"Yeah, well, that time isn't now." I growl back. She notices my venom and looks over at me.

"You know what I remember most about that day?" She asks and waits for my answer. Am I supposed to answer?

"Um, well, we left Thursday afternoon, so are you speaking of Thursday?"

She chuckles, which makes me sick to my stomach but brings me to smile too. Why would she chuckle?

"Yes, Cal. Thursday. I remember clearly what happened Friday and Saturday." She looks at me with I-would-never-forget-look.

Clearing my throat, I form a chuckle back to her. Guess we have a playful Jen in the car, which is a positive for me.

"Okay, Thursday. Hmm, what do you remember most?" Tapping

my chin and repeating the question out loud.

"Was it what we did at the cabin after everyone went to sleep?" Peeking over at her, butterflies emerge from my stomach when she blushes and looks down at her hands, still in between her lap. She looks at me as she leans her head against the headrest, covering her face in embarrassment.

God, she's still so beautiful.

"Calvin! No." I love that I'm making her laugh again. Especially while we talk about something so sensitive to us.

"Okay, okay, um, was it the gas station stop we made before we pulled into the cabin?" I look back over at her to see if I got it right this time. She looks out the windshield, pondering the memory.

"Hmm, I remember that guy. He was a creep, but I kind of forgot what he said to me for you to curse him out."

I switch driving arms again and take the wheel with my right arm. My left arm rests on the window dash. It makes me a little difficult to look at Jen, but it gives my left arm a break from being extended.

"He was weird. He was practically drooling over the color of your eyes. Said there was nothing quite like them and was trying to do some poetic shit, but then I walked behind you and heard him. I couldn't take it. Yes, your eyes are literally one of a kind, but he was making me gag. I told him to shut the fuck up and use his poems on someone else."

It's silent for a second until I hear Jen bust out laughing. She holds on to her stomach. Her face is turning red from laughing so hard. I can't help but switch driving arms again so I can look over at her better. I laugh with her and boy, I'm entering a good fucking place.

"Holy shit, I remember that." Her laugh slowly fades away, but she's still smiling. I want to grab her hand so badly and kiss the top of it.

"No, actually my most vivid memory of Thursday was when we were standing in my room and before we left, you kissed me and you told me you wouldn't let anything happen to me. Those words were so powerful; I trusted them completely. I trusted you with everything."

And what goes up must come down. The fun we were having is now overshadowed by guilt and pain. My mouth feels full of glue because I don't know what to say. No words are coming out.

"I'm sorry." I'm not good at apologies, and there will never be enough for her.

There will never be enough apologies for Jen. Ever.

I tense when her hand grabs mine. My eyes welled with tears as I looked over at her. I quickly try to wipe them before she sees. But Jen notices everything.

"I don't blame you. I should've not let anything happen to you, so I'm sorry I didn't promise that back to you." She wipes my face.

I don't know how much more of this I can handle. Each time she blames herself, my soul breaks more and more.

Jennie

After Calvin pulls into the parking spot, it feels like time stands still. I don't move to open the door, and he just sits in his seat, rubbing his forehead. I'm not sure if time is our friend or enemy right now, so I ask.

"Is time on our side right now?" Anticipating the coming heartache, I lower my head and clasp my hands. I don't know what to expect when I leave this truck. I'm trying so hard to hold my tears back. Glancing at Cal through my blurred vision, he looks right at me and grins.

Don't smile at me like that, you bastard.

"I don't want to jinx it or make it angry if it is on our side."

It's getting hot in this truck. My stomach is in knots and my mouth is quivering. I can longer hold back my tears. Unlocking my hands, I wipe my eyes with the palms of my hand, not sure why I'm becoming emotional.

Yes, you do.

I hate myself because we left the house early. No, I decided we should leave early.

I hate myself because I don't know what is going to happen between me and Cal.

I hate myself because I love this boy. And I shouldn't.

I hate myself because I don't want to say goodbye.

Once I list the reasons in my head, my eyes become "wet plants" as Cal refers to them. My soaking, saturated eyes.

"Jen... please..." His voice is heartbreaking, and I don't know what he's pleasing me for. Jen, please don't fuck this up for us? Jen, please don't cry anymore? Jen, please don't go?

Believe me, Cal, I want all of that.

I don't know why I'm not grabbing my bags and jumping out of the truck.

Just leave him be and he'll find his way to be happy without you.

I'm in a full sob, but Cal doesn't console me. I can't see what he's doing because my vision is blurred. As much as I keep wiping the tears away, they come back even stronger. He just lets me cry.

I don't know how much time passed, and I'd be embarrassed to find out, but once I compose myself and my tears subside, I sigh deeply and look at Cal. He's been watching me the whole time, silently crying himself. His face is blotchy, as if he's been wiping away his tears, too. His eyes are red and so painful to look at. I never knew how beautiful his wet plants could be, too.

"Do you have anything to say before I open the door?"

Just pull it off like a band aid. Once you get inside, you can cry your eyes, and heart and ass out.

I force myself to look out the window, anxiously hoping Cal wants to tell me the story about what happened in Easton. I prepare myself for whatever disaster happened.

"I'm sorry I wasn't him."

I jerk my head to look at him. *What does that mean? Like who?* Cal is leaning against the door, facing me. His fingers are making circles on his forehead, in clear distress. His eyes are staring into space, so I follow his gaze.

My ring. Cal's promise ring that sits on my middle finger of my left hand.

"Like who?"

"Glen. Andy. Jonah. Whoever got a chance to make you happy." He has yet to look away from my ring.

"If anything, Calvin, I'm sorry they weren't you. It doesn't matter how many guys there were, or what they were to me, whether a friend or trying to be something more, they would never be you. It was never a competition. The top spot was always yours. You've always been on the tallest pedestal. My heart belonged completely and fully to only you. Only you could give me the sun, moon, and stars. It didn't matter if it was day or night, because you were always shining the brightest. You were the only one who I wanted to be with. I found the purest happiness the first day I met you and I only got happier as our story unfolded. It wasn't until you left that, I lost everything. You were the only one who could make me feel whole again. There was no one else, Cal. It was only ever you." I twist my ring, hoping to distract him from a death stare.

Even though my voice was cracking through almost every word, I didn't cry. My body is craving to be comforted by him, but I can't let him. I need to move on from him, but I am too wounded, too destructive, too sad to be with him.

I leave Cal with my words, grab my bags, and open the door. Facing him, he avoids my eye contact.

"Is there some secret you're keeping from me? I want to say I'm sorry I couldn't be what you wanted."

And with that, I shut the door and don't look back.

As soon as I close my front door, I drop my bags and let myself drop behind the door and again, break down. The worst crying I've ever done in the past four years. The kind where your stomach hurts from expanding too much. Your throat is dry and you're gasping for air. Your head pounds and your temples feel like they're going to explode. My insides are breaking down, and I have no remedy. Cal was my relief.

Time becomes an evil thief. I don't know how long we were in the driveway. I don't know how long Cal let me cry in his truck. I don't know how long we sat in silence, waiting for each other's response. Or how long I sat on the floor crying. I don't know how long Cal waited in the driveway until he left.

Everything in me became empty. By the time I get myself off the floor, the sunlight streamed through my living room window, indicating the sunset was approaching. I had no energy to pick up my bags, so they stay by the door. I crawl onto my couch, letting depression greet me like an old friend.

I wasn't hungry, or thirsty, or happy.

I just wanted to rest. I wanted to sleep.

Jennie

Tuesday, April 17ᵗʰ, 2007

For two and a half days, I slept. I woke up here and there, groggy, feeling like someone drugged me. Although I stumbled to get to the bathroom or get a drink, I never questioned the time or day. I don't remember moving from the couch to my bed, but I must've gotten there somehow. I didn't care anymore. Time was no longer a companion. Time is the scum of the Earth.

I've grown used to how my face feels after falling asleep crying. It's that tight feeling around your entire face, how your eyes feel swollen, almost like an allergic reaction. I rub my face, hoping to ease the throbbing tension from my head. I stretch my arms above my head and point my toes down, trying to loosen all my muscles. Bringing my body close to my body pillow, I'm swallowed by the images and conversations that occurred before I slept. It felt like ages ago.

Leaving Cal.

Reaching over to my nightstand, I try to find my phone, but the table is unoccupied. I sit up on my bed, feeling more empty today than I did three days ago.

What is my purpose anymore? You weren't ready to meet him yet.

I'm not in the mood to hear Devil's bullshit. She wins.

Somehow, I get out of bed and walk to the front door, where I left my bags scattered on the floor. Sighing out loud at my mess, I spot my phone. There are smells that are familiar around my living room, and there's an overwhelming presence that someone is watching me, but I'm too tired to care. Checking my phone, there's two percent remaining. *Thirty messages. 16 missed calls.*

I walk back to my room, plug in my phone into the charger, and crawl back into bed before diving into reality.

{Sunday}

Cal: I'm not hiding anything. **8:46 AM**

Cal: I just don't think you are emotionally ready to hear that story. **8:47 AM**

Cal: please don't hate me. I will tell you what happened. One day. **8:47 AM**

Cal: text me later, okay? I miss you and I will always love you. **8:53 AM**

Pat: Did you make it home okay? I haven't heard from you. **3:34 PM**

Missed call from Cal **5:00 PM**

Missed call from Cal **5:01 PM**

Cal: I'm hoping you are resting. I will try you again in the morning. I miss you and I love you. Please don't hate me. **8:14 PM**

Pat: You alright? It's not like you to not get back with me for hours. **9:28 PM**

Missed call from Pat **9:30 PM**

{Monday}

Cal: Good morning. Couldn't sleep, AT ALL. I understand your pain. I feel I was run over by a truck. How are you feeling today? **7:02 AM**

Lydia: Hey, are you okay? You haven't shown up yet... **11:06 AM**

Missed call from Eva **11:20 AM**

Eva: Byrd's are worried about you. **12:30 PM**

Missed call from Lydia **1:15 PM**

Missed call from Max **1:16 PM**

Max: Jennie, hey. Are you alright? Do we need to send Evana over to check on you? You've never not shown up on a Monday. We know you spent the weekend with Cal (Lydia told me...) Did it go well? Let me know if you need to talk. I'm always happy to give the dad advice. **1:18 PM**

Cal: Wow, you must've been really tired, or maybe you're just busy at work today? I'm going to stop by your office so I know you're okay **1:57 PM**

Missed call from Cal **2:26 PM**

Missed call from Lydia **2:29 PM**

Lydia: Cal stopped by... he told me what happened this weekend. Where are you?? We can help you. **2:30 PM**

Cal: What the fuck, Jen?! WHERE ARE YOU **2:30 PM**

Cal: Jen... please say something. **2:31 PM**

Amanda: Hey girl! Are you able to cover my shift tonight at the shop? **2:37 PM**

Cal: I'm coming over if you don't answer me in the next hour. **2:38 PM**

Missed call from Cal **2:40 PM**

Missed call from Pat **2:41 PM**

Pat: Hey Jennie. Whatever is going on, please call me back. I'm short staffed today. Let me know if you could help us out. **2:42 PM**

Missed call from Lydia **3:04 PM**

Missed call from Lydia **3:05 PM**

Missed call from Lydia **3:06 PM**

Cal: Fuck it. I'm coming over Jen. You're scaring me. **4:09 PM**

Missed call from Cal **4:34 PM**

Cal: ANSWER YOUR DOOR **4:34 PM**

Cal: Jesus Jen, please let me in. **4:35 PM**

Cal: I'm going to get Pat. **4:36 PM**

Missed call from Pat **5:05 PM**

Pat: Jen, let us in. We are outside. We are here. **5:06 PM**

Cal: We are waiting outside, Jen. Please open the door. **5:06 PM**

Missed call from Lydia **8:57 PM**

Lydia: We are coming to you. **8:57 PM**

Cal: Oh you've got a party outside your door. You better wake up soon. I'm holding off calling the police because I know how tired you are. I'm praying to fucking God that I'm right. I'm trying to get rid of these people. **9:31 PM**

Pat: Jennie...we care about you. **10:45 PM**

Pat: I will call Jonah if I need to. You know he won't take any of this crap. **10:47**

Lydia: the most powerful thing you can do right now is be patient with yourself while things are unfolding for you. **11:11 PM**

Pat: I have to open the shop. I'll be back soon. If you're in there, call me back.

7:56 AM

{Tuesday}

Jonah: Jennie. **8:05 AM**

I'm lost in a pool of tears. Again. After finally getting some rest, my close friends are now overwhelming me. I'm struggling to breathe. How dare they bring Jonah into my mess! Dropping my phone onto the floor, I curl myself tighter into my pillow.

"Please make it go away. I want it to go away..."

My dad would be ashamed of who I am now. A coward.

I have failed everyone around me.

I am nothing.

The familiar feeling enters my body and forces me out of bed. I have tunnel vision as I walk to my kitchen and spot the very thing I'm looking for.

A knife. My favorite knife.

My dad bought me a purple knife set for Christmas the year Cal left. My dad wasn't a big present person. He just liked to have company and didn't care for gifts. Quality time was his love language. Again, I failed miserably in that.

With the small pear knife in hand, I return to my bedroom, shutting the door and head into the bathroom. Lifting my left sleeve, I feel my throat tighten. I cry at the sight of the damage I've done to my body.

Calvin

Yesterday when I got to Hilltop to harass Lydia about where she was keeping Jen, she harassed me, wondering where *I* was keeping *her*. We both tried calling her again, proving a point that we both didn't have any leads to her whereabouts.

I should've called Henry. He would've busted down her door in a heartbeat.

After Eva and Lydia told me she didn't show up, I went outside and punched the brick wall. Lydia followed me out. She saw my bloody knuckles and forced me inside so she could clean and bandage it. That's when I told her what happened over the weekend.

"I picked her up. We had dinner. We stayed at my parent's rental, but she didn't know that. She thought I booked a B&B for the weekend. Then we just started talking, like how we did back then. It was sweet and gentle. It was full of love. Our chemistry was natural. Then we started arguing about when she went to the hospital. I wanted to get information from her, but she was so closed off from me. I tried to be patient, but I just wanted to know that she was okay. Then we started kissing. It was weird, like a quick light switch turned on between us. Then she accidentally scratched me in bed, and I fucked up the rest of the night."

The alcohol was burning, but I was distracted by Lydia's eyes on me. *Please don't ask me to elaborate.*

"What did you do?" I glared at her.

Lydia was easy to talk to. Must be why she's a psych. And maybe it's why Jonah is already close to her. It makes me wonder what kind of relationship Max and Lydia have with him.

"What didn't I do?" I chuckle, reminiscing on all the things I ruined in a span of twenty-four hours.

"Her fucking scream..." Lydia wrapped my knuckles, and I stare blankly as she intertwined the gauze between my fingers.

"Good or bad scream?"

"The worst possible scream I've ever heard. I went outside to get some air and she screams at the top of her lungs. I find her in the bathroom having a fucking panic attack because she thinks I left her again. She thought I left her."

"That's part of her trauma. I hope you understand that."

I hear Lydia, but don't formulate the words of what she means. I so badly want to ruin the work Lydia just did on my hand so I can pound my knuckles into the wall, pretending my face is there. Lydia nodded, waiting for more details.

"I tried to calm her down, but I think I fucking failed. It just broke my heart, watching her be so distraught. Eventually I got her to bed and read her a poem I wrote to her. Then we were back in this cycle of talking sweet and cute to each other. I think she was even flirting with me. The next morning, I'm reading a couple of her letters, and she wanted me to read one to her. So, I do. Then the sweetness and cuteness just fucking evaporates because she wants me to tell her what happened after the camping trip. She's always wanting to know what the fuck happened to me."

"I assume you didn't tell her then?" Lydia finished up on the gauze, threw her trash away and put the alcohol back in the first aid container. We were in the employee bathroom, so I was leaning against the sink. She backs away, giving me space to finish speaking.

"No. We left early. Then..." I crinkled my nose, feeling the tickle that comes before I cry. I looked away to wipe my nose.

"You can cry, Calvin. I won't judge."

"She fucking lets it all out to me. Tells me there was no one else, that there will be no one else. That she will always wait for me. She thinks I'm keeping a secret from her, about why I'm not telling her what happened to me." My eyes burned, not sure if it was from the smell of the alcohol or holding my tears back.

"And are you keeping a secret?"

"Fuck no. I just... I hate myself for what I did that night. I was so drunk and pissed off. So impulsive. I should've just called her to pick me up. I have so much regret from that night."

"I don't know much about you yet, Calvin, but I know Jen loves you wholeheartedly. Every time I see her, there has always been some sort of comment about you. I know she won't stop fighting for you.

But she's been hurting for a long time, Calvin. I'm on her side because I think she has so much potential. But I have to admit something..." I was intrigued by her insight. Lydia reminded me of Pat, someone who tells you the truth no matter how hard it is to hear. I looked towards her.

"Yeah, what's that?"

"I'm rooting for your love story."

"Why? I'm not good for her." I ran my thumb over the gauze, feeling a slight prickling sensation. Lydia leaned against the door frame, holding the first aid kit in her hand. She ran her fingers through her hair.

"I don't think you realize how good you are for her. The smile that girl had on her face when she came in to work on the day she found out you were getting released early was just..." Lydia wiped underneath her eyes and shook her head, clearly feeling embarrassed.

"Tell me. What did she look like?" I stare hard at Lydia.

"It was like wearing the best sweater. It felt so good to see her smile that big. Just made me so happy because I truly had not seen something so beautiful and radiant. That day, gosh, that day was special for her."

My wounded hand was a good distraction as I pictured the way Lydia described Jen smiling. It's a mental image that doesn't take long to make me grin.

"Thank you." It's all I can say to her.

Before I called Pat for help, Lydia expressed concerned that Jen wasn't doing well. She and Max couldn't get to her apartment until later in the evening. She tried to tell me to go home and wait for them to be available, but I couldn't. Her words swarmed my mind all fucking day. *I don't think she's well.*

It was dangerous that I knew where Jen lived now. It was near dusk when I got back to her apartment and called Pat. He was annoyed that he had to leave the shop. How dare he say the shop was more important than Jen at the moment! Even though I still had my grudge towards Pat for ghosting me, I knew he'd help. We texted and called her for a while, but there was no answer. Max and Lydia arrived around nine at night.

It was at that moment Pat shared he had a key to her apartment.

I could have killed him.

He told us to go home and we could meet in the morning to let us into her apartment. I could've killed him twice. I don't know why the psych's didn't argue, considering her mental health could be at risk. Somehow, Lydia persuaded me to go home. Because I feared I would seriously hurt someone, or myself, if left alone, Henry picked me up from the diner instead.

I stayed with Henry last night. Didn't sleep or eat and paced his apartment all night. I should've convinced him to drive me to her apartment and break down her door. He would have no second thoughts. As soon as the sun broke down his windows this morning, I ditched him.

On my way to her apartment, I called Pat and told him I was on the way. He would be at her apartment around eight. I called Max and Lydia next. They were already on the way. Begrudgingly, I texted Anna if she was available to come. She agreed, however, I wasn't sure if she would show.

While we waited for Pat, Max paced on the front sidewalk, his phone glued to his ear. Was that how all doctors were? Anna sat on the front steps, talking quietly with Lydia. I leaned against the door, waiting and hoping to hear any fucking sound come from inside. The texture of the gauze was comforting, so I rubbed my fingers around my hand.

Pat took about an hour to arrive. My anger felt dangerous the moment I saw him walking towards us. Where was the freaking urgency?! If I wasn't stressed already, my shoulders tightened, my throat felt dry, and I wanted to disappear. I notice the nice-looking guy walking with him, carrying two drink carriers filled with coffees. I decide to not kill Pat.

Who the fuck is this guy?

Pushing myself off Jen's apartment building, I eye him up and down. He's wearing black scrubs and black non-slip shoes. He has an oversized rain jacket on and a baseball hat flipped backwards. His minimal hair showing from under his hat leads me to believe he is good on his upkeep. His beard reminds me of mine, but it's more tamed. He's almost as tall as me and even though he walked with confidence, his face was full of concern. His stare stays on me, but he speaks to Pat.

"Jonah! Glad you could make it!" Lydia prances off the step from Anna and engulfs Jonah. He has yet to take his eyes off me. The drinks tetter as he opens his arms for Lydia.

Jonah. The almighty Jonah.

When Pat finally unlocks the door, I push him in, wanting to see her first. But there's nothing except her bags by the front door, nearly tripping over them. Everything is in the same place from when I picked up her. Lydia leads the way down the hallway, only to find her door locked. Still trying to avoid a conversation with Jonah and Anna, I talk specifically to Pat and Lydia.

"Someone has to get in there!" I panic. For everyone else, this behavior might be normal. For me, it feels like life-or-death.

"Calvin, we are here in her space if something happens. Give her time to rest, okay? We will check on her soon." Lydia tells me.

Minutes feel like hours. Hours feel like centuries. Time is fucking torture. The tension was also torture. Everyone could feel the awkwardness of me and Jonah being in the place for the first time. We still had spoken no words.

I about lose my balance when I see Jen walk towards the door to get her phone. Leaning against the couch, she was completely unaware of my presence. Pat was sitting at the kitchen counter, making coffee, and she didn't realize it. She doesn't see Jonah was uncomfortably sleeping in the oversized chair by the window. Lydia stood by the wall, watching her. She didn't notice the front door was slightly cracked because Max was outside on the phone. Unbeknownst to her, Anna had spoken her name.

She was in a trance, not noticing anything or anybody.

All six of us look at each other when we hear sobbing coming from Jen's room after she grabbed her phone. Panic rises in my stomach as I pace around the room. Everyone explicitly instructed me not to go into her room. Max has kept an annoyingly close eye on me, reminding me to let her sleep.

"Is she okay? She didn't see any of us?" Anna said.

"We'll check on her in a minute. We don't want to alarm or overwhelm her. If something happens, we'll decide who should go in." Max announced, and I see Lydia nodding in agreement.

Jesus, how many times are we going to say that until she's doing something completely insane in her room?!

"I think we need to make a quick plan of who will be the first to make their presence known." Max offers again.

"Not Calvin."

Biting my lip until I taste blood, I scold at Anna.

"Fuck you, Anna."

"Fuck you, Cal. You're the reason for all of this." She waves her arms around the room, clearly annoyed at bringing a circus to the living room. I haven't seen Anna since the camping trip. She was a person I completely broke as well, and little did I know that her entire world came crashing down. Her anger was deep towards me. I had to keep some distance from her before spilling my apology to her.

"Okay, quiet down. We're not here to fight." Pat steps closer to me, nudging my body to sit on the couch to keep me stationary somewhere. My blood is boiling. Mostly towards Pat and Jonah. *Don't touch me, dude.* I want to be the first one to see her, and to make sure she's alright. I'm here to save her and prove I haven't failed her. God, those words still crush me.

"I don't want to piss you off Calvin, but I think Anna is right. You shouldn't be the first one." It's Pat's voice. He sits next to me on the couch. He's playing that father role I remember before I left. His voice reminds me of my father. That type of tone where he says straight facts. The sternness in his voice quickly makes my boiling level rise even more. As much as I respect Pat, he has no fucking business telling me I shouldn't see her. Out of everyone in this room, he knows how important I am to her.

"What the fuck is happening?" Clawing my hands through my hair, I'm irritated that I gathered everyone, only for them to eliminate me from her. I'm on edge when I feel Lydia approach me. I'm sandwiched in between Lydia and Pat—the real versions of Devil and Angel.

Jen would want me to stay calm. I'm trying my hardest to be as calm as I can, knowing she's barely holding herself together. Probably because of me, again.

"Hey, nobody is out to get you. I know what you're thinking. She's so fragile after the weekend you guys had. We need someone who can remain calm if she's hallucinating or hysterical. This is what

I was telling you about when you came to me the first time. She gets lost in her head and sometimes we have to wait it out. I know that's not the answer you were hoping for." Lydia talks quietly, speaking close to my ear.

Somehow, everyone has moved into the living room. Jonah is awake on the chair, watching the conversations. Why isn't Mr. Perfect speaking up about how we save our queen? Anna is standing by the window, still looking annoyed at the reason we are here. Her new dark brown hair still has me taking a double look at her. Pat and Lydia are on the couch with me. Max is still standing by the front door, arms crossed, and head tilted against the door, looking frazzled.

It's only been a few minutes since we heard the sobs but her door opens again. We remain speechless when we see Jen go into the kitchen. She's like a fucking zombie. Her face is so red and blotchy. Her hair is up in a messy bun, and she has my sweatshirt on. She still doesn't notice any of us. The placement of her bedroom door directly across from the kitchen allows her to walk straight into the kitchen. Not to mention a giant bookshelf obstructs a clear view if you're in the kitchen.

I look at everyone, monitoring their reactions. Max was already staring at me, holding his index finger to his lips to keep me quiet. *We don't want to overwhelm her when she wakes up.*

Max leans off the wall, analyzing her behavior. His eyebrows pinch together and his hands are in his pockets. Anna nervously plays with her lip. Her annoyance has clearly disappeared, and she looks nervous. Pat just watches her from the couch. Jonah's eyes look as if they are about to pop out of his head. Lydia tries to stand up, but I put my hand on her leg to keep her seated.

I don't think she's well.

My heart is racing. What the fuck is she doing? I want to get up and hold her. Whatever feelings she has right now, I want to take them away.

It's at this moment where I realize how much Jen is hurting. How broken she is. She's disassociating, just like I did at the cabin when I just wanted to leave my body. We are too alike, and I'm realizing how dangerous that might be.

As much as I try not to think about the stack of letters waiting for me at my apartment, those letters hold so much information. Part of me wants to leave here and read them so I can understand what else Jen has been through. So that we can put the past behind us, all the mistakes, the guilt, the regret, and I can just love the fuck out of her.

Then she grabs the knife and wanders back into her room. After the door shuts, everyone starting panicking and yelling. Lydia dashes off the couch, approaching Max and putting her hand on his chest. They talk secretly to each other as he puts an arm around her and runs the other through his hair. He nods in agreement to whatever his wife says.

"I have to go in!" I shout as I stand up.

"Calvin, no, please. You are not the best person right now." Max approaches me to keep me back from going down the hallway.

"She's going to think you aren't real. She has a past with self-mutilation. If she sees you, she will cut herself to reason with reality. A cut is permanent." Max mutters to me.

"I need to be the one, Max!" I resist shoving him into the wall; to hold his throat and tell him he has no idea how much I need to see her.

"Calvin, this is the reason. You are too impulsive. Too irrational. You are only going to make the situation worse. Please, man. Please don't do this." Pat has his arm on his shoulder as I'm trying to release tension in my fist.

"FUCK!" I move away from Max and feel Pat's arm release me, walking towards the window to straighten my mind. If Pat wasn't here, I could get to her but because he is here, I know he's trying to protect the both of us. Just like he always has. I'm pissed off about it, but I'm grateful. The damage I would do if Pat wasn't here would most likely put me in prison again.

"She won't know how to respond to me. I haven't seen her in a while. I wouldn't know what to say." Anna's eyes are wet and the big brother in me wants to console her. I realize how close I am to her, both of us by the window,

"I'd be too therapeutic. That's not what she needs." Lydia admits.

"I'm just here for support. I need to make a call anyway." Max says.

"I'm biased. I know too much about her life. Talking to me wouldn't do a damn thing." Pat mutters, helplessly.

And just like that, like we are playing Clue or playing Murder Mystery, all eyes are on Jonah. He's the one.

"Me? I haven't seen her in a couple months. I've had very little contact with her. Pat's the only reason I know what's been happening."

I round the couch and pull him up by the collar. Instantly, Pat and Max grab me.

"You need to save her. Please. It needs to be you." These are my first words to Jonah. I could've probably made a better first impression. My anger has turned into helplessness.

Jonah. Her ex-husband. Her nurse. Her confidante. The man who got left behind.

I can feel the earthquake forming in my body.

"Please, Jonah. Just this once, you need to save her."

I don't know what happened inside my body, but I feel no tension. Tears are leaving my body because I'm desperate. I don't know Jonah, but I know I trust him enough to be alone with Jen. He took over what I was supposed to do. He wasn't signing up to compete in a marathon. Jen is no marathon. She's a triathlon. It's not just her mind that needs tending to, which I think is what Jonah thought he was doing. It's her heart and soul, too. I will take on a triathlon any day for Jen if it means I can fix her mind, heart, and soul.

I don't know who pulls me away first, whether it's Max or Pat, but I pull Jonah into me and cry into his shoulder. Time is ticking, but he's my only fucking hope.

"Okay, okay. I'll do it." Jonah speaks out loud, but I wish he was only talking to me. Releasing Jonah, I try to regain my composure. I look like a pansy, crying in front of these people. Jonah moves down around the living room, down the hall, and I follow him until we stop at her room.

"I think you should wait in the living room. If you hear the words exchanged between us, I can't have you barge in. I will come get you when I think she can handle it, okay?" He whispers these words quietly, only for me to hear. My heart drops into my stomach.

Trusting Jonah with Jen feels easy. He's the only one I know that took the bull by the horns and tried to help her. I just don't know if I trust Jen with Jonah. If she needs someone to love, someone to hold her, someone to rely on, I want to be the one.

Angel responds for me.

"I love her, man. Please don't make me kill you." My face is serious, but Jonah lets out a small laugh. Realizing everyone stayed in the living room, it's just him and I.

"I love her too, Calvin. I'd do anything for her." He gives me a small, friendly shove to make my way back to the living room. I feel the eyes of everyone. The first interaction between her past and her present. Hoping nobody places bets on us, I can get competitive, especially with things I love.

Now at the end of the hallway, I watch as he opens the door, barely wide enough for me to see anything

Talk to me, Angel. Tell me good things.

He knows her. She was in the hospital because of this, and he was the one that was there. Trust him.

I want to trust him. His words felt like fighting words, though. *I love her, too.* There's no way she would choose between us. She'd always choose me. That's selfish of me to say, but it's the truth because it's what Jen had told me face-to-face, in her letters, in text messages. I'm the only one for her. Whether she's said the same to Jonah or not, I couldn't care less.

Annoyed that I'm stuck out here, I walk backwards to sit back on the couch. The tension seems to have disappeared, and knowing Jonah is with Jen has helped ease some of the awkwardness. Everyone has gone back to their form of fidgeting. Pat is back in the kitchen, cleaning dishes and making another pot of coffee. Max and Lydia are whispering in the corner. Their suspicious behavior is fucking with me, but I don't have the energy to confront them right now. I look at Anna, who is still by the window. She has her arms crossed and is scowling at me. She walks over to me and sits down.

My once dear confidante, she knew the best and worst things about me, the one who saw me on top of the world, now sees me swimming through the ashes of Hell.

"I'm sorry about what I said earlier. I mean, you are the reason for all of this, for Jen being this way. But I'm sorry I said it in such a bitchy tone." Anna leans back against the couch.

"No, you aren't. You meant every word with the intended tone." Chuckling at her words, I lean back into the couch and look over at her.

"Fuck you. That one I actually meant." She nudges my shoulder, making me feel a slim better.

"You're such a pain in the ass, even after all these years." I breathe in the air's lightness.

I reminisce about the devastation I left Anna with at Easton. That was the last time I saw her. Remorse overwhelms me. I rest my hand on her leg, a gesture out of the ordinary with communicating with Anna.

"I'm sorry about everything." My voice cracks.

Jesus, we have to do this right now?

"It's okay. I don't blame you anymore. We just need to get her better. Okay, we focus on that, so you guys can enjoy the rest of your lives." She grabs my hand and holds it, feeling connected in a way that I can only feel with Anna. She's always been on my side, my little cheerleader.

Jennie

I've been running my finger down the blade, contemplating the potential consequence of my choice. I feel like I keep hearing voices, and honestly, as tired as I am, I'm not sure if they are real or in my head.

I miss Calvin and my dad. I miss having a purpose. My purpose was to love them both endlessly. When I had them both, I felt like it was my high. I would leave my dad to get my fix of Cal, then I would leave Cal to get my fix of my dad. It was constant love. Even if it was for a short while, it was the best feeling I've ever felt.

Then I wasn't sure if God or whoever was my puppeteer decided I shouldn't be happy anymore. They decided I wasn't worthy to have the two best kinds of love. Whoever they were, they let me drop so far into hell that I feel stuck. And I feel like I'm burning alive.

I just want someone to save me.

A vision of Jonah interrupts my thoughts.

"Jonah?"

Is this real? Is he real? I feel guilty holding a knife if it is him. All the memories of Jonah reviving me from my deep cut incident flash through my mind. He was so careful when stitching my arm. He kept me engaged in a conversation about planes. Travelling. Airports. He said if he could be anything besides a nurse, he would be a pilot. I wish I could let Jonah take me anywhere I wanted to go. He could be my personal pilot.

He looks at me, then looks back at the door, closing it ever so quietly. He stands with his back to the door, almost afraid to approach me.

"I'm here." He whispers.

"What are you doing here?"

I haven't seen Jonah since February. My heart feels like it's skipping a few beats because he's so handsome. I remember when I started falling in love with Jonah. It petrified me to even have a thought of falling in love with someone else. I had been in the hospital for a couple of weeks and he became my constant. Every morning, whether he was on shift, he would drop off my medication and tell me what would come for breakfast. He realized I was not a fan of the garbage oatmeal the cafeteria served and put in a special request to the head chef to bring me blueberry muffins instead. Ugh, they were the worst muffins I've ever had. But anything was better than the prison oatmeal.

He just noticed things about me. Being in a hospital, there's only so many benefits you can get, but Jonah let me get away with so much. He brought me good smelling shampoo, he let me wear my slippers, he let me watch movies for an extra hour. God, he was just so genuine.

"Well, we've been worried about you. We couldn't get a hold of you. You missed work yesterday, and Pat needed help at the shop. You were sleeping for two days. Do you remember anything?" He's still standing by my door, looking uncomfortable, like he's waiting for an invitation to enter my room more.

"You can come sit." I never had to hide from Jonah. Feeling guilty to be holding this weapon, I place the knife on my side table. I know he can see it and he can hear it hit the table. Taking my invitation, he walks over and sits at the end of my bed while I criss-cross my legs.

"What did you say?" I look at him, knowing he asked me a question but wasn't sure what the question was.

He chuckles and looks down. "Do you remember anything that happened in the past couple of days? Or do you remember what happened before you went to sleep?" His voice is so mesmerizing. It's so calming. So neutral. I feel I'm on edge, waiting for Cal to lash out at me. I'm not talking to Cal, though. This is Jonah. Jonah is safe.

"Um..." I twist the ends of my blanket. *Yes, I remember what happened before I went to sleep.* I wish my sleep would help me forget.

"Cal and I came home early. I told him how I felt about him, and he didn't really respond, so I slammed the door and cried until I fell asleep."

It's impossible for me to look at Jonah when talking about Cal. Seeing the hurt in Jonah's eyes, plus the feeling I'm going to throw up, it's best to stay avoidant.

"How do you feel about him?" I stop twirling my blanket and blink my eyes up to look at him.

"Jonah, you know how I feel about him." My response comes off as rude. Anyone who knows me, knows how much I'm breaking myself to love Cal.

"Well, yeah, I know how you felt about him a couple months ago, but how about now? Now that's you've seen him. I want to hear the words. What did you tell him?"

Jonah likes to push buttons. He always pushed me. He always succeeded because he was confident, and knew I would crack under pressure. When my guard is nonexistent, that's how he wins. My eyes move back to look back at the blanket and I twirl again.

"There would never be anyone else to compete against him. Hell, you know that. No matter how hard I tried to love you completely, Cal had a part of my heart. All the way across the country. I told him he was the one I wanted to be with. The feelings I have when I'm with Cal are just... rare. Even though our relationship seems strained right now, I know that we'll be able to get through this. I don't want to struggle with anyone else. Whatever is happening between Cal and I, I'll fight for him. He's everything to me. I've never loved anyone as much as I love him. Including you."

I repeat myself without crying, which I take as a victory. It feels like I've cried all my tears out. It's so easy to talk to Jonah, but what isn't easy, is talking to Jonah about Cal. It's like talking about the best player on the other team.

"Jennie, you broke my heart once, remember? You don't have to do it again." I look up at him and he's smiling. He's giving me a hard time. Taking my pillow, I swat it at him. I couldn't imagine being in Jonah's shoes, having to hear him talk about another girl who was the love of his life. A girl that wasn't me.

"Hey, I never intended to break your heart." Saying those words breaks my heart.

You broke him though, you dummy.

Jonah didn't deserve me. Not in an arrogant, selfish way. No, definitely not. Jonah, being so loving and caring, shouldn't have tried so hard to help me. He deserves someone who has their shit together. Who doesn't constantly have to be reminded of their worth. Who doesn't have to talk someone off the bridge every time something goes wrong. He deserves better. So much better.

I think about all of this as I look at Jonah again. He is so handsome, especially in his black scrubs today, my favorite. He looks older and more mature in black. His backward baseball hat is really teasing me. Since I've seen him in February, he's cut his hair but he's also grown out his beard. I don't know what it is about facial hair, but it swoons me. Jonah only had a stubble of hair for the months we were married, and it concerns me if he hasn't been taking care of himself since getting divorced.

You broke him. All you ever do is break precious things.

I used to love when he came home, immediately changed out of his scrubs, and sat with me on the couch. I always thought someone who worked in a hospital would smell like a hospital. Smells of latex, cleaner, sterile. Jonah smelled so good, even after a twelve-hour shift. I hated how he felt he had to continue being a nurse once he got home.

He's been looking at me while I think about the past. It feels we are having a silent conversation with our thoughts. Breaking the eye contact because he makes me nervous, I look over at my door, curious who else is out there.

"I want to say I'm sorry."

I'm sorry you had to come out to save me-again.

"I'm not sorry. What are you sorry for, Jennie?" His voice is so calm. God, I don't think Jonah has a mean or annoyed bone in his body. His response startles me for a moment. I hear the echo of Cal's voice in my head for telling me to stop being sorry.

"Well, for this." I lift my wrist up, displaying my almost poor decision. "For bringing you here. For things not working between us. For dragging you into my messed-up mind." The list could go on and on. Jonah moves towards me, and he puts his hands on my leg. I didn't realize how much I missed his touch. It feels like a mini firework exploding in my heart.

"Like I said, I'm not sorry. I will never miss a chance to save you or being your Savior. You know how much I enjoy taking care of people, but you'll always be first on my list. No matter where I am or what I'm doing or who I'm with, I will always be here for you. Please never forget that. I have so much love for you, and it will never go away. You are special to me. You are special to a lot of people. And Jennie, goddamnit, I want you to know how worthy you are. If it's Calvin, then he's so lucky to be the one to take care of you. I will always wonder what more I could've done to be what he was to you.

I could never hate you or hate him, but I'll always wonder what more I could've done for you." He moves his thumb in circles as he spoke.

Just when I thought my tear canister was empty, they flow again. Jonah was always good at stitching me back together. I can feel my broken heart become slightly stitched, not only from his presence, but his words. His words were never a lie. He put me on a pedestal so high, I never knew what I did to earn that privilege from him.

The stitches were never permanent, but it was enough to make me feel complete. I brush Jonah's hands off my leg and pull him into me for a hug. I hated comparing Jonah's hug to Cal's, but Jonah's hug was gentle. Just enough of a squeeze to feel that someone was holding me, but I ached to feel the tight squeeze of Cal's hug. I hug him for a few moments. He moves his hand up and down my back. How fortunate I am to have such a constant companion who can make me feel better. My ex-husband. Bleh, I hate saying those words.

I sniffle and lift my head off his shoulder. He's grinning at me, enjoying the moment I could give him.

"Is he here?" I motion to the door with my eyes. My question immediately ruins our special moment. Jonah's grin disappears and he frowns. He looks down at his hands and moves away from me. He remembers he isn't Cal, and he's no longer my husband.

You ruin every good thing. Every good moment.

He clears his throat. "Yes. He contacted everyone here." My heart races. I don't have many people in my life, so who else could be here?

"Who else is here?"

"Well, I guess Pat informed us he was the only person who has a key to your apartment. I should've remembered that from the hospital last year. He's the one who let us in, but after he opened the shop this morning. Lydia and Max are here. They've been holding down our emotional forts, reminding us you'll be okay. Anna is here too. She looks a little out of place, but I guess Calvin thought she could be helpful to you if something was wrong. Pat and Calvin and me."

"Oh my god... I can't believe I didn't reply to any of your texts this morning. Were you guys here when I got my phone from the front table?" Jonah looks more relaxed now that Cal isn't part of the conversation right now.

"Yes. We were all here. We saw you come back out to get the

knife, and we had to come up with a game plan. I knew you weren't okay, but they volunteered me to come in first."

"Why didn't you want to come in?" I try not to sound hurt.

"Well, because one, Calvin was here. You would've wanted to see him first. Max and Pat got into it with him because he about barged in here. And second, I just wasn't sure if I was prepared to see you this way again. It was traumatizing the first time you came into the hospital. I will never forget how shaken up you were. I wasn't sure how bad you may have gotten." His voice cracks a bit. I can never not cry when he shares the truth. Even though I'm disappointed Cal wasn't the first one to check on me, I'm relieved it was Jonah.

"I don't know if I'm worse or better since then. Everything just feels so messy."

We sit quietly for a bit. It became uncomfortable because of Jonah's intermittent questioning. He always wanted to get information out of me.

"Do you want to see him? I told him to stay in the front living room until I tell him he could see you." He laughs for the first time since being in my room. He enjoys having the upper hand on Calvin at this moment.

"Yeah... I do."

"Okay." His voice is barely audible. That's not what Jonah wants to hear, but seeing Cal will make me feel better... I hope.

Jonah moves off my bed and kisses the top of my head. He stops at my door before opening it and tells me, "I'll always be here for you, Jennie. I'll always be rooting for you to get better."

Sitting in anticipation, I wonder what the conversations are like in my front living room. I think of the people who are in my corner. Anna and Pat, who have been in my corner since day one. The OG's. Max and Lydia, my step-in parents, really. The ones constantly rubbing my shoulders, praising me, lifting me up. Jonah, the lover. The one who just needs to give me a wink to make me melt. But none of them compare to the one who is walking down the ramp now. The one who I am always watching. My Cal.

Calvin

It feels like Jonah's been in her bedroom for hours, but it's only been twenty minutes. Twenty gut-wrenching, sickening minutes. What the Hell are they doing in there?! I tried multiple times to wander down the hall to hear their conversation, but Max or Pat always stopped me. Fuck them. I just want to see her.

My misery finally ends when I hear Jonah's footsteps before I see him. He looks sad. I haven't been able to sit still, so I've been pacing around her apartment, at least the places I have permission to be. I meet him at the end of the hallway, eager to get a run-down of the conversation.

"What happened? How is she?" I feel the group huddle behind me, looking at Jonah. We need answers, man!

He moves around us to head into the kitchen, staying quiet. I watch him slip the knife back into the block, looking clean and undamaged. He turns around and leans against the counter, the bar top separating him from us.

"She's fine. I walked in just in time. Didn't do anything, just holding it. We just talked." Adjusting his hands deeper in his pockets, his eyes move to everyone, then stop at me.

"She's ready to see you now."

I don't even say anything to him. I should have, though. He saved my girl. Again. Turning to walk down the hallway, something stops my shoulders. I turn back and see Pat's hands are stopping me from moving. He's never grabbed me like this before.

"Pat, get the fuck off me." I dig my fingers at his hands.

"Calvin, I'm warning you. If you do anything to upset her, I will literally end your life."

Pat was serious. I look around and see Lydia, Max, and Anna watching me. Their eyes are telling me the same thing. Jonah's demeanor makes me cringe. He looks distraught that I'm next in line to see her.

"I'm so goddamn serious, man. She's been through enough. She's so easy to love. Don't make this complicated for her."

Pat NEVER curses. I must be a bad influence. His grip loosens, but I remain motionless. Slightly offended by his words, I lock eyes with him, accepting that I deserve them.

I'm not a hero in her story. Jonah is. Lydia and Max. Even Pat himself. But not me.

"I will lay you on your ass if she gets upset, by any means." This time it's Jonah's voice.

What the fuck is happening? Has my Devil multiplied and instead of speaking in my head, is now speaking from my acquaintances?

I nod in agreement. Nobody needs to get hurt. I think I'm more nervous to see Jen right now than on the first day I saw her in Whole Foods. I don't know why...

Maybe because I know how fragile she is right now, and back then I didn't. I hate myself for being gone. I could've helped Jen become confident and proud. There are a lot of things I could've helped with. I shake off the bullshit in my head and stop at her door.

Don't make her cry, you prick.

I open the door and see Jen standing in front of her mirror. She smiles at me through the mirror. She's brushing her hair, and I can see an open container of makeup wipes on the corner of her vanity.

She was getting herself together...for you.

"Hey..." I smile and quietly close the door. I don't know if everyone plans to stay near the door to listen to my conversation, but I don't care. I'm with her now.

"Hi." Her smile is even wider now. "Sorry, just pulling myself together here. Didn't realize how terrible I looked with Jonah." Leaning against the door, I just watch her. She looks so much better. Sleep was a good friend.

"You look beautiful. You always do." She tears her eyes away and blushes. I walk over to her bed and sit at the end. It feels warm. This must've been where Jonah was sitting. I'm happy he was sitting so far away from her, but despise he was on her bed in the first place.

As my eyes wander in a circle around Jen's room, her eyes meet mine in the mirror again. She's done brushing her hair and has her arms crossed. She turns around to face me.

"Can I give you a hug?" She walks towards me. How could I say no? I don't question her. Rising from the bed, I meet her in the center of her room. My arms move under her armpits, gliding over her ribs until my hands clasp behind her back. I can feel her lift on her tippy toes, and she glides her own hands up my pecs and around my neck. She hides her face in between my neck and shoulder.

She feels so good. I squeeze her a little tighter, burying my face in her neck. I always hug her a little tighter.

We hold on to each other for quite some time. Pat and Jonah probably think we are making out or snuck out the window. I'm surprised they haven't busted through the door, considering we've been silent.

I hate the feeling of Jen releasing her arms around my neck. Quickly, I take her hands and wrap them around me again.

"No, don't let go yet." I whisper to her.

When I feel her hands secure together behind my neck, I let my hands run down her body until I reach her thighs and pick her up. She wraps her legs around me, and I take the short walk back to her bed. Falling back on her bed, she straddles me. She doesn't let go, but she moves her face from my shoulder to look at me. She looks even more refreshed up close. I remember thinking at the cabin how much more affectionate she would be if she had more sleep.

What's going on in your mind, sweet girl?

"So..." She starts. I put my hands on her lower back and stroke her back.

"So..." I mimic.

"I guess I should say I'm sorry for worrying you." She frowns and runs a finger over my eyebrow.

"You don't need to be sorry. I overreacted. I should have known you needed sleep, or just time away from me. I know I can be a lot." She smiles at my comment, but I don't. I'm disappointed in my reaction to all of her cries for help. I can be more than a lot, probably too much.

"I'm sorry I didn't stop you from leaving my truck. I should've responded to what you said, and I just didn't kno...." She puts a finger on my lips to make me stop talking.

"Let's not talk about the past couple of days." She's no longer playful. She doesn't need to hear any more of my excuses.

"Can I just ask you a question first? Please?" The desperation is strong in my voice.

She leans forward to connect her forehead to mine. Without looking at me, she says "what?"

Don't make her cry. There's an army on the other side of that door who is waiting to see you fail.

I lift her chin so she can look at me. Finally, I can look into the calmness of her forest.

"Were you going to hurt yourself because of me?"

I hate to ask that question. She didn't hurt herself, and that should be enough. But, it's not... She adjusts herself so she's just straddling. Her arms are no longer around me. Her face has separated from mine. She faces me eye to eye. It reminds me of the cabin when I wanted to know how bad she had gotten. Her reaction was just the same.

"Cal..."

"Please, just tell me." I'm not trying to upset her. My ego just needs to know if it was because of me. Do I get to give myself another tally for ruining her life?

"It was a mix of things. I wasn't in the correct headspace. It wasn't just you. I didn't even want to. I just wanted to feel the blade. Just wanted to see if it would make me feel better. But I knew it wouldn't. I didn't want to disappoint anyone."

"You wouldn't disappoint anyone. You have an entire room of people who care about you. We would've all barged in if we had to." She moves her hand to the nape of my neck and runs her fingers up and down.

Holy fuck, that feels good. I close my eyes in pleasure.

"Please tell me there's no more questions?" I open my eyes to her, and she smirks at me.

"You're the one who brought up the question!" I close my eyes again and she runs her fingers through my hair. It feels better when she goes slower.

"Do you have a letter on you?" She asks me. I open my eyes, not wanting to leave the euphoria of Jen showing her affection.

"What if I did?"

"Can you read it to me?" She tilts her head to the side and I'm trying to use every fiber in me to not kiss her. She's so fucking beautiful.

"Do you even know what letter I have?"

"Of course I don't. I want it to be a surprise." She stops rubbing her hands on my neck, and I let out a small whimper.

"What if it's a bad letter?" My heart races, thinking of the unpredictability of these letters. "I have people on the other side of that door who will kill me if I make you cry, so I'm really, really, really hoping I don't make you cry." I release a sigh at my words of honesty.

"Oh c'mon, I promise I won't cry." She brings her pinky finger right in front of my face. I laugh a little.

"Jen, I really don't want to upset you. You seem so peaceful and rested right now. I don't want to ruin that. I just want to enjoy this moment."

"I really want you to read to me."

She playfully pouts, and it makes me lose all restraint. I kiss her. A deep kiss. Putting my hands on the side of her face, I bring her close to me. A small moan comes from her mouth. Her hands are back on my neck, pulling me even closer. Her rapid breathing pushes her stomach against mine.

You should probably stop.

Thanks, Angel. As hard as it is to stop, I release my hands from her face and break my lips away. She opens her eyes.

"That reminded me of our first kiss."

She still has her hands on the back of my neck, and she awes at me. I kiss her on the cheek and lift her off me so I can get the letter from my pocket. She crawls under her covers and once I retrieve the letter from my wallet, she lifts the covers for me to join her.

I do. Of course I do.

She folds the covers over us, and I unfold the letter. She rests her head on my shoulder.

Please be a good letter.

April 2, 2004

Cal, I'm in the mood to tell you a happy story. Probably my most favorite moment in our story. Are you ready to hear it?

March 14, 2003. Do you know that date? I have it engrained in my mind. A permanent engraving.

For some weird reason, Pat had us scheduled an open shift. We got off at 2:30. You asked me if I was doing anything after work. I said I needed to go home to check on my dad, but I would be available in about an hour. So you asked me out to dinner. I cannot lie to you so I have to be honest that I smiled the WHOLE WAY HOME and THE WHOLE WAY TO MEET YOU. Honestly, I'm smiling now just thinking about the memory. We went to some pizza place that I can't remember. Maybe when I see you again, you'll know the name of it. I had that feeling in my stomach that I wasn't hungry because I just had so many butterflies that I didn't eat much. I hoped you didn't notice. This was the first night I realized how much you loved your truck. We had left my car at C&H and you drove us to the pizza place. We laughed so much during dinner. I'm not sure if I was but I felt I was blushing all night. You just made me so happy. We talked about customers who come in asking for the most complicated drinks. We talked about Pat's new love interest, Lizzie, who seemed to be coming into the shop every day but he claims she was a friend of his sister? Okay. But we just kept talking. There were endless things to talk about with you. So we finally decided we were done with pizza and you asked if I wanted to go mini golfing. You knew of this glow in the dark mini golf that was in the next town over. I said yes of course. I hope you had as much fun as I did! It was my first and only time doing glow in the dark mini golf. I hated that the night was ending. You held my hand in your truck all the way back to C&H so I could get my car.

We did a lot of talking in the parking lot after our shifts, keeping time on our side. You let me take your sweatshirt home. It started sprinkling as we parked, and we just waited a few minutes to see if it would lighten up. It didn't. Tt started full blown thunderstorming. Lightning flashed, thunder roared and just like two idiots, we watched the sky in awe. The storm didn't last long so once the thunder and lightning disappeared, we got out of your truck. Everything on my mental checklist was crossed off.

Delicious food

A first adventure of mini golf

Hand holding

Borrowing your sweatshirt

Watching a storm in the parking lot

You opened my door for me and as if there was one more lightning strike that happened, both of us tensed. You brushed a piece of hair behind my ear and left your hand on my cheek. You stared into my eyes. Even though I was warmer with your sweatshirt on, I was getting goosebumps all over my body. You were so close to me.

I don't know if this was part of your plan but I know it was part of mine. I wrapped my arms around your back which I didn't normally do. I liked putting my hands behind your neck. I pulled you into me and I swear, Cal, it's like someone was watching us. It started raining again and that was one of my teenage girl dreams – to be kissed in the rain. You looked down at me and we both leaned into each other and finally kissed.

Your kiss was magical. It was everything I thought it was going to be and more. You moved your hands from my cheeks and ran them through my hair. I hated that I had my hands on your back because I wanted to pull your neck, which would've pulled your mouth closer to mine. My hands hovered over your kidneys and I moved my hands into small circles. Ugh, I enjoyed this moment so much. We kissed each other repeatedly for a few minutes. It was perfection. To be kissed in the rain by you. If I would've died in that moment, I would've been okay with it. I felt your reluctancy to pull away but I knew one of us had to, and I can tell you this now, I had no intentions of stopping. I didn't want to stop kissing you, Cal. You still held my hair with your hands and my hands had now moved to your sides. There was only a sliver of space between us. I could see the wetness on your lips still. You said to me, I've wanted to do that since the first day I met you. I told you that was the best kiss of my life.

And it was, Cal. No matter who else I've kissed, your lips were imprinted into my soul. I checked off one more thing on my mental checklist.

Kiss the man of my dreams

It the most perfect night. It's a memory I will never forget. After this kiss, I feel like we never stopped kissing. It was constant.

I can't wait to kiss you again.

Waiting,

Jennie

"Wow." I said out loud, exasperated. Looking over at her, her eyes are closed.

"Yeah, wow." She says and opens her eyes. She keeps her head on my shoulder, and I let the letter sit on top of the covers.

"Is your version different?" She asks me and lays a hand on my chest, mocking me from when I called her the other night. I wonder if she realized how fast my heart is pumping, simply from the touch of her. Something in me takes over as I put my hand on her cheek and kiss her. Feverishly, she kisses me back. It's not something that last long but something she needs. Something I need.

"I'm sorry I don't have any rain this time." Feeing her grin under my mouth, I bite her bottom lip.

"I only needed that once."

I need to distract myself before I pull her on top of me and finish what we started over the weekend. I'd probably fuck it up, but she's so irresistible. All versions of her.

I pull the covers away and stand up from the bed, folding the letter and putting it back in my pocket.

"I'll keep that one forever." Jen sits up with her back against her headboard and criss-crossing her legs. I can't get over how much better she looks. All she needed was sleep. This is the Jen I remember; the one I can take care of.

Just as I'm about to sit back down and hold her again, the door busts open.

"What the hell Jennie, you haven't been taking your pills?!" It's Jonah.

Standing behind him is everyone. Everyone is staring at Jen, including me.

Jennie

I've never pinned Jonah for ruining things. But he just absolutely ruined this moment. Things felt so normal between Cal and me. It felt like old times where he was just hanging out at my house, and he crawls into bed with me and kisses me.

It's the first time I see all the eyes on me. Lydia, Max, Pat, Anna, Jonah and Cal. They look like a SWAT team. I can see the orange bottles Jonah is holding. I don't even know how to explain this to him.

"Is this true, Jen?" It's Cal.

I can't even bear to look at him. The disappointment is strong in his voice. My secret is out. Cal walks over to Jonah to remove the bottles from his hand.

"How can you tell she hasn't been taking them?" He talks directly to Jonah, and I'm really annoyed at their calm demeanor towards each other. Only Jonah doesn't respond, Lydia does.

"Her bottles show how many refills she has left and when the prescription was filled. These bottles were last filled in January. She hasn't been taking anything for three months." Lydia's voice is also full of disappointment and anger.

"I've also called your psychiatrist and dietitian. You haven't been going."

"Pat, I've seen you more than anyone. You know I've been okay. I've been normal." I plead for Pat to come front and center. To be my hero that I don't need the medications to be normal. All the eyes move to look at Pat who is standing near the back because he's tallest.

"Jennie, no. You don't get to gaslight me. Sure, there are days where you've been happy and good because it's because I thought you were taking your medication! I didn't think I had to monitor every freaking choice you made!"

Oops, Pat's disappointed and angry too.

"Is this why you've been so tired and haven't been eating and being so moody? Where is your Xanax?" Jonah shouts.

"What right do you have to go through my stuff, Jonah? You lost that right months ago. How dare you dig up my dirt." My voice cracks as I raise my voice at Jonah. I'm holding myself tight so that I think I'll leave marks on my arms later. But who will care?

There will be nobody to take care of you because you are a failure.

"You told me you stopped taking your Xanax because of the side effects." Cal's looking at the pill bottles but talks directly to me.

"Jennie...he's joking, right?" Jonah's disappointing voice is almost as heartbreaking as Cal's.

"What do you mean?" Cal looks at Jonah. I don't even have to know that his rage meter is quickly rising. If Jonah were smart, he would leave... like right now.

Cal isn't frustrated with Jonah. It's you. You are always the problem.

"She's supposed to be taking her Xanax every day with the other two. Her panic attacks were happening daily when we were married. She's been taking that one about four months now."

Jonah is just giving facts, but he's pissing me off. He isn't playing the nurse role right now. This is the controlling ex-husband Jonah.

Cal slams the bottles back to Jonah, then disappears from my room. "Cal, please. Don't go!" I try to chase after him, but my legs are cement.

He didn't fail you. You failed him.

I'm looking around the room, waiting for someone to save me. Who is going to be the one to tell everyone to shut up and go away? Who is going to be the one to tell everyone that I'm okay? Who is going to be my hero?

Nobody moves. Then I hear a cough, almost like a signal cough. Wiping my eyes, everyone starts to leave my room. All backs are to me until I see Max fully enter my room and shut the door.

Chuckling, I sit back on my bed and pull my blanket in my lap.

"Lucky you, huh?

Instead of sitting on the end of the bed like Jonah and Cal had, Max sits on my vanity stool. It's adjacent next to my bed. He leans forward and clasps his hands together.

I've disappointed Max too.

"What lovely, fatherly advice do you have to give?" I try to hide my sarcasm, but I can't. I don't even feel like talking to him.

"I just want to know why, Jennie? Why haven't you been taking your pills? I'm won't go all fatherly on you yet, first I have to be a doctor." Twirling my blanket, I find a piece of string and debate on wrapping it around my finger to cut off my circulation.

"I don't know. When I found out Cal was getting an early release, I wanted to feel normal for him. I knew he was going to come find me. I didn't want him to see how bad things really were for me. Or to know how much the past completely broke me because of his choices. But I told him about my medications this past weekend. I reassured him by saying that I was still taking them."

"So, you lied to him? You should know firsthand the purpose and benefit of continuously taking your medication. It's prescribed that way for a reason. You've been having panic attacks every time you work since the beginning of the year. Since the moment you knew he was coming home. You've been restless and moody and exhausted. Do you think stopping your medication will miraculously cure you? I had my concerns that maybe your dosage wasn't right."

There's hopelessness in Max's voice. There's hurt as well. He's a child psychiatrist, for God's sakes. He does this every day. Clearly, he would be the first to know if there were any changes.

I don't respond because I know I'll go down a terrible self-destructive path.

"How do you feel, anyway? Or how have you been feeling?" Max's voice is switching into his father mode, which makes me relax.

"Sad. Tired. Hopeless. Anxious out of my mind. The panic attacks have been hardest to manage without anyone noticing. Clearly, today was not a good day."

Max laughs. "Clearly."

"Do you want to be better for him, for Calvin? Do you think he deserves this side of you?" God, I hate the doctor questions.

I roll my eyes to look at him. "No, of course not. I want him to love the happy me." The moment I spur out the words *him* and *love,* I cry. I have never cried in front of Max before. "He shouldn't love me. I don't want him to love this version of me."

Max leaves his doctor form at my vanity and sits next to me on my bed. He pulls me in for a fatherly hug, and I grasp onto him with so much desperation.

Who is going to love me?

"I don't know him all that well but the amount of effort he put into calling all the people who love you, to be here with you, to make sure you were safe, I don't think it matters what version of you he sees. He loves all of you." I continue quietly crying into Max's shirt, hating how embarrassing this will be in a few weeks.

"I'm going to be honest with you. I think you disappointed him. We thought you were improving, Jennie, but I think you've let us all down. I don't understand why you think not taking your medications would make this better. You have chronic depression, post-traumatic stress disorder and with a cherry on top, you have panic disorder. Those are real things, okay? They unfortunately don't go away. We just want you to be okay, to be happy. You deserve that. Without or without Calvin in your life, you deserve all the good things."

"No, I don't." I say harshly. My depression speaks for me.

As if they are in sync, Lydia opens the door with my pill bottles and a glass of water. Ice cold water.

Only Calvin knows that about you.

She sits next to her husband on my bed, no doubt looking at each other, trying to come up with a plan to fix me. I probably remind them of their clients—children.

"Jennie, hunny. Let's start over, okay? Let's get you back to being happy."

Even now, I continue to hold on to Max as if he were my actual father. I attempt to regulate my breathing. All I think is how I don't want to be a burden.

Lifting my head off Max, he keeps his arm around my shoulders. I can't look at either of them, knowing how much of a failure I look like to them. Staring at my arm, I count how many times I've failed. When I get to twenty, I can't go on. I wipe away the remaining tears from my eyes.

"My dad told me once that my mom had severe depression and was bipolar." I feel Max remove his arms from around me, allowing me space to speak. I move away from him, to give myself space to share what I'm about to tell them.

"He said living with her was awful. Not sure which days were worse—the depressive days or the manic days. He said on the sad days, he knew no matter what he did to make her feel better, nothing worked. She threw his flowers away. She left her favorite food where he had left it. When he lit candles, she blew them out. When he tried putting on her favorite movies, he came back into a black screen. The defeat was the worst. But on her manic days, he knew he wouldn't win either. Everything she felt depleted of during her depression was just amplified that she wanted to feel it all. For hours, she would drive, listening to music way too loud. She would drink coffee from eight AM to nine PM and wouldn't fall asleep. She went all out on hobbies, purchasing a sewing machine for sewing, a treadmill for garage workouts, and gardening tools. My dad fell into debt because of her mania. He tried to get her into therapy, to get her to take her medications."

I bring my knees up to my chest and hold myself. I haven't shared this story with anyone. It brings back harsh memories, and a dark sadness of what my dad had to endure. From my mother and from me.

"He found her in their bedroom closet, hanging. Not sure if it was from depression or the mania. I don't remember any of it because I was only three. My dad told me the story when I started asking questions about her." I lean my cheek on the top of kneecaps, daring to look at Max and Lydia. Max is holding Lydia's hand, and she's still holding the glass of water with my pill bottles in her lap. Max has been looking at me, but Lydia stares at the ground.

"When my dad took me to a doctor because I told him I was feeling sad, like how my mom acted in his stories, I promised him I would be better. I wouldn't end up like her. That I would be happy, and I want to be happy."

Lydia wipes her face with her thumb, and Max's face is soft and empathetic. I wasn't expecting to have my very own double therapy session. I make a mental note to pay them back later.

Turning my palm upward, I allow Lydia to pour my cocktail into my hand. She looks at my hand for a moment and brings the water to me first.

"You aren't like her. You won't be like her." She opens my Zoloft bottle, shaking one pill out. I drop it onto my tongue and swallow. Max rubs the top of my back. A proud, fatherly moment. I bring my hand back to her and she drops my Valium next.

I'm sorry, daddy. I'm sorry I almost joined you and mom. It's not my time yet.

Finally, she hands me the Xanax. I wasn't lying when I told Cal that I don't like to take Xanax. It makes me feel weird. I know it helps with my panic attacks. It makes my earthquakes feel very weak. Then I'm reminded of him.

Cal.

"Do you think he hates me?" Max and Lydia look at each other as I finish the rest of the water.

"Calvin, you mean?" Max clarifies.

"Yeah. I don't want him to hate me." Max drops his hand off my shoulder again and Lydia kneels in front of me, placing the cup on my side table.

"That boy has gone through leaps and bounds for you in the past few days. The past few months, really. Hate is the last thing I think he'll ever feel for you." She grabs my hands for reassurance.

"I want to see him, but I know it's just going to end in an argument."

"Do you want me to tell him to go?" Max asks me. I look over at him, but he's watching Lydia comfort me.

I want a love like theirs.

"I think that's probably best." Lydia answers for me. I don't want him to go, but I know we need space. Again. The more space we keep needing, the further away we are going to become. The thought turns my heart is ashes.

"I'll go talk to him." Max leaves my room, leaving Lydia still kneeling in front of me, holding my hands. I try not to cry looking at her. She would've been the best mother. I wish I would've met her sooner in life.

"I know this is hard right now. Things are changing. Calvin coming back into your life. Seeing Jonah, I'm sure feels uncomfortable. I know this quote that I tell some of my clients. It's from C.S. Lewis. *You can't go back and change the beginning, but you can start where you are and change the ending.* You think your ending already happened with Calvin during that camping trip, right? That was just the beginning. Your story continues. And ..." she pauses and smiles. My eyes fill with tears again. Lydia always uses the best quotes.

"And what?" My voice screeches.

"When Calvin came to us to find you, I was tending to his almost broken hand, and we had a chat. Before he left, I told him I was rooting for your story. I want you to have a happy ending." She shakes my hands and tightens them. I can't handle it anymore. I let go of her hands and hug her fiercely.

Maybe it's just my head thinking the pills are working faster than what I remember, but I'm already feeling better. I regret bringing a knife into my room. Leaving my pills on the kitchen counter instead of by my bed was a silly mistake. And of all people, for Jonah to find them, makes me nauseous. I feel awful for lying to Cal. As my heart mends itself, I hear the shouting and the front door slam.

I look at Lydia for reassurance.

Please don't let it be Cal who left.

She lets me walk to my bedroom door first. I take in a deep breathe, preparing myself for the harsh reality I've created.

Calvin

The moment I left Jen's room, I smashed my already bruised hand onto the countertop. I must've reopened a wound because blood seeps through the gauze. *Don't let Lydia see this.*

FUCK, it throbs. My anger is at a level I never imagined was possible. Why would Jen lie to me?

Then it clicks.

When we were having the conversation about her being in the hospital, she said that one word that changed the context of everything. She was *supposed* to be taking her medications. She never said she was and I feel like an idiot that I didn't catch her mistake right then to corner her. Granted, that was only four days ago, but I expected her to be honest with me.

I might be impulsive and have a quick temper, but if I knew in that moment that Jen hadn't been taking her medication, I would've fought anyone who would get in my way to help her get better. We would have driven back to her apartment to get them if she didn't bring them with her. I would have found Jonah and ask for his advice. I would have asked Max and Lydia for their help. Hell, I would have asked Glen for help.

No. I wouldn't ask Glen for anything.

But besides that, I would have done anything at that moment to help her.

I hate my body is entering a mild panic attack. Jen is the only voice I want to hear to bring me back to reality. I've tried to do the 54321 technique myself, and it's no use. All I see is red and I'm so angry.

I have my fists clenched on the counter and my temples are pounding from the tension that is building up. My forearms shake as I try to release the tautness in them. My upper back feels like it's on fire with the amount of stress I have there!

Jonah, Anna, and Pat say nothing to me after I storm out of the room. Pat approaches me but keeps a suitable distance between us.

I don't know how long I've been standing with my muscles being strained, but I feel a large hand on my back and my muscle have become more taut. I don't want to be touched. Whipping my neck, Max stands next to me. Lydia isn't with him, which means she must be with Jen. If I had to pick anyone from this circus to tame the tigress we call Jen, Lydia would be my first choice.

"How is she?" My voice is full of irritation. Max leans against the counter, copying my body language. Everyone has left me alone. Jonah is talking quietly to Anna, which pisses me off because she's off limits to him, and Pat has gone outside.

"We think she'll be okay. She took her pills just now and told us about her mom. Did you know about her mom?" Max's voice is so doctoral. I find him intimidating, which says a lot coming from me. He was intelligent and fairly good looking. He had ample amounts of compassion. Not to mention he was level-headed. If I could trade places with him for a day...maybe he could fix my brain.

I'm more bothered by his choice of words than by his calm demeanor. *Did you know about her mom?* I push off the counter like those are fighting words. Max's body language copies.

"What do you mean, did I know about her mom?" My eyes are no longer seeing red. They are seeing the darkest crimson ever created. I want to punch Max in the face. Why is the love of my life building lies around me?

Max holds his hands in front of me, retreating from my fight. Staring forward, Jonah and Anna look in our direction. Are they wanting to get into a fight with me or what? Every slight movement they do just pisses me off.

"Woah, Calvin relax. I just wasn't sure if you knew the backstory of things. I'm sorry, man. It's just her mom had some serious mental health disorders and, well, Jennie just doesn't want to end up like her mom. That's all. She took her pills because she wants to be better for herself. Better for you. She wants to be with happy."

Max is so calm. He must deal with this shit all the time. De-escalation. The constant difficulties of his clients, even though they are children. Children can be unpredictable.

Sometimes I feel like I'm a child because of the unpredictability I bring to the table. In this moment, I'm so glad he has Lydia, who provides saneness and stability for him. I would bet all my money this is not the kind of day Max Byrd planned for himself—to deal with a suicidal employee and her incoherent ex-boyfriend. Current boyfriend? Stalker? Whatever he thinks I am.

The only time Jen brought up her mom to me was during her birthday in 2003. I had made Jen chocolate chip cookies. When she ate the first cookie in five bites, I only know that because I was obsessed with watching her. She said her mom would've loved my cookies. When I asked her why she thought that, Jen said, "I could tell you made them with love and happiness. The only ingredients my mom lacked."

I knew Jen's mom died when she was young, but I didn't know how or why. Jen never wanted to talk about her. Every strained muscle in my body could've snapped at the sound of Max's words.

She wants to be better for you.

I can't even form any sentences or phrases to respond to Max.

My heart is stuck in quicksand for Jen. I try to find a piece of paper and pen to write about what is happening in my heart before it's gone. I can feel Max watch me as I scavenge around the kitchen.

"We think it's best that you give her some space, Calvin. I know she wants to see you and have you stay, but she needs time to rest and recover. I'm sure Lydia will stay with her with for a while but please, give her some time. Can I be frank with you about something?"

I don't answer him. I just keep writing what's in my head.

"I know you saw me and Lydia look worried earlier. We've been dreading this day. The day where she would fall apart in front of you. It was bound to happen. We didn't realize it was because she wasn't taking her medication. I'm eighty percent sure her medication would have helped with her emotional stability, but seeing you and having you around, just a phone call and text away, God, we knew it was going to be like walking through a spinning tunnel. Ever since you busted through our door to find her a couple months ago, not only did Jennie talk about you nonstop, but now my wife was talking about you. You weren't at all what we expected you to be. Your intentions seem true and your love for that girl is unwavering. We want you guys to be together and reconnect and build the most enjoyable life together. But speaking from a doctor level, Jennie has experienced a lot of traumas in the short time you were gone. There is a lot she has not come to terms with. Lydia and I have been wanting to help her so very badly, but you have blinded her for the past couple of months. So, if there's any way for you to get through to her, Calvin, to get her better, we will no doubt have the utmost respect for you."

I hear bits and pieces of his words. It's like a lightning bolt is striking my heart and I have to get out of here fast or I'm going to explode. I planned to leave anyway because I'm going to fall apart. Jen is slipping through my fingers and I'm going to punch every fucking person in the face because I hate myself for putting Jen through this torture. Either way, I don't need an audience.

I feel like an asshole for not responding to Max, but I'm letting the words sink in. Helping her will be my priority. Having finished writing the poem that came to me, I re-read my words.

I care for you deeply

My heart beats for your slightest touch

Your voice sings so sweet to me, I want to be with you ever so much

I think about you always, sometimes with concern and despair

I want to mean something to you, a place in your heart

No matter what I heartache I can bear

You have such an aura around you

Once that make me weak in the knees

I get so nervous around you, it's hard to put the butterflies at ease

Your eyes reach inside me

I fear that you see everything

Opening my heart so wide

I can't help but hear your heartbeat

Wanting those moments to forever be mine

You have such a power within you

A responsibility not taken so lightly

To you I would give you everything

What an honest man I would be

To hold you

To kiss you

To take all of the hurt and set it free

I care for you so deeply

I sign my name, fold it into a tiny square, and smack it into Max's chest.

"I hear you. I need some space myself. Give this to her. I'm begging you." His hand takes hold of the poem and even though I desperately want to stay, I slam the door shut.

I take the longest walk back to my place, needing time to clear my head.

What is happening to us? What is happening to Jen? I find myself stuck in a sick, twisted game of Saw, but there's no escape. What is the fucking solution, God? Please help me save her.

I stop at the corner grocery store to pick up anything that sounds appetizing. Since dinner on Friday night with Jen, I haven't eaten anything. I'm wandering through each aisle, but everything is making me nauseous.

You know what you want.

I don't have to search long until I find her. She's beautiful and polished. She's calling my name.

Jack Daniels.

Jackie sounds better. Less weird. Jackie Daniels.

I stop right in front of her and idolize her. My fatal flaw. What I stare at is the masterpiece that cost me everything. My deepest desire.

You want to take her home.

It's almost like the bottle has venom and spits at me. The camping trip is suddenly tunneling my thoughts.

I hate you. You are nothing. I wish I never met you. You should just go fuck Glen and leave me alone. You make me sick.

Unexpectedly, a sudden pain shoots in my chest and instinctively reach for it. Wishing I could squeeze my heart to suppress the pain, it burns.

I'm getting sweaty and warm. My vision is getting blurry. My heart is going into tachycardia.

I hate you.

The words are spiraling around me. The words echo in my mind, but I can only picture Jen's face. I will always remember her face from that night.

My eyes remain fixed on Jackie.

You ruined everything I ever loved.

My mind is slipping into a new dimension, a black one. My chest is on fucking fire, and I'm losing my balance. I can no longer see Jackie anymore. She's gone.

Calvin

Wednesday, April 17ᵗʰ, 2007

I wake up in a panic, in a room I'm not familiar with. I smell eggs which smell like fucking heaven.

My head is pounding.

I didn't buy Jackie and drink her, did I? I try to sit up on this uncomfortable futon, but I sink down deeper. The curtains are slightly closed, but the sun is barely peeking through the slits of the blinds. I push the warm Sherpa blanket off my body. I look down at my clothes that are not mine. My pants are off, but my boxers are still on, and I'm wearing this hideous Boston Celtics shirt. It smells like laundry detergent. I rub my hands on my face, trying to piece the puzzle together.

I was at the store.

I found Jackie. I wanted Jackie.

I had flashbacks of the bar.

I was about to pass out. No, I did pass out? Someone drugged me? Someone knocked something across my head? I don't remember what happened after being possessed by the whiskey.

"Hey, you're up. It's about time. I was about to pull the curtains wide open to wake your ass up."

I know that voice. This isn't happening. This can't be real. My hero can't be...

Jonah.

I drag my hands down my face to see him standing in front of me, holding a plate of eggs and orange juice. He's already dressed for the day in his dark navy scrubs. I have no idea what time it is, but the sleep was much needed.

"Holy God, this can't be real. Jonah, what the fuck am I doing here?"

My body is still so tired, I refuse to stand up to intimidate Jonah. Instead, I sit normally on the couch. I don't take the eggs or juice from him, so he places it on the coffee table in front of the couch. He walks over to the oversize single chair and looks at me.

I remember yesterday, and how I pulled him close to me, practically begging him to save her life. I never met this guy before yesterday and only for me to discover he is the ex-husband of my girl makes me want to throw up, but there is nothing in my stomach to hurl. Instead, Angel soothes me.

This man saves lives. He saved Jens, and he's saving yours.

"Good morning to you too. I was worried about you when you left Jennie's apartment yesterday. So, I followed you." I'm eyeing him like he's a traitor. Angel and Devil are about to brawl like it's a WrestleMania main event.

He's a punk. You should knock his teeth out. Eat the eggs first and then leave.

He saved your life. You are someone who needs saving, too.

"What do you mean, you followed me?" My stomach barks at me at the smell and sight of the eggs in front of me. I try to ignore it, but I'm starving. Reluctantly, I pick up the plate of eggs and devour them in four bites. Jonah is watching intensely.

"You want some more?" He chuckles. He gets off the chair and takes my plate. Since when did this guy start call the shots? I hear him behind me in the kitchen, scraping the skillet with the rest of the eggs onto my plate. He brings the plate back to me as I still try to process what is happening.

"Thanks." *Stop being a dick for once.*

"Welcome. Yeah, so you seemed irritated when you left Jennie's. You shouted a little at Max and he was talking to you in the kitchen, but I couldn't hear what the conversation was about. You slapped him with something and then jetted out the door. I had to make a quick decision to follow you or let you get into whatever trouble you were looking for. Max and Pat both told me to go. I didn't know you, but in a way I did because of all the things Jennie told me about you. They told me you were impulsive, and that was what I was worried about. I couldn't live with you making a dumb mistake because you were angry at her. Trust me, I am still angry with her. Anyway, I swear I didn't ever think we were going to have a destination. You just kept walking, and I was getting so tired following you like a little puppy. We had been walking for probably forty minutes, at least, and we walked into this convenience store–Johnny's. You seemed familiar with it, but I let you walk in first and I came in behind a few moments later. You wandered around. I got distracted by the seafood. I wanted to make myself some nice halibut and broccoli and sala..." I clear my throat at Jonah. That information is irrelevant.

"Sorry, off tangent. I walked around to find you and saw you staring at a bottle of Jack Daniels. Like you were staring weirdly at it. As a bystander, you almost looked possessed by the bottle, and it was just weird to watch. I was going to approach you, but I feared you were going to knock me out. Then I don't know, man, something snapped in you. You grabbed your chest like you were having a heart attack and you were about to pass out, so I hurried and grabbed you, so you didn't hit your head on the ground. Cause that would've just been terrible." I finish the last bit of eggs as I hear the sarcasm in that last sentence.

I could kill you right now.

"I'm not one for making a scene, so I laid you on the floor and put my sweatshirt under your head. I assume the guy who runs that place, Johnny, knew you. He asked if you were okay, but I wasn't sure. You were breathing and everything, but you were like not there with me. I called Pat to help me bring you home. He and I had you wrapped around our necks and literally dragged you here. I lived closer. Johnny's is right down the street. Pat said you lived in the complete opposite direction of Johnny's, so I made the decision that I wasn't walking another fifteen miles with you. So here you are."

I'm frozen. For once, someone saved me. And to think it was Jonah. The ex-lover of my current lover. What a caring bastard.

Angel and Devil tussle with each other about starting an intimate conversation with Jonah.

You can trust him. He took care of Jen while you were away. Do you honestly think he would want to harm you?

He's just trying to distract you so he can swoop in to be Jen's hero. He isn't the fucking hero.

I decide to side with Angel.

"I got drunk on whiskey at a bar after the camping trip. There was this guy who was just fucking with me. He was asking for it.

Things just escalated. He went to the hospital and I went to jail. I wasn't looking at the whiskey last night to devour it. I was looking at it to destroy it. I want to smash every bottle of Jack Daniels. It ruined everything for me."

Although my stomach feels better with food, and the throbbing in my head is lessening, there is still so much emptiness in my heart.

I never had someone to talk to about the camping trip, besides my group leader and counselor. Let's see if Jonah is the right choice, I guess. Leaning back on the couch, I fold my arms and stare at the ceiling.

"If I would've stopped drinking, I would have just left, and I could've made it back to her." My throat feels tight.

No, you will not cry in front of Jonah. Absolutely not.

Devil wins this one. I form spit in the mouth and swallow.

"Did you think about anything else besides smashing the bottles when I said you looked possessed?" Jonah's question makes my throat dry again.

"Umm..."

With the dryness becoming too much and I can feel my eyes becoming wet, I blink the wetness away and pick up the orange juice on the table. I avoid eye contact at all costs, but I can feel Jonah watching me, waiting for me to crack.

"Um, I was thinking about the last words I said to Jen." Unable to hold it together, I feel tears leave the corner of my eyes, quickly wiping them away.

"They were brutal. I would do just about anything for her to erase those words from her memory." I say again.

"Yeah, they were pretty brutal." Jonah responds, his voice soft.

I drop my head to look at him, connecting point A to point B.

"Of course you would know what I said." I don't say it maliciously. More so pathetically. Until now, I forgot I was talking to Jen's ex-husband. The nurse who took care of her and her wounds, internal and external.

I don't know what washes over me, but I bring my hands over my face so I can quietly cry. It all becomes too much to handle. I hear

Jonah clear his throat.

"Dude, I want you to know... no, I need you to understand that no matter if I was her husband, or friend, or brother, or whatever I was to her, I was not you. She talked about you every day. Before marriage, during marriage, after marriage. Her world revolved around you. I was just someone to help keep the band aids on. You have no idea how awful it was for her and I. We both had our fair share of arguments, and you would probably kill me for the way I would raise my voice at her, but I just tried to be what she needed. It just never clicked with me that she needed you. You were the missing piece."

I can feel my heart drop into my stomach. Jonah. Pure, kind and patient. Everything I'm not.

"Why did you stick around?"

Feeling like an emotional teenager whose hormones are raging, I find the nerve to look at him. He has no tears on his face. Just sadness. He's running his fingers along his beard, thinking.

"I couldn't let her be alone like that. My grandma was sick when I was a kid, well, as a teenager. I had stepped up to take care of her and it just brought me joy even though she was dying. In a crazy way, I knew she would die with a smile because that's what I tried to do. I had to bring her soup and tea every day. Had to change her clothes. Had to learn how to braid her hair. As weird as it sounds, I just thought of my grandma when I was with Jennie. She needed someone."

"Did you think you were going to be married forever?"

The word *marry* burns on my tongue. If I marry Jen someday, I won't ever use her marriage to Jonah as ammo. This guy is constantly exceeding my expectations.

Jonah's reaction surprises me. When he laughs, I shoot him a look. Surprisingly, his laugh is contagious. I feel I haven't heard a decent laugh in a long time.

"What's so funny?"

Jonah leans back into his chair and kicks off his shoes. He props his foot to rest on his kneecap. He looks like he's getting comfortable. I thought he was leaving for work?

"I caught Jennie at a good time to ask her to marry me. Some would consider it coercion. It was a good day for her. I had to work fast or else I knew she would never say yes."

Everyone has their secrets, I guess. Jonah's secret intrigues me.

"How did you do it?"

I'm going to regret listening to this story. I don't really want to know how this man proposed to *my* Jen, but I want to know how he picked up my little bird and protected her. Jonah makes eye contact with me. He's just as surprised as I am. He shifts in the chair, now crossing his ankles.

"Well, Jennie came into the hospital last May. I don't know if she ever mentioned it, but she brought herself in. She had wrapped her arm in an old shirt, and said the blade went too deep. I'm so glad I was on duty that night. She didn't flinch once when I started doing the stitches. Her strength was clear, but I could tell there was something causing significant pain. Because people don't usually cut for no reason, you know? She stayed in the hospital for a month. She had a lot of suicidal thoughts, was underweight and was meeting with a psychiatrist, so that took up some time. I had developed a soft spot for her. Instead of the nasty ass undercooked oatmeal, I brought her warm muffins. I let her watch scary movies, even though she wasn't supposed to. I let her wear slippers and wear this smelly Vancouver Canucks hockey shirt. God, she never took that shirt off."

I had to interrupt him to give myself leverage.

"That was my shirt."

"I figured that out later. Thanks. Anyway, at end of May, she was getting much better. She'd been going to her group therapy, been regularly meeting with her therapist and psychiatrist. She was nervous about starting her depression and anxiety medication, but she was happy that she could have things that made her feel better, but said she was sad about it, too. Something relating to her mom. That part I never found out."

I nod my head, connecting with the conversation Max told me about her mom having mental health disorders. I wonder if Jen was sad because her mother didn't have access to medications, and if she did, she might still be here.

"Her release day was June 2nd. She was nervous, but more so excited. As delusional as it sounds, she was excited to be out to find you. She believed you would surprise her by coming home early. Of course, you didn't. I drove her home that day, then stayed the night with her that night. I didn't think she wanted to be alone, and she never fought me about staying. I had wanted her first official day home to be special, so the next day I planned everything to a tee. She slept in until ten, which she was appreciative of because she had to be up at eight-thirty every day. She took the longest shower possible, and I convinced her to let me wash your shirt. Once the dryer was done, she immediately put it back on for the rest of the day. I let her make coffee. She wanted to go to the *Coffee & Honey*, but I suggested we take it slow with the transitions and seeing people like Pat. She was okay with that. She picked Chinese for dinner. We picked out a fun pill organizer since she'd be taking her pills three times a day. I, um..."

Jonah repositions himself in the chair, looking mildly uncomfortable.

"I let her make the first move that evening when she pulled me to the bed." My eyes leave Jonah's face as I lowered my gaze. My cheeks get hot from... anger? Everything else in me didn't feel angry, though. I don't clench my fists. My stomach doesn't flip. I wasn't seeing red. It was something else.

Jealously.

I want to throw up at the thought of whatever Jen did to provoke Jonah into the bedroom. Until that point, I had been the only one.

"If you don't mind, I'd love to skip that part." My body is still, and I move my eyes to look back at Jonah.

"Yeah, yeah, don't worry. Anyway, the next morning I noticed she didn't have your shirt on. Um, well, because... you know."

"Get. On. With. It." I sneer through my teeth.

"She just felt like a blank canvas. There was always something connecting the two of you together. Whether it was the shirt, or the ring, or the memories she constantly shared. There was no imprint of you. So, I took it like it was the best dog bone I've ever had. I watched her wake up to smile. *At me.*"

His emphasizes on himself makes me sad. God, she played him good. Turning my attention back to him, my body squirms in discomfort.

"I said good morning. Will you marry me today? Her answer was quick, and of course, the answer I wanted. The pure happiness only lasted for a couple weeks. I planned to marry her soon so I could care for her permanently here. I gotta say the hardest part of that whole thing..." Jonah pauses, and I look away from him while he tells me this story. I have been listening intently to his words.

Finally, emotion. He wipes his eyes before anything falls from them. He notices me watching him but doesn't hide it like me.

"The hardest part of that point in time was walking in on her, looking at both rings. She had mine, a half carat small gold princess engagement ring. And your oval white gold promise ring. Each hand held a ring. The only time I never comforted her. I didn't know how to. When she emerged from the room a few minutes later, she had both rings on. Mine was on her left hand and yours was on her right hand. I would never be so cruel to make her choose. I took whatever I could get from her. I just wanted to be with her, so I took all her baggage."

I'm staring at the ceiling again, taking in the story of how my enemy married my lover.

"Let me get this straight. You knew each other for a month because she arrived at the hospital for a wound. After a month of being her nurse, you took her home, stayed the night with her and then proposed to her on the next day? Are you fucking with me right now?" I let out little quips of a laugh. The whole thing sounds absurd.

"Yes, Calvin. That's what happened. Like I said, I knew I wouldn't have much time to play my shot. The moment I realized she was stripped of you, both literally and mentally, I had to act immediately."

"Didn't it bother you though that she wore my ring the whole time she was with you? Or that I was probably the first and last thing on her mind? Did it not bother you she didn't wholeheartedly love you because she already loved me?"

My own words stab through my chest like a dagger. I'd hate to be Jonah, to hear those words sink into my soul. I let my eyes drift to look at him. His eyes are closed, like he's not about to crumble on my behalf.

Why would you say something like that to him?

"Does it not bother you that if it weren't for me, picking up your dirty pieces, she would probably be dead?"

Okay, okay, he's ready to fight. I've had time for my energy to recoup. As my fists clench, I feel the forming destruction coursing through my veins. I'm ready to take down this motherfucker. Before

I stand up from the couch, Jonah's voice starts again.

"I didn't force her to do anything, because like Pat said, she's so easy to love. Even though the bliss of her saying yes to me only lasted a couple hours until I walked in on her with both rings, I tried to remind myself that she was the one who decided to be with me. Could you imagine all the idiots she would say yes to? She was desperate, man, desperate to have you. I knew I couldn't be you, and you know what, I was okay with that. My goal was to protect her. My intention was to help you and keep her safe until your return. When you were coming home, I knew my time was over. I had a small sliver of hope that maybe, maybe one day she would be over you and she would love me instead. The day we found out about your early release, she came into the hospital, Calvin. The fucking hospital and handed me my ring. All the while, your ring still stayed on her finger. So, I'm sorry you hate me so much that I had to marry your girlfriend so these lonely ass predators wouldn't snatch her up, but I was holding her safe, for you."

As if someone pours holy water over me, I feel a demon leave my body. My hands relax. My breathing regulates. Awareness hits me like the hangover I felt after the camping trip.

Jonah *was* the fucking hero. He was holding onto what was mine, so that nobody would hurt her while I was away. Took care of her until I could again. For months, he allowed her to cry, scream, and panic over the memories I left her with. This Saint has every right to kill me right now. Everything Jen has turned out to be is because of him. I did nothing but ruin her. I ruined him. I ruined them. I mean, I finally find her, and she's bringing knives into her bedroom. Jonah almost certainly never encountered that problem.

I fall onto the couch, my mouth agape and my mind swirling with thoughts from Angel.

Apologize to him. Thank him. Tell him you owe everything to him. Tell him he can destroy your life.

"Fuck Jonah." I spit out while my hands run over my face. Pinching the bridge of my nose, I'm forcing all my water gates to stay closed. "I'm so sorry, man." My voice is tired. My mind is tired. I never realized how important this man would become to me.

"Did you ever read the letters about me? She explains all of it. She knew this was just part of the plan." Jonah's voice is calm.

My thoughts find Jen who has all these patient people in her life, and I slip back into her life to cause havoc. Patience is not one of my strong points. I can't imagine what everyone thinks of me, reacting so quickly. I'm kryptonite.

The letters. The fucking letters. Jen told me everything I'll need to know is in the letters. God, I should've never put up a fight about them. I should've finished them. That's what I need to do, just finish them.

I run my fingers through my hair and Jonah looks at me, completely aware how of stupid I'm feeling.

"No. I didn't finish the letters. Jen told me if I finished the 2003 letters, I could see her. That was Friday night. And we're here." I hear Jonah sigh in disappointment? In frustration? In anger? He has every right.

"Look, you can stay here for however long you need today, but you gotta get home and finish the letters. I'll watch out for Jennie until you're done. She told you to finish all of them, right?"

It's not so much a question as it is a statement. I feel like I'm talking to a male version of Jen. Their words are in unison. *Don't call me until you finish them.*

"Okay. Okay, I will. I'll leave now. I'm good." Leaping from the couch, I grab my pile of clothes. I've wasted enough time. I'll bring the letters in the shower if I have to. There's no reason for me to remain at Jonah's. He has saved me too many times already.

"Keep the clothes. I hate the Celtics." He gets off the couch also and smirks.

"I left a poem with Max that he was supposed to give her. Make sure she reads it. I'll find her soon. And Jonah, thank you." He purses his lips together and nods.

Time does not feel like it's on my side right now. I'm slowly losing her. If she hasn't already, she'll realize that Jonah was the one for her. Soon I'll only be a painful memory to her.

"Gotcha. I have a short shift today, but I'll stop by her apartment later. And Calvin..." Stopping at the door, I push my feet into my shoes and turn to him. He's gained my respect in the past thirty minutes.

"Please, just read all of them before you call or see her. I'm begging you. It'll give me time to get her back on her medication. I'll tell her you'll be back. Once I see you again, I'll know my time is over and I'll back away. I just need to say this before you go." He leans against the column that is supporting his kitchen. He crosses his arms and looks at me. For the first time, I feel intimidated by Jonah. I want to hide under a rock and wait for him to move to the next city.

"If you don't fight for her, I will. If you don't want to love her anymore, then I will. It won't be easy to love her after she's been crazy obsessed with you, but I'll do my damn best. She's the best thing I've ever known. I just know that she wants you. If you want her back, then I will know my place. I will know that I have to stay away."

I swallow the raw truth. Do I really want Jonah to leave her alone? Fuck yes, so I can step in and take care of her. As a friend, though, to both of us. He could stick around...

I nod. That's the only thing I can do. My mind is racing with setting up a plan.

Find a taxi. Get home and shower. Start reading and don't stop. No sleep, no alcohol, no texting or calling Jen. I dedicate my life to learning about her life.

Jennie

Alone on my couch, I'm shaking while holding Cal's poem.

To take all the hurt and set it free.

My Cal. You have no idea how I wish the hurt could disappear. It's not just hurt, though. There's sadness, anger, resentment, jealously, irritation. They are all sitting on my shoulder talking too much, talking too fast for me to understand anything.

When I heard the door slam, I walked out with Lydia following me. Max said he told Cal I took my pills and briefly mentioned about my mom. He said it was hard to describe if Cal seemed annoyed or angry, but he jotted this poem, slapped it into Max's chest, and left. Anna and Pat shared that Jonah went after him. He was probably concerned that Cal would make impulsive decisions, but he also knew how upset I'd be if something terrible happened to him.

Jonah. My hero. My heart smiles at Jonah finding Cal, talking him off the cliff, like he has with me so many times. I can only hope that's what happened.

After learning that Jonah was hunting Calvin, I politely asked everyone to leave. I feel... dirty, still exhausted, hungry (finally), confused and lonely. Sad and anxious. I realize I won't be cured overnight, and I'm upset with myself for not taking my medicine for the past three months. My emotions would be in such better shape right now.

Currently, my emotions feel numb. I want to cry so badly because I miss Cal. I hate that I lied to my entire circle of people who care about me. My favorite knife is calling my name, but I just feel completely empty.

I wander to the kitchen to find something to eat, but I'm not motivated to cook anything. I decide to order tacos. Tacos always make everything better. Back in my room, I grab my phone to set a delivery for Angelo's a few blocks away. I have several texts from Jonah, but nothing from Cal.

I feel my heart sink. *Please find him, Jonah. Don't let him get away.*

Jonah: Hey, I know u probably won't see this til later but I ran after Calvin. I'm following him now. I won't let anything happen to him. I'll keep u updated.

Jonah: still walking behind Cal. He hasn't noticed me. don't know where we are walking to...

Jonah: I got him to my apartment. He's safe. He'll probably stay the night here. Not drunk.

Jonah: Calvin just left. Not pissed or irrational. He's okay. He's going home to read the letters.

Me: thank you. For everything. <3

Why did he take him back to his apartment? There had to be some story to share about how Jonah convinced Cal to stay over. Or maybe Cal didn't have a choice? Jonah has a tendency to be controlling and highly persuasive...

Hearing my stomach grumble, I place a delivery order for my tacos that should arrive in about thirty-five minutes. Falling back on my bed, I pull up my texts again, tapping on Cal's name.

You shouldn't do this. I should leave him be until he follows mine and Jonah's directions and finishes all the letters. That's exactly what should've happened since the very beginning. But I hate how we left things. I hate what I did to him. I keep replaying the whole situation from this afternoon.

Cal read the letter about our first kiss. My favorite memory. We cuddled on my bed like teenagers. Jonah walks in to ruin the moment. Cal's face. And then he left again.

I feel it in my chest. I feel it in my throat and my eyes. Picturing Cal's face when he found out I wasn't taking my medication. It was utter disappointment. I try to determine which face was worse to look at; Cal's disappointment face from this morning or Cal's disgusted face from four years ago. They both burn a hole in my heart.

Me: Hey you...

Sighing, I wait for the ellipse to show.

He's going home to read the letters.

I bet Jonah told him to keep his distance given the circumstances from this morning, but because also, those letters are everything. All he has to do is read. Once he's done, he has the choice to love me for me, for all my mistakes and choices, or can choose to walk away and move on.

A few minutes go by, and I doze off. The knock on my door startles me, and I check my phone if there are any messages, but there's nothing. For some annoying reason, I think the knock on the door is Cal.

Jumping off my bed, I am greeted at the door by a young girl dropping off my tacos.

Well, not totally terrible, but I'm still alone. I decide to eat my tacos in the living room and find something to watch. It takes all willpower in me to not get my phone to text Cal again. The hole in my heart is only getting bigger. I guess, in a way, I'm preparing myself for when he decides he wants nothing to do with me.

I only watch romance on rare occasions. Although I prefer horror movies, I don't want to watch a scary film tonight. Flicking through Netlfix, I look into the romance movies. I've never seen *Pride and Prejudice* but have read so many novels referencing the love story between Elizabeth and Darcy. Honestly, I'm just a fan of anything with Kiera Knightley. Laying a blanket over my body, I lay the tacos in front of me and somehow prepare myself for a long night of silent crying, dreaming of my fairytale coming true.

Sniffling during the ballroom dance scene, my phone rings in my bedroom. I didn't realize I had turned my sound on. Throwing my pillow off to the side, I dash down the hallway.

Please be Jonah with good news.

As I get off the couch, I glance at the clock. 5:18. My phone illuminates on the bed and I see Cal's name. I hold in my breath. To answer, I slide my finger over and lift the phone to my ear.

"Jen?" Cal's voice. I'd recognize it anywhere. Sitting on my bed, I bring my legs to my chest. I totally forget that I'm holding my breath.

"Hey." My voice doesn't feel like mine. Why am I so nervous to talk to him?

"Are you okay? You haven't been responding to my texts." I bring my phone away from my ear to see five texts from him.

Cal: Hi there

Cal: What are you doing?

Cal: Ignoring me, I take it?

Cal: Don't do this to me again, Jennie Marie.

Cal: you are so dead.

His last text was one minute before he called me.

"I'm sorry, I was just re-reading through your texts. I waited for your response, fell asleep, then got food and watched a movie while I ate. My phone was in my room."

I haven't forgotten that I lied to Cal about my pills. It's been eating at me. I don't want him to feel I am keeping secrets from him.

"I'm sorry. I took a shower and needed to take a nap." He seems so distant and different; it's breaking me.

"What are you doing?" I don't want him to stop talking to me, so I'll keep the conversation going.

"I'm about to order some food myself and start reading." A smile forms on my face. *Good boy.*

"Yeah? What are you going to eat? I had tacos."

"Ooh, tacos from Angelos?"

"Only the best."

I hate how this conversation is going. Tacos? Really?

Tell me you miss me. Tell me you're going to come over.

"That actually sounds good. I think I might do that." He grunts as I assume he's getting off the bed or couch.

I want to be with you.

"Nice. Good choice." *Oh my god, say something smarter.*

There's silence for a few moments, and it makes me want to throw up my tacos. That makes it even more upsetting, considering I haven't had food in my stomach for a couple of days. I hate the discomfort right now.

I hear Cal's chuckle and then say, "I'm not supposed to be talking to you right now. Jonah would kill me."

A part of my heart breaks and disappears.

I shouldn't be talking to you right now.

What the Hell did Jonah tell him?

"Is that so? Why would your best friend Jonah be mad?" I hear him chuckle again. His laugh is making it hard to be annoyed at him and Jonah. I want to say anything to keep him laughing.

"First, he isn't my best friend, but he is a good guy. You did good picking him."

I didn't pick him. He picked me, but I picked you.

"Second, he told me not to call you or see you until I finished the letters."

"He'll get over it." I tease back, trying to fight back my tears. It didn't take long after the movie started, my floodgates opened. My eyes feel like a leaky faucet.

"So what do I have to look forward to in 2004?" I sift through my thoughts and memories back to 2004. It wasn't the worst year, but it wasn't the best year.

"Hmm, I tell you about my birthday, Pat's birthday, my next hobby. Oooh, the renovation at *Coffee & Honey*. I tell you about ..." Quickly, my voice closes and my nose tickles.

Be honest. He's going to read about it, anyway.

"I'll tell you about a party. But there are random letters in there that I hope will make you smile." I wipe the snot coming from my nose.

"How many happy letters do I have here?" His voice is breaking my heart. It's so guarded and sad. He makes it sound like he's about to enter detention and the only way he can leave is to read.

"To be honest, I don't know. But..." I bring the phone away from my face to regain my composure. Taking a deep breath in, my lower lip quivers and there's so much pressure in my chin to hold back my tears.

"Um, please just keep the happy letters close in case you need to re-read them for a refresher."

"Why do you say that?" His comment is almost instantaneous. It's dark and cold.

"Because 2005 is not a good year. And 2006 is pretty much a shit show. So please, just try to stay in good spirits."

Silence.

The kind of silence where I check my phone to make sure he hasn't hung up. The time elapse continues.

"Cal..." my voice is quiet, haunted by my past.

"Yeah, I'm here. I'm sorry. I just don't really want to do this, but I know I have to. For you." I try to think of anything to make him feel better. Just a minuscule thing.

"I want you to know that no matter what Jonah says about you being able to talk to me while you do this, just know that you can. Not sure how long you plan to take to read these, but I hope it won't be long. I, um... I really miss you." My voice cracks, and tears stream down my face, despite my efforts to stop them.

I should start digging my grave. Cal is going to hate what happens in 2004. I don't want him to be impulsive and get angry. And most of all, I don't want him to hate me.

"Jen, I plan to read these as fast as possible. I don't want to sit in this fucking misery any longer." He speaks in a matter-of-fact tone. His voice scares me, but I know he's not thrilled about this request.

"I should probably get going, though. Long night ahead. Don't stay up too late." His sincerity was almost there. His poem stares at me from my pillow. I pick it up with my free hand and read through it, trying to memorize it as fast as I can.

"I hope I'll see you soon."

"Me too. Goodnight, Jen."

"Goodnight, Cal." I barely get the L out before the call ends. Keeping my eyes closed, I hold back as much water as I can before it becomes a waterfall.

Calvin

Dropping my phone onto my chest, I sigh out loud.

Her voice was so fucking sad.

I knew I had to stay somewhat neutral in the conversation so she wouldn't think good things were coming. To be honest, I don't know what's coming.

I wish I hadn't asked about what's in next year's letters. I'm setting myself up for either several panic attacks or someone is getting fucked up. Lying here, I want to set these letters on fire.

I feel a whirlwind of emotions and I'm not used to it. I'm still upset with Jen for hiding the fact that she wasn't taking her medication. That should be part of her routine, and I hate she lied so easily to me about it.

I'm angry that I'm letting that ruin me. It makes me nauseous that she's lying about other things. Jen has never been one to lie to me though, so why is she starting now?

I'm beyond confused about the relationship I'm forming with Jonah. The moment I heard Jen was married to a guy named Jonah, I wanted to kill him. For taking what was mine. But God, I feel like a prick. He was protecting what was mine. If I could, I'd kiss him. I'm so eager to read these letters. I'm doing this for Jen. She was waiting for me this whole time. The least I can do is read the journey of her life without me.

I want to break something, so I decide to walk into my bathroom and punch the mirror.

Glass shatters everywhere and stupidly, it's the same hand that I punched the brick wall with the other day at the Bryd's office. Of course, my wounds reopen and blood is pouring from my knuckles. I feel a million times better though and turn on the water to run the blood down. I grab a towel, knowing it's going to be ruined, and wrap my hand.

I leave the pieces of glass scattered around my bathroom and turn off the light.

You make stupid choices when you're impulsive.

Thanks Devil, I'm fully aware.

I should probably look into a gym membership or getting a punching bag installed.

I walk to my kitchen where the stack of letter haunts me.

Trying to distract myself, I search for all the letters I've read and put them in order. *Fuck, that didn't take long.* I can't move past Jen's answer about how many happy letters I have left.

I don't know.

Great, just fucking great. I don't think my boiling level is going to take this.

I pick up the top letter. looking at the date in the corner of the envelope. For each letter, I've tried to pinpoint what memory happened that specific day. I've realized, though, she brings up the most random memories. Holidays are easy to expect the content, but other times, I have no clue what she is going to surprise me with.

The date on this envelope reads January 13, 2004.

I'm blanking. I thought I already read a couple letters from February and our first kiss letter was in April. Why am I going backwards? There must've been a mixup and some letters aren't in order. Who knows if the order even matters?

I know where I was on January 13th - stuck in a prison cell. I was probably bench pressing 160 pounds. My counselor thought it would help with my irritability. It did.

I debate where to sit. The kitchen table, the balcony, my bedroom, perhaps my spare bedroom for different scenery?

JUST OPEN THE LETTER YOU COWARD.

For once, I agree with Devil. I choose the kitchen table and run my finger through the sealable flap.

Here we go.

January 13, 2004

Cal,

Happy late New Years. I had the same thought I did on Valentines Day, do you guys decorate for New Years? I had this funny dream that the guards give out confetti poppers but all the inmates pop them at each other, like in the eye or in the groin. HA, I hope that is not the case. I'm keeping tally on how many New Years kisses I owe you when you get back.

||

We've never had a New Year's kiss and that depresses me. We met right when the year started so I'm going to add another tally because I think I deserve a New Years kiss from 2003.

I just started my second semester of school. First semester could've been worse but I'm glad it's over. I don't feel so nervous walking into an auditorium lecture or asking someone to be my partner for biology. I worked a lot during winter break just because there wasn't much of anything else to do. Pat is probably thankful to get a break from me. I think I torment that man without even realizing it. I'm sort of glad you are gone right about now so I don't have any distractions. I already know my statistics class is going to kill me. You were always so good at math. I should hire you as my tutor. If only I could send you my stats homework and have you do it for me.

I wish we could've gone to college together. It would have been fun to live with you and even have a couple classes together. I wish I knew what you were up to these days. I hate that I still have the need to call you and ask you to hang out. I haven't tried calling you, your phone is probably dead. When you do turn your phone on, once you're out, ignore the millions of texts from me. Literally, there is probably millions.

I miss you so much it hurts. I don't know how I'll survive for five years. I'm trying to convince myself that I'm just in school to help pass time while you're gone. That's smart right? Then when you come back, I'll just be able to recivilize you to the world. Have you hang on my arm while I show you off to everyone. Yeah, that's what I'm going to tell myself.

Waiting,

Jennie

I don't realize I was gripping the letter, crumpling it. It reminds me of the way Jen was holding onto my sweatshirt during the weekend.

When I finally relax, the veins and muscles in my hands throb. With a half-hearted smile, I refold the letter. They all won't be that easy to get through.

I hate she had to preoccupy herself with going to school instead of fulfilling herself differently. She could've worked multiple jobs. Or travel. She could've flown to South Carolina to see me.

I try to think rationally about the situation I'm in and these letters. If I don't plan on seeing or talking to Jen until I'm done reading these, I have to find the bright side of each letter. If I don't, I'm going to go fucking insane. There has to be something good, just a small minuscule thing to be thankful for. I also feel like it'll be helpful to write questions to get more clarification about Jen's life. I find a piece of paper and write the date of the letter.

January 13–Jen found something to keep her occupied. Why didn't you just keep working at the coffee shop? Pat would've taken care of you. He was supposed to take care of you...

Huffing loudly, I stack the letter on top of the others, then pick up the next one.

January 18th.

This date I recognize. It's Pat's birthday. Jen wasn't around the first year Pat and I went out for his birthday in 2003. She would infiltrate my life a couple of weeks later.

In 2003, Pat wanted to go to this hipster poetry/stand-up comedy gig in Tacoma. I didn't want to go. I begged him to have someone else tag along, but everyone in the shop was smart to come up with good excuses. Pat was smart too, considering he asked me last and therefore, I wasn't able to get out of it.

The show was fucking awful. I only laughed at the comedy because of how ridiculous it was. Thinking back now, I realize how much Jen would've LOVED going. She loves that dry humor. She laughed at everything I said, and I think I fell in love with her laugh the first time I heard it.

I'm trying to cover my heart with duct tape, hoping and praying to whoever that Pat's birthday is just a replica of that year. I hope and pray that Jen took my seat at that bar and simply enjoyed the presence of Pat. Opening the letter, I immediately realize that is not how his birthday went.

Disappointment shoots through my heart.

Well, that duct tape was useless.

January 18, 2004

Cal, I'm wasted.

I don't know how or when or what I drank but I feel dizzy. Pat had a little shindig at the coffee shop (after hours, TEHE!) It was me, Pat, Maggie, Angelina, Joey and then we hired another dude Corey. He just transferred to University of Washington as a junior. He's studying economics and needed a lil side hustle for some caaaaash. He's funny. Not like you, but he's funny. Maggie brought her boytoy, Sam. He was pretty intimidating but lightened up with a couple of drinks. We ended up being drinking buddies, along with Corey. You know Pat hardly drinks but Angelina and Joey thought it would be so hipster to throw Pat a rad-icle 35th birthday. Any who, we just started doing shots and Angelina's husband came with tequila and whiskey. Did you know how good whiskey tastes? At first, it was a harsh burn in my throat. I thought I was a dragon, about to breathe fire. It was disgusting but it made me feel powerful. After a few drinks, it started to taste like the forest. It had this tang of the woods. I can still feel it on my lips. I'm licking my lips right now. I wish I was licking your lips.

I ended up kissing Corey's lips. I don't know how it happened but yeeeaaah. You'll be happy to know that Pat was the one to pull me away from him and drive me home and tell me to stay home tomorrow since he thought my hangover would be exxcruciting (not sure how to spell that right now)

So I'm going to go to sleep and wake up tomorrow feeling like the biggest piece of shit and feeling like garbage.

I'm sorry.

Love, Jen

I rip the letter in half.

I yelled "fuck" so loudly that I wouldn't be surprised if the cops came knocking soon. Frustrated, I knock over my chair and run my fingers through my hair, tempted to rip out every follicle.

The urge to call Jen and curse her out is in the danger zone.

Don't be angry at her. She was just having some fun.

That's a pathetic excuse. She can't sit here and say she was waiting for you and kiss other men.

I want to rip out my soul and put it in a shredder, knowing Jen got drunk off *her.*

Fucking Jackie. In her case, Jack. He's a demon. The grim reaper. He makes you do cruel, foul things. Terrible things.

Yes, remember it's Jack's fault. Not Jen's.

I want to side with Angel. God, I know how good whiskey tastes. My mouth is salivating at the thought of having just one drink. Thankfully Henry helped me clear my stash, so I'm left with water and Sprite.

A glass of ice-cold water sounds good right now. I think of the many times I gave Jen ice cold water after her panic attacks. As I drink, I can feel my throat turn into a vial of liquid nitrogen. It's almost instant relief of the water creating a tsunami and destroying all the bad things I just read.

Find one good thing.

"There's nothing good here!" Screaming to the invisible Angel.

I'm certain the cops will show up. My neighbors probably think I'm having a Satanic ritual or an episode.

Hovering over the table, I pick up the pencil and scribble.

January 18–Jen drank whiskey and kissed a guy. Why did you have to kiss another guy? Why couldn't you have kissed Maggie or Ang?! Why did you have to pick up whiskey? You should've gone for the tequila.

Reading that letter, I need some time to process it. There's no way I can start another one, especially when my rage-o-meter is at a stifling 90. My heart is racing so fast, I don't know whether I want to cry or scream. I hate that confliction.

You should've been there to stop her.

I find my phone sitting on the coffee table and decide to make a phone call.

"Calvin, what's wrong?" I was expecting to hear her voice, but it wasn't hers. I check my phone screen to remind myself who I called. My mind is all over the place, trying to put all these pieces together.

"Hey, I uh, I hope I'm not bothering you... I just" Feeling out of breath, I can hear the breathing over the phone. He was always there, always listening to what I needed.

"You're never a bother. What is it? What do you need?" Pat responds.

"Where the fuck is Corey now? Does he still work there?"

Pat sighs on the other end of the line, almost relieved that I'm reading these letters.

"Corey?"

"Yes, Corey. I just read this stupid letter from your birthday from 2004 and she kissed him or he kissed her or whatever the fuck happened, but she said you pulled them apart from each other and you drove her home. Does he still work with you?" I spit out the words to Pat, pacing around my apartment to keep my cool.

If he still works there, what will you do?

I can't tell if that's Angel or Devil, but I don't care because the answer is easy–I'm going to rip his intestines out and make him choke on them, so he forgets about their kiss.

"Calvin, I fired that creep the next day. He tried showing up for his shift and I told him to leave his apron on the counter and go home." Gratitude eases my rage. Pat—the best guy I've ever known.

"Thank you, man." The words feel strange coming off my tongue. Conversations with Pat usually end with some sort of "I'm proud of you" or "I care about you" speech, but I'm not ready to hear those words from him. It's a dick move, but my hormones are raging.

Tossing my phone on the couch, I pick up the pencil.

January 18 -Jen kisses another dude but Pat and his Holy duty called to him, fired the dude

I smile proudly at the advantage of having Pat on my team. He was always on our side. At least, he was supposed to be on our side...

My rage-o-meter is lowering to a normal 65. I move this letter to the completed stack and reach for the next one. The date of this one says February 14th, 2004. I read this letter to Jen at the cabin. It was a letter I thought would make me smile because she missed me. My eyes move to the next letter, which was February 17th, 2004, the poem I wrote her. That letter after that was April 2nd, our first kiss memory.

Just keep the happy letters close.

Moving those letters to the other pile makes me feel a little better. After my heart's regeneration, I feel it break only at the sight of the next letter's date.

April 28th, Jen's birthday. This can't be good.

April 28, 2004

Dear Cal,

I only have one wish for my birthday. It's you. To come home. To kiss me. To cuddle with me. To hold my hand. To take me to our favorite places. To make me laugh.

That's all I want today. I hope you'll magically show up on my doorstep and make me happy.

I want to re-write the poem you gave me last year for my birthday.

I need something to make me feel good right now.

You mean the world to me Jennie

I can't bear the sight of myself without you by my side

We've been at it for two months, going on three, the best of my life

We yell and cry and even after it all we come out on top

You and I are like the moon and the night sky. We are perfect together

We have true caring and every day it grows stronger

Place your hand on mine and I shall do the same, for another wouldn't be the same

A promise we have made, to stand by each other's side

Faithful I will remain, never will I leave you

Until death do us part, reunited in a new world

And do say it I may, our friendship will never die

Waiting and missing you like crazy,

Jennie

The poem I wrote her instead of the one where I told her I loved her.

Cringing at my words, I smile anyway. Every word is still so true. I would do anything for her.

We yell and cry and even after it all we come out on top.

Those words are on repeat in my head.

We've been crying and yelling at each other for ONE WEEK. It's been one week since returning to Jen's life and all we've done is cry and fight. What happy moments have we created?

I feel defeated that after all these letters of Jen waiting for me, this is how I welcome her back. With angry words and tears.

That's because you are a piece of shit.

You can fix this. She has created a complex of you that involves romance, yearning, contentment. You were supposed to make her dreams come true when you came home. You were supposed to see her light up and smile and jump into your arms while you breathed in her smell, held her tight and promise to never leave her again. That's what you said you would do for her. What have you done since? You've made her cry more times in the last week than in the last seven months. Make it right for her.

My brain wants to explode from the bitching coming from Angel, but she's right. Plopping myself on the couch, I pick up my phone sitting next to me.

My fingers hovers over her name.

If you don't fight for her, I will.

That's the only motivation I need to push down on the green button. Jonah had her once. He doesn't get her again. I don't bring my phone near my ear until I hear her voice.

"Cal?" Her voice is fucking honey. I'm a honeybee and my honeycomb is depleted of its substance.

"Hey Jen." Her name runs off my mouth like Jackie.

It's delicious. Even more delicious than Jackie.

"What are you doing?" She sounds like she's been sleeping. I'm part angry at myself for waking her up because I can't imagine how sleep deprived she must be, but because I'm greedy and selfish, I'm also glad she woke up to answer my call.

"I'm missing you." Vulnerability is not something I like to feel, but with her, it's easy to lose control.

"It sucks, doesn't it?" Her soft giggle pierces through my heart.

"A million percent, yes."

Stay in the happiness.

"What are you doing?" I ask her, rubbing my forehead, trying to rid myself of the guilt for wishing I was with her in bed.

"I was taking a small nap. I need to get up, though. Jonah said he was going to stop by. He was supposed to come by yesterday but got caught up late at the hospital."

"Oh yeah, do you know why?" I hate that it's Jonah being able to see her. If only I could trade places with him.

"I think he just wants to make sure I'm doing okay." I hear her grunt, like she's getting off the bed or couch.

"Lucky him. Can I ask you something?"

"Have I ever stopped you before?" Picturing her smile form in my mind, I bite my bottom lip.

"Did you take your pills today?" My gut gets tight. I hope after our eventful couple of days, she'll be honest with me.

"I'm getting up right now to get them. I'm not used to taking them this late, but I'll slowly take them earlier so I can take them before I leave for work or school. It's tough right now with my summer break starting, but I'll be working at the shop and with Max and Lydia all summer, so it'll be to have it as part of my routine."

She shakes the bottles in the background, and the tightness releases. I pull my phone from my cheek to the check the time. 7:45.

"Good. I'm really happy to hear that."

"Yeah, I took them yesterday with my dinner before you called."

Keep being honest with me.

"Yeah? Shit, Jen, I didn't even ask about yesterday. I'm sorry, baby." Pinching my nose, genuinely pissed at myself. Yesterday was a rough day.

"Hey, it's okay. Trust me. I'll be better now." I hear a gulp, followed by two more. Good girl, she took all three.

"I do trust you."

Fuck, fuck, fuck, this is going sideways. Change the conversation!

"So, when can I see you again?" I blurt out.

"I'm not sure." Her uncertainty makes me clamp my eyes shut.

You've ruined it, asshole.

"I just finished reading your birthday poem. The one I gave you instead of the other one." I loosen the tightness of my eyelids and look up at the ceiling.

I'm triggered by a memory, so I talk again before she can even respond.

"Can I tell you a happy moment this time?" My whole body is sparking with euphoria.

"Yes, of course." A door shuts in the background. Jonah's there already? I ignore the thought because this memory is in my top three.

"Let me throw a date out for you. Do you know what we were doing on July 22nd?" There's silence for a moment and I enjoy being on the other end of knowing the importance of a date.

"I want to say yes but honestly, all the years sort of mesh together..." I can picture her frown. More leverage for me to make her smile even bigger by the re-telling of the story.

Adjusting my arm behind my head, I get comfortable.

"Well, you had told me you wanted to sit under the stars and..." I'm cut off by her.

"Eat Chinese food."

"And eat Chinese food." My smile is getting bigger and bigger. Angel is loving me right now.

"Do you want me to tell you this story?" I ask for her permission.

"Yes. I remember this day now. One hundred percent one of my top three favorite times together."

"Okay. Well, I can't remember exactly when you told me this was one of your teenage dreams, but I obviously had to take advantage of it. We were driving around in my truck one night, sometime in May or June. Whenever it wasn't raining, we would always try to drive around. Despite the chill, we had the windows down. God, you looked beautiful every time with the wind blowing through your hair. I was so distracted looking at you, but you hardly noticed. You looked over at me and suggested we get blankets and pillows, load them into the truck, find a park, and watch the stars. You wanted to eat Chinese food and eat my chocolate chip cookies. Do you remember that?"

"Yes." Her voice is quiet.

"I had to wait until after July 4th because, you know, I had to do the spectacular kiss under the fireworks. I had picked you up that afternoon after you worked. We already made plans to get Chinese food and take it to a park. I don't think you noticed the mound of blankets and pillows in the truck's bed, and I was worried you'd see or smell the cookies in the back seat. That night was supposed to be special for you. I wanted to make all your teenage dreams come true."

Bringing my arm out from under my head, I place it over my heart. Why can't she be here with me?

"I don't think you noticed the time, but I took the long way to get to the park." I chuckle out loud at the memory. Jen laughs with me.

Thank fucking God.

"I took us to Discovery Park, and we walked to the Bay. We rarely went to the west side of the city. I'll never forget your face when I got out of the truck to set up the bed with blankets and pillows. I think it was a mix of confusion, then recognition, then I don't know, but you had a giant ass smile on your face. You covered your face with your hands, and I stopped messing with the blankets and walked to your door. I'd never seen you do that before; you looked exposed. I brought your hands off your face and had you look at me. Do you remember what I said to you?"

"You said you loved me and quoted a poet. You said *out of all the stars, you were staring at me.*" I smile at her response. Verbatim.

"I only want to stare at you. There is nothing more beautiful." My heart feels like gold, and I can feel a teeny tiny Jen carry my heart along this invisible string to hers.

Don't drop it, baby.

I lose my grin when I hear a sniffle through the other side of the phone line. Of course I made her cry. That's all I ever seem to do lately.

"Jen, what's wrong?" It felt as if Angel was controlling my voice, talking lightly and gently.

"Cal..." She's sniffing through the one syllable of my nickname. I picture her tethering on our invisible string, balancing my golden heart.

"What's wrong, baby? Talk to me."

"I covered my face because I was blushing. My face was on fire that night. My cheeks were hurting so much from smiling that I thought my left cheek was going to make a dimple like my right. I loved you more than I thought possible, but you kept on exceeding my expectations every time we got together. It's like you took the words from my mouth, all my teenage fantasies, stored them in your pocket and then made them come true. I was the luckiest girl in the world." Her voice trembles and I feel the back of my throat become dry.

The only word I can focus on is *was*.

You can do this. You can have a tough conversation with her without getting angry and without her crying. Be gentle.

Angel doesn't realize that I don't want to have this conversation, but I also don't want to end the conversation. Fuck, why does Angel always have to win?!

"Don't consider yourself lucky anymore?"

Jen was a pretty predictable person. I always knew when she was keeping a secret. Always knew when something was wrong. Always knew when she found something out and wanted to tell me. But for the first time, Jen shocks the hell out of me. I was not expecting her reaction. Her infectious laugh startles me that I instantly sit up on the couch.

"Oh, that's a good one!" she's cackling over the phone.

I can't help but to chuckle myself. I'd do anything to make her laugh. It's one of her best qualities, probably second best to her eyes.

"What's so funny about that?"

"Cal...," she pauses. "You've seen my life, right? Seen how disastrous it's been. In what realm would I be lucky?"

Her words make my rage meter rise. She's more deserving than anyone to have good things happen to her. I'd turn the world upside down and shake all the shittiness from it, flip it over and hand it back to her.

"You deserve good things, Jen." Angel takes over my voice again. I'm glad because Angel's right. There's silence for what feels like an eternity.

"So do you, Cal." I ponder my next set of words, hoping Angel will take over to say something sweet and kind. Instead, Jen speaks.

"Well, Jonah has been staring at me like I'm a crazy person, so I better get going." I fall back onto my couch and let my head hang back on the top of the couch. A strange feeling enters behind my eyes.

"I hate saying goodbye to you."

Honesty and anguish don't mix. I can feel my golden heart crash into a million pieces, but not because of Jen. Because of me. We wouldn't have to hate goodbyes so much if I DIDN'T MESS EVERYTHING UP. Moisture has entered the corners of my eyes. I ignore Devil, telling me to suck it up.

"That's why we don't say goodbyes. We say goodnight, remember?"

I think my honeycomb will always want more. I could listen to her talk all day, every day. Especially when she says sweet things like that, the nectar is most sweet.

"I love you, Jen. I know that might be abrupt and crazy to say at a time like this, but I love you so goddamn much. There hasn't been a day that has gone by where my love has wavered. There are special moments in my life that I have fallen more in love with you, but it's only ever been you. I'm so sorry I fucked up. I'm trying to make this better. So I will say my goodnight, I will keep reading and when I'm done, I will come find you and love you even more. I will make you feel like the luckiest woman in the world again, and I'll do whatever it takes. Okay? So goodnight, Jen. I will talk to you soon."

I'm not entirely sure when courage and adrenaline entered the game, but I'm thankful they play. Jen needed to hear that. Especially at a time where she was in a good mental state. She needed to remember those words.

I sightly panic at the extended quietness.

Give her a minute, she'll respond.

Angel has yet to fail me during this conversation, so I wait.

I hear muffled chatter.

Jonah.

Fuck. He's going to kill me for making her cry.

Jen, give me the phone. What the hell did he say to you? Why are you smiling-crying? He isn't supposed to be talking to you!!

Jonah's word stampede through me. I want to be the one with her right now. Suddenly, I hear shuffling and hard breathing.

"Jen, what the hell is going on?" My heart rate rises. I stand up, pacing back and forth until I decide to go on the balcony. Jonah would never hurt her. I don't think he would...

Then I heard a *click.*

"Cal?"

"Jen, what is going on?! Is Jonah trying to hurt you? I swear to God I'll murder that motherfu..."

"Well, he was trying to chase me to get the phone, but I ran into my room and then locked my closet door, so I'm safe for now. I'll tell him you'll pick a fight later." I hear her smile. The teeny tiny Jen in my chest is picking up my golden heart pieces.

"Anyway, that was really sweet of you to say. I want you to know that I love you, Cal. I've only ever loved you. Jonah would literally die if he heard me say that in front of him and I don't know CPR." I laugh wholeheartedly. Can we please stay in this moment forever?

"And trust me, you aren't the only one who messed up. I have just as much a guilty conscious on me as you do, and I hope we can still love each other after all of this is over."

"After what is over?"

"You reading the letters? Just like I told you to keep the happy letters nearby, I will keep this conversation close to my heart. I know eventually, you are going to hate me and I'm preparing myself for it because I deserve it. But right now, just know that I love you."

Is she playing a sick trick on me? I'm going to hate her for what?

Get out of the storm.

"I gotta go. I'll talk to you soon. Goodnight, Jen." *Click.* See how she likes it when she does it to me.

I toss my phone across the room and shout my favorite word as loud as I can.

Just burn the letters. You know you want to. Pack your stuff and leave town. Leave her behind. Start over somewhere.

Should I? Do I let Devil win this fight?

Jennie

I look down at my phone at the abruptness end of the call.

Sulking, I pull myself together to prepare for Jonah's harassment. When I open the door, he's already standing there, his hand pulling me up. Without speaking, we walk back to my living room. I can feel Jonah's eyes pierce through me. Disappointment feels the air between us.

You shouldn't be talking to her.

His words replay over and over in my head. I sit on my couch and Jonah sits on his oversized chair. I find the willpower to lift my head and look at Jonah. My rainforest drizzles.

"Why would you tell him to not talk to me?" The words taste like bile. Jonah looks away from me, unable to answer me right away.

"Jonah, look at me and answer me. Why would you tell him to stay away?" I untangle my legs from each other and sit criss-cross on the couch. My heart rate is slowly increasing.

Did something happen when Cal was at his apartment?

"Because he keeps hurting you, Jennie!" He stands up angrily and puts his hands on his head. Jonah doesn't handle anger very well. He paces around my living room for a few moments. I let him do so, knowing he's feeling uncomfortable with this feeling.

Silently, I compare Jonah and Cal. Cal was never an angry person, he was just hot-tempered. He had a short fuse, something that was both a blessing and a defect. Jonah was the most patient person I've ever known. He finds joy in caring for people. He was level-headed and practical in dire situations.

I snap back into reality and realize Jonah is sitting at the bar facing me.

"You were thinking of him, weren't you?" That was one thing Jonah and Cal both shared, though. Directness. They wanted answers.

I wipe my eyes clear to see him better.

"That's not a fair question to ask. I was thinking of both of you." Mumbling under my breath.

"Yeah, but it's not the same. I told him to stay away from you to give you time to get better. You were better, Jennie. You were good for six months. Until the day you knew he was coming home. Why would you do this to yourself? To him? To me? You let me down, Jennie. I thought you were good, and I trusted you could do this by yourself."

"I just wanted to be good for him. My bandages weighed me down, physically and figuratively. Just wanted him to see that I had been okay without him." My eyes prickle with water again.

"Okay, but you weren't! You had to start medications *because of him*. You had to be stitched together *because of him*. Literally! You had to start therapy *because of him*. You had to marry me *because of him*." I shoot my eyes at him, sad to hear him say that.

"I don't regret marrying you, Jo. Was it my first choice? No. But I understand why you did it. Why we had to do it. I would have gone off the rails if I didn't have you to protect me. For those six months, I was in a safe haven. I know you would not let nothing bad happen to me. Cal is back though and I'm no longer your problem. We agreed to that. When Cal would come home, you would let us figure it out. You would let me go." My voice is weak and strained from trying to convince myself that I wanted Jonah to let me go. I want Jonah to pull me close and tell that he still loves me.

As much as I want that, Jonah is not Cal. Cal was always the missing piece I needed.

I sniffle and stare around my living room. It's been many months since we've been down the rabbit hole of arguing. This used to be the normal for us.

"Has Calvin told you anything about after the trip? What happened to him?"

My heart sinks into my stomach. The question I've wanted answers to for four years. I feel sick to my stomach, thinking Jonah has even a hint of information to give me. Without speaking, my eyes move back to him and shake my head.

"When I followed him the other night, he ended up at some corner convenient store. He stopped in front of the whiskey and just stared at it, like the bottles were talking to him or something. Then he crashed onto the floor, like something was hurting his heart. He was grabbing his chest. I obviously checked to make sure he wasn't going into cardiac arrest, but he was fine."

Jonah's story is haunting me. Is this what I needed to know all along? I'm clutching the pillow to my chest without realizing it, but I sense Jonah's story isn't finished, so I grip it harder, preparing my heart and soul for the worst.

"I told him about his behavior the next morning when he woke up at my place. He said..." Jonah stops mid-sentence and I contemplate throwing the pillow at him. He appears stressed.

"I don't even know if I should even say any of this to you. Calvin will probably kill me if he finds out I told you any of this."

"I'll protect you like you have protected me all these years. Tell me, Jonah. What did he say? Please tell me." My voice cracks and I'm on the verge of tears again.

My mind is thinking *he got drunk and knocked up some girl, he killed someone, he ran away from the police.* Jonah looks at me with sad eyes. I can sense the confliction he's feeling. But I'm hoping my puppy dog eyes are doing the trick for him to feel persuaded to tell me.

"I don't know the specifics but, I guess he just said that he got drunk after you guys left and something happened at a bar. Some guy was mouthing off to him and Calvin just lost it. He didn't go into details."

I feel dazed and confused.

A million questions have now entered my mind about what happened after we left Cal at the house. What the hell happened to him... My heart breaks for the both of us. Whatever hell he put himself through, I want to comfort him. The urge to want Cal to answer my questions at this very moment is dangerous. We just ended a conversation on weird terms, so I know he doesn't want to have this conversation right now. As much as it kills me, I will have to wait for my answers about what happened to him.

I release the pillow from my death grip and lay it on my lap. One of the best things about Jonah is how I never have to explain my silence to him. He lets me feel my feelings, never poking or prying me. I need to remind him I'm grateful he told me the parts of the story he knows.

"Thank you for telling me that. I appreciate it. I hope one day Cal can tell me what happened."

I give Jonah a weak smile. He walks over to me on the couch and sits down. He wraps his arms around me and pulls me close to him. Clamping my eyes shut, I feel all the bad energy leave my body.

Jonah's care and love are so genuine and sweet. He only wants to make sure I am okay and happy and healthy.

The feeling of being wrapped in his arms reminds me of our six months of bliss mixed with torture. Burying my face in his chest, I take in a deep smell of him.

"What did you like best about being married to me?" I mumble to his chest. He squeezes me, pulling me closer to him.

"Ah, Jennie. You really want to have this conversation?" He jokes.

I lift my head to look at him. His stubble is so attractive and new. Running my fingers along his jaw, he sighs, enjoying my touch. I realize how similar Jonah's eye color is to Cal's. My confliction trap eats me more. Staring up at Jonah for a moment, I get lost in watercolor pools of blue.

"The best part was this. Knowing that you were breaking and struggling, but when you would look at me like that, I felt like I had some sort of hold on you. I wasn't ever going to let you fall. I still won't. Knowing that you needed me gave me a high." He whispers to me, feeling the heat of his breath on my cheek.

I drop my hand from his cheek and lay my head on his chest again. Jonah made me feel alive. Made me feel like Cal was an idiot for walking out on me.

Again, silence falls between us. Jonah's heartbeat is pounding against my cheek. Even four months later, Jonah makes me feel like I'm his. I'm only his.

I pull his drawstring from his sweatshirt and toggle with it. Jonah brought a change of clothes over and obnoxiously slammed the bathroom door to change when I was on the phone with Cal.

After all the times of seeing Jonah in his scrubs, I still prefer him in his casual clothes. His light gray hoodie and black sweatpants complement him. Being a nurse, Jonah takes his nutrition and exercise seriously. I'm not sure if he still does, but when we were married, he went to the gym after his shift before hurrying home to me. His arms were firm and I'm not sure if Jonah liked buying a size too small or if his arms were just that big. I never asked. I just liked the look of them. Feeling more comfortable, I swing my legs over his thighs so I'm practically sitting sideways, leaning into him.

"What was the worst part about being married to me?"

My stomach flutters a bit because I hate knowing there is something bad Jonah would say about me.

In his eyes, I'm a glass sun catcher. I have no imperfections; except I can crack easily. I'm more beautiful in the light, just enough for sunlight to refract and illuminate my color and unique design. Jonah would hang me where everyone could see me, to make me feel important. I feel him sigh again, hating that we are having this conversation. Jonah only wants to talk about happy things. He's just a happy guy.

"Jennie, c'mon. Don't do this." His hand instantly starts rubbing up and down on my arm, coaxing me for hurtful words. *I have experienced more hurt and damage. Whatever you have to say won't hurt me.* I twist his drawstring around my fingers and find myself leaner closer to him. He's the world's best comfort.

"There has to be something, Jo. One thing you hated. That drove you absolutely bonkers." I lift my head off his chest to look at him.

Every time I look at him, I'm in awestruck. Confliction taps me in the gut, realizing how equally handsome he and Cal are.

I smile at him, brushing my hand through his hair. A gesture I did for both men. It brings me comfort to feel them in my hands. Jonah closes his eyes and I can only think he is thinking good things. He tilts his head in favor of my hand, caressing his hair.

"Tell me." I accidentally say this seductively. My voice almost felt like a moan, a want for Jonah. His eyes snap open at me, thinking the same thing. Without losing my stare, he cups my cheek with his free hand.

"There wasn't anything that I disliked about being with you. You were and still are perfect. My wildflower." I stop playing with his drawstring and stare into space, replaying the words in my head.

You were and still are perfect. My wildflower.

I wrap those words in tissue paper and store them in the safest part of my heart. Jonah brings me closer to him so that I'm fully encapsulated in his arms.

"Was there anything you liked about being married to me?"

The way he asks this question makes me fall apart. As if there wasn't anything special about us. That I would have to think long and hard about trying to find the smallest thing that I loved about being with Jonah.

Little does he know, there's an infinite number of things. From his level of comfort to the easiness of talking to him about the toughest things. From his morning kisses to his evening kisses, I was always excited for both. Jonah never made my hand sweat, so I never had to fear of removing my hand from his. The best, most rewarding thing about Jonah was his demeanor.

Snuggled close to him, I find the words to say.

"Jonah, the best part was and still is that you never bring me down from a high. You said that taking care of me was your joy. My dreamland is when you care for me and make me happy and want me to be better. You never bring me down like he does." The words slip unconsciously from my mouth.

Cal is the most important person in my life, but his biggest fault is his death grip on the rope he has to hell. I don't think Cal *enjoys* bringing us both down, but he does it anyway. Just like how he did ten minutes ago. How he suddenly ends a call, like he's lost in thought. Instead of talking to me about his feelings and emotions, or letting me care for his mind, he shuts me out and we both crash.

I don't want to spend the rest of my life in hell. Even if it is with Cal. Jonah brought me out of there, and whatever contentment I'm striving for, I want to bring Cal here with me.

"I hate when you think about him." Jonah breathes into my neck. This is the most intimate we've been since October. One of the worst months and I let Jonah hold me close every single day. My mouth quivers at his words.

"I wasn't thinking about him." I lie. Trying to unlatch myself from Jonah, my confliction is becoming a dangerous game.

"You get tense when you do. Your heart beats fast. Your eyes get super focused, like you're trying to piece everything together. You fidget with your hands. He isn't good for you. Let me take care of you."

This time, I separate from him. I stare at him, disappointed. Angry. Sad. He wasn't expecting me to move to the opposite end of the couch. He gives me space but holds out his hand, in case I might grab it.

"Jo, you don't get to do that. You knew I was waiting for him. You don't get to manipulate me to think badly of him and try to get me back. I love you, truly. I have from the moment I met you in the hospital and I still do, but like I have told you time and time again, Cal has always had a piece of my heart. I need to figure out if the piece he has ahold of will make me feel complete again. I deserve to feel complete."

Without hesitation, I grab his hand. Jonah brings me so much goddamn comfort. I yearn to be enveloped in his kisses, starting from my forehead and working his way down my body. I crave his embrace, to lose myself in thought as his arms wrap around me and let my world shatter. Even if it was for a few months, Jonah made me feel like I could be happy again. Right now, we could be happy again. I ache to sit on his lap while he showers me with compliments about my beauty, worth, potential happiness, and powerful future.

There's a part of me that's drawn to the idea of falling in love with Jonah again.

But I can't.

I blink back tears as my visions haunt me. Jonah is at my fingertips, and I could have him if I wanted.

"I think you should leave, Jonah."

Every fiber in my heart breaks. My inner devil is internally screaming and I can feel her twist my insides.

Don't let him go!

Jonah looks at me in disbelief. "What?" He says like he's sucking in more air.

I can't bear to look at him. If I do, I'll want him to stay. I'll see the pain in his eyes, and knowing how much pain I've caused him already, I'll fall under his spell.

Standing up, I wrap a blanket around my body, preparing myself for at least an hour of depression. Jonah stands up too, but he walks to me. I have no energy to push him away. Instead, I feel him envelop me. His chin rests on his head and I keep my hands in front of me, holding on to the fibers of the blanket. If I wrap my arms around him, then I'll keep him forever. He moves his hands up and down my spine, comforting me in the most delicate way.

"I will always wait for you, Jennie. I will keep fighting for you because you're worth fighting for. You understand me?" Without speaking, I sob instead. I carefully store those words, wrapped in five layers of tissue paper, in my heart box, hoping to protect them from damage.

I'm thankful it's Jonah who pulls away first, because I know I couldn't. He lifts my chin to look at him. My blotched face. Puffy red eyes. Swollen bottom lip from nervous biting. My cheeks flush, but blushing at the same time as I fall back into the feeling Jonah gives me. He brushes his fingers through my hair like claws, right above my ears, and when I think I couldn't take anymore... Jonah's lips press against my forehead. The most tender, infatuated kiss.

"I don't know that I trust you to leave you by yourself right now. You feel awfully ... sad." My face is resting on his broad chest and I chuckle out loud. Out of all the words, he chose sad.

"I'll be okay." I wipe my face with the blanket. God, I'm so tired of crying.

Jonah pulls away from me to look at me again. I feel embarrassed about how I look, but I know he doesn't care.

"Please, for the love of God, call me if you need something. Don't call Calvin. He'll make it worse." I laugh again, knowing Jonah isn't kidding.

If only he knew the conflict that was happening in my body. Team Angel is all for Jonah. She's buzzing around in my head, telling me to just let him stay. Devil is team Calvin. She would shove Jonah out the door if I let her take over.

"I promise I will."

Jonah continues to hold me. I know he's stalling, trying to stay with me for as long as possible. I don't want him to go, but I don't trust myself around him either. How I've had such decent self-control this evening with him is beyond me.

All good things come to an end. This I have lived.

Jonah pulls away from me and leans down to pick up his duffle bag. My eyes follow his bag, hoping something in me will be courageous to tell him not to go. Jonah looks at me, wanting the same thing. He moves to the door, and he pulls me by the hand. I follow him and stop at the door, hating myself for letting him leave.

"Call me tomorrow, okay?" His voice is low and quiet. I nod my head, unable to produce words because Devil is gripping my throat.

After I watch him leave and shut the door, I'm left with loneliness.

The worst of all the emotions.

Jonah's cologne lingers throughout the living room. I can feel his arms still around me. I can feel his presence sitting on the couch.

Depressed, I wander to my room. Instead of Jonah, though, it's Cal who overcomes me.

Cal's cologne now overwhelms me. I can imagine him holding me close on the bed, reading my birthday letter. I can picture his smile and the way he looked at me while I was changing. Desperate to want to hear his voice, I turn off my phone to resist the temptation.

You are getting better for yourself.

I pull the blanket over my head and cry. I mentally check off another day that tears have been part of my daily routine. As I silently sob, thinking of Cal, and how we were so much in love in the beginning, but now I fear there is no more love to share.

Calvin

I fell asleep after ending the call with Jen. Three hours have passed, and I wake up to the time showing ten minutes until midnight.

I wipe my eyes to get rid of the grogginess. I sit up off the couch and pick up my phone from the floor. There's only one text.

Jonah: I'll do anything for her, man. Let me take care of her.

Panic sets in. What happened after I got off the phone with her? As badly as I want to call Jen and make sure she's okay, I text Jonah back instead.

Cal: Is she okay?

If insomnia wasn't on my radar, it is now.

I grab some coffee grounds and make a pot of coffee. It'll be a late night reading these bullshit letters. What I wouldn't do for a drink of Jackie right about now...

I contemplate calling Henry and see if he wants to meet at a diner. I need to get out of this apartment or everything is going to be destroyed into a million pieces. Again, I remember it's midnight.

"FUCK" I shout to no one. I plop myself down on the couch when my phone illuminates. I reach for it to see Jonah's name.

Jonah: I was going to spend the night with her, to make sure she was going to be okay. Then she thought of you. You ruined everything.

Jonah: She's damaged BECAUSE OF YOU. I wish you were still in prison or just somewhere far away from her. She needs peace and happiness and love. I can give that to her.

Jonah: you have such a fucking hold on her, it's sickening to watch. You don't even know man...

This doesn't feel like the same person I was talking with yesterday and I'm slightly concerned he may be drunk. My hands tense around my phone. I consider crushing it in my palm. My rage-o-meter is in danger mode. I don't know what a suitable level of adrenaline is, but mine feels tripled. Blood is coursing through my veins. I re-read the texts a few dozen times.

I was going to spend the night with her.

She thought of you. You ruined everything.

She's damaged because of you.

You have such a hold on her.

I have to get rid of this anger. This feeling that I want to murder someone... again, needs to go. Grabbing my jacket and keys, I slam the door behind me.

I know who can make this better. I walk in that direction, hoping the cool air will bring down my rage.

After Henry helped me secure the whereabouts of Jen, I wanted to stay in contact with him. He was more than helpful. He helped me find the essential resource I needed to survive.

Walking towards the diner, Henry was awake and said he would meet me there. I'm hating myself for thinking that finding Jen was a mistake.

I turned her universe upside down four years ago. In the time I've been gone, she shifted it to being normal again. Then here I come, deciding to turn it upside down again.

She doesn't deserve that. She deserves a wholesome life that is full of warmth and happiness and normalcy. All I've done is give her coldness, sadness and unpredictability.

My throat feels like something, or someone, is strangling me. I pause on the sidewalk to collect myself. Grasping my throat, I wonder if I'm imagining a murder attempt. I'm likely high on the priority list of several people who want to harm me. My chest feels like it's on fire. I bring my other hand over my sternum, hoping by some miracle my touch will soothe the flames. It doesn't. My legs give out on me, and I fall against the brick building. My body is losing the spark.

There's only one thing that gives me light. One person who can relight my flame, to make me shine. No matter how many times I decide to be an asshole and blow out her light and give her darkness, she always brings me solace. And that's something I don't deserve.

A hand shakes my earthquake on my shoulder. Through my blurry, wet vision, I see a shadowy figure leaning over me.

Henry.

He crouches down to me, and it's only then I can clearly see him. It's close to one in the morning and the Seattle suburban streetlights flicker. They've never been good for night walking.

"Hey man, you good?" Henry gives my shoulder a squeeze, bringing me back to center. His sarcastic tone has taken a drastic turn since the first time I met him. I've had a mini panic attack in front of him about a month ago. I went down a spiral that we would not find her.

I try to catch my breath but only spit out Jen's name.

"Dude, no. We aren't calling Jennie. I'll get you through this. What the fuck does she usually do? If she does some sweet kissing shit, then I'm walking away."

I attempt to laugh, but my chest aches. To breathe hurts like hell. It reminds me of the first time I saw Jen coming into *Coffee & Honey*. She was so breathtaking. Then I remember when I saw her again at Whole Foods. I thought my rib cage was going to break from the amount of pressure aching in my chest. I didn't think she could get more beautiful, but she did. She was always shining, even when she wasn't trying.

I realize Henry has sat next to me on the wall.

"She does the 54321 technique." I say, still holding my chest. The pain is intensifying.

We could just call her.

Angel never misses the chance.

"I heard of that when I was doing therapy. How do I do it?"

Henry is a different good-heartedness. After being in prison with men who seriously don't give a fuck about anything, I thought all men were like that. Hopeless. Unempathetic. Cold-hearted. I begged to myself that I wouldn't become that way. Not for Jen. She deserved someone good.

Little did I know, she had someone good for her. I feel a twinge in my chest at the thought of Jonah. I grab my chest with both hands, hoping for any sort of relief.

"Fuck, just call her. Please. It'll make it better." I wheeze at Henry.

He believes in delayed gratification. I can hear his thoughts of *you'll thank me later,* circulating in his mind as far as calling Jen. But it's never been this painful.

The thoughts of Jonah being close to her in bed. Jen wanting him to stay makes my brain want to explode. The words of Jonah are strangling my heart.

She's damaged because of you.

That was never my end game. The brokenness of Jen is no fucking trophy. It's worse than prison.

We can make it better. We will be better for her. Angel to the rescue.

I get my phone out of my pocket and toss it to Henry.

"Please, Henry. Just call her. You can strangle me later." My eyes have been fighting back tears for several minutes.

I miss her. I hate the way I ended the conversation earlier. Henry sighs in disappointment as he unlocks my phone, and I can see his fingers slide on the screen to find her name.

"Your death wish, my dude." The screen changes to her name and he switches to speakerphone. The dial tone begins and Henry holds the phone in between us.

One second. Two seconds. Three seconds. Four seconds. Five seconds. Six seconds. Seven seconds.

Voicemail.

Someone should have just run me over because nothing else mattered except hearing her voice. Henry ends the call and drops my phone in his lap.

"Just keep breathing, man. We'll get through it."

As I let the wind brush against my face, I try to regulate my breathing. I close my eyes and reminisce about the friendship I've created with Henry.

After we met the first time, Henry disclosed to me that his had parents died to a drunk driver when he was fifteen. He had become obsessed with finding the son of a bitch. Not to get even or to make his life hell, but for closure. He just wanted to know that his parent's killer was amongst us and he would track him down until the worst karma attacked him.

Henry became a PI for that reason. He was driven by determination, and possibly obsession, that he would keep his eyes on the fucker who destroyed his life.

When Henry was twenty-five, the drunk driver met his fate. He discovered the guy was a dealer in the University District. Henry wasn't sure if they were students or not, but they cornered him in an alley and left him for dead.

He watched the whole thing from afar, thanking whatever gods for sealing his fate. Henry was going to quit his PI job after that, but a few individuals had reached out to him, desperately needing help.

He found comfort in wanting to help people.

That reminds me of someone...

My case was different.

When Henry asked if the person I was looking for was because of hate or love, I was the only person he'd met who was chasing someone for love. He could relate to hunting for a vengeance, but love was a different ballgame.

He asked so many unecessary questions about what happened between us, how we got separated, and why I was so desperate to find her.

Henry says he's never been in love. Naturally, this intrigued him.

He had never done hunting on someone for love and he felt the end goal was a different kind of victory. He said something like Lydia about rooting for us. Henry was on my team. He wanted to see me do better and be better for myself and for Jen.

I've been doing the 4,7,8 breathing without realizing it.

Inhaling for four, holding for seven, and exhaling for eight. Repeatedly until I feel my chest relax.

Until I can see clearly.

Until I breathe in the fresh air.

Until I can think clearly.

I drop my hands from my chest and look over at Henry. He's

smirking at me.

Told you we didn't need to call her.

I nudge his shoulder, thankful for his patience, for his stubbornness, and for his friendship.

I wipe my face clear of the attack and try to bring myself to get up, but I don't want to. Henry notices my lack of motivation to get up so we stay sitting against the building.

"Can I ask ya a question?" Henry blurts out. He pulls his hood over his head, noticing the drop in the temperature. I bring my knees close to my chest and rest my forearms on my kneecaps. I continue to keep breathing in through my nose and out through my mouth.

"Yeah, sure man."

I was an open book for him. Besides Lincoln, I didn't have many male figures who were close to me. Until I met Pat. Pat was much older than me, though. Even though Henry was a couple of years older than me, it felt like having a big brother. I didn't feel like I had to hide my past from him. He had a dark past of no parents, foster care, dropping out of high school. We connected in a way with having shitty luck in life.

"Do ya have a letter on you?" I drop my head, magically feeling a hole burning in my jacket pocket. I don't answer because I can't. Why do I even have a letter on me anyway? If something were to happen to me again, like returning to jail, I would have something precious to hold on to.

Who knows, you might have the worst of the worst letters sitting in your pocket. Good thinking, dumbass. You should've grabbed a letter that made you happy.

Henry takes my unresponsiveness as a yes. I can see him subtly shake his head.

"Can ya read it?" In disbelief, I almost snap my neck to turn to him.

"Fuck no."

"C'mon, why not?" Beneath his hood, I can see his grey eyes upset at my answer.

"Because some letters are intimate. There have been some that get me so fucking pissed off. Some make me cry. Some of them make me smile like a fucking teenager. I don't know what kind of letter I have. I never know what she's going to give me."

"So what? I know how much she means to you, man. I just want to hear what kind of hell you've been living in. You don't have to do this alone." I feel my pocket get heavier and heavier,

"Ugh, I hate you." My hand digs into my pocket and I lift the grenade. I'm not prepared to set myself off. Internally, I try to convince Angel to tell me that this is a good letter.

No response.

I read the date on the front of the envelope.

"Nope, we aren't reading this one."

I'm even more pissed off that I didn't check the date of the letter before I picked it up. I chuck the letter in front of me, Jen's handwriting still visible. To conceal the letter, I covered it with my shoe.

The worst possible letter is right here, right in front of me.

I told you, didn't I?

I wonder if Henry has any sedatives to shut Devil up?!

Henry pushes my foot and picks up the letter.

"Fine, I'll read it to you like a preschooler."

"Hang on, man. I need a minute before you start."

I feel my throat get dry and I'm wishing I had something to drink. *Jackie.* My nose has that tingling feeling and I feel my bottom lip quiver. I'm clenching my jaw, hoping to hold back the tears.

This can't be fucking real. This isn't happening. I let my head drop and I can no longer suppress what I'm about to hear.

I feel a hand on my shoulder.

"Hey man, it's okay. We don't have to do this. I was just curious, and that was wrong of me to do. You're supposed to be doing this on your time. I'm sorry, man." He's trying to return the letter back to me but I shove the letter back to him. I wipe my nose and try to get my emotions under control.

You need to hear this. This was her life that was shattered.

"Just read it." Anger and sadness are fighting for the spotlight.

"Are you sure?" Henry's voice is full of caution.

Angel, where are you?! Tell me this will be okay. Tell me I will be okay.

Nothing.

There's only Devil.

You'll have to read it at some point. Might as well read it with a friend.

"Yeah, just do it." I clench my fists, hoping I won't kill someone after this.

My breathing just ripples when I try a couple rounds of 4,7,8 breathing. I can't get it under control. For a few moments, I felt Henry's gaze upon me. He flips the letter back to the front.

Like Henry, I put my hood over my head as I prepare to enter the darkest dream I'll ever be part of. I let my tears silently fall as I prepare myself that I won't be able to stop them.

Keep the happy letters close.

Henry clears it throats and looks at the envelope.

"August 17th, 2004."

The year letter. One year without me.

Prepare to break, you son of a bitch.

August 17, 2004

Dear Calvin,

It's here. A year. A year without you.

First I want to say I'm sorry I haven't written you in a few months. The anticipation building up to this day kind of took a toll on me. I haven't been good. I haven't been taking care of myself. The past few weeks have been miserable. I haven't been eating. I have nights of constant tiredness and other nights of insomnia. I can't get my mind to turn off from you.

Despite knowing where you are, I never know if you're okay. I think that's the worst part about this. I so badly wish I could call you to make sure you are okay. I think about it all the time. I just...can't. I'd never be able to stop calling and I wouldn't want you to get in trouble. I'm okay with taking the brunt of the pain in order for you to be okay. We'll be okay when you get out and come back home.

Cal, I've been crying for days. Every day I think I'm going to be okay and all of a sudden, I'm not. I miss the way you hold me when I'm overwhelmed. I miss the way you kiss my temples when we are cuddling, watching scary movies. I miss the way you would kiss the corner of my mouth before you would full blown own my mouth. I miss the way your hand feels in mine, both sweaty and dry. I miss your sweatshirts. I miss the feeling of being the only girl in the world. Without you, I feel like I'm nothing. And I don't like this feeling.

I got fired from my child specialist position last month. Started missing too much work. I blame it on the depression, but Pat says I'm being irresponsible. He lets me work as much as I want. Lately, it hasn't been a ton. I can only handle a couple hours at a time each day. Until I start thinking about something funny or dumb you did while we worked, then I start having panic attacks and I have to leave. Pat understands but I know he's getting annoyed with it. I'm getting so tired of letting him down, Cal. He's all I have left.

I've watched Pirates of the Caribbean every day for the past two weeks. I'm waiting for you to rescue me like Will Turner saved Elizabeth.

I've been trying to watch happy movies. This movie White Chicks came out a couple months ago. You'd hate it because it's stupid. But I know you would probably just watch me laugh the whole time. I miss the way you look at me, too.

Cal, I want you to know that no matter how much I miss you I also hate you so much. Why did you have to do this to us? Why couldn't you just leave with us... what did I do for you to turn your back on me and hate me? Why would you let me go home with someone else? Why didn't you call me from jail? I would've bent over backwards to get you out. But you fucking didn't, you asshole. I'm not sure I'll ever forgive you for what you did. You left me. With this fucking ring as a constant reminder of our broken fairytale.

So yeah, I'm in this phase of I love you but I hate you. And I don't know how long I'll be stuck here. Maybe I'll always be stuck here, even after you get out because there is so much time we are wasting. I have nothing here. You have nothing there. Without each other, what is there left for us?

I've spent thirty minutes trying to write this next sentence but I had a panic attack.

Four years left.

I hate you so much. I also love you more than anything. Please be good. Please think of me. Please don't forget me. Please get home to me. Please just come home.

Waiting with a crushed soul and heart and mind,

Jennie

Every part of me is tense and it's becoming really uncomfortable. I've balled my hands into tight fists. Holding my breath has made my stomach sore. My teeth are causing my jaw to ache from being pressed together. My throat burns, as if I swallowed gasoline. The pressure from clenching my jaw and shutting my eyes is causing my temples to ache, and I'm desperately trying not to visualize Jen writing this letter three years ago. But I picture her.

My lonely Jen. Without me. Without her dad. With no one holding her close.

I picture her on her bed, the one I thought I would spend countless times on whether it was cuddling, watching movies, talking, kissing. Instead, she's curled in a ball trying to write me this letter but having to pause every few minutes to either wipe her eyes, or get more tissues, or curse at the heavens for being alone.

The image breaks me. My face is hot, and I can feel the streaks of tears beginning to dry up. I've balled my knees close to my chest and have hidden my face from looking at Henry. Every word was a bullet right to my chest.

"Shit, man. You're right, I wasn't expecting any of that." I can hear him fold the letter back together and slide it back into the envelope.

I can't bring myself to lift my head off my arms. My body feels like it's carrying a thousand pounds.

Henry lets us sit in silence for a while.

Words are swarming like bees in my head. The letter is on repeat.

I haven't been taking care of myself.

I got fired.

Depression.

Without you, I'm nothing.

I hate you.

Panic attack.

Waiting with a crushed soul.

Every time I think the tears are done, more continue to escape my eyes. She has no idea how lost I was without her. From seeing her every single day, seeing her smile, hearing her laugh. And then, in a span of a couple of hours, she was gone.

I stand up with purpose. Using the back of my sleeves, I wipe my face. Henry stands up with me, sensing my urgency.

"Where are we going?" He's still pressing the letter to me. I don't want this letter, but I take it anyway and place it in my back pocket.

"You are going home, or the diner, or wherever the fuck you venture in the middle of the night. I am going to see Jen." I walk in the direction of her apartment. By walking, it's at least thirty minutes away, but my adrenaline will help me get there in twenty.

"Wait, wait, wait. Calvin, what the fuck? No, dude." Henry jogs quickly to stop me from the front.

Don't make me angry.

"Move, Henry. Yeah, I know this isn't a good idea. I'm probably going to make her cry. We're probably going to say things hurtful and things we don't mean, but for Christ's sakes, I spent three and a half years away from her. I just want to see her. Nobody understands the calmness seeing her face brings to me. Just please let me see her." It's not a question, but a request.

"Let's just go to the diner, grab some coffee, process the letter and then, if you want to see her tomorrow, I'll let you."

Wrong answer.

I feverishly shake my head. My best confidante is not understanding. I spin in a circle, getting frustrated and irritated by each passing millisecond.

"From the very beginning, I told you that this love shit is complicated. I told you that Jen was going to have open arms for me or spit in my face. She's already given me both. I don't know what the fuck is happening between us, Hen. One second I'm falling in love with her all over again, the next moment, I'm breaking her heart. And it's a constant cycle for the past week. I just want to make things right, man."

I pace back and forth, grabbing the side of my hoodie with one hand and grabbing my stomach with the other. I know this isn't a good idea, but I have no control over being able to stay away from Jen. This doesn't feel like adrenaline. It feels like something more.

Fear.

The idea of losing Jen makes me nauseous. And literally.

I'm bent over the nearest public trashcan, emptying the remnants of my stomach. I'm hoping with each spew, the fear is exiting my body.

Henry keeps a steady hand on my shoulder, letting me know he's present. I stand up and wipe my mouth and try to regain my senses.

I try to do the quickest 54321 possible, but I'm only focused on getting to her.

I walk in the opposite direction from Henry.

"This isn't a good idea, man!" His voice feels further away, knowing he isn't walking with me.

I know it isn't, but when have I ever made good decisions?

I trace my lines on my palm until I reach her apartment. The owls and crickets are the only species awake and I'm praying to God that she's awake, and that she'll let me inside and she'll let me hold her. That's all I want to do is hold her close to me.

Jennie

I don't even remember changing my clothes, but when I wake up to use the bathroom at 2:30 in the morning, I'm looking at my favorite Vancouver Canucks shirt and black yoga pants. Somehow, I slipped on my favorite purple fuzzy socks. My feet feel moist as I'm sitting on the toilet, so I take off my socks and toss them to the side. I let my head hang and run my hands over my face, debating if I hate myself for letting Jonah leave or thanking myself for telling Jonah to leave. Either way, the depression still wins because I don't have Cal.

I clean myself up and wash my hands when I knock over the soap and find my heart rate increase.

Three knocks on the door. Gentle but loud.

There's no way Jonah would come back. He isn't supposed to get off until morning. Unless there are texts from him I haven't responded to, and he's been worried about me. He should know how wonky my sleep schedule is right now with my medication trying to set back in my system.

Convincing myself I'm overly tired, I pretend I didn't hear anything. I dry my hands and walk into my living room to clean up my depressive den.

A minute must've passed, and three more knocks happen again at my front door. I eye the door wondering who the hell, what the hell and why the hell. I double check the time on my clock in front of my TV that read 2:33 AM.

Hesitantly, I walk to the door and lift my toes to peek through the peephole. I see a tall silhouette with a hoodie on, but I can't see his face. He's looking from side to side, antsy. I keep watching him until he puts his hands on the doorframe and speaks.

"Jen..." I drop off my toes and gasp.

The only person to call me that. Without a second thought if this was a dream or a drug dealer or an axe murderer, I unlock the door and stand in front of the ringleader who has created the biggest circus of my life.

Clear as the first day I saw him walking into *Coffee & Honey*, my Cal stands in front of me. He lifts his head, relieved to find the door open. We don't say anything, just soaking each other in, staring at the person who left us behind.

I'm scared to talk, to ruin the moment of being ogled by Cal.

"Do you want to come in?" I squeak out.

Cal doesn't blink or seem phased as he walks through the front door. I don't lose eye contact either, as I shut the door and help him take off his jacket. And then, as if our worlds collide, Cal pulls me into him.

It's not a typical hug between two people. This feels different. It needs to be different. I want this to be the hug where Cal accepts all my baggage and mistakes and will continue to love me, regardless.

Crushing my face into his chest, I'm worried about his rapid heartbeat. My arms wrap around his waist, and I press my palms against his shoulder blades. I press my hips against him, fitting into his figure perfectly, as I always have before. Cal wraps his arms over my shoulders and rests his head on the top of mine. He's a mixture of both cold and hot. I can feel him breathing in my hair. He just holds me. So close that I feel I'm going to pass out from the lack of oxygen, but honestly, dying in Cal's arms would win a first place in cause of death.

He just feels... wounded. Fragile.

My strong, hot-headed Prince feels broken in my arms. How can I cure him? I'll give him whatever he wants to feel better. I try to pull away, but he's too strong, so I let myself relax against him. His smell is intoxicating. He smells like a masquerade–mysterious, enticing, and cloaked in danger.

I silently talk to Angel in my mind.

Give us the time. Give us just one night to escape from what's happening now. Let Cal be my Cal and let me be his Jen. All the years ago how we just knew what each other was thinking. Please hop to Cal's shoulder and tell him I am here and I will not let him go tonight.

I hug him tighter, hoping our Devils don't come out to play. He feels me squeeze and reciprocates, squeezing me just a little tighter. And as if Angel is talking to him, he releases me.

Unlike Jonah's eyes, which are pools of the lightest baby blue you'll ever see, Cal's eyes are a dark deep blue, reminding me of the ocean, lit up by a small tint of the moonlight. I've never noticed the speck of gold in his eyes. I'm lost in a trance. Cupping his cheek, I miss his stubble and skin.

"You have small pops of gold in your eyes. It's beautiful." I whisper up to him. I can slightly feel his head lean towards my hand, slowing letting himself go. He closes in eyes as I can picture his words traveling through his brain.

"You're beautiful. I must only light up when I look at you because usually my eyes are black." He remarks back to me, giving me a small grin. It's true. From afar, Cal's eyes look black. Up close, they're soothing to look at.

I breathe a sigh of relief when Cal shuffles his shoes off. He never breaks eye contact with me.

I drop my hand off his face, but he catches it and intertwines our fingers together. He kisses the top of my hand, sending an explosion of fireworks and shooting stars through my stomach. The simplest things he did, now and then, send me into a frenzy.

"Can I stay here tonight?" He rubs his lips over my hand, and I feel his other hand enter my hair.

My God, he's trapping me like a bear. How I missed being trapped...

"Yes." Within a split second of the *s* leaving my mouth, too many things happen for my mind to comprehend.

First, Cal lets go of my hand and claws the other side of my hair.

Then he crushes his mouth into mine.

Third, he lifts me effortlessly, so I'm wrapped around his torso and he's supporting my thighs. He carries me to my bedroom, as if he's been here multiple times already. He probably has my apartment blueprints memorized.

We are in sync with our kissing, twisting our heads back and forth to get better and deeper angles of each other mouth. His knees hit the mattress before my ass feels it. He lays me on my back, continuing to engross me in kisses. It almost feels like he's making up kisses for each minute he's been gone.

I want him to unravel me and make me feel like I'm on top of the world again. For months, I've been stuck in a freaking hole like a groundhog. Trying to weasel myself out, waiting for the perfect opportunity for fresh air.

It's now. I've been suffocating all this time for my moment of pure resuscitation. Cal is making me feel whole again.

I don't mean to, but I moan ever so lightly. Cal moves from my lips and stares down at me, clarifying he heard me right. With my hands in his hair, I pull him closer. He wasn't ready to be hauled to me because he pulls away again. He shifted, his hips on the mattress, forearms supporting his weight near my head. Only using his fingers, he plays with my hair.

"I have missed looking into your eyes. They make me feel safe and happy." He runs a finger over my eyebrow and I shudder for a moment, feeling so overwhelmed by a feeling of happiness. I thought I had more time to prepare myself for happiness, but holy hell, it's crashing into me. I bring my hand to his face, tracing my finger around his lips, savoring every word that escapes it.

"I'm happy and safe with you." I remind him.

I'll tell him over and over until our last breath. Nothing in this world beats the feeling of being in the arms of Cal Klenn. He kisses me hard again and I moan more this time. My hips are behaving badly as they lift to feel Cal. Lost in the morphine, I somehow feel Cal's hand slip through my shirt on my waistline. He's pushing me down, away from him. I try again to push my hips towards him. If he's torturing me, I won't play nicely. Again, I feel resistance as my hips get lowered to the bed. Then I no longer feel the moisture from Cal's lips. I open my eyes and he's beaming at me. The look I have engraved in my mind. I brush the little hairs from his eyes, but I like the feeling of his beard, so I run my hand down his cheek.

"Jen, as much as I want to fucking do that with you, I can't. You are so tempting, but I just want to cuddle and talk and be near you. Is that okay?" I can feel his thumb do circles on my skin.

Devil must've stuck her head in our business.

That bitch.

Internally I frown, externally I grin at him.

As long as he's here with me, I don't care what we do.

I nod my head, unable to accept that we won't be exploring each other. But the way Cal rearranges our bodies makes me smile inside and out. He big spoons me, my body filling the extra space of our bodies. He puts one arm under his head for support and wraps his other arm around me, pulling me close to his chest. I grapple his arm for dear life, wishing time would stop for us. I don't realize how close his mouth is near my ear until he spills his heart.

"I thought about this moment for so many years, Jen. This is how it was always supposed to be. Us two, nobody else around, fitted perfectly into each other. I thought about you every day." He kisses my temple.

I'm staring into space, gripping on to his words before they disappear. My heart feels so full. It's not heavy or empty or broken. All I needed was Cal.

"I've missed you, baby. All parts of you. I'm sorry I wasn't there, but I'm here now, and I'll be here forever. I won't let you go again." He kisses me on the cheek this time.

Every single butterfly is happily flying in my stomach. His words electrocuted my heart, and it's beating normally again. This moment will live in me forever.

I flip on my back to look at him. I can't seem to get rid of my smile, so I lick my lips. He notices and looks at my lips. Before I can even speak, he's kissing them. My hands are running their course in his hair and I'm groaning again. He's entering dangerous territory and quickly ends the kiss. My idiotic smile returns.

"It's only ever been you. Past, present, and future." He pecks my mouth. I turn my head around to cradle against his arm. He moves his hand up and down my arm, gently enough to form goosebumps on my arms.

"Tell me about prison."

I picked the wrong topic.

Cal's hand stops rubbing and I feel his body tense against mine. Shutting my eyes in embarrassment and shame, I kiss his arm in front of me.

"I'm sorry." I whisper, hoping he can hear the crack in my voice. My heart cracks, too.

Stay in the bliss, Jennie.

"I'm so sorry, baby." I kiss him repeatedly on his arm and flip to turn to him again, trying to prepare myself for his facial response to my stupidity. He's already looking at me. There isn't any emotion, though. Knowing I can bring him tranquility when I rub his cheek, I fully turn so I'm on my back entirely and use both hands to grip his face. I try to keep my tears at bay, but the humility is overpowering. I can feel my eyes become watery. He still stares, his eyes looking black despite how close I am to him.

"The rainforest is always so beautiful but heartbreaking." His first words to me are both an insult and a compliment to my eyes. A few tears escape the forest, but his thumb is there to wipe them away.

"Don't cry, please." His voice cracks as he tries to whisper his plea.

Get it together!!!

Angel doesn't normally yell at me, but I deserve it. I close my eyes for a moment to regain my composure.

"What are five things you see?" Cal's voice is calm and so lovely. I open my eyes to find him looking at me like I'm the eighth wonder of the world.

"I'm not having a panic attack." I tell him.

"I know. I just want to change the subject and want to hear your voice."

It's like a shot of chamomile. Cal's words are enchanting. I can make this fun and exciting instead of serious and self-loathing.

"Well, I see the handsomest creature to walk through Washington. I see that dimple on your lower cheek. I need to clean the mirror on my vanity. I see you haven't shaved your beard since the last time I saw you, and I like it. And let's see..."

I look around my room to find something purposeful. I can feel Cal gawking at me, his dimple only getting deeper. This is probably not a good idea to say, but I want to mess with Cal like I used to. My eyes move back to him, knowing he hasn't checked out the disarray of my room.

"I see Jonah left his pants here from earlier." Taking the bait, Cal immediately loses his smile. He snaps his head around my room, looking for the invisible pants.

"Kidding." I snicker and turn his cheek to look at me again, rewarding him with a kiss. Thankful he isn't as mad as I would expect, he kisses me back, dark and deeply. We get lost in each other for a couple of moments until he pulls away.

"Not funny." I don't take his seriousness seriously. I snap my tongue in my mouth and move on.

"Four things I hear, right?"

No, the next sense is touch, but I'll play along. I'm enjoying this game. Slowly entering our little heaven, Cal smiles at me and nods.

"Sure."

"I hear your heart beating fast. Like really fast. It's almost concerning. I hear the tv still on in the living room. I hear the car horns. And I hear your voice in my bed. And it's making me feel alive all over again."

I couldn't be *all* cruel. My feelings towards Cal were strong, and I was so far deep in love with him. He watches me in awe. He brings me close to him again, forgetting about the pants already.

"You make my heart feel like there's a stampede. And as annoying as it feels, it's the best feeling in the world because I thought those animals were dead. I don't care how many animals are running around in my chest, I'll gladly let them. Until I tell them to shut the fuck up and lay down." He makes me chuckle. My chuckle makes him chuckle and together, we are laughing together, just like when we were teenagers.

He pushes hair behind my ear. "Three things you can feel." I slowly stop laughing and look at him innocently.

"Cal..." Hearing his name makes him crinkle his eyebrows, lost in confusion at my hesitation.

"There are more than three things I'm feeling. Next question." I blush instantly.

Some feelings are innocent and others are .... Fiery. I put my hands over my face to hide my rose-colored cheeks. Cal pulls my arms down so he can look at me again. God, I'll never get over the way he looks at me. It drives me crazy.

"Just pick three feelings. I won't push you." I look at him, glaring at his determination. "Your favorite three feelings." He says again.

I hide myself again. My favorite feelings? I can't look at him while I answer this one.

"I feel happy. That's stupid and simple, but God, it feels so good. I feel in love. And I feel..." I pause because I can't say it. This time, Cal touches my skin where my shirt has ridden up, exposing my stomach.

NOT HELPING.

"What else, Jen?" His seductive voice is making me feel trippy. He is purposely making me lose control. I want to push his hand away to make the feeling go away, but lord almighty, it feels incredible. Under my covered arm, I feel my eyes roll as Cal moves in closer to me, still touching my skin but moving his hand up my shirt.

"Cal, stop." I plead, but it comes off as a whine.

"What, is there a bad feeling you're having?" My Canucks shirt is halfway up my body as I feel Cal kiss my stomach.

"CAL!" I scream this time. "You're making me feel turned on, but you don't want to do anything, so you better stop right now or I'm going to feel very angry at you."

I lower my arm but stare at the ceiling, hoping my words sink into him. His breath hovers over my stomach, and it's like pins and needles on my stomach. But I get the worst injection when Cal kisses my stomach again, but I feel his teeth bite me.

THAT'S IT.

I hop off the bed even though I don't want to, snatching a pillow to hit him with it. He's enjoying it too much as his smile is wide and his dimple is an eyesore.

"I had to get you back for scratching me and making me bleed." I put my hands on his hips, and I remember *that* feeling and my crazy reaction. Looking at him, I ponder his response. He's grinning and raises his eyebrow, waiting for me to accept his behavior.

"Fine. But if you want to make it out of my apartment alive, then don't kiss my stomach. Or even bite me. Please."

But if you want to, I won't stop you. I smirk at Angel's internal response.

"C'mere, I miss you already." He pats my side of the bed, and I can't resist. As I take the three steps to get back in bed, Cal removes his hoodie AND shirt. I gulp hard and stare at him, lost like a kid in a candy store. I sit on the bed, soaking in all the gorgeousness of this man. He's a nice-looking ringleader.

"How does it look?" He moves around on the bed so his back is in view. I cover my mouth with my hands and can't help but laugh.

"Oh my god, Calvin." I don't normally use his complete name, but I'm in shock.

"What?! What the fuck is it?" He grabs at his back, as if there's something physical he could get off, but I can't stop laughing.

"Your back looks like my arm."

He doesn't appreciate that comment.

"Stop, that's not funny. What does it look like? I haven't looked since it happened. Been busy..."

Busy being unhappy while you read through the shit show of my life.

"I could be a good abstract artist." I crawl over the bed to get closer to him. Using my index finger, I trace over the faded lines of my scratch marks. It's a maze. Perfect for our circus.

"Jesus." Cal laughs. I don't get through the maze until he turns and grabs me. I wrap my arms around his neck as he holds me by the waist.

"God, I love you so much." He says to me.

I can't help but to smile and blush and feel all the good feelings.

"I love you." I tell him. "Are we done playing? We still have smell and taste."

He lets go of me, only to pull me down to the bed where he spoons me again. The butterflies in my stomach have been multiplying by thousands. It's a feeling I never want to go away. A feeling I've been missing.

He hums out loud. I look up at him to identify what he's thinking.

"Taste is easy." He winks at me. "So just tell me two things you can smell and we can play another game." I move my body in a 180, so I'm lying on his chest. His bare, broad, warm chest. I trace random shapes on his chest.

"Well, the smell of you has been intoxicating since you arrived. Every room smells like you now." I push my nose into his chest, soaking in more of his scent.

It's literally the best drug I've ever known. He's twirling pieces of my hair as I feel his smile.

"What else do you smell?"

"I guess I smell the soap on my hands. Vanilla." I trace lines close to my face so I can get a quick sniff of the vanilla. It's the only soap scent I buy because it makes me feel 0.01% happy. But right now, vanilla scent mixed with Cal's scent is a perfect 100%.

"Perfect."

I try to comprehend his response, but I feel him pull me by the armpit towards him. Then he kisses me.

One thing I taste.

He keeps his arms wrapped around my body and I'm hoping he'll bring a hand to my face so he can stabilize me because I feel like I'm dreaming. And in this dream, I'm falling. I'm falling back in love with Cal. But he keeps his arms on my waist, and after a few gentle kisses, he moves away. I don't want to open my eyes because I'm disappointed he doesn't kiss me more. Instead, I keep my eyes closed and drop my head into his neck, sighing out loud.

"That wasn't easy." I muffle into his neck. Hearing his laugh slightly lowers my frustration. Holy cow, I've missed his laugh.

"Believe me, Jen... I wouldn't be able to stop myself." I flick my eyes open to stare into my bedroom, connecting each word together.

I wouldn't be able to stop myself.

"Do you remember the first time?" Cal stops rubbing my back and I feel a tightness in my throat. *Wrong topic.*

"I could never forget." He whispers. His hand rubs again. I pull myself closer to him, moving my head into the crevice of his shoulder and neck. He pulls me closer, which makes me smile. Thankfully, he can't see that.

"For once in my life, I was thankful my dad had a heavy, deep snore or he would have for sure heard us." The memory lights up a bright light in my heart.

"Uh, he would have heard *you*. I stayed quiet." His emphasizes on me makes me snap my head up to look at him. He's grinning and moves hair out of my face. He looks so relaxed, stress-free, handsome and exactly where I want him to be–with me.

"God, you're so beautiful. I'll never stop telling you that."

I keep hoping the color of red gets less every time he compliments me. Turning onto my stomach, I use one hand under my chin for support. I stare at him, getting lost in the sea. He angles his head to get a better look at me. He's rubbing strands of my hair.

"What?" He says with a smile. Watching his mouth move, I smile back.

"Nothing." I lie. Angel is knocking hard at my heart door, wanting me to express all the feelings.

"Don't lie to me, Jennie Marie." His fingers move to my cheek and feeling his fingers on my face makes me giddy inside. Angel is going crazy!!!

"I guess I just... why did you come here?" I can picture Angel and Devil having their ears pressed on the walls of my heart, wanting an explanation from Cal.

He's silent for a few seconds. It worries me, so I bring my lips to his, to reassure him I love him, no matter what his reasons are. I have missed kissing this man. He looks at me with sad eyes.

"I was with Henry. He read your one-year letter to me." I watch him intently, feeling relief for his honesty, feeling pain for what I wrote to him.

"He read it *to you*?" I clarify. He brings one of his arms to rest behind his head and the other hand comes back to my face, gliding back and forth along my jawline.

"Yeah. At first, I threw it because I couldn't dare read it, so he offered to read to me."

"I want to say I'm sorry, but I'm not sorry.".

"I don't want you to be sorry. It was my fault. I'm sorry you had to be writing that letter in the first place."

"It was such a shitty time, Cal."

"I don't deny that because it was shitty time for me, too." My neck is getting a kink from looking up at him, so I rest my head back on my chest. His hand moves through my hair again.

"I'm glad you're here."

"Me too, Jen. I'm not sure what I would've done if you didn't answer the door. Why were you up anyway?" I swallow hard.

Because I'm depressed and my sleeping pattern sucks.

"I just wasn't tired anymore, so I woke up." I lie to him again.

"Well, I appreciate you being awake. I'm tired now so we can go to sleep?"

He brings his body down onto the bed so he's laying flat. He brings both his arms around me, encapsulating my soul. I position my body so he's embracing me from behind, as I don't feel prepared to sleep just yet. I want to make sure I set myself up for a position from which I can easily get out of bed if necessary. Kissing his forearm, he groans in satisfaction.

"Cal..." I whisper.

"Hmmm.."

"I'm really sorry about everything."

Probably not the best time for that, but my heart is telling me to tell him. Not Angel or Devil, but me.

"I'm sorry too, baby. I'll always be sorry." He kisses the back of my head.

I want to keep talking to him about the past and the future, but I'm feeling guilty for the lack of sleep this man has endured for the past week, so I let him sleep. I keep my eyes wide open, staring into my bedroom.

All I think about is second chances. Of all people in the world who deserve second chances, why me? Don't get me wrong, I'm thankful that Cal came back to me, found me, still wants to love me, but I don't deserve this. I am broken. Into a million pieces, that I'm not even sure Cal would have the time or resources to put me back together. I hope and pray to whatever God gave me this opportunity, that Cal *can* fix me.

It's only been a few minutes, but I sneak out of his arms, leaving Cal peacefully in my bed. I turn off my light and let him dream.

"Have sweet dreams."

Calvin

I wake up in a sweat. *Where am I? Why does it smell like cinnamon and maple syrup? What time is it?* I scrunch my eyes to gather my surroundings.

Jen's room. Her blinds are closed, blocking the sunlight. Sitting up in bed, I take it all in. I pick up a T-shirt, hold it, and smell it. Jen's perfume penetrates my nostrils.

This place is a lot better than waking up at Jonah's place. I don't know where she is, but I miss her.

I've dreamt of this since the moment I knew I wanted to be with her, way back in the day. Waking up with her as my wife, living together, making memories, making mistakes, kissing and making up. It's all I've ever wanted. To start a life with her.

If only it were that easy.

I use her bathroom first before leaving the bedroom. When I open the door, a giant whiff of cinnamon and bacon fills my nostrils. Following the scent to the kitchen, Jen leans across the counter. She's reading the back of the pancake box. I sneak behind her, giving her waist a little squeeze. She jumps and shrieks, then hits my arm.

"Good morning." I kiss her.

Is this a dream? How did I get lucky enough to have someone as beautiful and perfect as her?

"Good morning. Did you sleep okay? I hope I wasn't too loud." She looks tired, almost as tired as when we went to the cabin.

"Did you sleep?" Concern builds in me. She looks at me, sad and ashamed.

"No." Her voice is low.

"Why?" Pulling her towards me, I'm eager to soothe her and free her mind from its heavy burdens that prevented sleep.

"I couldn't, so I read instead." I pull her back, making sure I heard her correctly.

"You what?" I give a little laugh, not because it's funny, but I didn't know that was a past time she was in to.

"Yeah. Here, let me get you some breakfast and I'll read to you. If that's okay?"

"Fuck yes."

I let her leave my arms to walk around the other side of the bar. Then I just watch her in pure awe. My future wife, making me a plate of breakfast. Sitting at the bar, I notice a full bottle of pure maple syrup sitting there. There's an empty glass and a fork and knife. I don't deserve this woman... She turns around from the stove with my plate FULL. Three pancakes, bacon and eggs.

Oh, this is only getting more and more better than Jonah's.

"I wasn't sure how hungry you are. Plus, I don't know how to make much of anything else." I realize she doesn't have a plate when she walks to the fridge to get orange juice. I eat, realizing how depraved of food I am. Henry and I never made it to the diner last night...

"You aren't eating?"

She fills my cups, looks at me like that was a stupid question. She puts the juice away. Still without answering me, she walks around the bar to sit next to me. She rests an arm on the counter and looks at me.

"I'm not hungry right now." Panic sets in as I drop my fork, realizing three-fourths of my eggs are gone.

"What's going on, Jen? You didn't sleep. You aren't eating. Are you okay?" I pull her arm towards me, resulting in her leaving her chair and coming in between my legs. I push hair behind her ears, my favorite thing to do so I can get a better view of her face.

"I'm fine. I just..." she hesitates, and I feel my stomach drop. I knew something wasn't right. Maybe this was too much for her... for me to be here all night.

"Tell me, baby. What is it? Did you take your pills today?"

"It's too early to take them. I won't take them until dinner, maybe a little earlier." She completely dismisses my concern about her, only answering the question about her pills.

"Talk to me. Why aren't you sleeping or eating?" I want to pull her close to me, but I don't want to hide her face.

"I don't want you to go."

Her eyes moisten quickly and a single tear falls slowly down her face. She grabs my waist, holding me for support. Cupping her cheeks, I wipe away her free falling tears with my thumb. I kiss her forehead, hating myself for being here, but loving that I'm here to comfort her.

"Hey, come here." Clawing my fingers through her hair, I wrap my arms around her head to bury her into my chest. I hold tight, but she holds me back tighter.

"I'm right here. I'm not going anywhere, okay? You get to call me. I get to come over. You get to make me breakfast. You get to wear more of my shirts, and meet me for dinner. I'm here now. We have all the time in the world. Even if I have to go, Jen, I'll be back. Okay? I came back the first time for you, and I'll do it over and over."

No matter what words I'm saying, they don't do justice for how I feel about her. I don't want to leave either, but we aren't in a state to stay with each other for a long amount of time yet. There are still wounds that have to burn before they heal... wounds I wish weren't there.

Jen is letting go in my chest. One tear has now multiplied. I hate so fucking much that she is feeling this way. As if she's never going to see me again. It breaks my heart. I want to stay here forever with her. It feels like we're in a little oasis, away from responsibilities, from mistakes, from other people, and we only have each other. That's all we ever needed.

"Can you read to me now?" Whispering in her ear and petting her hair like a wounded animal. I need something to ease the surrounding heaviness.

Hopefully, it's something good.

Fuck you, Devil. Cynical, pessimistic monster, who unfortunately lives in me.

Jen moves away from me and wipes her hands under her eyes. She's still so beautiful. Even with the wet rainforest, she's gorgeous. I don't want to stop touching her, to remind her I'm here. Longing to kiss her, she's already in the living room picking up a book of some sort.

"Well, they aren't like my letters, but they were prayers. I wanted to read them to you. I found my notebook that I wrote all my letters to you last night and just a few scribbles didn't make the cut."

I should probably finish my breakfast before I faint, because knowing Jen, her words are going to cut me. If she cuts me with no food in me, she's going to cut through my organs and then I'll die.

"Can I finish eating my breakfast?" *Thank God for Angel for taking over my vocal cords.*

"Yes! Can I take a shower while you finish?" My heart and stomach both drop in disappointment.

I was hoping we could shower together.

That's only going to make it more painful for her to accept when I have to leave.

"Good idea. I'll be right here. You can leave the door open if you want or I can bring my plate in the bathroom, and we can talk so you know I'm not leaving."

The past few days of seeing Jen's anxiety about my absence have been gut-wrenching. Her diabolical scream from the cabin could keep me awake for years.

I hear her chuckle as she walks to her bedroom, and smile as I hear a sign of life from her.

"I'll leave the door open, but please don't bring your food in here. That's weird."

I shove so much food into my mouth that I'll probably make myself sick, but I feel I haven't eaten since I went out to dinner with Jen. I'm starving, and she's a pretty decent cook.

So much has happened in the past week that if I were to tell a stranger my story, they would probably think I'm making all of this up.

I peer over my shoulder when the shower water starts. Jen has left the bathroom door cracked open a bit. I think about the future where she'll be able to leave the door wide open and never have to worry about whether I'm here.

I down my orange juice, which tastes a million times better than Jackie. Rinsing my plate off, it occurs to me how clean Jen is. Everything is in place, that it almost feels like a person doesn't live here. Her apartment feels like a model home.

Not sure how long Jen's showers are, and realizing I didn't bring any clothes to change into, my daily preparations are at a halt until I get back home. Sitting on the couch, there's an overpowering smell of Jen. She threw her blanket on the cushion next to me.

Did she try to sleep on the couch instead of with me?

I pick up the blanket and lay it over my lap, feeling any remnants of Jen on me. Devil is pushing me to get off the couch and enter the bathroom.... To peel back the shower curtain and see her. To step in the shower with her and clean her. To kiss her in the water.

I lean my head back against the top of the couch and yell out to Jen.

"Are you almost done because I have about 5% of resistance in me before I'm joining you!!!"

My voice tries to come off jokingly, but I'm not. My world feels a million times better when I hear Jen's laugh come from the bathroom. The door opens and Jen is standing in the hallway with just her towel.

"Oh, dear God..."

Jolting my neck up to look at her, an overwhelming feeling enters my vision—it runs to my cheeks, dripping down the back of my throat. I feel it run down my chest, making me completely speechless. The feeling explodes in all chambers of my heart, leaving me feeling like someone shot me in the heart. The feeling enters my stomach like I've swallowed the most expensive, perfect tasting medicine. Although I'm sitting, the feeling makes my knees feel weak and tingly. I can't even appropriately describe the feeling it has on me, specifically in between my legs.

If this moment was just for a millisecond, it was fucking heaven. I just witnessed an angel, and she's a phantom that I want to follow—simply just to see her beauty again.

I remember the first time I saw Jen naked. My body was shaking uncontrollably. It felt like my nerves were shooting fireworks off in my body and for fuck's sake; I wanted the show to end. Despite my attempts to remain calm while touching and kissing her, the fireworks proved overwhelmingly distracting. I apologized over and over to her, but she didn't seem to mind. She was only focused on me.

Right now, I'm not sure if it's the time that has passed between us or if my brain has completely forgotten what a woman looks like, but she's more beautiful than the first time I saw her naked. Even more beautiful than what I saw from her over the weekend. There's something so glowing about her. It could've been the shower. Maybe she used a special face wash, or she ate breakfast before me and the food was moving through her, fueling her body, or maybe it's her medication that was doing good for her, or maybe it's just me...

It's a love-hate relationship that I'm having with myself for the way she acts around me. Right now, it feels as if I'm living with Jen, but the teenage version of Jen and she's embarrassed but secretly wanting me to see her with only a towel on. It makes my heart hurt.

"Oh hush it, I'm changing!" Her voice disappears into her bedroom.

I can't help my raging teenage boy hormones. They are overpowering!

Quietly, I toss Jen's blanket off my lap and tiptoe down the hallway to her bedroom. She has her door wide open, but I don't see her. I hear shuffling from her closet and realize she's probably getting dressed in there. *Damn.*

Then she walks out of her closet with a matching bra and panty. A dark, lace maroon and somehow, I keep my squeal to a minimum.

Or so I thought...

I no longer think Jen was embarrassed to be seen in front of me. She lifts her head from holding a shirt and stares at me, posing her body as if it's the Stanley Cup.

I stop at her door, and it seems against the rules to enter her room, even though she's an adult and her dad isn't here... My eyes are the only body part that move–up and down, over and over, to fully capture the sculpture of Jen. There feels like an invisible fence blocking me from entering Jen's room.

It's Devil...

It's almost as if she turns on a home video in my brain. She makes me relive the moment of the last time I was in Jen's room, only a few days ago. It's almost like there's a giant pill stuck in my throat because I'm having trouble swallowing.

Remember the Jen that lied to you?! She's standing right in front of you. She's deceitful and won't think twice about breaking your soul again.

I'm still looking at Jen, wishing for her to turn into a fairy so she could summon me to her.

Then Devil plays the worst fucking game—connect the dots.

Jonah enters the room.

Accuses Jen of not taking said medications.

Jen admits she hasn't been taking her medicine.

Jonah continues to yell. I storm out of the room, this exact room.

I heard Max's voice, but didn't quite understand the words coming from his mouth. I write a poem and leave.

Jackie. Fuck, I remember wanting Jackie so badly.

Waking up at Jonah's apartment. Him telling me about asking Jen to marry him. I'm still struggling with erasing the visions of Jonah and Jen together...like together-together.

Jonah tells me she wore both of our rings and the fucking agony all over his face from reliving that memory.

How I went home so I could fix things between us. Then I missed her. But I called her and Jonah was already there.

It's pure torture. I hate this game with Devil. She does it on purpose to make me realize the shitty life I have created. There is a picture forming with Jen, but I'm not any of the dots!

She's creating a life without me. Devil will kill me playing this game.

I lean my head against the doorframe. How something so perfect is right in front of me, but I can't have it.

"This isn't fair..." I whisper and somehow my eyes move off her, looking at the floor.

"What isn't fair?" She whispers back, still only wearing her undergarments.

I thought she moved closer to me, but when I look back up at her, she's still standing there. She pulls a shirt over her body, realizing it's not my Canucks shirt. It brings me disappointment, just as much as I see disappointment fill Jen's face that I haven't attempted to move towards her.

Our dance of happy, then sadness just continues.

"I just want to make you happy and I just...I can't." I admit to her. This time, she approaches me. I'm stuck at her doorway, but thankfully she can pull me through. I'm trying so hard to avoid to eye contact with her and I'm biting my bottom lip to keep my impulsiveness in check. The feeling of her hand on my cheek as she nudges my face to look at her. I can't resist. She's so close to me. She smells fucking insatiable. I love being this close to her so I can enter peace as I look into her eyes. My face gets tight at the sight of how goddamn beautiful she is.

"You don't think you make me happy?" Her mouth even smells incredible. Every inch of this woman is flawless. Hearing her say the words makes my heart crash.

I drop my head, but she still has hold of my cheek. She brings her other hand to my other cheek and lifts my head, desperately, to look at her. My eyes are getting fuzzy and my jaw is aching from the tension of my teeth. The truth hurts.

No Jen, I already know I don't make you happy. It's clear as day on your face.

"Come here. Let me read to you."

She pulls me into her bedroom, and I'm thankful I don't burst into flames. She has me sit on her bed and she disappears to the living room. My eyes stayed focused on the doorway, waiting for her reappearance. When she comes in, she lays the journal on her vanity, then uncoordinatedly, she puts sweatpants on. She tilts her head to the side and smiles, settling onto the bed next to me.

"I started this journal when I first met you. Wrote to God about you, asking how on earth someone like you came to be and why He placed you in my life. Then you left, and I started writing your letters in this journal."

She lays a hand on top of the journal as if it's a treasure. It's large with colorful flowers on it. The edges are worn as if someone dragged it around, and a lavender string peeks out from the bottom.

"We were together for seven months until... you know... but I prayed to God and thanked him for every moment He created for us. Our time together was so special and I was just over the moon to be in the same lifetime as you."

"Go ahead, I'm ready." I reassure her. *You aren't though, but nice try.*

I can feel Angel and Devil sit down in a comfy chair in my heart, as if they are going to watch and listen to the best movie that ever existed. She looks at me for a moment, then back down at the book and finds the first page to start on. Before she reads, she sighs, then looks back at me.

"Cal, please don't ever say you don't make me happy." I can't respond because I don't know what to say.

"February 20 2003 -Dear God, Calvin is incredible. He has been so helpful the past couple of days with teaching me things. We have a strong chemistry but he could just be a good actor. Either way, I am so thankful that you brought me to him. He's funny, sweet, and just genuinely makes me happy.

February 27 2003 —Dear God, Calvin is feeling like my best friend. I stayed the night with him last night and he made me breakfast this morning. I woke up, thinking I was in another world. He's so funny that he makes my stomach hurt. He's so nice and sweet that I think his insides are secretly made of sugar and high fructose corn syrup. We have so much in common that it feels unreal. I feel like a nerd talking to him about our interests but he just listens to me and says he likes how my eyes light up when I talk about things I enjoy. We both LOVE scary movies and have planned for a scary movie date tomorrow. I can't wait!! God, he means so much and I can't thank you enough for how happy he makes me.

February 28 2003 —Dear God, we went to the movies tonight. It wasn't really a first date, more of just friends hanging out but when he grabbed my hand during the movie, I felt like spiders were crawling all over my body. Friendly, nice spiders. It was such a nice time. I hope there are more nights like this to come because I'm feeling on cloud nine. If there's something better than cloud nine, please take me there.

March 5 2003 —Dear God, you have taken good care of us. I feel like every time I see Cal (that's what I call him now), I get more butterflies in my stomach. He loves to be around me and he just makes me feel wanted. Thank you for giving me him. This feeling of happiness will never go away!

March 14 2003 —Dear God, we had our first kiss tonight I think I'm going to die from an overdose of euphoria. I never want to wash my lips again. It was just perfect in every way. My happiness level reminds me of that high strike game at carnivals and fairs. Cal pushes himself more and more to make sure I'm happy but I swear to you, he's been hitting the top of the tower since I've met him. He doesn't even have to try... I love being with him, God.

March 29 2003 –Dear God, Cal is my absolute Angel. I can't thank you enough for placing him in my life. I want to be with him, and I think he wants to be with me too. Nobody has ever made me feel the way he does.

April 23 2003 –Dear God, Cal is by far one of the best things to happen to me. He treats me so well that sometimes I feel like this is a dream. Is this real, God? I didn't think living on a cloud at 18 could be real!! He gives me feelings that I can't even explain. I feel safe and happy with him.

April 26 2003 – Dear God, I told him I loved him. He didn't say anything and I think I want to bury myself. It was so humiliating. Why would you have me do that?! My dad isn't doing well either, so I'm double mad at you."

Jen laughs to herself, but I can't seem to look at her. My eyes are swimming in tears. She continues without looking at me.

"April 27 2003 –Dear God, OH MY GOD. Did you know he was going to do that? That he was going to write me a poem that says he loves me back and bring me flowers and make me feel literally all colors of the rainbow?! I want to throw up thinking how fortunate I am to have someone like him be in my life. I don't care why you put him in my life, but I'm going to thank you forever. This is so unreal and I can't believe I get to be the one to love this boy forever.

May 14 2003 – Dear God, may I keep Cal forever? I don't want to let him go. I guess you can say we are dating even though he never asked me to be his girlfriend but it's okay. He's so amazing and I feel like a thirteen-year-old girl smiling at her first crush for calling me pretty but that's what it feels like. He makes me feel so special and so happy.

June 8 2003 –Dear God, I don't quite think you understand how happy you've made me with Cal. I've never thought a boy would care for me as much as he does, but it's insane how much he cares for me! He never lets a day go by where he doesn't tell me how much he loves me. My heart is full and healthy and happy!! THANK YOU

June 17 2003 –Dear God, how did I manage to get so lucky? I wake up every day with a smile on my face, from Cal. He just knows what to say and what to do. He's a professional at being a perfect boyfriend. Thank you for creating this masterpiece of a human being that I get to call mine.

July 2 2003 –Dear God, all I think about is Cal... I'm so glad it's summertime or else I would get no schoolwork done! I can't stop thinking about him and I want to be with him all the time. That probably isn't healthy but every day he just finds more things to compliment me about or wants to show me off to the world. I can't get enough of him! I hope I get to fulfill my teenage girl dreams with him kissing me under the fireworks. Do you know if he plans too?! Oh it would make my heart so happy.

July 22 2003 –Dear God, this life isn't real. Cal has to be an alien or some sort of robot because there can't be someone so perfect. I kiss him constantly to be sure he's real and well, he is. I'm just so happy, God. I'm smiling like an idiot writing to you right now because I can't get over how much he means to me. He took us to watch the stars tonight and I felt like it was a dream. Is this a dream, God? Is someone making a movie, secretly following Cal and I around? He's just a really good actor, isn't he? It's been six months though and this feeling is so strong in me. Everything about him is so perfect. Thank you for giving him to me.

August 13 2003 –Dear God, we are going on a trip this weekend. For the first time, I am really nervous! Cal and I have spent nights together but this just feels different... special? He's been acting different for the past couple of days. Still lovey and sweet but just wants reassurance that I want to go camping. I keep telling him yes over and over so I maybe he's just nervous about our first trip together? I don't know. I hope you look after us and keep us safe and continue to let our love flourish and grow. He's simply amazing. I would do anything for him and if something were to happen to him, God I swear I would just break apart. No more thinking like that because we are soul mates and we will live happily ever after!

August 24 2003 –Dear God, I hate you and I never want to talk to you again. I will never forgive you. You took everything.

August 30 2003 –Dear God..."

"Stop, Jen..." I hear her sigh, but then I realize she's trying to catch her breath from crying. I didn't realize she was crying.

Pulling her into me, I try with all my willpower to make her feel better, however I can. She throws her journal onto the bed and I can feel a sense of relief when she latches herself onto me.

I'm crying, she's crying. She's holding me, I'm holding her. My heart is breaking and I can only guess that hers is too.

This side hug shit isn't working. I pull her torso up from the bed and have her stand in front of me, in between my legs. She's looking down at me, grappling my face like its precious marble. Standing up from the bed, she moves back only an inch or so, but then I grasp my hands on her cheeks, forcing her eyes to stay on mine. She brings her hands up, placing them ever so gently over my chest.

"Jen..." The words get caught in my throat. I pull her face to my chest, just wanting to hold her instead. Her arms glide down my torso then reach around my back, where I feel her hands grip together as she pulls me close. My hands have intertwined in her hair and her face is a soothing cushion against my chest.

Dear God, just please let me hold on to her and never let her go.

"Let me read the last one to you, please." She sniffles and grabs her hair to lie behind her back. I don't know how much more I can handle, but if this makes her happy, as she is describing here right now, I'll let her do whatever she wants to be happy.

"Okay." I whisper.

I don't think it's a good idea, but we'll go with it. One more. I can handle one more. I let go of her, and we both sit back down on her bed. She holds her hand out for mine as she picks up her notebook again. Laying it on her lap, she turns a couple of pages. Interesting... I didn't think she would write to God anymore.

"January 16 2007 – Dear God, I haven't had much to say to you in the past couple of years but I want to tell you thank you. Today is the day. Cal gets to come home. I thought I was going to be waiting longer for this moment but I'm a feeling a mix of a lot of emotions right now. God, I need you to give some sort of sign that Cal is going to come here to Seattle for me. Anything. I just need to know that I was worth the wait."

I look at her, confused. Satisfied, she looks at me.

"So, what happened?" I guess this is the question I should be asking. I'm not really sure.

She closes the notebook and repositions herself on the bed. Her hand releases mine, and she throws her leg on the bed to face me.

"Cal, I know we say we love paranormal stuff, but you've always been skeptical about believing in it. I promise you I am not making any of this up." Looking at her through my eyelashes, my eyebrows crinkle and my heart rate rises.

"I get to the shop that morning after writing that prayer and sitting on the counter was an Americano. No customers were around the counter, and I asked Pat whose drink that belonged to. He was confused, thinking maybe Ang or Maggie had made it for someone who walked away. It sat there for thirty minutes, and nobody came to pick it up. Americano was your favorite drink, when you didn't want a black coffee. Then I was taking a break and took the trash out. I propped the door open like we usually did, and it seemed the trash was just collected so the dumpster was empty, except for one thing. There was a trash bag that was slightly torn open, but I could only see one thing. Only a sleeve of broken chocolate chip cookies remained at the bottom of the dumpster. I'm thinking it was just a coincidence. Not everyone likes chocolate chip cookies. I go back inside, and Pat needs help with the mid-day rush. There's a red truck through the front windows. I do a double take to make sure it's not yours, but it took my breath away. The rims were black, and the taillights were black and I could see something dangling from the rearview mirror, but I couldn't see it clearly. I thought it was your fishing pole. I had to stabilize myself against the wall for a moment. Then the ultimate thing hits me, the mysterious fourth cannonball. I'm taking orders from a group of gentlemen. You know Pat, he's making conversation with a few of them, and they mention they are from out of state– Montana, I think is what they said. They came into town for the weekend for the Seahawks game and decide to explore some of the city. Pat's ego busted when they said they read about his coffee shop on Google. Anyway, the gentleman I was helping wanted a macchiato. No problem, easy. Then I asked for his name. Calvin, he said. I dropped the mug I was holding, and it crashes on the ground. Pat and the other guys stared at me, wondering if I was having a seizure or something. Pat checks on me and my face is flushed. The odds of someone having your name, on the same day that I'm asking God for a sign... it just seemed bizarre."

I understand the purpose of the last prayer now.

For God to show her a sign. She got four of them. I always knew my lucky number would show itself somehow. I was coming to her.

That was always the plan.

Her memory not only makes me happy that she felt me in so many ways, but how sickening it must've felt for her it took me four months to find her. She was waiting for me the whole time, but I was the one who was slacking.

I blame Henry; he was the professional.

Surprisingly, I'm overwhelmed by God that I pull her close to me. He gifted me the most perfect and precious angel. She radiates the most potent strength of any human being I've ever met. She has the gift of love and care that I don't deserve, but she continues to build me back up, like a melting snowman.

Jen may have been deceitful, and she may be emotional and unstable, but God is she worth it. I can tell she's on a roller coaster that she just wants off and I'll do my damn best, with all the strength and determination, to stop it and get her off. To save her.

Jennie

He made me the happiest after the *third* day of meeting him. I started walking on the stairway to Heaven and I went up for seven months.

When Cal left after Easton, Devil pushed me off, like the little bitch she is.

I never wrote back to God until I found about his release. It felt easier to write to Cal instead, so that's what I did. I was so angry at God. He took Cal in August, then took my dad in November and left me by myself until I met Jonah.

All these years, I thought He wanted me to be happy...

I live with anxiety that God is watching the reunion of Cal and me these past couple of days, but He puts on the most demonic mask and begins the warpath of destruction for us. I partly wish this weren't real, because losing Cal again would shatter me.

Being wrapped in Cal's arms is the best place in the entire universe. It gives me hope we can make it, despite all the time we lost.

His hugs remind me of candy, being wrapped so tight in the plastic. Unwrapping the candy is disappointing when it leaves the candy feeling alone and exposed.

That's how I feel every time Cal isn't holding me.

At first, I was crying because I was reliving the pure blissful moments of Cal and me at the beginning of our relationship. Life was so easy and carefree. But now I'm crying because I know the inevitable has to happen–Cal has to leave.

I want him to stay with me and I hate this point of medication transitions where hormones are being bounced around like an amateur tennis game. I already feel that I'm going to enter a depression once Cal leaves, and I don't even want to think about ways to feel better. There's nothing that will make me feel better.

Cal is holding me so close that I feel myself grasping for more oxygen. I make a little noise and Cal backs his chest away for my mouth to breathe in more air. I keep my arms wrapped around him and he keeps his arms wrapped around me.

"I think you need some sleep, Jen." He whispers to me and then I feel his lips kiss the top of my hair. I close my eyes hard, hating that the end is approaching.

Please don't go.

I cry hysterically into Cal's chest, sharing my fear with him.

"I don't want you to go."

He's patting my hair and squeezing me a bit more as each second passes.

"Baby, I know, but I have to take care of some things so that we'll never be apart again. I'll be back soon, okay? I will call you tonight."

He kisses the top of my head, then my forehead, moving to my temple, and down my cheeks. He moves us apart, staring at each other.

He's going to take a piece of me with him right now.

He's cupping my cheeks and stares at me, *like he's staring at the stars.* He kisses me again with enough force to make me feel a tingly jolt of electricity jolt run through my body.

Calvin

I decide to walk home to give myself time to decompress and understand all my options right now. All I know is giving up on Jen isn't an option. Angel helps me process my options.

There's always Jonah. He understands this version of Jen. He'll be able to help you and her.

I know what Jonah would say to me if I ask for his advice. He would spit in my face about how I should've stayed away. He would say how he needed the time to get her better. Better for me. But there's no way I could live with myself to not be there to help Jen get better. I'm all in for her, every piece. Plus, I'm not in the mood to pick a fight with Jonah. I've seen his arms. He could probably knock me out in two hits. Next option.

Lydia and Max have been more than helpful. They understand the mental part of this. They specialize in this and could help you understand Jen's symptoms and medications.

Angel has a point. They have already done so much for Jen. Being her fill-in parents for the past year. Jen values them and their input. I don't want to create an awkward situation for them by having them care for an employee unprofessionally. I also don't want to affect Jen's future with them, thinking they need to hire her to monitor her. Her amazing, caring nature warranted recognition, securing her a position to show her skills. Next option.

Henry. Nope, fuck Henry. He'll want to read another letter and I can't entertain him right now.

That only leaves one person.

Thank God for Angels.

I walk toward *Coffee & Honey*, hoping to catch Pat.

I'm slightly nervous about seeing Pat. The person who was once a close friend, someone who kept a protective eye on me and Jen, but someone who has gotten too close to my face lately. I know Pat had to tuck Jen under his wing while I was gone. That was before Max entered the picture. She needed some sort of fatherly figure.

The bell jingles as I entered the front door of C&H around noon.

Great, the mid-day rush. Pat sees me, and I see his shoulders slump, almost relieved at finally seeing me without Jen. I sit on the far side of the bar, facing the door–just in case she shows up to see Pat, too.

"Calvin..." He greets me. I'm looking around, surprised the shop isn't busier right now.

There is a group of girls at the far corner table with books open, book club or bible study, maybe. By the front door, an elderly couple shares a muffin and coffee together. An oversized gentleman is reading the newspaper at the table next to the couple; his coffee and pastry dissolved. Once I walked in, the front door jingled again and in stepped a middle-aged woman. Maggie, who I try to avoid saying hello to, helped her.

"Pat, man, how are you? It's kind of quiet in here today." I shake his hand as a substitute for our hug. The bar creates a barrier between us. Pat has a dishrag in his hand and is carrying three mugs that are dripping with water.

"Yeah, it's Thursday and not much is happening in the area. It was a busy weekend so I'm kind of glad to have a slow day. We all kinda need that. Hey, thanks for coming in guys. Come back soon!" Pat looks back to the front door as the couple smiles and waves at Pat. He turns back to me.

"Where's Jennie? I thought she'd be with you." I move my head down, ashamed of everything that happened since I saw Pat a couple days ago at Jen's apartment.

"I'm actually coming from her place. Just need some space." I don't make eye contact with Pat because I don't want him to ask more questions.

"Americano?" I smirk a bit at the word, which reminds me of Jen's story.

"I'll just do a black coffee today. Thanks."

He turns away to grab a mug and heads to the coffee machine. I look around and admire the progress of Pat's shop. There are vintage pictures on every wall, side by side. You can't even see an inch of the wall. On the wall behind the bar is a picture I would recognize anywhere. It's me, Jen and Pat posing for Jen's birthday. I smile instantly at her picture.

How breath-taking she must look to a stranger.

Pat comes back over and follows my eyes to the picture. He sets my coffee down and brings me a brownie as well.

"How is she today?"

Pat moves a stool behind the counter to sit across from me. I take a drink of the coffee and it tastes just as I remembered. It's rich, and the temperature is just warm enough to continue drinking without burning my tongue. Pat's question gives me goosebumps though, as if he's waiting to hear the worst news.

"Um, she's okay, I guess."

Is there really a good way to describe Jen's emotional state lately? It changes every five fucking seconds. She might be okay for now, but when I talk to her again, who knows what version of her I'll get?

I try to avoid eye contact with Pat because I know he'll see through the bullshit. She isn't okay, but now with her medication becoming part of her routine, hopefully she will be.

"Calvin, I want you to know that I didn't know she wasn't taking her pills. I thought she was this whole time. When Jennie left the hospital and Jonah was taking care of her, they came into the shop a couple of weeks later. And boy, she was such a different person. She was just happy and alive. I thought for sure it was the beginning of a new Jennie. I didn't realize how depressed and moody she was before the incident." Pat talks with his hands and I can see them flying around in my peripheral vision. I still can't look him in the eye. The disappointment is strong in me.

"You were supposed to look after her..." It's all I can breathe out without shooting flames at Pat. I can feel him remove his glasses and pinch the bridge of his nose. I finally find the courage to look at him. He's pained.

"Jesus Calvin, she's a human being with real emotions! She isn't a robot whose feelings I can turn on and off. I did my best. When you called from jail and told me what happened, I didn't want to believe it. I remember holding the phone and picturing the absolute anguish on Jen's face when I would have to tell her the news. And when she came into work a couple days later, it was a million times worse because she told me herself. The look on her face, Calvin, you have no idea how scarring that was. That memory weighs so heavy on my heart, even till this day–for both of you. To lie to her the whole time was miserable. To be part of the conversations that she just wanted to hear your voice, and she just wanted to know that you were thinking about her, and here I am, having daily phone calls with you!!! I had to lie to you, Calvin, because there was no way I could tell you how God awful it was to have Jennie so unhappy. And then I knew it would make you unhappy, but I had no way of helping you from here! I'm sorry about everything. She did her best. I did my best. But you know what, Calvin..." I stop him there as he points a finger at my face. I grab his wrist, gripping it tightly. My stomach is in knots at the facts I'm hearing.

"What Pat.... I dare you to finish that sentence." My inner gremlin is emerging. I'm already pissed off that I had to leave Jen today, and so help me God, I have to deal with Pat's shit.

"It was your fault you left. There's no one to blame but yourself. Now let go of my hand."

The truth is the hardest slap I've ever received. Without hesitation, I release my grip on Pat, locking eyes with him. He lays his hand on the counter. I fold my hands together in front of my forehead and let my head drop.

"You don't get to come back and think everything is the same as when you left." Pat's voice is calm and nurturing.

He never made me guilty of my actions during our phone calls from prison. Hearing the words *it was your fault* from him is like getting drilled in my ears. It's hurtful but Devil and Angel are both standing front and center of my heart with their arms crossed and *we told you so* face.

It was always your fault this happened.

The guilt is becoming too much to handle. I squeeze my hands together, wishing I had enough force to break my own hands. Pat can see the tension building in my body and I feel his hands pull my arms down, trying to relax me. I don't know how he does it but he's out from behind the counter in no time and standing in front of me, pushing against my resistance, Somehow, I let him win and he wraps his arms around me, holding me like the brother, uncle, father, and friend he's always been to me.

"I just want to be good for her." I whimper to Pat. He's holding me tight, protecting me.

"You will be. You are good for her. You are all she's ever wanted. I was here to witness it. She put her soul into those letters. She thought she was helping you by sharing pieces of her life, whether it was good or bad. Even if you were here or not, there were going to be good and bad things to happen, right?" Pat should've been a preacher instead of a barista. He's got the voice for it.

I'm so fucking overwhelmed to have a friend like Pat. I told him to watch over Jen, to make sure she wouldn't do anything stupid. To keep her in Seattle. He updated me on her every week. I called him at 4:00 east coast time, usually on Wednesdays because it was typically the slowest day and time for him to have a decently long conversation. For months, he told me everything.

Until he stopped answering my calls last year. I think it must've been late March when he ghosted me. Talking to him now, I realize why. Jen went downhill, especially when she went to the hospital in May. He'd have so much information to tell me on how she was then, but if he wasn't even able to answer the phone and talk to me, I could assume it was a dark time.

So much of my anxiety about returning from South Carolina stemmed from Pat abandoning me with no information on her whereabouts. I pull myself together and pull away from Pat. He hovers over me, keeping a hand on my shoulder to support me.

Pat. Jonah. Max and Lydia. These are good fucking people. People who kept my Jen from falling apart–or at least they did their best.

"I guess I need to finish them, huh?" I wipe my nose with my sleeve and look at the ground. My emotions feel all over the place, and I blame Jen. Pat grips my shoulder a bit, trying to grab my attention.

Quit blaming other people.

"Yes. I know some of the shit is going to hurt, but there are so many good things that she talks about. Give her a chance to explain. Don't stop reading. I know you're going to want to. I know you, Calvin. You're going to want to call her and curse her out. You're going to want to call her and ask to see her. You're going to want to call other people and ask questions. Hell, you are probably going to contemplate drinking, but it's like walking through fire. Jen is at the end. She's already walked through the inferno, and she's waiting for you. I guess you have to decide if she's worth it."

Hearing Pat curse still makes my stomach flutter. It's something he hardly ever does, and you can tell when he curses at you, he's feeling strong emotions.

"She's worth it." I sniffle and look at Pat, my mentor, my protector, Jen's protector. We don't deserve him. He's such a good man and I hate that I have to leave him, too.

He brings my storm to a halt. And it's a peaceful feeling. I take in a big breath, absolutely fucking hating the job I'm about to do. But God, for Jen, I'll do anything for her.

She's at the end. She's waiting for you.

I've tried to set the mood in my apartment—locking the front door, trapping the evil within, and letting myself burn. All the lights are turned off except my side table lamp. Despite a chilly breeze and light rain, I have the balcony door fully opened because I already know I'm going to break into a sweat. I've changed into a black tank and black sweatpants. Sweatpants bother me, but I'm trying to be as comfortable as possible–if that's what you want to call it.

I stopped for food on my way home and even though I'm full, I already feel the burgers and onion rings coming back up. As much as I contemplated buying any form of alcohol to keep my nerves at ease and my brain a little foggy, I decided against it.

Jen put all her blood, sweat, and tears into these letters. It's only fair I do the same. I grab the stack of letters *to be read.* I'm clenching my hands to avoid trembling, but the strain is causing finger pain.

She's worth it.

You'll understand all of it.

You can move on with your life, with her, after you are done with this.

Don't be a fucking pansy. Thanks Devil, you always know what to say.

August 18, 2004

Dear Cal,

I wrote you a poem this time. I hope you like it – whenever you get the chance to read it someday.

It happened so fast, I didn't think it was real

Everything about you seemed wonderous and lovely and surreal

Your words were like sweet nectar, and I was the hummingbird

You became my home, a place I want to stay, a place I preferred

Your body was safe, like your arms were built only for me

You were my temple, a place I'd return to every day, undoubtedly

Your smell was a drug I didn't think existed

It made my stomach lock in knots, unable to get it untwisted

Your eyes drew me in that I got stuck in a trance

Even if someone tapped me on the shoulder, they didn't stand a chance

The best part about you though,

Were your words, the never-ending ammo

IF only I could give you a taste of your own medicine,

You took everything that was good for me – serotonin, dopamine, oxytocin

You left me drowning in my own blood, unable to heal the wound

I'm starving for safety and love, perhaps it got left at the campground

I hate you for what you've done and how you showed your love

But I'll never stop loving you, you're someone I'll never let go of

Continuing to love and hate you at the same time,

Jennie

September 5, 2004

Dear Cal,

I'm trying a new hobby this week. Pat thought I should try kickboxing with Ang. I really don't want to go because I know I'll hate it, or I'll look stupid doing it, but I have so much anger in me that maybe it'll help. Guess you never know until you try. Ang usually does three days a week but I'm going to go for one class and see how it goes. I'll probably update you about it.

I can't believe I made it to sophomore year. I didn't think I'd get through last year. I have no motivation to do any assignments. I just want to sleep. The past couple of weeks have just been a blur. I don't know idea what day it is, what time it is, the time I showered, the last meal I ate. I have no clue. Time is just one consistent minute, and it's not bringing me any sort of joy.

I'm trying to be happy and normal without you. I know there is still so much time that has to pass until you come home, but I'm struggling. Pat is worried. He's always worried about me. He forces me to eat at the shop and to lay off the coffee. I wish he had something that would make me sleep. Insomnia is an asshole, and I don't wish this feeling on anyone. I feel I'm just inside my body and someone is handling all my controls. I have no control and I just hate that. Anyways, going to figure out what shitty thing God has lined up for me today.

Still hate you,

Jennie

September 18, 2004

Dear Cal,

Kickboxing is stupid. I wish I could beat up a real person because that would make me feel a million times better. Instead, we just hit a punching bag. The bag bruised my hands the first time and then when we started doing kicks, I thought I looked like an idiot. Ang is a badass though. She grunts for every kick and at first it was hysterical, but then I realized how much I wouldn't want to get in a fight with her. She could do some real damage. So kickboxing is crossed off. Hopefully something helpful will fall right onto my lap.

*Pat is starting renovations at the shop this week. Can you believe he's actually going to close the shop for a whole week? Thankfully the weather is decent this week and we just plan to move the tables and chairs outside in the back so the painters can do their thing and the flooring can be installed. I'm most excited for the new bathrooms. They were disgusting and vile. He said I can decorate the women's bathroom. What a lovely duty. He wants to go deep hipster mode with putting signs and wall art on the walls, like every square inch. He wanted to add a neon sign behind the bar, but I told him absolutely not. We aren't living in the fifties. I told him we should look into getting a nice modern sign that says **Coffee & Honey** and put it on the back wall. There's a wood worker a few blocks away. He's most excited about the new bar. It's going to be twelve feet of butcherblock. I'm worried about the coffee stains but Pat says, "well if you make drinks correctly, it won't be a problem." Jackass. Everyone is a jackass. My professors. Customers. People on campus. You.*

We are approaching October and I'd rather throw myself off a bridge.

Still hate but you miss you like crazy,

Jennie

October 31, 2004

Dear Cal,

There was once a time that this day brought me so much joy and happiness. But now it brings me so much hatred and sadness. I told Pat I didn't want to come to the Halloween party this year. If I did dress up, it would be either a ghost or an all-black cloak. A ghost because nobody would notice or talk to me and I could just silently move around. It's not like anyone has noticed me anyways.... Only you did. It's like your attention was enough for a whole football team. I feel worthless now. But I'd dress in a black cloak because that's how I feel inside. Everything is black, so what better way to dress up then dress how you feel. It's a good idea, right?

What would you dress up as? Maybe a jailbird. Oh wait... that wouldn't be dressing up.

Tonight I'm going to sit in darkness and attempt to watch Halloween. I haven't been eating much lately but maybe the smell of Chinese food will seem appetizing.

Oh and Anna invited me to Andy's birthday dinner/party this weekend. I'm not looking forward to it, but Anna keeps pestering me every single day about what I'm going to wear. What has life come to...

Anyways, Happy Halloween, my black widow. I hate to look at you and you make my skin crawl when I think about you. But when you are around, you make me powerful and brave. I can't wait to have you back.

Miss you immensely today (and everyday),

Jennie

The party.

The fucking party she warned me about.

This won't be good. I mean, these past few letters haven't been good.

Where are the happy letters? Where are the good letters?

Her depression is gut-wrenching. I can feel it like powder exploding as I open the letter. It's brutal.

It's only going to get worse.

I don't think I can do this. My blood feels like it's disintegrating my muscles and bones, completely obliterating me.

You have to finish. Keep going.

FUCK.

November 5, 2004

Dear Cal,

I just finished getting ready for Andy's party tonight. I have a few minutes before I head out. I don't know what I'm getting myself into. Anna says they rented a limo, a private section of whatever club we are venturing to and Andy's older brother has gotten all the good alcohol. I didn't realize a 20th birthday was so... crazy. Wait, now I'm wondering if he's turning 18 and that's why we are doing this. That would make the most sense cause why else would they be going all out? Ugh, great... I don't think I have enough time to mentally prepare myself for all the drunkenness I'll encounter. I'm staying at Anna's tonight so hopefully I make it there in one piece.

I wish you were coming. I wish you were here, in general. To be able to hold your arm or hand and feel utterly and completely safe from creepy people. I don't know where I'm supposed to hide tonight. That gives me the most anxiety.

Anna has tried keeping me in the loop of things but I'm having a hard time remembering things lately. My attention to anyone and anything is just very minimal. I think about sleeping most of the time. There are supposed to be friends from Andy's cross-country team and then of course, his college friends. God, this is going to be terrible. I can't deal with college kids –even though I am one– but that's not the point. Everything is just so infuriating.

Part of me wants to just call Anna and tell her I got sick from something, anything. But she knows when I'm bullshitting her. Plus, I'm supposed to be her wingman tonight, whatever that means. I hope she stays sober enough to not leave me alone. I will absolutely kill her. There's just so many people I don't know and I already don't' want to be out and I don't drink often and I have to pretend to put on a smile and laugh and enjoy myself? Fuck all that.

Speak of the Devil, an obnoxious horn is beeping from outside. What would they do if I never went out there...

Anna would probably drag me by my ankles. So I guess it's showtime. I wish you were here and pulling me along, telling me we would have a good time, together.

Hate your guts so much tonight for making me go alone,

Jennie

November 6, 2004

Dear Cal,

I don't even know how to start this letter.

It's seven thirty at night. I've been throwing up all day. When I'm not throwing up, I'm sleeping or just curling in bed from the brightness of the world and the loudness of my neighbors. Or just wishing I was dead. Anna tried shoving a whole loaf of bread into my mouth at the first sight of consciousness this morning. It only made me throw up more.

I've been replaying last night over and over, putting all the pieces together, clarifying what was real and what was not real. It was all real.

Before I go on, I just want to stay I'm so fucking sorry. You can hate me forever after you read this because I deserve it. There is no forgiveness for doing such a despicable thing. My stomach is churning right now and I don't know if my shaky hands will be able to write this out.

Glen and I...

Cal, I'm so so sorry. I can't even breathe right now, and my eyes are so blurry. I didn't want to believe it. I still don't believe it.

I don't know how much alcohol I drank, and neither does Anna because she was trying to handle Andy most of the night. She said she tried to stay with both of us but Andy was just too much. Glen became my babysitter. I briefly remember him being around, but I didn't care because I was delusional and was looking around the club for you. Anna said I was drinking whiskey all night. She told Glen to take me home. I guess I ended up here? I have no idea really...

He just ... felt like you. He helped me change out of my clothes. His touch was gentle, not invasive on my body, or curious. Just so gentle. I remember him putting me in my bed and getting a quick glance at the "stranger" in my room. I remember your name coming from my mouth. Then he was undressing himself (except his boxers, that part I do remember!!!!) and getting under the covers with me.

His stubble felt like yours. His eyes were dark brown so I avoided looking at him. He brushed my hair out of my face, like you did. He kept saying my name, only he was saying Jennie over and over. I knew it was different because you called me Jen. It felt new and I don't even know how long it lasted or what happened afterwards, but I remember his lips on my forehead, kissing me goodbye and then I fell asleep and found Anna laying next to me.

Anna's face this morning (or afternoon?) was just...

Her version of the story was that Glen told her that he was taking me home. She agreed to it, as she was trying to get Andy home too. Girls should stay with girls and guys should stay with guys. She got a text from Glen when we got to my apartment and I was home but I kept telling him to stay? She showed me the texts, so it's hard to say that she was lying. Then she started reading me the conversation between them. I don't know how she had time to keep a conversation going with Glen, at the same time caring for Andy. This is what I briefly remember:

Glen: she wants me to stay.

Anna: do you want to? You don't have to. I just wanted you to bring her home.

Glen: I want to make sure she's okay.

Anna: Well, if you want to. Let me know when you leave so I can come over and hold her hair back. That's not an attractive thing.

Glen: Oh I'm already past that...

Anna: oh god.. I'm so sorry

Glen: she keeps touching my face and looking at me like I'm someone familiar

Anna: well she's known you for years and hasn't seen you in months so I'm sure you look different to her

Glen: I've missed her

Anna: I don't think it's a good idea to get involved with her right now, G

Glen: nothing serious, but I just want to be in her company. We haven't been this close since Easton. It's all too familiar.

Anna: don't bring that up to her for God's sakes

Glen: Will you be mad if I stay with her?

Anna: I think she needs to be okay with it. You can stay and keep your hands to yourself ONLY if she asks you. Don't stay willingly. You remember my birthday last year. She threw you on your ass

Glen: She just seems... I don't know, different?

Anna: Well, be careful with her. she's still hurting from him. I don't want this to get messy

Glen: you're so supportive

So I guess I wanted him to stay. I don't know. I don't remember any of it. By the time I woke up, he was gone and there weren't any calls or texts from him. I asked Anna if she's heard from him. He told her he needed to leave because I started talking about Easton... and how was glad I went home with him. How happy I was when he got close to me. How I wanted to spend time with him.

Things that make me vomit more and want to die the most tragic death. There's no way I would've said things like that, Cal. I promise you.

I don't know what to think. We just slept together, that's all. I mean I barely had any clothes on because he removed mine and he was only in his boxers but still. I know that doesn't make it right but nothing happened.

I'm so sorry.

I don't hate you, I hate myself,

Jen

December 25, 2004

Dear Cal,

It's raining today. It's been raining for two weeks straight. It feels like the weather is aligning with my life, a complete shitshow. A constant thunderstorm and no hope for sunshine.

I started a new hobby but I can't tell you because I know you'll get mad at me. Thank God you aren't here to badger me about it. It's not the most productive hobby, but it releases a lot of tension.

I'm falling behind in some classes so I have to re-take a couple courses over winter break. I haven't been working a lot either so I haven't seen Pat. The last time I saw him was for your birthday. This year it was just he and I at the shop. We sang happy birthday to you and lit a cupcake. We reminisced about you for hours. It felt nice to be in the presence of someone who saw the best of you.

Anyways, I miss you. And I'm sorry for everything.

Waiting,

Jennie

January 12, 2005

Dear Cal,

Adding another tally

|||

Happy New Year. Something weird and unusual happened today. It was the icing on top of my melting, crappy, disgusting coconut-infused cake.

Your mom came into the shop today. I about died. I saw her walking up to the door, so I ran into the bathroom. I didn't even have time to tell Pat to cover for me. He knocks on the door and says someone is here to see me.

I haven't met anyone scarier than Tracy Klenn.

I walked out of the bathroom, terrified that she was standing in front of the door with a butcher's knife, ready to cut my throat. But she was sitting at a table. Our corner table. Her back was to me, and she was looking out the window. I didn't even have time to do a breathing technique, so I walked to her. I greeted her but her facial expression was clear that she did not come to squash things between us.

She was annoyed at my enthusiasm (thankfully it was fake). She said she hasn't heard from you at all since being in jail, besides the first night. She harassed me if you had been calling me in prison and not her. I said I haven't had any contact with you and I'm not sure if anyone in Seattle had talked to you. Pat maybe? Andy potentially? As much as I hated having a conversation with her, looking at her did give me a breath of fresh air.

She resembles you, so for a few moments, I got a small piece of luscious, strawberry filled, lightly iced cake. You got your eyes from her, and it broke my heart to stare. Part of me knew I was being rude, by just staring, but it felt like you were there with me. Her nose and cheek bones are shaped like yours too.

She didn't stay much longer after questioning me. I told her over and over I haven't heard from you. I'm not sure if I ever would again. She spit the worst words at me, right before she stood and walked away. "You aren't good enough for him."

I cried for a while at our corner table. I covered my face with my hands, hoping nobody would watch me wallow in my own misery. Pat didn't even come to check on me. He was either probably busy, knew not to ask, or overheard the conversation and didn't want to involve himself. We had just gotten to a point where we weren't talking about you every shift.

She's right though. I'm not good for you. I'll never be good for you. I want you to find someone who is good for you. I'll always be waiting though, just in case.

I love you

March 29, 2005

Dear Cal,

I'm sorry it's been a while. Life still continues to suck. I'm trying to just focus on school right now so I'm working very little at the shop. My dad's savings is coming into good use at this time. I miss him so much.

I need to tell you something.

Glen came into the shop last week to talk to me. I haven't seen or heard from him since November. He sat at the bar and I stayed on the other side. He asked how I was doing and I just laughed without responding. I was falling apart, more and more each day. He, on the other hand, was doing good things with flight school. He's been travelling at lot along the west coastline. He's seeing someone and her name is Allie. Sorry, I know you probably don't care or want to know. He just needed closure before moving on, I guess? He needed to hear it from my mouth that I wasn't interested. The words I slurred to him in November have constantly been on his mind. I wanted to die from embarrassment.

It was never Glen. Could there have been potential? Sure, but nobody ever compared to you. I told him that he was absolutely okay to move on with Allie and that I was not interested. We could remain friends but that was all.

I hope that gives you closure from Easton. I know he was one of the reasons for things turning to shit, but in case you never knew, he was never competition. He was never in the same category as you. Of course, you may never read this letter again because of what happened between him and I, and you might want to disown me for the rest of your life but I just need you to know that.

He was nothing compared to you. You were, still are and will be everything to me. Even if I'm nothing to you.

Waiting for you,

Jennie

I rip up the remaining letters until I get to the ones I need to read.

The ones about Jonah.

About the hospital.

About how her life changed when she found out about my early release.

April 30, 2005

Dear Cal,

I was in Portland for the week. Thankfully spring break lined up with my birthday and felt I needed to get away from Seattle. I left Sunday afternoon and came back this morning. It was relaxing.

I stopped at this doughnut shop, Horror King. When you get out, we have to go back. It was incredible. He creates these doughnuts inspired by slasher characters, and I had the Mikey-Likey. It was a blueberry doughnut topped with white icing, but the icing was out of this world. I was talking to him for a while about how he started his business and his sister, who is the decorator, came up with the idea to open a shop. She makes all the toppers for the doughnuts. The Michael Myers inspired one has his knife punctured in the doughnut. The Freddy has his claw glove that stretches across the top. I felt bad that I was eating it without you there.

I tried something new – I went to a vineyard and did a couple of hours of wine tasting. I thought maybe, just maybe, I would finally start to enjoy the taste of wine but it was all disgusting. I took a sip from each stop along the tour so I felt nothing. I thought about going to an art museum but it just wasn't up my alley. I spent the day at Washington Park and that was fun. Lots of people. Lots of time to just think.

Currently Cal, this is what I think.

I think I lost you. And I'm really struggling with that.

I don't think you're going to come find me. I don't think you want to see me. I don't think you want to save me. And I can't say that I blame you. I have messed up so much of our story. There is absolutely no doubt that I'm the villain in your story.

For the rest of my life, I will punish myself for not saving you. You deserved better.

I will continue to hold you close to my heart and I continue to miss you more and more each passing moment,

Jennie Marie

Okay, now I rip up everything else.

The only reason that letter was important was because her birthday was in April, and I needed to know what she did. Each letter that has an irrelevant date, I rip to shreds.

The second half of 2005—the second-year letter, my birthday, Halloween/October, Christmas—I don't care about any of it. Well, I do but I don't have the fucking patience to waste my time with those letters.

I don't even care there isn't a trash can around. It's looking like snow in my living room.

Then I reach them. May of 2006.

May 6, 2006

Dear Cal,

I miss you so much it hurts today. I feel my oxygen level is barely functional. It hurts to be human. I haven't eaten in days. I've missed class all week. I've haven't showered in a week, I think... maybe longer. Pat keeps calling me, but I don't want to talk to anyone. I just want to talk to you. I only want you.

I never knew depression could be this bad. I mean, my dad told me stories about my mom growing up, but I never got to witness the brutality of what she was like. My brain hurts to think that this is what she went through. Lately, my brain has felt like ash. There aren't any happy thoughts anymore. All the good memories I've had with you are being submerged by a dark cloud. I can't believe we are going on almost three years with you being gone.

I haven't prayed often Cal but I hope you come and find me. I hope you haven't forgotten about me. I hope I still bring you some amount of joy or happiness. I often think about the possibility that you have forgotten about me. The chances that once you get out of prison, you'll stay in South Carolina or move somewhere far away from here, from me. That you'll never want to see me again. Those are the thoughts that kill my soul.

I've tried for months and months to understand where things went wrong during Easton. I wish you were here to tell me what I did wrong and tell me how I can fix it. I will fix whatever mixed emotions you are dealing with from Easton and you can fix my depression by coming home. Deal?

As much as I think you should hate me for what I did with Glen, I don't want you to hate me. I want you to continue to love me, the same or even harder than before. Is that possible for you to do? I'll pray to God for that.

Whatever part of me is left, it misses you.

Jen

May 10, 2006

Dear Cal,

I've been in the hospital for awhile. I gave a key to my apartment to Pat and asked him to bring a couple of my things. The first being my journal to you. So, I'm writing to tell you that I fucked up.

It wasn't supposed to be bad. It was supposed to be like any normal time but I don't know what force in me decided to push the knife a little more. I didn't cry or flinch or fear that I was going to die. I immediately realized the excessive bleeding wasn't normal. I grabbed the closest towel I could find and wrapped my arm and somehow managed to drive myself to the hospital. I must've been high on adrenaline because there's no way I would've gotten there in one piece if I was incoherent.

The nurse, Jonah, and the emergency medicine doctor, Dr. Nicks, were so patient and understanding. Jonah gave me stitches and Dr. Nicks asked me a couple of questions, I think to gauge my mental status. I explained to them what happened, how I've been cutting since December of 2004 (that was my secret new hobby). Jonah, specifically, asked a lot about you. Dr. Nicks, on the other hand, asked me if had intentions to hurt myself or end my life. I couldn't answer him because I wasn't sure. Because of policy, he referred me a twenty-four-hour suicide watch observation. Jonah asked Nicks if he could watch care over me, even if it was a different department. I don't know what all happened, but Jonah was there with me. He is so kind.

After the observation was lifted, a different doctor came in. Dr. Beckett (her first name, Tess as she wanted me to call her later on) was a psychiatrist, her focus was in anxiety and mood disorders. She is young, probably out of college in the past couple of years. She has long blonde hair, dark brown eyes and wears these cute clear framed glasses. She's short and always smells so good. She asked me so many questions, Cal. Questions I didn't even want to acknowledge or talk about, but she waited until I answered. We talked so much about you, it hurt my heart. I didn't see her again until the next day. By that point, I was able to shower and change my clothes, but I was still tired and not hungry. She said after looking at the results to the tests, I have major depression with panic disorder and mild PTSD. We established the plan for dealing with all of that. First, she wanted to know if there was someone I wanted to call, to let them know where I was and that was doing okay. (I don't know if okay is the right word...) I wanted to throw up at the thought of the panic Pat must've been feeling for the past couple of days (this was before he came to drop off my things). I told her we could call Pat. He answered on the first ring, and he started crying on the phone when I told him what happened and where I was. On the third day of being at the hospital is when he stopped by to get my apartment key and grab a few of my things. Before he left, he stayed with me for a while. He was so worried about me. He didn't realize I was "this" bad. We hugged for a long time. You know, Pat gives the BEST hugs.

Oof, I hate to end right here but I have to go. I'll write you tomorrow morning.

Jennie

May 13, 2006

Dear Cal,

Sorry, I just realized I didn't write you back the next day. I didn't have a good night. Panic attack. I'm not sure what caused it but afterwards, I just felt so lethargic, so I slept a lot. They are wanting to start me on some medications, but I'm not sure how I feel about it yet. I just want to feel happy. But you are my happy, and without you, I know it's not possible.

Anyway, it's sort of late here and I should have my lamp off but Jonah lets me stay up late. He's on duty tonight and has already checked on me four times. Thankfully he brought me some Starbursts (they were the only things that sounded appetizing, and he would drop the moon to find me any food, considering I'm not at a healthy weight right now.)

Can I tell you a happy moment? I feel like it's been a long time... I'm sure these letters have been so depressing to read.

So I know technically the first time I slept at your house was in February of 2003 and we made each other breakfast but I want to tell you about the actual first time I stayed the night with you. I think it was sometime in March. We had to wait until your parents were in a deep sleep because your front door creaked if you opened it too wide. I remember waiting in my car down the street —I don't even know why I was down the street. I think I was nervous if they looked out the window and saw a suspicious car sitting in front of their house, they would come out with some sort of weapon. It was definitely after midnight, and you texted me a "all is clear." I got my bags and so very quietly shut my door. My heart was pounding so fast!!! I saw the front door opened, and just like every time I saw you since I met you, my stomach fluttered with a zillion butterflies. You were already smiling at me, and standing at the door, having it opened as much as it could open before squeaking. I slipped my body through like I was Kim Possible. The next challenge was getting up the stairs. Unlike last time, your brother was not as generous to let us stay in the basement so we had to come up with a plan to get up the stairs. You instantly grabbed my hand and put a finger up to your lips, nonverbally telling me to stay quiet. I nodded and squeezed your hand as a response. You pulled me close to you, as if we were walking as one. You stepped on the first stair and eagerly yanked my arm to get my attention —I needed to step on the first step too. We were going to step simultaneously.

Despite your parent's bedroom being at the top of the top of the stairs, the excitement was the most fun. I was definitely hoping we wouldn't get caught but playing a game of risk was quite exhilarating! We completed the climb of the fifteen steps –AKA– fifteen piano keys of roulette. If one of the steps made the slightest of noise, your mother would be at the top of the stairs, pushing us back down. You warned me she was the lighter sleeper between the two of them. Still holding my sweaty, anxiety-ridden hand, you pulled me to your room. It was actually the first time I entered your room. Talk about nerd! There was a second amendment poster, a poster with different types of knives, a large Michael Myers poster and then randomly taped to the side of your bed was our first date movie ticket stub and the photo booth polaroids. Your room smelled of you. I swear to God I think I entered the space between Heaven and Earth –a place so peaceful and intoxicating. I wanted to melt. It's like you were a cloak that wrapped itself all around me.

I must've been distracted because I felt you take my bags from my hands and set them on the floor. You grabbed me by the arms and pulled me close to you. Our first kiss was only a few days prior but kissing you in your bedroom felt so intimate. We'd kiss many, many, many times between then and now, but the way you held me that night and the way you grabbed my waist and pulled me close to you... it was different. We kissed for a while (as we always did) and when we both let up for air, you clawed your hands through my hair and looked at me like ... like I was the only girl in the world.

Even though I brought my own clothes, I liked to wear your shirts. They smelled like you and they were a little bigger on me so I liked the baggy-ness. I don't think you realized but you threw me your Vancouver Canucks shirt. And little did you know that I never gave it back after that... (I'm currently wearing it now). You changed into your basketball shorts and no shirt... the giddiness inside of me was not the least bit tired.

You had dark blue cotton sheets and a giant black comforter that I thought was going to make me sweat. You pulled the comforter down for us to get comfortable and I crawled in, of course, away from the door, and you pulled me close to your side while pulling the comforter back over us. It was at that moment, I fully entered Heaven. Your bare skin was on fire but my oxytocin was making my blood feel like a desirable, well-aged form of whiskey. From that, I started to sweat. I know you will continue to apologize for this, but I don't mind that it *happened. As I'm trying to fill my head with less detailed thoughts on what I wanted to do to you, I feel you slump towards me. I look up at you and your eyes are closed, peacefully and beautifully. So I watched you sleep for a while. I waited for you to do something crazy in your sleep like snap your eyes open or make funny noises so I could make fun of you in the morning, but you are one of the most quiet and undisturbed sleepers I've known. It's like nothing bothered you —as if you were in your own Heaven. Watching you made me sleepy, and I found myself in the perfect, most comfortable spot in your arms and drifted off.*

We woke up in the exact same spot as we fell asleep. We woke up before your alarm (the one where I had to leave before your parents woke) so we cuddled for a while, enjoying our paused moment of pure bliss. That was the start of my love-hate relationship when sleeping with you because it was one of my favorite things to do with you but I also hated when it was time to leave. Not to mention, I had to leave at like five in the morning but thank God for us working at a coffeeshop.

I dreamt of the days where we wouldn't have to leave each other, and we could stay in bed all day.

I hope those moments are still on your bucket list.

I miss you, and everything about you (including your posters, your shirts, whatever magic spell you use on yourself to smell good, and everything in between.)

I'm trying to be better for you, even if you don't want me anymore.

Jennie

May 30, 2006

Dear Cal,

I get to leave in a couple of days. I'm working with Tess (my psychiatrist) on a plan to start some medications, group therapy and setting up some one-on-one therapy sessions with her. I also have to follow up with a dietitian. I'm thirty-four pounds under my average weight.

My medications might change here and there until they find out which ones work for my situation. For right now, I'm starting an antidepressant and anti-anxiety. The dosage seems kind of high, but time will tell if it's helpful. I have to attend weekly group therapy for grief. Tess believes I need to change my mindset as if you have passed away because there is a high probability that you may not come back, so I have to treat the situation like death.

I've thrown up five times thinking about the idea. It's not true –I know you'll come back, but it's part of my safety plan and I want to be happy while you're gone. Right now, Tess wants to meet twice a week for individual therapy. We've been meeting here at the hospital but she has an office near the park so it's not totally out of the way.

I hate that this is happening to me. My world feels like it's falling apart and tumbling down on me. I could've been okay.

Jonah, the nurse, has been really helpful and patient with me this entire time. He checks on me frequently. I think he has a crush on me, and it's flattering. He looks at me differently. In a good way. It's like he doesn't see all the brokenness and damage. He makes me laugh constantly and he's even allowed Pat to bring some of my favorite things, things that aren't even allowed!! I think you'd like him for caring for me the way he has. I hope you get to meet him someday.

To be honest with you, I'm scared about leaving the hospital. I fear of returning to reality –the life that still doesn't have you here with me. I miss you so much Calvin Louis. I think about you every morning, and every night. I try to keep myself occupied during the day but you still cross my mind every once and a while. So much has changed about me and I fear that when, if, you come back to Seattle, I won't be the same person. I'll do whatever I need to do to be enough for you. You've always been enough for me.

Waiting for our fairytale to begin again.

June 1, 2006

Dear Cal,

I'm leaving in about fifty minutes, so I thought I'd write to you real quick.

I met with my dietitian yesterday and we came up with a meal plan and to meet weekly for a check in. Jonah said he would drive me to all my appointments. He's actually going to take me home today. He has been such a blessing to have around. Every day he has checked on me —literally. He sneaks in blueberry muffins for me and lets Pat bring my own shampoo and my slippers. I'm not sure why he's clicked with me so much but we've talked A LOT. A lot about you. I don't know why he's so interested in you but of course, I don't mind. We talked for a while one night about our first kiss in the rain and he muttered under his breath something like "wow he's a lucky guy". It made me blush. For two reasons —I was the lucky one to have you and to think that there is someone in the universe who feels lucky enough to have me in their life. He uh, was very open about not being your biggest fan after finding out what happened after Easton. How you could leave someone like me behind.... I still wonder.

But I'm hopeful that I'll be better for you by the time you come back. That is if you plan to come back for me. I'll do whatever the hell I have to do for you to love me again. I'll continue to break and repair my mind, body, and soul over and over until we are in sync again.

I love you and I miss you and I'm waiting for you,

Jennie

June 2, 2006

Dear Cal,

As weird as this might sound, I'm writing you in the bathroom, behind the locked door, away from Jonah. I'm also profusely crying. Seems my medication is not working right now, or maybe they are because it's like I can hear silence in my head instead of all my feelings shouting to me at once. It's calming...

Cal, I know you hate me. And probably for many things. I unfortunately have to add another thing to the list.

I'm getting married to Jonah. He proposed to me this morning. At first, I was shocked and I didn't want to say yes but he told me to hear him out. Let me try to explain it to you:

It was obvious he cared about me and he wanted to be with me genuinely but he also knew that you were someone so important in my life. We had two more years to be apart and he thought it would be safer to my well-being to be married to him so that I was unavailable to other people. He bragged for a good ten minutes about how beautiful I was. I mean, Cal, there's no way I could've looked beautiful being in the hospital for almost a month. I hardly looked at myself but he looked at me like the way you did, completely oblivious to my flaws. He was candid though and said that even if I didn't believe his truth about my worth, he was a male and I was any male's dream. He was very protective of me. He wanted to protect me from any person out there that wasn't him or you. Cal, he wants to marry me until you come home.

That kills me. I only ever imagined getting married to you. The fact of marrying anyone who isn't you makes me sick to my stomach. But I feel the need to explain this you. Jonah brought up this idea to essentially "watch over me" until you get home –if you do come home. Just having his added protection for the time being seems appropriate. I don't want to navigate this life alone anymore. Jonah is in a good, stable place in his life. He knows that my heart is like a tombstone with your name on it, but it doesn't seem entirely crazy to have someone care for the tombstone until you return, right?

God, I just hope you don't hate me for this. Please don't ever think for a moment that I want to spend the rest of my life with Jonah because I don't. I want him to be part of my life but not in a legally binding way.

I am yours, and you are mine. Until then, I'll be Jonah's, and he'll take care of me, okay. I hope you trust us in this decision and know that by the time you get home, I will get a divorce from him and have my hand ready for you.

I'll never let you go.

Jen

Jennie

Thursday, April 18th, 2007

I haven't heard from Cal since this morning after he left.

My anxiety has been playing tricks on me. I'm replaying every word, phrase, sentence, and conversation over and over from yesterday, piecing together what I said wrong. My brain is feeling like a burnt piece of toast–completely black. I'm trying so hard to figure out when things took a turn.

For the first time since Cal has returned, last night was the best night we've had. It was carefree. There was so much love. So many kisses and cuddling. He left my apartment happy and said he would call me later.

It has to be those stupid letters. I don't know what letter Cal just finished or is currently reading, but it's tearing me apart.

I'm tempted to tell him to just burn them. There is nothing in this world more important than him. Not even my story, my memories. I'll just pretend none of it happened and we can start over.

It can be that easy, right?

Jennie

Friday, April 19ᵗʰ, 2007

He still hasn't called.

I'm having a breakdown and make calls to Jonah, Lydia and Pat by nine o'clock in the morning. They all come, trying with all their willpower to calm me down.

It was fortunate that my first panic attack occurred upon Lydia's arrival. I was a mad-woman; talking fast, going through the million reasons of why Cal hasn't called, pacing my apartment, trying to keep my body moving. She just sat with me, helping me to breathe.

The next one comes a couple of hours later. By that time, Lydia, Max, Pat and Jonah were at my apartment. Lydia suggested I lay down for a while. She gave me a sleeping pill, but I kept it on my side table. I didn't want to fall asleep. I was afraid of missing his phone call.

Unlike my first attack with excessive talking, pacing, sweating, this attack was just one loud scream. It felt like the same scream when Cal and I were at the cabin and I thought he left me.

I'm not sure which situation is worse...

Every goddamn second that passed, it was torture.

Jennie

Saturday, April 20ᵗʰ, 2007

Still nothing.

Jennie

Sunday, April 21ˢᵗ, 2007

I've been laying in my bed all weekend, exhausted from crying so much.

I pick up my phone, which has become an annoying habit to check for messages or missed calls. Of course, there's nothing.

My face feels like there's dry stained streaks of tears. I can tell my eyes are puffy. My temples hurting from crying so hard.

Jonah left early this morning for his shift. I overheard him talking to Max–who was next on watch-over-Jen duty–that he was fine with calling into work. Max fought with him about that. He could watch me like a vulnerable newborn puppy. I'm sure Max is reading on my couch cause that's usually what I find him doing when he's over here.

I gaze over the dozens of unread texts to Cal. I have nothing to lose if I text him again. My fingers are shaking. My mouth is trembling. Everything in me is broken, and I'm not sure what's keeping me together.

Hope maybe? Hopeful that Cal is putting himself through Hell so we can be together.

Jen: I'm not a fan of the silent treatment. Talk to me, please. I am under constant supervision because you are making me a lunatic. I miss you.

The butterflies are about to escape my stomach when I see the three dots on my screen. I sit up in my head so fast that my brain joggles back and forth a bit, making my screen look fuzzy.

He's alive. He's going to say something to me.

Then the dots disappear, and the butterflies die in my stomach like the worst plague that was created.

I couldn't take it anymore. The silence was killing me.

Knowing Max would refuse, I called Pat instead. I beg him to drive me to Cal's apartment. I knew he wouldn't take the conversation well. It was a back and forth of him telling me to be patient and that Cal would reach out when he was ready. I yelled back at him that I couldn't stand to wait anymore.

Something felt wrong. Cal wouldn't ignore me for a straight week. I sobbed hard on the phone and with the harsh sigh on the other end of the line, Pat agreed to pick me up.

It wasn't a pretty sight when Max answered the door to find Pat. The conversation wasn't pleasant either when they both went into full dad rage mode on me for lying. I didn't tell Pat that it was Max on duty, and I didn't tell Max that I called Pat to bring me to see Cal.

Honestly, I have a distorted view of reality. I don't have a sense of time, what is real or not real. It's all a blur.

An hour passed before they both agreed. Pat felt uneasy that something serious was going on with Cal, and he couldn't live with himself if he knew something happened to him. I wouldn't be able to live with myself either. I put the guilt on Pat and Max, too. It wasn't a fair move, but I was running out of options.

Under one condition, I had to eat. Max and Pat watched me eat my chicken and rice before we left. I guess they weren't playing fair either.

The drive to Cal's apartment was silent. Pat felt like my parent who knew I had a drug problem and, well...Cal was my drug. I had been clean for years. I just couldn't let him go.

When Pat parked on the curb and looked out the window at Cal's apartment, the worst anxiety came over me. I fidget with my sleeve. I feel my breathing get heavy. My leg shakes.

I'm thankful Max suggested taking a Xanax before doing this. My earthquake feels like a small tremor, and for a moment, I think I can handle it.

A small part of me contemplated telling Pat to take us back to my apartment and keep waiting until Cal was ready. I had no clue what I was about to find... and that scared the shit out of me.

I felt a hand on my arm and looked over at Pat, who was sadly grinning.

"Want me to go with you?"

I can't speak, so I shake my head no.

Just give us a minute.

"Call me if you need me, okay? I'll be close. Don't do anything stupid."

I couldn't even respond because my stomach was churning over itself and my tongue felt like it slipped down my throat. I nod my head, understanding his request.

I walk up to the broken main door and pull it open. My feet feel like concrete, so I stare at the stairs, mentally preparing myself to climb them.

I will save you.

I reach the fourth floor, and my eyes immediately fixed on his door. Tears welled in my eyes as I prayed for an answer at the door, fearing the worst.

Please, just be behind the door.

Knocking softly, I barely have enough energy to knock louder. I won't leave until I see him. After a couple of seconds go by, I get nervous.

Okay, you'll wait.

Then I hear the door unlock. The butterflies that I thought were dead have slowly come back to life. I don't feel them flying with pride or enjoyment. It's almost like all they've done is open their eyes.

The door opens and I want to die, or maybe I do die because every happy thing that I love turns black and cold. The man who opens the door is unrecognizable and I can't help but let my eyes become waterfalls. I weep into my hands that are covering my mouth, nose and partially my eyes.

Cal looks fucking terrible.

His eyes are rimmed with red. Underneath his eyes, the red fades to a black and blue discoloration, presumably from a lack of sleep. Something—a cat, bird, or devilish sex—tousled his hair. Bile rises in my throat at the thought of sex.

Please don't have someone come up behind him.

His shirt is wrinkly, and he's in sweatpants. Cal NEVER wears sweatpants.

He leans against the door and rests his head against it, looking utterly drained. He takes in every inch of me as his eyes travel from my eyes down to my body and back up. For a moment, an elixir seems to have revived him. I wish I could say that I cured him by my mere presence, but I can clearly see that is not the case.

He looks angry. His eyes betray a deep bitterness. Torment and anguish are fully present. I can feel it all around me.

He rolls his eyes at me, switching emotions to annoyed, and walks away from the door, leaving it open a bit—what a wholesome invitation. I push through the door and hold it to prevent a slam.

I turn around to witness the tornado mixed with a hurricane and a hint of a tropical cyclone. A gasp escapes my lips, and I quickly cover my mouth.

What have I done?

Some furniture has been overturned. Paper shreds are everywhere. I see the first aid kit open on the kitchen table with items sprawled everywhere. A red stain disfigures the wall, but I can't ask what it is because my mouth is stapled shut. It's not until I fully look at Cal, who has gauze wrapped around his hand again and band aids line on his arm.

"Cal..." I squeal.

He's leaning against the counter in the kitchen. I walk a bit more into his apartment to look around the corner to see him. He has his head slouched, and doesn't even look my way when I say his name. I walk closer to him, hoping again that my presence will calm him down. Hopeful that it will bring him a sense of comfort.

"Don't Jen." He walks around me, out of the kitchen, and sits on his couch that is jumbled with blankets and pillows. The only piece of furniture that is in place.

You deserve this, remember? You wanted him to hate you.

I'm sucking in my tears, trying to keep them inside for however long I have.

"Which part was it?" I'm still in the kitchen, facing the empty presence of where Cal just stood. He huffs behind me, making me feel like I asked a stupid question.

"November letters. The hospital letters. All of it." Frustration fuels his response. Turning around to look at him, he's leaning forward on the couch, running his fingers through his hair.

I try to remember the letters. There were only two in November, when everything went to shit. I remember what happened with Glen.

And just like that, my heart cracks. My bones snap. Some force has cut the invisible string between us. There's nothing left for us to discuss. I know what I did. He knows what I did. This is where we end. Forever.

"I'm sorry." I gasp out, running my sleeve under my nose and feeling every neuron in my brain turning off.

I turn the corner to head for the door and place a limp hand over the knob. I'm trying to figure out if I have enough energy to twist the knob, but it doesn't budge.

My heart races as I can sense his presence. His bloodshot eyes met mine as I lift my gaze. I wish I had the same reaction to pull him close to him like he does for me. I see that he's using his hand to keep the door closed.

Say it. Say you don't want me to go. I'll stay here with you forever.

"Don't go."

I've never seen Cal so vulnerable before. He looks miserable and I want to ease the agony as best as I can. I feel my soul crash into his as I wrap my arms around him and pull him close to me. His arm falls from keeping the door shut that engulfs me until I'm lost in the past of being with Cal.

I'm lost in a moment of no secrets, no pain, no hurt. Just the best, most unconditional love. The strength of his arms makes me feel safer than I have felt in the past week. I lay my cheek against his rib cage but I can hear his heartbeat like it's beating in an amphitheater. It's soothing.

Thank you time, for being on our side.

And just as quickly as Cal and I can enter paradise topped with a feeling of ecstasy, we can quickly crash to the darkest depth of purgatory.

"Why did you do that to me, Jen?" He pulls me away to examine my face, using his thumbs to erase my tears. He seems conflicted, wavering between anger and wanting to comfort me. He's looking for answers to understand why I would jeopardize our relationship, and friendship, with Glen. Of all people.

"Jesus, Cal. Do you still not get it? You have no idea what life was like without you! It's not like I wanted to do anything with Glen or even Jonah! I waited and waited and waited... hoping that every single day you would come back so I wouldn't have to wait anymore. My heart was breaking more and more each day. Five years, Cal... I had to wait five fucking years. When I found that out, I had two options—I could find a bunker and bring all our zombie apocalypse necessities and wait underground for you. Literally just pause life and then start back where we left off once you got home. Or I had to move on. I had to take care of my dad and go to school. Just try to create a life worth living. You and I said it before, time is a thief and it doesn't stop for anyone.

As you can tell, Cal, I did neither. I took care of my dad for as long as I could until he was no longer alive, and then my purpose just fell off the Earth. There was no one left to love and nothing left to live for."

I'm sniffling so much that I get a headache. To give us some space, I leave Cal by the door and walk towards the kitchen.

"There were only two people I let take care of my heart. Obviously, there was Jonah. I hope the letters made it clear that he cared so much. He was a nurse, so I think a lot of his love was just natural because he had a passion for wanting to help people. I continued to feel like his patient even after leaving the hospital, and I freaking hated it. He was always getting my pills together, making sure I was doing something productive with my time when I wasn't working. I tried so hard to let him take my whole heart, but I couldn't. I couldn't give it all to him. He had a minuscule, broken piece of my heart. Our marriage was a sham. It was a joke. It was a label because Jonah wanted to protect me from all men in the world. He wanted to keep me under his wing until you came home. I swear to God I did not expect to get married for six months. And I hate that all of that happened, but I didn't know what to do. What I did to Jonah, that wasn't fair to him, and the added pressure of marriage weighs heavily on me."

I take in a big breath of air as I fall apart in front of Cal. Guilt tings me as I shout at him. Along with the long list of emotions I'm feeling, I'm so tired. I'm so tired of failing him. My rainforest feels flooded.

Cal looks at me like he's in pain. Deep physical pain.

It felt impossible to save him.

"The other person was Glen, wasn't it? To take care of your heart." His voice is sad. My frustration builds and I hate that I have thoughts of slapping him. Shaking my head with betrayal, I look away from him.

"No." I bite my top lip, licking the tears that have fallen to my upper lip.

"A piece of my heart was always with you, Cal. When will you fucking realize that?"

Feeling uneasy and dizzy, I lean against the kitchen counter while Cal stays put in the center of the living room. I let my head fall and run my fingers through my hair. My rainforest is not ready to lighten up.

Several minutes of deep, uncomfortable silence fill the room. I take advantage of the silence to get my heart rate back to normal.

"You can say what you need to say. I can handle it." I blubber through my sniffles, using my sleeve to wipe my nose. Three years of being away from Cal was torture, but there is nothing more or less torturous than the pain I just caused him.

He glares at me as I watch him move to sit on the couch.

Just hate me so I can let you move on without me bringing you down.

After all these years, Devil might actually win this war.

"What do you want me to say, Jennie?"

I snap my eyes shut and flinch at the way he says my name. *Don't call me by my name.* He only does that when's upset, which was hardly ever. The sound of it from his mouth feels unfamiliar. The sound of my name makes my stomach fold over itself. I wipe the last couple of tears with my fingers and look at him.

"Tell me you hate me." I say it with sincerity and truth. If he hates me, he won't want to love me anymore.

I don't deserve his love.

I watch him flinch in pain. The sight of his tight fists appears that his rage meter has entered an F5 get-the-Hell-out-of-dodge warning. He is trying so hard to control his temper right now.

Speaking through his teeth, he says, "54321."

What the Hell?

"What?" I watch him awkwardly adjust to the couch where flashbacks secretly haunt me.

Sweat is building on his hairline; his eyes are snapped shut; his shoulders are tense, and his leg bounces up and down like it's being hammered.

No, not a panic attack. Not right now. Please, for the love of God.

I'm torn between wanting to comfort him and leaving him to console himself. If I were to leave with him like this, I would hope a bus would run me over. He wants me to help him calm down? Do I have enough strength for this?

Instead, I walk to the couch and start talking because it's Cal, and I'd do anything for him. Maybe I can distract him. I don't know how to get him through a panic attack.

Our relationship is so messy. Being two poisonous snakes, we suck deeply, without ever reaching the venom. A witch and a pirate, we are putting each other on trial to die. Continuously attacked, we remain like a bulletproof vest, wounded but not truly hit.

He's rubbing his temples, trying to soothe the tornado in his head. I've done that gesture so many times, and I want to tell him that it won't help.

The back of his head is leaning on the top of the couch. His shoulders look stiff, his face looks sad and angry, and I just want to make it go away. I will take away his pain and inject it into my veins and live with it forever if I could.

Just try it.

"What are 5 things you see?"

His body shakes and his uncontrollable bouncing leg is making his trinkets vibrate on his glass coffee table. He takes in a big sigh, almost gasping for air. Trying not to bother him with my presence, I sit next to him on the couch. Heat and anger are radiating off him. I internally panic that I won't be able to disarm this bomb of Cal.

"I want to punch Glen five times. Each time, being a different strike to his face."

That's not how we play this game. We never play what we see in our mind. That's the whole point of this technique is to regain yourself to stay in the present moment.

Sometimes when you are in the panic, any feeling can set you off even more. Even though he's upset with me, I gently wrap my hands around his fists.

Please Jesus, whoever is up there, please let me be the one to bring him peace.

"No, what do you see? Around you, Cal."

I've never experienced trying to calm down Cal down when he's over a level 10.

Then my stomach flips over itself again.

A second chance.

Do I get to rectify Cal? I don't know if he's doing this on purpose, allowing me the opportunity to calm him down—the very thing I never had the chance to do.

Telling him to hate me was a mistake.

No, don't hate me. Let me do this. Let me help you.

I try to pry his fists open so I can hold his hand, but he's strong. I close my hands around his fists, like a nice cozy sweater.

"Tell me what you see around you." I keep my voice calm, intimate so that his senses only feel me.

I'm in control. I will not fail him. Not again.

He crinkles his eyebrows and opens his eyes to look at me, almost surprised at the change in my voice. Maybe he doesn't realize what he's allowing me to do. I don't care. I'll do whatever it takes.

For a moment, I feel his body relax and look at me with that look. His 'I have hope that we will get through this, even though I hate you right now'. He gave me that look after Jonah interrupted us the other night. With my hands still wrapped around his fists, they relax, then unravel and interlock my fingers with his. He moves his eyes around the room, soaking in all the visual inspiration.

"I see I turned this place into a fucking disaster. I see the red stain from the wine bottle I threw at the wall yesterday. The sunset is happening. You're wearing my sweatshirt." He side eyes me, looking at my chest.

"One more thing." I urge him. My throat becomes dry when his callous eyes meet mine, almost trying to look deep into my soul.

"The most beautiful green rainforest in all of Washington." Trying to hide the change of color in my cheeks, I look away and lick my lips.

"What are 4 things you feel?" Letting go of his hand, I flip it over so I can trace his lines, creating a curvy letter m.

"I feel a giant hole in my heart because I haven't seen or talked to you. Anger is pouring through my veins, even though I'm trying really hard to stay calm. I'm thirsty, and I feel you tracing my lines." He moves his eyes down to his palms. I watch him smirk, and for a second, I feel like I'm winning.

He charmingly maneuvers his hand to snatch mine, so I'm no longer tracing.

My heart. Oh, my heart is feeling something...

Watching him making circles with his thumb, I'm getting lost in his touch.

Angel distracts me by tickling the back of my throat.

Stay with him. What else does he need?

"What are 3 things you hear?"

"Your voice is my favorite sound, even though you're breaking my heart. The car horns from the street. I hear noises from the hallway." He keeps his fingers interlocked with mine, but I want to rip mine away. I want to run to the bathroom and cry.

I wasn't trying to break your heart.

Ignore Devil. She's angry because you are winning. Keep going. You're saving him. You're doing what you never got the chance to do.

My voice cracks and my eyes are moist.

Keep your shit together.

"2 things you can smell."

"Burnt bacon and jasmine." His answers were quick. The bacon's scent hit me quickly as I walked in, but my other senses were preoccupied. And jasmine, my shampoo scent.

"1 thing you can taste."

"Blood."

"Blood?" I blink a few times to make sure I heard him right.

"I bite my tongue right before you got here. That's why I kept my mouth pretty still. It hurts so bad."

"Let me get you some water." I try to remove my hand and stand, but he doesn't let me.

"No, don't go. I'm fine." His hand tightens around mine. The same tone when I was trying to leave here. Desperation.

Letting Angel continue to guide me. Twisting my body to face him, my free hand moves the hair from his face, stroking my fingers down his cheek. I watch him breathe deep at my touch on his face. With his other free hand, he takes my wrist, brings my hand to his mouth and kisses my knuckles. Tenderly and sweet.

I watch him intently. *Please, please stop messing with my heart. I don't know what you want.*

"Thank you." He opens his eyes and holds my gaze. Suddenly the room feels small, and he adjusts himself to face me. Our hands separate and my hands feel cold, so I clasp mine together in my lap.

"For what?" I squeal out. I'm nervous that he's going to kiss me, not that I'm opposed. His unexpected kisses always make me nervous. He's still so close.

He reciprocates my gesture and runs his fingers down my cheek, making my insides twirl like a ribbon baton. I flutter my eyes in pleasure.

"For saving me. For a moment there, I thought I was going to bust the balcony window. You deserve a chance to save me. All those times before, when I just ran away from the problem, I didn't think it was fair to do that."

"All I've ever wanted was to save you, Cal." I whisper back to him, feeling like he's sucking all my oxygen. I take my gaze off him, trying to not give the impression that I want to kiss him. Even though I want to so very badly.

I feel like gambling all of my poker chips. It's time for both of us to lay all the cards on the table.

"Calvin, I need you to tell me what happened to you after we left Easton. I think it's time I hear it from you...Please." Begging isn't a good look on me. My body feels weak, and he's taking so much of the oxygen between us that my voice is barely loud enough. It shakes with fear and anticipation. It was a story that was constantly pushed under the carpet. I need to hear Cal's point of view of how the best weekend of our lives turned out to be the most traumatic and depressing weekends that would change our lives forever.

You aren't ready for this story yet. I think it's time we leave.

Something happened to him all those years ago... The boy who I left behind is not the same person he is today.

Cal drops his gaze to the ground. I watch as he traces his own palm lines, and it sends the worst pain in my stomach that I'm not doing enough.

I knew asking this of him was about to set the grenade off. He looks calm on the outside, but he's still a ball of fury on the inside.

He's quiet for a couple of minutes. There's a part of me that is hoping his anger is subsiding. But I'm preparing myself for disappointment that he won't tell me the story; just like all the times before.

He doesn't care enough about you to tell you the truth.

Then he spits the words out. I feel Devil inside fall over as she receives the best bitch slap from Angel.

"I almost killed him, Jen."

SUMMER OF
2003

Calvin

Thursday, August 14ᵗʰ, 2003

I had a disgusted feeling inside of me. Jen was just ogling over Glen, right in front of my fucking face. Everything he said, she laughed. Every suggestion he made, she agreed. Every comment he spoke, she responded. Every time I caught him looking at her, she was already staring at him. It made my blood boil, and it made my heart break.

At first, I crumbled, then something snapped in me.

I don't know what hurt more—the thought that Jen was just fucking with my feelings to get back with Glen or that Glen was enjoying this. He knew how much I was falling in love with her. I really hope he wasn't testing my limit because I'd beat the living shit out of him. Jen was here with me. She was *my* girl. Not his.

I tried hard to control my jealousy with Jen. At C&H, there were so many times I would catch boys (and men) flirt with her. How could you not? She was a gorgeous gem. She didn't even think twice about the message they were giving.

But when Glen flirted with her, it's almost like she was in a different dimension–one without me.

She and I rode together in my truck to Easton, and things were normal. We held hands in the car, almost making it the entire way without letting go. We laughed about how Jen was going to shower in the woods, and I heckled her over and over about the nightmares she would experience for her first camping trip.

Bad fucking karma on my part. How a joke about nightmares in the woods would escalate to real life for her.

The moment we got to the house; Jen was still in a good mood. She even walked around the truck to find my hand again, even after the long drive. Her hands weren't even close to being sweaty.

I knew she was nervous to camp, but I'd been camping plenty of times with my family, so I wanted her to know she was in good hands.

I consider myself a semi-expert.

We left our bags in the truck just so we could see the house first. Anna planned this trip and booked the house, but I gave her explicit criteria so the place would make a good impression on Jen. None of them knew what to expect, including me, but I knew Anna wouldn't disappoint.

Walking to the front door, I was pleasantly surprised by the modern weekend home. The purpose of this house was to settle in before making our way to the campground in the morning. I hoped it would help with Jen's nerves. There was another purpose for this place also, but that is for sharing later.

When I looked back to check on her as we walked, she appeared relaxed and smiled widely at me.

Then I heard the first warning.

Glen called from the top balcony, "I call dibs up here!"

Jen says, "aw."

What the fuck.

I remained silent towards her, unsure whether my anger or sorrow manifested first. Either way, I didn't like her reaction to his comment.

I tried to keep my focus on the weekend ahead. As we got closer to the house, the details are pretty spectacular. Six large glass panel windows face the side of the house. Andy and Anna are walking through the glass double doors. The other sides of the house are a solid oak wood finish. To the left of the front doors is a lovely, overgrown garden. It's filled with wildflowers. All of Jen's favorites-daisies, tulips, forget-me-nots, dame's rocket. I peek at Jen to see her smiling at the flowers. *Nice job, Anna.*

Near the garden, there is a small firepit and four Adirondack chairs. That area is definitely screaming my name later. I gesture to Jen to walk inside so I can have a moment to peek around the back. I walk on the freshly paved sidewalk to the backyard. It's there I see the first thing I asked Anna to find as part of her criteria. The sidewalk curves down a small slope to the gazebo. It's a perfect shade of white and I'll be sure to leave a tip for the owners for the addition of the string lights.

It's romantic and perfect. *Really nice fucking job, Anna.*

I bite my bottom lip in joy. Even though I haven't fully made my decision, I'm satisfied with the setup if I follow through.

I get to the front doors, eager to see the view from the inside. My eyes search for Jen but I don't see her. Her perfume lingers in the front room, and I hear Glen's voice complimenting something. By the time I get all the way inside, all I hear is "so beautiful."

He better not be talking to Jen.

I grit my teeth and watch Anna and Andy ooh and awe at the grand living room. It's open and white and... large. There's a tan couch and a light brown coffee table. More windows surround the fireplace, making it the focal point of the room.

I twist my neck toward Jen's laugh coming from behind some wall in the kitchen. Douchebag right on her tail. She stops when she sees me and her grin slowly fades. She seems guilty of something.

She dances over to me, painting a smile on her face and wrapping her arms around my neck. She kisses my cheek and I'm swept under her spell again. I bury my head into her neck, letting her aroma penetrate my nasal cavity.

She lets go of me and we play tug-of-war with each other-she's pulling me towards the windows in the living room and I'm tugging her towards the stairs so we can capture our room. I let her win for three reasons; even though I'm in a slightly irritated mood, I'll always let her win her games. I also love her, and I want to see this view.

We stand at the windows that look at the view of the Wenatchee Mountains. I bring her in front of me and wrap my arms around her shoulders. I rest my chin on top of her head and enjoy the moment. *The first of many perfect moments this weekend.*

"Okay, all the couples here need to find their bedroom and leave all the cute shit in there." Glen mocks from the kitchen. I glare at him as he comes next to us to look at the view. My view is garbage now.

"What's your problem?" Glen looks at me and loses his smirk.

I don't care that Anna and Andy are giggling as they climbing the stairs. They are probably grabbing the best room, but I'm bothered by other things.

"You. Just because you didn't want to invite another human being here doesn't give you the right to suck the fun out of this for everyone else." My rage meter spikes. I wrap my arms tighter around

Jen's shoulder, protecting what's mine.

"Cal, stop. Glen's date was .... Unavailable." Jen twists a bit, facing towards me. She puts a hand on my chest, trying to keep me tamed. She appears cold towards me, but then laughs when she talks to Glen.

Again, what the fuck? I look down at her, bewildered.

"I don't give a fuck who he did or didn't invite. He'll be spending this weekend alone if he pulls that shit again. Anna and Andy are already banging the headboard against the wall. I don't hear ya complaining about them!"

Glen looks at Jen for some sort of help on how to respond to me. I'm done looking at his punk ass face. I take Jen's hand and pulled her towards the stairs to claim whatever bedroom was left.

"Fuck off, Glen."

I don't see it, but I can feel it. Well, I think I heard Jen whisper an apology to him, but I also feel this weird chemistry between them. Almost like she wanted to stay in the living room with him. Like I didn't matter.

I win at tug-of-war now, pulling Jen up the stairs, trying to keep my wrath inside. The bedroom Andy and Anna picked was a stupid choice. They have no bedroom door, and it's set up more like a loft overlooking the living room. However, they have a giant king bed and a connecting bathroom.

That room is not the privacy I want for me and Jen.

Suckers.

Jen's calling my name and I'm happy to hear my name escape from her mouth. The room in the middle of the hallway that is an immediate no-go. It's about the size of a closet and has a single bed. This belongs to Glen. He can sleep in the closet. I slam the door shut, hating that Glen occupied my thoughts again. Another door is about seven feet down the hallway.

"Fuck! I scream. My patience is wearing thin. Not to mention the concoction of hunger and sleep are entering the equation.

"Stop pulling me, Cal. Jesus, you're going to rip my arm off!" Jen's voice feels miles away, but I ignore her. I just need to get her in our room, by ourselves, and kiss her.

We pass a bathroom before approaching the next bedroom. Andy and Anna must've scoped this one out and denied it. Stupid choice.

I push the door open, eager to examine our haven. We have four wide glass panel windows that overlook Kachess Lake. I chuckle because we picked the room with bunk beds. No wonder Andy and Anna ditched. We won't be using the bunk beds, anyway. We'll just need one bed.

I look back at Jen, who is gawking at the view. This view is definitely better than the living room view. Quietly, I close the door. Smirking to myself that I kept myself from exploding, I approach her from behind. I glide my hands up her waist and turn her around to face me. *Finally, our moment.*

I look down at her and brush a piece of hair behind her ear. She gives me a weak smile, but when she closes her eyes in pleasure, I know I've won. I always win.

"I want this weekend to be perfect for you." I whispered in her ear, then make a trail of kisses from her ear, down her cheek until I kiss the corner of her mouth. Moving away, I grant her the opportunity to make the next move. She traps me like a bear and kisses me hard. Grappling my hair, I pull her closer to me. Our tongues mesh and she tastes so sweet. As she dragged her nails down the back of my triceps, every goosebump on my body activated. *Jesus Christ.* Desperate to pull her down on the bed, I move her back gently there. In between kisses and groans, she says, "stop being mean to Glen. He's nice."

She's laying on the bed, propped up by her elbows, and I stand above her. I think someone just blew an air horn in my ears because I can't believe what I just heard. However, I don't need her to repeat what she just said. I bite my bottom lip hard, then pace around the room.

"Glen's a fucking idiot and he's annoying. I'll be mean to him if I want to." I say my piece and move back to kiss her again, but she rejects me. She side- swipes my kiss and our cheeks caress. My stomach fills with paranoia.

"What?" I shrug my shoulders, pretending I did nothing wrong. Jen stands from the bed and walks to the window, crossing her arms to look at the view. I stay put, unsure whether to follow her.

"Glen just got out of a crappy relationship. He's trying to be pretend everything is fine, but he's not doing okay. I wish you were nicer to him. You're making him feel worse about himself than he should." I stare daggers into her back. What I want to say is something so cruel and sickening that Hades and Menoetius would judge me. Instead, I ask, "how do you know that?"

Fuck, jealously has come out to play. I cross my arms, impatiently waiting for an answer. Jen turns to stare at me.

"We talk occasionally." Her entire voice level drops. Ashamed? Embarrassed? I can't tell, but her entire demeanor has changed, too.

"What do you mean, you talk occasionally?" I use my fingers as air quotes when I say *occasionally.* Not only is jealously getting fired up, but I scrunch my eyebrows in confusion. I'm with Jen practically ninety percent of the time, and she's hardly ever on her phone, so does that mean she's sneaking behind my back?

"Like we talk here and there. It's nothing serious. We have history, Cal. I can't just not pretend his feelings don't matter to me. He's still important, okay? Just needed some advice after Emmy broke up with him. Anna and I both talked to him about it."

She's getting defensive and I'm not having it. It's also not a time I want to pick a fight with her.

Where did the romance go?

"Well, those conversations are over, and so is this one. Let's go get our bags." I huff and unfold my arms. The tension in my shoulders hurts as I turn around and try to relax. My body tenses more when Jen's hands wrap around my torso.

"Hey, stop."

I've compared Jen's voice to so many things. It's just poison, and I'll always want more of it. Unable to move, I freeze and turn. Her eyes are getting glossy and she's holding back her tears. I don't have a habit of making her cry, and I don't want to start now.

I am not a controlling boyfriend. While I never want to dictate her friendships, Glen is strictly off-limits. I love she wants to care for his emotions, but that isn't her responsibility anymore. Jen has the biggest heart and always wants to put others first, but it's Glen I don't trust. He's a snake, and at any moment, he could wrap himself around my perfect Jen and manipulate her. I'm not in the mood to turn on my predatory instincts.

I express my feelings with my face, but doubt my apologetic look is convincing. She pulls me close and lays her head on my chest. I don't even hesitate about wrapping my arms around her. The comfort she brings to my life is in-fucking-describable. Kissing the top of her head, I breathe her in. Jasmine and peach nectar. Her shampoo and body spray. Singularly, they are fresh and waken my soul. Together, though, they are exhilarating and activate all my goosebumps. Every inch of her is perfection.

She lifts her head off my chest to stare up at me. Her intense gaze makes me want to jump off a cliff. It's pure magic to my self-esteem.

"I love you. I know you are only watching out for me, but he's just a friend. Swear to you. You are everything. Stop fighting with me because I don't like it."

Laughing, I rub my fingers up her chin, holding her face still as I lean down to kiss her. Softly and intensely at the same time. My Jennie. The only one for me. We break apart and I let my teeth bite my bottom lip to salvage her taste. I want more. She bites her bottom lip too, which only makes me bite mine more. I think she might pull me towards the bed, at least, I hope she does. Instead, she pulls me towards the staircase.

Well, damn.

When we get downstairs, Glen isn't around, which I'm thankful for. Anna is in the kitchen, putting away a few snacks from the drive. I send Jen to retrieve our bags. A few minutes apart will do the trick for us to become in sync. I hand over my keys to her and wait for the door to close.

"Pss, Anna." Her back is to me, and on cue, she jumps. My favorite hobby is scaring Anna.

"Damnit Calvin! I thought you went outside with her." Her aggressive towel toss makes me laugh. Anna has a really beautiful smile. The first time I saw her smile, I thought she had to either be a cheerleader or dancer or even a model. It's one of her best features.

Anna and I have been friends since elementary school. Her mom was a reading specialist, and I needed extra help with reading starting in second grade. I had a difficult time summarizing parts of a story. I could remember the story, but I would sequence the events incorrectly. In second grade, her mom formally introduced us and thought Anna could help me with language arts homework. Throughout elementary school, she was my reading partner. In middle school, she helped me with English papers, and anything related to the English language while I helped her with math. It was an even trade.

"So when are you going to give it to her?" Anna's loud ass mouth makes my insides twist. I look behind me to see if anyone was listening.

"Shut the fuck up about it. I'll do it when I think it's the right time. Anyway, what are we doing tonight? How do you call this a camping trip when I feel like we're in a mansion?" I twiddle my fingers together, feeling antsy and irritated about the reason I brought Jen out this weekend. I hate it when someone ruins surprises.

Anna turns around from the counter, looking hurt at my questions.

"You were the one who gave me this crazy ass checklist of amenities this place should have. You're welcome, for one. Two, I didn't realize I was the one planning the entire weekend, but since I'm so smart, I decided I should do it, anyway. There's this treehouse excursion that I made reservations for at seven. After that, I figured we could find a place to eat and then around nine, I found this lantern festival. I don't want to spoil the details for you, but it's pretty romantic." My hands find their way to the edge of the counter, and I grip hard to calm myself down from gripping Anna's throat.

"If you mention one more goddamn thing about my plan for this weekend, I will haunt you for the rest of your life. I'm not fucking kidding, Anna. Talk to me in private if there's something romantic you want to plan. I have a list of things too, so I don't want to overwhelm her with too much love shit." Quietly, I yell at her, making sure not to startle Andy or Glen should they be in the house.

I glare at her, hoping the look frightens her when she closes her eyes. I hate threatening Anna, but sometimes she needs it. The jingle of keys makes me break eye contact with her. I peek over my shoulder, seeing Jen struggling to get through the door. Standing up quickly to help her, I look back at Anna. She has her arms crossed, but her eyes look pitiful. Deep down, I know Anna is only trying to help us, but she needs to take a back seat. I don't even know if this is what Jen wants—if she even wants me.

"I'm serious." I mutter to her again, walking to the front door.

I open the door and chuckle at Jen, who is trying to pick up both our duffle bags and her small tote bag dangling from her arm. Taking the duffle bags from her, her face eases with frustration.

"What the hell did you pack? Your bag feels like a bag of rocks."

My insides twist but then release butterflies. *You have no idea, my girl.* I don't respond to her to prevent myself from spilling any secrets. We turn towards the stairs to take our bags to the bedroom. Anna has been watching us from the kitchen with her arms still folded. I scold her from behind Jen.

"You haven't mentioned what we are doing tonight, Anna." Jen pauses at the base of the stairs. Anna briefly glares at me before she responds to Jen.

Is that a threat? Please don't spoil this, Anna. I am begging you.

"Once everyone is settled, I'll share the details! It'll be fun."

Anna was always so good at changing personalities. I thought she was bipolar in middle school. The mood swings were scary. I even told her mom that I didn't think she was normal. She thought we were too flirty, and that Anna acted that way toward me because she liked me. She did it all the time around her mom. We'd have heated arguments about math and English homework. She would call me a dickhead or punch my arm so hard that I would bruise. Her mom would knock on the door and ask how things were going, and as if she had a split personality, she would angelically smile and say we were having the best time.

It's déjà vu right here, right now. Standing behind Jen, I'm mesmerized by Anna with how she could pull off being an asshole to me and be a friend to Jen, all in the same thirty-second time frame. If she were anything less of a friend to Jen, I'd have to do some damage.

"I can't wait to hear what it is!" Jen adjusts her bags on her arms and walks up the stairs. Being the jerk I am, I wink at Anna for behaving herself and pick up our bags and follow Jen.

I check my watch on the way up the stairs to determine how much time we have. 3:57.

I follow Jen down the hallway to our room and lay our bags on the floor while she tosses her bag onto the bed. Feeling slightly warm from the adrenaline between Anna, my weekend plans, and the weather, I take off my sweatshirt. Jen is standing at the windows again. I make a mental note for our future home to have large windows like these.

"I like the view here. It's so peaceful." I smirk behind her, taking in her words, but in a different context.

"I like the view too." Whispering as I approach her from behind, letting my hands grab her waist. She lays her head back into my chest and holds onto my hands.

"Oh, shut up." She grumbles back to me. I turn her around to get a better look at her. Seriously, I could look at her for hours. She's so fucking breathtaking.

"Come here, lay down with me for a bit."

Walking backwards to the bed, I pull her. She's following me easily, almost as if I'm just barely tugging at her fingertips. Falling on my back, I pull her up to my chest. I play with her hair, enjoying the quietness and each other.

Devil and Angel bicker in my mind, right as I enter tranquility, as always.

Thought we were going to get some action here, buddy.

Oh hush it, let him hold her and cradle her and make her feel special.

Our libido is running high. Why doesn't anyone ever care about what I want??

You just saw her naked yesterday! Not everything has to be rated R now. Shut up and let them enjoy this moment.

God, I wish I had an on-off button for them. They annoy the hell out of me, even if they are both right ninety-nine percent of the time. As much as I want to see Jen naked again, I'm perfectly content with her in my arms. My hand moves down her hair to caress her arm and she snuggles close to me, grabbing me like it's our last day together.

A crash from downstairs springs Jen and I off the bed. We fell asleep for a while, and I'm annoyed as hell that something interrupted my dream. I move my groin off Jen to hide the hardness in my pants, and thankfully I get more time because Jen darts out of the room.

"These people are going to be the death of me." I mutter to myself. Or to Angel and Devil. Who knows?

A few seconds is all I need before I'm dashing down the hallway to make sure Jen isn't entering havoc. I skip down the stairs and see Andy on the couch, flipping through a magazine. My eyes search aimlessly for Jen. My nose is trying to follow her scent.

"What was that noise?" I ask Andy. He looks at me and points a finger towards the kitchen.

Jen and Anna are crouched in the kitchen, picking up pieces from a shattered lantern.

"What the hell happened here?" I walk towards them and Glen is coming in from the laundry/closet room holding a broom.

"I was getting our camping shit ready and forgot I had two lanterns in the bag when the bag fell off the stool. So, I guess we really have to tell ghost stories in the dark." Anna shakes her fingers in a spooky vibe manner towards Jen.

"Shut up, Anna. You're annoying." I grumbled, running my hands down my face. She raises her lip and gives me an annoyed look.

We've all been giving Jen Hell for this trip, considering she's the only one who has never been camping. Jen knocks Anna in her arm, standing up to take the broom from Glen.

Okay, fuck face, you can stop staring at her like that.

I walk towards them to grab the broom from Jen and to break eye contact.

"I'll get it." Irritation is clear in my voice.

Glen walks in the opposite direction from us, towards Andy, to sit on the couch. Jen gives me a small glare and washes her hands from touching the floor.

"Okay people. You have an hour to get ready. We are leaving at six-thirty. Shave your balls, or mustaches, wear deodorant, don't wear thongs, and get ready to climb on all the wood!"

With my eyes wide, I hold the broom still. Did she just say that? Jen's also staring at Anna. Glen has his jaw dropped on the couch and Andy is the only one making noise, laughing hysterically.

"You got it babe!" He shouts back, even though we are all ten feet within each other.

"What? Someone has to get the party started." She shakes her shoulders up and then leaves the kitchen, going up the stairs. Andy following tentatively right behind her. That leaves me, Jen, and Glen... again.

I'm too afraid to walk away to put the broom and dustpan away, thinking they'll have a secret conversation, so I stand it in the corner, next to the fridge. Jen opens the fridge to grab a water, but I don't think she realizes I'm standing on the other side, so I close it. She jumps and I smirk at her.

"What are you going to wear, Jennie?"

Excuse-fucking-me?

"Why does it matter?" I spit back. My grin disappears and my blood boils. Jen touches my arm, hoping that will help me calm down.

"I was just curious if we were dressing casual or comfy or active." Glen stands up from the couch, making his way to the stairs.

"Cal, stop. Let it go." I think that's what Jen says to me... I feel her hand on my chest, trying to get my attention, but all I see is red.

"Glen, I honestly don't know. I think I might just do causal. Lucky for you to be a guy, you can wear whatever you want, but us girls have to be strategic when choosing an outfit."

Jen's touching me, one hand on my chest and the other trying to loosen my fist. I feel her heat radiating off her body. I want to look at her so badly, but my target is Glen. As soon as I hear her voice, my rage lowers. She brings instant relief.

Until...

"You look beautiful, no matter what." Glen speaks.

I about jump over the island to reach his throat. Glen moves only a little up the stairs, barely flinching at my reaction. It's Jen who stops me again, yanking my shirt and grabbing my face. I'm breathing heavy and my fists are tight.

"Hey! Enough."

Her voice is stern. I only get that tone every once in a while. I hate I let this prick get under my skin, but he's up to no good, I fucking know it. Jen's back is to the stairs, ignoring Glen and trying to give me a hug, to keep me grounded. I wrap my arms around her shoulders and pull her close, never letting my eyes off Glen as he walks up the stairs.

I about lost my shit when he smirks and winks at me.

He's messing with me. This fucking prick wanted me to get riled up. Holy shit. This motherfucker is going to get buried right here, in the middle of nowhere.

We wait until Glen is fully up the stairs when I let go of Jen and walk towards the front door. I need some air or I'm going to die. Jen follows me.

"What the hell was that about? Someone can't compliment me?" Jen snaps as she slams the door.

"That's not the point. He's provoking me, Jen. I swear to God, he won't like what I have in store for him if he wants to play this game." I swing my fists around, practicing my left hook.

"Why do you hate him so much? He's done nothing to you." Her voice feels so far away, and for a moment, it hurts my heart that I hear sadness in her voice.

"Uh, have you not been paying attention?" I motion my hands towards the house where Glen is inhabiting. "He's pulling some ugly trick of making me jealous. I don't play those fucking games."

"Well, clearly, he's winning if you need some fresh air to calm yourself. Or do you always have bulging veins after every conversation with a male?"

"That's not fair." I drop my hands and turn towards her, realizing I've been pacing away from the house and she's standing by the front door. There's a good fifteen feet between us as I walk towards her.

"I don't mind if people compliment you. Hell, I would encourage it because you're one in a million and you deserve to know that, but don't react like you've never heard things like that before. I compliment you all the time, so it bothers me when you react like it's hearing a goddamn symphony."

My honesty lingers between us for a moment. I've never said anything so hurtful to her before.

"I didn't even react to him, though." I pause when I'm about an arm's length from her.

"You can't see yourself."

My voice breaks, and I'm embarrassed that I'm reacting so hostile to this. I want Jen to feel on top of the world when someone notices her. It felt like though, Glen complimented her, and she didn't feel on top of the world... she went straight to the Heavens. As if she enjoyed hearing *his* words.

"You blushed and your smirk was something I've never seen before. I've never gotten that reaction from you before." I watch her react to my truth. Her face falls, caught in the lie that she "didn't react." She knew she did. It was clear as day.

She walks towards me and grabs my hands. For a split second, the feel of her is annoying me, but it's so incredibly soothing.

"I'm here *with you*. Only want to be complimented *by you*. Only want to be touched and looked at and adored *by you*. I'm sorry if I made you think anything otherwise, okay?"

She pulls my hands to her face and kisses each of my knuckles, making my legs shake. Her breath on my body always makes me feel shaky. It's like her words are a spell and I forget everything that just happened. I pull her up, holding her ass while she locks her ankles around my back, and I kiss her.

God, she drives me crazy.

"Take me upstairs so you can help me figure out what to wear." Her voice is soft, but so fucking provocative. I don't know if she means to come off that way, but I walk as soon as I hear the last word leave her mouth.

Being the nice guy that I am, I tell Jen where we are going first and reveal Anna's stupid riddle of climbing on wood.

"Oh my gosh, that sounds awesome!!"

She's pulling every shirt and pant out of one of her bags and tossing every article of clothing onto the bed. I grab a pair of boxers so I can take a quick shower. I beg Jen to come in with me, but she knew it wouldn't be quick and after the whole altercation downstairs with Glen, we were running a little behind. Jen still had to use the bathroom and get herself ready.

After clothing myself in my khakis and a black long sleeve with a black widow on the back, I head back to the bathroom to brush my teeth, even though it's near six o'clock at night. It's a weird habit I do after I shower. I want to make sure every part of me is clean.

Someone pushes the door open a bit, and I hold on to it to avoid being hit.

It's Glen.

"My bad, man. Wasn't sure if someone was in here. Pretty stupid there's only one bathroom for us and the two lovebirds get their own en-suite. I think Anna planned that shit."

I'm glaring at him the entire time he speaks. Where is the small talk coming from? Rinsing and spitting into the sink, I stare back at him. For a moment, I want to laugh at his comment because it's something Anna would totally do.

"Does Jen need any help?"

"What?"

"Oh, I wasn't sure if Jen needed help with anything."

There's a tornado happening in my stomach and all the blood is rushing into my fists.

"What would she need your help with, you fucking pig?"

"Eh, she may need help to get her ass into her pants. Or maybe a hook broke on her bra, and she needs some help there. It's been a long time since I've seen her bra. What designs is she into now?" He's moving back from the bathroom, towards the closet with the most smug grin on his face.

I can't help it. I slap him across his left cheek. When he looks at me, his lower lip is busted and there's a slight cut of blood. He touches the cut, bewildered that I let my impulsiveness win.

"You're psychotic, dude. I hope she leaves you."

I watch him enter his room and close the door behind him. There is so much fuel brewing inside me. I move back into the bathroom and splash some water on my face.

Get yourself together. If you continue to let him get under your skin, he will win.

I'm standing in the doorframe watching Jen struggle with an outfit. She's holding shirts up to her body in front of the mirror. Thankfully, she can't see me yet.

Glen's words play on repeat for a minute or two. *I hope she leaves you.* I clamp down on my bottom lip to keep my trembling chin steady.

She looks at me, her eyes lighting up. It's the only medicine that would cure a fearful heart.

Be better than him.

"You are going to look incredible, no matter what. You can always wear something of mine if you want to."

When I approach her, I trace her jawline and watch her eyes roll. Just from a simple touch of me, I watch her melt. While it should melt my heart, it only strengthens my spirit.

She doesn't look at him like the way she looks at you.

"I like when you say it." She purrs to me. I dig my fingers into her hair, right beneath her ear, and pull her into me. I kiss her deeply, reminding her of my lips. She moves her hands around my sides, then I feel them move up my torso and chest until she places her hands on my collarbone. Goosebumps light up my body. The way she makes me feel should be illegal. But I'd let her do it no matter the consequences. I feel her teeth as she smiles under my kiss.

"We have to finish getting ready. You know Anna will leave without us." I drop my forehead to hers, disappointment in the ending of this. She pecks my lips one last time until she moves away from me. Smirking like an idiot, I'm falling more in love with this girl.

She grabs a handful of clothes and heads to the bathroom. I take the time to check out the view of the mountains. I debate with Angel and Devil about what I should do this weekend as far as the surprise goes.

Are we moving too fast?

We want her. There shouldn't be any second guessing this.

Lost in thought, the door opens, and Jen appears. I bite my lip at the look of her. God, she can pull anything off. She's wearing these tight black biker shorts with *my* Rolling Stones shirt. It's baggy on her, but she looks so irresistible. She probably would've gone through my clothes even without my invitation...

"I need to do my hair and makeup!"

She seems panicked. Jen HATES to be late, plus there's the added pressure that we both know Anna will indeed leave without us if we aren't downstairs at six thirty. She can be cruel like that. I walk over to my bag and check my phone for the time. 6:18. Yikes....

I sit on the edge of the bed and watch Jen add more sparkle to herself. She sits in front of the mirror with her makeup bag in her lap.

She doesn't need makeup and her hair is always in good condition. I'd be proud any moment, of any day, to walk with her on my side.

I'm considering surprising her right now. She'd be shocked, but I know how excited she is to climb in the treetops.

I want to give her everything, and I hate I can't.

One step at a time, Angel tells me.

Either I was in a trance for a while or Jen is just fast at her makeup because she switches off the light.

"All set! With two minutes to spare. Get your shoes on, let's go." She slips on her purple Nikes that I bought for her graduation present and pulls a sweatshirt from her other bag. I'm tying my suede Vans, then grab my sweatshirt on my way out the door.

"Take mine." She tilts her head in appreciation and doesn't hesitate to throw her sweatshirt on the bed. She cradles mine against her chest.

God, she's fucking beautiful. I can't stand it. She's got a nice layer of mascara on, making her eyes shine like two leprechauns. Lucky me... She's touched her cheeks with some blush and her lips have a shine to them from some sort of gloss or ChapStick. It takes all the resistance in me to not lick it off. Again, she's pulling me from my thoughts, literally.

"Byeeeeeeeee" we hear Anna echoing through the living room.

Jen is pulling me down the stairs, even though I'm full force coming down the stairs with her. We make it out the door as everyone else is piling into Andy's SUV.

"Ha, suckers! We made it." Jen snarks at them.

"Oh my god, Glen. What happened to your lip?" Jen's concern makes me want to throw up. I slightly turn my head in Glen's direction, but he avoids eye contact with me. If he throws me under the bus about slapping him, all bets are off the table and I don't mind doing more damage.

"Oh, my phone dropped on my lip. Hurts like a bitch."

Confused, but grateful, I side smirk to myself. Hmm, must have some common sense to not mess with me.

I hate the fact that Jen is sitting in the middle of Glen and me.

I double check that her leg wasn't touching his or any part of her, for that matter. He's already buckled in, leaning against the door and looking out the window. *Fuckhead doesn't even compliment her.*

I buckle myself in and grab her hand, interlocking our fingers. Jen lays my sweatshirt on her lap and angles her body towards me. I wish I could hear the thoughts running through Glen's mind right now...

Andy drives for about twenty minutes, bringing us back to civilization. Anna is barking at him, giving him directions on when and where to turn. Meanwhile, I'm getting car sick at the sudden turns. Anna was never good at explaining shit.

"Jesus Anna, give him more than ten seconds before the turn or else we are going to throw up back here." I growl at her.

"You don't speak for everyone." The first sentence Glen has spoken since the drive.

Immediately, like a fucking bear, I glare at him. My eyes notice his fresh cut on his lip. I feel Jen squeeze my hand, bringing me back to the moment. I suck in my cheeks to prevent myself from going off.

The one time I'll bite my tongue, but because we are in close quarters, and Jen is in the middle of us and I don't want her to get hurt.

"Turn here." Anna snaps. Andy whips the car, and all our bodies sway to the left.

"Jesus fuck." I speak.

"Dude, Andy, teach your girl how to give directions." Glen shares.

"Oh shut up, nobody died." Andy says as he puts the car in park.

The sound of five clicks occurs at once and four doors pop open. I hold out a hand for Jen to grab. There's already a slight chill in the night and Jen puts my sweatshirt on as we walk towards the entrance. I'm too busy idolizing the string of lights twisting up the trees, at least sixty feet. I hear a grunt come from behind me and realize Jen ran into Glen's back. They are giggling and I stop in my tracks to turn around. His filthy, rat hands are touching Jen's arm. I'm pissed off that I'm not into cannibalism or else I'd eat this motherfucker alive. I snatch Jen to put her on the other side of me and imagine punching him in the face with his nose getting broken.

Glen says nothing. His face says it all. That fucking wink he does to me again. Jen adjusts her sleeves and grabs my hand to pull me behind Glen, Anna and Andy.

How do they always miss the confrontations? Or maybe there are really good at ignoring us...

I halt Jen to prevent her from continuing to walk.

"What the fuck was that?"

She's looking right at me, her eyes still glowing like two granny smith apples, crisp and delicious. She somehow fills them with guilt and shame.

Why are you yelling at her? Because she accidentally bumped into him... because she totally planned that, you idiot. I shake my head at the argument from Devil.

"I'm sorry. It was nothing. I bumped into him, and he grabbed my arm, so I didn't fall over." Her voice breaks my heart, pleading with me she did nothing wrong.

I wipe my face with my hands, trying to be rational that it was nothing. *BECAUSE IT WAS NOTHING.*

I don't respond and grab her hand to meet up with the others. I get the tickets for me and Jen and ascend the tree.

The stairs spiral around thick oak trees. We follow the path of string lights. Thankfully, it's not too busy and for several feet, it's just us five climbing. I hear Anna laughing at the front of the pack. Andy right behind her. Glen is taking his sweet time to enjoy the view from the trees. The sky feels like a painting. It's a light grey with the stars beginning to twinkle. Hardly any clouds are in sight, which makes the air cool.

I'm behind Glen because I'm not waiting for another "accidental bump", so I let Jen be a caboose. I have my arm behind me, holding her hand as we trail the steps around and around. There's a landing every thirty steps or so to rest and take in the view. It's pretty romantic when it's just Jen and me. When we reach the landing, Andy and Anna are climbing again. Glen is right on their heels.

Jen's arms dangle over the barricade, and I stand next to her, enjoying the moment.

"Everything you thought it would be?" I nudge her, then smile.

"It's incredible. I could do this every night." I make a mental note to make a tree house with string lights at our future house, to commemorate this moment. We'll have it forever.

Looking down, I noticed my shoes were untied. As I kneel to tie them, I'm lost in thoughts of our future dream house. I've never asked Jen what kind of house she prefers—something small and cottage-looking or something grand that makes a powerful statement. I can imagine us in both. When I stand, Jen isn't by the barricade and when I look around for her, she's hurrying up the stairs.

To him.

For a quick moment, I think about jumping over this barricade. Or at least imagining Glen getting thrown over the barricade. Better him than me...

I rub my lips together and feel my heart beat fast. I run my fingers through my hair, trying to understand what the fuck is happening.

She just ditched you for him.

I'm sweating despite the breeze. Only a few moments ago, the breeze coming through the trees was peaceful and enchanting.

"Jen!" I shout to her as I climb again, skipping every other step. She turns around, like she's surprised I'm calling her. Almost for a split second, she looked confused on why someone was calling her name. When I reach her, my breathing is heavy, and my fists are tight.

"Hey, sorry! Glen called me up to see something, and I didn't want to miss it." Again, her voice is pitiful, like she has done nothing wrong.

I snicker. "You couldn't have waited for me so I could see too?" She doesn't answer. Glen is a few steps in front of us and I can feel him looking down at us. I don't dare look up at him because I know I can do more than a slap. But I hear his chuckle, and I lose my shit.

He's enjoying this and I'm going to fucking kill him.

He's had enough chances to fuck with me. I lunge towards him and grab him by his collar. Taking him by surprise, I watched his ugly smirk fade. Behind me, I hear Jen calling my name, trying to get me off him. Then I hear Andy's voice trailing down the stairs to us. He's pulling at Glen, but there's something in me that can't let go of him.

He deserves punishment for being a dick.

"Cal, get off him!" It's a mixture of Jen, Andy, and Anna's voices. Unfortunately, something in me gives in and I let go. Glen falls back into Andy, who's holding his shirt. Lucky for him, I didn't hit him. Only held onto his collar. Jen pushes me back. For the first time, she pushes me.

"That is not okay!" She shouts at me.

I've done it. This is where she leaves me.

I should've just let him keep walking, but goddamnit, he was testing me.

"C'mon, we are almost at the top." Anna tries to de-escalate. Andy and Glen follow. Jen tries to, but I stop her. She looks...

Fuck! She looks sad and angry and disappointed and annoyed.

"I'm sorry, baby. I don't know what came over me. I had no intention of doing anything. He just gets under my fucking skin. I don't know why. I don't like how he looks at you, like you're a lollipop."

We're stopped on stairs, and the next landing is maybe fifteen steps. We can see the top of the trees. She doesn't respond to me, instead she crosses her arms and looks at the ground. I go to lift her chin to get to her look at me.

She's crying. It's the second time already I've made her cry.

"Hey, no. I'm so fucking sorry Jen." I pull her into me, to hold her, to comfort her. Whatever the hell I need to do to get my girl to stop crying. She buries her face in my chest and hides her face in between her hands, even though nobody is around. I kiss the top of her head to give her more comfort. I just keep apologizing.

"Stop fighting with him. Just be with me."

Her voice is full of pain. As if I've been ignoring her and giving Glen all my attention. Have I? Fuck, I hope I haven't been. She's right. I'm here with *her*. She's all that matters.

I kiss her head over and over.

"You're right. I'm here with you. I want to enjoy this with you. Come on, we're almost at the top. It'll be easier and quicker to go back down." I hear her sniffle and wipe her nose on my sleeve. She looks up at me. The rainforest... the wet rainforest will always break my heart. Using my thumbs, I wipe under her eyes.

"That isn't the only thing going down..." It's like some angel sprinkled pixie dust on us. She's grinning and my mouth gapes open.

"You dirty dog." I kiss her as she allows my tongue to enter her mouth. She grabs my face, pressing me towards her. We have a moment for a ten second makeout session. *We needed that.*

We reach the top in less than five minutes. There's a platform that circles around several trees, probably for more support. The view is just indescribable. Now the sky is just a blanket of darkness, speckled with teeny tiny fireflies. The outline of the Wenatchee Mountains looks surreal. You can barely pinpoint the peaks of the mountains, but you can tell there's something incredible out there. We move around the platform to get a good view of the moon peeking through. It's hanging low tonight, waxing gibbous. I would've guessed it was a full moon if Jen wouldn't have told me. She stands in front of me and I surround her, entering a state of contentment.

Her and I.

I move close to her, kissing her cheek, giving her my attention. She leans her head back, relishing me. I look around the platform to scope our group. Anna and Andy are taking pictures of each other, stuck in their own world. I know those pictures will go into Anna's scrapbooks. That's been her thing for a few years now.

A few people have joined us, and we hear them oohing and awing at the view. I look in the other direction and see Glen standing by himself, overlooking the trees. As if our thoughts were talking to each other, he looks over to me. He looks miserable. Truly pathetic looking. For a moment, my stomach churns for him. I have everything he wants. Then the selfish part of me internally smirks and I turn to kiss Jen's cheek again.

I have everything I've ever wanted.

We marvel over the view for a couple more minutes. Anna huddles us together as we prepare to descend. To change the order, I announce Jen will lead us down. I'm behind her and by the grace of God, Andy follows behind me, then Anna and Glen. Those two have been chatting quietly. I clench my jaw, hoping Anna isn't sharing my surprise with Glen. That would be the worst possible thing to happen. I try ever so hard to eavesdrop, but the wind makes the leaves brushes together, and it overpowers.

The way down felt much shorter compared to going up.

Somehow, Jen beats us down and is patiently waiting for us. Andy and I haven't said a word to each other, and still talking to each other privately, Glen and Anna emerge from the steps. Simultaneously, they look at me as if I'm a suspect. I ignore it and walk over to Jen, who is reading the information board about the treetops.

I barely get my arms around her as I hear Anna shout for us to follow them back to the car. Jen grabs my hand, but she's quiet for the short walk.

We load the car, and despite my lingering resentment towards Glen's presence, I unwind as Jen rests her head on me. I want to look over at Glen and wink at him. *I've got her.* But he's looking out the window, completely oblivious to our affection.

When I say we are in the middle of buttfuck nowhere, we are. Somehow, we end up in a town called Roslyn. Anna is still barking "turn left" and "turn right" at Andy. He's so whipped.

He pulls into a Waffle House and it doesn't hit me how hungry I am until I connect the words waffle and food. My mouth salivates.

Seatbelts click and four doors pop open again. I help Jen out and she looks so cute right now with her sleepy eyes. I wrap myself around her shoulder and tuck her into my side. We walk through the door and there are a couple of guys at the counter and a younger couple in the corner. Andy leads us to a table on the opposite side of the couple.

Like Tetris, everyone tries to decide how to arrange themselves.

Just keep us away from fuckface.

It's these moments I'm grateful to have a friend like Anna who can be so controlling. She pushes Andy to the end of the table and has Glen sit next to him. I sit across from Andy, Jen is across from Glen and Anna sits at the end of the table, trying to be the middleman. It's not ideal but it'll do. I'd rather look across at Andy than look across and see Glen. However, I hate the fact that when my eyes leave the menu, Glen is staring at Jen. Jen's head is looking at the table, preoccupied with her menu. I clear my throat, which makes everyone stare at me.

"Sorry, my throat is dry." I talk directly to Glen, who rolls his eyes and looks around the place to find our server approaching. This little old lady has her snow-white hair wrapped in a bun, being kept together by a pencil. Her lips are bright pink and must still use the same lipstick from the sixties. Her white uniform is clean and crisp, and she smells like a grandmother.

"Hello lovelies. How are we doing?" Poor lady could use some water. Her voice sounds dry.

"Hi! We are great. How are you?" Anna cheers.

I lean back and put my arm on Jen's chair, glaring at Glen, who lifts his eyes to my action. He crosses his arms and he takes a deep breath in, his chest expanding. His shirt collar looks wrinkled, and his stupid face still has the cut on his lip.

In a circle, we tell Lettie our orders. She leaves us be and leaves the scribble of orders to the cook. I watch her take a pack of cigarettes out of her apron and walk out the front door.

It's quiet for a couple of seconds until Anna cuts the tension. I lift my eyes to check on what Glen is looking at. He's watching the water droplets fall from his water. If I had to be critical, his eye level was a little too close for staring at Jen's chest. She's playing with her hair, looking happy, and talking to Anna. *Finally.* Andy is leaning forward with his hands balled together, listening to Anna and Jen talk about the weekend and probably a bit irritated his girl is at the end of the table. *I get it, dude. Sucks for you.*

"I'm going to the bathroom." Everything seems calm. I push my chair back and kiss the top of Jen's head.

I continue to strategize my surprise for the weekend. How much do I involve Anna? If I do, do I risk Andy finding out and spoiling something? Do I take all my items with us to the campsite, or should I leave it as a surprise for when we return? I really should've had a better plan. I dry my hands and open the door with the paper towel and throw it away.

For once I have a feeling that maybe we could have a relaxed dinner and Glen understands his place, but then my world comes crashing down.

Looks like we've done a round of musical chairs... Devil whispers to me. There's nothing in my stomach to create bile, but I feel something turn and burn.

Andy sees me first. In a split second, he's reading my thoughts and meets me at the table, holding me back from pounding Glen's face.

His hand was resting on top of hers. AND SHE WASN'T EVEN

MOVING IT AWAY.

"Hey, hey, hey, stop. Go outside, come on."

Andy is strong. I didn't realize how strong. By himself, he forces me outside without being able to say a single word. Glaring in the direction of the group, I realize I wasn't looking at Glen. Jen is standing up at the table, fear painted on her face.

I'm sure she's trying to come up with some stupid excuse for letting him touch her.

Anna was standing up too, trying to keep the peace like always. The only person who doesn't move is Glen. He took Anna's seat, claiming head of the table status. His back was to me, so he would've never known I was coming for him, had it been for Andy. He doesn't look at me. He sits stoic in that seat as if he's won a shutout.

I shove the door open with all my might that I wish I could've broken the hinges off. I feel Andy's presence behind me.

Andy and I have an interesting relationship. He transferred schools in eighth grade and joined the basketball team right away. Anna was a basketball cheerleader, and that's when they met. Anna and I helped each other with homework until graduation. I was terrible at writing; she was terrible at math. We had each other, so why set ourselves up for failure?

Of course, I intimidated him. Anna and I would stay after school and explain assignments to each other in the gym bleachers. He assumed we were dating, and I guess she never explained that we were friends. She must've told him something interesting because they started dating freshman year. When it was basketball season, she and I would *try* to do homework in the gym bleachers, but she was annoying because she just watched him. Don't get me wrong, he was a good defenseman, and I certainly wasn't upset to be writing English papers, but I knew he was trying to show off for her.

Tenth grade was the worst. I hated when it was offseason for them because she would ditch me after school for him. The infatuation between them was nauseating. When it was basketball season, my grades slipped badly in junior year. I was trying my best to do homework by myself, but Anna would usually double check my work. My mom called Anna's mom and I don't know what words were exchanged, but I knew Anna had received the message.

Senior year was a breeze. I completed my credits a semester early, so lucky for Anna, she had all the time to be with Andy.

We didn't talk much to each other. There wasn't much to be said. I had no feelings whatsoever for Anna. She was just a friend and tutor. The same goes for me, to her. Were there times when we had deep, meaningful conversations? Sure, but there was never a connection between us. I've just known her to be my non-biological little sister. But there was always an unspoken language between us to protect Anna. She was our common denominator.

In this circumstance, though, Anna isn't the problem. But Andy understands... to watch someone you care about, be around someone that you hate. I was the guy he used to hate at one point, and he knows I feel that way towards Glen.

I put my hands behind my head and pace the parking lot. I have such a strong desire to scream at the picture-perfect sky to break it in half, just as I'm feeling. Like a mirror that is cracked.

I turn around and pace towards Andy, who has his hands in his pocket, giving me space.

"Nothing happened in there, Calvin. I promise you. Jennie said something like she was glad he was okay, then he put his hand on hers. That's it." He tells me.

I spit my words out to him. "That's not the fucking point! Am I delusional or is something going on between them? I feel like the third fucking wheel, and I don't understand!" I'm shouting now.

Jen and Anna are looking at us through the window. I see the back of that son-of-a-bitch, wondering what kind of bullshit he's telling them. I continue to pace, hoping to lower my blood pressure.

"What can I do, man?"

My body feels like a bomb, ready to explode. My nose and throat are both itchy and my vision is blurry. I'm nauseous. There is so much tension in my shoulders and arms. I just feel my body falling apart. I put my hands behind my head and lean my head back to stare at the sky. Is this what a broken heart feels like?

Dropping my hands, I move to the side of the building where they can't see me from inside. I don't need the fucking audience right now. Falling onto the curb, I rest my forehead in my hands. The sound of gravel crunches around me, and I feel Andy approach me.

That's another thing about Andy. We've had so many silent

conversations over the years. We don't have to talk for us to know how we're feeling. The many times both of us waiting for Anna to change after practice. *She takes forever, doesn't she?* The times he would meet us at the coffeeshop, and she would leave us to get drinks or use the bathroom. *If she drinks coffee now, she'll be up all night.* The only thing we verbally agreed on was Anna's driving. It was horrific.

"What does she see in him? Am I not enough for her?" My vulnerability slips through the cracks as I confide in Andy. It feels weird, but I need some sort of reassurance.

"I'm sure you're aware they dated, right? Before he transferred. They went to the same school up in Lake City." I only nod because I'm aware of this.

"I guess I'm the one to blame for bringing Glen into the picture. When he transferred in the middle of sophomore year, he joined the team. By that time, he tagged along with me and Anna. It was kind of annoying because I wanted alone time with her, but I was too nice to him, so I let him." His story telling is calming. It puts things in perspective for me.

"I didn't know they dated until Anna invited Jennie out with us one day. It was clear there were still mutual feelings between them. I'm honestly not sure how often they hung out after that. I didn't ask because it wasn't my girl. She was single, so it didn't seem like a problem. But I'm sorry, man. He's a good guy, but there's definitely something about you that attracts his temper."

"I guess I'm glad she stayed at a different school. If I were to have met her at school, I would've been so distracted. I think Anna mentioned that time, where Jen ran into an ex-boyfriend and she thought they were going to get back together."

"Did Anna ever talk to you about Jen, or how did you guys meet?" This is the longest conversation I think I've ever had with Andy. He's good company.

"Anna and Jen worked at the daycare together. She talked now and then about her co-workers, but not specifically about Jen. She started at the coffeeshop in February and then left the daycare in April. It was funny to see Anna's reaction when I introduced Jen to her. It was the only time I had the upper-hand on Anna. She had no idea. By the time Jen and I were a thing, I was out of school, so I hardly saw Anna, thankfully. She'd stick her nose in my business."

"Oh, okay. That makes sense. Funny how paths can cross sometimes like that."

My body is so much more relaxed now.

"So, was Glen dating someone from school?"

Not that I was super popular, but I knew a lot of people.

"Emmy Hune. She was on the yearbook committee. They broke up at the end of the year."

For some reason, Devil inflates itself and whispers to me *ask questions and get leverage on him.*

"What happened, do you know?" Peeking at Andy, he doesn't notice me staring, then he chuckles, which hardly ever happens. Andy is a tough guy to crack a smile if you aren't Anna.

"Yes, I know, but you don't want to know."

YOU NEED TO KNOW.

"Come on, you can tell me."

I won't stop pushing until I get my answers. This time, Andy lets out a sigh.

"He told Emmy that he may have feelings for someone else, and he wasn't sure how he was feeling about her or the other girl, but he wanted to be honest with Emmy."

I'm struggling to swallow. *Another girl.*

"Who was the other girl?"

"Come on, man. You already know."

He nods his head to the building. Certainly, he can't be having feelings for Anna. That woman is psychotic. So that leaves...

"Jen."

I wish someone would put me out of my misery because it's too fucking much to feel all of this.

"He wasn't originally going to come with us because he thought it would be awkward. At first, he asked Anna for advice on what to do. Of course, she said to come. I'm not sure how Jen got involved, but she knows. She knows that he's feeling conflicted right now. To be honest, man, she isn't helping."

He and I both look at the door as it opens and we see Jen standing there, hesitant to approach us.

"Hey J." Andy says, and he stands up. He leans down to me and gently slaps my back.

"Don't let her go." He whispers.

In my peripheral vision, they pass each other and switch positions. Andy goes back inside, and Jen is standing on the curb, holding her body. I can't look at her, feeling betrayed because she's allowing Glen to flirt with her on purpose.

"Can I sit?" she whispers. I nod my head up and down. As soon as she sits, though, I turn my head away from her, knowing her gaze will bewitch me.

"Do you want to be with me?" I despise having to ask, but I need something. I need some hope to hold on to.

She tries to touch my arm. At first, I flinch. For the first time, I question if I want to be touched by her. But I miss her touch, so I let her.

"Of course I do." Her voice is barely audible.

"Then why are you doing this to me?"

She has her arm fully around mine and part of me wants to move closer, but I need her to be the one to make the first move. *Show me you want me.* On cue, she brings herself close to me. The left side of my body is reawakening.

"I'm sorry. You're right, I haven't been playing fair. I want you. I want only you."

The feeling is overwhelming, and I look down at her. She takes her other hand to graze across my cheek. I feel like I'm being reborn. The fire burning in me is being washed away. I connect my forehead to hers.

"Please promise me you'll stay away from him. Please." I beg for mercy, as if my life depends on it. As badly as I want to lift her up and put her on my lap, I need to hear her promise. I need to hear that she wants *this*. That she wants *me*.

"I promise. I will do anything for you."

I closed my eyes, feeling cleansed by her words. It's that easy for me to get lost in the world of Jennie, and it's not fair.

I swing her over my legs so she straddles me on the curb. It's not the most comfortable, but I need to feel her engulf me. I bury my face in her chest, into my sweatshirt. She wraps her arms around my head like a wounded cocoon. I just hold her. I internally beg for time to pause for a minute or two so we can just hold each other.

Love is hard. Fighting the urge to push back other people who love you is hard. As much as I despise Glen, I don't blame him for any of his actions. Jen is a goddess, perfect and unique in every way. If I were him, I'd flirt with her too. I'd want to touch her. And make her smile and laugh. I'd want to be near her. Jen is so easy to love that for a split second, I feel sick at all the other guys in Seattle who could be in love with her. I mean, for God's sakes, look at her?!

But she wants *me*. She wants me to be the one to touch her, to make her shine, to love her endlessly. I won't let anyone take that job away from me. Not even him.

She leaves her fingertips on the back of my head, moving them ever so gently, and beams at me. Her eyes light up like I'm the only one to give her that glint in her eyes.

"They've probably finished eating by now. I told Lettie to make yours to go in case you were hungry later." She lightly scratches her fingernails on my neck, and I can feel every single fucking nerve explode in my pants. Jesus, when did that feel so good?

"Thank you." I kiss the tip of her nose.

A few seconds pass when the door opens, and I hear the voices of our friends. Jen stands up and holds out a hand to help pull me off the curb. I'm back on top of the world again. She's fully devoted to *me*. Making eye contact with Andy, I see his half grin as he pulls Anna toward the car by the hand. I watch the interaction between Glen and Jen, but she pulls me towards the car, completely ignoring him. He's watching her, disappointed.

Sorry but not sorry, man. I've captured her heart.

My grin widens as I follow the force of Jen and wrap my arm around her shoulders. She smiles up at me.

There must've been some sort of conversation that happened inside because Anna is getting in the driver's seat. Jen tells me she gets passenger side. Glen opens the back door on the driver side, but lets

Andy get in first to sit in the middle seat.

These people are true fucking blessings.

Although I hate Glen has a good view of Jen's profile, at least I'm behind her to have easy access to touch her.

The ride back to the house is entertaining. Someone let Anna have coffee and she rambles about nonsense. Really, just nonsense. She talks about why there's a difference between a blinking red light and a blinking yellow light. She doesn't obey either and just slowly cruises through the intersections.

We are in the middle of nowhere and it's close to eight, so few cars are on this dark road. Then she attacks Andy, who is quietly minding his own business, that his car doesn't have a GPS system. I don't know why she doesn't ask Jen for help, but she throws her TomTom navigator at Andy to help her get back to the interstate. Like I mentioned earlier, she is a HORRIFIC driver. I wouldn't have minded anyone else to drive except her.

I close my eyes to prevent getting car sick. After two minutes of her voice, I pinch my nose and decide if I need to tape Anna's mouth shut. After her hearing her voice for over a decade, every single fucking day, I hate I would recognize her voice anywhere.

I lean my head against the window and envision setting up the surprise for Jen this weekend. *The perfect weekend.* It hasn't started off very well, but I can be optimistic.

After Andy helps Anna get to the interstate, we are back at the cabin within fifteen minutes. Everyone seems pretty tired, and I come up with an excuse for Anna to stay behind.

"Hey, I don't think anyone has the energy for this lantern thing. Are you still planning to go?"

I keep my voice low, trying to be respectful of the secret plans Anna had arranged. I'll give her credit for the treetops. Even though there was a moment I thought I was going to kill Glen, it turned out to be a pretty cool experience. Anna leans against the car and folds her arms.

"I know. Didn't realize we would have so many arguments and middle school fighting matches. I mean, Jesus Calvin, is there just one fucking day where you can keep your hands off people?" I choke on my spit and my eyes get wide. Okay, I didn't realize I made Anna this mad tonight...

"Shit, I'm sorry Anna. I wasn't trying to ruin things tonight."

The best part about Anna is her ability to forgive. I've made some bad choices, and she's been with me through most of it. Countless times, I've betrayed her. I've used her. Raised my voice to her. I haven't been kind to her. She always lets bygones be bygones.

"I know you weren't. You are just so hot-tempered, and it ruins the mood so quickly. I spent weeks trying to find exciting and adventurous things in this shit city. Just stick with Jen, leave Glen alone and do what you came here to do. Alright?" She unfolds her arms and lets them hang on her side. I don't respond, but nod instead. She deserves that.

"We'll just talk about leaving tomorrow afternoon for the campsite. Everyone could use some time away from you. Shit, I feel bad for Jen that she has to sleep in the same room, but I guess you guys chose the bunk beds so she doesn't have to sleep next to you." She nudges my shoulder as she heads towards the house. I roll my tongue around my mouth. This woman is maddening.

I walk behind her as she leaves the front door open for me. I lock it and find the living room empty and quiet. There's a nightlight coming from the kitchen that illuminates the room enough to find the bottom stair. At the top of the stairs, I look over to see Andy and Anna hugging awkwardly. Sucks they don't have a door, but at least I get to close ours to block them out. I pass the closet and hear rummaging coming from it. Sucks to have a small room, but I'm not letting Glen take over my thoughts. I reach our room and see Jen sitting on the bed with her phone. I shut the door and lock it, just to be on the safe side that nobody intrudes us in the middle of the night. Just me and her.

"Everything okay?" I keep my voice low. Her neck snaps up and then she relaxes. Her head falls to the side, glad that it's only me.

"Yes, I'm just checking in with Rosie on how my dad is doing tonight."

I want to strip off my clothes of the humiliation and anger that I'm carrying around. I hate that I've created so much turmoil, but I blame Glen. He's should know his place. Jen is with *me*.

I lift my bag off the ground and put it on the bed, trying not to bother Jen as she awaits good news from Rosie. My shirt gets thrown on the chair in the corner. Trying to unbutton my pants, I don't realize how tired I am. Facing the wall, I'm only in my boxers and socks.

Then I feel her. She moves quietly, like a mouse. I didn't even notice she got off the bed. Her chest presses against my back, and this is the feeling I've been wanting. For her to want me. She rests her hands on my chest, holding me close to her. I rest my hands over hers, feeling like we are entering a new level of intimacy. As if I didn't think she could get closer, I feel her cheek on my bare back. Right on my spine and the shivers electrocute me. I can't stand to be looking away from her, so I free myself from her gentle hold and turn around. I grab her face and just look at her. That's all I want to do. She's the only thing that keeps me grounded, that keeps calm, that makes me feel alive. I never want to leave this moment and I desperately take a mental image of the way she's looking at me and move it to the top of my list in my memory.

"I love you." I whisper to her before covering her mouth with mine, unable to let her repeat the words back to me. Our mouths are in sync, opening more and more to taste each other. Our tongues dance with one another and I'm pretty sure the first sound comes from Jen, but the moment becomes all too foggy.

All I remember is the need to get her into the bed. Keeping our mouths attached, I turn her around and lightly lay her down. I climb on top of her, but she pulls me down, destroying the gentleness of the moment. Better for me. I'm feeling greedy.

I can't elaborate on this moment too much because some things are better left unsaid. All I can tell you is that there was a lot of sweat, saliva, and groaning.

I felt bad for our housemates as neither one of us could contain our noises, but I could also care less because it felt like fucking ecstasy. I'll leave it at that. This night gave me all the confidence and signs I needed to move forward with my intentions.

I wanted Jen, forever.

Jen was laying on my chest when I woke up, and the sheets were halfway off her body. Her gorgeous, perfectly sculpted, naked body. I wanted to just lay there and gawk, but figured I'd already acted on most of my animalistic tendencies last night, so I pulled the sheets up to her neck. She moves a bit, cradling closer to me. I remember looking at the ceiling, smiling like an idiot. Or maybe I was smiling at God.

Someone gave me my most prized gift. I would do anything to protect it. To protect her.

She shuffles again, and I look down at her. Her eyelids flutter open to adjust to the light.

Yeah, we probably should've closed the blinds, but things happened so fast...

"Good morning." Her morning raspy voice tells me.

I swear when I think all the butterflies in my stomach emerge every time she speaks to me, there's more that escape. Morning Jen is my favorite Jen. When she grunts and throws the blankets over her face, when she rubs her eyes, when she sits up and runs her fingers through her hair.

The way you look in the morning is usually the most disheveled, less appealing time of the day. For Jen, though, she was most beautiful. It's like she was a white dove, full of innocence. I loved that my love for her was already at a hundred and twenty percent in the morning. That was usually a baseline for me. Most of the time, my love only went higher and higher.

"Good morning, beautiful." I kiss her upper shoulder as I sit up next to her. She leans her cheek into her shoulder to look over at me. Things like that make my love for her jump to a hundred and thirty. She's so fucking cute.

"I hope you're rested. It's a big day for you!" I tell her again.

Camping is something I've been looking forward to. I haven't gone camping since freshman or sophomore year with my family. The first thing on my list today though—find Anna and get her help to distract Jen so I can prepare. This moment is everything.

Jen gets in the shower right away and I wait a couple of minutes to make sure she isn't escaping. Then I text Anna to meet me outside by the firepit. She immediately texts me back with an "okayyy". Oh great, over-exaggerated Anna is the version I get this morning.

I grab a shirt from my bag and slip on my gym shorts that were on the floor. I sneak out our door and walk downstairs. It seems like nobody else is awake yet, so the living room and kitchen look the same from when we came home last night. I unlock the front door and feel a push behind me. I stumble out of the doorframe and try to catch myself. Then I hear Anna's diabolical laugh. She doesn't even make my blood boil anymore. She just fucking annoys me. I'm on all fours, probably looking stupid as hell. I bite my lip and smile to the ground.

"Whoops." Anna's voice sings as she walks towards the fire pit. I lift my head to watch her walk.

God, I wish I could fucking tackle her. I would destroy her. She's the most annoying non-biological little sister.

Okay, so maybe she makes my blood boil because I can't attack her like I could Lincoln, so I guess we'll start trash talking. I push myself off the ground to follow her.

What were we coming out here for?

I forget, but priorities have changed.

By the time I reach the fire pit, Anna is already sitting down in one of the dark brown Adirondack chairs. She has a leg-crossed over the other and a bright pink robe on. Her pink moccasins are bouncing from her leg. She has thrown her hair up in a bun.

I walk swiftly to sit in the Adirondack across from her.

"I didn't realize it was trash day." I mirror her posture and lay my left ankle over my right leg. Rubbing my chin, I try to hide my smirk.

"Oh right. I didn't realize we all signed up for the moaning and groaning getaway, you pigs. We barely got any sleep last night." She rubs her eyes, exaggerating her tiredness.

I put my arms behind my head and relax my shoulders.

"Ah, that sucks. I slept fantastic." An enormous grin widens on my face.

"Whatever. What do you want?" She crossed her arms and looks at me, annoyed, like always.

My smile fades as nerves overtake my body.

I remember why I wanted to talk to Anna.

I clear my throat, drop my hands from my head, place both my feet on the ground and lean forward to Anna.

"I, um..." The words are stuck in my throat. I *know* Anna will help me. She's helped me for my whole life. I see the vision, but I'm nervous something is going to get fucked up. Or someone...

This needs to go perfectly.

"Spit it out." Anna is not a patient person in the morning. We made sure NEVER to do homework in the morning.

"I need your help to surprise Jen with the thing..."

Anna reacts as if I've said the most genuine, nicest thing to her. Her face lights up like she's seeing Christmas lights for the first time. She gets up from her chair and sits right in front of me on the stone pavers surrounding the fire pit.

"Really?" Her voice is quiet, but she has the biggest smile on her face. Her smile makes me smile.

"Yeah, I'm ready to do it." My nerves are slowing down and are popping inside me with joy.

"Okay. Okay. Okay. Oh my gosh, I can't believe this. You've been talking about this for months. Okay. So, what do you want me to do?" Anna's arms are flaying around.

"I don't know. Do you think you should take her with you to the store to get food and supplies and I stay here to set it up? Or should you and I stay behind a bit and have the others set up the tents and shit later? I don't know what the best option is, but I just don't want her stuck here with Glen."

Anna is watching me intently. She squints her eyes, thinking... I think. It feels surreal to talk about this out loud to someone. I've only had ideas and thoughts in my head. I've briefly mentioned a couple ideas to Anna when we were studying.

"Hmm, good point. Well, I think it would look suspicious to Glen and Jen if you and I hung around here after they left for the campsite. It was always the plan for you and me to get food and supplies because you're the pro here, so I was going to pay and you were just going to tell me what to get." I nod slowly, agreeing with her. We sit in silence for a couple minutes, trying to fit different puzzle pieces. Something has to work.

"I guess Andy and Glen could check in to the campsite and wait in our lot. You could take my credit card and do the shopping, and I'll take Jen somewhere into town to distract. I don't know with what." *A closer piece than before, but not quite right.*

"Then we'd have three vehicles. I don't know if we'd have enough room. Plus, I feel Jen would be suspicious."

"I guess we could still go to the store as normal. You and me. I'll have to have a chat with Andy about keeping the peace and keeping his fucking eyes on Jen. Then we could come back, get all the shit together in Andy's car. At the last minute, I'll say that we forgot something, and I'll run up to the store in town and meet you guys at the campsite."

I'm hopeful this piece fits. *Please fit.*

"Yeah, that's good. But you know Jen will want to go with you instead of us."

"Then that's your time to shine and get her excited to get to the site. Make her feel guilty that you don't want to be left alone with Andy and Glen. I promise I won't make it long." I look at Anna, who looks pleased. She likes control. Almost as much as I do.

"I like that idea." She rests her index fingers against her mouth, thinking.

"Anna, I really need you to convince her to go with you. We both know she's going to put up a fight to go with me, but we can't let her."

"So you plan on getting the house set up and when we come back Sunday night, it'll be ready for her?"

"Yeah. I think that's what I want to do." I rub my hands together, nervous but excited about this next phase for us.

"Okay! Well, I'll get breakfast ready. You and I will head out to the store. I'll talk to Andy so that he and Jen can do something productive. Then we'll be on our way hopefully by one thirty. Does that work?"

For once, Anna feels like a supporter. We've bickered for years, constantly getting under each other skin. I always felt that she never approved of my choices. She judges me, whether verbally or by facial reaction. It's hard to make her happy, to even please her. But looking at Anna, she is the most supportive I've ever seen her. For once, she feels excited for me.

I let Anna go back inside first, hoping that nobody was awake yet and trying to dodge the questions of why we were both outside. Looking out, I see the Amabilis Mountains to the East. I'm proud of myself for having a five-minute conversation with Anna without losing my temper.

Boy, the future me is going to thank the present me. I wish the plans were set and ready, and frankly, I wish we were already returning from the campground, so I could see her reaction. God, I can't wait to see her expression.

Standing up and walking back inside, the aroma of bacon and eggs has filled the house. Andy is hovering over the stove, appearing to supervise the eggs. Anna is at the counter, cutting strawberries. When she hears the door open, her eyes meet mine for a split second, as if we have a secret.

"Jen not down here yet?"

Anna shakes her head no. Then, as if Devil lights my ass on fire, she and Glen walk down the stairs together. His hip clearly touching hers. I don't move and I clench my fists and my jaw and walk towards them.

"Calvin, make us some coffee! You do it best!" Anna's fucking distracting voice. I flutter my eyelids and look over at her. She's talking to me with her eyes, coaxing me to the kitchen, away from them. From *him*.

I ignore her. I meet Jen at the bottom of the stairs and pull her into me. To prevent Glen from flanking us, I position myself so he stands awkwardly behind Jen, slightly elevated but at my eye level.

I will kill you. I mouth to Glen. He bites his bottom lip, a scab forming. He scolds me. *Be careful what your next move is, punk.*

"Good morning. Did you sleep well?" I kiss her temple, still holding the gaze of Glen.

"Nobody slept at all, you prick! You kept everyone up all night." Andy shouts from the kitchen. Jen laughs. I wink at Glen, acknowledging that if Andy and Anna had a hard time sleeping, then he certainly did. I move from in front of her and allow her to walk into the living room.

"Not my problem that you picked the shitty room without a door." I shout back to Andy as I turn around to follow Jen. She sits on the couch, her legs folded behind her on the cushion. She leaves an open space for me and I take it. I wrap my arm around her and bring her close to me as we wait for breakfast. Glen walks depressingly to the kitchen, ignoring us on the couch.

"Are you making the coffee or what?" Anna bitches at me again. I sigh and tilt my head backwards, annoyed. Jen places her hand on my cheek and easily gets me to look at her.

"Please make us some coffee, you grumpy bear." She brings her other hand to my face and squeezes my cheeks together. I gently slap her hands away and get up. Pat taught me everything I need to know about creating the perfect cup of coffee.

"Jennie, doesn't Glen have an amazing view from his balcony?" Anna yells from the kitchen. She's taking the pan from Andy, who appears to be in the way. When I realize what Anna just asked, I'm about to go into cardiac arrest. I brace myself on the counter and look back at Jen, who is already looking at me, fucking guilt written all over her face.

"What..." I barely get out.

"She came into my room and I showed her my view." Glen sits on the adjacent couch, smirking at me. He's pleased with himself that he got Jen into his room.

So this is the move you want to play?

"You went into his fucking bedroom? Are you insane?"

I misdirected my anger toward Jen. It should've been aimed at Glen's idiocy and Anna's provocation. Turning to Anna for a moment, I see how she's handling my tantrum. She's getting plates out, not having a care in the world that she brings out The Hulk in me.

I don't know what force in me walks outside and slams the door. I'm amazed the windows don't break from how hard and fast the door slams. Running my fingers through my hair, I try to understand what part of "stay away from him" she doesn't get.

Did I say something to her to make her feel like I didn't want her? Did I make her feel a certain way that she doesn't think I love her? I'm playing every sentence over and over in my head, deciphering where I went wrong.

Why would she break a promise to me...

Somehow, I walked down the steep driveway. I would've kept walking, but this town is small and creepy. There's nothing around us. I look around at the end of the driveway and barely see the top of the roof. I sigh out loud, wishing I could leave. It seems apparent Jen has no interest in staying away from Glen and I'm not about to sit here all weekend in fucking fury watching them interact. I trudge up the hill, my body radiating with anger. When I get to the top of the hill again, she's waiting outside.

Her short caramel hair is blowing in the wind. She's sitting by the firepit. I chuckle to myself at the very thought that less than an hour ago; I was sitting there with Anna, planning my future with Jen. There is such a huge part of me that wants to walk in her direction and console her. To grab her and lift her into my arms. To tell her I'm sorry for vanishing. To promise to keep my anger in check.

But what do I get in return?

She's going to continue seeing Glen when I'm not around. To continue feeding into his crush on her. I don't think that's fucking fair.

Again, some force pulls me away from her direction and I head towards the front door. The magnetism between us is strong.

"Cal, come here." She speaks loud enough for me to hear. I lower my head, Angel and Devil both arguing about whether to walk towards her.

Her words are not sincere. She clearly doesn't care about you. You aren't the only one she seems to think about.

This is YOUR Jennie. She loves you.

I shake my head at the shitty arguments Angel and Devil come up with. I turn my body and walk towards the fire pit. She has her arms wrapped inside the sleeves of my sweatshirt. I don't look at her for too long because it hurts. When I do, her eyes look like she's been crying. I bite my cheek instead of punching myself if I was the reason she started crying.

I sit in the same Adirondack chair from earlier. Jen doesn't move as she sits stoic on the concrete pavers. Her body faces the driveway, away from me as I sit in the chair.

"What the hell, Jen?" My voice cracks. I'm exhausted and sad. I never knew I had to compete for her attention. God forbid, it's Glen's attention I'm competing against.

"Cal, I'm sorry." She breaks down after saying my name. She covers her face, hiding her tears from me. I move my eyes to watch her cry. Devil whispers to me *what is she even crying for?* But Devil is an idiot and I decide to wait for Angel's response to her tears. I watch her for a few seconds, growing more helpless that Angel isn't telling me anything. Jen's sniffles and cries are making nauseous.

Fuck it. I stand up from my chair and approach her. I pull her up from the bricks and hold her. All I ever want to do is protect her. To be the one to hold her and make her feel better. I worry and hate at the same time that I might not have that opportunity. Glen is clearly doing something to her I am failing at.

I pull her closer to me, wishing for her tears to stop. My comfort makes her cry even harder into my chest.

"I'm so sorry, Calvin. It was nothing. It wasn't supposed to be anything." She weeps to me. I feel my chin tremble and my eyes moisten. Running my hands through her hair, I hate this feeling of us drifting apart. I sniffle for a second, trying to keep myself together. Her embrace was unexpected, but as her arms enclosed me, a tiny spark of hope ignited within me.

She still wants you.

I pull myself away from her to look at her. She keeps her stare on my chest. I move my hands to her cheeks to force her to look at me. Her eyes make me want to die. Every time she cries, it makes me want to be buried alive. Both of us are crumbling, right in each other's arm. I'm trying to understand why I'm forming a habit of making her cry? Then she closes her eyes, avoiding me.

"Look at me, Jen." All the anger in my body has escaped.

"I can't." She pulls back, enough for my hands to fall from her face. She keeps her arms around me, barely a couple of centimeters of space between us.

"Baby, what more can I give to you? What does he have that I don't? Tell me whatever you want, and I'll find it and give it to you. I just want to be the only one." I rake my fingers through her hair.

I don't know what part it is, but Jen finally looks up at me. Her face is a light shade of red and her eyes are lighting up my soul. She puts a hand on my cheek, taking in the feel of me like she's depleted of oxygen.

"You are everything to me." She breathes. Her words are the world's most addicting potion. I want to float in a bathtub, letting those words soak through me. *You are everything to me.* That's one of my favorites.

Overwhelmed by my emotions, my eyes fill with tears and I feel a couple seep out.

"I want to do everything in my power to keep it that way." I blubber at her. God, we've never been this vulnerable and transparent with each other. I've always been authoritative, and Jen has always been submissive. It's as if we've both fallen through the cracks and allowed each other to get swallowed in the harsh reality of love. Love isn't always pretty.

For the umpteenth time, I kiss her forehead, sealing the promise with a kiss to forgive her. I choose to believe that she will continue to pick me, over and over, no matter the bullshit Glen is feeding her. Our love story is the real deal. I'm trusting that talking about my future with Jen is not karma causing trouble for me. Maybe I should've kept my plan a secret and left Anna out of it.

I surround Jen, pulling her closer and closer to me. She holds tightly onto my shirt.

"You are all I've ever wanted, okay? I'm not leaving this life without you." I tell her and then plant another kiss on top of her head.

We hold each other and sway back and forth for a few minutes. All we need is just a moment to be back in sync with each other. I hate this cycle we've entered of anger spurts (on my end) followed by consoling a damn toddler. I hate the look in her eyes that she feels I'm going to just walk away from her. Sure, I may have had the thought earlier, but knowing me, and the powerful charm Jen has on me, my ass would've walked right back up the hill to her. I would do anything for her.

She is the sun, the moon, and the stars—all wrapped in one majestic universe that I get to live in peacefully. Just me, alone. If Glen were gone, I'd have less blood clots and lower chance of onset hypertension. If Anna were gone, I wouldn't be going prematurely grey. And with Andy gone, the personality of a sloth, we might have more excitement in the world. We could let Pat enter our mini universe, only to deliver coffee, but I'd happily kick him out.

And this is all I've ever wanted in life. To be just be in this moment, with the girl of my dreams, holding me so tightly that I feel she'll rip my skin off, and just pretend that we live in a different world.

The rest of the day could've gone by better, but people who were slowly making me blow up surrounded me. At breakfast, Jen and I ate in the living room, away from everyone else. Anna, Andy, and Glen sat at the bar in the kitchen, quietly talking amongst each other. Jen thought it would be smart if she made our plates while I waited outside by the firepit. It bothered me I couldn't see if there was an interaction between her and Glen, but I had to trust her. If I had any more doubts about the two of them, I think I was going to lose my shit. Again, I wanted to believe that I was the one she wanted.

After breakfast, I hopped in the shower and got myself together. The hot water was refreshing over me. As I was getting my clothes on, I told Jen the plan that Anna and I were going to the store to get food and supplies. She picked a fight about wanting to go with us, but I couldn't let her. I needed time with Anna to go over certain details.

I also had to teach Anna a lesson about bringing up the fact of Jen going into Glen's room earlier, because she doesn't get to say shit like that and not have consequences.

"I don't want to stay here, though." She folds her arms and walks to the window. I pull my shirt over my head and push my arms through. Running my fingers through my damp hair, I walk to her. Guilt is penetrating my soul.

"Hang out with Andy. That's all I ask." When I get to her, my hands steady her shoulders, noticing her hair and makeup were done already. She looks and smells immaculate that I want to lose myself in her. Turning to face me, I see worry flood her features.

"It's not me I'm worried about." It's the fear in her voice that I'm instantly regretting not taking her with me. My jaw tightens as if I'm sucking on the world's most sour candy. I'm half-tempted to punch a hole in the wall because I that Glen has made her feel this way.

"Hey, look at me." Her face fell after she confessed her truth about not wanting to be here with Glen. She slowly lifts her head to look at me. I smile at her, hoping that it gives her something to be happy about. *You make her happy.*

"I'm going to find Andy and tell him you guys are spending the afternoon together. I'll threaten him to not mention a word to Glen so that Glen has no option but to stick around the house. It'll be an hour, max. I won't be long, okay?" I can feel Angel and Devil fighting in my heart—pitchfork versus magic wand.

Take her with you. She wants to be with you!

You have nobody to blame but yourself if something bad happens between her and Glen while you're gone.

I want to throw up at the comment by Devil. That asshole.

I pull her close to my chest and wrap my arms around her head, cradling her like she's the most expensive piece of china. When I close my eyes, I picture Jen and Glen being together, and it makes me want to kill them both. I'm counting on Jen to avoid Glen while I'm gone; she's been warned twice about him. My insides are being constricted with barbed wire, hoping that she just listens to me. Despite what Andy says, Glen is not good guy. Quickly, I pull away to find Andy.

Andy—either the best thing to ever to have lived or my next addition to the shit list.

I walk down the hallway to their bedroom. Anna is standing in front of the standing mirror, brushing her hair. She's wearing hot pink athletic shorts with a white tank top. I see her shoes are on, which means she's about ready to go. Thank fucking God.

"Andy, I need to talk to you."

I still feel so much tension in my jaw and I glare at Anna while I walk in. She's just as guilty that I have to have this conversation because she's the instigator who brought up the show-and-tell moment.

"What's up, man?" Andy is laying on the bed, his arms folded behind his head, watching the television that is barely audible from the corner.

"I don't care what you have to do, but please, I'm begging you, keep Jen occupied while we go to the store. Do not let Glen get close to her." I take a couple of steps forward to the bed, my fists tightening at the thought of *him.*

How can one human being have the power to make me feel so utterly defenseless?

"I'll try my best but..."

Wrong way to make me feel better. I grab his shirt by the collar and force him to stand up in front of me. Anna's brush drops to the floor and her pathetic gasp fills the room.

"You're dead if I find out something happens between them."

I feel these weak, gangly arms try to push us apart, but Andy remains unphased. In fact, it looks as if I've pissed him off. His cheeks are turning red, and I can slightly see his chest puff out.

"Cut it out. What the fuck, Calvin?" Anna finds the leverage to push me away from Andy, looking like his bodyguard. At the sound of her voice, I forget Andy is in the room. My eyes jump to look at Anna.

"I'll deal with you later." I point my finger at her.

"Threatening her?" Andy enters my bubble and for a moment, I feel a twinge of intimidation. No, no. Everyone should fear what I'm capable of if something happens to Jen. Jesus people, it's one fucking hour and nobody can help me out?!

"I'm not threatening anyone. She knows what she did." My eyes ping-pong back and forth between him and Anna. She's staring at me, with that expression on her face, silently begging me for mercy to spare her. As I mentioned before, I've done and said some cruel things to Anna throughout the years.

"I'll be in the car. We're leaving in five minutes. Give me four minutes to cool down."

I turn my back on them and walk down the stairs, too mad to say goodbye or I love you to Jen. I'll regret that later. If this is karma, I may as well just jump into a pool of lava because nothing is going my way. I wanted to do something special for Jen. For my Jen. And these monkeys had to tag along and mess everything up. This can't be a sign that Jen and I shouldn't be together, right?

I don't realize Glen is sitting on the couch in the living room until I slam the door and look back at him through the window. Although I should warn him to avoid Jen while we are away, I am certain he will do the opposite.

I trust Jen. Right? I need Jen to prove her trustworthiness to me.

Slamming my door shut in anger, I punch my steering wheel, sending a throbbing pain through my knuckles. Was there something that could help with the tension? I'm feeling like a balloon, over-inflating with emotions that are becoming too much. Looking down at my cupholder, I find exactly what I need.

My black American Lawman utility knife feels cool to the touch. The blade flips open, and I grasp the handle tightly in my right hand.

I don't know what comes over me, but I press the blade into my left wrist, dragging it across my wrist for a few seconds. As I sense the balloon slowly deflating, I hold my breath. Wow, that feels good. I rest my head back on the headrest, feeling the blood trickle down the side of my wrist. I snap out of my daze to grab a napkin from the glove compartment to wrap it.

Shit. I didn't mean to do that. Within a second of wrapping the napkin around my arm, the passenger door opens.

Double shit. That was a quick four minutes.

"Ready." Anna already sounds irritated, which means this shopping trip should be disastrous. She doesn't look over at me until she clicks her seatbelt.

"What happened to you?" She lays her purse in her lap. I look over at her, trying to read if her concern is genuine. She looks down at my lap to see my pocketknife laying open. Her eyes move back up to mine and I witness a new emotion wash over her face.

Sorrow. She's not even trying to hide it. Her eyes are slowly filling with tears. I roll my eyes in disappointment. I'm preparing for the lecture of how a stupid idiot I am, how I never make smart choices, how much I fail her.

"Anna, please. I don't need your acting shit right now." Out of the corner of my eye, I watch her hands cover her face, then she shouts at me. Not like a brother to sister shout, more like a mother to son shout.

"Damnit, Calvin! I'm not acting. Why do you always have to be such a dick? Why the hell would you do something like that?"

Her words cut out, trying to gasp for air. When I look at her, her makeup is smeared on her face. She's wiping her fingers under her eyes, but it's only smearing black lines more.

"Since when do you care about what I do?"

My voice shocks me. Really though, since when has she cared about my feelings? I've spent over a decade of her nagging me, trying to control me, telling me how to do things, telling me what not to do. I swore up and down that Anna's heart was lonely and black, sitting miserably in an ice chamber. As I run through the reasoning of why Anna should care, I realize we've been sitting here for a while, in silence. She startles me when she opens the door.

"I'll be right back."

You can tell she's been crying and I'm curious how she's going to get past Andy if she's going inside. She's back out in less than two minutes. Even if her heart is a black icicle, she's superhuman. She hops back into the passenger seat with a white first aid kit in her hand. Her composure seems to be back to normal. She adjusts her body, so she's facing me as best as she can. She opens the aid kit and rests it on the cup holders. Without speaking, she grabs my arm and starts cleaning my wound.

I watch her intently. She looks like a pro. Not realizing she had a wet paper towel in her hand, she removes my red stained napkin and lays it in her lap. I don't think that's sanitary, but growing up with a girl; you cross many boundaries. She drags the wet paper towel over my cut. She squirts a dime size of Neosporin onto my cut and uses her index finger to smear it in a straight line. It appears I didn't do any significant damage to my veins, or enough to require stitches. She wipes her index finger on a clean napkin then grabs a roll of gauze.

"Where did you learn to do this? I didn't realize you were a secret nurse." My voice is quiet, not trying to start shit. Genuinely, I'm impressed.

"My grandma Dez was a nurse in World War II. Taught me everything I needed to know." She says confidently back to me, wrapping the gauze around my arm a few times. She rips it and tucks the end tail beneath itself.

"Okay, all done. Up to you what you want to tell Jennie." Anna continues to not look at me. She cleans up the first aid kit, putting the cream and remaining gauze back in it. The kit goes on the floor, obvious she's not planning to go back inside.

"Anna, look at me." I watch her bite her bottom look and scrunch her face again, clearly holding back her tears. She shakes her head back and forth, answering my question without words.

"I don't enjoy being around the controlling, jealous, vicious version of you. It's scary. It's uncomfortable. It's not you."

She talks to her hands, playing with her hair tie around her wrist. I think I blinked for every word. I'm hoping for further elaboration from her. Remaining silent, I look at her. Then she pulls her head up and meets my stare. Her face is streaky again and red. I haven't seen Anna cry many times in my life—something I'm thankful for because I'm clearly not the best comfort—but I would never add this image to my *best views* list.

"Why are you trying to ruin this for us? We just wanted to have a good time." My actions filled her eyes with so much pain.

"I'm not trying to."

"Bullshit. If you weren't trying to, you would just walk away from Glen. But you choose not to. You choose to fight with him every single damn time, Calvin. Like why? Why do you let him get inside your head?"

I hate Anna has the compelling charm to tell my emotional operator when to pull the curtains. Jen is usually the only person I've ever felt I could let my guard fall with and see the sensible guy in me, but man, Anna knows how to claw her way in.

"I'm afraid she's going to leave me for him. The way she smiles around him, Anna... fuck, it kills me. It's just a different smile that I have never seen before."

The verbal truth hurts worse than the internal truth. There's something about having faith in Angel to use her magic wand to make those thoughts go away, but when you actually say the words out loud, you don't believe in angels.

"Calvin..." Anna sighs. I grip the bridge of my nose, trying to hold myself together.

"I know it sounds stupid, but I just can't shake the feeling that something is happening. It's taking everything in me to not barge into the house to make sure they are in separate rooms. I can't lose her, An. She brings me so much solace and calm that I don't think I'll ever be able to find anywhere." I feel a hand touch my arm. I'm not used to gentleness from Anna, considering she punch-buggy-no-punch-backs me every single day of our lives.

"She loves you. It's clear as day on her face every time you enter the room. She lights up like you've been gone for years and suddenly you've returned. She talks about you consssssstantly: I usually want to drill a screwdriver into my ears. But that's not your fault. She's just so in love with you. I'm rooting for you, Calvin, I really am, but you have to trust the process that when things are ready to fall into place, they will."

Spoken like a literature tutor.

I look at her, my truest and realest best friend.

There really isn't much left to say. Letting her words sink into my soul, I start my truck and head into town for the store. Anna makes a few suggestions here and there for snacks to get but I remind her of the game plan–I get the supplies, she pays. It's all taken care of.

As planned, we are back at the house within an hour. Andy was already sitting outside and promptly jogs to us to help unload the bags.

"Where is she?" I holler at Andy as he approaches us.

"She's been in the back, reading, I think. As soon as you guys left, she went out there."

"And Glen?"

Andy rubs the back of his neck nervously. Immediately, I stop in my tracks.

"What does that mean?" I hear the shuffling of the grocery bags behind me, presuming Anna is picking them up. Andy tries to get around me to help her, but I stop him.

"I haven't seen him all morning, so I don't know." Anna stands next to me, facing Andy, and I look over at her, confused why she isn't telling me to ease up on him.

"Andy, you were supposed to make sure they weren't around each other. Why was that so hard for you?"

I'm pleased Anna is standing up for me. I'm also satisfied with the reaction from Andy that Anna is supporting me, and not him. She turns to me and grabs my arm.

"Go find her. We'll take care of the bags."

My Holy Savior they call Anna. Bless you. It's weird to run full force from my truck, but I don't stop until I see Jen sitting on the swing, the gazebo only a few feet away from her. She's barefoot, and her hair is in two French braids, falling down her back like two waterfalls. Her black tank top clings to her body and shows a little skin from her lower back. From the looks of it, she has jean shorts on.

I swear, no matter where she is, she's a fucking dream. It doesn't appear Glen is around, which is a good sign. Quietly, I approach her from behind. I grab hold of the swing to prevent it from moving back, and it makes her jump.

"Hey, that was quick!" She says to me. From behind, I make a path of kisses, starting with her temple, down her cheek, until I reach her neck. I ponder the words Anna told me prior to our trip.

"What happened to your arm?"

Crap, that was quick for her to notice. What do we tell her? Devil says to lie. Angel says to tell the truth. I look around the yard, trying to determine which path I want to take.

"Oh, I scraped my arm when I was getting in the truck. Anna cleaned it up for me. That's why it took us some time to leave. Not sure if you were listening to when my truck left."

My stomach turns from the lie I spit to her. There's no way I could tell her the truth.

I shoved a knife in my arm because I'm jealous of a boy that I believe is trying to steal you away from me.

She kisses the bandage. "I'm sorry, babe. Glad she could help you out." I wrap my arms around her neck and breathe her in. I nestle my face in between her shoulder and neck. *God, I love this girl. This girl is all mine.*

"We better get inside and start packing. We'll be leaving soon. Feeling better about it?" I kiss her neck, which makes her squirm and giggle.

"Nope, so you better bring all your arsenal to protect me."

"I won't let anything happen to you." I kiss her cheek, then allow her to stand up to put her shoes on. As much as I don't want to leave the moment of peace and paradise, I'm excited about entering a new adventure with her. I hold my hand out to help her up. She grabs her shoes and walks close to me, back to the house.

Thankfully, Jen doesn't notice him, but I see Glen leaning over his balcony, watching us. Not really us, but more so her. I scowl at him, hoping that fire comes out of my eyes to burn him. I try to remember Anna's words again... *just let it be.*

In the kitchen, Anna and Andy are repacking the food in reusable bags Anna's mom lent to us. I make eye contact with Anna and Andy, hoping the tension has diffused.

"Hey!" Anna cheers. *Thank God.*

"Need any help?" I offer. Jen remains at my side. She seems...

nervous? She doesn't normally hang on to me for this long, but I won't complain. I bring her to my side as we approach the bar.

"Nope, I think we mostly have everything. Everyone just needs to get their stuff together soon, and then we need to stop for ice on the way." Anna says as she throws three paper towel rolls into the last bag that looks to be full of paper plates, cups, and cutlery.

"Sounds good. We'll get our stuff ready now." Jen is the one to talk this time.

"Anyone know if Glen is ready?" Andy asks, plopping all the bags on top of the counter. I couldn't care less. He could stay here by himself if we want to change plans.

"Not sure. I'll check on him." Anna responds. For a moment, I feel a tightness of Jen around me.

"Are you alright?" I whisper to her to prevent the eavesdropping of my nemesis and her boyfriend.

"Yeah, yeah, I'm fine. Just getting nervous."

She doesn't look nervous, though. There's something else in her eyes. Trying not to ask question or pry because I'll go down a rabbit hole, but for a moment, it looks like guilt.

Without getting myself stir crazy, I pull Jen towards the stairs. She walks with me, obedient as always.

Once our bodies enter the room, I close the door behind her. When I turn, her arms are crossed, and she's looking at me as if I'm in trouble.

"What?" I chuckle. Is she messing with me right now? I walk towards her, trying to embrace her playfulness, but I'm met with two hands that shove me away.

I crook my neck, widen my eyes, and bite my tongue.

"Uh, okay. What the hell, Jen?"

"What do you think you're playing at? You want to sit here and accuse me of sneaking around with Glen when clearly something is going on with you and Anna? Don't you dare make me look like an idiot!" She's flailing her arms around. Tears well in her eyes, and her voice is breaking.

I'm bewildered.

"I hope you're not fucking serious right now." I rub my chin to piece together how she made up this connection. She recrosses her arms, holding herself like a wounded animal. Tears now fiercely fall down her face. My heart feels torn. I don't know whether to comfort her or walk out the door.

Angel versus Devil.

"Don't play with me. You two have been awfully intimate since we got here. This morning you were outside with her by the firepit. We have large windows facing that direction, asshole! Then it was just you two going to the store and absolutely nobody could go. She tends to her arm. You guys have been giving each these looks like you want everyone to disappear so you can do..."

She chokes on her words. She brings her hand to her mouth and starts whimpering. I try to move closer to her, but I'm afraid I'm not welcome in her bubble right now. I cannot believe she has this notion in her head. But I challenge her instead, continuing to move close to her and she doesn't retreat.

"So we could do what..." my voice is low. I squint my eyes to feed into her crazy thoughts. There's about two feet between us. I can see her shiver as she grips her arms tighter.

She doesn't answer. Cause she knows it's delusional. I stand in front of her, chest to chest. Her breathing is more like a pant. I run my fingers down on her braids and see the change of her eyes from betrayal to lust. Moving my hand down her neck, trace the outline of her waist until I stop there when I feel her skin. I pull her closer, shifting from chest to chest to pelvis to pelvis.

"Are you jealous?" I moan into her ear. I place my other hand on her waist, ever so gently pushing up on the bottom of her shirt to expose more skin.

"No." She moans back. I get a look at her face. "You don't get to play me like a fool," she spits back at me. She doesn't move her body, but she pulls her head back to look at me. I snatch the back of her neck to hold her gaze to look at me.

"I've known that psycho blonde since the second grade. I find her repulsive. She's controlling like a dictator, and, frankly, I feel bad for Andy. She puts on way too much perfume and makeup, but I guess if she wants to look like a clown, that's her problem. The sound of her voice makes me want to become an alcoholic. Everything she touches,

I want to clean with disinfectant at least three times." Jen's eyes are wide at me. I'm not finished, either.

"There are words in the dictionary that I would highlight and underline over and over to describe Anna. The only thing good thing she offers is her patience with teaching me how to read. But guess what? I'm done with school, so thankfully I don't have to see that witch every day. Trust me, baby, I hate the simple fact that I've spent so much of life with her. I didn't have a choice. My mom was up my ass about passing English and her mom was my reading tutor. It was really our parent's fault. There was this stupid string always connecting us together and for the life of me, I wanted to cut it off every freaking day I was around her."

I try to regain composure because I find my blood pressure rising. My hands, somehow, traveled from her captivating waist to her face, holding her expression to keep her focused on me. I still have more to say. She picked the wrong topic for me to go off about.

"She is absolutely nothing compared to you."

More tears leak out of her eyes and I'm thankful to have my fingers close by to wipe them away so quickly.

"Then why the secrecy?" She mumbles.

Because she's my secret keeper. And what I have planned for you–for us–I need the help of this maniac.

"She's got some shit going on with her mom. Again, I've known her mom since second grade, so I guess she feels she can trust me with it." Jen blinks away her tears, looking down at my chest.

"You sure that's it? I swear to God, Cal, if I found out something is happening between you two, I can be very cruel." She pokes me in the chest. I could get used to feisty Jen. It's pretty sexy. I smirk at her bravery at challenging me. Part of me wishes she did it more often.

"C'mere." My hands slide from her cheeks and tangle at the base of her neck. She wraps her arms around my waist and lays her head on my chest. Kissing the top of the head, I can't help but chuckle out loud.

"What?" She laughs into my chest.

"I just can't believe you thought something was happening between me and Anna. It's absurd." I'm laughing more with each word.

"Hey! Flirting doesn't always have to be sweet and cute like Glen. There's flirty banter." My laugh turns into licking my lips, and my muscles tightening. I unclasp my hold on her.

"We should get our stuff together." I paint a grin on my face, trying to hide my anger... and my sadness.

I turn around to pick up my bag off the ground and shove it full of my clothes. I set my bag on the bed, knowing that I'll be leaving after everyone. As Jen fumbles around with her stuff, I focus my brain on my complete, well-organized plan. At least, I hope it's well-organized. Half of my plan falls into the hands of Anna, who is getting more under my skin. Because I hoped Jen wouldn't put her bags in my truck, I left the rest of my supplies in the back.

"I'm going to wait downstairs. Do you need any help?" I pick up my bag anyway, so she isn't suspicious.

She shakes her head no and continues to shove items in her bags. I close the door behind me, giving her some privacy.

Fuck me.

Glen is the only one downstairs, rummaging in the kitchen. I glare at him as I turn around the staircase and set my bag by the front door. His bag is already there. I think about kicking it. Fuck him for being punctual. We are supposed to be leaving in the next ten minutes.

"What's up, man?"

I turn my back to verify the words are coming from the person I think they are. Glen is leaning against the counter, eating a pack of Nutter Butters. Chuckling, I turn my back to him, wishing I had something to occupy myself with.

"Jennie and I had an interesting conversation while you were gone."

I almost break my molars from the pressure of biting down. My heart is pumping so fast, it makes me a little scared.

Just ignore him. He's trying to get a rise out of you.

I clamp my eyes shut as I lean against the large windows, looking at anything to distract me from murder. Not sure why I don't leave the room, I stay put, hoping he doesn't continue.

"Yeah, she uh told me she thinks you and Anna are a thing." I can see my reflection in the mirror and I show my teeth, ready to bite his head off.

"It's been dealt with." Not that he needs an explanation, but I snarl back at him.

"Oh, is that so? She seemed pretty upset about it. I'm glad I was there to console her. Seems you're too focused on ripping my head off instead of caring for her." I tug at my hair; wish I could've saved my cutting moment for right now. I'd cut this obnoxious fool's voice box out and let the wolves eat it.

"Fuck. Off."

"Hey man, I tried to stay away, but she came to find me." When I look back at him, having enough of his bullshit, his hands are up in the air as if he was innocent. My mind is racing with questions, and I'm filled with rage toward him.

Andy said she was in the back the whole time. Was she not? Did Andy lie to me? Did Jen really go seek comfort in Glen .... Over something that wasn't even true?!

My body is radiating with fire. Glen must've had an angel hovering over him because Andy and Anna come trolling down their stairs. The tension is thick, and it's obvious for them.

"Everything cool?" Andy asks. Anna immediately looks at me. *You always pick a fight with him.* I can see the words on her forehead. If I don't fight back, he continues to talk.

I JUST WANT HIM TO SHUT UP.

Not even a minute passes and Jen comes down the stairs. God, she's beautiful. I hate that I'm supposed to be upset with her. She's redone her braids, looking tighter. Unfortunately for me, she's put a jacket around her tank top, no sign of skin. Her face looks clear of any redness or tears.

I forget Glen is in the same room as me. Approaching her, I take her bags out of her hands. I want to pick a fight with her so badly. To ask if she really saw Glen while I was gone. But I can't. This morning has already been a train wreck. She smiles at me when I approach her. I kiss her hard on the lips, hoping it gives Glen nightmares. *That's right you prick, she wants me.*

"Okay, everyone got everything? Are we ready to go?" Anna looks around nonchalantly, then stares at me.

This is it.

I raise an eyebrow, just a hair to give her the signal. She looks through the bags that she meticulously sorted. Canned foods. Cold items. Drinks. Paper goods.

"Oh, crap!" She yells out.

"What is it?" I say my line.

"We forgot to the get the good toilet paper."

I hated her excuse, but whatever. Andy, out of everyone, starts laughing.

"You're joking, right?" There seems to be some sort of uncomfortable tension between Andy and Anna. He's standing by the front door, preparing to put the bags in the car. Anna is by the bar. When I look at him, he rolls his eyes at her comment. Perhaps he's heard the same stupid rumor about her and me, only their conversation didn't go as well as mine and Jen's.

"I'm not using port-a-potty toilet paper, Andy." Anna shrieks.

"What?! You said there was a community bathroom, Anna!" Jen enters the living room to be part of the conversation. Glen, smugly, stays behind the counter of the kitchen. *Good place to stay.* Anna looks apologetic.

"I'm sorry..." She brings her hands together, giving the universal praise to Jen, begging for forgiveness.

"We need good toilet paper." Jen demanded.

Yes, that's my girl! Get fiery!!

I smile back and cross my arms. I'm delighted that Jen is bothered about the toilet paper. Inside, Angel is secretly giving the bowing down gesture towards Anna. I would too, but then it would blow our cover. When I do a look around of everyone's faces, I stop at Anna's who is trying to hide her eyes widening at me.

Oh, right... my next line.

"I'll grab some on the way. I'll meet you guys there."

Please end the conversation there.

"I'll come with you."

Disappointment shoots through me. Literally any other time in my lifetime, I would absolutely say yes. Just this once, I can't let her. Anna and I have a conversation with our eyes again.

"While you're at it, you can drive back to Seattle." Glen says.

Anna is standing in view of Glen. My eyes move past her to look at him, thinking of a murder plan. Set him on fire. Push him into the water. Poison his food. Scavenge fire ants and put them in his sleeping bag.

I feel the comfort of Jen grab my arm.

"I'll come with you." She whispers only to me. She's a wonderful distraction.

"Jennie, come with us! It's bad luck if you show up late and we don't explain anything to you." I try to hide my smile.

That was pathetic.

"Cal is the only one who knows a damn thing about camping. I'll learn everything from him."

"Andy knows how to set up a tent. He'll need some help since it's family size one. Each of us will have to hold up a corner."

Hmm, that's convincing. Let's see if she takes it.

"We can put the tent up when we get there. We won't be long." She looks at me for reassurance.

"Jen, putting up a tent is frustrating as hell. The more people, the easier. Plus, it would be sweet of you to have the tent ready for me with our sleeping bags and blankets." I hate that I have to be gushy in front of everyone, but I have to keep pushing this. I brush a piece of hair behind her ear and kiss her cheek. *Please, please go.*

"Then we have more time for adventuring!" Anna adds from behind us. I chuckle to Jen.

"She's right. More time for adventure." Jen looks at me, as if I'm going to be taken away by the police. She licks her lips, debating. I can see the wheels turning.

"I don't want to go without you." She innocently discloses to me. She pushes her head towards my chest, and I run my hand over the back of her head. I kiss her forehead again, consoling her in any way I can.

"I'll be there so fast, you won't even notice. I promise."

"Ugh. Fine."

Thankfully, Jen's back is to the rest of them, and I smile right at Anna. I try to be sure Andy and Glen are not looking to give her a wink as a cherry on top. *Job well done, my friend.*

"Yay, so glad we are done with that conversation."

Glen's sarcasm makes me realize that not only am I glad Jen is going with them, but I need some much-needed time away from this asshole.

"Okay, great. Let's get everything in my car." Andy's annoyance is still prominent. Everyone, as if fueled by caffeine, moved quickly to pick up all the bags—sleeping bags, groceries, and everything else.

I make a mental note to repay Anna somehow for this. I'll owe everything to Anna if this goes successfully. So far, we're making good progress. Step one is complete.

With the help of ten hands, we take no time to get everything neatly stacked in the Andy's SUV. I pretend that I'm getting in my truck and following behind.

"I just gotta pee right quick. I'll meet you there, okay?" Before closing the door, I kiss Jen. Anna gets another brownie point for sitting in the back seat with Jen so that Glen is in the passenger seat.

"Okay. I love you."

"I love you too."

There is nothing that I love more than this girl in front of me.

Walking back towards the house, I watch the White Trailblazer head down the driveway. To be safe, I count to twenty to make sure Jen doesn't convince Andy to reverse and come along with me instead. I have wholesome faith in my bratty friend to force Andy to keep driving.

The biggest smile appears on my face when twenty seconds are up. I leave whatever altercations or misunderstandings that happened in the last 24 hours on the front step like dogshit. Unlocking my truck, I get all my goodies from the backseat.

Flowers. Flower petals. Marquee lights (we got lucky with a craft store up the street). I wish I could set up candles, but there's no way to keep them lit until Sunday evening, nor is there any way I could come home early to light them. I couldn't trick Jen twice for staying behind without me.

I kick the door shut, leaving behind the good toilet paper in the backseat. There was no way I was going to drive in the opposite direction of the campsite to get toilet paper.

Carrying everything in my arms, I open the door with my thumb and index finger. Gently, I lay everything on the counter.

Starting at the front door, I scattered at least ten boxes of rose petals through the living room, around the kitchen bar, out the back door, and along the concrete path to the gazebo. In the center of the gazebo, I sprinkle the remaining rose petals, right where I want her to stand. Then I bring out the marquee letters.

I know we are too young to get married. Hell, we just finished high school. I stand each letter next to each other. Marriage will come later. For now, she gets this.

I PROMISE YOU.

I make the promise that she is the only person I want to be with. After these next couple of days, I won't ever have to worry about Glen again. Honestly, since the day I met her in the coffeeshop, I knew things would be different. She was different.

Knowing this place is in the middle of nowhere, I'm not worried about anyone trespassing. I probably shouldn't leave the ring outside, but it's the first thing I want her to see when we get back. I spent all my C&H savings on the most stunning ring for her. When I get back home, I can explain to Pat why I was desperate to work every single day.

Right now, it's all I can afford. She deserves something better, but for now, this is what I could give to her.

A white gold thin band topped with an oval cut diamond. The diamond was large and flashy-just how I pictured it to be. I admit, I'm nervous if Jen will wear something so large on her finger, but I figured if it was from me, then she absolutely would.

I double check the weather to make sure there's no chance for rain. It's Washington, there's always a chance, but until Monday, it's clear skies. Thank God.

I leave the flowers on the counter, filling the biggest cup I can find with water, and setting the flowers in there. A mix of yellow carnations, red roses, blue delphiniums, baby's breath, and pink dahlias. Jen loves wildflowers. I would do this in a field of wildflowers if we had something remotely romantic like that in Washington. This will have to do.

Following the path of petals and internally pretending to be Jen, I ponder if I need to add more pizzazz to this. When I get to the gazebo, I realize it's perfect.

Thankfully, I find a clear vase to put over the ring box as I set it down in the middle of the gazebo. It reminds me of the enchanted rose from *Beauty and the Beast*. I walk backwards to the back door to get a wider view of the scenery I've created.

I promise to love you forever.

Feeling satisfied with my work, I walk back through the house to my truck. My future is on my mind. Our future. But for some stupid reason, I let Devil take control of my emotions.

What if she doesn't want you? What if you aren't what she needs? What if she's sucking face with Glen right now...

I punch my steering wheel, which sends a throbbing vibration down my wrist when I cut myself earlier. Looking down at my wrapped wrist, and for some whatever reason, Devil continues to discourage me.

She is making you hurt yourself. She is only going to continue to hurt you. As much as we want her to light up your life, she is burning you.

I shake my head feverishly to get rid of the thoughts. No, no, she's perfect. Right Angel...

No answer.

Feeling incredibly annoyed and pissed at the thought that Glen is making moves on Jen, I start my truck and haul ass down the driveway. Turning up the loudest rock music to drown out Devil's shit, I keep envisioning the gazebo, trying to spark a jolt in my heart that Jen will choose me.

The drive to the campsite is in Naches. It's supposed to take an hour, but my adrenaline is pumping to get to Jen, which gives my right foot some energy to press down on the gas. I take about fifty minutes. I call Anna to get directions to where they are located.

"Well, where are you now?" Anna says.

"I'm about to turn into the main entrance." I have her on

speakerphone with my phone laying in my lap. From the looks of it, the main entrance seems quiet.

"Turn at the first right you come across and then head down that pathway for a while. Glen, hold up your side a bit more!" She yells at the phone.

"Sorry, the phone is in between my shoulder. We're trying to get the stupid tent up." I continue driving down the pathway, looking side to side at the occupied spaces of people.

"Keep going?" I sound irritated because Anna sucks at giving directions.

"Oh yes! Sorry. We are practically at the very end of that path. The lake is like so close to us!" She's breathing heavy through the phone.

"Nice. Hey Anna..." I drive a little slower, hoping to not come across a fucking nightmare.

"What?" She sounds annoyed, but I don't care. I need to know what I'm walking into.

"Are they..." I can't finish because I'm afraid I'm going to break down or scream.

"I'll be right back. Well then, drop it, Andy! Everyone can stretch their arms, Jesus!" I hear her panting.

"How honest do you want me to be?" My throat goes dry that no amount of swallowing is making it feel better.

"Just tell me."

I thought I had more time, but the back of Andy's trunk open with him leaning against it comes into view. Whatever words Anna is saying is useless, but somehow, I hear the last couple of words from Anna.

He's with her.

I push my foot down on the gas a bit to get to them faster.

GET YOUR HANDS OFF HER.

I slammed my shift handle into park and jumped out of the car. Anna's words are meaningless now, so I end the call. Devil *was* right...

My adrenaline literally feels like its serum, making me invincible.

I slam my door with all my might and trudge to them. Jen and Glen are sitting in the small patch of grass under a perfectly placed oak tree. She's drinking a water, and he's pushing hair behind her ear.

She's not pushing him away. She's smiling. Granting his permission to touch her, almost identical as I do.

She sees me first and immediately jumps up, looking at me like I'm a ghost. *Yes, I still exist.* Then I feel like a million and one things happen.

I hear Andy shouting my name.

Anna calling my name.

Not her normal sweet voice, but Jen screams my name.

My knuckles feel broken, but I don't care.

All I see is red.

His fucking brown eyes make me want to throw up.

There is tension pulling me from every direction, but I can't stop.

I'm completely overcome with rage. Left punch, right punch. Over and over until I feel better. But I don't feel better.

"Get off him, Calvin!!" I think it's Anna's voice, but I don't know because everything around me feels like it's crashing down.

He was touching her, and she allowed it.

Yes, Devil, I'm aware of the narrative going on. I was gone for less than two hours, and this is the bullshit I get for setting up something romantic and promising for this girl?

Left punch, right punch. Wetness is smearing over my hands.

"Stop, Cal, please!"

Jen's sobs make me want to die. Her voice, pleading for me to stop mid-murder, is the most prominent force to destroy me. My hits stop and I look down at the bastard, who barely looks recognizable. A busted lip. Blood oozing from his nose. His eyes could barely stay open.

"Fuck you." I squeeze his face and shove it down as leverage to push myself off him. I don't even look back as I move towards the lake.

"Cal, wait!"

If you want me, come get me. I'm tired of chasing after you, Jen.

She must want me, as she stops me in my tracks. I move my head around, annoyed at the pause. Trying to get around her, she moves to stay in front of me.

"Are you serious right now?"

Her sobs are the most prominent they've been. Her face is full of streaks and her eyes are bloodshot, with only the green of her eyes glowing. My insides twist at the look of her right now. *You made her like this.* She pushes against my chest to get my attention, but I'm lost in the rainforest. I reach my hand out to touch her cheek, but she slaps me away.

"No, you don't get to pull that shit and think you can touch me."

I drop my eyes to get out of the trance. Pinching my lips, I struggle to formulate anything nice to say. With a snicker and a head shake, I get past her and head to the lake. Calm and peaceful. That's all I want.

This time, she doesn't follow. Her sobs get further away, and if that isn't the seal from the Devil to send me to Hell, I don't know what is.

You shouldn't leave her like that.

I fall into the rocks. Bending my legs and gripping my hands in my hair, I stop myself from screaming. I resist the urge to grab a handful to feel ... something.

I want to hurl at the hurricane of emotions happening inside me.

The obsession with ruining Glen's life is strong. Jen's betrayal has me considering driving back to the cabin for the ring and going home. The anger I have towards Andy and Anna for allowing the two of them to weasel their way into our relationship makes me want to spit in their faces. The fucking disrespect. Everything Anna told me earlier was bullshit. She was never on my team... If she was, she wouldn't have let him get close to her.

I remove my hands from my hair and look over my shoulder at the sound of rocks moving. Speak of the devil.

She approaches me, hesitantly, and with her arms crossed and a sad look on her face.

"Fuck off, Anna."

Of course, she doesn't. She continues walking towards me, then sits beside me, keeping a safe distance. At this very moment, I don't care if she possesses the XX chromosomes, I could punch her.

"Calvin." I try to block her out and look back at the water again.

Please bring me peace. I can't hold my tongue, though.

"I can't believe you. How could you betray me like that?" Shaking my head, lost in so many thoughts of when things took a turn.

"I didn't betray you." Anna comments. Her voice is confident, in control, like always.

"Oh, so you just normally let your guy friends flirt with your best friend when she has a boyfriend?"

"I didn't realize you guys have titles. You never mentioned it." Her response reveals a snarky attitude.

"I've been completely captivated by her since February. Was I supposed to call you to get your approval or something? Is that why you're trying to ruin this for me? Jesus, can I get your blessing now?"

I can feel my face getting warm. What, are we twelve years old that I have to ask permission again to date her best friend? Maybe this is payback for breaking Claire's heart. Anna didn't talk to me for weeks and I failed so many assignments back then.

I hear Anna chuckle to herself. "No, this isn't about permission, Calvin. I have yet to see Jen smile or enjoy herself around you. You get all weird when your girlfriends spend time with my friends."

"Gee, I wonder how you would react if we brought an ex-girlfriend of Andy's on this trip? Wouldn't you be so thrilled?" She's quiet for a moment. When I look at her, she's resting her chin on her knees.

"You're right. I'm sorry. Sometimes I forget that Jen and Glen have history and that must be tough for you." She sniffles, and I hate she's putting me in this situation. Consoling Jen is not something I've ever succeeded at.

"You've dated a few of my friends before, and I want to believe things will be different with Jen. I'm not sure if this is typical of your relationship, but..." I'm watching a worm slither through the rocks as Anna hounds me.

"But what?" I breathe out.

"I enjoy seeing her laugh and smile when she's with Glen. She just glows. You don't know how badly I wish I could see *you* make her react that way, but every time she shines and looks perfect, you find them together and then she looks... empty. Like you drained her soul of happiness."

My world instantly goes dark.

The love-hate relationship I have with Anna is a never-ending nightmare. One minute, she is on top of the world to help me plan this gesture for the woman I want to be with. For a moment, just one small freckle of a moment, I believed she was on my team. And then somehow, she has these magical powers to wipe everything from under you. To leave her hovering over your own body, forcing you to realize what a piece of shit you are.

"I just want her to be happy, Calvin. I want you to be happy, too." She pokes my arm harshly.

"As much as you drive me insane, you are like a brother to me. I've only ever wanted good things for you. Ever since we were kids, I wished every year on my birthday that some new girl could come along to help you read and write." I look away from her so she can't see my smile.

"Am I right though? Do you think Jennie looks at you the same way she looks at Glen?"

"No." The response is immediate because I see it every time I see them together.

"I know you've had some crappy relationships. Girls like Britt and Ramsey absolute broke you. I mean, you didn't come over to study for almost a month. You just get in your head about things, Calvin. She isn't like the others. You need to trust her. Relax on the obsessive, controlling shit. You are going to lose her if you don't. I know you probably don't believe me, but I am on your team. I want you to get the girl. Stop messing it up."

And just as quickly as she appears, she stands up and leaves me alone with her advice–if that's what you want to call it. Currently, I call it bullshit, but maybe in the next ten minutes when I allow my brain to recenter itself, I'll consider it advice.

We don't want to lose her. She is everything to you.

I don't know how long I was in a trance of putting the pieces together. My mind felt like a spider web, tangled in different avenues of forming an apology for Jen.

The smell of jasmine and peach nectar traps me in a glorious bubble. For a few seconds, all I do is breathe in and out of my nose until I find the courage to face her, using every muscle in my face to open my eyes. I don't think I can bear to face her.

But like always, she saves me. She wraps herself around my arm like ivy. I feel my body shudder at the feel of her. My sense of completeness comes from her, resting her head on my bicep. I don't know how many doses of Narcan she's used to rescue me.

For a while, we just sit in silence. Silence that we need. To process the events and emotions together. She's been moving her hand affectionally up and down my arm. I've been too drunk from inhaling her smell. Even if I said any words, I would probably slur because she has that sort of effect on me. I'm thankful Angel takes over my control panel because she deserves an apology. I kiss the top of her head and whisper into her ear.

"Let's talk a walk."

Compliant, like always, she unravels her ivy-like hands and stands up. I still can't allow myself to look at her, so I stand up, looking at the ground the entire time, and hold my hand out to her, hoping she'll take it.

Of course she takes it. My insides smile with glee, but my brain can't seem to shake the tension that is still surrounding us. I walk us towards the opening of a path through the trees. I don't look back at my friends because the moment I look at Anna and her beaming optimism, I'll want to plan her death because she's faking it.

I squeeze Jen's hand as I can feel her heartbeat pulse through her hand.

SAY SOMETHING–ANYTHING.

I'm trying to, Angel!! The invisible tape over my mouth feels like it's super-glued on. I'm nervous to speak, fearing I'm going to say the wrong thing for the millionth time. Devil creeps into the conversation.

Jen has every opportunity to speak up and apologize, or say she loves you, or say that will say away from him, or just say anything. She doesn't get a free pass here!

We continue following the dirt path, being absorbed in the willow trees. I'm staring at my feet, and I can slightly see Jen look out to her right.

If only it were this easy... to just enjoy the blissful moments.

My anxiety (and blood pressure) rise when we reach the end of the dirt path and there's four picnic benches in front of the lake. We must've walked in silence for twenty minutes, just walking around the lake perimeter.

My throat is becoming more and more dry as Jen leads us to one of the picnic tables.

You better figure out what you're going to say...

She lets go of my hand to turn around and sit down with her back towards the table. I stand awkwardly, looking down at her for the first time since ... then.

"You can sit. I won't bite."

Goosebumps and butterflies get awakened by her comment. God, I've missed her voice. Careful to not bother her, I sit down next to her. For the first time, I don't know what to do with my hands, with my eyes, with my mouth. What am I supposed to say? I close my eyes for a few seconds to form any sort of sentence, but I get nothing when my eyes open to find her giving me a hard stare. She has somehow twisted her body towards me, her right leg resting on the bench and her right arm holding up her face. God, she's ...

"What?"

The one syllable word I croak out to her after almost two hours. *Two hours fucking wasted.* I can't keep eye contact with her because it makes my heart hurt.

She smiles and looks away from me, towards the water. The light breeze moves some of her stray hairs and *my god, she's beautiful.*

"You think hard." She says to the water and not me.

"What does that mean?"

Okay, good, adding three more words to your vocabulary.

She looks back to me, looking like a goddamn ray of sunshine. Someone walking by would never know that she witnessed her boyfriend beating the shit out of her ex-boyfriend.

"You just always look lost in your thoughts. I'm sure Anna could give some good advice for you."

A dagger straight to my back. Or manhood. Or soul.

The sarcasm just rolled off her tongue like spit. I wonder if that's why the word is called spiteful...

"What's that supposed to mean?" I stare down at the ground, avoiding eye contact. She lets out one obnoxious laugh, and her head tilts backwards at my comedic response.

"You are something else, I swear." She adjusts her body, so she's no longer facing me. She plants both of her feet on the ground and crosses her arms. Looking away from me, I'm tempted to pull her face to mine.

Okay, I guess we weren't walking into a positive conversation.

"Just say what you need to say, Jen. I'm tired of this game with you. I'm tired of fighting with you." My voice is tired because I *am* tired. I must've lit the end of the firework because Jen does not appreciate my response.

"What game are we playing?! I didn't realize I signed up for this game. Jesus, Cal!" Her arms flail around us and when I look over at her, her face is red... and wet.

Of course, it's wet because all you've done is made her cry.

"We have never, ever fought like this before. You're obsessed with Glen and then you want to sneak behind MY back and disclose all your emotions to Anna. Am I nothing to you?"

Oh great, the narrative of thinking me and Anna is a thing is still relevant. I snap my eyes shut, hating that she is right and wrong. I sit up at the table and find the nerve to face her this time.

"Look at me."

I don't have any idea what I'm going to say back to her, but my heart craves her attention. At first, she continues looking the other direction, nervously licking her lips. But then she slowly makes her face known to mine. Trapped in her spell, my hand touches her cheek. *To feel her again.* Her eyelids slowly flutter with peace.

"Open your eyes, look at me." When she does, two teardrops fall from her eye.

"What do you want from me?" Holding my own tears back, I'm hoping there is something, one goddamn thing, that Jen can tell me she wants.

Please don't say nothing...

"I want you to fight for me." Her response comes out like she's had that answered planned. Like she's been waiting for me to ask that question. I look deep into her eyes, confused about what I've been doing all weekend already.

"I have been, have I not?" I drop my hand from her cheek, slightly offended.

"You call all that shit fighting for *me*? It felt more like you were fighting for you. To not burst your ego. Never once have you just come up to me and whisked me away. You want to fight Glen because he flirts with me? I would be more in love with you, Cal, if you just managed your anger and told Glen to piss off while grabbing my hand. Instead, you leave me in the dark while I watch you unravel. And then you expect me to apologize. What exactly am I supposed to be apologizing for?" I hold a gaze with her until I can no longer handle the sadness I've created.

You were fighting for you.

"Answer me. What do you expect me to say sorry for? You give me these puppy dog eyes, or the silent treatment, or completely ignore me. But you were the one who started the fights. You always are." Her voice is shaky, like she's scared to stand against me. To be in control.

"I guess I want you to be sorry for being around him. I asked you multiple times to just say away, and I caught you both times." I drop my eyes to the ground, hating myself as each minute passes. How insecure and jealous I've been.

"So you want me to say sorry for being around someone who makes me feel better?"

"Fuck, Jen. No. That's not what I'm trying to say." I can't take the honesty anymore. Moving off the bench, holding the back of my neck, I try to think of any other explanation for my behavior.

Her sniffles destroy my fucking soul as I pace around the picnic table.

I want you to apologize for not putting me first.

There's silence between us while we both cool down. I was not expecting the conversation to take such a deep wrong turn.

"Cal... come here." Her voice is calm, patient, lovely. Taking in a few deep breaths, I'm preparing myself for a right punch.

I sit back on the bench, unsure if I should face her, if I should hold her hand, if I should touch her. The inside of my cheek bleeds as she repositions herself to suit herself in front of me. She squats in between my legs, facing up at me. She holds my face in between her hands, lightly making circles with her thumbs. Her face is free of tears, but still blotchy. Unable to keep my hands to myself, I place my hands over hers.

"You make me the happiest, most loved creature in the world. You make me laugh until my stomach hurts. I smile so much because of you that I'm self-conscious about my dimple. In indescribable ways, you make my heart race. The feeling I get when you enter the room and immediately find me makes me woozy. You give me butterflies every single time I see you, whether I'm mad at you or not. You are so perfect and handsome in every way to me. I'm sorry if I ever made you feel you weren't important to me because you are the most important person to me. Glen never wanted to hold my hand, but I want to hold yours forever. I never want to stop kissing you. I never want you to not lead me through life. You are everything to me, and I'll do anything for you. What can I do for you, baby?"

I absorb every word, letting it linger in my mind. My lips are feeling sore from the constant lip-licking to distract me from wanting to kiss her. I interlock my fingers with hers, our foreheads touching and my hands covering hers on my face.

How did I win the lottery to have *this girl* as I the one I get to spend the rest of my life with? For a moment, I let my mind wander to the house. Should I tell her the plans I have for our future?

I promise you.

I promise to love this girl for the rest of my life, no matter how uncomfortable or tricky things get, because she's fucking worth it.

"Jen..."

Whispering her name, my eyes are stuck on her mouth. I can't fight the urge anymore as I've been eyeing her lips for several moments. I pull her up from her squatting position, moving her legs to straddle me. Resting my hands around the base of her neck, I drift my hands upward under her ears, then I connect our lips together. She doesn't refute. My shirt sleeves feel like they are being tugged. And for a couple of minutes, we just kiss. When I pull away, I have the words ready to share for her.

"I just want you to stay away from him. He brings out the ugly in me. He turns me into a version of myself that I don't like. Nobody enjoys being around that version, it appears. I get it, baby, you are a goddamn saint and you want to be kind to everyone to meet in life, but just please, this one person, I need you to just avoid."

Vulnerability doesn't suit me. My voice shakes like crazy. The muscles in my neck constrict my words, and the amount of tension I hold in my jaw to release my truth is agonizing. It makes me feel like a coward.

You are a coward.

However, the feeling in my stomach is light. Since arriving at the campsite, I don't feel a clenched tightness eating away at my insides. The tension in my shoulders is also becoming loose. I'm not used to sharing these intimate heart to heart conversations with Jen about how we feel about each other. For months, we've just ... known.

Perhaps I've failed Jen by not *telling* her how much she means to me.

I watch Jen study my face, her eyes moving back and forth between my eyes.

"Then be my boyfriend, who is going to make me feel better all the time. Not just after we have a fight. I haven't enjoyed fighting with you lately."

The sweetness in her voice is like freshly squeezed orange juice. I want to keep drinking her in.

I stand both of us, my hands resting on her waist. She's the perfect height for me. Her hands rub up and down my arms and I didn't realize how much I've missed the goosebumps.

"Boyfriend, huh? Guess we never made that official for all these months." I purr my face into her neck, sucking in my jasmine high.

She runs her fingers up my shoulders, dragging her nails on my neck, then through my hair, making my head spin.

"I'm sorry, baby. I'm so sorry." Apologizing while planting kisses from her neck to her chin.

"I'm sorry, too." The pressure of lips is subtle through my shirt as she kissed my chest.

And for a while, things were good.

We walked back to the others, where Jen stayed by my side until dusk. I gave Andy props for taking charge of setting up the tent. Jen and I got the rest of our things out of my truck and unraveled our sleeping bags and mounds of blankets.

We sectioned our tent into thirds, with a zipper door creating a personal space for me and Jen. Audibly, we could all hear each other breathe but knowing I was the only one who could see Jen made my heart happy. After settling our belongings, we laid in the tent for a couple of hours. She had her head on my chest as I stroked her hair, feeling like a complete lunatic for causing such chaos this morning.

This girl is worth every bit of a psychotic breakdown.

Angel and I secretly came up with a plan that we would indulge in the presence of Jen for the rest of the night and then tomorrow, our adventures would begin.

My energy level was low, so I let Andy and Glen take charge of the food prep for the evening. Classic hot dogs and burgers on the grill.

Jen and I stayed in the tent, staying wrapped in our cocoon. I kept cursing the Gods that this trip wasn't just for her and I. Things would've gone so differently.

"What time did we want to see *Freddy vs Jason* Friday? I think we both get off at three, right?" She mumbles to me and I smile internally at the idea that I missed hearing her voice.

"Yep, we're off at three. Did you want to get dinner before or after?"

"You know I don't make the plans." I stop stroking her hand and laugh, causing her head to bobble on my chest.

"Then why did you ask me?" She brings her hand under her chin and looks up at me.

Jesus. She's an illumination that is as beautiful and bright as the Northern Lights.

Tracing her jawline, I tuck a strand of hair behind her ear. I watch her feel my touch, enjoying the sensation.

"I love you."

She deserves to know every second of every day.

"I love you." She tells me.

And as all good things end, Anna calls for us.

"Get out here, love turds. Food is done."

I close my eyes in annoyance, wishing someone kidnapped Anna for a couple of hours. Jen chuckles at my reactions and jumps up. She holds her hand out to me, helping me to my feet. She unzipped the curtain barrier. The sunset was peeking through the willows, painting the sky an amber hue.

I give myself a pep talk before coming face to face with the culprit of my bad mood. Well, I guess I allow Devil and Angel to pep talk me...

Focus on Jen. She's the only thing that is important.

Let's try to stay out of prison and not get kicked out of the campsite for reckless fighting.

Of course I follow the words of Angel.

I find Jen's hand and intertwine my fingers through hers, hoping to stay in the solace.

I make a plate for her as she sits at our picnic table. I already know that fucker will try to sit next to her, but I try to keep my eyes on things I can control. When I turn around to sit, he's there. Right in front of her, gleaming and *trying* to have a conversation, but Jen is already looking for me. I grin and my heart feels like the sky—glowing like a supernova.

"Scoot over."

I want you to fight for me.

Stop picking the fights, you prick.

Willingly, Jen moves over, so now I'm in the center of attention for Glen. I watch his face fall and his eyes roll.

Take that. I can play dirty without using my hands.

Anna squeezes next to Jen and Andy sits next to Glen. Thank God I can't see Anna because there's only so much I can handle of seeing her hypocritical face.

"So tomorrow..." Anna squeals and taps her fingers together like she's holding onto secretive information.

I continue to eat, trying to tone her out. I'm too busy enjoying the effect I'm having on Glen, intimidating him. He glares at me like I've taken something that belongs to him. I take a drink of my beer, continuing to have a staring contest. Part of me hopes he looks at Jen, even for a split second, just so I can insult his manhood.

"I've rented kayaks in the morning." Taking my eyes off Glen, I look over at Anna. Instantly, she looks at me.

"I told the place that you've kayaked practically your whole life, so they were okay with you leading us."

I was completely fine with leading the group around the lake, but I wasn't okay with the look on Anna's face. After all these years, I can tell when she's keeping shit from me.

"But..." I speak up. Jen looks back at me, confused, then back at Anna. Andy and Glen are also looking at Anna, waiting for her to spill the secrets. I can feel my insides twist, knowing the information she is about to throw at us isn't good.

"Well, the guy said that because you're the experienced one, he recommended for you to be the one to give us a shove off the dock, but that means you'll be in a kayak by yourself."

I was utterly confused at first. What's the big deal? Andy rides with Glen and Jen and Anna ride together. But from the looks of Anna, that isn't her plan.

That manipulating wench has it out for me.

My fists instantly ball into a fist as I feel the surrounding energy become tense. Everyone else is understanding the problem...

Glen would ride with Jen.

I sneer through my teeth, loud enough for Anna to hear from the other end of the table.

"She's not riding with him. I'll make it work by pushing you all off, but it's not happening. Either you ride with her, Anna, or she doesn't go."

Then shit hits the fan.

"Cal, stop." Jen's voice.

"Fuck off, Calvin. She can do what she wants." That was Glen.

"Watch your tone with her, Calvin." Andy threatens.

"I didn't realize it until I booked the number of kayaks." Anna's pitiful excuses.

Unable to keep my temper in check and wanting to prove to Jen that I can keep my shit together, I grab my beer and walk away from the table.

If I stayed, someone would have their head ripped off.

I walk the opposite direction of the path Jen and I walked earlier to get a different scenery.

She'll come to you. She'll reason with you.

I continue walking towards the main cabin, keeping my sights on the *information/rental* sign that hangs outside.

Don't worry, she'll come to you.

I want to look behind me to see how far away she is. Am I walking too fast for her to keep up? Has she been calling my name?

When I get to the stairs of the main cabin, it's closed. *Of course it's closed.* I let out an exaggerated sigh and decide to sit on the stairs and wait for her.

There's nobody in sight.

She's coming. Don't worry, she'll be here soon to make you happy again.

You were supposed to bring her with you, you idiot. That's what she asked you for.

I finish the rest of my beer and lean back on the steps, allowing the breeze to take away my wrath. Using the steps behind me as support for my elbows, I stretch out my legs. My head falls back into the most uncomfortable position.

I don't know how much time has passed, but I've somehow missed the change of the sky's colors. The once orange and yellow ribbons in the sky have changed to the color of my heart—black. Just a blanket of black with small gems of the stars trying their best to compete against the darkness.

Shaking off my unconsciousness, I look around, my fight response activated.

There's still nothing. Nobody.

She's back at the site with him.

No sight of Anna to apologize for her stupid plans. No sign of Andy to check if I've killed someone. I thank the Heavens for keeping Glen away because I wouldn't hesitate to hurt someone. Not even my Jen.

I pinch the bridge of my nose, wondering what the fuck happened. Where did I go wrong? I kept my cool, right? Instead of resorting to violence, I walked away. My mouth had a metallic taste, realizing I bit the inside of my cheek. It was painful to not go off on everyone, but I tried to keep my shit together *for her.*

I chuckle out loud, wondering what sort of Edgar Allan Poe gothic twisted tale I'm starring in.

"What the fuck is happening..." I direct to Angel and Devil.

My body can't move.

Why wouldn't she come find me...

Whatever spark in me lights my ass on fire to get off the steps and start walking back to our site. I put my hands in my pockets, feeling overly devastated and hurt. I question every word and action I did, over analyzing where I went wrong...

It doesn't take me long to find our site. My red truck and Andy's white SUV sit side-by-side a few feet away from our tent. I see the silhouette of bodies, but I'm too far away to tell whose.

For the millionth time, I contemplate packing my stuff and just leaving.

She'd be better without you. They all would be.

Andy catches my eye first, sitting on the far side of the fire. I'm impressed by the intensity of the flames. Bravo again, Andy.

See, they could do all of this without you.

I see Andy first, sitting tall, facing me. Everyone must've noticed because Anna jerks to the side to look at me, pity painted all over her face. Glen, conveniently sitting next to Jen, glares at me like I'm a plague that has come back for more. Jen's back is to me, wearing my sweatshirt—a noticeable change since I left earlier.

She's the only one who doesn't look at me. It breaks my fucking heart.

You're losing her.

"Hey man, we were giving you some space to chill." Andy dares to say. My eyes shoot him daggers.

It seems you were all so fucking concerned.

"Jen..." I approach her, trying to keep everyone else in the background. She's the only thing face I want to see.

As if I insulted her, Glen immediately stands up to protect her.

From me. As if I'm a monster.

"Calvin, she doesn't want to talk to you right now." I stop in my tracks, praying to whoever that his words are just bullshit.

"I thought you were the one who said she can do whatever she wants." Spitting back at him.

Just then, everyone watches as Jen stands up. Catching my gaze with her rainforest drenched, she walks towards the lake.

"Jennie!" Anna calls after her. Glen tries to take a couple of steps in her direction. Andy just sits and watches. How I despise his position in all of this.

"Don't. Both of you sit down and shut the fuck up." I point a finger in their direction, warning them to not move.

Time to pick up the pieces again and save your girl.

I put my hand in my pocket and follow Jen. By the time I reach her, she's sitting on the outskirts of the water, her legs close to her chest and her chin resting on her kneecaps. She had taken out her braids, and her hair is flowing beautifully down her back.

Have your speech prepared.

What is he apologizing for?

I hate to admit it this time, but I side with Devil. What am I apologizing for? Watching her from afar, I get try to lower my internal temperature.

I watch the girl I'm crashing over. My insides turn and my heart feels like a liquid detonator. Longing for her taste, I lick my lips. I should just flee this oncoming inferno. The walls we've built from the outside world are crashing down on us.

She is worth every blazing wildfire. Both of you hold an extinguisher, and if this isn't what you want, then put out the fire.

Quietly, I moved next to her, head down. How did we end up in this position again? I attempt to grin as she jumps to my arrival, however I'm fearful that she won't want to see me right now. Instead, she looks at me with wide eyes and a smirk.

Like I was wearing shining armor.

Her smile could light up the whole goddamn state. Finally, I let my shoulders relax and let the butterflies find their way up to my heart. To bring me back to life.

"Hey." She nudges me with her elbow and then rests her chin back on her kneecaps like a gorgeous, perfect golden retriever.

"Hi." I grin at her like a child. "Are you mad at me?"

Extending my legs out, my hands rest in between in legs. Trying to not look uncomfortable, I'd rather not start a difficult conversation. Moving her head towards me, she rolls her eyes and chuckles.

God, she's beautiful under the stars.

She's beautiful all the damn time.

"Cal..." She sighs.

Creating a new position for herself, she extends her legs out like me and her arms behind her. She leans her head to the side, looking out at the water. Looking exquisite. All I can do is stare.

"I'm sorry for whatever I did."

You did nothing wrong. You shouldn't be apologizing.

Brushing away the bullying from Devil, I tell myself I'd rather put a million band aids on her than break her.

To my surprise, she scoots to me. Our thighs are touching and there's a fire coming from my insides. Only a couple of hours have passed, and her touch is a drug, and I'm ready for my next dose.

"It's just been a little much for me. All the bullshit from everyone."

"I know, I'm sorry." I choke out.

"Sometimes I think it would be better to go home. This was supposed to be fun and a first for us, camping. But everyone keeps fighting and shouting at each other. It's just... too much." Her head turns in my direction, and I stare back. I can see her eyes form a thin layer of moisture forming.

Please don't cry.

Instinctively, I wrap my arm around her waist and pull her even closer. I soak in her smell, her arm wrapping around me and her head laying perfectly in the crevice of my neck and shoulder.

"Do you want to leave?" My voice shakes because I won't hesitate to pack our shit and take her home. I'd rather she not be unhappy for the next two days.

"I want to be wherever you are, Cal." She moves her hand on top of my heart, grounding me. Pulling me from the agony and dejection. I kiss her forehead over and over, relieved that I am not the full culprit of this camping trip going wrong.

Then I hear her laugh.

And I want to cry.

The beautiful fucking melody of her laugh entering my soul is creating a Hypernova inside me.

She loses balance of her elbows, falling backward as I hover over her. I admire her like it's the first time I'm seeing her.

Her pair of piercing emeralds. Her dimple. Her infectious smile. Her wavy brown hair.

"I'm sorry all of this is happening."

Pressing her hand back from her forehead, she looks so tired. If we make it out of this weekend, she deserves all the rest. Looking at me with innocent eyes, it's hard to remember the battles we've encountered over the past two days already. She doesn't deserve this.

"It's not your fault. We all seem to have some sort of cutthroat tendencies with each other." I laugh at her honesty.

"Who is your beef with?"

"Anna. Glen. You. Andy." She smiles at me, then winks, making my insides curl around each other.

"Anna and Glen, I completely understand. Fucking psychopaths. What has Andy done?" She laughs at *my* truth this time.

"He's just always up Anna's ass. Everywhere she goes, he goes. I wanted time to spend with her and with you, but both of you are so preoccupied with everyone else. I just feel like an extra. Like I'm not supposed to be here."

Her flirtatious behavior has stopped twisting my insides, but I feel as if someone has filled my stomach with rocks. My instincts step in high gear and I pull her off the ground so she's facing me. I rake my fingers through her hair, pulling her close to my face.

"Baby, if I could tell you how much I want everyone else to leave so it's just you and me, I would shout it from the top of Rainier. I mean, Jesus, it feels like three brick walls are preventing me from getting to you. Only when it's just you and me, am I at my calmest and best. I swear to you, Jen, I want you here with me. We just have to push away the distractions. Can you do that for me? Can it just be me and you for a while?"

She's breathing heavy on my lips, giving me a warm feeling inside. She looked me in the eye as I confessed by truth. Eventually, she grabs my shirt, clenching it tight so that I could feel it pull against my body.

She plants a kiss on the corner of my mouth, making me lose all control of myself.

I pull her fiercely to my face and kiss her so hard and deep.

My drug.

Give me all of you.

The way she kisses me back makes me feel like something has equally depleted her supply of her drug of choice.

It's you. She wants you.

She pulls me down to the ground, crawling on top of her as we continue to exchange passionate, powerful kisses. She's moving her fingers around my hair, tousling it like a wild lion. I can't help but groan at her intensity of lust towards me.

"We could go to the truck." I try to advise to her, but her hands wrap around my neck, making it hard for me to breathe.

Not that I'm complaining. She gives me life.

"Hmm-mm, stay here with me." She moans on my lips. I lower myself down to her and she's quick to wrap her legs around my waist.

Fuck.

This is what I was imagining when I wanted to go "camping" with Jen. Being completely lost in the darkness with her, and only her. Emotionally and physically. She was quick to turn off the background noise and lose herself to me.

That's because all she needs is you. You are her light. She'll follow you blindly.

After a few minutes of detangling from each other, someone has painted a stupid ass smile on my face that I can't seem to shake off.

It's about damn time.

I was feeling like I was getting wrinkles in my forehead from the frowning and pissed off expressions I was constantly having since we've arrived.

This is what love and peace feel like.

Jen clears her throat as she pulls her pants back up before standing up. I pull my shirt back over my body, feeling refreshed and rejuvenated, and looking up at Jen as if she was trying to get my attention.

"You can stop smiling at me like that." She bites her bottom lip as she slips my sweatshirt over herself. I pick up my shoes and decide to carry them back to the site. Her comment only makes me smile more. I was already standing and staring the moment she popped her head through the sweatshirt.

"Smiling like what?" I keep her close, my arm slung over her shoulders as we head to our location.

"I don't know, like you just ate your favorite snack after being banned from having it." She grabs my hand that's dangling over her shoulder.

"I mean, didn't I?" Holding a kiss to her temple, she nudges her hip against mine.

Finally, I've missed being back on top of the world again.

I hate so much that we are walking back to the people who have brought us so much irritation and clear disgust for our relationship. Later, I'll be giving Anna a piece of my mind for betraying our friendship. I can never trust a word that comes out of her mouth again.

I'm on your team, my ass.

The first person I deal with is fucking Glen.

The moment I see him perched on the picnic table by himself, staring at us, has me wanting to hurt him badly.

Jen stays snug to my hip to me as we get closer to him.

"Jennie..." he announces.

"Hey Glen." Her voice, monotone.

"What the fuck are you doing out here?" I intercept. His eyes slowly move from looking at Jen to me, clearly annoyed that I'm speaking to him.

I'd rather your eyes burn to stare at me than to look at her, your filthy sleazebag.

"I was making sure Jennie would make it back in one piece. You know, considering you are an irrational idiot who just walks away from her whenever things don't go his way." I clench my free fist so hard that my muscles and tendons are aching and pleading for some relief.

Jen turns to face me, trying to block my view from him, but he's sitting above her head and she's so adorably cute and short that it's doing absolutely nothing.

"Hey, look at me." It surprises me when she grabs my face roughly to stare down at her. The sight of her comforted me, causing me to loosen my tight fist.

"Block out the noise, remember? He's just noise." She makes patterns with her fingers around my cheeks, quickly bringing me down to a safe level.

"So are you riding with me tomorrow, Jennie?"

You fucking prick.

"Don't speak to her. She's not going anywhere near you."

Despite Jen still touching me, trying to bring me comfort, the words from Glen are confetti laced with toxic chemicals that he's trying to kill me.

Perhaps I should just kill him.

"Pretty sure she doesn't need your permission to speak for herself."

He moves off the bench, approaching me. Jen doesn't notice his approach, so I give her a little nudge on the shoulder to move her aside.

It's time for the boys to play.

"Pretty sure nobody wants you here." I move closer to him but feel a tug on my wrist.

"Cal, please don't. Don't do this. He isn't worth it."

Glen is still approaching me, leaving only a couple of feet between us now.

"I'm not worth it, Jennie? Did you really just say that?" I squint my eyes at him as he speaks directly to Jen.

Okay, now you're really pissing us off.

Jen's head turns to him, concern in her eyes of Glen's questioning.

"Caught you in a lie, didn't I? Don't worry, we don't have to lie to him anymore. You said if Calvin wasn't a part of your life, that would want to be with me instead. Remember that? I mean, you only said that to me earlier when he left you behind."

Come again?

Feeling completely blindsided, I take a step away from both. Like watching a slow-motion scene, Jen's head snaps back in my direction, aimlessly moving to me, tears swelling in her eyes.

"That is not what I said." She barely chokes out to me.

I'm seeing red.

This double-crossing is turning into a triple-crossing. First Anna, now these two?

My tongue feels like it's being gripped by a force I have no control over. I can't even speak to her. Somehow, my eyes move to Glen, who is grinning, amused at my turmoil unraveling in front of my eyes.

You are a joke.

To him.

To her.

To all of them.

You are nothing.

Feeling queasy, I back away. No matter where I go, hell seems to follow me. I don't know where I plan to go, but I turn my back to my girl and walk aimlessly towards .... Well, anywhere else.

"Cal, please don't go!" Jen's voice is running after me, crying my name.

I stand still, waiting for her to come into sight. It's a torrential hurricane in front of my face. There are so many tears falling from her face. I am torn between wanting to kiss away the tears and wanting to shout at her. Does my heart not matter to her?

"Cal, please. I swear to God I said nothing like that. He's manipulating you because he knows how to get under your skin."

Her pleads are making my throat clench.

Don't cry, you pathetic excuse for a human.

"Leave me alone."

It's all I can say. I don't know if I'm speaking to Jen, the others or Devil. I just want all the voices to shut up.

Glen may be a pain in the ass, but I wouldn't put it past him to be a liar.

If Calvin wasn't a part of your life, you would want to be with me instead.

Maybe Jen is the one who is lying...

The words replay over and over in my head.

She would want to be with me instead.

Anger fills me like gasoline. It fuels my system, making me feel in control again. My rage was so intense that when I punched a tree, my knuckles immediately bled. I don't even bother using a piece of cloth to care for my hand. That felt so unbelievably good, although my hand is pulsating with pain.

Why the fuck would he say something like that to me?

I don't know how long I had been walking or exactly where I was walking to. My mind was playing tricks on me. Angel had completely checked out of my mind. I have had no reassurance of anything for hours. Devil was maddening. I was seriously concerned I was having a mental breakdown. A few tears escaped but sadness wasn't the problem; it was the betrayal. Whether the words coming out of Glen's mouth were true, or the words from Jen were a cover-up, I was still a fucking human being with feelings.

How many times did someone have to be betrayed until they eventually break?

My phone had been ringing nonstop since I left Jen earlier. When I found the courage to check the time, there were fifteen missed calls and over twenty texts messages.

It was 10:45 P.M. The crickets and owls had become pleasant companions.

I terribly wanted to talk to God—to question his karma, to understand his creation of a person like Glen. But the only person to overpower my thoughts was Devil.

I told you she wasn't good for you.

You should have never come here. She wanted to be with him.

You look like a fool for the stupid surprise you have for her.

You don't deserve love. You don't deserve her love.

Glen could love her so much better than you ever could.

My body was collapsing in a matter of seconds. Somehow, I found my way back to the site. I came from the opposite direction, so our cars were blocking the tent. Unsure if anyone sitting by the fire, I opened the driver's door and scooted myself in.

Nobody can save you from the person you are.

The amount of strain in my body was equivalent to getting run over by a semi-truck. At least, that's what I felt was happening to me. Losing all control of my senses, I find my pocketknife in the cupholder where I set it earlier.

You'll never be able to love her the way he can.

I flick open the blade as I feel my heart is about to take its last and final beat.

She doesn't love you.

With no target in sight, I press the blade to my wrist, dragging it slowly to release the tension inside me. To bring me back to reality. However, the visions of reality are simple—Glen and Jen want to be together. She doesn't want me. Anna has been a shit friend. I am all alone.

Reality only makes me push down further into my arm. I've been holding my breath the entire time, creating a red stream on my right arm. Compared to the damage I did earlier when Anna helped me, this cut is a mammoth. My face feels swollen from the heartbreak that has shattered my world. I close the knife, not minding the residue of blood, and allow my body to rest.

You are alone. Nobody is coming.

And as if the sun and the moon collide, I hear knocking on my passenger window and that's when I realize I'm back in reality.

She'll always find you. She's the one who is supposed to save you.

Turning my head only, I'm feeling too much for my body to react. She stares back, clearly distraught by the look of her face being blotchy and red. When I make no movements to allow her in the car, she disappears from my sight.

Only a second passes when my door opens and I feel her hands on my arm, gentle but shaky. I can't bring myself to look at her, disgusted in myself for how shitty I've let her be loved by me, but disgusted with her for being so verbally sensual with a man who I would kill in broad daylight. Disgusted at how quickly our love is vanishing right in front of my eyes.

"Cal..." she whines as she steps closer to me. It takes too much energy to keep my head up, so it falls, looking down at my open wound on my arm. Jen's head drops to look at my arm.

Tenderly, she lifts it and tries her best to smear away the blood with her thumb. Her sniffles twist my heart strings to suffocate me.

"C'mon."

One word to cast me under her spell. As much as I want the

bricks in my stomach to keep weighing me down so I can't move, Angel's wings are much stronger and powerful. I turn my body to hop down the truck, following the gentle tug of Jen as she moves her fingers into my mine.

She won't ever hurt you.

Clenching my teeth, holding back the words I want to say to her, I just follow her. We get to our picnic table where thankfully it's vacant of ugly-looking, jealous rats. She moves me to sit on the bench but continues to stay quiet. I watch her move around the tent, entering the main opening, hearing a mumbled "no" and then watching her exit with one of her bags.

She sets the white bag on the table next to my leg and opens it, moving items around. All I can do is look at her. God, she looks so fucking broken.

You just put her through hell. Give her a little piece of heaven back.

Releasing the tension of my jaw, I separate my lips.

"Jennie..."

She doesn't look at me. A wetness streaks my arm. When I look down to see if there was more blood, it's a cotton ball soaked in water. Lightly, she drags the cotton ball back and forth, removing the semi-dried blood. Looking past her working hands, there is a Band-Aid on the top of her bag.

She'll always take good care of you–if you let her.

"Jen, look at me. Please." My voice quivers over itself. She continues wiping my arm, shaking her head.

"I can't." She croaks back to me.

She takes the band aid, cuts it vertically to make two thin pieces and gently lays them over my wound. As soon as she crumples up the trash, she tries to move away from me, but I catch her. I feel her tense around my grasp.

"Look at me." I plead again.

She rubs her lips together, contemplating my request. She keeps her eyes closed as she lifts her head in my direction and then opens her eyes. The rainforest is active. My heart continues to break repeatedly.

"I'm sorry, baby."

Knowing this time that I have something to apologize for, I pull her into me. Still sitting on top of the picnic table, her body moves in between my legs and I wrap my hands on her shoulders, but she doesn't reciprocate.

Give her a moment, she'll grab onto you like she has so many times before. You are her lifeline.

I don't know how Angel knows, and frankly I don't care, but on command, Jen brings her arms around my lower back and pulls herself close to me. She buries her head into the crevice of my shoulder and neck and lets it all out. My neck is wet within a few seconds. Her sobs are probably waking everyone up, but I'm hopeful everyone can stay the fuck away from us while I fix this.

You can fix this. Make it right. Tell her you won't leave her.

"I'm,"

Kiss her temple.

"So,"

Kiss her temple.

"Fucking,"

Kiss her temple.

"Sorry."

Kiss her temple.

Her body is stagnant as I force my lips onto her, and I'm forever wishing that she'll be able to say something, anything, back to me. I hold her close to me, letting her think, or breathe, or just rest.

Just as long as she's with me, I don't care what she does.

She continues to cry into my chest as I do my best to console in the right way.

You left her.

I want to crack the neck of my internal Devil and watch her burn in misery.

"Where did you go?" She finally whimpers out at me. Or more specifically, to my chest.

I take in a big breath, relieved she has words left in her to speak to me. We'd be in big shit if she had nothing to say. My mom always told Lincoln and I that when females have nothing to say, you've done something drastically unfixable.

I continue to stroke her hair as I come up with excuses for disappearing from her.

"Just had to get away."

"You left me here... with him."

I don't know if she's trying to make me guilty, but she's sure doing a damn good job. There's such a big part of me that wants to walk away again from her.

"I'm sorry, baby. I just..." I lick my lips, trying to find the right words to make her understand she isn't the problem. It's that fucker who I wish would get kidnapped in the woods. It's maddening to be around someone who brings out the worst in you. I never knew I had this side of me, and I hate that I'm letting it affect my relationship and my friendships. This was not the type of guy I was expecting Glen to me.

"I just can't be around him anymore. I don't know what his problem is with me lately, but ever since we got here, he's been on a mission to destroy my life." Her cries have lessened, and we have synchronized our breathing.

"Again, though, you just left me in the dark. You could've just grabbed my hand, and I would've gone anywhere with you."

And that does it. She nails the dagger another four inches into my heart.

She's not making you feel guilty. She's proving her point.

YOU DON'T FIGHT FOR HER.

Realizing what Angel is trying to say, I bring Jen as close as I can to me.

"I don't want you to cry anymore. I don't want to keep hurting you." Biting the inside of my cheek, I'm holding back tears of my own as I hear Jen sniffle again.

"I don't know how to fix that for tomorrow, but for right now, just come to bed with me and hold me. Just don't let go, okay? Can you do that until morning? Can you just not let me go?"

God, I want to absorb all the doubt she has about me.

We could never let you go.

I can't even speak because I'm afraid that any words that come out of my stupid ass mouth are going to drive her away. Instead, I give her another kiss on the temple and just nod my head as she hugs me.

She's just as eager to get out of this metaphorical disaster we've created since arriving at the site. She pulls me by the hand, and I follow her into the tent.

Thank the Lord that the barrier to Anna and Andy's section is closed off because I would give Anna a piece of my mind. I'm even more thankful to the Lord that Glen zipped up his area; otherwise, this tent would become a bloodbath.

I zip our little piece of normalcy and calmness as she tugs off my sweatshirt. The shirt I've been wearing has dried blood on it, so I remove my shirt as well. Sifting through my clothes in my bag, I feel Jen's hands snake up my torso. Instantly, I feel like a hyena, my body erupting with piloerection.

I'm too tall to stand without my head hitting the top of the tent, so I move to my knees. Jen stands over me, my mouth breathing into her stomach.

"Come here, lay down with me."

Not sure if she heard me, but she massages my hair and I swear, all my senses are peaking.

Just enjoy this moment with her. Enjoy this time with her. Just for tonight.

The sight of her makes my mouth water. Every detail of her is perfect.

"God, you are so beautiful. I'm such an idiot for leaving you behind." She falls down to our sleeping bag and I can see a bashful smile appear on her face as she maneuvers the surrounding blankets.

She's stripped down to her panties and has my Vancouver Canucks shirt on. My pants are uncomfortable from the growth happening between my legs, so I grab gym shorts from my bag. My temperature is scorching, so I keep a shirt off for now. Getting under the blankets sends me to the moon. I pull Jen to the front of me, pushing her ass against me, and I try to silence my moan. Holding myself up on my elbow, I kiss the beauty mark on her neck, which makes her squirm as she leans to flip off the lantern. Before she turns the switch, I grab her arm. Peeking at me over her shoulder, an insatiable throb shoots in my groin. I rest my mouth on her shoulder, looking at her.

"I love you, Jen. I love you so much."

"I love you too, Cal. It'll only ever be you." She flicks off the lantern and pushes herself more against me. My arms wrap around her waist, and when I feel her fingers intertwine with mine, I finally enter dreamland.

The best feeling is falling asleep next to Jen.

As I try to enter the tranquil quietness of Devil finally being asleep, I should've known better than to doubt her.

She won't want to ride with you tomorrow. She'll want to be with him.

They'll be in the same kayak. Laughing and almost touching. He's going to be touching her and you'll be in a whole other boat, unable to teach him a lesson.

And she'll realize how much she likes his touch.

She'll crave his touch more than yours.

She'll want more thana simple touch from him.

"STOP!" I shout, and my eyes snap open. I'm drenched in sweat and I'm clenching on to Jen for dear life. Startled by me, she sits up to see what's wrong.

I have my hands pressed against my forehead, wishing Devil would shut the fuck up.

"What's the matter?" Her soft voice brings me back to center. Dropping my hands, she's laying down with her half-opened eyes. She must've been sleeping peacefully, and I'm trying to steady my nerves before talking to her.

It's okay, tell her how you feel.

Sitting up now, she rubs my arms to comfort me.

"Please don't leave me for him." My voice cracks as I tell her my truth. My nostrils flare open, and I can feel the dams in my eyes open.

"Hey, look at me."

She runs her hands all the way up my arms, around my shoulders, my neck, my cheeks until she lightly forces me to look at her. Her eyes are wide open now. I'm clenching my jaw so fucking tight, holding on to dear life to hold in my emotions. I keep my eyes down to avoid her gaze but turn my head anyway, allowing her to take control.

"Look at me, Calvin."

Wow, the authoritative Jen is incredibly delicious. I uncover my eyes, looking at the most perfect ice cream sundae. She just looks at me for a while, trying to hide her smirk. Her hair is messy; fly aways going in every direction. Her makeup her slightly smeared under her eyes and the way her eyelids are not fully open remind me why I love morning Jennie. When I see the dimple form on her right cheek, it sucks me in and I'm a goner.

"I won't ever leave you. We're going to save each other, right? You're the only person who I want to save me. He is nothing to me. I swear to you."

She lays a gentle kiss on my lips, but I can't help but to add a bit more to it, so I grab her shirt and pull her onto me, so she straddles my hips. Still with no pants on, I run my hands over her thighs. Soft like butter, she presses against me when I get to her hips. I press the back of her head towards me, pushing my lips to hers, like they were lined with the finest cocaine.

Desperate that I'm going to lose her with one look from Glen at any moment, I give myself to her.

She coils around my body, one leg over mine, the other around my hip. Her arms are moving in every direction, moving through my hair, down my arms, around my shoulders. Her touch is keeping my arousal on full blast.

Don't get me started on the continuous motions her pelvis has been doing to me for the past fifteen minutes. I wish I could absorb her somehow and get her closer to me. I'm afraid I'm pushing too hard, but fuck, I just want to be close to her.

Her panting and my sweat are making our small oasis turn into a greenhouse. Very hot and moist.

While I continue a trail of kisses from her mouth to her stomach, I keep her words at the forefront of my mind–at least I try to.

I won't ever leave you. He is nothing to me.

Before this trip, she's never given me a reason to doubt her. Her groaning brings me back to reality that she wants my mouth, so I work my way back up her torso, in between her breasts, right on her beauty mark–AKA the sweet spot because she coils into me every time I kiss there–then back to her lips which eagerly invite me in.

As we finish each other, we lay together as we drift back asleep. Part of me is forcing myself to stay awake so I don't have to deal with the torment of my thoughts about Glen's warnings. I am so tired. Is there anyone who can give Devil a well-deserved vacation because I need her to leave my mind?

With Jen snug to my side, I realize for a moment that I fought with the group five different times already. They don't deserve this mess I've created. Part of me tries to stay awake because I cringe at the sights of leaving Jen behind on every occasion since arriving in Easton.

We just want to make her happy and smile. You can do that. Let her save you and she can be the brightest star in your world of darkness. Just let her do that for you.

The feeling of having her nestled in my arms just brings me so much peace and calm that I eventually drift off.

"Let's go fuck buddies. We are leaving in twenty minutes. I'm being nice by giving you time to get ready." Anna shouts and cat scratches at our zippered barrier.

I snap my eyes open, but the brightness burns my eyes, so I snap them shut and try again until I'm accustomed to the light. Jen squirms under my arms and groans at the words of Anna. She isn't a morning person. I stretch my back around and twist my torso from side to side to get the kinks out of my body.

Wow, the ground is uncomfortable. I rotate my neck in circles and crack my knuckles and ankles. Feeling all my bones and muscles feeling less tight, I hover over Jen's body and kiss her arm.

"C'mon baby, we gotta get up." I press more kisses down her arm until she is moaning from my annoyance. I chuckle when she pushes my face away. We could've used more sleep, but I'm waking up feeling satisfied with the other fun extras we did last night, so I'm not one to complain.

"I'm going to the shower, so I'll be back in about ten minutes. You better be up and ready to go or I'm throwing you over my shoulder."

Groan.

I unzip our side of the tent, and when I have enough room to stand, I lift my hands over my head and twist my body some more.

"Well, well, well, look at who rose from the ashes."

Prick. I wasn't expecting such a harsh morning greeting from Anna, but she was already on my shit list, so I didn't bother to acknowledge her.

"Morning Andy." *Take that you asshat.*

"Uh, hey man. Jennie awake?" I'm rummaging through my bags to grab my shampoo, bar of soap, and my swim trunks.

"She's getting there. Rough night." I laugh and look over at the three pairs of eyes looking at me.

"Joking. Jesus, everyone get their panties out of a twist. Anyway, I'm taking a shower. I'll be back. Told Jen to be ready, or at least up, when I get back." I head toward the community shower and bathroom, which is roughly thirty feet away.

"We will leave without her, Calvin!" I hear Anna shout at me, but I could give two fucks of what she had to say to me.

Go ahead and leave without us. I'm not leaving her behind, you crazy psychopath.

Even though the water pressure of a camping site community bathroom is weak, I feel extremely refreshed and clean from the dried blood, sweat, and tears that have been lingering on my body.

If it were up to me, I'd pick a campsite that didn't have community bathrooms to get the full effect of not showering for a whole weekend, but I'm glad it's here. I won't enlarge Anna's ego, but I appreciate her for picking this place.

Carrying my dirty clothes, shampoo and soap, I see two females at our tent, confirming Jen is up. She's already changed into a purple tank top and black shorts. I can see her bathing suit under her tank top.

Damn, she was supposed to be sleeping so we would have to miss out on the fun with everyone else.

Jen is squatting on the ground while Anna braids her hair. I keep my eyes on Jen, who immediately smiles and winks at me when I'm in her line of vision.

I bit my bottom lip, already feeling on cloud nine this morning. Speaking of which, I need to find some chap-stick. My lips hurt badly.

Okay, it's possible that this camping trip won't be a total shit show.

You have a lot of making up to do.

I ignore the request of Devil because I'm not making up to anyone unless it's Jen. Nobody else is worth the reconciliation.

Dropping my things in my bag, I pick up some sunscreen and mimic Andy's actions by rubbing my legs and arms.

Glen is fixing his sunglasses to attach them to one of those straps that he can drape around his neck. He looks like a college frat tool and I just want to punch his face already.

Easy tiger...

"So we need to figure out who's riding with who..."

Anna announces as she's tying the bottom of Jen's hair. Deep down, I knew the conversation was bound to still happen. I was hoping I made more time to stay within the calm. With her hair done, Jen stands up and meets eye contact with me. My stomach is filling with rage, and I think Jen can sense my ticking time bomb. She comes over to me and caresses my arm.

"I have a suggestion, but I don't want anyone to get mad or upset. I'm tired of everyone yelling at each other."

"What is it, Jennie?"

Glen speaks to her, and I watch him sit on the picnic table next to Anna. Andy is standing near the tent with his arms crossed, listening to the conversation from afar. I continue to rub sunscreen onto my face, hopeful that I don't have to squirt any lotion into my eyes to blind me...

"How does everyone feel if Cal leads the way by himself? Anna, you ride with Glen and Andy and I can ride together? That seems to be the only pairing where someone doesn't get killed."

Her mention of Glen nearly gave me a heart attack—my heart

raced uncontrollably—but this plan is better. Closing the sunscreen and applying my chap-stick, I look at everyone's reactions to her.

"As much as I want to ride with you, I'm fine with that." I speak directly to Jen and kiss her forehead. Over her head, Glen rolls his eyes and stands up from the table.

"Why can't Anna and Jen ride together and I ride with Andy?"

I bite my tongue to tell Glen to shut up because clearly there's tension between Anna and Jen. They could use some time apart from each other as well. Not to mention the subtle tension between Andy and Anna as well.

"Glen, as much as I want to ride with Anna myself, you have been making this trip awful. I'm vetoing your idea, and I'm agreeing with Jennie on this."

Andy. Where the fuck did that come from?

We all shoot eyes at Andy, who comes forward to join the group. Anna lowers her eye level from Andy and starts packing her backpack. Interesting—no smart remark from her? Are they experiencing the same frustration and betrayal as we are, or do they have their own issues brewing?

Glen tilts his head towards the sky, completely humiliated and shocked that the closest person to him on this trip moved him to the back burner.

"So everyone besides fuck face is good with this? Again, it's not ideal, but we all want to enjoy the fun." I try to mediate, but Glen moves in front of my face.

Please hit me. I've been waiting for my shot to knock you out.

"Fine." Anna says with her back to me.

"I'm good with it." Andy confirms.

"Yes." Jen smiles at me. Satisfied in her authority.

"Whatever."

He steps away from me, shaking his head back and forth, clearly disappointed that he doesn't get to be co-pilot to my princess.

"Cool, let's get the show on the road."

I slip on my water shoes, feeling bouncy and happy as hell that

Jen is avoiding an explosion with Glen. I trust Andy with her. Plus, that leaves Anna and Glen to bitch and complain about me to each other. Maybe it'll put them in better moods afterwards.

It was about a two-mile walk to Naches River where the kayak dock was. It felt like Jen and I were the only ones excited, and also on speaking terms. Anna and Andy walked separately, Glen trailing them. It was shitty to think, but I'm glad they were the ones dealing with uncomfortable feelings instead of us. We've done our fair share.

Trusting Andy would look after Jen, Anna and I checked our group in while the other three waited by the kayaks. I hated I didn't know what kind of bullshit Glen was pouring into Jen's mind, but it felt like a small victory to know that Andy would put Glen in his place if he needed to.

It took us no time to get our gear and head towards the river.

Andy and Anna were hardly exchanging words and immediately separated from each other when we reached the water. I stayed close to Jen to help her into the kayak. Andy kept the boat still as I leveraged her into the small seat. In my peripheral, I could see Glen copy my behaviors for Anna.

I reciprocated the gesture of holding onto the kayak for Andy to get in the back seat, hovering over Jen.

"Take care of her." I gently punched his arm then walked away.

Ugh, the sight killed me inside, but I'm so thankful it's Andy and not Glen. Thank all the Gods.

Even though I wanted to avoid the two snakes, I walked over to them, anyway.

"Guys good?" As much as I wanted Glen to drown or have a malfunction from his vest, I also didn't want his blood on my hands. And Anna. Jesus, Anna... I would never forgive myself if something happened to her.

"I think so. Are you going to show us how to paddle once you get in?" Anna says to me, cool as a cucumber, tightening the straps on her vest. Same as Andy and Jen, Glen is sitting in the rear behind Anna. The weight distribution prevents capsizing.

I walk to my kayak as I answer Anna.

"Yep! It's fairly simple." I hop into my small cubicle and get myself situated in the seat. I'm enjoying the control of leading the pack.

"So you both want to make sure you tell each other which way to paddle. Left or right, doesn't matter as long as you stay synchronized. If you don't, you won't move, or you'll just going to go in circles."

Dropping my sunglasses down, I push myself with my paddles until I'm coasting in front of them as I watch them try to move. I laugh because it's like watching a game of *Survivor*. Overhearing Jen tell him to paddle right, left, right, left makes me proud. They make a good team.

That's my girl.

Anna and Glen are having a hell of a time moving. Anna is trying to paddle to the left, but Glen is paddling to the right.

"Together, you guys. Move together." I shout toward the idiots.

The natural current of the river pulls me around a bit, but Jen and Andy are close to me, continuing to move beautifully, like professionals. I rest my hand on my chin as I continue to watch Anna and Glen struggle to move. I shake my head, currently wondering how I let these morons make me feel less of myself.

After a few minutes, they finally move in our direction. I check on Jen and Andy, who have sat stagnant in the water, waiting for the others. They seem deep in conversation and I smirk on the inside, knowing Jen is having a decent conversation without arguing or name-calling.

I move my paddles backwards and then, using only my left paddle to turn myself; we head towards the mouth of the river. I take the lead, glancing back at my gang every so often. Jen and Andy are on my right side, casually paddling in sync and looking around the natural scenery. Anna and Glen, on my left, are still trying to paddle in sync but seem to enjoy themselves. Anna keeps laughing when she pushes off, but Glen does the opposite. Surprisingly, Glen is smiling too.

Huh, it's not a bad look on them. It sucks they are fucking vultures, because from the outside, they look like they would be nice, kind people.

We spent a couple of hours drifting on the water, enjoying ourselves, as we should've been all along. Every time I peek over my shoulder to make sure nobody has gone overboard, everyone has a huge ass smile on their face. And when I'm not looking, my ears fill with Jen and Andy's laughter and Anna's shrieking from Glen swatting water at her.

Damn, we should've done this bonding activity first thing yesterday instead of the treehouse excursion. Perhaps the rest of the weekend would have been different.

When the sun is at its highest, I'm sweating like crazy. We're probably five miles from the check-in dock, but this has been relaxing. I let my paddles rest and dip my hands in the water, slapping a bit of water around my neck, down my arms (which are unfortunately getting red) and on my cheeks.

And when things were perfect, Devil decides it's time for a tsunami and wants me to drown.

Opening my eyes to check on my beginners, I find myself in a cutthroat line of being quadrupled blindsided.

Andy is lathering sunscreen on Jen's arms.

Not in friendly fucking way.

Jen seems to enjoy the feel of his hands pressed to her arms.

He's rubbing his hands up and down her arms, wanting to keep his hands on her body for an extended period. His head is resting on her shoulder, close and fucking intimate that I think I want to carve out my heart and feed to whatever species are beneath me.

"Hey!" I shout at them. Jen immediately looks at me, startled to know that I've been there the whole time.

"What the fuck is going on?" I maneuver my kayak alongside theirs. If I leaned over enough, I could tip them over.

I should tip them over. My boiling point is literally in a fucking danger zone. And it's not even from the sun.

Andy is conveniently resting back in his seated position, his hands gripping the sides of the kayak and purposely looking the opposite direction.

"What the fuck was that?" My eyes ping-pong back and forth, but I'm speaking directly to Jen.

She bites her bottom lip nervously and looks away. She's the only one not wearing sunglasses, and it's not hard for me to notice she's trying to bat away her tears.

"Jennie!" I shout loudly to her. Loud enough that she jumps when I yell her name.

"Hey man, relax. She needed sunscreen on her shoulders, and clearly she couldn't reach." Andy defends her, but I don't bother to listen to his reason.

She continues to look down at the water as my kayak gets knocked. Glen and Anna in my proximity, concern on both of their faces.

"Oops, sorry. What's going on?" Anna says out loud.

"Jennie, why are you crying... again?" Glen's observations make me want to light myself on fire.

Perfect fucking timing for Glen to save the day.

There is something in me that just snaps.

I've spent the last twenty-four hours being fucked over in so many ways that I don't even recognize who I am. Whatever kind of poison my so-called-friends have given me is working. To the fullest potential.

I turn my eye level to Anna. She needs to be the first one I hurt.

"You should probably ask your boyfriend why his hands are touching your best friend. It seems to me there was some sort of conspiracy to Jen's brilliant idea of pairing with her new buddy. So, looks like I'm not the one who looks like an idiot. Fuck you all, get back to the dock by yourselves."

There's so much I want to spit out to each of them, but I would say some hurtful things.

You don't want to hurt Jen.

Putting my paddles back in the water, I push off, heading in the direction of the dock.

Don't do it. Don't look at her. It's going to ruin you.

But I can't. She's a magnet that I have to make sure she's okay. I feel like there's a crane grabbing my head to force myself to look at her. Andy's trying to reason with her to stay put in the kayak, even though she's trying to paddle towards me.

Yes, come to me. Come, save me.

I'm curious about Andy's persuasive words that kept her from coming to me because she suddenly stopped paddling and buried her face in her hands.

There you go, breaking her heart. Again. Just go home. All you do is ruin things for her. For everyone.

I can't handle the bullying from Devil. There is a small piece of hope in me that is preventing me from jumping over the side of the kayak and letting myself sink. To feel nothing. Replaying the flirtatious five seconds between Jen and Andy is on repeat. On top of ripping my heart out, I want to snip the connection between my eyes and brain so I can stop seeing the chemistry between them.

I paddle hard on the way back to the dock. Sweat is dripping from my forehead, and my back is extra moist. I feel like a fucking Olympian and bypassers are probably wondering what is chasing me.

Evil.

When I see the check in flag, I let the boat idle to the dock as I stand up and jump onto the small port. Removing my vest, I throw it in the kayak's seat.

Every fiber in me is shaking with fury. I walk the two miles back to the site, hoping it's enough time to regain my composure before they come back. It's necessary that we all talk about what the fuck just happened.

My hope is dead when I get back to our area because I feel even more pissed off. I replay Jen's request to ride with Andy as I walk towards the picnic table where the first red flag occurred.

My molars are going to bleed from the tension I'm clamping on them.

Then I just completely disassociate.

I get my hands on whatever I can to throw. Everyone's bags, the coolers and trash and the tent. Things are flying every which way that I don't even care about anymore. My "friends" want to destroy my life, well I'll take property destruction to a whole new level!

I don't know when the screams started, but in the middle of tossing someone's bag in the fucking dirt; I scream so hard and long that it burns my throat.

Once my inner Hulk feels some sort of relief, I take a walk to the lake. As I back away from the disaster I created, I continue to show no remorse.

You fuck with me, I will fuck with you.

Jen doesn't deserve this. She wasn't part of it.

She has openly flirted with the two other males on this trip! She is just as much as an accomplice. She deserves to feel his pain.

I shake my head, trying to side with Devil that Jen maybe, just maybe, deserved some sort of retaliation for stomping on my heart. After how many times?! I plop myself on the lake where we were yesterday.

My body hurts. I look down at my arms, noticing the sunburn and lack of re-applying more sunscreen. On my right arm, there's still a band-aid over my cut from last night, as well as a scab forming from my other cut. I can't imagine how much damage my brain has endured.

I try not to let myself slip into the happy moments because they feel like a complete hoax.

Did she even love me at all? Where the fuck did all this go wrong? This isn't us!!

I let myself sit in misery, for I don't know how long. The sun in moving down to the west, so I can tell it's been a couple of hours.

They should be back by now.

Why hasn't she come to save me...

I hear the movement of someone behind and my heart feels like it's about to be resuscitated.

She's coming. She's coming for me.

I've been laying down on the ground, looking at the sky transform around me. When I sit up, the silhouette of a short, blond girl with her arms crossed over her chest stares at me. She's changed out of her clothes and into grey sweats and a bright pink hoodie. Her hair is up in a messy bun and she looks like she's been crying as she gets closer to me.

My heart immediately drops into my stomach.

"Hey." I say to her first.

She stops in her tracks at my conversation starter. I can see her hold her arms closer to her chest, looking uncomfortable. I stare at her, feeling her disappointment radiate off her. She knows what I've done to the site...

My throat is getting tight, and my eyes move away from her.

"So Jennie doesn't feel comfortable staying the rest of the weekend. She wanted to leave tomorrow morning. What do you want to do?"

I say nothing, only shrugging my shoulders. The sadness in her voice is unbearable to listen to. I'd rather listen to her controlling, annoying voice over this shit. I can't stand that Jen is ready to leave without me.

But I also don't blame her.

"Why does she want to leave?" Pinching my nose, I wish someone would just kill me.

"She's scared of you, Calvin. We all are. You've never done something like this before." I stay silent at those words.

She's scared of you.

Anna moves closer, but still stands near me.

"Trust me, I'm beyond pissed off at Andy. Things haven't been right between us for a while. You wouldn't know because you don't ask about other people."

I've had enough. Turning my head towards her, my eyes are blurry as I stare at her.

"I'm sorry."

My behavior has led me to fail my best friend. The number of times she showed up for me, to support me—when it was genuine or not—the countless times of sharing my fears about the future. She's always been there. Always been a constant for me. And I completely failed her. I stay silent as I sniff in my snot. There's no way I can hold myself together anymore. Every person I've loved, I've failed them.

Anna sniffles are so close. The ache in me physically hurts. I wish I could get myself off the ground to hug her, but I don't move. It's been about five minutes of us weeping.

"Okay, well, I think we are going to head out tomorrow. Let us know if you want us to wait for you or if you'll drive back by yourself."

My throat feels like the Sahara Desert. There is so much temptation to just let it out to Anna. My closest confidante. My longest friend. I can't get past the mistrust and doubt she had in me.

"Anna..." She turns when I call after her.

"I'm sorry."

I wish she knew how much guilt is swarming in my stomach. Looking at her takes a lot of nerve, but she just stares back. She bobbles her head up and down, wiping her eyes, then walks away.

Nothing. You deserve nothing because you are nothing.

I stay on the outskirts of the lake until night fall. After my explosion, I'm unsure how I will face my group again. The blame is mine. I'm the one who should be apologizing. That I'm the one who got left behind.

But the pieces don't go together.

Glen egging me on since the moment we stepped foot in the cabin.

Anna almost ruining the surprise in the kitchen with her loud comments.

Jen and Glen frolicking at the treehouse.

The musical chairs shit at Waffle House.

Parking at the site and with my own two eyes, watching Glen and Jen continue to be immersed in each other.

Anna sharing her truth that she enjoys seeing Jen be happy when she's with Glen.

The fucking plot twist of the weekend that Jen believed Anna and I were a thing.

Andy's hands were on her.

AND THEY WANT TO CALL ME THE IRRATIONAL ONE? HOW MANY CHANCES DID THEY THINK THEY DESERVED UNTIL I LOST MY SHIT?

I run my hands over my face, wishing there was some sort of comet that would appear in the sky to change the rest of the weekend. What would I wish for?

Glen to fucking disappear. That's obvious.

For Anna to be a genuine, kind friend that she always was to me when we were younger.

For Andy to disappear as well.

As for Jen...

I want to scratch my eyes out. God, I just want to Jen to love me fiercely like she did before this stupid trip.

Over twenty-four hours of pure torment, Jen is slipping through my fingers. Two days of being on a fucking roller coaster that isn't fun. I like roller coasters that have hills and where I can put my hands up because I'm having the time of my life. This roller coaster inflicts spikes, stopping our momentum at our best moments. The random corkscrews are making me sick with the bickering. The sudden stops are the worst. It's like reading your favorite story, and then suddenly, the book is over.

I don't want this to be over.

I love this girl more than anything, and I don't think my love will ever waver. My heart, in its entirety, is hers–perfect or imperfect– because I trust her to protect it.

I don't know how long I've been daydreaming, or night dreaming, about fulfilling Jen's promise. Our promise to each other to save one another.

Again, footsteps approach me and I close my eyes in fear that Jen is arriving. To tell me it's over.

My heart isn't ready. I lick my lips as I sit up and face the water, waiting for the shadow of her to appear behind me.

But it's not her.

Fuck me, my worst nightmare has taken over.

Please let me go back to night dreaming!!

I look up at the two figures standing close together, one watching me and the other staring at the water.

Glen and Andy.

"Can we sit?" Andy is the one who has been looking at me while Glen is avoiding eye contact by looking at the lake. Like Anna, they've changed their clothes since this morning. From the looks of it, they had some clothes that were salvageable from my destruction.

With a silent hand gesture, I motion for them to sit. Andy sits closest to me, leaving a few inches between us. I'm thankful for the space because I have little left in me to fight these two imbeciles. Glen sits on the other side of Andy.

"Look, we know you probably don't want to talk to us, and it's fine. We just need to share our feelings with you. With all the shit so far, you deserve some sort of explanation for things. Can you just listen to us for a moment?" Andy says again.

I bring my legs up and hold my hands together in a fist, hoping to hold myself together as I prepare to hear the truth.

"Fine." I spit out.

"First off, we should tell you that Jennie is not happy about what you did to the camp area. She was furious. Still is furious, really. She hasn't said much since we've gotten back, but it's clear as day on her face that she is holding herself back to come find you. She sobbed to Anna that she wanted to leave tonight, but Anna thought she could convince you to... I don't know, be better? Second, we tried to keep Anna from approaching you, but she felt she'd be able to reason with you best. She was pretty upset about the whole thing, really. She's been keeping herself in the tent since she came back from talking to you. I haven't had the chance to explain myself to her."

Andy's voice is pissing me off because he's talking so causally.

"Fuck explaining yourself. It was clear as day that you were enjoying touching Jen. Don't try to gaslight Anna for your fucking actions." I bite back.

"Fuck off, Calvin. Quit giving yourself a pity party!"

Glen.

I swear to God if there were a million shooting stars that passed, I would wish for a different way to off this guy.

"Shut up, will you?" I look over to make sure he isn't talking to me. Thank God it's directed to Glen.

"Look, this isn't about Anna. It's about Jen. This is hard for both of us to say, so please just keep your cool for five minutes."

I try to swallow, but I'm having a tough time working any of my automatic responses. Angel and Devil have been MIA, but the silence is deafening. As with Anna's voice, I'd rather have them bicker back and forth than nothing.

"Jen is ..." Andy starts. My eyes glance in their direction. They are both looking down at the sand, clearly very uncomfortable.

"She's what?" I sneer through my teeth, praying they only have good things to say. Better yet, I hope they don't have anything to say.

"She's different, man. She's so different." Glen peacefully says. My eyes shoot at him as he finishes the sentence. My brain is going into hypervigilance. I don't want to hurt these guys, but they better start explaining themselves.

"She's funny and warm. She's so fucking kind and smart. She has the best laugh. She smells fantastic. She's just different." I blink several times to understand the words coming out of Andy's mouth.

"Ever since I started dating Anna, there was something different about being around her. When we all started hanging out, I was so jealous of how easily Jennie made you smile and laugh. It was so effortless. I would read Anna's text, not in a snooping matter, but just to pass her phone along. I'd get a glimpse of the pictures she would send of the things she made for you. I wished Anna would do things like that for me. It got hard to be around her, well really both of them, really. To breathe in the same air as her. It was suffocating to know I had to put on my lying face on and wrap my arm around Anna. The girl I didn't want."

I don't realize I've been holding my breath, listening to Andy.

"And what about you?" My eyes shoot to Glen, who immediately fixes his posture. I don't really want to give him the time of day to explain himself, but here we are.

"I don't think you realize what kind of girl you have." His eyes meet mine, so full of jealously and truth. A simple statement. It doesn't take a rocket scientist to understand that Glen is agreeing with all the things Andy just said.

"How come you both aren't ripping each other in half because of her?" I ask them. They both chuckle and look at each other.

"Oh, we have. Early on, before you were around, Glen caught on to me that I was interested in Jennie. He would send me stupid texts when we would hang out together in front of her. We've had our moments, plenty of them. I guess we just knew she didn't want us. When you came along, she only wanted you."

The only sound you could hear was the gentle movement of the lake water.

"It doesn't feel like she wants me."

I hate my vulnerability shows to these guys. A mix of emotions is churning inside me. I'm trying to not let my ego inflate at the fact that Andy and Glen are jealous-of me! They want what I have. Andy's actions have made me furious; he's been stringing Anna along, keeping himself unavailable while not genuinely loving her. All the excessive flirting from Glen has left me agitated. I don't understand the motives for being assholes. To understand my predicament, I remain silent.

"From a distance, since Jennie started bringing you around more, I've had to watch her fall madly in love with you. Glen had to stop hanging out with us because it infuriated him. What was so special about you? We thought Glen could get under your skin to convince Jennie to leave you so one of us could swoop in and save her. I couldn't be part of that, considering I had Anna's feelings to worry about, but it was hell to watch. We thought we were winning, especially when Glen said Jennie wanted to be with him, and not you. She didn't budge, though. Whatever stupid shit you get yourself in, she never leaves your side."

I should feel grateful, right? Should feel on top of the world that there are people who want what is mine. This precious piece of life is mine. But Devil wraps her talons around my heart and electrocutes me.

"Has she ever done anything with either of you?"

Devil masks herself so beautifully sometimes. She must feel insecure right now. My jaw tightens and fists clench with each passing second of silence from them. If there's any skin on my bottom lip, I bite at it.

"Which one of you? What the fuck happened?" I stand above them, my fight response activated.

When they stand, it's clear as day which one was the recipient as Andy stands in front of Glen, protecting him.

"Put your hands down, dude. We aren't doing this tonight."

"What the fuck did you do!?" I shout as my eyes fill with moisture.

How could she... Why would she...

"It was one kiss, dude. I swear. She regretted it immediately. I never forgot about it, and tried to force her to not forget. I wanted more. It was a long time ago, right after you guys met." Glen timidly hides behind Andy, but he has his arms up, ready to catch my right punch.

"And you?" I wipe my nose with my sleeve, looking at Andy. Devil just devoured my heart and I'm left with nothing.

They both say nothing. My anger and ache are not getting along internally. I'm furious with both of them, Glen especially, and Andy, for shielding that son-of-a-bitch. The ache is just flooding throughout my body.

"Tell me."

"Our graduation." Andy eventually says.

"I don't remember what came about, but she had to grab something from Anna's car. She looked so beautiful that day, considering she wasn't in cap and gown with us. She had this baby blue dress that just clung to her body like latex. All her curves were on show. I just had to be alone with her. Just for a minute, so I followed her to Anna's car. Of course, she shut me down because she had you. Gave me a nice slap across the face, and I had to explain that to Anna later on. You just..." he pauses, running his hands through his hair. "You just have a hold on her that no one will ever be able to break through."

I relive that moment at graduation, putting the pieces together in my head. Anna and Andy's brief argument caught my eye, but I stayed out of it. I've encountered too many fights with Anna over the years, that for once, I was glad it wasn't me again. Then, when Jen found me, she felt different. There was no mention of Andy trying to make a move. To want to throw up at the memory that maybe, just maybe, she lied to me, and something happened. *No, she wouldn't do that.* My mouth gapes at the revelation. Unable to hear any more, I walk away from the grim reapers.

"Calvin, wait, man!"

She wanted to be with someone else. Someone who wasn't you.

No, don't believe the lies!! It's only ever been you. She would walk through fire to be with you. Don't listen to her!

I jog, building up space between us, but I hear them both breathing hard behind me.

Go to her and protect her. HE kissed HER.

I run even harder as Angel wants to make her fucking voice known now.

I see our fire from a distance and Jen sulking in a chair, wrapped in a blanket. For a split second, I want to save her. I imagine grabbing our bags and driving to my parent's cabin, just us two. Picturing her reaction to putting my ring on her finger and promising me I'm the only one makes me change personalities.

She doesn't want you.

Someone else can love her better than you.

My face feels hot and drenched in tears as I approach her, no longer jogging. I hear the hard footsteps stop behind me as Glen and Andy have caught up to me.

It's too late.

"Cal!"

She throws off the blanket, and I think I see a smile appear on her face. When she notices my emotional distress, she frowns. Not a minute passes, and the tent opens, and Anna appears. Seeing her face, and having the revelation that she was a fucking pawn to Andy, makes me even angrier.

"What's wrong?" Jen walks towards me, her expression confused on why Glen and Andy are standing behind me.

This time, I bite my top lip, looking at the fire.

Is she worth burning for?

Don't do this. Don't leave her.

"What's fucking wrong? These assholes decide to tell me how they are both in love with you. Were you aware of that? They purposely tried to break us apart, flirting and getting you alone from me. And you fucking let them! You wrongly assumed Anna and I were romantically involved; in reality, someone has manipulated Anna for years. What's wrong is that you've given your time to each person here, except for me."

Running my fingers through my hair, I pace back and forth. Anna has her mouth covered as she hears the most disturbing news about her relationship. I glance at Andy and Glen, who look like fucking toddlers that walked into the wrong classroom. My eyes move to Jen, who has stopped moving towards me. I have a moment to see her. She's holding herself, like Anna was earlier, and she's wearing my sweatshirt. Wearing my clothes always brought her comfort. Her hair is being blown to the side by the slight breeze. For once, she has no tears on her face, even though my tone was harsh. I'm trying to regulate my breathing, but the thoughts are too much.

"Cal, please. Just listen to me, please."

Just hold her close, and don't let her go.

"I hate you. You are nothing. I wish I never met you. You should just go fuck Glen and leave me alone. You make me sick."

My cheeks are about to explode from the instant regret. I walk backwards from our camp. Everyone around me is indistinguishable.

All I hear is sobs. All I feel is heartache.

I drive for a while, not sure which direction I'm headed in. My guilt has taken a sick, twisted turn, making me nauseous enough that I pull off the side of the road to empty my stomach. It doesn't help that the scent of Jen captivates my cabin, so I leave the door open.

Why would you ever say that to her...

I dry heave until I spin my wheel into the gravel driveway of the *Diamond's Beast Pub.*

For a while, I just sit, crying into my hands. Desperation overwhelms me—*you should go back for her and tell her you're sorry.* I blame Devil for every single word. Devil lives inside *me,* and if something happens to her, something happens to me.

Guilt overwhelms me more, though. I sift through my glove compartment and pull out my fake ID from the end of my junior year that my friend Chris made me before he moved states. Wiping my eyes, I try to conceal my indifferences. Mostly, I look the same except my hair being shorter than the photograph, and my face looks fuller.

After I pull myself together, I drag my feet to the front door, fearing they might kick me out because of my age. It's about 8:15, and the parking lot looked empty. I doubt many people would drink this early, but there's nothing else to do in this town. I just need to silence the thoughts.

The inside of the bar almost feels the same as outside. It's dim, almost too dark. It would most definitely make for an obstacle course once you're intoxicated. TV's are on low volume, as I'm moving my head around the place to pick my seat. Mariners and Dodgers. Pass. Giants and Cardinals. Pass. Local News. Pass. Reality television. My chest tightens. Jen would watch as I drink myself to death. Pass. Cops. Yeah, sure.

There's an open seat at the far end of the bar to get a good view of a speed chase, and away from people. Why do people have to suck?

"What's up, kid? Got an ID?"

The bartender, a Santa-looking guy with a long white beard and white hair with a trucker hat, approaches me. He's got a black t-shirt on, both of his arms covered in tattoos. I can see the veins popping from his arms, clearly ripped and beefy.

I pull out my ID and I play it cool when he looks at me and the ID. He does a small squint and I rub my chin, waiting for him to give me the green light to order.

"Whatcha having?" He slides my ID back to me.

"Uh, I'll have a shot of whiskey, please." I ball my hands in front of me, hearing the chatter get loud around me, and for a moment, I want to tell everyone to shut the fuck up. Even though Devil is in time-out in my mind, I let her guide me.

You will die if you tell anyone here to shut up.

The bartender brings me my glass and I stare at it for a moment.

God, I miss her. The way she sobbed after me, begging for me to stay, makes me want to throw the drink across the bar. The pent-up aggression I have is dangerous for anyone who crosses my path. I clench my jaw at the idea of Glen and Andy consoling her. Would she let them? I should go back and find her. To take her home with me. What will she do when she sees me? We need some time apart, and we can discuss what happened when we get home. It's not a conversation I'm excited to have, but whatever makes her happy, I'll do it. Pulling out my phone, I find her name.

Cal: We'll talk when we get back home. I need some time.

"You gonna drink up, or are ya just gonna look at it?"

Pushing my phone back in my pocket, I only move my eyes to look at the jerkhole sitting a few seats away, facing towards the Mariners' game.

You don't want to mess with us right now, man.

I tilt the shot down my throat and let the burn linger for a moment. The guy is watching the game, so I take a quick moment to scope him out. He looks like he's in his mid-thirties, sitting alone with a Yuengling in front of him. I recognize the Seattle Pacific University logo on his shirt. His five o'clock shadow looks unclean. How can someone who attends a prestigious private school look like this? He looks a little too comfortable, like he's been here before, or he's just been here for a while. He has a bowl of unshelled peanuts in front of him, the bowl practically empty. Four empty bottles of Yuengling sit on the counter.

"Ya got a name?" He takes a drink of his beer, looking at me. Quickly, I drop my eyes on the counter and twirl my finger to get the bartender's attention to get me another shot.

Before I answer the guy, I'll wait to take the next shot. I didn't come here to make friends or have a conversation about my crisis with a fucking stranger. Can people not get a hint that I don't want to be bothered?!

"Carl." I tell him.

"Carl? The fuck, your parents make you in the eighteen-hundreds? Don't hear that name often." He talks to me while he watches the game.

I twirl my finger again.

"You here by yourself, boy?" He asks me again.

Jesus, shut the fuck up.

I sigh, hoping he'll get the message.

"Yep."

I don't want to be alone. I want to be with her.

"My girlfriend kicked me out again, but I'm sure she'll be calling me here soon." He rests his phone on the counter, taking another drink.

I'd kick you out forever if I was your wife.

I take my third shot.

"What's the meaning behind the bar's name?" The bartender, who is wiping glasses at the bar, looks mildly bored. He's standing closer to me, so thankfully I don't have to use a lot of energy to talk to him. I didn't check what he was watching, but he didn't seem too interested in it. Stepping a little closer to me, he chuckles, then puts the glass with the others.

"Diamond, my lady. She passed away about eight years ago from breast cancer. She always knew I wanted to open a bar. It was something we were saving up for before we had to tap into our savings for treatment. We had our fair share of arguments over fifty-five years together. She would put me in the doghouse when I was acting a fool. I turned our garage into a little workout area and when she needed space from me, I would go in there. "You're going into beast mode," she would say, finding me in the garage. So, I'm Diamond's Beast. Best investment I made. This is all for her."

He pours me another shot as he talks, and I let the last five words marinate in my soul.

This is all for her.

Not much time passes until I'm thinking about Jen. Pushing my glass towards him, hinting another refill.

"It's great in here, man."

"Not the best place for kids, though." The Yuengling guy asks for another beer.

"No kids here."

I'm becoming more relaxed with each drink I take. The whiskey isn't helping so much with the tension in my shoulders and jaw, but my thoughts are drifting away from Jen. It's not her I want to forget about it, but everything else that has caused us to separate.

"You just look a little young to be in here by yourself, boy." Yuengling guy leans forward and lets his arms rest of the counter, interrupting our conversation. His peanut dish is completely empty now.

"I'm just minding my own business. Why don't you do the same?" I twirl my finger. How many have I had? I don't know, but I just don't want them to stop. Yuengling guy is pissing me off, and I'm hoping I can get a little more tipsy so I can tune him out.

"Who the fuck you think you're talking to, boy?" Yuengling's voice gets louder that I see some heads turn towards us. Trying to keep my cool, I nod to them for reassurance, then take another shot.

"Ian, let up a bit. The kid has barely spoken ten words to you."

The bartender takes his empty bottles away and replaces it with a new one. Hmm, not contributing to the situation as we switch out the bottles, right? To be fair, I'd want him to keep refilling my glass, no questions asked.

Assuming his name is Ian, I replay the last five minutes wondering when the screw fell out of him. Do I have a sign on the back of my shirt that says <u>please be a dick to me</u>?

"No, you kicked out my buddies last weekend who were probably younger than this guy." I continue to mind my own business, taking another shot.

You should probably wait a couple of minutes for the next one.

"Your buddies were belligerently drunk and mouthing off. Kind of like how you're starting. If you don't watch yourself, you'll be out of here."

Moving my attention to the TV screen, a cop uses his taser gun on a man trying to jump over a fence.

Could someone tase me now, or at least have Jen bring an AED with her to shock my heart.

"You listening to me?" My eyes feel a little dizzy and heavy, but I look at Ian, anyway.

"What?" My tone comes off rude, but who cares?

"What the fuck you mean, what?"

For some reason, my appearance clearly annoyed Ian at the bar. He hops down from the bar stool and moves to the end of the counter before it turns into my side of the counter.

"Ian, hey, back off him!" The bartender moves to our side of the counter after cleaning up some glasses from the other end.

Twisting my body to face the guy, Ian, I can't help but picture Glen and Andy's smug faces instead. Unfortunately for Ian, I throw the first punch.

Then I just become possessed. I can hardly remember what

happened next, or for the following hours, because rage consumed my mind.

All I saw was red. I wanted to kill him.

I didn't know I had that much anger. The weekend I had envisioned two days ago did not involve this shit.

The lights burned my eyes, and my back was in so much pain. When I finally opened my eyes, I was sitting on a cold ass metal bench behind metal bars. *Shit.* I don't remember my fingerprints being scanned. Or my mugshot being taken. I wanted to look at Jen's picture, to make sure it was safe, but also because I needed some sort of guiding light that she was real and this night wasn't turning into a shit down. But when my pockets were empty, I knew I was in deep shit.

I just wanted to fucking see her again. I would beg to any police officer to give me whatever fines I need to pay or to apologize times to Yuengling guy just to get the hell out of here.

"Klenn, lucky you. Your court appearance is tomorrow morning at nine-thirty."

Jesus, why is the police clerk is shouting at me? Closing my eyes in irritation as the vibration of her voice rumbles through my brain, I rest my head against the cinderblock wall.

"What time is it now?" I croak out in agony.

"It's about twenty minutes til ten." She says back to me, shuffling papers around. There aren't any other "criminals" in the booking cell, so it's just the officer on the other side of the bars. I gently bang my head against the concrete wall. *How the fuck did I end up here?*

According to the police report, I fractured Yuengling guy's zygomatic bone, dislocated his eye socket, broke his nose, and busted his lip enough to give him stitches. My actions completely transformed his face. Police also told me I must've had some cooped-up anger because it took the bartender and three other bar-goers to get me off him.

Leaving Jen at the campsite felt like days ago. I wish I could glue my eyes open, because every time they close, I see the poor, broken version of her. Her face is engrained in my mind. The way she looked at me as I told her the most hurtful words, God, it looked like she was dying. I feel like I'm going under without her. My biggest fear is coming to life.

Unfortunately, sleep has not been on my side for the past couple of nights, so I'm left with the nightmares.

"When do I get a phone call?" My chest is hurting, my stomach growls, and it's hot as shit in here. Huffing out my request to the lady, I stand to stretch my legs.

"You can't call anyone until they arrest you or return your belongings. That won't be until after your arraignment tomorrow."

"Fuck."

"Just sleep it off for now. I know it's not comfortable, but it'll make the time go by faster. Not to mention you look like shit."

She continues to mess with paper and hasn't bothered to look at me while she talks, so I'm not sure when she got a look at me.

Not only do I probably look like shit, but I feel like shit. Yuengling guy must've gotten a couple punches on me because my left cheek is throbbing. I look down at the band-aids Jen put on my self-mutilated cut. The edges are peeling up and I run my fingers over it. I'd do anything to go back to that moment, to have her next to me. The cut Anna tended to is now a long scab. Blood splotches cover my shirt, and my neckline is stretched. Other than the lights giving me a blistering headache, I lean against the bars and close my eyes to avoid the brightness.

"Angel, where are you?" Barely move my lips, I speak out ever so lightly so the officer doesn't think I'm hallucinating.

Nothing.

Two of my best girls removed from my life in a matter of moments. Removed from my soul because I couldn't fucking walk away.

No, that's the problem. You did walk away because you're a coward. You lost everything good, and I'll make sure you remember that for the rest of our life.

Clamping my eyes shut in torturous pain, Devil is still alive. Jesus Christ, how do I get rid of her?!

Eventually, I must've walked back to the bench and fallen asleep because I wake up to a kink in my neck and my body cold as hell.

"Klenn, let's go."

The female officer's voice has been replaced by a deep male voice. When I blink open my eyes, a short, dark-haired Hispanic middle-aged lady holding a briefcase is standing in front of my cell. I regret moving so quickly because every fucking fiber in my body feels like glass and I lean against the wall to hold myself up. Massaging my temples, I wait for the bars to be unlocked.

"Good morning, I'm Tara Rodriguez, your appointed attorney. Let's have a chat about your case."

The officer is already walking down a hallway to a new room, where he opens the door for Tara and then for me. My eyes are still adjusting to the light and my brain feels like it's cracked into a million pieces. There's only a table inside and she's sprawled her briefcase on the table, grabbing a stack of papers.

I hesitate, unsure what the entire process is of having a lawyer.

"Come in, Calvin. Sit down. We have lots to go over." The officer shuts the door, and I'm aware enough to know of the two-way mirror on the adjacent wall.

She doesn't move for a minute, then hands me two white pills, and pushes the glass of water towards me. Sitting down at the table, I hesitate to trust this lady.

"It's Excedrin. You'll feel better in a couple of minutes. Sit down, please. I don't bite." I do as I'm told.

"So..." Swallowing the pills and drinking the entire cup of water, I watch as she sorts through several piles of papers. Hopefully, the Excedrin will help with the ache in my cheek. Stretching my jaw to mask the pain, I don't want this lady to think I'm a wimp. This room feels smaller than the freaking holding cell!

"Calvin, may I call you Calvin or do you prefer a different name?"

I lick my lips and then bite my cheek at the urge of wanting to hear Jen's voice to call me Cal. For a moment, I picture watching her tongue roll behind her teeth when she says the *l* in my name. God, she's so beautiful and I miss her.

"Calvin..." A blink a few times in a row after hearing Tara's voice. It brings me back to reality. Shitty reality.

"Sorry. Calvin is fine."

"Okay, Calvin. I have to be honest with you, things aren't looking good..." She sits opposite of me, organizing all the papers until she finally looks at me.

Searching her eyes for some surprisingly good news, I rest my hands on the table, nervous for the first time since being here. I twiddle with my fingers, eager to hear the bad news. She clears her throat and looks at her stack of papers.

"Calvin, you severely harmed another individual in which that individual is resting in the hospital and may have to undergo facial reconstruction surgery. The family is moving forward to press charges and they are demanding a maximum sentence for the damage you caused. That brings me to the bad news."

That's not the bad news?!

Frozen in my chair, my stare falls from her. I put someone in the hospital, and they may have to get fucking surgery to fix what I did?! I refrain from responding and allowed her to continue decaying my soul.

"Not to mention, you assaulted the victim with several objects. I've listed here the objects you assaulted the victim with: a broken beer bottle, a bar stool, and, after the fight moved outside, a parking sign."

Having no recollection of that happening, I run my fingers through my hair, disturbed by the news I'm hearing.

"Fuck."

"Calvin, I don't work a lot with young gentlemen like yourself. Not to mention, you had a fake ID on you, drinking underage. Your blood alcohol concentration was a 0.17%. The police report states that you were intoxicated at the time of your arrest, hence your headache. Good news is you were pretty compliant with the officer's directions, after they finally pulled you away from the victim. We would have double the work if you did anything to assault the officers or resist arrest. So, thank you for making my job such a tenth easier. Do you want to tell me what you were doing a bar by yourself, anyway? Diamond's Beast is a remote bar along the highway."

What was Yuengling guy doing there?

My mind spirals and I swear it would be better if I were in a coma.

How much do I wish to disclose to a stranger? Would she think I was a controlling psycho boyfriend? Would she think I was in the early stages of becoming a serial killer? I didn't want her to think badly of me.

"I got into a fight with my girlfriend."

It wasn't a complete lie.

You spit out the worst, most vile words to your girlfriend and left her behind.

"Hmm, I see. What happened?" Tara closes the top folder and scoots her chair close to the table. I take my hands off my head and look up at her.

"Uh, what didn't happen is the question? Just a fucked-up trip." I run my hands over my face, completely helpless.

"Oh, no!" I drop my hands on the metal table, which makes the outsides of my hand pound from pain, but it's incomparable to the pain I have pumping through my heart and brain.

"What's wrong, Calvin?" Tara's concerned voice seems in the far distance.

"Oh no. No. No. No. No." I stand up from the table and pace the room, feverishly running my fingers through my hair.

"I have to get out of here. She's going to find it." Stopping at the table and ignoring the pain, I punch my fists onto the table. Desperate, I look at Tara for help.

"Who is going to find what?" Tara's composure is impressive. I can have my moments of intimidation, but she's not moving, just watching me intently.

"My girlfriend, Jen. I left a ring for her at the house where they were staying. Oh, my fucking god. No. I was supposed to be there when she finds it." I hyperventilate, grabbing onto my chest. My heart rate feels unstable.

"Hey, Calvin. I think you should sit down. Let me get you some more water." Tara stands up and knocks on the door to get the officer's attention. This room is suffocating! Breathing harshly, I think I might have a heart attack. Trying to get Tara's attention to call 911, my voice doesn't work. Moving backwards until I feel the wall, a weird sensation presses my shoulders down as I glide down the wall until I'm sitting on the floor.

"Here, have some water." Tara is crouched next to me. A whiff of vanilla hits me, and I wish it was enough to re-center me. Tara assists me to hold the cup to my mouth, but my hands are shaking uncontrollably and I spill some of it.

"I can't." My voice breaks and the pain inside me is intensifying. "Make it stop, please." I plead with Tara to make the unbearable pain disappear. The pain that is invisible to everyone else but feels like it's tearing me apart inside.

"What can I do? We can help you."

Two officers stand in the doorway behind Tara as she holds a glass of water. They don't seem too concerned, but my onset panic attack definitely troubled Tara.

"This is going to sound bizarre, but it's the only thing that works. My girlfriend would do this for me. I need you to trace my lines." Tara's eyebrows divert together, confusion clear on her face.

I hold out my hands in front of her, palms up.

"Oh, your palm lines." Without hesitation, she readjusts herself so she's sitting on the floor next to me, legs straight out and her ankles crossed. It must've been a good sign because the officers move away from the door.

She has enough of a fingernail to trace over my lifeline first, the one closest to your thumb.

"Did your girlfriend know about palmistry?"

The mere feel of the touch instantly eases my heart rate.

"What the fuck is that?"

Tara laughs as she moves on to my money line, the one that goes vertically starting at your wrist.

"Palmistry is palm reading." She chuckles.

"Oh. No. It was just something she started doing, and I liked the feel."

Tara says nothing as she moves on to my head line, the one usually in the middle of the life line and the heart line.

"Do you?" I don't even have to watch her trace over the lines to know which one she's doing. Jen has done this so many times that I just know them now.

"My sister tried it once. She did readings on me and my younger sister often." She moves on to my heart line.

"Do I just need to trace these once?"

"Just one more time, please. I don't know why it helps so much, but thank you. I know it was a stupid request."

"No, not stupid. Everyone has their thing. I like to run a piece of yarn in between my fingers." She finished with my marriage line, which is very faint, then starts again.

"What's going to happen to me, Tara?" Leaning my head against the wall, pondering her potential responses.

"It's hard to say. Sometimes it just depends on the judge. In your case, we already know the prosecution is going to push for maximum sentencing. I know it doesn't feel right, and it doesn't feel real, but from person to person, unfortunately, we have to endure our consequences. You seem like you good kid. A young kid with so much potential in your future and I can tell from the looks of it you just want to get home to your girlfriend. I'll do everything in my power to get you back to her."

She finishes tracing, and I let my hand fall. Pulling my legs up to my chest, I hide myself from her. This is fucking worse than detention.

This is what you get. This is your karma. You should've just stayed with her.

"I just want to do whatever the quickest option is for me to get back home. When can I make a phone call?"

"Let me see what I can do. Hang tight."

Tara stands up, and I hear her heels click as she opens the door to find an officer. I can't hear the conversation, but just some mumbling outside the door between Tara and another officer. They both come back to the doorway, where I look up at them.

"C'mon. One phone call. Use it wisely. Not sure when you'll get the next one."

Tara smiles at me and holds out a hand to help me out. The officer leans against the doorframe as I get myself together. The officer leads me to the phone stand as I hear Tara's heels follow me.

"Are you gonna call her?" Tara asks me. Picking up the phone, I freeze. I would assume her reference to *her* is Jen.

Nope, because she wouldn't answer you, anyway.

Calling Jen makes me want to throw up. Picturing Jen's face absolutely destroys me. Not that I have much left in me. Instead, I dial the only number I know.

"Hello?"

"Mom. Hey, it's Calvin. I, um... I fucked up." I rub my fingers over my eyebrows, thinking of how to start this conversation with my mother.

"Where are you?"

"Cle Elum."

"Calvin Louis. That's almost an hour and a half away. It's Sunday morning. We are about to leave for church. What am I supposed to do now?"

The fury in her voice was the only reason I didn't want to call her. But I knew she could try to help me.

"Did they give you bail?"

I look at Tara, who is leaning against the wall near me, looking through the papers again. I tap her on the arm and mouth *bail* to her. Tara's facial expression immediately frowns when she whispers back, *don't know yet.* I roll my eyes in annoyance.

"I don't know. Hopefully, I can see a judge soon." Tara is back to shuffling the papers.

"Mom, I just need to you please not tell Jen anything. If she comes around to look for me, make something up. I have to be the one to tell her and I'll call her when I find out more information. Just please, I'm begging you to not tell her." It's hard to swallow when I feel like rocks are stuck in my throat.

"What did she do to you?"

Her comment makes me want to hang up, but I remember this is my only phone call until God knows when.

"We just had a fight. She did some things, and I said some things. They were going to leave early, but I decided to just drive off to a bar. Some shit happened there that I don't fully recall."

"I knew she wasn't good for you." My mom tries to mutter this to herself, but clearly, I'm the recipient on the other end.

"Mom. Don't go there. Not fucking now. Just please keep this between us." Tara motions to me it's time to end the conversation, putting her black notebook in her oversized bag. "Look, I have to go. I'll call you soon when I know more. Love you, mom."

"Okay, love you hunny. Be safe. Call me soon." I hang the phone back on the receiver and move to Tara.

"Come on. Our hearing is in fifteen minutes. The courthouse is just next door. Let's head over there and I'll prep you."

My heart falls in my stomach at the thought of seeing a judge and potentially earning several years behind bars. I say a silent prayer to my mom for her to pray to the big guy to let me off easy.

Following Tara down a hallway, I unexpectedly found myself in an archway that turned out to be the courthouse entrance. The station and courthouse seem to be attached.

"Come on. Keep up. We don't want to miss your name."

Tara is hurrying down the hallway, her shoes clanking against the tile floor. I push my hands down in my pockets, feeling more anxious that this is happening to me. I'm going to court because I assaulted another human because I got drunk after telling my girlfriend to fuck off. It seems impossible.

Tara holds the double doors open to me. There are a few people sitting on the benches as the judge to speaking to a blonde attorney. It appears the person she is defending is an overweight, bald, short male with creepy circular glasses and a black mustache. His shirt is barely covering his stomach, and I can smell him from where we decide to sit.

"Just remain calm and let me do the talking. Only respond to him when he speaks to you. Okay?"

Tara gets out her black notebook again and crosses her leg over the other while we wait. I hate people are going to be listening and looking at me, judging me based on a mere fifteen-minute interaction between a guy who was pissing me off after a terrible night. I drop my eyes to stare at my shoes to show the respect that if I don't want them to look at me, I won't look at them.

It felt tortuous to sit there and wait. I had to keep intercepting my thoughts from Jen. Her voice echoed in my mind, suffocating me.

I want you to fight for me.

You're the only person who I want to save me.

It's only you.

Over and over, I just hear her promising me she's going to save me. Secretly, I say a pray that I could use her saving right now.

"Klenn. Case number 002172013."

"Head through the little gate right there and stand next to me."

Tara stands as I walk out of the pew. Her shoes follow me as I push through the miniature doors. I try my best to not look around at my audience. Instead, I take a moment to just be eternally grateful that I have Tara to represent me.

At the stand, I watch her for a moment while she gets herself situated. She's effortless as she grabs a pen and that black notebook. Her long black hair is slightly curled and before she talks, she flips it back, so it lies on her back. She's a little shorter than me, even with heels on. With her hair out of the way, I get a view of her profile. Her eyelashes are long and dark. There is a hint of eyeshadow behind her eyelashes and her cheeks are pink. She has full lips that are lined with a faint pink color. They remind me of Jen. Noticing my staring, Tara looks at me and smiles.

"Klenn, Calvin. Age 18. Date of birth, December 27th. Charges are as follows: intoxication, disorderly conduct, unlawful card identification and assault in the second degree with a deadly weapon. How do you plea?"

I bow my head in shame. Fuck, that all sounds terrible being read out loud. Tara had a pleasant, unbothered way when she read that to me earlier. I feel a small jab in my side and look at Tara, who is nervously eyeballing me to answer the judge's question. Oh right.

"Not guilty, sir."

"I have it noted from the prosecutor they wish to have maximum sentencing because of Mr. Sonder's physical injuries as well as accumulating hospital bills. Defense, your thoughts?"

"Thank you, your Honor. Mr. Klenn is turning nineteen in four months. He has a blank criminal history. He plans to attend college next fall to study business. He has a younger brother who is watching his every move in life. Tracy and Bill, his parents, are devoted Christians who raised a fine young gentleman. With all due respect, sir, Mr. Sonder was verbally harassing and antagonizing Mr. Klenn at the Diamond's Beast bar. There are several witness statements that confirm this. Mr. Klenn was at a nearby campground with some friends and, because of unfortunate circumstances, he departed his friends and was on his way back to Easton, Washington. My client fully accepts taking on the financial responsibility of Mr. Sonder's treatments, however, it seems indecent to punish my client for the maximum sentencing. My client was simply in the wrong mindset and as we humans sometimes have no control over the way we react. Mr. Sonder was the unfortunate recipient of Mr. Klenn's repressed anger. We are asking for the minimum time and possibility of early release after eighteen months."

Shit, she's good. Intelligent too. For a moment I have a brief wind pass through me that I may get to go home early.

"Ms. Rodriquez, I understand wanting a lessened sentence. Mr. Klenn seems to have his head on right. However, as you said, sometimes we interact with the wrong people at the wrong time. Part of my duty is to create a fair sentencing for all parties. I'd rather not waste anyone's time and complete the sentencing now.

The sentencing is as follows. Disorderly conduct constitutes for six months in a federal correction facility. Public intoxication constitutes for six months in a federal correction facility. Unlawful card identification constitutes a penalty of two hundred dollars. Assault in the second degree with a deadly weapon constitutes thirty-six months. Mr. Klenn will be financially responsible for the hospital bills of the victim. I am also mandating him to complete a twelve-month behavioral program."

I stabilize myself on the table in front of me as I feel the wind get knocked out of me. Tara lays a hand on mine for comfort. If I'm doing the math right, that is sixty months. Five years.

A five-year sentencing for merely punching a guy a couple times?

I try to keep my balance, but collapse on the ground. My chest is on fucking fire and my fingers are tingling. The whole courtroom is blurry. My whole fucking world just pulled out from beneath me.

"Calvin. Hey. Stay with me, okay?" I can barely make out Tara's voice as it goes in and out.

I'm not exactly sure what happened, but I ended up in a clinic back in the jail. My meal resembled dog food, however, the side of dinner roll and green apple looked appetizing. Feeling parched since the bar, I chug a cup of water.

"Hey, you feeling okay?" Tara appears around the curtain where I bite my teeth into my roll.

"Um, no." I talk with my mouth full, but I'm going to be behind bars, so who the fuck cares what I do?

"Calvin. Hey. I'm sorry that sentencing didn't go as planned. I heard from the grapevine that Judge Hornsby is a friend of Mr. Sonder's father. Seems a little fishy to me, but it's the law. Sometimes we can't fight it. When's the last time you ate?" Tara watches me intently as I shove spoonfuls of the fruit cocktail into my mouth, the juice seeping out from my mouth.

"I honestly don't remember. Must've passed out from a mix of that, the sentencing. Just everything."

Tara sits at the end of my bed and rests a hand on my ankle.

"I'm not technically allowed to do this, but I'll let you call someone off my phone. You'll get your personal phone call when you arrive at the facility." She moves items around in her purse and pulls out her Blackberry. Classic lawyer phone. She hands it over to me, but I just stare at her.

"Why are you doing this for me?" I put the spoon down, wondering why this gracious person is being so... gracious.

"You remind me a lot of my brother. Lost. In love. Impulsive." She chuckles to herself as she puts her arm down, still clutching the phone.

"Where is he?"

"He died three years ago. Drunk driver. Everything I do, every case I have, I always try my best to get a fair fight. His killer got off with a slap on the wrist because he had money. Lots of money. I just want you to be okay, and I want you to get back home to your girlfriend, to your life and continue living."

Her face turns sad when she looks back up at me. She no longer wears the professional, intimidating, lovely lawyer mask. She looks fragile and I hate to look away because she reminds of Jen.

The face Jen had on when I walked away from her.

"Can I call my boss?" I lick my lips, trying to keep the water gates closed. I look at Tara for a moment and she lifts her phone to me.

Because of natural habits, Jen's number forms. All ten digits and I look down at the screen. I fucked it all up. Everything we had, everything we were going to be, I ruined it. I erased the numbers and redialed Pat's number.

"Hello?" I take a breath of relief at the sound of Pat's voice. It feels like months since I've heard his voice. It's only been a few days.

I clear my throat, feeling it get clench and dry up. I shake my cup to Tara for a refill, but as a signal to give me some privacy while I destroy my best confidante.

"Pat, it's Calvin."

"Hey man. How's the trip going?"

"Um, not good, actually. Jen and I got into a fight. Um, Pat, I'm going to be away for a while. In prison." I hold my face in my hand, feeling my breakdown about to happen.

"What? What do you mean? Hang on. Let me go out back." I'm thankful for the five seconds of silence as I get a handle of myself.

"Explain it all to me, Calvin. What happened?"

I give Pat the short version run down of the past three days. The building friction between Glen and me. The way Jen let Glen flirt with her, and how Jen wanted me to fight for her. The constant disagreements between Anna and I. Andy. I completely lose it when I tell him about the ring I left for Jen at the cabin.

"She's going to think I'm not coming back, Pat." I heave after every word.

"I just need you to watch after her. Please. If she leaves Seattle, I need to know. If she gets bad, I need to know. If she starts dating, fuck, I don't want to know, but I need to know. I will call you every week when I get to the facility. I just need you to hold her until I get home. Please."

"Where are you now?" Pat's voice is cracking, and I can tell his emotions are getting the better of him.

"I'm in a clinic at the jail. I just had my hearing, and the judge sentenced me. Recovering, I guess, after I passed out. Although I'm not sure how one is supposed to recover from this."

"Jesus, Calvin."

Again, the disappointment in Pat's voice is obvious, and I feel an overwhelming imbalance of my emotions. I cover my face again, crying into my palm.

"What do you want me to tell her if she asks?" Pat asks.

Breathing into my hand, I wipe my face with my shirt's collar.

"I don't even know. I told my mom to lie in case Jen comes around looking for answers. But she's at the shop every day."

I feel my armor disintegrating, becoming one with the air.

You can't protect her.

"Hey it's all good, man. I'll think of something. So you're going to call me every week and you just want to know how she's doing? You won't call her yourself?"

"Pat, I wish I was dead right now. I hate what I said to her. I left her. And I didn't go back for her! The idea of even hearing her voice makes me want to do terrible things."

My chest is completely empty. There is no heartbeat in me. Nothing. Without her, I am nothing.

There's silence for a while as I fear Pat hung up. I swallow the ball of spit that has formed in my mouth.

"Pat..."

"I'll protect her, Calvin. I'll keep her safe for you. You just get better and come back to us. You call me the moment you can again, okay? Don't worry about anything here. I'll take care of her." I clench my eyes shut, forever haunted by the words that Pat should never be saying.

I'll take care of her.

Those are my words. No one should ever take care of her besides me. I wanted a hundred billion people to take care of her. I just didn't want her to crumble without me.

"Thank you. I'll pay you back whatever it takes. Just don't let her fall." I can't stand the thought of saying goodbye to Pat, so I hang up.

Tara must've been waiting for the conversation to end and I appreciate her respect for letting me have a personal conversation. I wipe my eyes as she walks back in. She picks up her phone and places it back in her bag.

"Well, you rest up here. Probably in a few hours, you'll receive the name of the correctional facility you'll be going to. I'm rooting for you, Calvin. You have an entire future to look forward to. Don't let this hold you back, okay? Do good in there and get home to her. I can see that she means so much to you." She holds my arm as I look up at her.

"I'll be in touch if I need to be. Other than that, good luck. I hope our paths cross some time."

Something clearly bothered Tara because she left in a hurry. It's weird sometimes how quickly a relationship with a stranger can form. It sucks how quickly loneliness just swoops in to ruin your life. I lay my head back on the pillow and try to allow myself to rest.

A few hours must've passed because I wake up and there's a new plate of food and more water. I feel hands on my arm and my body shutters, but it's just the nurse.

"Hey. You've been out for a while. Making sure you didn't die on us. You just got this from the judge." The nurse rests a hand on my shoulder, undoubtedly giving me a comfort squeeze because she knows what that envelope contains.

I let the envelope rest on my legs before opening it. With no interruptions, I let Devil ruin whatever is left of me.

She won't be here. She's going to find someone better.

The damage is already done. You won't be able to fix this, no matter how long it takes.

She's gone. She's done with you and she'll find someone better.

I plead for Angel to have the last word before I open the envelope.

Save yourself so you can save her.

I take in a deep breath and rip the top of the manilla folder.

"Fuck." I mutter to myself as I pull the papers out. Searching for my destination, I ignore all the unnecessary information. Would it be okay if I called the nurse back to inject me with poison because I wish I was dead?

Kersaw Correctional Facility. South Carolina.

Almost three thousand miles away.

Seriously, there wasn't anything fucking closer?

Date of arrival–Wednesday 20 August 2003.

I have spent all my energy, and I want to curse the Gods terribly, loudly, and with the vilest profanity. But I have nothing in me.

Angel is right, it's time to reset so that when I get back, perhaps I might use less profanity. I hope not, cause fuck, I love that word, but so I can be the best version of myself for her. Someone who is understanding, patient, rational. A person she is proud to have beside her. That's all I want.

When I board the flight a couple of days later, the rest is history.

Jennie

Sunday, April 21st, 2007

I've completely drenched my sleeve in snot, and the continuous wiping has made my nose raw. I blink a few times to grasp the full story of everything, to let it all marinate. Okay, yes. He was one hundred percent correct the other day. I would have not been prepared for that story. Even now, I'm don't feel ready.

I pat my cheeks with my soggy sweatshirt, trying to bring life back into my face, and rubbing my lips in circles, trying to respond with a word, phrase, anything to tell Cal.

"Cal..." my voice croaks like a frog.

Neither of us has moved in the last two hours of storytelling. As I return to reality, my left foot is tingling because it's asleep, and I've cramped my legs close to my chest. I extend my legs in front of me to get blood circulating through my whole body. Cal has been sitting on the opposite end of the couch, facing forward, looking at me only a few times to gauge my reaction. Watching his reactions was the worst part. His muscles tensed, especially his temporal vein. I noticed his forehead sweating, especially during the bar fight. The anguish in his voice when he thought he was going to lose me to Glen and Andy. Every part of that weekend was a jab into my heart.

As I move closer, I'm afraid he'll distance himself; we both know about those who've pursued me. He doesn't move away, thankfully, but he doesn't show affection either. I wrap my body around his arm and wipe away the remaining tears falling from his face. He looks down at the ground, probably trying to rest his vocal cords.

"Hey, thank you for telling me all that. I can't imagine how incredibly challenging that was for you. There is so much I understand now. And there is so much that..." I bite my tongue, hating the reveal the truth.

"There is so much you know now. With Glen and Andy. I never intended to keep secrets from you, and whatever they tried to do, it was nothing because I wanted nothing from them. And when I tell you that arriving back at the house and seeing the flowers and the petals leading outside and finding that ring, Cal, it was the most confusing day ever. I had mixed feelings about everything all weekend." I rest my chin on his shoulder as I whisper into his ear. Our intimacy has entered a whole new quarter now.

He dips his head into mine, closing the gap between us.

"I'm sorry I wasn't there. I'm sorry, Jen. That should've been the first fucking thing I should have told you when I saw you." He cries again, and I hold his face, offering whatever love I have left.

"It's okay. It's all okay now. Not everything was your fault. I need to take fault, as well. When we did kayaks, I should have told Andy to fuck off, and I should have just ridden with Anna. There are so many what-if's and things I should have done differently, but I just... I don't know. There's no excuse for the things I've done."

Cal swiftly moves his body, so he's facing me, and he rests his forehead against mine, holding my face in between his hands. He is so close that I could kiss him.

"We were both in the wrong, okay? I'm not letting you take all the blame."

His answer shakes my insides. He took on far worse punishment than what I had endured. What would have happened if I had been the one imprisoned? I wouldn't have lasted... But I know Cal would've done everything and anything to get me home. That's where I failed him, because I crawled into a hole and never attempted to get him home. Instead, I wrote him letters. Pathetic letters, and because of that, I failed him.

We were silent for a while, our foreheads resting against each other until he speaks.

"You know what this means, though, right?" He pulls back slightly, but his fingers remain on my cheeks. I already feel cold with the gap he's created.

"What?"

"Remember when we left the house because I didn't want to tell you what happened after you guys left? You said if I tell you the story, you would tell me what you regret about our relationship. Well, I held up my end, so now it's your turn..."

I back my head away because I'm fearful I'm going to throw

up. We still haven't left the tornado yet. I breathe out of my mouth, trying to prepare all my organs for malfunction at the next hardest conversation. As if I didn't hate myself enough already...

"I just didn't know how to help you. Your mood swings were new to me, and I didn't know what was happening with you. Seriously, I thought you were bipolar or something. One minute, you were fighting, and just so pissed off, then when you saw me, you were calm and happy. You were cutting yourself. I just, I regret not getting you help or figuring out what was bothering you. I know you won't want to hear this, but being around Glen and Andy brought me solace. Did I want to be around them? God no. But I knew they were protecting me and wanted to keep my safe. I didn't know what to expect from you."

It pains me to share my truth with Cal. How does one human being have the emotional capacity for all this?!

His temporal vein is tense, and he's clenching his jaw. I yearn to comfort him with a touch, but that would only worsen the situation. My touch doesn't have the power to comfort him anymore.

"I was supposed to save you."

"There's still time, I promise." Unable to restrain myself, I touch him and the tension releases from him.

"Would you have stayed with me if things turned out differently?" He stares forward and I watch him bite his bottom lip. Dragging my hand down to his lip, I give his lip a tug.

"Leave your lips alone. And by differently, do you mean you staying the rest of the weekend or me going home with you?"

"Yeah. Knowing that you were having these doubts about me and my behavior, would you have stayed with me?"

"Yes. I would have stayed no matter what because I'm supposed to save you. Remember? I would've done everything to help you. Cal, I hate with a burning passion that you went to prison. Especially because of something I did! I'll never forgive myself for that.

For four years, the thought that I let you down and that you hated me constantly haunted me. I can't tell you how much that ate me up, day after day, year after year. Sitting here, I believe I have failed you. I let you go under, and it kills me. The guilt almost killed me.

But honestly, I think you going to prison was the best thing to happen to you. You got the help you needed. You could figure your shit out, talk to people, have time away from me. When I saw you again both at Whole Foods and meeting for coffee, I knew you were different. In the best way possible. I could feel something different about you and I could see something different in your eyes. But I suffered here, Cal. Every day, I wrestled with whether you loved or hated me. I saw your promise ring daily, a symbol of your desire to be with me, yet I constantly replayed your hateful words in my mind. That you wish you never met me. I became so unstable, but I thought I could handle it. The moment you walked away from me in Easton was when things changed forever. That was my biggest regret—not running after you. I waited for you to come back, but deep down, I had a feeling that you didn't want to see me anymore."

My nose hurts from my sweatshirt material, wiping against my skin.

"I hate I didn't stay healthy for you. I wanted to be the same person for you, but the camping trip changed everything. For you. For me. For us."

Before I share my deepest truth, I breathe deeply. I don't know how much more I have left in my gas tank, but I rotate my body to face him. As much as it hurts to look at him, my hands find his face so he looks at me. His eyes are wet and beautiful, and I fear I may create the worst hurricane here.

"I want to love you forever. God, I don't know how I got so lucky to be the one to love you. You're the only person I've whole-heartedly loved. But right now, I don't think this version of myself can love you as you deserve. I want you to stay until I'm the best version of myself to love you deeply, unconditionally, and healthily. I don't want you to leave my life because we can't be together right now. I'm hoping for time to be on our side as it continues at a normal pace, allowing us to get to know each other again, allowing us to fall in love with each other again and allowing us to heal our demons. You are someone I need in my life. I've experienced trying to live without you and it's ... it's true fucking torture. I would pick anything else to deal with rather than trying to survive without you. Even though these past couple of weeks have been like climbing to the top of Mount Everest and realizing we've stepped foot in a landfill of deep, unresolved emotions, you have been someone stable. You've been there every single day, whether it was making me cry or laugh or smile. You make me happy when I'm sad. You make me feel safe when I feel alone. You make me feel special and important when I feel useless and unworthy. You make me feel seen and heard. We were so young when we met, but I always knew in my heart that nobody would matter as much as you. You are the most important character in my story right now. You always have been. Edgar Allan Poe once said, *"Tell me every terrible thing you ever did, and let me love you anyway."* I will love you forever, regardless of what you or I have done, because you're worth it. Please stay, Calvin. I want you to stay here with me while I try to save myself. You were brave enough to save yourself, and I owe it to you and myself that I allow myself the chance to do the same. And when I'm strong enough to climb Mount Everest again, I want you to be up there waiting for me. We deserve a happy ending, Cal. Right?"

I finish my long-awaited spiel for Cal. An enormous amount of tension releases from my shoulders, even though I'm awaiting a response. This man swept me off my feet at the first sight of him. He's carried me effortlessly. Dragged me through the dirt, leaving me bruised. He's put me on his shoulders, allowing me to touch the stars. But he's never let go. He's always been my krypto-knight.

He brings his hands over mine and grips them tight. I don't pray often anymore, but in this very moment, I pray Cal understands what I'm asking for. It's been hard for me to speak up, to share my thoughts and feelings, but I hope the message is clear. I want him to stay while I remove all my band aids and fix myself. I want him to understand that I've been breaking myself for the past four years to keep my shit together, but I can't do it anymore.

Calvin

I pull my face away from her hands because it's too painful to look at her. Jen makes me feel things I've never felt before. I've never had her break-up with me before. Were we still together once I came home? She's giving me false hope that we'll find our way back to each other. What if she doesn't get better? What if I ruined her for the rest of her life? She's optimistic that we'll get our happy ending. Maybe a good, kind-hearted person has our voodoo dolls and wants us to fall in love again. Above all, though, she's making me sick.

You love her. You love all versions of her, and you will take her in any condition. But she won't give you the broken, damaged version of herself.

It's probably the worst time to fall more in love with her because she says we can't be together. Having to love someone from a distance is a fucking death sentence. To watch her from afar, already chest deep in love with her, and knowing that she's only going to be better, and get better, for herself (and for me), I think I may drown from devotion. To watch her sculpt herself into something even better than what she is, even though there's no need for it, it makes my stomach turn. She's a perfect twelve—she always has been. To keep my distance from this masterpiece feels impossible, and I want to jump off whatever mountain we've been climbing.

Let me love you exactly how you are.

My eyes swell up after Angel cheers me on, trying to give me the courage to tell her those words. I look down at our feet, sniffling, and wiping my nose with my sleeve. I grab her hand from her lap and give it a squeeze. That's one thing that will never change-our physical signal that I'm here, that she is safe with me.

"Jennie..."

I don't even know what to say, but I just need to say her name. Reliving that story reminds me of all the things I *didn't* do for her. She squeezes her hand back, waiting for my response.

"I know you think I've been your Prince Charming, but in this story of ours, I think I have missed the opportunity a long time ago to be that for you. I don't think I'll ever be able to play that role for you, no matter how desperately I want to be. I've made too many mistakes."

I pause for a moment, feeling overwhelmed that I have the most perfect Queen of Hearts in my living room.

"I've hurt you a lot, Jen. And you've hurt me. I want you to know that I'm not going anywhere. There will never be anyone else. I will continue waiting for you, just as you did for me. I will be whatever you need me to be. A friend, a boyfriend, a listener, a midnight kiss, whatever you need, I will give it to you because you deserve everything good. I will love you whether you're cracked or stitched together or perfectly whole again. No matter what condition you are in, Jen, I will always love you. I told you that from the very beginning and nothing has changed. You've been the only one for me. Yes, I want to know all the terrible things you've done, and I want to love you even more."

She leans against me, wrapping herself around my arm. I kiss her forehead. How twisted has this fairytale of ours has become?

"I understand your request, though. We need to get you better, in every way possible. I've loved the version of you when we were teenagers, when all that shit happened and I doubted you, I still loved you. And from the other side of the country, God, I loved you then. And I still love this version of you." I bite my bottom lip and pull her head towards my lips. While lost in thought, my lips linger on her forehead.

"I suppose it's only right that you shatter my heart now." I playfully nudge her shoulder to let her know I'm teasing. Kind of.

Four years ago, I broke her heart. Not even broke but disintegrated it. There was nothing left inside of her. I left her with the words *I hate you*, but that was never the truth. This girl in front of me holds my heart; she's been the only one to. Day by day, she gave me hers. And I fucked it up. I deserve this.

"When you find yourself again, Jen, I'll be here waiting. The message you came back to in Easton is still very much true. I promise you; you don't have to do this alone. You will never be alone."

THE END

Dear Kevin – also known as *Calvin*,

I have written you so many letters in my lifetime. I have a journal just for you. There are letters I have set on fire, hoping to eliminate the embarrassment and pain you caused. There are letters that I've written the same thing over and over again, hoping to come to terms which how things ended. There are letters that only say your name because I can't even manage to write anything. And there's so many blank pages; mental letters I wanted to say but never made it to paper. But this is the one that matters most because there's potential you may see it someday.

This story was for you.

While most of this story is fictional, the idea of you was very real. There are so many things I still remember about you. Your temper for one, the way you smelled, your khaki pants, the way you loved Halloween and *The Walking Dead,* your short, soft, blonde hair, your blue eyes, your weird obsession for knives, your red truck, all the poems you wrote me, your chocolate chip cookies and the way you made me feel like I was the only girl in the world.

That was the best feeling of all. For seven months, I was lost in a euphoria I didn't believe existed. And I will never forget falling in love with you. I'll always never regret it, either.

The day we left from the camping trip was the absolute worst heartbreak I've ever encountered. Even after all this time, it was the most traumatic thing to ever happen to me. I thank God I only had to experience that once, but I paid dearly for it. I have put so much work into repairing my mental health because of that. You turned my world upside down. When we got into separate cars that day, I had no idea that would be the last time. I wish I knew a better word than shattered, because that's what you did to me.

I had the idea one day to write a story about what happened to me—to us. The hardest part about writing this book was trying to come up with some sort of plot regarding how the camping trip went horribly wrong. I wanted to use the real-life experience to help with the healing process. For the last eleven years, I have pondered every single scenario of why things turned so badly, so fast. The frustration was real because I don't think I'll ever know what happened.

I've held on to our chapter for so long that it has eaten me up inside, kept me wondering for years why I wasn't enough for you.

That affected me for a long time because I felt I wasn't good enough for anybody. You ruined so many good things for me, and I didn't deserve that.

I wanted you to be my Prince. You were supposed to be it for me. You were the first person who made me feel like I wasn't invisible. You were going to save me, and I was going to save you. That was always the plan for us, remember? You had your own demons, and I had mine, but we thought together, we could conquer anything. Funny enough, you left me with more demons than what I started out with.

You were actual kryptonite, though. You blew up everything good in my life. I stopped watching *The Walking Dead* because it reminded me of you. Every time I saw a red truck, my stomach and hands would clench in panic, and I got scared to leave the house. I had to bypass all the places we had dates because I thought maybe you'd be there with someone else. Whatever confidence I had (which wasn't a lot to start off with), you destroyed it and made it almost impossible for people to get close to me. I built the tallest, thickest walls because I didn't want to hurt again.

I want to tell you that I wish in real life we could've stayed friends and you could see the person I am today. After all this time Kevin, I saved myself. I hope after all these years that you saved yourself too and you found someone who is good, kind, patient and loves you wholeheartedly. You deserve good things–you always have.

After I contemplated suicide in 2013, I got my second tattoo that represents Jennie's scar on her left arm. *You are enough* was a reminder that because of you, I was capable of being loved. At the time, I didn't believe it. I didn't think anyone would love me. You made me believe I was nothing. You weren't coming back to save me and really, this was the first step to saving myself. It took over a decade to fix so many things that you caused for me.

Have you ever read the quote that says, *I had to forgive a person who wasn't even sorry...*

I know it's been a long time, but I am sorry. I'm sorry I couldn't be the one for you. I'm sorry I couldn't fix you. And I'm sorry I wasn't ready to grow up and help you be better. But you never apologized either.

I'm ready to say goodbye to you. There has always been a corner folded down in my life to mark our story, and I've been holding on to you for so long, that I have to let go now. So many of the things I remember about you and about that night are slowly fading and for the longest time I was scared to forget. I swear to God you were real, even though there are times where our time together felt like a dream.

Thank you for inspiring me to tell our story. It was so incredibly hard to relive such a heartbreaking, humiliating, broken fairytale. But writing this story as granted me so much peace that I feel an abundance of confidence and optimism for the future.

I can do this without you.

Whether our paths cross again or not, I want you to know I'm glad I had you in my life, even if it was for a short time. You taught me some of the best lessons of life. Because of you, I have found people who care and love me, exactly for who I am, despite the scars that are visible and invisible. I was ashamed of both for a very long time. Because of you, I understand that it's a terrible idea to love someone when your self-love gas tank is on empty. That should've been red flag number one. We were desperately seeking love from each other, but had nothing to give in return. Because of you, I have made it a mission of mine to validate that ANY experience someone thinks "wasn't a big deal" or "should've gotten over quickly", that it matters!! I never realized how dark and twisted and demented this little piece of heaven would forever change my life.

You changed my life, both for the good and the worse. You were my inferno, and I was killing myself by staying there. I'm ready to leave this place now.

I'm no longer waiting,

Jamie/Jennie

Acknowledgements

I'd like to acknowledge and thank the real-life beings who inspired the characters specifically of Glen, Jonah, Andy and Anna.

Glen – this character was inspired by the personalities from a couple guys that comforted me after Kevin left. JMC, AW - thank you for making me feel special again. I had absolutely nothing to give to you because Kevin took it all, but you made me feel like I was on cloud ten. Even if things weren't serious, I am grateful and appreciative for the attention you gave me and the time you spent listening. The beginning of my healing process started with you.

Jonah – Oh, Jonah. He has such a journey to share in the future, but this character was inspired by the qualities of my husband, JC, and another man who lifted me up so far into the sky that I was scared to come down, JD. There were moments that felt like someone like Jonah couldn't be real, but they are. It's a one-in-a-million type of person who makes you feel cared for, safe and protected. The way Jonah protected Jen is the same way JC and JD cared for me, and it really, really sucked to pick one. To you both - thank you for reminding me that even in our darkest times, people like you are willing to shine the flashlight on us to bring us out of darkness.

Andy – a person I've known since I was seventeen, RC. I want to make it known that nothing ever, ever, ever happened between us (that's the fun part about writing fiction) but thank you for just being who you are. I admire your laid-back attitude, before the camping trip, during the camping trip and after the camping trip. I felt you were most excited about this than any of us. Thank you always for taking care of the real-life Anna, also. I will forever appreciate your loyalty of getting Kevin home safe that night. If he would've stayed, I'm not sure what may have happened to him...

Anna – my dearest and oldest best friend. DC, you were there for all of it. You witnessed *all of it*. You expressed your concern about Kevin and I getting together from the very beginning. You saw me enter a "love high" being with him. You saw me fall flat on my face.

You helped me rebuild myself and continued to cheer me on. Thank you for being the most perfect rock in my life. I'm so glad you picked being friends with me over being friends with him!

I also want to acknowledge those affected by mental abuse. It's so easy to get lost in the words of someone you love. They tell you how much you mean to them, how they will never leave you, how you are their perfect fit. As I went through my healing journey of this experience, I learned so much about mental abuse. Before you let someone love you, I encourage you to find love within yourself–raw, true, genuine self-love.

You are worth the best kind of love. Please, don't settle for the first person who shows you love.

I am an avid supporter of promoting positive mental health. The following are services I subscribe, follow, support and wear proudly.

988 – Suicide and Crisis Lifeline

To Write Love on Her Arms – Crisis text line: 741741
www.twloha.com

Own Your Stigma
www.ownyourstigma.com

National Alliance on Mental Illness
www.nami.org

Call: 1-800-950-NAME, Text: 62640, Email
helpline@nami.org